CRY KOREA CRY

A NOVEL BY TY PAK

Cry, Korea, Cry a novel by Ty Pak
The Woodhouse, Inc.

Library of Congress Catalog Card
Number: 98-094006
ISBN 0-9667458-0-9

Cover and book design: Hoon Lee

Cry, Korea, Cry a novel by Ty Pak

The Woodhouse, Inc.
69 Bank St. #103
New York, NY 10014
(212) 741-6637

other works by Ty Pak

Guilt Payment

Moonbay

I.
Mercy Home

I entered the fenced compound of the Mercy Home, holding the hand of a beautiful lady in blue scarf, to whom I had the tenderest feelings that only a child could have toward its mother. The date of this entry was May 22, 1953, the date of birth on my Korean passports and ID's, and the beginning of my life, because that's the earliest event I could recall in the blank of infancy. I never regarded this discount of a few years from my real age as a loss or disadvantage, for it served me in good stead. At school, for example, maturer than my official age, I outperformed my peers and was considered some sort of a prodigy, a moral boost I certainly needed to sustain my self-esteem growing up as a mixed-race orphan in the racially homogeneous Korean society.

In my youthful imagination my father was usually a prince who came from America incognito to look personally into the devastation of the Korean War and fell in love with my Korean mother, herself a princess whose nobility and beauty caught his discerning eye in spite of her reduced circumstances. Invariably I killed off my gallant father in some heroic battle against the Communists but backed away from the painful dilemma of this great lady in blue scarf, whose recurring image my conscious mind quickly suppressed, falling so low as to desert her child of love. I couldn't bring myself to entertain the more realistic script, a sex-starved American GI raping or buying a hungry Korean whore for a can of pork and beans or a stick of gum, with me as the unwanted byproduct.

At that time, however, for all I or anybody else knew, I might have dropped from the sky. In a rare display of fancy Jongman Bag, the humorless Director of the Home, named me Chundong Bag, the first character chun standing for "heaven" and the second character dong for "child." Unfortunately, the character chun can also mean "low born" if its vowel is lengthened, so "heaven child" can be easily corrupted to "gutter snipe," a corruption that occurred often enough as it seemed to fit the subject better. Moreover, the consonant d in dong can be given a glottal click, which then means "shit." Few dared to go that far for fear of my instant reprisals, but out of my hearing I am sure I was more often "dirty shit" than a human being, let alone a "heaven child." The last name Bag was of course that of the Director, who had visions of founding a dynasty of Bags and gave the name to every child that came to the Home without some definite documentary counterproof. We were his children, not different from those he had sired biologically, and owed him love, loyalty, and gratitude as to our real father, he reiterated, though he never quite got around to mentioning his end of the bargain, to love and cherish us like his own.

Occupying a sloping hillside in the outskirts of Daegu, most of the Home's residential buildings were positioned around a courtyard that served as a playground with swings, slides, and a volleyball court near the gate in the level part at the lower end of the property. On the higher side, separated by a hedge and a stand of bamboos, stood overlooking us what we called the Big House where the royalty lived, Director Bag and his family. The ground beyond tilted upward gradually but steadily to the fenced limits at the crest of the hill and served as pasture land for the Home's considerable livestock holdings. Near the Big House were ranged the stables, barns, and pens for the cattle, horses, goats, hens, and pigs. It was the Director's ambition to own and operate a combination ranch and farm on the grand scale of the American west. If he lacked the scale or style, at least he had one thing going for him that no American rancher or farmer could boast, unlimited supply of free labor, of which he took ruthless and unrelenting advantage, making us graze and feed the animals, clean and brush them, cut, dry, and bale hay, collect and bag manure, and toil every waking hour in fair weather or foul.

From the cattle the Director got milk and from the pigs meat, but I do not recall tasting any of these goodies. The livestock and accessory facilities, including the pasture land, were originally purchased with American CARE funds to balance the diet of the orphans, but the Director had his own idea of 'balanced diet', which definitely excluded dairy or meat products. For breakfast we were given a ball of steamed barley and for lunch and supper a bowl of corn meal or flour broth, so thin we could gulp it down without the aid of spoon or chopsticks. There never was any seasoning, nor any side dish to relieve the monotony of starch. We were always hungry and constantly on the lookout for food of any kind, grasshoppers, fern, berries, even lizards.

As far as I know the Director had never been in the service but had a fetish about military organization, perhaps born out of the Japanese militaristic mores that had dominated his generation as they grew up. He saw his Home as an Army brigade and himself as its commander in chief. Hence his official title, Director General. From among the boys 20 years or older he appointed his officer corps, headed by a colonel he trusted most. The 18- and 19-year olds made the sergeants. Those 17 years old or under formed the body of enlisted men. The Director General's dearest wish was to make his Home a division, so he could call himself a bona fide general, but his vigorous recruitment and collection efforts netted only a couple of thousand orphans even at its peak. The number averaged around a thousand. In spite of 24-hour vigilance and the horrid punishment meted out to anybody caught escaping, the children still ran away, not believing his talk about our being his children. We never saw his own children eat with us or wear the rags we wore. They went to a private school in Daegu to which a chauffeured car took them, but we walked to the run-down cow school in the valley.

The Director's six children, the aristocracy, were strictly segregated from us, the peans. We could not go around the hedge into their separate gated driveway: the gate was latched inside. But they could come over to us any time if they pleased. Meeja, Director Bag's youngest daughter, used to stray over to our world against her father's explicit orders. A girl named Yoonay and I were her particular playmates. One day we were playing family. I was Dad, Meeja Mom, and Yoonay the daughter. Under the elm tree we built a small smoldering fire with dry leaves and grass and roasted a large nut the size of a plum from among the jimsonweed plants that grew in abundance along the hedge. The prickles burned off and the greenish nut turned brown. The skin cracked open and a perfect 4-celled pod came into view. Each split open in the heat, disclosing numerous black seeds the size of millets, which gave out the sweet aroma of roasted sesame seeds. Though perpetually hungry and sorely tempted, I was deeply troubled by the mathematics of division. If each of us had a cell, one would still be left over. As the Director's daughter Meeja would undoubtedly claim it as her due, as she did in everything else. Suddenly I loathed the injustice of her prerogative. Yoonay was entitled to it just as much as she was. Pale-faced, shy, and retreating, Yoonay definitely needed encouragement and preferment. Otherwise she would retreat and sink out of sight. I had to make sure she got the extra cell. The only way to effect this was to give her mine.

"You girls have them all," I said in grim self-denial.

At the moment I was distracted by a bumble bee that had tired of exploring the bluish purple pentagonal jimsonweed flowers and strayed over to where we had our domestic scene. Once stung by the vicious creature, my face swelling horribly and closing the left eye for a whole week, I ran with sudden fright to the middle of the playground where boys were playing with a tennis ball. From the goodness of his heart, the Director had set this one aside for us instead of selling it like the others in the CARE stamped boxes. I tossed and chased the ball with the other boys, forgetting all about the fireside dinner.

"Hey, you Foreign Boy!" called to me one of the sergeants coming from the Big House. Stopping in my tracks I bridled up, ready to settle a long-standing score. Because of my blue eyes, high nose, and blond hair, they called me a foreigner, flagrantly ignoring my other features which made me as much Korean as they, such as the slit of the eye, squareness of the jaw, flatness of the cheeks. But the boy's message disarmed me at once.

"You are wanted at the Big House," he said.

"Why?"

"The Director's daughter Meeja and Yoonay are sick, very sick."

"I am no doctor."

"The doctor is there already. Come on. There's no time to dawdle."

At the Big House both girls lay doubled up and convulsed on the shiny waxed floor, their fingers digging in vain into their bellies to tear out the excruciating pain. As soon as Director Bag laid his eyes on me, he let his tightened fist fly at me, sending me to the floor with a bloody nose.

"Why did you give them jimsonweed seeds to eat?" he yelled between slaps and kicks.

"I know nothing about jimsonweed seeds," I whimpered, hugging my head defensively.

"Weren't you with them playing house?"

"No. I was with the boys playing ball."

"Meeja went out to play with you."

Apparently no eye witness had come forward to disprove my alibi and I decided to stick it out. Bag would have beat the truth out of me, in the meantime braindamaging and mauling me, but was called away by the screams of the suffering girls.

They died before midnight, Yoonay gaining a place of equality next to Meeja's in the house where she could not be admitted alive. Every jimson weed in and around the compound was uprooted and burned. Though nobody had seen me with the girls at the fatal play, an unshakable suspicion had settled on me. I was bad luck, a jinx to be avoided, if not eliminated. The fact that I had not died with the girls was proof enough for them, and nobody thought about my own close escape, as if my partially Caucasian features made me impervious to poison or other harm. I was repeatedly beaten by the entire officer and noncom corps with cowhide belts and baseball bats or inch-thick rods. My skin ruptured and I was covered with open festering sores for months. But I welcomed them, which seemed to atone my implication in the girls' death, of which somehow I was convicted and felt genuinely guilty. I would have willingly had all my bones broken, if it could bring them back to life. I particularly mourned the dark-eyed Yoonay with a natural curl to her hair. Those blows with the bat or rod could have potentially broken all my bones and I made no attempt to dodge them, making myself as vulnerable as possible for my penance, but mysteriously no bone was broken. As I shed secret tears for the melancholy child Yoonay, an abandoned orphan so untimely cut off, I sometimes wondered if I was not the foreign devil they called me.

From the day of his daughter's death the Director hated my guts and would have starved me to death, if he had his way. My food allowances were generally more stringent and niggardly than those for the other children, but I still grew like a weed, perhaps thanks to the American genes from my unknown father. At age ten I was as big as a full-grown Korean male. Not only was I tall and tough, but had a reputation as a dangerous scrapper. For this I owe to the officers and noncoms who battered me cruelly from my tenderest years. I knew exactly where it hurt and how to inflict the most telling blows. At the elementary school, to which we went marching in columns as a body, we were a holy terror, wild beasts let out to pasture among the gentle flock.

"Home boys" we were called and were deferred to and given special privileges. At the cafeteria, for example, the line that had formed ahead of us disintegrated and reformed behind us. Attack against one of us was attack against all of us. No child dared to stand up to that kind of solidarity. We might have our internal problems and rivalries at the Home, but once outside we stood together like one family against the hostile and contemptuous world that had abandoned us.

However, even this solidarity did not protect me from the universal curiosity in my person. I was relentlessly ogled at by the whole school. When I went to the bathroom and unbuttoned my pants, heads craned to see if I didn't have a tail or lay golden eggs. Some hardy urchins climbed the window for a frontal view. Naturally I hated school, though I excelled academically. The classes were too easy and boring anyway. But both the Home and school had a strict policy regarding attendance, automatically equating it with education. Director Bag packed off to school all children between ages 6 and 12 and prided himself on cooperating in full with the law on compulsory education, though he could not care less whether they actually learned anything. Likewise the school authorities boasted and tried to achieve 100% attendance, putting one man full time in charge of tracking down truants, but showed little concern for such an intangible thing as scholastic achievement.

From time to time representatives of CARE and other foreign aid agencies came around to check us out. We literally lived for these occasions. A few days prior to the visit we were fattened up on pressed rice or lard. On the day of the visit we were given decent, balanced meals - steak or short ribs of beef marinated and broiled, fruits and vegetables and huge bowlfuls of rice. Impressed, the visitors nodded their heads approvingly. On the same morning we would also be issued new clothes - jeans, striped or plaid shirts, sweaters, shoes and socks. When the American visitors came near us, we were told to smile and thank them and say we were all very happy and considered ourselves lucky to be the beloved children of Director Bag, the personification of mercy and all the other Christian virtues. These plaudits were amplified by their Korean interpreter, apparently to the satisfaction of Director Bag, who kept smiling and bowing in deprecation. Invariably, the visitors had a package of gifts for each of us - chewing gum, pencils, crayons, socks, handkerchiefs, toys - at the sight of which we were to beam silly with joy. They clicked away with their cameras, pleased at the glowing reports they would be sending to their sponsors and donors in America. As soon as the gate swung closed behind the visitors, we were marched to our rooms, lined up, told to strip, then to step aside. The new clothes and gifts were taken away and our old clothes put back on us. Truly we learned early on the transience of worldly belongings.

A correction is due here. Though I've used the pronoun we above, it did not include me. Director Bag must have known about the US Foster Parents Program for Mixed Race Orphans of Korea. The wild oats sown by the GI's during the Korean War were being harvested to appease the conscience of the American nation. White blood being preferred to black, I would have been among the first in line. But Director Bag, to whom I was still his daughter's killer, could not bear to see me adopted by some good American family and grow up a normal child. I was confined during the visit in one of the closets in the basement of his house with no room to lie down or stand up, no ventilation or light. He locked it from outside, quite unnecessarily it seemed, because I had been thoroughly brainwashed to dread the visitors like the devil. The thousands of mixed-blood children, rounded up from the streets, orphanages and homes of Korea and never seen again, had been sent, so I was told, to various medical centers and laboratories of America for vivisection and other experimentation in the interest of medical science. How else could America achieve such rapid progress in medicine? During World War II Germany had the Jews to work on at Auschwitz and Belsen and Japan had the Chinese and Koreans at Pingfang and Nanking. Now America had its opportunity with the mixed-race Korean orphans, who were less than human and therefore beyond the protection of the American Constitution. Did I want to be shot up with the bubonic plague, cholera and syphilis germs? No. Sitting cramped and smothered in the black hole, I actually thanked Director Bag for hiding me so effectively from the bloodthirsty monsters, little suspecting that these possible distant cousins of mine would have rescued me from the living hell I was in. I envied the other children for the gifts they received, the food they ate, the clothes they wore, however temporarily, and hated the Caucasian portion of my blood.

Director Bag took pains to prevent us from learning

English, which automatically translated into money and power in Korea at the time. He was an eloquent example of this truth. It was his understanding of English, however meager, that had given him the advantage and connections necessary to own and operate an orphanage business on this scale. To ensure his exclusive control of this 'open sesame' he did not want anybody speaking English around him and discouraged us, his beloved children, from having any opportunity to learn it. No Home child went beyond elementary schooling, which was compulsory and free, to secondary school, the curriculum of which included English and for which the student's family had to pay. Bag was not about to do any such thing. In my case his indoctrination had succeeded so well that I needed no urging to have nothing to do with the Americans, let alone speak their language.

Some of the Director's 'beloved' children repaid their benefactor by breaking into his barred and locked house and helping themselves to the valuables, including the repossessed gifts. When an item was thus found missing, the whole regiment was ordered to line up in the yard and stretch out in pushup position. On the Director's orders his officers went down the rows of horizontal bodies, striking them mercilessly with baseball bats, until the culprit should step forward. This was a mighty bizarre procedure because we all knew it was the officers themselves, perhaps even the colonel himself, who were beating us, that had committed the burglary.

"You are all responsible," Bag barked enforcing the punishment for hours without result.

One winter morning some woolen blankets had been stolen and the regiment had to fall out in the yard as usual. In the ankle-deep unswept snow that had fallen overnight, we were stripped down to our underwear shorts and stretched out on our hands and toes. The cold slashed through our blotchy skin and shook our intestines angrily. Next to me was Chuldoog, whose left leg was a couple of inches shorter than his right, who had been always good to me, sharing his food with me when I was put on a starvation diet and got into fights with other children in my defense. His facial muscles began twitching, then twisted into lumps, closing one eye and wrenching his mouth into a grotesque sidewise pucker. Any more exposure would kill him for sure.

"I did it," I cried, jumping to my unbending feet, my knuckles numb and stiff.

Brought before the one-sided court martial I was asked what I had done with the blankets.

"I've sold them," I said after a short reflection.

"Where?"

This was a tough question since I had not been anywhere outside the compound except the school.

"At the West Gate Market," I said remembering the overheard conversation among the kitchen staff about the bargains and rip-offs on their shopping trips.

Bag ordered a delegation consisting of four officers and one of his clerks to get to the bottom of this.

"Get the merchandise back from him," he said. "Tell him the fence is just as guilty as the thief."

I was supposed to lead them to the fence in the market but their enthusiasm got the better of them and they ended up leading me. Once at the crowded market place with its noises and smells, all eyes turned to me to direct the group to the fence. Across the square I noticed a store with piles of blankets, sheets, quilts and pillows in front.

"There!" I said, relieved.

Feet firmly planted before us, the owner stood as if a tank could not push him over and heard us through with imperturbable calmness. He was certainly not the type to be moved, let alone frightened, by our wild story.

"So you are the one who came here and gave me blankets?" he asked, half amused, eyeing my mixed features curiously.

"Yes, you took them yourself," I said.

"When? Yesterday? The day before?"

"Yesterday."

"Ha, Ha," he guffawed. "I was in Seoul yesterday and came back by night train this morning. I don't blame you," he said, turning to the others. "I know his kind. He may have a

Caucasian face but can't be different from the rest of them. I wasn't an intelligence officer for nothing during the war. They'll swear to anything, sending you on the wildest goose chase, just to avoid being beaten. Go back. I won't press any charges."

On one occasion the entire payroll was found stolen at the Home. The bat and belt routine applied to me as the first suspect produced no result. The regiment was put on joint responsibility and the whole compound was turned upside down. Even the yard was dug up here and there and the sewers dredged, but there was no trace of the money. The brutal group punishment, carried out by the zealous officers and noncoms, would have gone on forever, but it was census time. The Director had to devote his entire energy to arranging loans of children and busing them from other orphanages just a step ahead of the official inspectors, because aid allocations depended on head count.

The orphans were always running away from the Home, fully realizing the danger of getting caught in the attempt. In the books of the Home escape was the worst crime. Runaways caught and brought back were so brutally punished that they ended up crippled or dead. One boy was hit in the head with a baseball bat while dodging the blow on his back. His skull literally cracked open and he never regained consciousness. Doctor Moon of course fixed up the death certificate so the boy would be buried, unmourned and unmissed, with no further repercussions. I had known Byungdoo rather well, a sensitive boy. He had confided to me before his escape that he was running away because he was sure he could find his way home and persuade his parents to take him back, however poor they might be. He wouldn't eat their food, and wouldn't crowd them in their one room hut by sleeping under the eaves. He would be no burden to anybody, he had reiterated to me passionately. Well, he certainly was none now.

The severe beatings resulted more frequently in permanent maimings and cripplings. One boy had his tendons snapped at the heels and limped for the rest of his life. Another had his thigh bone broken, which never healed properly. He moaned and suffered for months, bedridden, as no surgeon came to set the bone. The whole leg was swollen for weeks and he ran a high fever. We all gave him up for lost. Some suggested amputation of his leg, but that was a luxury the likes of him could not afford. Miraculously he recovered, however, and was up and about, but his thigh bone was out of shape and his right leg twisted outward at a grotesque angle. With every step he took with that leg he kicked out sideways.

In addition to the baseball bat the customary instrument of torture was the cowhide belt. At least in theory the bat was to be used on the back, buttocks and legs, but the belt was considered applicable to any part of the body. One slash of it would cut the skin open on the face and make the blood spurt in a geyser. After being flogged with it, one's body would be all raw with bleeding welts. The victim would first be gagged, then either tied to a post or spread-eagled on the floor, four limbs sat upon and held down by the assistants, so the punishment could be meted out in an orderly and leisurely fashion, without having to deal with the victim's unseemly resistance or screaming.

Generally the Colonel or Lieutenant Colonel would be in charge of a major beating project but he never lacked for assistants and spectators from among his junior officers and noncoms, who got so excited at the sight of the victim's suffering that without invitation they would join in and fall all over him with kicks and punches. Perhaps these were far more damaging than the more or less systematic bat and belt. In one instance of such a free-for-all the boy collapsed. They poured water on him and he seemed to come around, but as days passed his face turned the color of grass paper, while his stomach grew bigger. Then on the last day he coughed up blood and died. His guts had split open and the poor boy had been bleeding internally all the while. Of course no inquest was ever made.

A more recent example of internal bleeding must be mentioned. A boy named Jungshig Yoo and blind in one eye was caught in the village nearby where he had been hiding after escaping from the Home. Dragged back bound like a pig, he was beaten by a ring of sergeants and officers, until he passed out. He regained consciousness and seemed all right, there being no outward wound or bleeding. We all thought they had gone easy on him because of his one-eyedness. Two days later he complained of a headache, then suddenly blood gushed out of the empty socket of his blind eye, through the nose, and ears. He fell to the ground, lifeless.

So anybody who wanted to escape had to do so literally at the risk of death. I was prepared, though I was not quite ten when I came to this resolution, a record of a sort, because nobody had ever attempted that young. Perhaps my physical precocity may have had something to do with it. The morning after Jungshig's burial we were herded into the chapel and knelt on the floor without breakfast to hear the Director's post mortem sermon, while our intestines groaned on mournfully.

"Let us remember Jungshig," said he, pious and solemn as usual. "Pray for the salvation of his soul. His body might have been dirty and corrupt, but his soul, given by God, is as clean, sweet and spotless as a lamb's wool...."

I would have puked if there had been anything to throw up in my stomach. How could a man be so devoid of conscience that he would let a helpless boy get killed and yet next moment mouth those sanctimonious sentiments? Wasn't he afraid of the avenging ghost? How could he own and operate a crime ring and serenely go on being a church elder and pray long and loud condemning the sins of mankind, the weakness of the flesh? By what crooked paths do men arrive at such double standards and distorted perceptions? It was at this time I developed an irreconcilable lifelong distrust and hatred of religion or any high-sounding dogma or principle, organized and ritualized with public proclaimers and officiants, ministers and elders, hypocrites like Director Bag. My determination to quit the place of iniquity at the earliest opportunity became a religious commitment, no matter what the consequence.

As we were leaving the chapel, one captain buttonholed me and asked, "You won't be so foolish as to try to escape?"

"No," I said, shaking my head vigorously.

He broke into laughter. "Of course you won't. How far can you go with that American face of yours?"

I could have punched him on the nose, making it flatter than it was already, but remembered to hold my temper. I could not let a small thing like this get in the way of my escape project. Not to incur any suspicion I had to be on super good behavior. Besides I should be grateful to the flat nose for reminding me of the important circumstance I was almost forgetting in my preoccupation. My chances of detection and capture were doubly greater and I had to be extra careful in my planning.

But unexpected events kept popping up setting me back. After school one day they sent me to fetch hay from the high ground on the boundary of the meadow. I cut busily with the sickle and loaded armfuls into the two-wheel pushcart. As soon as the hay filled up to the brim, I jumped on it to pack it down according to the instructions and the hay sank back to the floor. It seemed as if it would never fill up the way they wanted even if I should work till midnight. But I couldn't be late for supper, because they never saved any food for one who was not there at the time to eat it. At sundown I put up my sickle and started homeward, dragging the handle bars to the ground to brake the slide. When I reached a straight downhill path, I had a sudden impulse to ride the cart instead of following it. Nearby lay a log a foot in diameter and a couple of feet long. I rolled the log in the path and placed the handle bars on top, making the cylinder the third wheel. I jumped on the tricycle and coasted merrily down, gaining momentum to a breathtaking speed. Just then one of the cows grazing by the side took it into her head to walk straight into the path. There was no time to stop the hurtling vehicle or evade. The collision shattered the cart, spilled the hay everywhere, and threw me twelve feet, bruised and cut. The hay could be gathered up, the cart pieced together, and I would heal, but not the cow, which died from the impact delivering a stillborn calf. She had been the Director's particular favorite on account of her plentiful milk and the expected calf. I had dashed his great plans about improving his herd through her. Of course my own considerable wounds got no notice, let alone sympathy or medical attention. In fact new ones sprang up under the blows generously laid on by his minions. Across my back still remains a strip of scar tissue inches long from the beating I took on that occasion.

At first I was accused of sabotage, of deliberately creating the accident to hide my laziness. The quantity of spilled hay quashed this line of thinking, but was powerless to prevent the revival of the myth that I was bad news, a general disaster area to be avoided. The pleasurable task of milking the cows was permanently taken away from me, which seemed at the time the greatest misfortune. I had loved the soft resilience of the teats as my hand cupped over them and squeezed. The stream of milk shooting into the pail had been reassuring music to my ear, proclaiming in clear accents the triumph of life over adversity, the flow of life-giving milk in spite of the exploitation and brutalization of the cow, whose lot symbolized mine. Of course there was no drinking any of the milk, even on the sly. The overseers watched our every move. Also it was common knowledge that the Director had a powerful telescope installed at his window to observe everything that went on in the pastureland.

From the cow sheds I was demoted to the pig pens. I had to rake up manure and soiled straw and take them out to dry before bagging. The floor was then swept and hosed down and new straw was brought in and spread out for the porcine highnesses. Every night I returned to my room to be taunted and shunned by my fellows as "stinking pig ass wiper". I couldn't put off the escape any longer.

The school was like a prison with a high fence and guards but was still easier to run away from than the Home. In the confusion as everybody headed for their classes after the morning assembly, I made my way unobserved to the toilet, a separate building across the playground near the gate. The old custodian who took the first watch, with a glass of hot tea in hand, was engrossed in the sight of the student body disintegrating like ants milling in a pan. I went behind the outhouse and climbed over the fence, jumping ten feet to the street below. A man in a dark blue suit and a red tie looked up startled but resumed his walk, hands in his pants pockets and eyes on the ground. A bean curd vendor with a stack of square boxes on his back watched me throughout but went on shouting "Freshly set bean curd!" without the slightest change in his inflection. I cleared the alley and came to a wide thoroughfare, momentarily expecting the heavy hand of law to be laid on the back of my neck. I ran in the direction of the West Gate Market which I remembered from the last trip. The road curved and hid the school. Nobody was in pursuit and I breathed with relief, tasting the joy of freedom.

The marketplace was crowded, noisy, smelly, and dirty, especially where the groceries were sold. The unpaved road was wet and muddy, very much like the pigsties I cleaned. A produce shop owner was struggling with an oversize crate of cabbage. I went over and helped him carry it inside. But as soon as we put it down, instead of thanking me, he looked me over suspiciously.

"From an orphanage?" he asked.

"What does it matter if I am?" I said. "I need a job. I can work for you. I am strong and you won't regret it. Just feed me and make me sleep in your store."

"I can't hire you," he said. "The police will be all over me for harboring a runaway orphan, especially a GI orphan. Why don't you go to Seoul? It's a big place with thousands of homeless and you won't be recognized."

"How do I get there?"

"By train. Go to the railroad station."

He did not give me any money but was generous with the directions. Perhaps they were too detailed and I got lost. It was dark when I reached the station. I went to the edge of the vast rail yard where the fence ended and the tracks issued bound for their ultimate destinations. I followed the tracks to the station, diving into a ditch or under a platform at the approach of trains or lantern-swinging linemen. The whole yard swarmed with rolling stock - chugging and whistling locomotives, dark freighters loaded with lumber, coal, cattle, grain, lighted coaches with passengers dressed for travel and talking excitedly. I did not dare go near them and ask where they were going. The platform by the station building was crowded with people craning their heads for the next train, which must be north-bound from their lay. The train pulled in, Seoul-bound night express, with a piercing whistle. The crowd on the platform tensed, repositioned themselves, and picked up their luggage unnecessarily. The express came to a stop and a mad rush started for the entrances at both ends of each coach, pushing, shouting, swearing. A long freight train stood between me and the express. I decided to crawl under a box car. Just as I emerged on the other side, the mountain of steel above me screeched and lunged forward. I jumped off, startled as never before at the close call. I could imagine my head and body crushed like a tomato between wheel and rail with the spilled brains and guts draping the ties. The freight train came to a stop as suddenly as it had started and remained stock still like the dark earth itself, indifferent to my pounding heart. Cautiously I went down the aisle between the two trains until I reached the steps at the end of a coach. I could see why the station platform was so high. The bottom step came to my eye-level, and the conductor on the opposite side was wholly occupied with the people jamming the entry from the platform. Nevertheless I thought it prudent to wait until the train started and the vestibule was clear of people before I jumped aboard.

The locomotive of the express shrieked and the train started moving. I ran along, holding on to the banister and stumbling over the ties and rocks of the railroad bed. When the conductor went inside, closing the door behind him, I pulled myself up and rested my weight on the elbows, feet dangling, ready to duck down at the first sign of train personnel or passengers nearing. An hour went by, but there was no traffic along the passage and I became bold enough to come up and sit on the steps. It was December and the night air, wind-chilled and dipping lower with every mile of the train's northward progress, cut through my light clothes and laid siege to every molecule of water in my body. I suffered miserably, fighting the temptation to sneak inside the car, where, though dank, it was at least above freezing from the body heat of the press. But I persevered, stomping my feet, thrashing my arms, jumping up and down, rubbing my numb knuckles and toes to bring back the circulation.

The sky was breaking when the train pulled into a huge bay of railroad tracks, from the size of which I judged it to be Seoul Station. I waited for the train to slow down to a safe speed. My legs, drawn up between my arms, were stiff. My whole body felt like a foreign stump. After bending the knees a few times I jumped off. The impact nearly killed me, because somehow I landed head first. I couldn't breathe however hard I pushed my diaphragm. Sweat broke out all over me and I was sure I would die of suffocation. Tears of anger rose to my eyes, as I protested the unfairness of it all. Then the breathing came back slowly. Nothing could be sweeter than the morning air that filled my lungs again, spreading its cleansing, nourishing influence throughout my body. I breathed greedily, shedding tears of gratitude to God. After brushing off the dirt from my hair and clothes, I dragged my still groggy body over the tracks and went into the street.

The usual staring began and the pedestrians, all in a frenzy to outpace each other during the rush hour, would slow down or halt to have a better look and verify what their hasty glance had told them. But whenever I went near and tried to speak to them, they all scurried off. I managed to detain one man long enough to hear my request for directions to the nearest marketplace. Though I could not have spoken more clearly in Korean, my mother tongue and the only language I knew, he did not understand me and kept giving his version of nescience in English, snorting out "I don't know." This curious exchange of Korean and English persisted for some time, before my Korean got through to him at last.

"GI orphan!" he spat scornfully and walked off, without telling me how to get to the marketplace!

But I did not mind. I was in Seoul, free, away from the claws of Director Bag and his blood-thirsty crew. The taste of freedom was sweet and energizing, and my weak body was inspired with new strength. A song broke out of me spontaneously. I felt a little lightheaded, and my stomach growled, having nothing to work on since the day before, but I skipped and hopped, singing just about any tune that came to my head, hymns, army songs, popular songs I had heard snatches of on the radio. The ravages of war were still evident everywhere. Little of Seoul had escaped, as it changed hands four times during the three years before cease-fire. Reconstruction was under way with US aid but not nearly fast enough. I rambled all day long, looking at whatever buildings or monuments that had been spared or rebuilt. I might be penniless, starving, in rags, and the scene one of devastation and chaos, but no tourist could have enjoyed the nation's capital with keener appreciation.

In the square before Seoul Station I stood admiring what remained of the ornate brick and marble Victorian architecture with the clock tower lopped off at the middle and the endless crosscurrents of people arriving and departing in the huge lobby under the gaping, bombed-out skylight dome. One block away to the north rose in the center of a rotary the quaint South Gate without the stone wall that used to stretch to the left and right of it, surrounding the whole city. The eaves, gray with the grime of the centuries, yet described energetic, jaunty curves, and the mythic creatures in clay still sat astride the tiled ridgelines in their eternal laughter. The concrete fortress of City Hall, with several sections knocked out, loomed behind the fountain in the plaza. I walked down Broadway, lined with new government buildings, some finished but mostly still draped by scaffolding, National Assembly, Central Post Office, Ministry of Internal Affairs, Foreign Affairs, Commerce and Industry, Transportation, National Arts Center, Bell Pavilion. Lost in the wonderland and dazzled by its grandeur, of what it had been or would be, as much as what there was of it presently, I was afoot all day, forgetting hunger and cold. After a brief spell of sunlight at noon the sky became overcast. The biting wind gusted, raising eddies of dust storm that blinded, choked, and whipped.

Long after dusk I crawled under a staircase by the side of a building to rest, not to sleep. By instinct I knew it would be deadly to fall asleep in mid-winter, with the temperature hovering near zero. But, hungry and weary, I had less and less strength to stem the tide of sleep that rolled in inexorably. As the night deepened, a sweet voice whispered and urged me to yield and stretch out, only for a few minutes, just to get the wrinkles out. I pinched myself, gritted my teeth, and tossed violently from side to side, to ward off the temptation. The night seemed never to end. I kept telling myself that I should stand up and get a move on, but my body was gripped in a paralyzing lethargy. I heard the rats squealing, cars screeching past, dogs barking, and other numerous night sounds louder than those of the day. Stiff and shaky, I longed for the comfort of the Home, where at least I could sleep soundly and wake up in the morning refreshed.

I must have dozed off. The fierce rays of the morning sun blinded my eyes. Busy steps tramped up and down the stairway, and the building was alive with its daily tenants, opening windows, cleaning up, getting ready for the day's work. Already pedestrians were abroad and vehicles roared past. I tried to stand up but my legs gave way. My hands and feet were numb, like detached stumps. Frostbite? In terror I hooked an arm around the banister of the stairway nearby and pulled myself up, sweat dripping off my forehead. I put one leg forward to take a step, but crashed to the frozen ground. As I lay struggling helplessly, panting, who should I see coming toward me but a Caucasian, in gray woolen sweater and slacks! My heart skipped a beat. All that desperation to escape from the Mercy Home only to end up in the hands of an American body-catcher! Nonetheless I would have fought him to the death and given him a run for his money, except no part of my body obeyed the simplest command of my will.

"What's the matter, boy?" he shouted, extending his arm and pulling me up. "Where do you live?"

Of course I had no idea what he was saying and only quaked in anticipation of my imminent transportation to some collection point for shipment to a flesh-cutting laboratory. Disgust and anger at my impotence and futility in the face of danger, as much as fright, made me pass out.

II.
Evacuation

I woke up to find myself in bed flat on my back, my arm tied to a long IV cord and my whole body bandaged and strapped down. My eyeballs rolled dazed. Everything in the room was white, the ceiling, the walls, the door, and the furniture. For a moment I thought I was dreaming. Then I decided I had died and was in heaven already, maybe in a waiting room until my papers got processed. It took me a full hour before I was certain of my being alive and began stirring. An American nurse came in and smiled brightly.

"So you are awake, John?" she said, though of course I had no way of understanding even such a simple sentence in English or noticing the mistaken identity.

I only perceived her as an American, someone in the medical profession, who had or was about to conduct a vivisection on me. The American male I had laid my eyes on last must have brought me here. I expected decapitation and other gruesome operation any minute, but the nurse changed my bandages and applied soothing salve on my swollen, inflamed skin. Everyday a team of nurses and doctors changed the bandages, took the temperature, listened to the chest, and palpated. Plainly they were trying to heal, not kill me. Some of the doctors were psychiatrists trying to coax me to talk. Modern antibiotics had done wonders and no finger or toe fell off in spite of the advanced frostbite I had sustained when found. However, as healing progressed, the wounds itched horribly but I was told by unmistakable signs that I should not scratch.

But why all the trouble to restore my health when their ultimate purpose was to cut me up? Maybe they were not going to experiment on me after all. But how could it be? Couldn't my finder figure out that I was a runaway half-breed orphan, exactly the kind they were looking for? Maybe he got fooled. I hadn't spoken a word of Korean to him, and, for all he knew, I might be a full-blooded American somehow stranded in Korea. Alan Heyman, which was his name, came to look me up at the hospital, though I gave him no sign of recognition or encouragement. Come to think of it, there was something naive and gullible about him. He got fooled and so did the others. Let them be. Certainly, it won't be me to disabuse them of my mixed blood, not when I was in a hospital near all the surgical instruments which would be turned on me the moment they discovered the truth. So I found my safety in catatonic mutism, which lasted for weeks, months, long after my physical wounds had healed.

The hospital was in no hurry to discharge me. Having unlimited access to US Army medical facilities as a veteran of the late war in Korea, Alan had taken me to the 8th US Army Evacuation Hospital in Yongsan and put me down as his brother with the name John in the admission papers. The fiction was perhaps aided by an uncanny coincidence: the remarkable resemblance between Alan and me. It could be his Indian blood, for he said his paternal great grandparent was a pioneer who married a Navajo squaw. Our likeness was so great, especially as I grew older, that people often mistook me for him and vice versa. Anyway, nobody on the staff at the Evac Hospital asked any more questions, even about the curious circumstance of my being away in Korea instead of going to school at home. Perhaps being with big brother Alan was explanation enough. Regardless, from a strict legalistic viewpoint, what he did may be fraud, falsification of an official document, or something like that, but justice is a balancing act, the harm versus the benefit of an act. No harm came from the irregularity Alan resorted to in the performance of his Good Samaritan deed. As its direct beneficiary, my assessment is probably self-serving but one thing is certain: no wounded or sick GI had to give up his bed or proper medical care at the hospital on account of me. The troops had been going home since the Armistice a few years back and there were plenty of beds and hands to go around, eager for some occupation. I was a godsend, particularly to the unemployed psychiatric staff, mostly brand new graduates and trainees on the lookout for their paper topics to set the world on fire. In no time I was transformed into a modern-day equivalent of the Wolf Boy. From my ignorance of American table manners, sooner eating with my fingers than with the awkward fork and knife (they didn't think of offering chopsticks!), from my noisy open-mouthed slurp and belch, they concluded that I had reverted to an infantile, primitive state, not suspecting that these might be acceptable behavior in a different culture, Korean, which surrounded them. Diagnosed as a case of radical amnesia with verbal loss, under stress of extreme physical trauma, I was launched on a comprehensive rehabilitation program, linguistic, social, cultural, aesthetic, a perfect guinea pig to try out their various pet theories on. Later I learned that no fewer than seventeen major papers and doctoral theses had come out of me, John Heyman Phenomenon.

For example, English was taught from ABC with illustrated readers, blocks, tapes, films, and other state-of-the-art teaching aids suggested by the latest research on language acquisition. Of course they all labored under the illusion that I was a reverted infant, not a foreigner trying to learn English as a second language with the added handicap of interference by the pronunciation and grammar of my native tongue. But it was just as well. Had they known the truth, they might have come up with a totally different approach, which probably would have been slower, though less taxing. In consideration of the great speed of learning shown by infants, especially in learning languages, they duplicated the imagined infantile situations and bombarded me with information, clues and signals. Intense concentration and ceaseless practice was necessary, forcing me to memorize my daily assignments even in sleep. Somehow I managed to live up to their expectations, learning to speak and understand English with native fluency in a few months to the delight of my tutors. Once mastered, English was the magic key that opened the door to every field of knowledge. I read greedily, and did not put down a book until I finished it. With every mile of my broadening intellectual horizon, I was elated with a sense of freedom and power, like Genghis Khan overlooking his latest conquest, only to be cast down next moment into chasms of despair over my vast ignorance, the infinity of darkness that beset the speck of light.

My rehabilitation included music, and the teacher was Alan himself, a music minor. It was a revelation to relate the musical notes to their corresponding sounds on the piano, filling me with the same kind of wonder as the savage feels on first learning how to write. In my ignorance I had always thought the tunes of songs as spontaneous embellishments, features of pitch, accent, or length added to the syllable, somewhat exaggerated maybe, which the black and white of normal script for the spoken language did not articulate anyway. Alan was an accomplished pianist and I swooned when he first played the rippling cadenza in Beethoven's Concerto No. 3. With such an excellent example to inspire me, I practiced piano hard in the hospital auditorium, but a Mozart I surely was not, and had to relegate this interest behind my other academic priorities.

One evening Alan had permission to take me out to a movie theater on the Yongsan base, a city within the city, where the hospital was just a part. The movie was "Enchantment". I was enchanted, mesmerized, broken-hearted. The romance was so sad and touching that I couldn't keep my eyes dry. I wanted to see it again so badly that Alan took me back to the theater the next few days early in the evening, so I could watch the first and second showings. I must have seen it a dozen times until the theater changed to another title. Once tasted, my appetite for movies was unquenchable. The more I saw, the more I wanted to see, and once we took a US Army bus to the 25th Division Headquarters at Dongdoochon near the Demilitarized Zone about 50 miles north of Seoul where they were showing "Jane Eyre."

"How does one make a thing like that?" I asked.

"With a movie camera, film, and a cast of actors," Alan explained.

"That's what I want to do, make movies, when I grow up," I said firmly, having made up my mind.

"In the States one goes to Hollywood to be in the movies, but I don't know where you would go here. We'll look into it when you get discharged. But perhaps you should go to school and finish your education first."

"I don't want to go to school," I protested passionately, recalling the vapid waste of time at the cow school in Daegu. "This is real school, reading books, talking to you, going to the movies. I don't need to sit in class with a bunch of stupid kids."

I began to read reviews about movies and studied books on the film art. Now every movie was more work than entertainment as I analyzed it as if I were its producer-director. So when the opportunity to be in a movie presented itself by and by, I was quite ready to seize it, though I had no practical experience.

One of the first things I looked into following my literacy was the practice of vivisection on mixed-blood children, but I couldn't find anything even remotely related to the topic, except a vast literature on the barbarous experimentations by the Nazis on the Jews during World War II, with such vehement outcries of denunciation. What consummate hypocrisy was this, denouncing Nazi cruelty while they themselves carried on experimenting on mixed-bloods? I kept looking, certain that somewhere somebody would slip up and give away the game. Maybe it was so classified that it could not be printed, in spite of all the vaunted freedom of the press and information in America. Naturally my investigation was carried out entirely alone. Nobody could be consulted, let alone taken into confidence, lest he or she should betray me.

As I got to know Alan better, I became convinced that he was a true friend, that if I couldn't trust him, I could trust no one, which seemed rather like a bleak prospect, like having to cross a vast desert alone, with nobody to ask for directions or keep company. Still I hesitated, as no less than my life depended on such confidence. Then, after watching a particularly moving Western portraying trust and loyalty between two friends, who confided in each other completely, I finally told him about my long-standing concern. Predictably, he was beside himself with indignation at Bag's knavery, the basest kind, to practice so vilely on a young mind.

"He should be vivisected," cried Alan. "Where is this Home located? I'm going after him."

"No, please," I implored. "Let bygones be bygones."

Not out of magnanimity, but lest Bag should take me away, if he found out where I was. I was afraid that he might still have some hold on me as father or guardian, as he had repeatedly claimed.

"Maybe later then," Alan said. "In the meantime don't be afraid of anything. Remember I am your brother and will protect you. Don't make a liar out of me."

"Do you have other brothers and sisters?"

"No, my parents died in a car crash when I was five. I was an orphan like you and have no family. Fortunately, I didn't have to be raised at an orphanage, because they had left just enough money to see me through boarding school and college. So it is fate that has brought us together as brothers, to be family. Maybe Bag did us a favor by saving you for me. Otherwise you would have been adopted a long time ago and be living in America now."

"How did you happen to come by and find me that morning?" I asked, freshly struck by my extraordinary luck: without his timely intervention I would have perished for sure.

"I was taking a morning walk."

"Did you live nearby?"

"Yes, in an inn. I still do but perhaps I should find a permanent place somewhere big enough for both of us after you get out of here."

"Aren't you married?"

"No."

"Have you been in Korea long?"

"Yes, since 1950. I was a GI during the war."

"But most GI's have gone home."

"I re-enlisted and stayed on. Only recently I left the US Army."

"You did not reenlist?"

"I tried to, but they wanted to send me to Europe. I didn't want to leave Korea."

"You must like it a lot," I said, surprised, because I couldn't imagine an American preferring to live in Korea.

"No, I don't care for it that much, either."

"Then what keeps you here?"

"I am under a curse and can't leave Korea, even if I want to," he said, pensively.

"Curse by a moodang?" I shouted, wondering that this tribe of women should have such influence even on somebody from America, the fountainhead of enlightenment and modern science. The moodang were sorceresses, exorcists, mediums with self-proclaimed psychic powers. Their most frequent function was to drive out or appease the ghosts of some dead relative who haunted those left behind in the form of sickness or other trouble. Otherwise they were called in to bless a birthday, wedding, or business opening, by offerings or other propitiatory gestures to the spirits. Of course, modern education put it down as superstition. But I could not understand Christianity, or any other religion for that matter, when they violently attacked and condemned the indigenous practice as "demonic," one being as spirit-oriented or demonic as the other as far as I could see.

"She is more powerful than a moodang," Alan said, who knew about this priesthood, as well as other facets of Korean life and culture. "She was a young Communist partisan woman, about my age or younger, who got caught and killed, along with a dozen others, her followers. I was at their brutal execution, and I didn't do a God-damn thing about it."

"But it wasn't your fault."

"She thought it was, said so loud and clear for the whole world to hear moments before she died, and I believed her. I still do."

Poor Alan, the incident had seared his soul! Her image followed him everywhere. He was no longer master of his own will and Korea held him in thrall, demanding atonement. He had tramped the woods and plains, the highways and lanes of Korea like the bewitched knight in Keats' La Dame Sans Merci. The ugly truths revealed by war had been too much for his uncommon sensitivity and idealism, but hadn't embittered him. Sweet and kind, he would go out of his way any minute to rescue a waif like me fallen on the wayside, dying. Nor did they snap his mind, as some thought. He was as sane or intelligent as the next man. His obsessive memory of someone long dead was therefore a tribute to his purity and goodness, not a sign of derangement or deficiency.

III.
Jinny Bay

"Her name was Jinny Bay," Alan narrated. "It happened during the Wonsan Retreat in the winter of 1950, about half a year into the war."

For an overview of the war scene at the time: by August of 1950, a month after invasion of the south, the North Korean Army was in control of the whole country, except for a small perimeter of resistance around Pusan. In a desperate gamble to avert a Dunkirk, General MacArthur landed in September a huge amphibious force, the largest since Normandy, at Inchon 150 miles northwest on the west coast, right in the enemy's backyard. The gamble paid off handsomely and the success was hailed as "the last gift of Mars to an old soldier." But nobody is content with a last gift, least of all MacArthur who wanted to trap and crush the main body of the North Korean People's Army fleeing north along the Taybag Range by launching another amphibious operation at Wonsan on the east coast. Detached from the Eighth Army, Alan's 10th Corps was sent by ship clear around the peninsula. Timing was of the essence. Unless they landed at Wonsan in 36 hours and connected overland with the forces on the west coast, it would be impossible to bag even the stragglers, let alone the main body of the People's Army.

MacArthur might scream and swear all he wanted but the X Corps couldn't land. When finally dumped ashore after yo-yoing up and down the Sea of Japan off the Wonsan coast for three weeks to give the minesweepers time to clear a channel through the "cabbage patch", the Corps found Wonsan already liberated by the South Korean Third Army, "the roaring ROK's" as they were called, bent on beating the Yanks to it to make up for the months of their craven retreats and defeats. They were already roaring up the coastal road to liberate some more. There being no work left for the Corps in the lowlands, MacArthur and Almond, Corps Commander, decided to proceed as originally planned: march northwest across the mountains and effect the link with the Eighth Army to close the pincers on the North Korean remnants, as if remnants still remained to be closed on.

So the men of the X Corps started hiking, but it was no picnic, with snowdrifts and hills blocking their way everywhere. The winter had come early to these forbidding heights, covered in deep snow and every bit as tricky as climbing Mt. Everest. But the word from MacArthur's GHQ in Tokyo was still to push on, snow or hill, to the Yalu, the China border. In the post-Inchon euphoria MacArthur's staff simply ignored intelligence reports of massive Red Chinese troop movements heading for Korea and scoffed at the "face-saving" Oriental gesture of Chou En-lai who had declared that Red China wouldn't stand idly by while her neighbor North Korea was being overrun by a foreign power. US patrols had caught dozens of Red Chinese soldiers who admitted under interrogation that their field armies, some 15 in number, had already crossed over and dug in the hills of North Korea by mid-November, but Tokyo wouldn't believe it. The maps and plans found on the POW's, spelling out the strategy of retaking Korea from the imperialist clutch of America, stuff known only to general officers in the West, were dismissed as a practical joke or a piece of deliberate dysinformation to diffuse and confound the offensive thrust of the UN Forces. Little did they know that the peasant army had a different philosophy about how to conduct a war: inform the lowliest private of top-level plans so he would fully appreciate his role and improvise and adjust as he went along in pursuit of the big goal.

Up and up the men went, deeper and deeper into the primeval forests and rocky peaks rising higher and ever higher until they camped on the solidly frozen Lake Jangjin or Shoshin as it was called then, because only Japanese maps were available and that was how it was pronounced in Japanese. Even if they had planned it all along, the Red Chinese couldn't have had it better, with the Americans walking right into their trap. The Corps got caught with their pants down. Drooling at the prospect of slaughter the Red Chinese hordes came crashing down, blowing pipes and beating drums.

Wonsan was the only salvation, where the LST's waited to transport the GI's to Pusan. The distance, 50 miles as the crow flies, from Jangjin to Wonsan, became ten times that, the road meandering with hairpin turns, up and down gorges and crests, the enemy firing point blank from high ground. Certainly there was close-in air support, with fighter bombers dropping 2,000 pounders with pinpoint accuracy on the enemy, often only a few feet away, but the foot soldiers did their share on the ground, too, breaking out in sorties of attack up the cliffs to knock out machine gun nests and trenches. They were awesome, these Americans, each equal to ten Chinese, who weren't backward either in raw courage or skill of artillery. They had orders to die killing at least one Yank, because with their numerical superiority they'd surely come out ahead.

"Poor bastards!" Alan reminisced. "I recall taking a trench filled with frozen Red Chinese, stiff like logs, leaning over the wall or crouching, faces pink under a film of frost, stiff hands still firmly grasping rifles."

The North Korean cold, no respecter of race or color, dealt much more harshly with the peasant soldier, padded though he might be in quilted cotton uniform, heavy with unwashed sweat and grime. So the GI's reached the sea, "attacking in the opposite direction," in the celebrated words of Marine Corps General Smith who refused to admit that he had retreated, licked.

"What happened to the Korean Third Army?" I asked out of idle curiosity, during a brief hiatus as Alan sipped his tea. We had been sitting at a table on the sun deck of the hospital cafeteria.

"They got decimated. Only a handful returned of the Army that had roared right up to the Tumen, the Soviet border. We were not out of the woods yet ourselves. The Red Chinese pressing close behind, we had to hightail out of Wonsan."

Before evacuation, however, steps were taken to leave nothing standing. Demolition teams were detailed all over the city to set up charges and blow up bridges, buildings, or anything of military value. At the last minute whole blocks were to be blown up by remote control and it was necessary to warn the local population, what was still left of it. Most had fled the city. US LST's had moved them out by the thousands but could not accommodate all. Turned back from the Navy docks, the refugees sailed in their own makeshift boats, leaky tubs that mostly perished in the stormy Sea of Japan. Others left on foot or by ox carts to starve and freeze on the road. Still there remained in the city pockets of people, the aged and the young abandoned by their families, the sickly or resigned. There wasn't a whole lot the Americans could do, and they should have just set the charges off and cleared out, but some commanding officer's conscience was troubled. Because of his ability to speak some basic Korean (he had a Korean roommate while at NYU and dated his sister) Alan was picked to go into the various sections of the city and make the broadcast about the impending holocaust.

With a complement of Korean Marines, loaned to the Corps for liaison from the ROK Command, his truck set out into the moonscape of Wonsan, weaving its way through the bombed-out dwellings, bumping along the cratered, chewed-up roadbeds, the loudspeaker mounted in the back blaring away the Korean messages. At the southern edge of the city, completing the circuit, they would turn and head back to the docks to flee the doomed city.

Rounding the half-crumbled wall of a house, Alan braked abruptly, almost running his head through the windshield. Armed with spears, sticks, long swords, and old bolt-action shoulder rifles of Japanese make captured from the North

Korean Army, a dozen Korean males, wearing armbands that read "Anti-Communist Self-Rule Team," stood around a knot of about as many young women, in their teens or early twenties, stripped naked.

Sgt. Cha, the ranking Korean Marine and a native of Wonsan, who also acted as Alan's backup interpreter, jumped off the vehicle and walked over to the men, unshaven, sunken-eyed, ragged, with whom he was already acquainted. Formerly hunted by the Communists as "reactionaries," these men had just returned from the south or resurfaced from underground and tracked down their previous tormentors. During the evacuation of the refugees by US vessels, they had acted as a screen, weeding out and preventing the wrong elements from obtaining passage south.

"These are Young Women's League partisans," explained Hur, a bearded Self-Ruler, "vicious hard-core Reds, who had the nerve to sneak aboard an LST as refugees to sabotage and wreak havoc on our rear."

Every gust of the wintry wind whipped up a few more welts and bumps on their pale skin. Alan stared out of his hooded parka at their tiny tits and scantily-haired genitalia, fascinated. Totally oblivious to their indignity and discomfort, the naked girls shouted their Communist slogans and screamed profanities at their captors. Irked by the absurd ritual, Sgt. Cha told the Self-Rulers to finish them off. But the Self-Rulers were adamant, though Alan couldn't quite see the point: the partisans had to be made to recant and confess their crimes before they were put to death.

Prodding with sticks and spears the Self-Rule people tempted the girls to curse Stalin and Ilsung Kim in return for their release and enlistment in the South Korean Women's Army Corps. For the trouble they received a barrage of colorful invectives. Cha cocked his automatic and shot a clip over their heads. That got him attention. He told the girls to shut up but was told in turn to shut up himself by Jinny Bay, their leader, who went on inspiring her naked comrades, certain to die by either freezing or shooting, to be defiant to the last. When she told Cha to shut up, something in her tone or idiom Alan couldn't quite catch triggered a general merriment among the Koreans, including the Self-Rulers and Korean Marines, apparently at Cha's expense. Noticing his face turn red and his arm lower his automatic, the men all became still, but the girls kept laughing and taunting. The men expected him to fire momentarily but he didn't. Handing the automatic to a corporal, Cha walked deliberately over to Jinny and raised his hand to seize her hair. In a lightning reflex her hand went up and scratched his face under the eye, drawing blood. Wiping his cheek, Cha unsheathed a bayonet and plunged it into the palm side of her forearm between the two long bones, radius and ulna. The blade went clear through. One twist of the steel and the pair of bones parted with a loud crack, snapping the binding ligaments, popping the carpal bones and phalanges out of alignment, shattering the evolutionary masterpiece, neuromuscular coordination of the human hand that can stroke a lover's face or play Paganini's Fantasia. Her maimed hand slumped below the wrist, fingers curled into a claw.

"Want to try the other one?" Cha mocked, wiping the blade.

"Slime!" she yelled, simultaneously her other hand flicking out and knocking him down. A Marine raised his M-1 and was pulling the trigger. Staggering up, Cha pushed the barrel aside.

"Let me take care of her my way," he muttered. "Oh, she's asking for it."

Jinny dodged and shifted so fast and deftly in spite of her handicap that it seemed for a while Cha would not be her match. Then she tripped and fell. As she tried to prop herself up on the good arm, down swung Cha's bayonet slicing through the forearm as before. There was the same crack of the parting bones, as she fell on her back. Even in this position she kicked, bit and spat, holding the men at bay. Finally overpowered, she was tied to the top of the exposed studs, first by her crippled hands, then by her feet, to hang spread-eagled above the other prisoners, somewhat in the manner of the Nazarene on the cross.

"We all know you are a Rusky whore with a big cunt," Cha jeered. A "Rusky whore" was as low as a woman could fall in North Korea, like her counterpart, "Yankee whore" in South Korea. I should know, for my mother must have been one, though I refused to acknowledge it and was always romanticizing about her person or status.

Jinny spat, bloody sputum landing on Cha's face. Wiping himself, Cha announced his intention to give her the "broomstick ride", because "she's itching for it." With a fused stick of TNT, a foot long and an inch in diameter, he went up to her, his eyes coming level with her crotch.

"You stink like a good Rusky whore," Cha said, fondling and sniffing at it in appreciation. The men laughed with lewd comments. Jinny pulled and struggled against the bindings on her limbs and spat at him. As he dodged playfully from side to side, fingering her mound erotically, a steaming jet of urine caught him smack in the eyes. Temporarily blinded and gagged, Cha jumped aside hugging his face. The crowd roared with laughter.

"They all piss and crap before they croak," Cha said, laughing nervously to hide his discomfiture. Stepping cautiously back up to her, he spread her legs farther apart and shoved the cylinder of TNT up her vagina, hammering the end in with the flat of his palm, until the peg tore its way the whole length into her abdomen. Blood dripped as from a faucet with a defective washer and thick drops of sweat rolled off her cold-blistered skin, her whole body shaking and writhing in pain, but not a groan escaped her lips, bleeding where her teeth had bit down. She took hold of herself somehow. From her elevated position she spoke in a hoarse yet penetrating Korean mezzo-soprano, thrilling not only her comrades with a new conviction in their cause, but their captors, war-hardened and insensitized men, who stood listening transfixed, in suspended animation.

All of a sudden, directing her gaze straight at Alan, she said in a cavernous voice that was to ring in his head as long as he lived: "You are responsible, and will pay for this."

There were others around him, Self-Rulers and Marines,

but nobody, least of all Alan himself, the only American, doubted who she meant. Nor was there any need for translation. His Korean might be spotty but intuitively he understood the full import of every syllable of her accusation.

"Yes, I know," Alan nodded, crushed by the burden of guilt for the macabre farce enacted before him, for the war, the hate, cruelty, inhumanity that filled the world.

"Don't mind the bitch," Cha said, steering Alan away and ordering his men to light the fuse.

The fire sputtered its way an inch a second, a corporal standing by with a pair of scissors.

"Say Ilsung Kim did a blow job on Stalin," Cha offered. "You will all go free."

In reply she and her comrades burst into the exultant melody of the Glorious Leader, a hymn to Ilsung Kim. Only a foot remained of the fuse. The men, including the Corporal with the scissors, had moved to the other side of the prisoners, away from her.

"This is your last chance," Cha yelled, cocking a pistol and aiming at the crackling ever-shortening fuse.

"Long live the People's Republic of Korea!" went up Jinny's frenzied chant. "Long live Ilsung Kim, our Leader! Long live Stal...."

The Soviet's name got truncated by the explosion. A blinding shower of bloody particles rained down in a twenty-foot radius, dabbing the prisoners with wild splashes of red. But singing their song of martyrdom deliriously none of them even blinked their eyes or wiped themselves.

A convoy of trucks pulled up, GI's in Demolition on their way back to the docks, gloriously drunk and in the best of humor. No other branch of the service enjoyed a higher morale. Nothing went to one's head quite like sheer destruction. For that brief moment one felt what every child feels when burning books, smashing glass, hammering a Rolls Royce, a sense of power in being able to erase the fruit of thousands of man-hours, the thrill that perhaps the assassins of Lincolns or Kennedys feel, overgrown children with arrested brains, who see in the fall of their renowned victims a transformation of their own drab existence into something equal or grander than those they undo.

"Why waste all the good meat?" protested the Top Sergeant, Tom Cades, a hulking Virginian. "Let's each grab one. There's enough to go around."

"They are confirmed Reds, murderers, and these people want to execute them properly for their crimes," Alan tried to explain.

"These little weanlings? You've got to be kidding. Cunts are cunts, man, mostly red inside anyway."

"You'll outrage these men, damage our image as fighters for freedom and justice...."

Disgusted by his naivete, Tom and his buddies were about to help themselves, pushing Alan aside, but in the sullen watchfulness of the armed Koreans they sensed trouble and delay. As it was, they were all running behind schedule and were due back at the ship that very minute.

"Tell you what, friend," Cades said after mollifying his disgruntled companions. "We'll take the problem off your hands. We'll tie them each by a rope to the back of our truck and drag them."

Liking this course of action as much or more, for sexual passion can turn into violence and murder at a snap of the fingers, the GI demolitionists pawed over and handled the squirming Asian female bodies that still put up a resistance, kicking, biting, scratching. At last, ankles tied to ropes hanging from the back of the vehicles, most of the girls lay on the icy ground in an exhausted swoon but some struggled up and sat on their haunches or tried to stand. Before any of them could reach and work at their tethers with their frozen fingers, not that it would have done any good, the trucks roared off, bumping and thrashing the bodies over the uneven terrain. By the time they reached the docks, none of the ropes bore any trace of their original burden, shredded and scattered over the countryside.

IV.
Tadpole's House

The free ride at the hospital came to an end at last and Alan took me to the house he had just rented atop Gahway-dong Hill. If this suggests a choice view lot, think again. The only access was by roads that zigzagged between abutting houses, forcing one to walk uphill nearly an hour after getting off the bus or taxi. The high elevation meant low or no water pressure. There were other disadvantgages galore, but Alan felt lucky to have found it. Seoul was still digging out from under the rubble of war and housing was at a premium.

Our house was a square doughnut, the open courtyard in the middle surrounded by eight rooms, every one of them rented. The owner of the house, nicknamed Tadpole because of his outsized head, had seen better days with important connections all the way up to the Blue House, as he was quick to point out, but the war had wiped out his wealth, forcing him to stoop to the indignity of renting out the rooms. Still, occupying the main wing, consisting of anbang, the main room, with attached kitchen and maroo, the hall, and sarangbang across from it, his family of six, including his wife, two children, and two unmarried sisters, could keep up the facade of aristocracy relative to his tenants, each family of four or five crammed into one room, less than half the size of the anbang.

So it was not without resentment that he and his family gave up the main wing to us and moved into the room next to the kitchen, just vacated. Alan had made an offer he couldn't refuse, two years' rent in advance. But, behind our backs and sometimes to our face, Tadpole never ceased to denounce American imperialism, malign us as yangnom, Western louts, and play mean little tricks, except nothing could faze either of us, a Jinny Bay retainer and a graduate of the Mercy Home.

Alan had the anbang naturally and I the sarangbang, all to myself, a luxury I had not known before. Above all I could read in it undistracted. The wall was adobe and the doors were literally paper thin, grass paper pasted over a wood frame, and kept nothing out. So one could hear even breathing in the next room, let alone loud talking and arguing, of which there was aplenty. But once I picked up a book, the world disappeared. After I went through Alan's private collection of books, none too small, he kept me supplied with loans from the US Army library in Yongsan. My room was my university and sanctuary, insulating me from the chaos that reigned outside, though at times they became too assertive to be ignored.

Every family had a radio, which they played at top volume all day, sometimes all night. Children cried and adults fought. The worst of the lot was Tadpole's household, a keg of dynamite ready to explode at any second. One of his unmarried sisters he lived with was a mental retard, whose only joy in life was eating. She ate and ate, getting bloated, and would fight back like a tigress when frustrated. Tadpole's wife, stingy by nature, couldn't tolerate the parasite, and did her best to keep food out of her reach, often coming to blows. The other sister would then join in, sometimes on her sister's side, sometimes on her sister-in-law's, as her mood dictated. Then Tadpole's two children, 3 and 5, fought with each other or hurled themselves against the fighting adults, the brawl often becoming a mass of five bodies tearing at each other five ways, which Tadpole was apt to make six when he was around.

Although the families did almost everything in their respective rooms, sleep, eat, cook with a hibachi, excrete into a chamber pot, there were a few things they had to do outside. For example, serious cooking like boiling rice in the cast iron cauldron had to be at the fireplace fitted to the underfloor flue outside the room under twatmaroo, a wooden ledge one stepped on to enter the room a couple of feet above ground.

Only our main wing had an enclosed kitchen of its own, but we had to access it from outside, by going down a couple of feet below ground, as its fireplaces were also connected to the underfloor flues of the main room, to make sure the cooking heat went to the warming of the room, too. No resource was wasted in Korea.

Also adult defecation was performed at dwidgan, the toilet catering to some 30 residents. Consequently, patronage was heavy and one had to use something akin to military vigilance and celerity to occupy it. Even if an opening developed and one gained entrance, one wasn't allowed to go about his or her business in peace, as the next user would come dashing and yank the door open. To prevent such rude exposure, the inside of the door had a hook to catch an eye driven into the jamb, but the pulling was so hard, especially by Tadpole, that the hook seldom stayed in place for long.

Not to mislead by the term "toilet," a description of its construction is in order: a 3 by 10 foot cubicle by the gate with a plank floor fitted over a cement tank below, though the concrete might not be leakproofed. This was the norm or better than the norm for most Korean homes at the time, with only a pit in the ground for an "outhouse", but after a few months of the flushing toilet at the hospital I was as snobbish about it as any American fresh off the plane and setting foot in Korea, "a pile of shit from one end to the other." But Alan's example humbled me. Uncomplainingly, almost cheerfully, he submitted to the smelly, fly-blown, maggot-crawling abomination. After entering, one stepped gingerly on the creaky boards, rotted and loose, and squatted over the 10-by-20-inch rectangle cut in the middle of the floor. To save money on the number of night soil buckets to be hauled away, Tadpole strictly enforced the "chamber pot rule", that is, collecting urine in the family's chamber pot and emptying at the drain in the courtyard, no matter how it stank in consequence. As a result his tank did not present the unpleasantness of "splashing" often encountered at other places. But it created other problems.

The rats, for one, that crawled and scavenged on the

firmer mass more surefootedly. Because of high usage, the tank filled up quickly, bringing the rodents into brushing proximity to the occupant's buttocks. The city sanitation crew came around once a week, hoarsely shouting "Empty your tanks!" at the top of their voices to herald their presence in the neighborhood, as if not already obvious from their signature, the reek from the pair of 10-gallon buckets slung on a pole balanced over their shoulder. These men, lowliest of the lowly, merrily trotted from house to house, filling their buckets and carrying them at a run to the night soil truck, parked at some central collection point on the street, to be paid so much per bucket. Naturally they preferred the watery mixture to the thick, and were apt to skip those that were particularly gummy, as in Tadpole's establishment. In winter the mass froze like stone, contributing even more to their reluctance to come to our house.

After feeding, the rodents showed a definite preference for the ceilings in the main wing, above our heads, as their playing field. So rambunctious were they in their antics that I feared they might fall through the holes in the paper ceiling any time. With paste made out of flour I papered over the holes several times, but each time, as soon as the glue dried, the rats chewed up the new closure, as if it were some special wafer prepared for their particular delectation, exactly retracing the old holes.

A rusty water pipe stuck out of the ground in the courtyard but there was hardly any pressure. What little dripped out of the faucet was monopolized by the Tadpole family. So we had to go down the hill to the public faucet, a half mile distance, and wait in line with two 5-gallon buckets, paying 10 won per bucket. Sometimes the wait could be as long as one hour, but I didn't mind, as I could spend the time reading. I dissuaded Alan from this task: an adult and full-blooded Caucasian, he was more likely to attract attention.

Theoretically, the house had electrical lighting, a quantum leap from kerosene lamps or candles in most homes of post-War Korea. But we had to have the backup ready anyway, as the transformers on the poles were apt to blow out all the time. Blaming them on illegal use of appliances like irons or heaters, though I couldn't imagine anybody in the neighborhood rich or temerarious enough to own such luxury contraband, the power company took their time repairing. Even when there was power available, it provided the most perverse kind of illumination, dimmer than the glow of a firefly during the early hours of the evening when it was most needed and piercingly bright when it was time to go to sleep.

The biggest chore in winter was tending the briquette fire. Briquettes, cylindrical blocks of black anthracite mixed with mud and saw dust, 7 inches high and 8 inches in diameter, with 29 vertical holes, heated the room by burning slowly, about 20 hours each, in the underfloor flue. The trick was not to let a briquette burn out before it got a new one started, because it took a lot of charcoal or firewood to kindle anthracite, the only abundant domestic fuel but the least combustible of coals. A new briquette had to be placed on top of a glowing one, holes lined up, so by the time the bottom one burned out and had to be removed the top one had caught and glowed, ready to pass on the heat to the next one to be placed on top. The ash, dumped everywhere illegally, became a dust storm and raised the street level several inches each winter.

The inconvenience, ineffeciency, and mess of handling anthracite was nothing compared to the lethal toll from its fume, carbon monoxide. Despite the care the builders must take to leak-proof the mud floor and cover with oiled paper, cracks developed and the deadly fume seeped into the room, generally made air tight against the arctic cold. In Seoul alone thousands died every winter, and many more became brain damaged. The fume, no respecter of persons, cut down people in the upper echelons too, like Jaypil Kim, a banker known to be Syngman Rhee's favorite. He lived, though the whore he slept with in the inn died, only to become a drooling idiot for the rest of his life. Nevertheless, before Korea began importing natural gas and oil, millions in Seoul and other cities survived the six or seven months of winter through this primitive and dangerous method of heating, still considered modern and urban compared to what they had in the rural areas, smoky firewood foraged from the already denuded mountains or rice straw with its other important uses such as rope making, sacking, roofing, fertilizer.

V.
Foreign Language Institute

A frugal man with no extravagant habits, Alan had been living in Korea on his savings from his army pay without having to work since his discharge, thanks to the lopsided exchange rate that made a US Army private wealthier than a Korean cabinet minister. But his money wouldn't last forever and it was time he looked for a job. Looking in the Korean papers, I found an ad by MOR, Ministry of Reconstruction: native English speakers wanted to teach at FLI, Foreign Language Institute, under joint management of MOR and UNKRA, United Nations Korean Reconstruction Agency. The language program was a big part of the US aid to rebuild Korea, meriting higher priority than power or fertilizer plants. American education opened all doors, cabinet minister, corporation head, privileges and immunities. But to go to America one needed English. FLI was therefore like the first stepping stone to success and fortune, outranking in importance any other academic department in the whole of Seoul National University. In fact, it was housed in the only decent brick building left untouched on campus, whereas the President of the University had to be content with a temporary wooden structure across from it.

"You are one hell of a finder, John," Alan said jubilantly, but soon he had reason to regret acting on my tip: he should have applied, not to the Korean Ministry, but to UNKRA, which he could have done as an American national. He was forever to be a local hire, which meant dirt cheap. George

Molinbeck, its Director, could have put Alan on UNKRA payroll without lifting a finger but wouldn't. Actually George was duty bound to tenure a foreign employee within a few months, regardless of the origin of hire. Months would pass but Molinbeck left Alan untenured, temporary, on tenter hooks, so he could bleed Alan dry and spit him out at his pleasure. Each time Alan asked George to make him an UNKRA employee, George said Alan was not qualified, never specifying his criteria for qualification. In no respect was either of George's pet boys, Lindenberg and Kyelsen, who wallowed in security and luxury as UNKRA staff, better qualified than Alan. In fact, Alan had a B.A. in English from NYU and knew at least as much English as either of them. Of German birth and Jewish descent, Lindenberg had come to the States when he was in his teens and did not know how to put a decent sentence together in English, but was a tenured English instructor. Kyelsen, a New Zealander and geography dropout, was also tenured and on UNKRA payroll.

Molinbeck, who owed his position to his friendship with General Kubal, head of UNKRA, derived from the Institute, his private fief, a staggering salary of $12,000 per annum, tax free, when a Korean worker was lucky to make $300. His two henchmen drew $9,000 each. Other employees, foreigners and Koreans, were locally hired, some getting paid from the UNKRA expense account and some, like Alan, by the Ministry. Alan's pay in local currency was the exact equivalent of $1,000 a year, one-twelfth of Molinbeck's. This was particularly unfair because FLI had been getting two for one. I had been Alan's unofficial teaching assistant, interpreting between him and his Korean pupils in class when the going got rough, as it often did, perhaps because of the huge size of our classes, over 100 in each, more popular than any in the whole Institute. Under the FLI charter only government and military officials going abroad on business or for training and education were to be allowed in but there was a genius on the administrative staff, Registrar Gwon, who knew all the loopholes and enrolled anybody who could pay. Molinbeck knew about it but, whenever Gwon's name was mentioned, he hastened to extol him as "the only honest Korean you can trust completely."

Small as Alan's pay was, he didn't get paid the first three months. Whenever Alan raised the subject to Molinbeck and asked for assistance, Molinbeck said it was none of his business.

"But you are my employer," Alan would point out.

"Most certainly not," Molinbeck shouted. "MOR is. Go to MOR."

Alan had to chase down the buck-passing Korean MOR officials and dun them daily, who hugely enjoyed dangling the carrot before a needy Caucasian, saying that there was a glitch in their budget allocations. Alan threatened to write to the Blue House or the White, without impressing them much. Finally, in the fourth month, they reluctantly paid up, "from our Special Fund," as if they were doing a big favor.

One day Alan brought home a stray mongrel, dirty, mangy, ribs sticking out, hair matted by blood from abuse. Obviously its poor condition had been its protection to date from the attention of dog catchers.

"I was waiting for a bus when she came around and licked my shoes, tail between her legs, fearing a kick," Alan said.

Alan washed, fed, and pampered her as if she were a human child, until she regained her health, her hair grew glossy, and her temperament revealed itself as playful and cuddly.

"Let's give her a name," Alan said. "Any suggestions?"

"No," I said. "We can't call her Spotty or Spots because she has no spots. Nor a Goldie because her color is closer to gray...."

"Why so many negatives? I'll name her Sonia after a girl I once dated back in the States."

Alan couldn't bear to part with her long and took her everywhere, except to FLI. When he did one fateful day, he was to regret it forever. He had never been Molinbeck's favorite, but the Sonia incident doomed any hope of improvement in their relationsip.

Mrs. Waters, the Institute secretary, sat near the door, pounding away at her typewriter, not deigning to acknowledge our entrance. We went to Alan's desk by the window. There was yet half an hour before his first class.

A big late model Cadillac drove in at the gate and parked in front of the FLI building. Who should step out of it like royalty on a state visit but the Institute Director Molinbeck! Just the day before Alan had seen him driving around in his Buick. Molinbeck always kept his own private car, though there was an UNKRA vehicle for his exclusive personal use.

"When did he buy the new Cadillac, Mrs. Waters?" Alan asked.

She came over to the window and looked at the black, sleek beauty.

"Hm, it's his fifth," she said, turning down the corners of her mouth. "I wonder how much he got for his Buick this time. Probably $10,000."

"Ten thousand dollars for that pile of junk?"

"He bought it originally for less than $300."

"Oh, no," Alan moaned.

"Don't you know this automobile resale business is the biggest racket in the whole world?" she said, with a disdainful glance at him. "Koreans jump at you if you have any kind of car to sell. We may give them a billion dollars in aid but we sure take five or ten back this way. So it works out fine and dandy for all the parties concerned. The whole business is just appalling. I would never allow my husband Stanley to do such a thing even if he could. You see only those with diplomatic privileges can do it. They can bring in two cars, but somehow people like Mr. Molinbeck can manage to bring in six or seven. Don't you think it's a little unethical?"

With that query ringing in the air she strode back to her station to go on punishing the typewriter. It was time for us to go to class. We were just stepping out the door with Sonia when Mrs. Waters looked up.

"Are you guys taking that dog with you to class?" she asked.

"Yes, why not?"

"If you don't know, you'll soon find out."

Every student was present and waiting. The class was

packed. I took the seat the students reserved for me in front before the platform, on which Alan stood, facing the class, Sonia in his arms.

"Good morning!" Alan greeted.

"Good morning!" the class returned, averting their eyes from Sonia.

"Isn't she pretty?" Alan asked, stroking Sonia affectionately.

Nobody made an answer, puzzled by his making so much of something they ate as part of their regular diet. They might as well be asked to get excited about a stick of turnip. Alan had intended to base the English conversation part of the day on dogs, their being men's best friends, and so forth, but, not getting an enthusiastic response exactly, he had to put her down and change the subject to the one in the textbook, something about democracy at work in the US. The students were no superachievers by a long shot and we would be lucky to get through a whole page in one hour, translating and explaining even the simplest sentences over and over. No wonder Sonia got bored and pattered off to the stove in the middle of the room with a sand box next to it where people threw scraps of paper, empty cigarette packs, or candy wraps. At once she was at home and started tearing the rubbish to bits.

Intuitively guessing that the class was over from people starting to talk, rising from their seats or moving around, Sonia scooted back up to Alan, who picked her up as well as other class material and exited the room hastily. There was no time to lose, because Molinbeck himself would be walking in any minute. Originally Molinbeck was to teach three or four classes a week but gradually this number dwindled down to two, then one, and finally none, as befitted the dignity of the Director. This was for now his one weekly class. Alan headed for his office, past the stairs.

"We'll be downstairs," I called out to Alan, referring to Wansong Char.

We had met at the Aran Ham Center for Korean Folk Music, where Alan had been a serious student for some time, with me coming along for company and for lark mostly.

"Okay, guys," Alan said, waving to Wansong.

We both liked him a lot. Everything about him was delightful, his nimble gait, fluid body movement, engaging and sweet personality, witty Jolla speech, for he came like many others at the Center from Jolla Province. Already a master of folk dancing and music, though in his early twenties, he had opened my eyes to this dimension of my Korean heritage.

No sooner had Wansong and I begun talking at the foot of the staircase than Alan came bounding down, Sonia in arms, Molinbeck in tow, fist raised. At the upper landing Molinbeck gave up the chase, but not without letting out a blood-curdling yell, "Alan!," that reverberated throughout the building. No doubt he would have gone on yelling at undiminished volume, but for his notice of the attention the commotion was attracting. For days the students at FLI talked about nothing but the Sonia Incident.

According to eyewitness reports, as soon as he stepped into the room, Molinbeck saw the shreds of paper littered around the sandbox, which he kept staring with a severe frown for ever and ever.

"All right," he said finally, pointing at the offense. "Which one of you did it?"

Nobody answered because they thought it a trivial matter, which was doubly reprehensible in Molinbeck's view: there was something downright sinister about the amorality, insensitivity of this inferior race without the benefit of the civilizing influence of America. Accordingly he went on and on about the virtue of tidiness and cleanliness which was only second to godliness.

"Let me tell you something," he said. "In America no one throws a piece of paper or spits on the street. Here you throw paper and spit. I saw ten people spitting on the pavement as I drove to school this morning. You all know how uncivilized littering is and how unsanitary spitting is...."

When he thought he had made a sufficient impression, he paused and surveyed the room with the serenity of a conquering general. Though he paid lip service to debate and invited people to offer opinions, only a fool or a total stranger would take him up on his word, for by opinion he meant consent. Doubt or argument of any kind was anathema. If anybody dared to contradict him, that person got either sacked or divorced. After divorcing his American wife Melinda for talking back, Molinbeck had married a half Korean, half Japanese girl who did not.

"Now for the last time, which one of you did it?"

One of the students decided to speak up.

"Mr. Heyman's dog did it."

Face turning red as a ripe tomato about to burst, he strode out of the classroom, boiling with rage. Stomping into the faculty room, he pointed his finger of damnation at Sonia, screaming, "Alan Heyman! Take that canine home."

"What did she do?" Alan asked, taken aback.

"Take that damn bitch away or I swear I'll kill it with my own bare hands."

Sonia whimpered and hid behind Alan, as Molinbeck lunged at her. Hadn't Alan made a timely escape in the manner described, Molinbeck would surely have choked them both to death.

There was another untenured Caucasian on the FLI faculty under Molinbeck's tyranny, Henri Cerviet, a Frenchman born in Belgium, teaching French. Upon discharge from the Belgian Battalion that had fought in Korea during the war, he had married a Korean girl, and was employed like Alan as local hire. But he had a tougher time making it than even Alan. French not being in much demand, few students signed up for his class. Unable to afford a place any closer, he lived in Yongdungpo south of Seoul across the Han in a miserable slum, apparently full of thieves who constantly robbed him of what little he owned. In the morning he had to commute by bus a distance of about ten miles. Any bus ride at this time from any point in and around Seoul was an experience in body compression that only the fittest survived. Especially at Yongdungpo the teeming population jammed the streets and mobbed the buses, until they fairly carried them on their shoulders. Clawing and kicking was the standard method of getting aboard, but once inside it was luck if one did not get crushed to death or suffocated. There were pickpockets on the bus and Cerviet was always picked. Besides the buses broke down halfway across the bridge over the Han or, still worse, dived off into the river or sand. To show up for work at all by this means of transportation was a minor miracle, a triumph of will power, which should excuse trivial circumstances like being late for class. But Molinbeck did not look at it that way and was mighty unhappy with the Frenchman, who had, incidentally, scuttled for good Molinbeck's pet theme about 'Korean time'. It was to be Koreans, without the benefit of European civilization, that did not have a clear sense of chronometric time, not Americans, certainly not West Europeans, which Cerviet was.

One day Alan took the liberty of asking the UNKRA driver Shim to pick up Cerviet before anyone else in the morning so he would not have to take the awful bus. The 15-seater van was after all for personnel working at FLI and ran half empty most of the time, so nobody made a fuss about Alan making me ride along for the morning commute from time to time. Alan had felt certain Shim would not mind obliging him with this favor, a purely altruistic one as he could plainly see. Shim owed Alan and me one, if anybody did. Of all the Koreans eager to practice English on us, he was probably the most aggressive and monopolized one of us whenever he had the chance, for free pronunciation and grammar corrections. But Shim did mind. To go all the way to Yongdungpo he would have to wake up half an hour earlier in the morning. Friendship or not, he reported the matter to Gwon, the all powerful Registrar, the "only honest Korean," who in turn duly reported the irregularity to his life-giver George Molinbeck. Alan was at his desk reading a newspaper when Molinbeck stormed into the faculty room in a fit of rage. Cerviet was in class.

"What right do you have to tell our driver to go to Yongdungpo?" Molinbeck roared. "You are not even an UNKRA man. This car belongs to UNKRA."

"I know that," Alan said. "But this Frenchman has a serious problem getting here to work in the morning.

Yesterday morning he lost his watch for the third time."

"What concern of yours is that?"

"Purely humane."

"Stop being a joker. You are not your brother's keeper."

The suffering of a fellowman never moved Molinbeck. He might talk suavely about tremendous aid to Korea, the conscience of the United Nations, Christianity and brotherly love, but would, without batting an eye, walk right over a man who was actually falling dead. His own private Cadillac, never intended for use to begin with, was garaged securely at his big, luxurious house in Shindangdong, waiting for the right buyer to come along. Shim went to him at eight and waited at least one hour till nine o'clock or often later when the Director felt like sleeping overtime. But that was all right. To divert the vehicle to Yongdungpo for Cerviet before it came to Shindangdong was too much. Poor Cerviet could not cope with the rigor of life in Korea for too long. Korean diet did not agree with him and made him constantly sick, but Western food was way out of reach in Korea to a person of his income. Finally, by miracle, he managed to save enough to take his wife with him home. We didn't hear from them except for a postcard from London a year later, which made us wonder because we thought they were living with his parents in France.

Before leaving Seoul, Cerviet had introduced us to two other Belgians, both formerly of the Belgian Brigade that had fought in Korea under the UN flag. One was Bergson who stayed on in Korea after discharge to marry a Korean girl he had met during the war. She was willing to sell herself to buy food for her family, parents and siblings who had been driven out of their farm near Pyongtak during the war. While in the army his salary enabled her family to return to their farm, except for her who remained behind to live in a room near Bergson's post, so he could visit off duty. Now married and together full time but incomeless, they suffered from poverty worse than even a Korean's. His previous trade, stone masonry, was not much help, being oversupplied with local talent. Still they were happy, carrying on as if they had not a worry in the world, though neither spoke the other's language and they communicated in a pidgin that jumbled English, French, Korean, and Japanese. Unable to make ends meet in Seoul they moved to Pyongtak to live with the wife's family and work on the farm. Whenever he came to visit us in Seoul, Bergson looked ghostly, coughing, sunken face covered with beard that reached down to his chest, uncut, uncombed hair straggling from under his beret down his back. Then we heard he had moved back to Seoul to work in a construction crew for the Eighth US Army Corps of Engineers. He started at the bottom, getting the same wages as a Korean laborer but, strong and honest, he soon got promoted to foreman. At night he went to the US Army Education Center and got himself a college degree. Next time we saw him, he was visibly prosperous, on a motorcycle, his full, florid face clean shaven, fine suit, hat, and shiny shoes betraying no trace of the man who had kissed death only a few months before.

The other Belgian was Hans Kohler, a sharp dresser and an engaging rogue, who never stayed put in a job or a marriage and, pursuant to an avowed philosophy that it was unmanly to work for an honest dollar, aggressively engaged in blackmarketeering, selling smuggled US Army PX goods to Koreans, a business most foreigners in Korea went into at one time or other. Not Alan, though, who hadn't done it when he was still in the Army and had access to the PX and certainly didn't now as a civilian with no such access. But not a day would pass without some Korean offering Alan double or triple the PX cost of fountain pens, watches, radios, stereos, refrigerators, even apparels and footwear.

Alan and I were walking home after a concert at the Folk Music Center when we ran into Hans, who hugged and spun us around, insisting that he treat us to a boolgogi (broiled beef) dinner at a restaurant. He had just been paid $10,000 for marrying a Korean girl.

"The easiest money I've ever made," Hans said, rapturously. "She flew off to Japan, as soon as her Belgian passport came through!"

When we met Hans a few days later, he was still riding high on the tide of good fortune.

"I have finally met a girl from a good family I really like," he said, praising her merits to high heaven.

But at an UNKRA reception on UN Day soon afterwards, where practically the whole foreign community was invited, we found him crestfallen. The girl of his dreams would have nothing to do with him, not even a chaste kiss, before their marriage, another sure sign of her good breeding. But his application at the Belgian Embassy turned up his previous paper marriage he had forgotten all about. He tried every means to locate his nominal wife in Japan, Belgium, all over the world, but there was no trace of her whereabouts. Meanwhile, the one true love of his life lost patience with him who couldn't deliver and married someone who could, none other than our friend Lindenberg at FLI.

Like every tyrant Molinbeck had his toadies and stooges, among whom Lindenberg and Kyelsen were the top captains. Particularly invaluable to him was Lindenberg, an ex-Army CID man with extensive police and military connections, both Korean and American. It was Lindenberg who had helped straighten out the incredibly complicated paperwork for Molinbeck's marriage to the half Korean, half Japanese wife, Yoko. Though he was now out of the Army and the CID, Lindenberg never got over his former occupational habit, and busied himself with investigations of all sorts, generally uncalled for, both for himself and for his employer Molinbeck, just to be in practice. No doubt he would have found out about my real identity, had he put his mind to it, but neither he nor his boss saw any point in that, and I was allowed to hang around, unobtrusively, as an attachment or other to the local hire Alan Heyman. Besides at this particular juncture our detective happened to be occupied otherwise.

A confirmed bachelor for a long time, most probably because no woman could stand a sneaky ex-sleuth, Lindenberg suddenly took it into his head, at the age of forty-four, that he must have a son and heir for all the money he was making. By applying to a regular Korean matchmaker, he got himself a twenty-nine-year old bride. His wedding was the highlight of the year, a social, cultural sensation that people talked about for a long time. Nothing was good enough for him except a genuine Korean royal wedding. He ordered the elaborate costumes not only for the royal bride and groom but for the carriers of the flower-covered litter, the musicians and dancers, those in the procession, and other sundry attendants. Bribing just the right places he managed to open up for his wedding one of the more private royal palaces, the Secret Garden. On that day the high roofed gate, firmly closed to the public, stood open with uniformed guards in profound obeisance bowing to the royal parade. The ceremony was held by the side of the pond in the middle of a thicket of birches and spruces that perfurmed the air. The weeping willows along the edge of the pond dipped their branches in the water, dragonflies hovered and darted, frogs skipped from one floating lily pad to another, fish of all colors leapt to snap at unwary victims, and songbirds sang more throatily than ever in the branches, as if in commentary on the solemn buffoonery below. The total bill was so enormous that even with his inflated income Lindenberg had to pay in several installments. Because of his precipitate departure from Korea, for reasons to be shown below, he could never quite clear the debt.

Lindenberg was very much enamored of his bride Yonghee, and had the habit of singing her virtues loudly in public, obviously unaware of the Korean dictum, "One who brags about his child is a half fool; one who brags about his wife is a whole fool."

One day the FLI staff had to attend a ceremony at the Ministry of Education and Alan and I got in Shim's van, assured that the UNKRA brass had found other means of transportation. The van was stopped at the gate and the security guard told Shim to turn around and pick up some more passengers, who turned out to be Molinbeck, Lindenberg, Kyelsen, and others. Those sitting in front hurriedly vacated their seats and moved to the back. Fortunately, Alan and I had been far back to begin with and didn't have to move. The dignitaries installed themselves in style, barely glancing at the back, and started talking loudly among themselves, as if none of us existed. Soon the conversation moved to the topic of yangban or Korean aristocracy.

"My wife is yangban," Lindenberg said suddenly in his booming voice, jumping up, as if he dared anybody to contradict him.

No Korean owned up he or she was anything but yangban, everyone having some great ancestor, real or fictitious, to boast somewhere along the line. The elongated lineage, clan origin and spread, and other profundities would be displayed at a moment's notice to anybody who showed the least interest. Lindenberg did not give any such particulars to support his assertion but reiterated his wife's aristocracy, using the same words, punctuating the conversation which had by now moved on to another territory. I caught the driver Shim grinning surreptitiously and nudged Alan.

"I couldn't help it," Shim said when we were alone. "I have known Bongja for a long time. Her real name is Bongja Min, not Yonghee Kim, as she calls herself now. She was a gisang, a geisha entertainer, the kind you can get by the dozen if you throw a twenty-dollar party. She is thirty-nine years old, not twenty-nine, and was once married, but was thrown out because she couldn't bear any child."

"But Lindenberg married her expressly to get a son," Alan observed.

"Well, Mr. Lindenberg may do better but her former husband had no such luck. Nor any other man either because she never takes any contraceptives. I am pretty sure something is wrong with her rather than with all these men, at least a legion I assure you. I know her former husband. He would have screwed her a hundred times a day if it worked, but it hadn't."

Shim chuckled over his own bon mots, as we stood wondering at the irony of it all. Lindenberg was detested by many Koreans for his arrogant, abrasive, racist manners. His English classes kept shrinking, until only one third was left. With no notion of what class teaching was meant to be, he spent the whole hour telling his opinion of life, which was too much even for Koreans lapping up any swill like Holy Writ, provided it was from a foreigner. One day Molinbeck called

Lindenberg to his office and had a long conference. After this Lindenberg was to teach a German class instead of English, but his German was limited. Persecuted for his race he had left Germany at a young age, retaining very little of the language. Probably Molinbeck's logic was to assign him where he would do the least damage, because registrants for German classes could be counted on the fingers of one hand.

Perhaps to console the hurt pride of his lieutenant, Molinbeck invited the entire faculty to dinner one night at his palatial Japanese mansion in Shindangdong. The ostensible reason for the occasion was "testimonial for Lindenberg," a lie if there ever was one, but everybody was glad to come for the food, even Mrs. Waters, who disdained dishonest money but never refused to accept dinner invitations from whatever source. Of course, I was not there: Molinbeck's hospitality wouldn't extend beyond Alan, whom he barely tolerated. Even if asked, I would have hesitated, lest my presence might set off the investigatory interest of Lindenberg, the guest of honor and ex-gumshoe. Nor did I miss much from Alan's vivid description.

Lindenberg and his wife Yonghee occupied prominent seats. His usual self, Lindenberg never shut up, thinking that his talk thrilled and edified his listeners. Yoko, Molinbeck's wife, sat at the end of the table opposite to her lord and master, wearing an elegant kimono in the distinctive style of a Japanese noblewoman. She never admitted to the Korean half of her blood and was perhaps Molinbeck's inspiration for belittling everything that was Korean and lauding everything that was Japanese. To Molinbeck Korean kimchee was an abomination, smelly, rotten, unfit for human consumption, and all Koreans were dishonest, unethical, immoral, amoral. In fact, he thought Koreans a subhuman species. That evening it pleased Molinbeck to again engage his mental energy in his favorite pastime, denigration of Korea. From the venom and force of his vilifications one might have thought he would be on the next plane out. But no. He stayed on. He never thought of relinquishing his lucrative estate and did everything to keep it under his tight control, when, for example, the newly-instituted American aid agency, OEC, Office of the Economic Coordinator, tried to take over FLI from UNKRA as the latter was soon to be scuttled.

Molinbeck was the most inconsistent man on the subject of sex and morals. Hearing him deplore the depravity of courting gisang and permitting concubines, one would have thought him St. Paul himself, especially from his straight, aristocratic bearing. But in the presence of the fair sex his tongue suddenly loosened up as if by a magic key and unmouthables, the most direct and colorful variety, gushed out of his mouth, while with keen relish he watched from the corner of his eye his female audience squirm and blush with embarrassment. After the dinner that night, the guests went to the living room, sat around and talked. There were of course a few ladies in the circle.

"Jim boy," Molinbeck turned to Lindenberg abruptly. "What have you got to show for screwing your wife all these months? I imagine you to have been at it day and night, knowing you. Where is your son?"

But Molinbeck was the boss, whose goodwill none of the distinguished company could afford to jeopardize. Even Mrs. Waters, one of the ladies there, affected a smile instead of a frown, her usual facial expression with beings of lesser order. Lindenberg defended his wife instantly, saying that he had become a romantic lover and his wife's barrenness did not matter so long as he loved her. Feeling uncomfortable at the general drift of the conversation Alan looked for a chance to get away unnoticed without success. At the moment the phonograph played hillbilly. Jumping up on his two lanky legs Molinbeck began jitterbugging in the middle of the room. The fast raucous music grew louder and louder and the tall man became more and more animated. When one record was finished, he asked for more of the same kind and danced as if for the benefit of the whole assembly, never suspecting what a ludicrous figure he cut.

Yonghee Lindenberg got bolder, as she became used to her husband, getting herself, among other things, a Korean boyfriend, and drove to his house in the UNKRA car, sometimes making the driver Shim wait outside. No one told Lindenberg about her infidelity, nor would he have believed it, if told. So single-heartedly was he devoted to her. Like many other enterprising women of Korea Yonghee belonged to a mutual loan society gay, and soon enough managed to get Lindenberg involved in a tremendous debt from which not even Rockefeller could have extricated himself. One day Lindenberg took his chum Kyelsen with him on a drive in his Volkswagen. Lindenberg did not tell Kyelsen where they were headed and kept his attention occupied by incessant talk, which stopped when they were at Kimpo Airport.

"Why are we here?" Kyelsen asked in surprise.

"Because we came here," Lindenberg said handing his friend the key to the car. "I have to catch the plane that leaves in half an hour. Please sell the car for me. Keep half of the money for yourself and send the other half to me. This is perhaps the last favor I'll ask of you. This car is all I have left. Good-bye."

That was the manner in which Lindenberg had to leave Korea. A few weeks later Yonghee Lindenberg turned up at the Northwest Airlines office in the Bando Hotel, wearing dark glasses. After paying the airline office enough money to arrange a ticket and a visa in a hurry, she flew to the States that afternoon. The next day a mob of screeching women came to the airline office, her creditors who wanted to know what had happened to her. When told she had left the previous day, they put on a war dance, howled, and almost tore down the place, while the frightened manager stood trembling by the telephone, ready to call the police in case it got really out of hand.

Not too long after Lindenberg's departure, Alan was called to Molinbeck's office. Alan thought Molinbeck had finally realized how unjust he had been and was about to put Alan on UNKRA payroll, now that Lindenberg's slot was vacant.

"Heyman!" Molinbeck said gravely. "May I be frank with you?"

"Yes."

"You are unfit to live in Korea."

"Unfit? How do you mean?"

"Physically, not to mention the moral and other aspects which are strictly your own business and I don't want to pry into or talk about. Look at you. You look real seedy, beat, down and out. You look terrible, worse than the miserable Korean beggars we are out here to help."

Alan almost said that if he drew $12,000, took a two-week vacation, all expenses paid, every two months to Japan, one month home leave every year, again all expenses paid, and three kinds of holidays, Korean, US, and UN, he would look peppy and fit, too. Instead for about $100 a month, he taught six classes a day, five days a week, which would have worn down even a cocky dude like Molinbeck. But Alan held his peace, lest he should be instantly fired, and tried to appear grateful for Molinbeck's concern for his welfare. Molinbeck took Alan's meekness for intellectual concurrence.

"Looking shabby like that," Molinbeck went on, looking Alan over in distaste, "you disgrace the American image. Remember each of us represents our country, sort of ambassador in miniature."

An American had to live exactly as at home, getting everything from the PX. If an American ate Korean kimchee and slept on the ondol floor, he was just as miserable as any Korean, whom Molinbeck and the likes of him had come to civilize. Molinbeck was indeed amazed to see Alan still alive and kicking instead of falling dead with hepatitis or some infection a long time ago. That Alan was alive at all was another proof that he was not his kind, Molinbeck's, that therefore Alan was unfit to live in Korea. Molinbeck was sincere in this assessment and did everything to make Alan more miserable, more unfit, so Alan might go where he belonged, out of Korea, no matter where. This was an insult even Alan could not live down.

"All right, I quit," Alan said, stomping out of the room. "Rule on, King Fit!"

That's how Alan's and my relationship with FLI ended. But even King Fit did not get to enjoy his fiefdom forever. Shortly, President Syngman Rhee fell in a bloody student uprising. After a short interim military rule began and its leader, Junghee Park, who had a grudge against FLI for flunking him when he tried to go to the States as a junior officer, stripped it of its privileged status by no longer requiring its certification for passport application. Enrollment shrank rapidly, forcing Molinbeck to seek employment elsewhere.

For a whole week I didn't learn about Alan losing his job, critical though it was to our livelihood: it happened while I was still out of town on an assignment of Molinbeck's arranging, for which we had thanked him. In hindsight, seeing how I almost didn't make it back to Seoul alive, one might suspect it was part of his sinister plan to get rid of us both: I was probably as much an eyesore to him as Alan, though I had done my damnedest to avoid his sight. But perhaps that's stretching, because at the time he called on me he had probably no intention of firing Alan. In fact, even at the last meeting with Alan, it's possible that all Molinbeck wanted was to dress him down, not fire him. Also, unless psychic, he had no way of knowing or suspecting what would happen to me on the trip a week later.

It was exactly four days before Alan's termination that I went into the FLI faculty room with Alan to help him carry the student exam papers and other stuff.

"Alan," Mrs. Waters said, "the Director wants you to come and see him with your brother."

"I am leaving," I said, dumping the papers on Alan's table and bolting.

"Mr. Molinbeck has a guest, who might need you, John," she said, blocking the way.

The visitor was Rev. George Epstein, a Southern Baptist missionary in Seoul, who needed someone to interpret for Brother Edward Bronson, a famous revivalist visiting from Tulsa, Oklahoma, on a two-week preaching tour of Korea.

"I hear your little brother here is quite a linguist," Epstein said.

"He is," Alan said. "Why don't you ask him directly?"

"Well, what do you say, John? You'll travel with Brother Edward and be his mouthpiece. Besides we'll pay you one hundred US dollars."

It was as much as what Alan made a month at FLI.

"I am not a Southern Baptist," I said.

"You are a Christian, aren't you?" he asked.

"I suppose," I answered, uncertainly.

"That'll do," he said confidently. "Brother Edward, a powerful man of God, will make you one of the chosen."

Though I didn't share his assessment, I agreed, chiefly because it looked like an easy way to make money. How more wrong could I be! First, my bilingual skill was most severely tested. Language representing the accumulated experiences of a culture, food, clothing, shelter, disease, many concepts simply defied translation. For example, how on earth was Korean kimchee to be translated into English and American hamburger into Korean, when neither food had been eaten by the other linguistic group? Apart from this basic untranslatability we had to deal with the logistics of delivery. Brother Edward wanted simultaneous interpretation, with the romantic notion that though two separate bodies speaking two different languages, he and I act as a unity in God, speaking with one mind and therefore at the same time, our lips opening and closing simultaneously.

"I had it done that way in Spanish while in Mexico," he said. But it soon became clear that simultaneous interpretation between Korean and English was a logical impossibility because of their radical structural difference. For example, the polarity (negation or affirmation) of the sentence, determined early on in English by not or other negative signs, could not be given until the end of the sentence in Korean. If one progressed simultaneously with the original, as perhaps between the Romance languages, the English negative could only be accommodated by a Korean equivalent of the type: "What follows is not to be: to wit, ..." Of course such a translation mutilated the structure and flavor of the original. Unless the text were known in advance or consisted of short and simple sentences with frequent pauses, as often occurred in unrehearsed speaking situations, simultaneous translation could not be attempted. But even if it were feasible, in our case the interference between original and translation would be too distracting. Consecutive interpretation seemed the only answer.

"But I don't want to pause after each sentence for the translation," Edward complained. "Any kind of emotional buildup would be impossible."

"You finish speaking first then, and I'll give the translation next."

"But how can you remember all? I don't speak from a prepared text."

"I'll make notes, mental notes."

Though skeptical, Bronson went along with the idea. The first tryout was at Epstein's church in Shinchon, where Edward spoke first for about half an hour and I followed, improvising and ad-libbing at will. I managed to make the congregation laugh and cry around the general theme the speaker wanted to convey. Now and then Edward, seated next to Epstein on the platform behind me, leaned over and whispered to his friend, no doubt to check on the accuracy of the translation. Perhaps it wasn't translation in the strict sense of the word, but at least he supplied the body and I gave it a Korean cloak of sorts, loosely fitting. Luckily, I had been exposed to enough Christian services and sermons since the Mercy Home days to use the right lingo in my translation.

"We'll work together all right," Edward said enthusiastically afterwards, pumping my arm. "I've never had the audience respond so positively in a translated situation."

If I had qualms about the authenticity of my translation from the point of view of language, the outward form and clothing, I was genuinely distressed about its inner substance, my purported Christianity of the Southern Baptist persuasion or otherwise. It was the height of hypocrisy to pretend holy zeal and prate about God and salvation through His only begotten Son, when all along I thought the whole thing nothing but solemn bunk. When in trouble I was not slower than the next fellow to fall on my bended knees and pray for help to God Almighty, but when healthy and prosperous, as I felt when I embarked on the bilingual ministry with Bronson, primarily inspired by the big fee I was getting, I was a roaring skeptic and agnostic, ridiculing gods, all made in man's image, necessarily ethnocentric. I had noticed early on how Jehowah looked remarkably Jewish, Jesus West European, Allah Arabic, Buddha Asiatic. At their sublimest and profoundest, humans were inextricably racist. So I, a mixed-race, had another ax to grind against all religion. But cynicism never stopped me from playing the clown when called upon as now. As our ministry gathered momentum, I almost thought I was a born again Southern Baptist and Edward called me Brother John with fervor.

Halfway into the second week we were in a farming village near Choonhyang. It had snowed and was bitter cold. Stooping through a low door into the packed room of the country church was like crawling into a cave. The ondol floor, heated burning hot for the occasion, cooked the unwashed bodies, and the resulting concoction of odors was enough to knock out an elephant. Nonetheless Brother Edward never showed offense either by word or frown, whereas I, one time resident of the Mercy Home, squirmed and snorted. Even more disconcerting than their smell was their appearance, stolid country folk, work oppressed, sullen, suspicious, to whom the only real thing in life seemed three bowls of rice a day. One might as well try to move a mountain as this crowd with promises of the next world. But we accomplished the impossible. At the end of the first service we had them jumping on their feet, singing hymns and shouting Hallelujah. But I had my comeuppance that night, divine retribution for my hypocrisy and arrogance.

After the service near midnight, we were taken to our separate lodgings, Edward to the pastor's house which had a spare room, and me to the church elder's with new guest quarters. To ensure a sufficient supply of heat overnight, the elder's family had put in new briquettes of anthracite instead of letting the old ones burn out. At night a crosswind caused the fume in the flues to back up and seep into the room I was sleeping in. As if in a nightmare I knew I had to get up but could not stir. Tons of weight seemed to have pinned me down. With superhuman effort I managed to kick the paper door open before passing out. Edward had me rushed to the nearest hospital ten miles away and oxygen pumped into my lungs. The returning consciousness brought on unbearable pain all over my body. My head seemed to split open, my intestines, twist and snarl. My aching legs wobbled and wouldn't support me. Fortunately, my mind was unimpaired and I spoke without impediment. But the muscle aches persisted and I could not get around. I had come inches to death or being a vegetable for the rest of my life. The fragility of the human condition was chilling.

VI.
Aran Ham Center for Korean Folk Music

I owe my subsequent recovery from the crippling effects of gas poisoning to the devoted ministrations of not only Alan but everybody from the Folk Music Center. At first they came to the house, bringing food but, predictably, Tadpole objected to the increase in traffic. At their insistence I moved to the Center to stay in one of its rooms during my recuperation.

"To help us," they said, "because we will visit and take care of you no matter where."

It was the Evac Hospital all over again, except for the all-Korean staff and the setting that might be Korea a century ago before the advent of the West. They sang, played instruments, and danced, continuing in the unchanging folk ways of Korean music they had learned since childhood. But they had no pride or conviction, no militant creed or sense of identity in doing what they did. On the contrary, in moments of self-reflection, they saw themselves as pathetic dropouts from the march of modernization to which Korea was inexorably committed. Feeling the contempt of the society at large, they had yet no choice but to go on plying the only trade they had learned from parents who, themselves bred to the hereditary caste of entertainers, the untouchables of Korea, had not known any better, not even to send their children to regular school to learn math, science, languages, arts, including music. Calling themselves musicians, they couldn't read music, school-taught music with its bars and notes that embodied the great symphonies, concertos, études, and airs of the West.

Making their living from the grudging pittance for performances at restaurants or parties, they could never have put together enough money to build and maintain a center like this at a central location in Seoul, where they congregated to socialize, give lessons to whoever cared to learn their discredited art, and even organize occasional concerts other than as entertainment for a drinking party. The Center, named after Aran Ham, had been endowed by her family, one of the most prominent in post-Liberation, pre-War Korea, who had had all the modern advantages. In particular, Aran Ham was a professor of music, Western music, at Seoul National University.

"She has synthesized the best of Korean and Western music," said Wansong Char, who, unlike the rest of the Center crowd, had the benefit of modern education, gaining admission to Liberal Arts College, Seoul National University, though he quit in the first year for full-time dedication to his art.

"What is she doing now?" I asked, offhand.

"She was taken by Ilsung Kim the moment Seoul was captured," Wansong said. "It was rumored that Kim made war on the south specifically to get her, who had fled south, refusing his advances. She hasn't been heard of since."

That's as far as we went regarding the subject of Aran Ham at the time. Even if I had been more curious about this personage, Wansong wouldn't have dwelt on her, as he had other priorities on his mind. Besides his art, Wansong had one other obsession in life, emigration to the US. Whenever I met Wansong, he was "on the point of leaving for the States." When I teased him the next time we met that I thought he was in the States already, he would reply, the incorrigible optimist, "A minor glitch soon to be straightened out."

To leave Korea one first needed a passport but to get a passport one had to be checked out by the South Korean police, whose chief interest was to screen out Communists or their sympathizers. Wansong had an elder brother, Wanyong, a newspaper reporter, who was serving time after capture as a partisan in the Jeeree Mountains. Wanyong was among the last of the partisans to surrender, having survived two years of starvation, freezing, and constant running from the South Korean special forces, which decimated the Southern Army of the North as the partisans called themselves, though abandoned by Ilsung Kim. Because of his brother Wansong would never pass the security check for his passport, unless a revolution occurred in the mind set of the South Korean government.

Besides the Communist blot in his family, Wansong had another formidable obstacle to overcome, official anti-Jolla bias, exacerbated by Junghee Park, the military dictator, in an attempt to telescope the popular demand for return to civilian rule, led by Daejung Kim from Jolla, into a conflict between their respective provinces, Kim's Jolla versus Park's Gyongsang. Though the bread basket of South Korea, accounting for a quarter or third of the population, Jolla always got left out of Park's 5-year plans, highway projects, capital allocations. When a Jolla petitioner went to a Ministry for anything, his papers got shoved down to the bottom of the stack. In contrast, the Gyongsangites got everything. In the division of spoils after his coup d'etat that had installed Park in absolute power, the Gyongsang people got all the government jobs from cabinet post down to city clerkship, bank loans, contracts, special licenses. Overnight, in the name of industrialization, new billionaires sprang up, the dictator's teacher's son, his wife's nephew, his concubine's cousin, his high school chums, all born in Gyongsang. An iron rule was clamped down on the country by his bodyguard, KCIA, lush with confiscated fortunes and exclusively staffed with his Army buddies and coup engineers and supporters, again from Gyongsang. Except Hyongwoog Kim from Soonchon, South Jolla, the undisputed king-maker, whose position as KCIA Chief seemed secure for now, though my Jolla friends at the Center were betting on how soon he would be ousted.

Like Wansong, many Jollanese naturally wanted to get out of Korea, a homeland that wasn't home, and wanted to immigrate to the US, but they couldn't even get started because the government wouldn't issue them passports: the approval rate for passport applications was 50 Gyongsang versus one Jolla. The Gyongsangites had the lock on everything desirable and immigration to the US was definitely desirable to most Koreans at the time. So the Jollanese, harassed and put down at home, couldn't emigrate either, and had to suffocate in the demeaning pressure cooker that was Korea.

"This happened when I first came to Seoul from Mokpo upon admission to Seoul National, heart brimming with joy and pride," Wansong recalled with bitterness. "I had the darnedest time trying to find a place to stay. The room for rent sign might be up, but after hearing my Jolla accent the landlady promptly took it down, saying the room had just been taken. So many of our people try to drop their accent and adopt Gyongsang dialect."

Indeed, Gyongsang dialect had become the shibboleth of privilege and immunity, as whole villages and counties had transplanted from Gyongsang to Seoul.

"When you get arrested for anything," so went a popular saying, "just mimic Gyongsang accent, and the cops would beg your pardon and let you go."

Unlike these Gyongsang swaggerers, the Jollanese, reduced to the status of second-class citizens, became the paupers of Korea and lived in their ghettos in Seoul. As a whole Korea was slowly sinking into a serfdom. The masses got poorer and poorer. Ninety percent of the people were grateful to eat salted rice three times a day, not tasting meat or produce in months, while the new tycoons did not know what to do with their money and banked in Switzerland, bought in America.

"By the way, how did you get your Gyongsang speech?" Wansong asked.

"I love Jolla better," I said, hastily switching the accent. Since my acquaintance with Wansong and others at the Folk Art Center, I had taken pains, ashamed of my Gyongsang origin from the Mercy Home in Daegu, Junghee's hometown, to eliminate traces of Gyongsang accent from my Korean, substituting the Jolla patois. But the native element was apt to pop up at unguarded moments.

"I have to go to America, the land of the free, with no such stupid prejudice on account of one's place of birth. The Statue of Liberty beckons, the Lady in White with the upraised torch, to the oppressed and downtrodden of the world, so they can all be free and equal. Downtrodden I sure have been and I am bound for America."

"But what will you do in America?"

"Perform and teach Korean dance, put down here automatically as some low thing, certainly not a man's profession. I hear male dancers are as respected as any artist or professional. I want some respect for my work and Americans will give it to me. They'll know true art when they see it. Like your brother."

"But he is not your garden variety of American. In fact, many Americans might be crass, vicious bigots, worse than Koreans."

"But look at Mr. Alan and you!"

"Please count me out," I begged, discomfited each time by a reminder of my deception. I wanted but couldn't tell the truth about my real citizenship. They might send me back to the Mercy Home or put me in prison. It was amazing how the fiction had worked this long. Simply nobody had bothered to check up on me by a phone call to the US Embassy. Of course it was my youth and the fact that I had not figured in anything that might trigger official interest, such as application for an ID, license, or a job. But the day would come when I would have to, though I wanted to postpone it as long as possible. If I were in the States, where I belonged by virtue of my paternity, then all this conflict would dissolve. But that would never be. Like Wansong, I would never get off first base with the Korean security check. Nor the US one, because they would spot me out instantly. On a visit to the US Embassy I glimpsed at the consular section, chillingly orderly, no pushover like the slipshod Evac staff.

Completely recovered, I had returned to our Gahwaydong house and was visiting the Center with Alan for his hojog flute lesson from Ilsob Hong, a tall gaunt figure with sunken cheeks and eyes, indisputably the country's best hojog player in spite of a reputation as a drunk.

"Ruined his life, never got where he could have gotten," the other musicians observed clucking their tongues in pity. "Women and wine, you know."

The lesson was interrupted by the entrance into the room of some Ministry of Education officials on an inspection tour of the Center for accreditation. The visitors seemed impressed to see no fewer than two foreigners as students, though I had been only looking on. Coming closer, they handled the instrument curiously, incredulous that anybody, especially foreigners, should give the time of day to such a toy.

"How many lessons do you have a week?" one of them asked in strained English.

"Depends," Alan said and I interpreted. "These days we come every day, but even when we have other work to do, we try to get in at least two a week. That's not including my own practice to get ready for the lessons."

"It's almost like learning to play violin, then," commented another official, skeptically.

"Every instrument demands lifelong devotion for mastery."

"But why this particular instrument?"

"Because of its brash, forthright, honest clarity, its versatility and range, almost like a clarinet. It makes beautiful music and expresses the soul of Korea."

"Can you play something for us?" they asked, after doing a double take at such an extravagant accolade for something worthless.

Alan obliged, flooring them with his spirited rendition of Arirang. No further inspection was necessary: the Center got the accreditation on the spot. After the officials' departure, everybody came around to thank us. The accreditation was necessary for the Center to continue to operate as a school and charge tuition.

"You get the Best Student Award, Mr. Alan," somebody said.

"No, he gets the Best Teacher Award," Alan said, holding up Hong's hand, flustering him no end, for he was a shy man, not given to attention, despite his extensive performance experience on stage.

Finally, screwing up his courage, the old man paid Alan about the highest compliment he could have wished from anybody: "Mr. Alan is an artist."

"You are a true artist yourself," Alan said, embarrassed.

"No, I am a tradesman," the old man insisted. "You pay and I play. I am a tradesman."

Hong declined Alan's heartfelt praise decisively. No modesty was intended either, for the others joined in the chorus: "We are only tradesmen."

They would not admit to being artists, which meant to them something pure and exalted, free from monetary taint. Penniless and living from day to day, the folk musicians always sold their talent and could not afford to give away anything free, but in their estimation this automatically disqualified them as artists, a title arrogated by much less qualified and more mercenary people in other climes. Korean musicians would probably not hesitate to murder a welsher on their pay but were true artists in every sense of the word. Especially this old man Hong was. He had music in every fiber of his body, his voice, his fingertips, his toes.

On our way home that day we ran into Hans Kohler, who was now his old cheerful self again, congratulating himself on escaping the clutch of Bongja, Mrs. Lindenberg.

"So where are you teaching now?" he asked Alan.

"Nowhere," Alan answered. "I only have a few private English classes to keep us going."

"I am working at the Yongsan PX now. My former job with the Wilcox Co. is still open. I can introduce you to its partners if you are interested."

"What kind of business are they in?"

"All sorts. Mainly military supplies, you know, refrigerators, club equipment, and recently even insurance. They are the subagent of Gray and International. If you are good as a salesman there, you can net over a thousand dollars a month easily."

The Cold War was still at its height and the US

maintained a big military presence in South Korea, which meant an attendant army of servitors, the military contractors, who generally had a bad reputation, but Alan decided to give it a try, make a quick buck and get out. The company was a partnership between Maple and Hessler, both Americans, to whom Kohler took Alan one day for introduction. But when they arrived at their office, the partners were just leaving on some urgent business and told Alan to come back by himself.

"Where did you meet Kohler, Heyman?" Maple asked, when Alan did.

"At FLI," Alan said.

"Oh, yes, FLI, Molinbeck's outfit," Maple said, grinning and nodding.

"Do you know him?" Alan asked, alarmed.

"Do I know him! We were good pals, Molinbeck and I. Real good pals. I worked in UNKRA, in charge of the motor pool. I remember those days very well. We had an agreement between us. Whenever he had any young chick coming to the Institute, he was to send her over to me for private instruction in the evening. I was to select one who was most qualified to go to America. I received four or five at a time and managed to narrow the field down to one most desirable. Then I worked on her. If she gave me a hard time, all I had to say was 'I won't recommend you to go to America.' It never failed. My good friend Molinbeck kept me in steady supply. No one could have said any girl recommended by me didn't get a thorough examination. Of course it worked both ways. He scratched my back and I scratched his. He got all the mileage and gas he wanted and extra car import allocations. He got the dough, I got the doll."

Nobody could say Alan did not receive a good introduction to the character of his prospective employers. The conversation got around to the subject of contributions to the Korean economy made by UNKRA, a byword among Koreans for inefficiency and corruption. At one point Alan was tactless enough to refer to General Kubal, former head of the agency, by the epithet he had been commonly known, "White-haired errand boy of Syngman Rhee!"

"Watch 'em words, boy," Maple growled instantly, looking daggers at Alan, as if he had said something seditious. "He is a good friend of mine."

Maple, coming from Georgia, got his motor pool job with UNKRA thanks to his acquaintance with his great fellow Georgian General Kubal, who had become a millionaire in Korea in the space of a couple of years, whose brazen statue in commemoration of his selfless services to help reconstruct war-torn Korea stood at a prominent rotary in Seoul for all generations of grateful Koreans to bow to and venerate. Maple's loyalty to his friend was touching. Alan was sure he would never get the job because he had insulted Kubal, but Maple and Hessler decided Alan might be good as an insurance salesman.

"You look honest and talk clean," Hessler said. "That's what we need in selling insurance. We haven't been doing too well in that department."

Apparently nobody could trust their faces. They looked and talked like the bruisers and heels they were and decent people shied away from their approach. Naturally all their business came from the US military, where they were in their element, entertaining and bribing club sergeants and officers. We were not sure whether he got a job or joined a gang of hoods.

His employers wanted him to come along with them to Dongdoochun to entertain the club sergeant and lieutenant there. Working for them during the day was enough; getting drunk on their nightly jaunts and hobnobbing with their friends was just a bit more than Alan had bargained for, though that was the accepted modus operandi for anybody doing business in Korea at the time. Maple forestalled any refusal or hesitation on Alan's part by spelling out the rules of the game.

"Day time is when you make it look legal," Maple said. "Night time, that's when you do real business. Are you coming or not?"

"Ya, I am coming," Alan replied, meekly.

There was one man every foreign wheeler-dealer looked up to, Jack Burns, formerly of the merchant marine, who had jumped ship in Pusan and made a great fortune in Korea. His big brick hotel on Ujooro, near West Gate, was a pleasure palace with thirty apartments, all liberally stocked with whisky from the PX, steak from the Army commissary, the tax-free outlets for US products, and prostitutes recruited from all over Korea. Club sergeants came and spent their weekends as guests at this bordello. Maple and Hessler could not do business on this scale, but they tried their best to emulate with what resources they had, hopping from one club to another in their rundown jeep. What little money they had went out in entertainment. The money must come back somehow but the two partners stuffed it all in their pockets. On pay day the Korean employees, insulted and browbeaten in every conceivable manner, got paid whatever happened to be in the safe, which was not much. Bookkeeping in that outfit was all guesswork. Nothing was regular. Being an American, Alan was on a different pay schedule: he was not paid even the amount that was in the safe.

The company never paid any taxes. Tax officials came and always had a big row with the Korean accountant Kim. One day he clambered upstairs and told his bosses that the visitors from the tax office were particularly persistent this time and could not be brushed off with the usual evasions and pleas, hints at bribery or concealed references to the higher connections.

"Bring 'em up," Hessler shouted.

The tax officials walked in cautiously, all five of them for they never traveled alone, especially when treading on foreign territory, to face the towering figures of Maple and Hessler, swinging their arms and fuming as outraged victims of injustice. Alan never saw a more accomplished pair of character actors capable of such instantaneous transformation. Only a moment ago they had been asking him to come along with them to Ujongboo that night to bribe the club lieutenant to replace all the ventilators, still practically new, at the Division clubs. Now at a moment's notice they posed as martyrs of saintly virtue, fighting against tyranny and lawlessness.

"We are American citizens," Hessler said in his stentorian bass. "We are under our country's jurisdiction. Our country is here to help your country. How can you ask us to pay tax when we are giving up everything to help your country get back on its feet?"

Not understanding a word of this oration and somewhat cowered by the physical size of their hosts, the visitors decided that no purpose would be served by staying in the executive suite and backed out one by one to argue it out among themselves with the accountant downstairs. Alan sat at his desk, feeling ashamed and guilty. To be identified with them as fellow countrymen! Hessler suddenly stood up and took off his striped tweed jacket.

"Let's go down and clear 'em out," he announced.

One tax official, probably their spokesman, was coming upstairs to present some final compromise. Through the door Alan saw Hessler grabbing him by the back of his collar. Next moment there was a tremendous crash at the bottom of the stairs. The banister broke and the man suffered compound fractures in both legs. It was horrible just to think of the disruption in his private and official life such injury would entail. Puffing angrily, Hessler still posed as the wronged party. With the good Uncle Sam as protector, he was safe. No criminal prosecution followed for assault on a government official, a capital offense for a Korean national. On the contrary, when it came time to fix the staircase, he and Maple were thinking of getting money from the Korean government for repairs and other damages.

Long after the end of the month, after waiting in vain for days for some gesture on their part, Alan had no alternative but to go up to the partners and ask for money. Guessing his purpose, they took turns to keep him off the subject. It was a full hour before Alan found an opening and asked for his pay. Alan had not earned a red cent since he joined the company. Stopped in the middle of their marathon relay of talk, they acted as if Alan had asked for the impossible, then gave him $25. Alan was lucky even to get that, for they had made up their minds some time ago that he should be rid of because he would not shape up to their standards. But Hessler had a more dramatic method of termination that suited his vicious nature. That night he forced Alan to go with him by the company jeep to a military club on the Yongsan compound, ignoring Alan's plea to be excused: we had to be at the Center for a concert. At the club there were the usual lot, club sergeants, hangers-on, prostitutes, all of whom Hessler knew familiarly one way or other. But he acted strangely that night, speaking loudly, attracting as much attention to himself as he could, pretending drunk on two glasses of Scotch. Then he grabbed Alan by the wrist.

"Let me see your watch," he said.

The watch, a Rolex worth $100, had been given to him by a girl student he had tutored, in appreciation of her passing the English test for students going abroad. Her father, a member of the National Assembly, seemed to have a truckload of those expensive watches. Alan thought Hessler wanted to see the time, but next moment Hessler had it yanked off Alan's wrist and was banging it on the counter top before dashing it clear across the room against the wall. As Alan sat stunned, Hessler's coarse face lit up with a diabolical grin, basking in the attention he was getting from the crowd for his bizarre behavior. Humiliated and shocked, Alan stood up to pick up his watch. One Korean hooker got up and brought it over to Alan. It was a total wreck - the crystal broken, face smashed in, both hands missing, and even the metal rim dented. Hessler snatched it off her and banged it a few more times on the counter. Others were laughing. By now Alan had completely lost his reason. Not seeing or hearing anything else, Alan picked up a beer bottle and raised it, determined to obliterate the reptile's face. At the moment another Korean hooker standing behind Alan pulled the bottle out of his grip.

"Don't do something you'll regret for the rest of your life," she said in a calm, gentle voice.

Suddenly Alan came to his senses and listened to her. Shuddering at the closeness of the disaster he had almost fallen into, he walked out of the bar and told the jeep driver to take him home. If Alan had hit Hessler, he would have either killed him or injured him severely. In either case he would have been criminally prosecuted. Also, if Hessler survived, he would have come back with all he'd got to exact his double or triple vengeance.

The next day Alan went to Allen Kean, an Australian, representing the Korea branch of Gray and International. The few times we had met him briefly he looked like a decent man one could trust. Feeling the way Alan did at the time, brutalized, dehumanized, Alan would have turned to a wall to air his grievances. He told Kean everything, the wicked business practices of Wilcox Co. and the violence he had witnessed and been subjected to in the course of a month. Kean said he had been thinking of taking the franchise away from Wilcox and asked Alan to come and work for him.

"I lived in Japan many years," Kean said. "I went there to study Buddhism, especially Zen, you know, the meditative sect that flourished around 1,000 to 1,300 a.d. I lived several months in a zen monastery. But there came a point in my life when I had to set down my priorities. I had to decide whether I should be a perpetual student or pick up a trade and become a useful member of society. I chose the latter and here I am today."

Kean stopped and lifted his hand to point the index finger at Alan.

"That, I think, is what you had better do, too," he said with the solemnity of a prophet.

"You are right," Alan said.

Finding him such an agreeable auditor, Kean waxed even more oracular.

"I have no competition in the insurance field except Caker and Lopp. If we can sell insurance to the American Embassy, USOM, US Operations Mission, and above all the dozens of US Army clubs, we will make thousands of dollars. We'll be rich."

Though the whole thing sounded like a scam, Alan had no alternative but to take his offer. Again he thought he would clear out after making a quick buck. Also there was the small matter of evening up the score with his previous pals, Hessler and Maple, who predictably threatened to kill Alan for having taken away the franchise from them. Whenever a stranger appeared, we tensed up, thinking he might be the hired assassin. We looked back and forward before crossing a street and took a roundabout way to reach our house at night. After a month of this we decided Alan should have a talk with Kean.

"They are out and out crooks and thugs," Alan said. "I want to expose them. Everything they do is illegal. For instance, they never pay taxes."

"So what do you have in mind?" Kean asked, rather icily.

"I was thinking of going to the police and blowing the whistle on them."

"God, no!" Kean shouted, jumping up, his face red with anger. "So long as you are with this outfit, don't ever report anything to the police. The moment you do, you are out, fired. Do we understand each other?"

Alan nodded, wondering whether he had not changed a coyote for a jackal as his master. Such antipathy to the police could mean only one thing: Kean had more things to hide than tell.

For the first few months the policies sold well. One month Alan made as much as $400 and thought we might really hit the jackpot soon that was to emancipate us once and for all financially. One of his clients was Admiral Whitwall, retired, US Navy, President of the Korea Gold Mining Corporation, which took out full-page ads in the two English dailies, Korea Times and Korean Republic, urging every foreigner or Korean for that matter who could read English and had the money to "Invest Now". From these ads we had formed of him the image of a sage financier who out of the goodness of his heart wanted to share the benefits of his business acumen with the less astute. Alan went with great expectations to his office at the Bando Hotel, the swanky headquarters of all important foreign businessmen who acted as pathfinders for the commercial and industrial development of Korea. Whitwall was stooped, a trace of dried saliva down his chin. It was hard to visualize the admiral or benevolent tycoon in the Neanderthal features of this lumpy, deteriorating face.

"Where did you work before?" Whitwall rasped.

"I taught at FLI for a while," Alan said.

"Oh, that one," Whitwall said. "I used to sit on its budget committee, when I was with UNKRA."

So here was another one of the UNKRA gang. It seemed Alan would never get away from them as long as he lived in Korea and wondered whether he should not retreat while he had the time. But it was too late. The former admiral had placed his signature on the application and nothing would induce him to withdraw. The policy was on his car. Weeks and soon months passed but the purchaser procrastinated and never paid a cent of his premium. Alan gave him calls, wrote him letters, but the admiral would not surrender. After two months of this Alan was ready to cancel the policy. Suddenly a call came through from Whitwall one day.

"I have a claim," the hoarse voice said. "Somebody has scratched up my car badly."

"But, sir, you've never paid any premium," Alan said, wondering at his gall.

"The premium can be deducted from the claim," the admiral said.

Alan was about to explain to him the basics of insurance, when Kean interrupted.

"Tell him we'll look into the matter," Kean said. "After all he is a big shot around here and we can use his name. Tell him that we need a police report on the accident."

Insurance was a publicity business and when a prominent person, an actress or a high government official, had a claim, the company paid at once. But if a nobody had a claim, he or she might have to wait until they dropped dead of old age to get paid. Swallowing his conviction and pride, Alan told the gold miner what was needed, almost hearing his chuckle of triumph over their servility. Instead the admiral grumbled and stammered.

"I don't want too much trouble," he said. "Either you pay me for my claim or you don't. If you don't pay me instantly, I'll change to Caker and Lopp."

"But, sir, it's a simple formality."

"No, I don't want the police to get involved."

Alan became suspicious and made an investigation at once. An amazing fact turned up. The Korean police reported that Admiral Whitwall had scratched up the side of his own car with a sharp instrument. There were several witnesses and other substantiating evidence. Alan called the admiral and told him the plain truth, barely suppressing his indignation. Whitwall flew into rage.

"I'll sue everyone of you crooks, from top down," he fumed.

Of course he did nothing of the sort. When we saw the next full-page ads about gold investment appearing in both papers day after day, we couldn't help wondering how many suckers had been taken in.

In addition to Caker and Lopp other small insurance firms began invading Alan's territory. Especially Caker and Lopp had become most aggressive, paying any claimant instantly in dollar checks, though this was against the foreign exchange regulations of Korea. No one, except persons with diplomatic privileges, was allowed to issue a dollar check or receive one. In that respect Alan's company was law-abiding and gladly went through the regular channels, Bank of Korea, Ministry of Finance, etc., etc., holding up payment three or four months, by which time the claimants had left Korea or forgotten about their claims. The company did everything to discourage people with claims. In addition to selling policies Alan's duties included convincing people with claims that they had none. Many were the times when, against his conscience, he had to talk people out of their rights. In practically all cases, except people like Whitwall, Alan ended up siding with the claimants he had set out to dissuade and argued for them to the company. Kean was predictably upset.

"Tell them they have no claim," he roared.

"But they have facts in their favor," Alan duly pointed out.

"That don't matter," Kean said. "It's always how you look at it. Try more persuasion. Make them see it from our point of view."

The company's reluctance to pay began to cost it business

as people went to the others who had a different philosophy about it. Alan felt obliged to talk to Kean after losing the Seoul Area Command NCO Club to Caker and Lopp.

"Treat the sergeants and officers in charge," Kean suggested. "Slip in a buck here and there."

"All right," Alan said. "Give me the money."

"That comes out of your pocket. You are trying to sell, right?"

"What do you mean? I am broke as I am."

"That's your problem," Kean said. "But remember we can't go on losing business at this rate."

Alan could have observed that the company had to pay the claims once in a while instead of evading all the time. But such pointedness would mean his instant dismissal. He tried a different tack.

"We can beat Caker and Lopp," he said. "They are issuing dollar checks on the spot against the law of the Republic of Korea. Let's stop them."

"How?"

"Let's report their violation to the police," Alan said, forgetting Kean's reaction to a similar suggestion on another occasion.

Kean's face reddened. Jumping up, he pounded his fist on the table.

"How many times do I have to tell you?" he yelled. "Don't ever think of reporting anything about anybody to the police. Do you understand?"

What could it be that set him so viscerally against the police, his ancestry traceable to some transported convict or his own unpleasant contact with the law? As our financial prospects darkened, Alan bitterly regretted having joined the company.

At this time Wol Bang, one of the better known senior musicians, died and the Center undertook his funeral, to attend which many people had come from Jolla. Wansong brought several of them over to our place and asked us to put them up. Of course we were glad to, though it meant mollifying Tadpole with extra won or two that we didn't have to spare.

That night, after the funeral, my out-of-town guests wanted to take me to a cinema to see the latest hit by the Jongnan Film, Rock Hill, starring Nanyong Song, who was a sensation among Korean moviegoers at the time. Nevertheless this was the first time I had seen her on screen or, for that matter, the first Korean movie I ever saw. I had only seen American movies while at the Evac and had not been to one afterwards. There were theaters around, showing mostly American imports and occasionally domestic productions like Rock Hill which had run for weeks. But for one reason or other we couldn't find the time to go to a movie, nor did I miss it, especially the domestic kind, toward which I had a snobbish attitude: they couldn't be much, mostly imitations of American models, as they had to be. But that night's outing changed everything. I was totally under the spell of the lead actress, Nanyong. Her beautiful face, austere, almost statuesque, was yet capable of expressing with subtlety and poignancy the deepest, minutest nuance of emotion, not found among the best American actresses I had adored, Deborah Kerr, Maureen O'Hara, Vivien Leigh.

"She is from Jolla," Wansong said proudly. "From Haynam, on the other side of the bay from Mokpo."

"Where is your gripe about Jollanese discrimination?" I asked.

"She is an exception," he answered. "Besides a woman has a better chance than a man in general and the film is a world apart anyway."

"I wish I could meet her in person, talk to her, look her in the face, feel her hand,..." my fantasy made me blush unknowingly.

"Hey, you must have a crush on her," Wansong teased. "Don't worry. You are in good company, the company of about ten million."

I knew this infatuation was stupid and hopeless, but after that introduction I went to see every film in which she appeared, regardless of the title or subject matter. I went to see her, not the movie. The setting she was in was incidental. We had a rendezvous, a love tryst, and I was her magnificent male lover she desired and deserved. The real male character playing opposite her in the piece, invariably despicable and unbearable, was replaced by myself in all the splendor and substance that imagination could supply. This was true even when she played an old woman or a lowly serving maid. Her outward form or circumtance could be anything, because her inner self remained the same, the fixed pole star of my unalterable love.

Lately Alan had been taking lessons in the janggo drum, which gave Korean music the kind of rhythmic freedom unknown in Western music. Syncopation was the rule rather than the exception and metric transitions were frequent, sometimes from measure to measure, which the drummer had to signal and lead like a conductor. Soon after this Alan developed an absent-minded habit of tapping with his fingers in the middle of whatever he might be doing. Once at the Gray and International conference room, the conversation stopped. Preoccupied with memorizing a janggo sequence, Alan had not noticed that they were all staring at him and his fingerwork.

"Are you through jerking your fingers?" Kean asked.

"Sorry I forgot," Alan apologized.

"You'll be a lot sorrier if you don't shed that habit and spook our customers."

That was a demeaning threat but Alan didn't care. If he were to be sacked, then he would be sacked. What right did he or I have to live in security, when our friends at the Center were content to live hand to mouth, not knowing where the next meal was coming from?

Whenever he had the chance, Alan's boss Kean entertained Sergeant Wigby who had become immensely wealthy as director of the NCO clubs in Ascom City, the sprawling US military complex with its support and residential systems in Boopyong halfway between Seoul and Inchon. Eventually charged with corruption and embezzlement, he was indicted but with his money he knew how to grease the right places in the wheels of military justice. The charges were dropped and he was reinstated to his rank and position, back in charge of the clubs.

Early one morning Alan went to the International Hotel

where Kean stayed, and found him at breakfast with another businessman, named Mill.

"Isn't it Sergeant Wigby's car parked outside?" Kean was asking Mill.

"Yes," Mill said. "He came here last night with a big businessman from the States."

"I must see him," Kean said. "Who is the sergeant sleeping with?"

"Miss Korea's sister," Mill said.

"Who is his businessman friend sleeping with?" Kean asked.

"Miss Korea," Mill said.

"Oh, no," Alan couldn't help moaning. "It's not possible. You are surely mistaken."

Only a week ago he and I had watched the Miss Korea Pageant pass City Hall amidst the cheers of the adoring throng three or four deep lined along the street and waiting for hours from early morning for a glimpse of the queen of Korean "beauty, chastity and virtue." This madonna of the modern age be nothing but a cheap harlot to foreigners capable of paying big cash because of the vastly slanted foreign exchange rate! It was just too shattering to be true. Both Kean and Mill stared at Alan, interrupting their breakfast.

"Why, it's not the first time," Kean said. "Don't you know Miss Koreas go to bed with foreign businessmen on a regular basis?"

"Well, I guess I am just as gullible as anyone else in this country," Alan said to his informed associates.

Kean's partner, Thomas Lotter, was a distinguished-looking man with a spotless silk tie held down by a diamond-studded pin and silver-white hair parted on one side. Neat, clean, handsome, he struck one as a nobleman walking out of a Life magazine advertisement. Alan thought he was at least a duke when he first met the man. Supposedly Kean's best friend, as well as his indispensable business associate, Lotter was in charge of push-button cash registers, supplied to all the US Army installations by Gray and International. One day Alan was having lunch with Lotter and Kean at the Seoul

Club, the hangout of foreign businessmen in Seoul. The sum of a thousand dollars was mentioned in some connection. Lotter, the nobleman, who had been eating accurately and elegantly in the best Emily Post manner with his back straight like a rod, raised his head.

"Why, for a thousand bucks, I'd do a blow job on any man," he said aloud in all sincerity and seriousness, without a flicker of his facial muscles.

Alan looked at him amazed. It was like looking at one and the same thing, which was black and white at the same time. Lotter went on eating undisturbed, as erect as ever. While pretending to be Kean's best friend, he had been plotting to take the Army franchise on cash registers for himself cutting Kean out of the deal. His wife, a good-looking but ambitious woman, was secretary to General McCoy, C-in-C, UN Command, and promoted her husband's cause energetically and effectively. Finally, one day Lotter walked out as sole agent for all Army cash registers and established the International Register Company. It was the greatest blow to befall Gray and International. Kean was immediately summoned to Japan. We thought it would be the end of Kean's career with the company, but after some weeks Kean returned. But Alan had to move out.

"It's been one hell of a losing streak with you around," Kean said, naturally finding in Alan a ready-made scapegoat for all the business losses.

It was a coup de grace, though. Alan had lost all interest in insurance salesmanship and had been hanging around for lack of a good excuse to quit.

Again through Kohler's introduction Alan got a job at the Yongsan PX as Korean concession supervisor. Soon Alan became the regular talking well for the Korean employees to air their grievances, especially on the bus to and from work every day, chiefly about their job insecurity and degrading treatment at work. They were bullied and abused, especially by the Japanese Americans, niseis, from Hawaii, who somehow held most of the PX jobs and could fire any Korean at the drop of a hat. So long was the waiting list for a job opening that a Korean worker could lose his position without notice. There was no grievance procedure, no compensation. Among these Koreans who came into daily contact with Americans the prestige of the US was not worth a dime.

Alan went to work one morning and learned that three PX trucks, loaded with women's lingerie and convoyed by an armed MP jeep, had vanished during transit from Inchon to Seoul. It was physically impossible for these trucks to simply evaporate into thin air on a well-trafficked highway. The whole thing was clearly an insider job and the Korean employees knew it, too. In that place nobody was fooling anybody. The Army Major in charge of the PX came in and made a big fuss over the loss, estimated to exceed one hundred thousand dollars.

"I'll fire all Korean drivers and use only GI's," he blustered, pounding his fist on the desk.

But of course he did nothing of the sort. Such "disappearances" would simply multiply tenfold if GI's took over. With Jesse James or Bonnie and Clyde as their exemplars GI's were generally more daring when it came to banditry. Using their Caucasian faces as safe conduct they would ram through any roadblock or dragnet the Korean police might throw. American managers and officers screamed about the theft and fired several Koreans, who tried in vain to appeal. Some were writing to the C-in-C, UNC himself but nothing came of it and their grievances were mysteriously suppressed.

A Korean operated the concession for snack bar delivery service. His boys carried food by brand new Yamaha bicycles, each of which worth its weight in gold on the local market. Every week, in a manner nobody could explain, one or two of the bikes disappeared, but the managers did not care to go into the matter, merely firing or not paying the delivery boys for the losses. The delivery boys went on strike to protest, saying that they were not the thieves, but it did not do them any good.

"We must do something about it," Major Buckley said, pounding his fist as usual and pointing out that another bike had disappeared.

"Cancel the contract and get a new operator," Alan suggested.

Buckley did nothing of the sort. The concessionaire, Mr. Han, a stocky man with a perpetual smile that could be either ingratiating or sneering, was the Major's pal. In fact Alan had often heard Buckley sing Han's virtues: "Han is the only Korean we can trust one hundred percent."

One day Han called Alan at his office.

"The bikes are not fast enough for delivery," he said.

"So what do you have on your mind?" Alan asked.

"We need to bring in motorbikes."

Alan thought he was joking. When Alan met Buckley, he mentioned it in passing, certain that Buckely would take it as a joke, too.

"You know how absurd it is," Alan said. "Bikes have been disappearing but Han has the cheek to ask for motorbikes. The minute they are brought in, we'll lose them wholesale."

"You know, Alan," Buckley said, jumping up in glee, "that is a capital idea. We can provide a more efficient service with motorbikes. Put in a requisition for them."

"What? With all our past experience with pedal-driven bikes?"

"Well, we'll get a new concessionaire."

The same man, Han, got the contract, because no one bid lower than he, who just seemed to know the next lowest bid down to the cent. Motorbikes were sent for from Japan, the general and total subcontractor for all US defense business in whatever size or form. As expected, the motorbikes began to disappear the moment they arrived, Han gladly reimbursing Uncle Sam for the loss, what it cost the US Army to import from Japan, so the replacement could be ordered. Nobody seemed the loser but our long-suffering victim, the hundred percent honest Mr. Han. Except for the minor detail: every single motorbike fetched about ten times as much on the Korean market because of the steep tariff.

Han had another concession, refuse collection and removal from the Army compounds. His trucks got caught three times, carrying out radios, TV sets, and even refrigerators under the trash. Each time Han extricated himself adroitly. It was criminal to allow a crook like Han to prosper and Alan submitted a strongly-worded recommendation to Buckley that Han be replaced. A new bidding was held. Alan knew a man, Sanggil Song, who had assured Alan that he could present a much lower bid. Song was himself a garbage collector and represented his fellow workers, who all wanted to eliminate the middle man and profiteer Han and do honest business to earn their just salaries. Identifying himself totally with Song's cause, Alan encouraged Song sincerely, promising all the help in his power. But before the day the bids were to be turned in, Song came to Alan.

"Gangsters are threatening me to join a fix-up," he said. "I don't know what to do. They want to pay me off for about ten dollars or else beat me up and kill me."

"Oh, don't worry," Alan said confidently. "If they do anything like that, I'll take legal action. By God, this country must have some policemen."

Song went ahead and won the contract. Han's, the next lowest among a dozen others, came in about eighty percent higher. Song's trucks went to the snack bars to pick up the empty cardboard boxes and cartons, as well as the garbage and trash, for sale to the recycler. Song and his collectors had counted on this extra revenue to break even. To their horror, all the boxes had been crushed and shredded. They asked the American sergeant in charge of the bar what had happened.

"We don't have to give you boxes," the sergeant said. "We give you trash."

When Song's trucks went to the Wangshimni dump, his men were assaulted by the army of rag picker-cum-beggars, who then proceeded to put the torch to all the US Army collection as soon as it was unloaded from the trucks, instead of sorting them out with the customary diligence, the American trash being more valuable than the Korean for its rich pickings. Song retaliated by bringing extra hands, but there were three times as many beggars waiting, all armed with pitchforks, knives, and other dangerous weapons. After spending all his savings, Song had to give up the contract. Alan could not take legal action as he had promised. Simply he did not know where to start. Bitterly remorseful, Alan resolved never to give any business advice to other people. Song's replacement had to be found right away, because refuse collection was something that could not be postponed. It was of course our good old Mr. Han again, stepping in to save the day. His connections were so widespread and entrenched that cooperation with him was the only alternative. Alan learned that it was Han who had managed to dispose of all his predecessors in the position of concession supervisor, that this position had been vacant for some time before he had stepped in. Everybody had been betting on how long Alan would last, now that their differences had come to a head. The expected ax fell the next day. Buckley called Alan to his office.

"You seem to have difficulty getting along with the concessionaires," he said.

"I don't," Alan objected. "It's just with Mr. Han."

"Well, he is the most important concessionaire. The others don't count much. Good public relations are essential to your job. I don't think you are working out exactly. So I am sending you to a warehouse."

"I was hired as a supervisor," Alan said. "I won't go to a warehouse."

"Either that or you have no job with the US Army."

The rent was due and so were other bills. Alan went to the cold, clammy warehouse at the northern end of the Yongsan compound right by the Wonhyo sewer main drain. Surrounded everywhere by ceiling-high piles of surplus military supplies to be auctioned off or destroyed, Alan felt the isolation and loneliness of exile. The work went on with the thieving and cheating usual in this line of work, and everybody, forklift drivers, maintenance personnel, laborers, foremen, wanted to keep him out of the way. They were a close fraternity, thick as thieves, huddling, whispering among themselves all the time, quickly shutting up whenever Alan went near, and ignoring him. Alan could feel he wasn't wanted, a figurehead they didn't need but had to put up with because the table of organization called for the position. All Alan could do was stand around, bored.

VII.
Fulbright Commission

Unable to bear it any longer Alan went to talk to Gregory Mendelson, cultural attaché at the American Embassy, who was deeply interested in all aspects of Korean culture and history and an avid collector of Korean antiques ranging from Goryo celadons, Yee dynasty silk screens and chests of drawers to coins, rings, and other personal ornaments. Our acquaintance with him began when we arranged a Korean folk music program through the Center for Mendelson and his foreign service dignitaries and visitors at the Korea House, with Alan providing the English commentary. Mendelson liked what he saw then and gave us more opportunities to organize traditional Korean dance and music shows for the foreigners in Seoul, who seemed to be about the only ones interested in the authentic Korean stuff, not caring much for the symphonies, ballets, and other half-baked Western imitations the Koreans were so eager to exhibit.

Mendelson was shocked to hear about what went on in the PX and advised Alan to quit his job at once, saying that the Fulbright Commission, just being organized in Korea, was looking for a program director. Alan was the very man for the job as far as he was concerned, a member on the organizing council. Alan quit, glad to leave the thieves and bullies behind and to work in his element, with decent, educated, cultured people. About time his luck had turned and something like this had come along, we told ourselves.

But we found out that Alan had quit too soon. Mendelson

was only one of the members on the council and not always the most popular or influential at that. The main hurdle was George Mahler, head of the USIS in Korea and chairman of the Fulbright Council, who was jealous of Mendelson and objected to anything Mendelson might bring up. After waiting two uncertain, harrowing months, Alan finally got the job, but was soon to learn never to be sanguine about changing jobs or about anything at all in life for that matter.

The first assignment he was given was to make a comparative poster for all the Fulbright grant applicants and grantees, showing a bird's eye view of their age, schooling, field of interest, occupation, place of origin, family, and other relevant background material. Having no examples to guide him Alan had to work from scratch, planning and revising over and over to arrive at the ideal of total presentation, a Herculean task, reconciling the two irreconcilables, outline and detail, the very feasibility of which was in doubt. After a day's concentrated labor, the end was still not in sight. When Alan arrived next morning, Dr. No, Director of the Fulbright Commission, which had to be a Korean by the US Fulbright Act, came over and reminded him of his tardiness. No, former Vice Minister of Education, had the degree from some American university.

"The chart is a priority job," No emphasized. "It's urgent. His Excellency, the American Ambassador himself, wants to look at it right away. Please finish it before five o'clock this evening."

No was so awed by the American Ambassador and so eager to please his Excellency that he did not care how many backs he broke to do it. Five minutes later he had a guest, who walked into No's glassed-in office next to Alan's. The visitor looked like a decent sort but had the habit of leaning over and whispering in No's ear, which the latter apparently relished. A pair of plotting thieves couldn't have looked cozier together. Now and then they turned their eyes to Alan and went back to their whispering, annoying him no end as the subject of their discussion seemed himself. Soon No came over, holding a letter in his hand, his friend in tow.

"This requires an immediate reply," No said. "It's got to be finished within thirty minutes. It's urgent. I'll be downstairs for a little while and then come up in exactly thirty minutes for the reply. Please have it ready without fail."

Putting the all-important grantee chart away Alan went to work on the letter. It was so convoluted that after two readings Alan still couldn't make head or tail of the writer's intent, let alone figure out an appropriate response. For one thing it called for some subjective response on the part of the addressee, some Kim he did not know. Already 25 minutes had passed, during which Alan had tried to cast himself in a dozen possible character roles for this Kim to come up with a suitable answer. Alan had typed as much as Dear Sir, but that was as far as he got, when in walked No, followed by his whispering chum, probably the addressee of the letter.

"Do you have the letter typed up and ready for signature?" No demanded with the hauteur of Julius Caesar expecting unconditional surrender from his vanquished Teutons.

"I could not answer. I did not know what to say."

"You don't have the letter ready?" No blew up. "I told you this is top priority."

His extreme agitation, out of proportion to the matter at hand, must have come in no small measure from his not being able to show off to his slimy friend that he, a Korean, could command an American slave, titled Program Director, who would, if pressed, wipe his behind maybe. The letter was clearly unrelated to the Fulbright program.

Subsequently Alan finished the letter, eliciting the relevant information as necessary, but had to labor under the most uncomfortable circumstances. Both No and his friend sat at his desk, breathing hard and turning around to stare at him impatiently and indignantly every time his typewriter stopped clicking. In the course of the afternoon two other 'top priority' jobs popped up and dumped in front of him, preventing him from giving another look at the grantee chart for the Ambassador.

Five o'clock struck. No stepped up to Alan's desk.

"Did you complete the chart?" he asked.

"No," Alan said puzzled. "You kept giving me those urgent jobs. You didn't seriously expect me to finish the chart today, did you?"

"Oh, Christ," No swore, shaking his head. "I told you this morning that it had to be finished by five, didn't I? There is only one thing we can do. I am sorry to say so but you must stay until you finish the job."

"No, I can't," Alan said. "I have an appointment to perform at the Center at 5:30."

"Oh, your Korean music!" No sneered. "That'll have to wait, I am afraid. This job is really important."

It was always like that. Alan had to work overtime, until ten or eleven, of course without any extra compensation. To return home before midnight curfew, the legacy of the Korean War, Alan had to take papers home, presumably to work on and finish before he turned up next morning at the office. Otherwise No would have kept him at work overnight. No wanted Alan to eat and sleep Fulbright, to devote his whole life to the worthy cause of selecting a percentage of these America-obsessed Korean youngsters for the American campuses to turn them into cultural sycophants. Most of them never returned to Korea, engineering their niche in America by means of incredible legal acrobatics against the explicit prohibitory clauses in the laws of both countries or in their notarized oaths, and the handful that returned dedicated the rest of their lives to turning Korea into a mini-America. No proposed to install a telephone at our house, courtesy of the American Embassy. Though a phone was a valuable asset worth thousands of dollars in the strange economy of Korea, Alan had to decline. We could visualize the Director calling Alan at midnight and three times subsequently in the course of the night to ask about some absurd detail concerning this grantee or that, this orientation schedule or that. Not only would we be deprived of privacy; we would not have a life at all, period, for lack of sleep.

Alan attended meetings of the Council, and they were a riot. At one meeting they discussed grantees coming from

America, for the Fulbright program was bidirectional. One Hill and one Goldberg were under review, both students of the Korean language on their own in Korea where they had come previously as draftees like Alan and stayed on after discharge for more than two years. More interested in the statistics, the total number of people on paper coming to Korea from America under the program, than depth or reality of cultural exchange, Fulbright had a rule that no one, who had stayed more than 18 months in the country, would be eligible for Fulbright grants. Under this rule both of the gentlemen proposed were to be automatically excluded from consideration. But before this technical point was brought up, the eminent Horace Becket came out with destructive rhetoric against one of them, Goldberg.

"That man Goldberg will never have my vote," Horace said. "I cast my veto right here and now."

"That's surprising," Mendelson observed. "He's been studying at your university and I thought you would be all for him. What's the problem?"

Becket was president of Wonday University, bequeathed to him by his far-seeing ancestors, who had come to Korea as missionaries to do good and had done indeed well. Many thousands of acres of prime city land belonged to the family, and under the new zoning laws, in which he had a hand, the prices of this land jumped twenty times. In addition, a whole beach belonged to the Beckets on the west coast, where he had cottages and hotels built for profitable rental during the peak summer months. But above all a huge hospital, probably the country's largest, was part of Wonday University, as well as other foundations and enterprises, supposedly philanthropic. Becket lived in a palatial mansion behind the campus, reached by a paved driveway nearly a mile long through luxuriant greenery. As a self-sacrificing missionary laboring in backward Korea he was entitled to the US Army postal service and PX privileges.

"The problem?" Becket reiterated distastefully. "Among others, he has been seen at drinking houses with disreputable Korean students. All the faculty hate this man Goldberg. He is a disgrace to America. I'll kick him out soon."

Becket went on denouncing Goldberg for 45 minutes, never allowing anyone else to speak. His first name Horace was pronounced by him and those bred in his dialect as "Horse", which aptly described him. There never was a more dogmatic or self-righteous man. The rather corpulent Unho Jo, representing the Korean Ministry of Foreign Affairs, tried hard to get a word in edgewise. In desperation he lifted a glass and banged it on the table, shattering it. Horse had to stop.

"I know he is a diligent student of the Korean language," Jo said. "If anybody deserves a grant from this organization, it is he. He has a Korean wife and a daughter and lives in a small rented room, with no regular job."

After hearing Jo quite a few of the Council members were moved to a sympathetic decision. Alan for one thought the poor man needed a drink now and then. Horace Becket looked at his watch and interrupted Jo.

"My God!" he exclaimed. "It's time to move on to the next topic on the agenda."

This was characteristic of the Horse, who monopolized every topic on the agenda, then looked at his large watch to lament the swift passage of time and urged the Council to move on to the next item. Having an unusually robust appetite, he uttered this call for forward march in more rapid succession as lunch time approached. Alan could not help looking at this confident, vociferous, opinionated missionary with awe. A man starving to death did not bother him in the least, but a man drinking to drown his sorrows affected his religious sensibility to a point of venomous hatred. In speech he stood fiercely by his Jesus Christ; in action he totally missed the point of his teachings. Horse never helped his neighbors.

At one meeting Becket was not present: as Moderator of the General Assembly of the Presbyterian Church in Korea he was dispensing his divine wisdom to a plenary session of the thousands of pastors and elders from all parts of the country, the Presbyterian Church being the most numerous and powerful among all the Protestant denominations. When he was absent, Mahler, the Chairman, filled his place. The only thing Mahler knew or valued in the world was mass media or journalism as he had learned it in college, everything else being trash. Mendelson, Alan's ally, suggested that Fulbright bring over some American archeologists to Korea.

"There is no decent course in archeology taught anywhere in Korea," Mendelson began. "No one knows how to conduct archeo-logical research or excavation. So many historical relics have fallen into ruin or been vandalized or destroyed. I have traveled to the Gyungjoo area recently. At one farmer's house I saw chickens feeding from a 2,000-year-old Shilla bowl! I saw drunken farmers throwing around like dirt pottery and shards worth ten times their weight. Farmers plow right through precious relics in the field. We must preserve them."

Outranking Mendelson in the American foreign service hierarchy, Mahler squinted at him impatiently. It was Mendelson's misfortune to have Mahler working in the same field, information, and to be opposed by him at every turn whenever some new proposal had to be made. Mahler found the young, brilliant Mendelson with a real enlightened passion for his work a serious threat and a constant source of irritation.

"Archeology!" shouted Mahler disdainfully. "Gregory, don't be ridiculous. Archeologists are a bunch of useless parasites in this world. There are so many urgent, necessary things to be done and taken care of in Korea, and you pick of all things a remote, impractical thing like archeology for crying out loud!"

"What does Korea need then?" Mendelson challenged.

"Good heavens, not archeology for sure," Mahler said. "Well, for instance, well, er, ..., mass media, for example. We can bring in journalists to Korea and make them teach Koreans how to gather news and disseminate through the media."

"You are always harping on journalism," Mendelson derided.

"Well, what of it?" Mahler glared angrily.

Their eyes locked together and sparks flew. Perhaps the meeting might still be described as having ended peacefully because no blows had been exchanged, but the tension was there and the two would have flown at each other's throat, if they could have done it decently, without all the witnesses around.

At every meeting No acted so servilely that he did not look Director but more like a page boy. His servility hit a new low whenever the American Ambassador was pleased to sit in at one of the meetings. Once he almost put his head through the glass door, as he pitched forward head first, to open it for the Ambassador. Had his Excellency stepped but two inches closer, poor Dr. No would have run his head through. On another occasion No nearly fell down a long flight of stairs in his eagerness to see the Ambassador off. Fortunately he was saved by the banister that cracked under the impact but mysteriously held.

There were other members, both Korean and American, as the Charter required, among whom Dr. Ingyong Chay, former President of Seoul National University, must be mentioned. A tall, handsome gentleman with firm eyebrows and pronounced nose, he never spoke a single blessed word at any of the meetings during his entire tenure of twelve months. In contrast, Julie Hayes, the recording secretary, who had legally no voice at the Council, presumed to put in her two bits. Every time she spoke, Mahler, the Chairman, who was interested in her in more ways than one, did not fail to encourage her. The blonde secretary, with her husband working at USOM, was well aware of her slim figure, narrow waist and long legs, and used them to good advantage. Moreover, she had the notion that superior intelligence was one of her endowments, which gave her a right, nay a duty, to speak up and meddle in other people's affairs.

At Mahler's insistence a journalist was finally brought over to Korea. Dr. Harman, a solemn bearded man with a recent Ph.D., arrived with his wife and adopted son, a Sioux Indian, who looked remarkably Asiatic. Harman was assigned to Central University, whose president had clamored for a Fulbright scholar, promising among other benefits a good house with all the modern amenities. When the Harmans and Alan went to this dream house, it was not habitable, not even by

Korean standards. Alan had to look for a house in a hurry for the three Harmans whose hotel bills were running up fast, depleting the Commission's emergency funds. Through the ubiquitous real estate agents a suitable house was found in a good, typically Korean neighborhood in Nagwondong, which was near Harman's school. This was dandy because it also met the requirement that, instead of isolating themselves in the guarded foreign compounds with Western comforts, all American grantees live on the economy, mixing with the local population, the only way to learn the host country firsthand. I thought scholars like Harman would welcome new experiences, new ways of life, new perspectives. In my naivete I had envisioned Fulbright scholars as the modern version of pioneers setting out into unknown territory.

After the Harmans moved into the new house, the phone at Alan's office never ceased ringing. Both Harman and his wife called alternately.

"Our son has been kidnapped," they screamed. "Alert the Seoul police. We'll write to our Congressman. Why don't you do something? You put us in this house, Heyman, and if anything happens, we'll hold you directly responsible."

The fact was that their adopted son, looking like any Korean boy in the neighborhood, was well liked and spent whole afternoons and sometimes days at some friend's house. Alan tried to explain but they would not listen, bitter as they were about living so close to the Koreans they had come to learn better and help if they could. If it was not the child problem, other complaints brought them promptly to the phone. For example, the Harmans claimed they had been robbed. Sometimes Alan's phone rang every twenty minutes and he was accused of irresponsibility for not dismissing the Minister of Home Affairs. The phone calls stopped only after the Harmans were moved to UN Village, part of Little America, as it was called derisively by the Koreans watching from outside.

The same was true with all the other American grantees, who uniformly and absolutely refused to experience Korea except across a guarded fence. I wondered whether these grantees could have been cut from the same material as the Pilgrims or the frontiersmen, who had slept in the open, spurning security and bodily comfort like the plague. Whenever they visited the houses of other Americans in Seoul, diplomats, businessmen, and well-to-do missionaries, these pioneers of American learning, the exponents of the outreaching American spirit, became green with envy. One look at the PX and the Army commissary was enough to send them clamoring to Alan to arrange the same privileges for them. After deliberately creating trouble at the Korean houses they had been billeted, the best Korean-style homes with de luxe Korean accommodations, they maneuvered their way to one of the colorless Western houses in Little America, in UN Village, or the bungalows on Itaywun Hill, which didn't diminish their conviction that they embodied the good old American pioneering spirit, roughing it in Korea, officially designated a 'hardship area' where those in the military and diplomatic services drew a higher rate of pay.

One of the Fulbright grantees was a woman sociologist Mendelson brought over to Alan one day.

"Alan, this is Dr. Mary Boone, probably granddaughter of Daniel Boone."

"What do you mean probably?" the lady in her sixties flamed into white heat. "Daniel Boone was my great great grand uncle."

Alan wasn't sure how to react to a female Daniel Boone. But one thing was certain: she wasn't any more pioneering than her other countrymen with less exalted names.

"I don't want to be put in a stinking Korean home," she made it clear at the outset.

Alan had to put her in a house on the Baptist Mission compound to live with the American missionaries, including my old acquaintances, the Epsteins, who proved congenial company, listening to her one-sided, long-winded conversation.

August came, the month when all the hard-working missionaries took off for a month-long vacation at the luxurious Mallipo or Daychon Beaches, owned and operated by their spiritual leader Horse Becket. The telephone at Alan's office did not stop ringing. The tough-grained relative of Daniel Boone sometimes almost wept with misery.

"I am alone," she said, whimpering. "There is nobody to keep me company."

"Aren't there any Koreans?"

"A couple of servants but I can't talk to them. They don't speak my language. I need someone to talk to."

"Why don't you try learning some Korean?"

"Learn Korean?" she shrieked hysterically. "That's the worst insult I've ever heard."

"I beg your pardon," Alan quickly apologized. "I'll try to find somebody to keep you company. If necessary, I'll be over myself."

He could not deliver, however. Nobody was free to go and talk to her. Alan could have sent me but knew how I couldn't stand her bad breath, as she kept pulling me to her, to hug and kiss her "pet", all innocent perhaps but still repulsive. Alan really meant to do the errand himself but got tied up at work as usual and had to be at the Center afterwards, making him forget about Mary Boone. But not with impunity. After waiting until one a.m. that night, her disappointment turned into violent animosity that had to exact its pound of flesh. To the very day she left Korea she never stopped asking Alan to do the most demeaning personal chores for her. Instead of gratitude, however, she brayed so loudly at the American Embassy about his inefficiency that some of it echoed all the way to his normally unsuspecting ears. As a parting gift she made Alan write over a hundred letters, her own private letters, to the various places she wished to visit after Korea and lecture at. This was before computers and word processors and Alan had to pound out each letter on the typewriter. Though she had the illusion of being a world-renowned authority in her field, she was realistic enough to suspect that not too many invitations would be forthcoming from the campuses around the globe. In fact, she was not sure whether she would get even a single invitation. To compensate for this Alan was ordered to consult the catalogues of all the universities on the seven continents and type the letter to each sociology department, making sure to address the chairman by name and include other details specific to that institution to avoid the impression of an impersonal form letter. Only the part citing her kudos and merits in superlatives need not be varied. We never found out how many invitations she got, because she had taken care to make her own residence the return address.

Yoonchol Ho, the newly hired director of the Aran Ham Center with some background in business, had a brain storm - start a tourist guide training program for the budding tourism industry of Korea. The school could not survive without outside support, the original Aran Ham endowment having been exhausted a long time ago except for the land and buildings, and was always begging one organization or other for help. The Korea Tourist Bureau had just been incorporated with government funds to attract foreign tourists and money seemed to be no object. If the school could identify itself with the Bureau's aims, subsidies and donations would flood in. Once the vision was there, the vision of money, the details and methods worked out by themselves in quick succession. What was more logical than that the Center be the tourist guide training school, because foreign tourists came to see the real Korea, its unique folk traditions and arts? he argued. Enough people had been returning from America to tell him that most foreigners did not want to see a replica of America in Asia, and now he saw himself as the leader of this new movement to show the real Korea to the outside world. The training program had suggested itself rather readily to his mind because the school had a resource it could count on, available for free or at a minimal cost perhaps, namely, Alan and me.

"Please teach English to the tourism class," Ho said. "The two of you as a team just as you did at FLI."

So Wansong must have told him, the traitor! But, then, Ho could have found out about FLI anyway. Neither of us wanted to hear even the name of FLI spoken again, but they wouldn't know that. On the contrary, it was to them something to write home about, on the order of the Academy of Science or something similar.

"But Alan has a job, nine to six or later," I pointed out.

"But you don't," Ho said, with alacrity. "You carry on weekdays and your brother helps on weekends. Our Center will be known as FLI Resurrected, and the whole town will flock to us."

"No way. We want none of it."

"Please help," Ho pleaded, seizing our arms as we rose to leave the room. "This will entitle the Center to an allocation in the Bureau's annual budget. We know you won't let your friends down. I'll have them all come one by one to beg you personally, Ilsob Hong, Gwayryong Shim, Choran Bag,...."

"Okay, okay," Alan agreed, knowing when he was licked and appealing to me.

"A small class, once a week, on Sunday," I said.

But I ended up teaching almost everyday to classes double the size at FLI, big as they had been. They were held behind the school building proper, in a warehouse, next to the caretaker's unit where I had stayed for recuperation. At this time Choran Bag, one of the more vocal and powerful directors on the Center faculty, was between houses, having sold her last home, with her new house still under construction. She moved into the dormitory with her tribe, which included grandmothers, aunts, children, maids, and her husband, Byongwon Yee, the daygum or horizontal flute virtuoso. He was also on the faculty of the school but lived completely in her shadow, happy to leave her all the family finances so he could live a carefree, boy's life. Though ranked among the top daygum performers in the country, he could not be relied upon for anything. His idea of participation in a public recital was to take off after five minutes of performance and have a swig of wine at some drinking house he had marked out before, making the producer or director run all over the neighborhood in search of him for his next appearance.

Madame Bag decided to hold her classes in the room she slept. Being next door all we could hear was her girls tapping on the janggo and bursting out into loud singing, led by her own booming, hoarse voice that did justice to her 300 pounds.

My students could not keep their minds on the lessons, but I did not really mind, because I found her comical. Also I tried to catch Bag's musical enunciation and phrasing, anything to divert myself from the monotony of teaching. Because her voice was husky, a first listener with no real understanding of Korean music was apt to think poorly of her ability. In fact, at a performance Alan and I had arranged for RAS, Royal Asiatic Society, Korea Branch, a social and cultural organization of foreigners in Seoul, a Hawaiian neisei said, "That blimp can't sing." But anybody who knew what pansori should sound like appreciated the intense dramatic artist behind her unprepossessing exterior. She could literally paint the opera with her singing. My students, who thought themselves modern and sophisticated because they spoke some English and were being trained to meet American tourists, had of course no idea of what Bag represented and were loud in protest, at last lodging a formal complaint with the school administration.

"We have our pride," they delcared. "We didn't sign up to study in a gisang and moodang school. We'll talk to the Bureau about it if this elephant of a woman does not stop making all that horrid noise, disrupting our class work."

Any mention of the Bureau brought on the jitters to Director Ho. On the other hand, he was equally timorous of the big lady's ire. Halfheartedly, the school administration sent a particularly diplomatic delegation to ask her to quiet down or move to some other part of the campus. She blew up like an over-blown balloon and stormed into my class. Shaking her fists, stamping her feet, she harangued in her enormous voice, unopposed and uninterrupted for two hours, at the end of which the saucy young men and women, as quiet as mice before a cat, forever renounced any thought of complaint so long as they wanted to come and study at the Center for their diploma.

VIII.
Impressarios

When I came out of class one day at the Center somebody was waiting, Changno Won, owner of a theater in Jonjoo, North Jolla, who wanted me and Alan to put together a Korean music troupe to perform at his theater for a few days. I was thrilled and so was Alan. Previously we had acted primarily as interpreter and go-between for presentations to private parties of foreigners. Now we were being asked to take charge of the whole production, from hiring the musicians to deciding on the content of the program for paying audiences at a regular commercial establishment. Luckily all the people we wanted on the program happened to be between engagements and consented to come along when we approached them with the proposal. The cast included Choran Bag, her husband Yee, Sunhee Kim, another pansori singer with a touch of refinement and class about her, Wansong Char, the dancer, who was still straightening out a glitch in his American immigration, Gwayryong Shim, the bald-headed and gaunt gomungo player, Ilsob Hong, Alan's flute teacher, and Wonjee Goo, his gayagum teacher who was also the nation's top shijo poet. All agreed to go on one condition, full payment in advance, which I duly mentioned to Won.

"Of course," he said. "I should have foreseen this. How thoughtless of me not to bring along enough cash! I can kill myself. All I had to do was stop at the bank and bring a roll."

"How much cash do you have?"

"Only about half."

"Can't you go to a bank here?"

"No, I left my passbook at home. I could go home and come back, but that would delay everything."

"Yes. Some of our people may have other plans and won't be able to come."

"We are in a jam. I have an idea. How about you putting up the other half of the cash needed? We'll be partners on this venture, splitting the profit fifty-fifty, fifty for me and fifty for you brothers."

That seemed like the only alternative. Besides, it seemed like a generous offer, because Won was providing his theater as well. I explained the situation to Alan, who had just been paid by Fulbright and decided to invest the larger part of his pay in what seemed like a foolproof deal. The musicians were all of the first caliber and were sure to draw. In all modesty, we two Heyman brothers were also the added attraction, Americans in a regular Korean folk band in a country town where many people had not even seen one Westerner before. All went well except for two things.

With a brimming heart Alan went to his boss No, Fulbright Director, to ask for the two-week leave with pay he was entitled to according to the articles of employment.

"No," No said. "You can't leave."

"But I am entitled to...."

"It doesn't say when you can take the leave. As your supervisor I say you can't take it when the office needs you. Besides in your kind of job you can't go strictly by the letter of the contract. You've got to be more flexible."

"That's why I have put in the many, many extra hours and days into this job."

Of course it had never occurred to No that some compensation might be due Alan for such flexibility.

"It's a job in which results count, not the number of hours."

"I haven't asked for overtime or anything, have I? All I am asking is a short leave so I can meet my commitments to perform...."

"You should have consulted me before you made those

commitments."

It was an impasse. Finally, after reviewing the metaphysics of leave-taking several more times No gave grudging approval on condition that all of Alan's future leaves be forfeit. Alan agreed, thinking he would cross that bridge when he got there.

The other problem was our disagreement with Won about the price of admission. Won wanted to charge 30 hwan, about 23 cents, hwan being the new unit of currency in the monetary reform carried out by the military government, and Alan and I wanted to charge only 20 hwan.

"Country people are too poor to pay 30 hwan," I argued.

"No," Won countered. "We need a prestige appeal. Selling cheap is not the way to go about it. Do you know what the trouble is with you Korean music people? You sell yourselves too cheap and get treated like dirt. People pay 100 hwan, 200 hwan, sometimes even 500 to go to a Western concert, jazz festival, circus, and think nothing of it. They think they have spent the money for a good cause. This low self-image got to change. Besides if we charge too little, the riffraff might come and disrupt the atmosphere."

He seemed to have everything figured out and we gave in. After all 10 hwan more wouldn't make that much difference even to a Korean farmer, we told ourselves.

On the appointed day we all assembled at Seoul Main Station to catch the train to Jonjoo. To my surprise Madame Bag turned up with her two children and her maid, which was above and beyond the stipulations of the contract. Since all expenses were paid by the sponsors, Won and us, these additions meant extra expenditure of approximately ten dollars a day. I wanted to object but Ilsob Hong stopped me.

"You'll only waste your breath," he said. "You can tell her seven times seven and she will still bring them along."

I learned that to invite her was to invite all her dependents. Nobody liked it but being indispensable she was invited nevertheless. She knew it and took ruthless advantage. The older child was in elementary school but the younger one was barely a year old, but neither of them resembled her in any way.

"It's a wonder how she dotes on them," Ilsob Hong said with a quizzical expression on his face.

"She is an affectionate mother," I said.

"But neither of them is her own. She can't have children."

"Whose are they then?"

"Her husband's."

"From his former wives? I didn't know Byongwon had other wives than Bag."

"You don't have to be a wife to bear children. Any fertile female would do. Bag wants children and gets women for him. I bet he likes it. What man wouldn't? She goes to the country for the purpose, sending a runner ahead to spread the word. After looking over the lot that has been assembled, she chooses the healthiest, pays her parents off, and brings her to Seoul to be bedded down with her husband in their bedroom."

"In the same room?"

"Yes. In fact she supervises the copulation to make sure nothing goes wrong. The girl stays until she delivers the baby and nurses it. As soon as the child is weaned, the surrogate mother is sent away. Bag has two now but plans to have several more that way."

We lost close to $200 on the venture, wiping out about all of our excess cash flow. It was a costly, sobering experience, making me think twice about musical entrepreneurship.

"You were right," Won said remorsefully. "We should have charged only 20."

But triumph or recrimination was out of place.

"No," I said, surprising him with this reversal of position. "You were right. We should have charged more in fact. It's not the price. Even if it had been free, we wouldn't have had any larger crowd."

I was understandably bitter. By painstaking persuasion I had most of the performers agree to necessary excisions and modifications in the repertoire, except Choran Bag who almost knocked me over for suggesting the elimination of the long prelude to the Bird Song. Fast-paced and coordinated without the frustrating waits and fillers the total program had artistically satisfying variety, balance, and cohesion. But all the hard work and planning had been wasted on a provincial city full of yokels just catching the snobbery of the capital against their indigenous musical heritage, when the capital itself was slowly awakening to its value, at least among the more enlightened minority. It was sad to see this happening to Jonjoo, the home of the Choonhyang lore, Maiden of Spring Fragrance, and much valuable musical tradition. Instead of romantic pavilions and pastoral lovers I saw only a crass miniature of Seoul where cheap pop tunes of some foreign inspiration were the craze to the exclusion and neglect of the native element.

About a month after the Jonjoo fiasco the city of Jinjoo in South Gyongsang Province invited the Center to come over and help celebrate its annual Sky Fest kicked off on the first day of the tenth moon. Drawing up a cast of 30, among whom Alan and I were included, the Center put Choran Bag in charge. This was another occasion Alan simply could not miss but because absence from the office was required he had to clear it with Director No. Under the contract he was still entitled to a week's leave, but since their last confrontation he didn't know whether he had any coming his way. Then, opportunely, No himself had taken a 10-day leave and returned looking chipper with glowing reports about the 700-year-old Hain Temple he had visited deep in the woods of Mt. Oday.

"I feel ten years younger," he said. "You can't exaggerate the restorative effect of a retreat in the pollution-free mountains."

Alan had to seize this opportunity when No was in such a rare mood. Besides, unless he was totally inconsistent, he would recognize the same need for rehabilitation in other frayed bodies, too. Perhaps all this excited talk about the virtues of leave taking was his own way of saying that he had changed his mind about their last talk on the same subject, occasioned in the heat of the moment and totally lacking rationality.

"I was thinking of taking a leave like that myself," Alan said.

No's bushy eyebrows jerked up and his whole body stiffened as if he had been stabbed. Not a trace remained of his bonhomie.

"You promised you wouldn't take any more leaves," he said gruffly.

"I said I wouldn't when we are busy," Alan said. "I don't think we are that busy now."

"Not busy! How can you say such a thing? You have no sense of responsibility, or else you won't be saying such a ridiculous thing. I say you cannot take a leave. We are too busy, period."

"When are we ever not busy, then? It's always like that in this office. I cannot miss this opportunity. It is too important to me."

"I don't care what it is, how important it is," No said stamping his foot. "If you are serious about continuing to work here, you cannot go this time."

"I must."

"All right. You may be as obstinate as you like. But I warn you. If you don't show up for work next week, I won't keep this matter quiet any more. I have had all the nonsense I can take from you."

It was an insulting threat. Alan decided to show the little tyrant that he did not own him and left for Jinjoo with the group, not caring what might come next.

Though promised the best theater in town before departure, upon arrival we were shown to a third-rate cinema house, more like a barn, damp, dirty, and cold with no heating. There were seats of sorts for the patrons in the auditorium but backstage, bare of chairs, desks, or partitions, we had to sit on the cold cement floor while changing costumes or waiting for our turns. I had a mild case of piles but after the first day at the theater it flared into painful, bleeding sores which the ice cold floor at the inn did not help either. Alan had a cough and a temperature, that made him dizzy.

Featuring many other forms of entertainment in addition to our folk music, the Festival had attracted large contingents of visitors from all over the neighboring counties and our accommodations became necessarily more cramped with four to a room instead of two as promised, though the rooms were barely the size for one man to move around in. But that was being spacious compared to what went on in the other parts of the inn, which happened to be inundated by high schoolers on a group excursion to the city. A hundred of them slept in some dozen rooms, probably on top of each other.

High-strung and traveling for the first time in their lives, these adolescents were so excited that they chatted, laughed, sang and carried on until two o'clock in the morning. I could get only one hour's sleep at most. By four I had to be up and finish my morning toilet. Otherwise I would never get the chance. The kids stormed the limited facilities and laid siege until the next kingdom come. To obtain any kind of water took as much determination as stealing Helen of Troy. The inn's entire supply came from a well, which the sleepless early risers surrounded from about five o'clock and hogged until it was bone dry. The well had a singular construction, its bottom disappearing in a dark abyss that probably went through to the antipodes. A bucket had to be pulled up by a rope, but after drawing on it for about five minutes what came up was just a handful of brackish water at the bottom, the larger part having leaked through a dozen holes. But the management never thought of replacing or repairing it the whole time we were there. With this limited supply of water the guests, young and old, washed themselves down from head to foot, and laundered their travel-soiled socks, handkerchiefs, and underwear, which were then hung up on doors, windows, closets. Particularly singled out for this purpose by our leader Choran Bag was a stand of stunted evergreens in the middle of the courtyard, which never saw the light of day while we were there. What with her numerous entourage and her own large person, she naturally had a good deal of laundry to contribute, which no sooner washed than promptly draped the poor plants top to bottom.

These distressing circumstances might still have been tolerable, if the food had been decent. It was barely edible even to me. Alan could not touch most of it and became convinced that Jinjoo people as a whole did not know how to cook. Their brew, called dongdongjoo or floating wine, was an absolute abomination. The other performers drank it and came down with the trots. Alan wouldn't have touched it, except Ilsob insisted that it would help relieve his cold. Weary to the bones even before the performance Alan feared he might not be able to go on at all with his hojog solos, which took a lot of lung power. The last straw, however, was Bag's decision to put on three shows a day instead of the two originally planned and bargained for.

"The theater is small and we cannot make enough money with only two a day," she said.

That was final. The commander in chief had made up her mind, to which she would brook no dissent. Grumbling and whining the rest of us went along. Predictably we all got sicker. On the second day my throat was so sore I could not swallow even my own saliva and felt as if I might drop dead any minute. After the second performance of the day Alan and I went to the inn for a snack and a rest before the evening performance scheduled at seven. In our room our bags lay open, with its contents spilled out. Gwayryong Shim, with whom we were sharing the room, was seething with rage.

"That bitch has searched all our bags," Shim said.

On discovering in the morning that her jade hair pin was missing, Bag took the time when everybody was at the theater to open and turn all our bags inside out, not coming to the afternoon show until she was quite done with the search, which yielded no hair pin. Finding the bags so violated during their absence, the members marched en masse on Bag's room, flailing arms and threatening to bring down the roof over her head, though the sight of her formidable person filling the doorway and confronting them quelled their spirit somewhat.

"Your husband probably pawned it," Ilsob Hong suggested in indignation.

In a paroxysm of anger that surpassed in intensity anything she had displayed previously, Bag almost tore the small, enfeebled old man Hong to shreds, though the timely intervention of the group averted this calamity. Before the stronger will the lesser broke and the demonstrators retreated to their separate quarters. But tempers still flew high and the whole group was for discontinuing the tour right then and there. By six-thirty, with the curtain to go up in thirty minutes, everybody was firmly resolved not to go to the theater. Finally one thing led to another and people began to take conciliatory positions. The show was saved.

The three shows a day schedule strained us to the limit. It was nothing less than heroic that we had endured as much as we had. On the last day, however, everybody broke down. Alan and I went to the theater for the last show near curtain time. Only five assistants were there. Not a single performer had showed up yet. It was time to raise the curtain. I told the assistants to get dressed and go on stage with Alan to open the show. They thought it madness.

"Without the principal singers and instrumentalists?" they asked.

"But the audience is getting restless," I pointed out.

"They'll riot if we go out by ourselves."

"No, we can hold them off for a while by just being on stage, and Alan can give his hojog solos."

While we were arguing in this fashion, fifteen minutes had passed curtain time. The theater manager came, shook his fist, and demanded his money back. It was thirty minutes past, but not a soul showed up. The angry crowd stamped their feet, whistled, and screamed.

"Let's begin, principals or no principals," I declared. "I am going out there no matter what. I'll beat the janggo. You girls sing and dance. I'll dance, too, if necessary. Are you ready?"

It was worse than hitching five mules to a yoke. No sooner had I pinned one down on the stage than another slid off like melting butter. In the fourth or fifth attempt, with split-second timing, the curtain went up, freezing them to the spot as they were about to flee. The show was on, hamstrung or not. Considering the obvious handicap we labored under, we did rather well on the whole and succeeded in holding the fury of the audience at bay for a while. Our number was finished, but still no one turned up. It was 45 minutes past. Alan went out again and played the Farmer's Song on the hojog. Just as he was finishing and I was worrying about what to do next, Wonji Goo, the gomungo master, stumbled in backstage. Greatly relieved, everybody pounced on him and dressed and rushed him to the stage, with me in tow to play the janggo. Few others, including Wansong, drifted in. It was one hour past, but still half the group had not arrived. By the close of the program we were all there, except our leader Madame Bag, the genius behind our extreme exertion, who had seen nothing wrong with pushing us beyond the limit.

Early the next morning, there being some free time before departure by bus to the train station about noon, Alan and I asked Wonji Goo to go sightseeing with us to a Buddhist temple on a mountainside near the city, reputedly built a millenium and a half ago during the Shilla Dynasty. We weren't disappointed. Small but clean and well tended, it exuded character and dignity found only in true antiquity. The abbot in gray coat and shaven head was an obliging guide and narrated its history. By and by he brought out a guest book and asked us to sign our names or write down anything we pleased. Neither Alan nor I could think of anything appropriate for the occasion other than our names which we put down one after the other, but Wonji Goo, a shijo poet, sat down and wrote out a beautiful quatrain to the effect that the temple was the embodiment of the nobility and idealism with which the ancient kingdom of Shilla had been imbued. The abbot seemed bewitched, his eyes glued to the calligraphy. At this point I thought it only proper and fair to enlighten him as to the writer's identity.

"Your visitor here is the great shijo poet and gomungo master Wonji Goo," I said.

"I have heard your high name before," the abbot said falling to the floor in deep obeisance. "Please forgive my ignorant rudeness in not recognizing you. Would you mind, sir, singing a shijo poem before the altar?"

"Not at all," Goo said without hesitation.

Goo rarely sang anywhere informally like that, but he was

in the mood and the inspiration was on him. The abbot rang a bell and the monks poured out of their cells into the main sanctuary where they sat on the floor before the altar in the lotus position with palms joined in front of them. Goo composed and sang a twelve-line syllabic ode on the spot, both the words and the music flowing out of him impromptu. From a solemn bass passage the melody soared to heights reached only by falsetto, followed by light staccato movements, probing a wide range of emotions. Everyone was in rapture. It was a revelation. I had always thought of poetry writing and music composition as a laborious process with constant revision and recasting toward the final product. To write and sing one's own lyrics at a moment's notice and move a sedate, religious audience to such a degree of ecstasy was something I thought only the legendary Homeric bards were capable of. When the singing was over, it was hard to descend from the heights of poetic exaltation to workaday existence.

"You have done us a great honor," the abbot said almost in tears. "Take anything you want from this temple."

Goo could have walked off with the treasure chest of the temple.

"I'd like to make a good bamboo flute," Goo said. "I saw bamboo shoots behind the temple. Can you let me have one?"

They cut down and trimmed the five best. From the persimmon trees growing in their garden large, sweet Jinjoo persimmons were plucked, filling three large panniers, too heavy to be carried by any one man. The monks would have gladly carried them to the end of the earth, but their religion prohibited their leaving the temple grounds. A stretcher was devised by weaving the bamboo sticks together with vines and the baskets of fruit were lashed securely to it. Reeling under the weight Alan and I lifted the ends, refusing Goo's offer to help, and gingerly picked our way down the mountain trail with the grateful monks still standing and waving to us from a vantage point. By the time we reached the inn with our trophy we were half dead but the sensation we created among our confreres alone seemed to be enough recompense. Livid with jealousy, they all stormed out of the inn and bought up all the persimmons at the market place that day to take home with them to Seoul.

A bus was to come to the inn to pick us up and take us to the train station. Worn out and suffering from one malady or other, everybody was quite desperate to go home. Train time was nearing. Bags slung around shoulders or wound around hands, we stood on our toes outside the inn or paced the street restlessly, anxiously peering into the distance for a sign of the promised transportation. The bus never showed up. We were all impatient to know what was holding it up. Finally, a messenger arrived to announce that the bus had broken down on the road and could not take us to the station at all. Panic and hysteria set in. No plague or invading Red Chinese army could have triggered a worse confusion. Somebody dashed inside to ask the inn keeper about calling a cab and returned with the news that the city had no taxi service. Even if one or two could be hustled up, not all thirty of us with our loads could have fitted in. Finally Goo, Wansong, Alan, and I, about the only ones who were not shouting, beating chests, and jumping, arranged an open truck to take us to the station.

When the truck pulled up at the inn, Bag promptly took the cab seats with her children. All the others threw their bags, inflated with the soft ripe persimmons, onto the back, then jumped right on top of them. Obsessed with the single thought of reaching the station in time for the train, they trampled on each other's bags and did not care. In vain I tried to tell them not to sit on the bags. Goo and Alan were up but I was still on the ground to hand up our baskets of persimmons. They both extended their hands for the baskets but plainly there was no place for them in the press, unless we shoved them underfoot like the other bags. The truck started moving and I had to climb aboard.

"Please take them," I told the innkeeper, pulling myself up the tailgate and pointing at the baskets.

The usual bumpy ride along the Korean road began. We were knocked about, left to right, back and forth, up and down, colliding into each other, banging against the sides, thudding on the floor. By the time we got to the station our clothes, faces and heads were plastered with persimmon syrup, but nobody stopped to think about such trivia. The train was leaving in two minutes.

"Let's go!" Bag yelled in her foghorn voice, leaping out of the cab.

Each grabbed what looked like his or her bag and made one mad dash for the entrance. Aboard, my friends squeezed their belongings into the overhead racks already filled with other luggage. Alan and I found seats several rows apart next to our people scattered in the car. As the train started moving, they sat back, breathing contentedly. Just then I noticed a streak of thick, pink liquid slowly working its way down the wall. But this was just the preamble. Soon the persimmon soup seeped and dripped everywhere, in dribs and drabs, streamlets, landing on the hats and clothes hung on the pegs, then on the heads of the passengers below, who began screaming, at first thinking it was blood dripping from some murdered body stashed above. Eyes were raised and the culprits identified, the persimmon-soaked bags of our group, creating an uproar of indignation.

Misoog Han, one of the assistants, had no persimmon left, except seeds and pulpy skin.

"Why did you throw your bags on the truck first?" I asked. "You should have gone aboard first, then have the others hand up the bags."

"There was no time for all that," she said.

"I bet it would have taken just as much time to do that way as the other. Anyway you have no persimmon to bring to Seoul."

"Nor you."

"But at least somebody else has the benefit of the goods."

"That was a dumb thing to do."

"Not any dumber than...."

"Who cares!" she said, smiling and taking the whole thing as a big joke, as did the others. "Anyway my family can see I have tried. Meanwhile I can travel lighter."

But it was no joking matter to the other passengers, who brought the matter to the attention of the train conductor.

Upset at the mess, the latter swore to throw us all out at the next station. When necessary, Choran Bag could turn on her charms, somehow irresistible to the Korean male. The determined official was soon prevailed upon and at last turned away, smiling and urging the other passengers to exercise the virtue of tolerance and mutual accommodation.

After the first hour of doing nothing, my companions began to feel bored. Soon several gathered around Choran Bag and played cards, shouting at each other, calling names and shrieking. Madame Bag always started these sotta games, the Korean equivalent of poker, and ended up holding all the money in her lap. At one corner Ilsob Hong, Misoog Han, and others started drinking distilled spirits. Soon Ilsob Hong felt drowsy and stretched himself out, his legs digging into the opposite seat to the disgust of its occupant Gwayryong Shim who, not liking the encroachment, frowned and muttered incessantly. Misoog Han, who made her living as a gisang at one of the big restaurants in Seoul, soon got out of hand, and began singing, drawing everybody's attention to our section. Those around her gave one excuse or another and moved away from her. Finding herself so rejected Misoog came right up to my side. Holding my arm, she began sobbing and recounting her sad life story. All the eyes in the car seemed riveted on us, and I blushed, not knowing how to extricate myself from the awkward situation. At this moment Gwayryong Shim, sitting across the aisle from me, jumped up suddenly from his seat.

"What is this?" he shrieked, brushing his pants and jacket.

One side of his suit was wet and so was the seat, with a distinct odor. Gwayryong and others shook Ilsob Hong, sleeping obliviously. After much shaking and even pinching by the others, Hong opened his eyes at last and rubbed his face. Gradually coming to his senses, Hong saw what he had done. Overwhelmed with shame, he hid his face behind his hands and ran out of the car to sit the rest of the journey to Seoul on the steps, perhaps the only way to dry his pants, having no change. I could understand what people meant when they said he had come to no good because of his drinking in spite of his obvious accomplishments.

When we returned to Seoul, Alan found an icy reception at the office. In his absence No had been blabbing to Mahler at the Embassy that he could not work with him, that either Alan or No would have to go. There being no love lost between Alan and Mahler, the latter decided to let Alan go and keep No.

"Free at last," Alan said, as he could now spend more time at the Center, both teaching English and improving his skills with the various instruments. But he seemed to take the loss of his job harder than he let on. He spoke fewer words and brooded often, preferring to be left alone. I did not intrude, letting him work it out.

Contacted by his friends in his native town Booan, North Jolla, on the west coast, to organize and bring over a performing group, Gwayryong Shim was putting together a cast of performers that included Choran Bag, her husband Yee, Ilsob Hong, Wonji Goo, and other big names, who would have normally disdained to go to a small town like Booan. Somebody was throwing money around. Alan and I were asked to come along too for a pay of $100 each. We had not seen that kind of money for some time. When we agreed, however, he paid only half, saying the balance would be paid later when we got there. The expenses were to be paid by the sponsors, as was the custom. I persuaded Alan to deposit all the money in the bank, finally adopting the practice of our Korean colleagues in this respect, though Alan had misgivings about traveling without cash. All Korean musicians adhered to the doctrine that they should go on a tour penniless, because that way if they returned home without making any money, as it often happened, they could still say they had not lost anything. In fact, they had earned their keep in the meantime, while any extra money they could bring home would be net profit.

The theater in Booan was literally a stable, with no seats for the patrons except dirty backless wooden benches, as narrow as saw horses, half of them teetering and falling apart with loose nails. There was no backstage or dressing room. In spite of these obvious physical deficiencies the tour was to prove an unforgettable experience to Alan and me in many ways. To the packed audience of country folk Choran Bag sang with the deepest emotion and richest artistry we had ever seen in a pansori singer. The theater might be a cow shed but the quality of her art made it something greater than La Scalla or the Metropolitan. The simple peasants were moved, applauded rapturously, and called her back to the stage for many more encores. She might be coarse and mercenary, but was an artist through and through, and in her turn she responded cordially to this genuine outpouring of affection and appreciation.

On the day of our departure from Booan the manager of the theater, Shim's friend who was the financial backer of our jaunt, was not to be located anywhere. None of the group had been paid the balance of the money promised and so no one had any money to buy a single ticket. As we waited in the inn for the manager to show up with the money, some old friends of Shim's in town came over to treat him to a drink. Though responsible for the group, he was not above such temptation and left the inn, assuring us that he would be back soon.

"We'll never see him until tonight," predicted Choran Bag, shaking her head contemptuously.

It was about 10 a.m. A bus was to take us at 12:30 to Gimjay, where we would board the train bound for Seoul at 2 p.m.. There being still some time, Alan and I went out sightseeing with a few girls in the group, stopping at the market place where the countryside had turned out with their merchandise, piglets, hatching eggs with new-born chicks pecking at the shells, produce, fruits, grains. Most of the people, farmers as well as some professional merchants, had come from miles around, some having left their homes at daybreak with heavy loads on their heads, so heavy it was a wonder their spines had not collapsed. From the market we went to the old school where Chinese classics used to be taught, an institution found at every country town or village. Unlike other modernized towns eager to shed old vestiges Booan also had a moodang shrine, Great Earth Temple, colorfully painted and adorned, still preserved in a prominent corner. But its days were numbered: on the opposite side, cater-corner to it, they were building a Presbyterian church, dedicated to the destruction of idolatry and superstition which the moodang cult was made out to be.

We returned punctually at noon, expecting everyone to be ready and waiting, but couldn't see a soul. We looked in the rooms and they were empty. In our room our solitary bags were in a corner, lids open. I went to Shim's room and found his bag left lonesome in the middle of the room.

"The others have all left already and are waiting for you at the bus station," said the inn keeper.

"Holy mother!" the girls panicked, ran to their rooms to fetch their bags, then dashed past us out of the yard, without saying a word to us.

"Wait, girls, wait!" I yelled running after them all the way to the depot, where the bus with all our group aboard, except for Shim, Alan, and me, had its motor running, ready to depart. I saw Choran Bag sitting near the front entrance unperturbed.

"What are you all doing?" I asked.

"Isn't it obvious?" she rumbled. "We are going to Gimjay to catch the train for Seoul."

"But what about Mr. Shim?"

"Oh, that son of a bitch," she broke out in passionate imprecations. "He ran away somewhere to have his second and third drink. Get on quickly. The bus is leaving. We have no time to lose."

"Wait. Alan is there. You can't leave him."

"All right, go get him."

I ran to the inn and the bus slowly trailed. I stopped.

"I have no money," I shouted back to Bag. "Who is going to pay for the train fare?"

"Hurry and get Alan and your bags," she ordered without answering my question.

"Madame Bag, we have to wait for Mr. Shim. Someone must have the money to buy the train tickets. We have to wait for Mr. Shim."

For the moment I was thinking only about the train, not the bus that must be paid for, too, somehow.

"We are already late for the train. Bring Alan and your bags quickly if you want to go back to Seoul at all."

"Will you buy our tickets?"

"No."

I did not know what to do. I ran towards the inn, but turned back again to the bus to argue and entreat with Bag, but, seeing no point in that, I turned again to the inn. After bouncing back and forth like a tennis ball I came to my senses at last. I knew I had to wait for Gwaryong Shim. In the first place neither I nor Alan had money, thanks to my smart finance. Shim had to give us the balance of our pay. Even if we had the money, we shouldn't be deserting him to be left behind alone. Besides, from my past experience, I knew Shim to be not the sort of man to let another man down like that. He had always come through at last, though maybe after some detours and delays.

"Go first," I told her. "We'll wait for Mr. Shim."

"I warn you he'll never get back in time."

I almost changed my mind and would have gone for Alan, shuddering at the prospect of two of us being stranded indefinitely in a strange town, but stuck to my announced course of action. The bus coasted down the street and rounded the bend out of sight. It was forty past noon. I went back to the inn disconsolately and gave Alan the news. We sat in our room with a sense of doom.

"What sort of life have I gotten you into?" Alan asked. "Is Korean music really what we want to pursue to put up with the type of people we are associating with for the rest of our lives?"

"I don't care," I said, comforting him. "If this is what you want, I am here with you."

"I am more than patient, perhaps ten times as much as any ordinary man, always willing to give a man the benefit of the doubt, always looking at the bright side, but I have a sneaking suspicion that my philosophy, my outlook on life and people might be all wrong, like a badly designed car destined to break down on the highway of life within the first thousand miles. I keep telling myself that I know Mr. Shim well, that he would not let us down, but I don't know any more."

As I looked at the clock tick away, I didn't know either and the skeptic voice inside me became more strident, mocking us as two gullible, trusting fools. The clock struck one. Shim came in, smelling like a barrel of maggoli, but with a worried look on his face.

"Where is Choran?" he asked.

"She took all the people with their baggage and went to the station," I said.

"That bitch! I hate her guts. She is a mean dirty bitch."

What had happened was this. During our absence Shim's friend, the missing manager of the theater, had come with a sum of money enough to pay for our fare back to Seoul and a promissory note for the balance to be paid in Seoul. Of course the note was not worth the paper it was written on, but he had been decent enough to make sure that we got back home. The money was for 15 tickets, which was the number of our party proper, not counting Bag's usual retinue of dependents. Being the only person at the inn at the time when the manager arrived, Choran Bag promptly appropriated the whole amount for herself and took steps to vacate the inn before our arrival. We could go on cursing Bag forever, but this was certainly not the time. Pooling enough change between us, we raced after a bus leaving the depot for Gimjay Railroad Station. Dashing through the gate, we ran to the platform out of breath and out of our wits, certain that we had missed the train. But the train had not come in yet, it being still 15 minutes before 2. Our friends were among the crowd waiting for the train. Boiling with rage, Shim charged straight at Bag, only stopping short of actual collision.

"Buy our tickets," Shim shouted.

"I won't," she replied haughtily. "I don't have to wipe your ass. Buy with your own money."

"You have the money for our tickets."

"I have spent all the money buying tickets for my children and maid."

"You should pay for them with your own money, not with the money for our tickets. You stole our money. Give it back."

"Imbecile! I got what was mine. You never paid me for the rest of the money I was to receive the moment I arrived here. Do you still have the nerve to say anything about that? You screwed up the whole thing from the beginning."

The argument seemed never to end, and every minute some violent clash was imminent. Needless to say neither of the combatants was the least bit concerned that all the eyes of the station were focused on them. At this juncture the train came in thundering and screeched to a halt. Like the rest of the group Shim, Alan, and I ended up borrowing ticket money from Bag at the dollar rate, one percent per day interest, compounded daily.

We all got on the train. The memory of their latest fight still rankling, Shim sat at the other end of the car as far away from Choran Bag as possible. The others of the party were also bitter about lots of things and sat morosely apart from each other, neither talking nor looking at each other. After being clickety-clacked for ten minutes without occupation, however, the tide of boredom bore down every barrier of resentment and they began furtively to reach out for some diversion, any diversion. The mood of the party was ripe for Choran Bag's timely call to a game of sotta to which they responded enthusiastically. Shim had begun casting longing glances at the players and became restless every minute. Finally, he rose.

"Well," he said, "I know she is mean, but I must go and win back the money I have lost to her."

"Don't," I said. "You'll only lose more. She is always lucky."

"No. This time I'll fix her."

"She'll fix you, more likely."

"Watch me."

Shim went and played. After some time he returned to his seat, dejected. Not only did he lose all the small change he had but ended up owing her five times more than the original debt.

"Mr. Shim," I said. "I know now why you are so bald-headed."

"Why?" he asked.

"You lost all your hair to Madame Bag."

Shim smiled wanly and did not reply. I could not imagine his ever being her bedfellow, but that's what they said, nor would it be anything out of the ordinary among these people. Not only could their love today transform into a violent hatred tomorrow, but they were uniquely capable of both loving and hating intensely at the same time. For instance, many hated Bag and told us so in private, using the most colorful terms of denunciation. But if we ever agreed with them, in two minutes she was sure to hear about it. A would come to our house and heap curses on B but if that B stepped in at the time, A would run over and embrace B. They would call each other "Big Sister" or "Little Sister" with an affection that seemed every bit genuine. It was a strange community, always on the brink of falling apart but somehow holding together. Never in my life had I seen a more closely-knit society of enemies.

IX.
Moodang Opera

On a tip from Wansong Char I went to the Pagoda Park one weekend to see the Hongjoo Kim Singers and Dancers perform as part of their repertoire the moodang exorcism called Babangee Opera. Though almost obscured by unrelated instrumental and dance impromptus, and excesssive horseplay, the sequence had a good dramatic potential: Old Woman, a hardened cynic and misanthrope, ugly and despised by her neighbors, has one redeeming feature, absolute devotion to her only daughter Babangee, a young maiden of exceptional beauty and charm, who attracts suitors from far and wide. The widowed king himself hears of her and seeks her hand in marriage. Then on the eve of her wedding, she sickens and loses her sight. The moodang consulted says it is the jealous spirit of the king's dead wife who causes the mischief. An exorcism is in order. What follows is a ferocious fight between the spirit and Old Woman, hair pulling, biting, scratching, providing slapstick, buffoonery, and robust peasant humor at its best. In the end the spirit of the stately queen reveals her true colors, uglier and coarser than the exterior of Old Woman, who wins the sympathy of the audience and the gods. The queen's spirit is driven back to the Hades, and Babangee, her vision and health restored, marries the king and lives happily ever after.

I thought the play, if properly organized and sequenced, would make a great presentation to the foreign community in Seoul, which often didn't get to see the real side of Korea, and also give Korean moodang the recognition they deserved. To me the moodang cult was just another religious expression, pantheistic, animistic, and indigenous, neither better nor worse than its imported competition, Buddhism, Confucianism, Taoism, Christianity, but most Koreans thought it some kind of national shame and spat on its ministers, the moodang, perhaps arguing a schizophrenic, masochistic streak in the Korean psyche. For example, a family might beg a moodang to come and heal a sick or dying member, after trying all other alternatives, then dismiss the moodang most ungraciously even when their ministrations had worked. Ostracized, reviled, and spat upon, they were the untouchables, pariahs of Korea. A moodang's children could not play with the neighborhood kids, go to school, or get married properly later in life. Any taint of the moodang blood was fatal to one's career. Since the advent of Christianity to be moodang was a high-risk occupation: in the name of their jealous God, Christians felt free, nay, duty bound to inflict any atrocity on these Satan's agents. Not too long ago a frenzied mob of hymn-singing, chanting churchgoers in Gangnung had burned down a moodang shrine, stoning to death those who tried to flee the flames.

With some hesitation I presented my thoughts to Alan, who listened attentively, then brightened up, agreeing with me completely, with a spark of enthusiasm I had not observed in him for some time. Previously we had never disagreed seriously on anything. Not only did we look alike but thought alike. But because of his deepening depression since Fulbright I had not tried to test it, lest I should be disappointed. How warm and good it felt to reaffirm the unique bond between us!

"I'll do all the legwork," I assured him. "I am going now to this man Kim, leader of the group, to sound him out about a presentation. Great to have your approval, Alan. You just plan and tell me what to do."

If I had expected Hongjoo Kim to jump up and down with glee at the opportunity, I was gravely mistaken. Suspicious and arrogant, he apparently decided to punish me for all the shabby treatment his class had gotten these many years from Korean society at large.

"We'll need a rich sponsor," was his first reaction, "because we have to rent the National Theater, where the stage is right and the lighting is ideal."

"The National Theater it is then," I agreed, though I knew there were cheaper and equally adequate places.

"We also need to be paid in advance, so we don't make other commitments."

"You'll be paid."

The theater cost about $1,000. Being a government-owned public service agency it charged no rental as such but there were other expenses the user had to take care of, custodians, engineers, security guards, and a host of other servitors, which added up to more than what a fair rental would have cost. The price tag for the all-male cast of Hongjoo Kim's performers cost another $1,000.

"Shouldn't we have some females to be more authentic, because most moodang are women?" I asked.

"We can act the women's parts authentically," he said testily. "Besides any substitution would cost extra."

Costumes, scenery, and other incidentals cost a great deal more. We needed a rich patron indeed to take care of all these expenses.

When I explained what I had found out so far, Alan suggested that we go see James Reed, Managing Director of the American-Korean Foundation and a music critic, who was well-known for his interest in Korean culture. Alan had met him when he was with Fulbright and they had maintained a cordial relationship. We felt we could at least discuss the matter with him.

As we entered the carpeted hall of the Foundation, I wished we did not have to come as beggars, especially as I saw a charming, elegantly dressed couple leave Reed's office, having finished a social call. In the way Koreans dressed, postured, or walked there was certainly a charm, the charm of anybody being what he or she was. But there was a style to White Americans, at least the better specimens, tall, blond, slim, laid back, cosmopolitan, that belonged to an order all by itself, like the American eagle soaring in the blue sky. Alas, I would never be that. One had to be born and raised in America, in a "free and open" environment as Wansong imagined it, to have that air and bearing natural to Americans. At least one had to live in America but, as it was, I could never do that, neither as the nonexisent John Heyman nor as the half-caste Foreign Boy of the Mercy Home. When unmasked, I would be stuck in Korea to be permanently stateless, marginal, outcast, imprisoned. These melancholy thoughts were dispelled by Reed who greeted us both with sincere welcome.

"Ah, the Heyman brothers," he said, holding our hands at the same time. "Or twins, more likely, because I can't tell which is one and which the other. One in two or is it the other way around?"

As my adulthood neared, our resemblance grew even more striking, so that our Korean acquaintances regularly mixed us up. This was partly the source of my anxiety. We would have to be sorted out officially, and that meant loss of my alias and fictitious identity.

"So what can I do for you?"

"Well, we didn't want to bother you but...."

Alan began laying out the proposal, ready to meet all opposition. To our complete surprise, Reed approved it at once. There was a growing interest in Korean music and culture in general among the foreigners in Seoul and an authentic presentation of moodang ritual might attract enough people to pay for the expenses and at the same time give publicity to the Foundation, which was in the middle of a big fund raiser among the US military personnel throughout Korea.

I went to Hongjoo Kim to break the news, which he received with anything but joy. A moodang's son, he did not wish to parade this background before a foreign audience. Having made a commitment to me because of the money, he now wanted to cut out the moodang element, the very thing I wanted to present. As work progressed, Kim opposed us in every little detail and disagreements soon threatened to wreck the whole project. He wanted to throw in all the dances, gayagum and gomungo performances and other tits and bits in the first part and show last as a second thought a watered-down version of the moodang dance and ritual proper. To me this would hopelessly compromise the show. I could have gotten the regular dances and instrumentations from better qualified people at the Center. What the foreigners wanted was the artistic synopsis of a typical moodang exorcism. The Babangee Opera with a good story line and strong character interest would be just the thing but Kim wanted to prove to the world that his group could play instruments and dance and sing as well as the next legitimate Korean folk artist, and was blind to his own inimitable strength. With great reluctance Kim agreed to our program.

The National Theater was booked for Saturday, September 28, MacArthur's Inchon Landing Day, and programs were printed according to schedule. Alan would read the program notes in English before or sometimes during the scene to provide a running commentary. To promote the show better, tickets were printed at a considerable expense and distributed among the US Army service clubs, diplomatic missions, aid agencies, and other organizations. Arrangements and rearrangements had to be made for the costumes, props, stage property, transportation, and a hundred other minor and major details, none of which we could count on as settled until the last minute. This hectic running around was disastrous to our English classes, private as well as at the Center, on which we depended for our income. Several classes had to be canceled altogether, for which nobody was going to compensate us.

September 28 neared. We had to see the group rehearse but suddenly Hongjoo Kim became incommunicado. For two days we called or went to all the likely hangouts of his but were unable to locate him. On the night of the 24th, Tuesday, we went to his house with a guide after getting the address from an acquaintance. It was in Hyunjaydong. His wife was jittery the whole time we waited sitting on the maroo. Apparently we were the first Caucasians in her house. It was nearing midnight but Kim did not arrive. Our guide said he had to cross the river to get home. Our place in Gahwaydong was also several streets away on the other side of the hill.

"Come to Tea Room Mountain at 10 a.m. tomorrow or come to the National Theater at noon," I wrote, marking the message as urgent, and had it read to Mrs. Kim a couple of times.

We had to make a run for it to beat the curfew unless we wanted to spend the night at a police jail or return and sleep at Kim's house, which was an unacceptable alternative, even if Mrs. Kim should let us. Its two rooms were bursting with their children and dependents.

The next day we waited until 11:45 a.m. at the tea room and had to run to the National Theater where we had an appointment with the Director of the Theater, about seating and other arrangements. The conference lasted only fifteen minutes. We waited around until two, but Kim did not show up. Thursday morning I left the house as soon as the curfew was over and reached Kim's at seven to find him still sleeping. I had his wife wake him up. It was pointless to waste time on recriminations.

"We must have a stage rehearsal, maybe two or three," I demanded.

"Yes," he replied irritably. "We are going to have one this afternoon at four."

I felt stupid and apologized for having been so concerned and anxious. Since he seemed to be in ill humor, probably because of his shortened sleep, I decided to leave for now and meet him at the Theater and talk about further rehearsals and other matters.

"We'll see you at four at the theater, then," I reconfirmed our date, leaving.

Kim did not respond one way or another, the morose son of a bitch. It didn't matter. He would be there to rehearse. He had said so himself.

We went to the Theater at four, skipping an English class at the Center that had been rescheduled about the tenth time, but neither Kim nor his people were there. Upon inquiry we were told that they had their schedule changed and had finished the rehearsal already.

"They really had a rehearsal?"

"Well, they were here," the guard said. "I didn't watch. They said they would have another Friday morning."

"Do you know what time?"

"Eleven."

We went there at the appointed time and found that they had it at nine. We were getting really nervous and apprehensive now, and looked for Kim all day long but could not locate him.

It was Saturday, the day of performance, for which we had been running around so many days. The show was scheduled to go on at 3 p.m. We were craning our necks to see if Kim and his friends were arriving, as they were supposed to for the rehearsal promised. Finally Kim turned up with his group at the Theater about eleven a.m.

"Without our seeing the show it shall not go on," I said, putting my foot down.

Kim muttered and said that he could not go on if he was not trusted and given full authority to manage his own group. Finding us inflexible, he agreed to give a rehearsal for our benefit. Just as it was about to start, somebody came with an urgent message, telling us to come to the Theater office at once.

"We are inspectors from the tax office with the tickets for admission of your patrons," said one of the black-suited men.

"We don't need any of your tickets," Alan answered. "We have our own."

"What do you mean your own?"

"We have had them printed and distributed already, weeks before," I said proudly.

The inspectors looked at each other, with an expression far from admiration for American efficiency and planning.

"Nobody can print and sell theater or entertainment tickets except the tax office," their spokesman said. "They have to be stamped with a tax office seal upon purchase."

"Sir, this is our show," I explained patiently. "Our people have rented the Theater from the Ministry of Public

Information, paying for all the expenses. We have every right to manage the event as we see fit."

"Have you sold the tickets, collected money for them?"

"Yes."

"There, you have already violated Section 366 of the Entertainment Tax Law. You shall go to prison for it."

"No one has told us about it. Look, we are not doing this for ourselves or by ourselves. The American-Korean Foundation is behind it. Surely you have heard of it and the great work it has been doing for Korea. The American Ambassador and the Commander in Chief of the UN Command and many other dignitaries are on its Board of Trustees. By the way they are all coming to see the show today."

"We don't give a damn who," said the official defiantly. "We enforce the law without respect to person or rank. No one shall enter this theater using anything but tax office printed theater tickets. That's the law. Don't you Americans have any respect for the law?"

"But people will start arriving at four, in four hours, with the other tickets."

"We'll alert the police if anyone tries to force his way in. That goes for everybody."

We were going out of our minds. Someone came from the stage to say the rehearsal was about over.

"We have to be excused a second," I said, turning to go.

"You are not going anywhere until this matter is resolved," said the tax men, blocking.

"Talk to him," I said, indicating Alan, as I pushed one of them out of the way and ran to the stage.

They were doing the concluding part of the opera. I had completely missed what had gone before, but I could not stand there watching the rehearsal either, when the whole program might be scotched for an absurd technicality. Alan's Korean was good but might be at a disadvantage in dealing with intransigent Korean government officials. It was horrible to think of the people, who had paid good money, coming to the gate to be turned away because they held the wrong tickets. I ran back to the theater office to find the deadlock still there. The situation was critical. I ran out and went to the nearest telephone. The Foundation lines were all busy. I dialed a dozen times rapidly but they were still busy. Dialing every other second didn't help matters either. I had to send somebody by taxi with a message to Reed. About forty minutes later Reed and other Foundation officers arrived with worried faces and went in a body to the theater office to argue it out with the Korean bureaucracy. Our increased number made no impression on our adversaries, however.

"We never told you or anybody to print tickets," the secretary of the theater pointed out, judiciously.

"But you should have told us not to print them," I said, interpreting for Reed.

"Why should we mention something so obvious?" Tak said, the Director. "It's like telling somebody to drive on the right hand side of the road or keep breathing not to suffocate."

"It was not obvious to us," Reed retorted.

"It is a point of the law, an established practice," Tak concluded. "Ignorance of the law does not excuse its violation."

Meanwhile, it was over 1 p.m., way past lunch time for the performers, who came to me to ask for lunch money.

"We must eat a good lunch to perform well," Hongjoo Kim said.

"But that was not part of the bargain," I said.

They all looked at me as if I had cracked a dirty joke. One of the theater staff nudged at me and whispered that it was customary to treat the performers, another established fact I didn't know about. I wanted to ask Kim to put on another rehearsal before they broke for lunch but, knowing his temper, I was afraid he might pack up and leave. He and his men were certainly not above it, especially having been paid in advance according to the golden rule of all Korean performers. Besides we had not settled our differences with the tax office and the crucial conversation could not be further interrupted by such an insignificant little thing as the players' lunch money. Shelling out the last penny in my pocket and getting some more from Alan, I dismissed them, swearing them to a prompt return for another rehearsal.

After interminable wrangling it was agreed that when the guests arrived with the tickets and lined up, we should exchange them for regular theater tickets, which would then be presented and collected at the gate. The other obvious alternative, that the guests turn in the tickets they already had as they arrived and the theater count up later and exchange with that number of regular tickets all at one time afterwards, was rejected out of hand.

"The ticket-takers are not allowed to take anything but tax office tickets," was the authoritative ruling. "They go to jail otherwise."

The crowd started arriving. There was no line and everybody converged on the entrance from all directions. The throng increased and pressed to the gate. Minutes passed but nobody was getting in. Tempers flared. Genteel ladies, grave generals, staid diplomats, high-ranking officials, all in their sparkling formal attire, began grumbling and complaining in language that got stronger by the second, especially as the clouds that had hung like a wet mop over the city all day long began shedding droplets. Finally a triple line had formed with much coaxing, and about nine extra hands had to be specially hired to change the tickets to the loud protests of the ticket-holders, each of whom had to be told about the Korean tax law through interpreters before reluctantly giving up the ticket with colorful comments on the absurdity of the whole thing.

"The show had better be good after all this flip-flop," snarled an irate infantry officer.

The process, already slowed down, got bogged down further by the Korean alphabetical and numerical seating orders, VIP sections, and other complications. Each clearance through the gate seemed to take ten minutes or more and there were hundreds to get through. With a distracted look, beads of sweat on his forehead, Alan was returning to the gate after directing an elderly couple to their balcony seats. We needed ten more of us to sort out the tangle in time for the show.

Suddenly I realized that neither Alan nor I had seen a

rehearsal through. It was imperative that one of us have a last-minute rehearsal and confirmation with the performers. But the tax people were on my heels all the way to the stage.

"We must settle the tax rate right now," they cried. "Otherwise we have to take half of all the receipts in taxes."

I felt as if I was being torn to pieces by a thousand yelping hounds.

The curtain lifted nearly an hour after four, the published opening time. Alan needed a microphone to give the English commentary. The theater people said the regular audio system, too late to fix now as they pointed out, made too much static and gave him a small hand-held, battery-operated megaphone, which made almost no amplification and did not carry his voice beyond the first few rows when he tried. Alan had to shout to the limit of his lung power.

The opening scene of the Babangee Cycle was announced according to the printed program. Out jumped a dancer doing a sword ballet. The second scene of the opera was announced, and out strode someone doing a gayagum impromptu. Perplexed, I went backstage and got hold of Kim.

"What's going on here?" I asked, suppressing a scream.

"Oh, we forgot to give you changes in the program," Kim said.

"What?" I yelled, almost fainting. The changes he gave me were exactly what he had first proposed and we had rejected.

"Why did you do this?"

"The audience always likes it that way."

"What audience? They are foreigners. We know them better. That's why we've made the changes. We printed the program and people are expecting to see what's on the program. You have no right to change so suddenly. Don't you know who is sponsoring the program? American-Korean Foundation! You must change it back right away."

"No, we can't. We have no scenery, and everything will be messed up."

"But why did you not tell us that before? Why did you not rehearse it before me as it should go?"

"We rehearsed this morning, don't you remember?"

The gayagum impromptu was over and Alan had to announce the next scene, another string impromptu Hongjoo Kim had wanted but we had rejected and stricken from the final English program. Puzzled by the incongruity between what they were supposed to see and what they actually saw, the audience became restless, whispered, then broke into laughter and catcalls. It was like going to the gallows but go Alan must to make the announcements, as Kim would have them, for he refused to do anything else. Would our audience, who had paid good money to see an operatic performance of an exorcist ritual by authentic Korean moodang, spirit women, understand and forgive if we explained that these last minute, arbitrary changes were made without our knowledge or permission?

Dorothy Reed entered backstage through the side door and came to me, waving in her hand a note from her husband addressed to Alan. On her face was etched an expression that almost said a best friend of ours had just died. Trembling, I took it to Alan. Written in an angry flourish was the declaration:

"Heyman! I have left the theater in a state of nervous breakdown. I am heading for a shot of morphine. General McCoy, Ambassador Marconi, and all the Trustees of the Foundation have left!!! [In addition to the three exclamation marks Reed had underlined the last word three times.] I don't want to hear another word about moodang as long as I live."

Alan flopped down on the floor. I could see him struggling to his feet but his legs gave way under him like jelly. Half leaning against the wall he stood up finally and climbed the steps to the upper floor. I didn't know what to do, whether to go after him or pick up the megaphone and offer some kind of explanation to the unruly crowd. Another glance in Alan's direction and I raced after him. Like a drunken man, unseeing, unhearing, he was approaching the rail at the highest point of the balcony, about fifty feet above the ground floor.

"Alan!" I shouted, grabbing him as he was about to pitch himself into the stormy sea below. "Anything but this. It's not worth it. Come to your senses."

"Let me go," he fought me. "My whole life has been one miserable failure. I am an embarrassment and liability to you, to my friends, a burden to society. Let me be. Give me self-respect by ending my life right here and now."

"Look, if anyone is all the awful things you mention, it's me, the fraud. Besides I got you into this, inciting and urging you. But I am not killing myself. We'll try to explain, tell them...."

We were shocked into silence by a thunderous applause that shook the whole theater. The eyes of the audience were riveted on the dancer on stage, someone I hadn't seen before, who hadn't been in Hongjoo's cast. She pirouetted and jumped, cotton stockinged feet kicking the air, flaring broad-sleeved coats parting open in front, as if her whole body had levitated and moved on an invisible plane above the floor. Spurts of balletistic extravaganza to the beat of the janggo drum were followed by intervals of plaintive intoning to the accompaniment of the ajang strings. Her body and voice were one living portrayal of the deadly struggle between the evil and guardian spirits, which culminated in the transformation of the ugly, blind, shrewish Old Woman into the beautiful, sensitive lady that she was before her possession by the evil spirit. Both Alan and I remained glued to the balustrade, mesmerized, watching her perform to the triumphant finale.

In the confusion after the show I lost track of Alan but was no longer worried about him. He was safe. I greeted guests left and right, eyes filmy with relief and gratitude. Who was she, the unknown benefactress who had turned disaster into triumph, saving Alan from certain death, for I had lost grip of him and felt his weight shift to heave over the balustrade when the timely applause came? I should look for her and thank her. Maybe Alan was doing that already. Someone tapped my shoulder. It was Reverend Wilson of St. Michael's Anglican Seminary with a visiting scholar from Berkeley.

"It was about the most wonderful thing we've ever seen, Alan," said Wilson, probably the best Korean historian among the foreigners in Seoul with several books to his credit.

"Very authentic," chimed in his friend from Berkeley.

At that moment Greg Mendelson of the American Embassy came over to me. He and Alan had been friends despite Alan's dismissal from Fulbright.

"Congratulations, Alan or is it John?" he said. "No matter. You guys did it again. For a while everything was out of whack but turned out all right. Where did you get your prima donna?"

Still stunned and unable to get over my bewilderment, I only smiled and mumbled thanks. As soon as I could get away from my well-wishers without appearing to be rude, I went in search of the mystery lady, but was hampered by the theater management who wanted me to sign some papers. One of Hongjoo's men was passing by.

"Sprung from nowhere, vanished into thin air," was the pert answer to my inquiry, with no sign of remorse or apology.

Then I noticed Alan walking out the gate, arm in arm with the dancer, in the company of several men, her escorts. I ran after them, trying not to lose them in the evening crowd on Bright Street, and barely caught up with them at the end of the block as they turned the corner at Loyal Arms Road.

"Alan, where are you going?" I yelled, pulling his other arm.

"It is she, Jinny Bay," he said, awe-struck eyes fixed on hers that blinked but did not move. She was blind!

"Are you out of your mind?" I said. "She can't be. She died at Wonsan."

"But is reincarnated in me," the lady said, in an ethereal, cavernous voice. "She will no longer haunt him but will help him, live with him. So the spirits have willed."

"Will somebody tell me what's going on?" I said, none the wiser, turning to one of her entourage.

"The lady is Queen Moodang of Korea," he said, taking me to the side as Alan and Jinny Bay carried on a deep conversation, oblivious to the world.

"What's her name?" I asked impatiently.

"Her name changes with the spirit that possesses her," he said. "She is Jinny Bay now. We had an exorcism ritual backstage for your brother and the transmigration is complete."

"So fast?"

"It's not how long it takes but the intensity of it that counts, the power that is brought to bear. I haven't seen anything more potent and real. Your brother was charged irresistibly with the moving spirit and she was equally wound up to receive him. It was a perfect match."

"Match, like husband and wife?"

"Yes, they are married. We have to hurry up not to miss the tide. The wedding will be properly celebrated at our kingdom on Moon Rock Island, 5 miles northwest of Inchon. That's where her grandfather and his followers had moved for sanctuary at the turn of the century. Over the years more moodang families joined in, buying out the few non-moodang families on the island, until the population became entirely moodang, the untouchables of Korea, as you know. Her father ruled after him but died recently. So she is now the Queen."

"But she is blind? Was that hereditary, too?"

"No, her father blinded her by giving her some potion."

"Her own father did that?"

"He had to make sure she didn't leave the island to pursue some worldly career like pop singing. She is a born singer, as you saw tonight, but her succession to the throne was critical for the survival of our community. We needed her insight, wisdom, leadership. Already she has set in motion a bill in the National Assembly to guarantee us equal protection as a religion under the Constitution and has instituted a hierarchy of internal government to police all moodang activity nationally and locally. A seminary is under construction to train and certify our future priests and priestesses. Her loss of physical sight has given her psychic and spiritual vision given to only a few great leaders in history."

"How did she happen to be by today?"

"Her responsibilities generally keep her on the island, but today was an exception. Somebody told us about your show with this charlatan Hongjoo Kim. We had to prevent him from dishonoring our religion worse than it is already. He almost succeeded, that scoundrel."

He stopped and stepped aside as Jinny Bay made way to me, Alan at her side. She stretched out her hand and felt my face, as I stood breathless at this novel experience.

"You do look like Alan," she said, removing her hand. "He is going with us to Moon Rock, to be dead to the world. But he leaves you behind as his reincarnation, his alter ego. Be him, like I am Jinny. Nobody will know the difference. Use his papers, go to America, or wherever you want to. I see a lot of travel and adventure ahead of you. You'll be going to unknown lands, take on dangerous missions, but you'll come through okay. You'll meet the lady of your dreams but there may be some trouble. You'll also meet your mother."

"My mother! Is she alive?"

"You'll see. We must get going not to miss the tide. Come visit us if you can, but you'll be too busy and soon forget us."

"Me forget him?" I cried, hugging Alan. "Are you sure this is what you want to do, Alan?"

He nodded impassively, then gently pushed me away and took his place by Jinny's side. Without another word the group walked away and went out of sight in the dark among the evening crowd of Myongdong.

I woke up with a start. It was one a.m. I must have slept nearly an hour. I had come home near midnight but couldn't sleep, despite the physical exhaustion from the stress of the day. It just was not real. Alan could not be absent in his room. We had never been apart ever since he had saved me. He was part of me and I couldn't exist without him. He wouldn't leave me now. I got up and went to his room. I knocked at the door and called his name. There was no answer. I slid the door open. The room was undisturbed. The bedding had not been taken down for the night. He was not there. The emptiness hit me like a physical blow, causing me to reel.

"Alan! Oh, Alan!" I moaned, leaning against the wall and wiping my eyes.

"No, it can't be," I protested next moment. "It just can't be."

The whole sequence of the day's events was too bizarre to

be real. Maybe I was dreaming or got bewitched by moodang spirits. But it wouldn't last. I would wake up and find everything back the way it had been, with Alan in his room.

Where was this island, Moon Rock? I would leave first thing, as soon as the curfew lifted, and bring him back. It was madness for him to up and leave everything, everybody he had known all this time. "To be dead to the world" my foot! The moodang witch had cast a spell on him. I must rescue him, cure him of this dangerous infection of the mind, just as he had healed my sick body. When I got there, this island of nuts, he would have come to his senses on his own and come away with me without persuasion. I closed the door and was heading back to my room, when I heard the rap on the gate.

"There! It must be Alan," I told myself, running across the courtyard and undoing the latch. It was James Reed.

"You mind going for a short ride?" he asked.

"No, but isn't it curfew?" I asked, puzzled.

"My car has a diplomatic plate, exempt from curfew," he said. "You don't have to change even."

Did he mean to shoot me for the afternoon's miscarriage of the moodang opera? Involuntarily, I frisked him with my eye, though I never thought of him as a violent type. At the car was waiting another man.

"Meet Al Edwards, an associate of mine."

"Hi, Alan," Al said, shaking my hand with a cordial smile. "I was at your show this afternoon and liked it."

"About the show, fellows, I'll explain to every member of your Board personally, make a public apology in the newspapers, do anything to clear your names and that of AKF. That villain Hongjoo Kim took us by surprise as much as anybody else."

"No, forget it. James told me about his note. It should be him and his friends who should apologize for walking out on the meat of it."

"He is right, Alan. I apologize. But we are not here to discuss that. We have an important favor to ask of you in connection with something totally unrelated. You are the only person who can do it for us, because of your bilinguality and other qualifications. I am asking as a friend. It's urgent."

"You know I'll do anything for you, James. Just name it."

"How much do you know about the Soogun Yee affair?"

"What I read in the papers," I said.

The south had rolled out the welcome mat, giving Soogun, the North Korean superspy, medals, money, house, even a wife. Then he gave his hosts the slip. The whole country had been hoodwinked, but it looked particularly bad for KCIA, which had flaunted him as a major victory in the intelligence war with the north, sending him on speaking tours all over the country. Thousands had come to hear this eloquent convert to freedom and queued up for his autographs. None of the KCIA agents assigned to him, largely for his own protection, suspected that these autographing sessions might be an excellent conduit of communi-cation between him and his contacts. Under a forged passport he fled to Hong Kong, which KCIA discovered largely by luck with US CIA help. KCIA sent a plane load of agents to Hong Kong to bring back the fugitive but was unsuccessful: the Hong Kong government, which held him under protective custody, refused extradition and was sending him to Phnom Penh by Air Cambodia for transshipment to North Korea via China.

"So are there any new developments?" I asked. "Does KCIA have Soogun Yee back?"

Normally politics didn't interest me but this spy caper did, because my friends at the Center were rooting for Hyongwoog Kim, a fellow Jollanese, the only exception in the all-Gyongsang power structure of Junghee Park.

"No, not quite, but they are trying and we want to help," James said.

"Help KCIA? Since when has AKF been in Korean politics?"

"Always," James said. "You see, Alan, Al and I work for the CIA."

The revelation fairly took my breath away.

"US CIA?"

"Yes, Al is head of the Korea Branch and my boss."

So all that I had heard or read about covert CIA

operations must be true, because I would never have imagined that James was an undercover agent, nor Al, who looked like a businessman or professional of some sort, not particularly distinguished either. But that must be the mark of real agents.

"Our friend Hyongwoog Kim, Chief of KCIA, is in a bit of a jam because of this Soogun Yee business," Edwards said. "We want to help him out. We think we can get Soogun with your help."

"Do you want me to just go up to Soogun Yee, shake his hand, and ask him to come along for a second tour of Seoul?" I asked when they finished briefing me on Soogun's status and what I was expected to do.

"You may have to use force."

"Kidnap and transport a healthy superspy over a thousand miles!"

"You will have some help at the other end. With or without help, we know you can pull it off, a survivor of the Wonsan Retreat."

There it was again, Wonsan Retreat! I felt a certain fatality. Jinny Bay, the partisan, was haunting the wrong Alan Heyman. On the other hand, this disclosed the limitations of CIA intelligence, its apparent ignorance of our switch.

"We'll have to give you a new name," Edwards said. "You are to be known henceforth as Dr. Archer Torrey, a surgeon from St. Paul, Minnesota, on your way to your new post at the American Red Cross Hospital in Phnom Penh."

I almost pounced on it, if only to evade the ghostly attention the old name seemed to attract. Whisked to the airport, I was put on a special military jet, given a hair cut, shave, shampoo, white suit, blue tie, white socks, shoes, dark sun glasses, instructions on the use of a revolver, stethoscope, aerosol can of ether, folding spyglass that worked like a periscope, camera, safecracking kit, and other tools of the trade, as well as a bundle of greenbacks.

At Hong Kong I was driven in a sirening ambulance to the DC-10 that was about to leave and was waiting for the last arrivals including me. My seat was near the door. I had hoped it might be in the back so I could observe the whole plane unobtrusively. When airborne, I left my seat to go to the lavatory in the back and looked for my subject without appearing to do so. There was nobody aboard matching Soogun's description or photograph. Only at Phnom Penh I noticed an Oriental woman dressed in pink, lips painted carmine, wavy perm to her head, an alligator purse in hand, walking down the aisle in high heels. She was every bit a rich Oriental lady tourist but there was something odd about her, a hint of stiffness in the exaggerated sway of her hips. I followed her at a distance to the lobby. Two Korean males greeted her, in telltale North Korean accent, reassured that no Korean-looking face was around.

"Dr. Torrey?" a blonde Red Cross nurse came up to my side.

"Yes," I answered, waking up to my new identity.

"I am Jane Shaw from the hospital. Welcome to Cambodia."

The Koreans were getting into a limousine waiting at the curb outside the terminal.

"Where is your car, Jane?"

"Right there across the street."

"Let's start tailing that vehicle, discreetly?"

She did as bid, without asking questions. Our quarry pulled up at the Phnom Penh Hilton.

"Bring an ambulance around as soon as you can and wait down here," I told her, sending her on her way.

At the front desk I saw the three men go off with the key, heading for the elevator. The clerk was finishing up the paperwork for Room 937, its occupant Mrs. Junghee Park! If intended for public notice, it failed because nobody on the hotel staff recognized the name. More likely, counting on its anonymity in Cambodia, Soogun did it as a private joke on the spur of the moment. Or, in hindsight, he could have meant it to stand for Widow Junghee Park.

"I would like a room on the ninth floor," I said.

"That's the top floor, and a suite costs $295 a night," the diminutive Cambodian said in nasal English.

Dismissing the bellhop with a $100 tip I took stock of my

suite, three doors down the hall on the same side as Soogun's. Leaving the door open a crack I stuck out the spyglass and watched. In less than 10 minutes the two North Korean Embassy employees left.

"Room service?" I called. "Bring me a cart of Cambodia's choicest food and drink. I might be in the shower but the boy can come in without knocking. He has a passkey, doesn't he?"

"Yes, sir!"

My reputation as a generous tipper must have gone forth like a trumpet call. Three men came instead of one. I gave each of them a $100 bill, flustering them out of their wits. As they were busy setting out the feast I took the ring of keys from the side of the cart. When they were about done, I held the door wide open and bowed, sweeping my arm down theatrically in exaggerated obeisance, which unsettled them even more. Hurriedly they kowtowed their way out, pushing the cart and forgetting all about their keys. I went to Room 937 and listened at the door with the stethoscope. Soogun was inside, snoring. The passkey opened the door but the chain was up as I had expected. With a wirecutter I snapped it off noiselessly.

Everything had worked like clockwork, paramedics wheeling Soogun out on a gurney, transportation by ambulance to a pier in Sihanoukville, then boarding the 50-foot freighter chartered. The prisoner was securely locked in a cabin aft. The weather forecast was good. All I had to do was relax and enjoy the 500-mile voyage to Singapore, where a KAL plane would be waiting. Nothing could go wrong in between. Except the Cambodian skipper started drinking the moment we left port.

"In sorrow for my wife and children killed by the Khmer Rouge," he said, crying.

"But you are responsible for navigation," I pointed out.

"Don't worry. I've been to Singapore hundreds of times and know the Gulf of Siam like my backyard."

Indeed there seemed no cause for concern. After a few hours we were already in the open sea with no land visible in any direction and nobody need go near the steerage, the course being set due south on automatic pilot straight for the

Equator. With nothing to do the entire crew, engineer, cook, and boatswain, copied their master and kept swilling. Not a single hand remained sober on that boat, but the passengers, me and my prisoner.

On the third day islands and coastlines began to dot the horizon. The captain got drunker by the minute, perhaps in anticipation of the big payoff, $10,000, the balance due on arrival. After supper, unable to bear his sniveling, I moved my cot to the poop, directly above Soogun below deck. Warmed by the orange glow of twilight and caressed by the gentle landward breeze I soon fell into deep sleep.

It was past midnight when the impact woke me. One of the drunks on duty at the helm had driven the boat smack into a reef, staving the hull. The boat started sinking almost instantly and it was all I could do to jump off and swim clear of the widening maelstrom. In the darkness I could not tell whether anybody else had survived. In vain I looked for a life preserver or a piece of wood so I could hang on. Toward daybreak I saw a dark spot bobbing in the waves seemingly an infinity away. Swimming closer I found it to be Soogun slumped over a door with a bleeding gash in the back of his head. I tried to stanch it with a wad of cloth but, no matter how hard I held it down, the blood oozed out and saturated the cloth.

"It's useless," Soogun said barely audibly. "I'm done for. Before I die, I want to pass some valuable information to you. Junghee Park is to be assassinated on March 1 at the Citizens Hall during the Independence Day ceremony."

"How? The place will be combed from top to bottom and nobody will be allowed to carry any weapon inside."

"That is why elaborate planning was necessary. We have the seating arrangements of the local representatives. Every year it has been the same, the front row assigned to the delegates from Daegu, Junghee's hometown. The seats will be taken out for repair at an upholsterer's to be returned with pistols and bullets sewn in. During the ceremony the delegates, agents of mine, will cut out the weapons and shoot."

"Why are you telling me all this?"

"Because I want you to stop it. I don't believe in assassination any more. You kill one and another equally bad or worse will promptly step in his place."

"Then why did you take all that trouble?"

"To prove to Jungil Kim, my pal Ilsung's son, that I could still do it. I have done it..."

He was dead.

For four days and nights I floated and drifted, hanging on the waterlogged door for whatever buoyancy it offered, without a single island or landmark to guide me. During the day the sun beat down mercilessly like a hot iron sizzling my skin and hair. At night small fish came nudging at me and strange lights and sounds played on the undulating darkness. At one time a huge mat of seaweed and algae entangled me for many hours and I had to fight my way out of the gooey mess. I was free at last but the door was gone. Totally unprotected, I dreaded being chopped up by the saw teeth of a shark, getting coiled in the tentacles of an octopus, or stung senseless by a sea snake or jelly fish. Boats and sampans sailed past but were either too distant to hear me or my voice failed. Finally a fishing sampan came within hailing distance and I shouted at the top of my voice, which got through. But the fishermen aboard apparently thought I was some kind of sea monster and rowed off for their dear lives. A few hours afterwards, however, perhaps ashamed of their cowardice or out of curiosity, the same sampan returned with a few more hands. As soon as I was fished out and put aboard, I passed out and slept for days.

When I woke, I was in a fisherman's hut. The host fed me and restored my strength. The whole village was solicitous of my convalescence and visitor after visitor brought gifts of food and drink. Sided by rocky cliffs the island in the Lingga Archipelago right on the Equator was unapproachable except where the village was, a bay through a narrow opening in the rock. Because of their isolation the villagers were quite primitive, dark-skinned, kinky-haired Polynesian aborigenes who went about naked. It was a forgone conclusion that a white-skinned, blue-eyed marvel like me should be promptly inducted into their pantheon of gods, a Poseidon whose emergence from under the waves was a good omen to their tribe. But my divinity did not relax their caution. To insure my continued presence among them sentries armed with poisoned arrows and darts were posted around my hut and followed me everywhere, making me a virtual prisoner. By and by, however, I got to talk to one of them, a toothless good-natured fellow in his late sixties, who spoke some English, which he had picked up while working in Singapore as a forced laborer for the Japanese during World War II. Then one fine morning he pointed at a faint shadow on the horizon.

"Singapore!" he exclaimed.

That was all I needed. Biding my time I stored food and other valuables for the long journey ahead. The opportunity soon presented itself. One full-moon night the villagers had a big party. Everybody, including my guards, went down to the beach and drank and danced, until they fell asleep, exhausted. I stole out of the bay paddling the swiftest canoe I had marked out before, the one that belonged to the chieftain.

"Passport?" asked the Ministry of Justice official in English upon my arrival at Pusan by a Malaysian freighter.

"I was shipwrecked and lost everything," I said. "Please put a call through to Al Edwards, Chief of the American CIA, Korea, or Hyongwoog Kim, Chief of Korean CIA. I have urgent information that can't wait."

Already banners and posters were everywhere in commemoration of Independence Day only two days away.

"CIA?"

"Yes, my last mission was specially performed for the KCIA Chief."

In my impatience I had spoken in Korean, quite flooring him. In undiluted, breezy Gyongsang accent, too. The months of not using a word of Korean had eroded away the Jolla patina I had so painstakingly cultivated, leaving only the coarse native grain. After staring at me as if I had been a Martian, he put a call through to his superiors. Half an hour later a sedan took me to a mansion on Yooldong Hill. The iron gate opened electronically and the concrete driveway led to a columned porch. I was taken to Director Shin of the Pusan District,

KCIA, who sat behind a glass topped desk.

"Now what was the mission given by Chief Kim?"

"The capture of Soogun Yee."

"So did you catch him?"

"He died in a shipwreck on the voyage to Singapore from Cambodia."

"That's just too bad. If you had him with you, you may be able to reinstate Chief Hyungwoog Kim to his old job. As it is, he had to resign under pressure. The loss of face was just too much even for him. We have now a new Chief, Jaygyoo Kim, one of us, a Gyongsang man. So any information you have will have to go to him."

"No, I want to talk to Chief Hyungwoog directly."

"We'll see about that."

Flashing a dome light the sedan tore through the new Seoul-Pusan Expressway, completed while I was away. After a few months Korea looked like a foreign country I came to visit for the first time. For one thing, the unit of currency had reverted to won from hwan in another monetary reform. Reaching the South Mountain Citadel, another name for the CIA Headquarters, under five hours, my hosts led me down a winding stairway to the cellar, furnished with grim instruments of torture.

"We don't have to use them," one of the interrogators I had been turned over to said.

"You can't do this," I shouted. "I am Dr. Archer Torrey, a US CIA agent. Chief Al Edwards will vouch for me. Call and verify."

"More likely you are an agent from North Korea."

"Do I look like a North Korean?"

"Maybe you are KGB. Tell us all the truth about yourself before we make you."

I was silent, debating how far back I should unravel my past. Apparently my captors took my silence for recalcitrance. Flopping me down into a chair, they tied my wrists to its arms, pulled down my pants, and connected an electrode to the scrotum.

"For the last time, won't you speak?"

I shook my head, not so much from any kind of heroic determination to refuse as from indecision coupled with a stunned, idle curiosity to see how far they would go with this insanity. A switch was tripped. I screamed but no sound came out of my mouth. The excruciating pain had stopped my breath.

"Shall we go on?"

I couldn't speak, though I was willing to tell everything, including my metamorphoses. The dial was moved up a notch and next moment my whole lower body shattered away, as if trampled by a thousand horses. Numbed and overcome by extreme pain, I looked forward to the next shock that would finish me off as a welcome relief. But it did not materialize. After untying me, they helped me put on my clothes and led me upstairs to a room where Hyongwoog Kim was waiting.

"I am glad I got here before they hurt you more," he said, seating me.

"How did you know I was here?" I asked.

"I still have men loyal to me in the Agency. Let's get the hell out of here."

It was our first meeting but I was instantly made at home by his guileless openness, a typical Jolla characteristic, which made me wonder how he could have ever been the top intelligence officer of the nation. He kept a 7-room apartment in Gangnamgoo south of the Han. All his children, two sons and one daughter, were in the US going to school and recently his wife had left too to look after them. So he was practically a bachelor. His comfortable but modest lifestyle belied the rumors that as CIA Chief he had siphoned off millions of dollars from the Agency's funds.

I remember him ordering on the phone some food from a restaurant but I passed out, not waking until five p.m. next day when I heard him enter.

"Congratulations!" he said, pumping my hand. "Your story checked out. The seats at the theater have all been inspected, and indeed those in the front row had the artillery. The grounds and buildings manager who had ordered the repairs was found to be a North Korean agent. The upholstery shop where the work was done was raided, a command post and nerve center for espionage in the south, complete with wireless sets, code books, and directories. Your information has led to over 100 arrests, the biggest sweep since the war. I cannot thank you enough for vindicating me and putting my enemies to shame."

"Are you going to rejoin Junghee Park's government?"

"He wants me to but I want to be on the sidelines for a while. The moral triumph is enough. That reminds me. The President wants to see you tomorrow at the Blue House."

"Me! Whatever for?"

The whole undertaking had been to help Hyongwoog Kim as a favor to James Reed to whom I felt I owed it for the embarrassment I had caused with the moodang show. I was glad that Hyongwoog could use the information I had supplied to strengthen his political position but frankly I wouldn't have cared if Hyongwoog hadn't done a thing to save Junghee Park from the plot. So strong had been my hostility toward him, though I had never met him before, on account of his well-known anti-Jolla stance.

"You've saved his life, and he wants to express his appreciation. Incidentally, where did you pick up that Gyongsang accent? Was your Korean teacher a Gyonsang person?"

I nodded. Clearly, neither US nor Korean CIA had delved into my pre-Heyman identity, my early years at the Mercy Home in Daegu.

"His Excellency has this weakness about anybody with Gyongsang accent, which must trip some hidden switch deep down in his libido. So watch out. He may never let you go, once he latches on to you. The Soogun Yee affair has chastened him a bit: those who were to do the shooting were all from Gyongsang. But I doubt it will really change anything."

There was bitterness in his voice, a bitterness I fully shared.

"I can speak Jolla as well as you or anybody else," I said, speaking in the dialect.

"That is remarkable," he said, surprised. "Where did you

learn it?"

"My best friends, folk musicians at the Aran Ham Center for Korean Folk Music, are from Jolla and I feel I am one of them."

"Believe me they can use friends like you. But this is a fight between us Koreans and does not concern you, an American, an outsider."

"Injustice concerns me no matter who I am, where I am."

"I appreciate your noble feelings," he said after some reflection. "But can I ask you to hide them around Junghee Park? Don't even breathe a hint of your Jolla accent, lest you should remind him of Daejung, his mortal enemy. Even I try to moderate my accent, a hybrid anyway. There is no point in distressing the man, when we know nothing is going to change him."

"What's the point of meeting him and going through an elaborate masquerade?"

"To get paid. You've done something for him and he owes you."

"But I didn't do it for him."

"I know that. Al has told me all about it. But it's a case of unjust enrichment and Junghee owes you in a big way. Do you refuse to pick up your pay check at work just because your boss doesn't measure up to your standards? It's as simple as that."

I was silent. He must know all about the shady characters Alan, my alter ego, had worked for, Molinbeck, Hessler, Buckley, Kean, No. Who was I to be so finicky about who I worked for all of a sudden?

"By the way, how do you want to be introduced, Alan Heyman or Archer Torrey?"

So Junghee knew only what Hyongwoog chose to let him know. Were all masters so dependent on their servants?

"Archer Torrey," I said, decisively.

X.
Blue House

"I owe you my life, Archer," the short man with a plain swarthy peasant face said, receiving me in the Octagonal Room of the Blue House.

"You owe me nothing, Your Excellency," I said truthfully.

"I've never heard a foreigner speak so perfectly, with the right accent, too. You must be an exceptional person."

"Just a combination of circumstances, Your Excellency."

"I understand you are unattached. It would give me the greatest pleasure if you make this your home, like family. Maybe you can teach my children English, though I loathe the language."

I saw no reason to decline. In fact, the offer was most timely because I had no place to stay. The lease on the rooms at Tadpole's had run out and I had been looking for a new place to move to. I was assigned a room in the dormitory of the Security Building with a bunk bed and a desk, no better than a military barracks, for which however many would have given their eyetooth. To my relief the President didn't follow up on my English tutorship. In fact throughout my stay at the Blue House I only saw the three children, aged 15, 13 and 9, a couple of times in passing. The first family lived in the Inner Court way back behind the office complex with little contact with the staff or visitors. Escorted by armed guards, the children went to a special private school for the exclusively rich and powerful where they had American teachers for their English. With a one-to-one teacher-student ratio for almost every subject and long hours, from eight to five, they had a fill of schooling and didn't need any more at home.

I had a car assigned to me but seldom had occasion to use it, because there was no need to leave the compound. The cafeteria provided the food, and the barber cut my hair. For any personal needs I had to only tell the supply officer who got them for me. I didn't know exactly what my status was. Though at the beck and call of the President and physically close to him, I wasn't a bodyguard. Nor was I an advisor. He had a slew of them with degrees and titles running around all the time. The best description might be that I was a house guest of indefinite duration the master wanted around as long as he pleased, showing off to his friends now and then.

Such an occasion was a reception given in honor of Gen. William Wainwright, the new C-in-C, UNC. Thank God for the change of command, for the other one, Gen. McCoy, might still recognize me from the moodang ritual at the National Theater in spite of my new name. Being near the President I was among the first to greet the guest of honor, who looked like a prize fighter with his crew cut and big hands.

"I wouldn't be here to greet you, General," the host said, "had it not been for this young man from your country. He swam the Gulf of Siam to save me."

"I also swam in the Gulf of Siam, Archer," Wainwright said, squeezing my hand in his mitt. "The plane I flew during World War II got shot down by Japanese shore batteries. We all parachuted and hit the water, but two crewmen drowned. The rest of us managed to stay afloat and got rescued within the hour by our Navy. We wouldn't have made it if it had lasted longer."

The entire west wing and the lawn crawled with US and Korean military brass, cabinet members, ambassadors, and other dignitaries and notables. The aroma from the barbecuing meat filled the evening air. Dishes prepared by the best chefs in all conceivable cuisines, Korean, Chinese, Japanese, American, European, filled the tables, and the bars kept replenishing from cases of vintage whisky and wine. The KBS Band played soft music, to which the guests danced.

I was still apprehensive that some of the company who had been at the Theater, notably Ambassador Marconi, might remember me or rather Alan, but nobody did. Who would remember a two-bit emcee at a local moodang show, who hadn't even made sense! Besides the label was everything. And the presentation, because by no stretch of imagination could they connect me, groomed and well-fed, standing next to the supreme ruler of the land, to the inept drifter, outcast and hungry. Even I couldn't believe it sometimes, and had to pinch myself to be convinced that it was all real. But as the reality sank in, I recalled the misery and anger of the millions outside, deprived and excluded from the feast of life for no fault of their own. The falsehood of the opulent occasion and my rather prominent place in it began to oppress me.

Unobtrusively I slipped away from the invidious circle around the President. It was odious to have my Cambodian odyssey rehearsed to every guest that approached him, as if it was some genuine accomplishment instead of a lucky chain of events that happened to have a happy issue. No adventurous heroism and certainly no personal loyalty to Park had motivated it, as it was made out.

"Dr. Torrey," somebody startled me, putting his hand on my shoulder from behind. It was Al Edwards with his usual polished, pleasant manners. "Sorry I was away and could not meet you at the wharf. But I gather everything has turned out all right, better than expected."

Hyongwoog came over and congratulated Al on a mission well accomplished. Before I could learn what it was exactly that Al had done in Tokyo, he was called away to wait on his Ambassador. Left to ourselves, Hyongwoog pointed contemptuously with his chin at a meticulously dressed three-star general talking to a group of officers a few feet away.

"That is Giryong Yoon, the Fashion Model. As Commander of the Auxiliary Division he did absolutely no fighting in Vietnam but came home in triumph, by default, with the returning expeditionary force as the Vietnam War wound down. He must have looked sleek and good as usual to Junghee, who promptly gives him command of the Capital

Security Division. Look at him talk and move about like a fashion model. Of course he has Gyongsang accent like 98% of the Koreans here."

He blinked an eye to signify exclusion of mine under the pact between us. A mountain of a man waddled over to shake my hand and congratulate me. But on seeing Hyongwoog he departed abruptly after the barest nod.

"He is Geeyung Jang, Chairman of the Economic Planning Board and Deputy Prime Minister," Hyongwoog explained.

"A Rocky Mountain grizzly," I observed.

"No, the tamest of pussycats."

Hyongwoog narrated the break-in of Jang's office he had authorized because the man was getting out of line. A hidden safe disgorged perfumes, Gucci bags, Pierre Cardin ties, diamond rings, cuff links.

"It looked very much like the cache of a smalltime burglar, not that of the Economic Planner of a nation, I tell you. He owns hotels, a whole strip of the prime beach at Daychon, blocks of homes, commercial and industrial buildings, but still loves it when people give him these trinkets. I took the whole evidence to President Park, who was ready to fire him, but Jang cried and begged, reminding Park of his previous services, especially the flour deal he pulled off with Mitsubishi that brought timely relief to the famine-stricken countryside and saved Junghee's first presidential election. After promising to shape up and swearing his undying loyalty, Jang could retain his job. I can still see him whimpering."

Hyongwoog stood chuckling at Jang's backside until he was distracted by a short man sidling up to His Excellency past us.

"See that mousy runt with glittering little eyes, Changsoon Yee, Class 9, Military Academy, currently our Ambassador to Britain. I bet he is here to line up for the next Washington appointment. Right after the coup he was one of the beggars who came to my office swearing loyalty unto death. He spoke tolerable English, so I sent him over to the Foreign Ministry. My one phone call made him Planning Controller, then

Ambassador to Mexico and West Germany successively, but now he avoids me as if I had the plague."

A stocky muscular man planted himself in front of us, eyeing me with curiosity.

"This is Gen. Jeechul Cha, Chief of the Secret Service," Hyongwoog introduced.

"What exercise do you do?" Jeechul asked.

"I don't exercise, sir," I replied, surprised at the abruptness of the question.

"No jogging or sparring?"

"No, sir."

"You should. Fitness is not something you can put away on a shelf. Come down to the gym in the basement. My boys spar every morning at 5 a.m."

"Thank you."

"Tomorrow morning?"

"Come on, Jeechul. Give him a break. He's just been through a war."

"The day after then," he said, leaving hurriedly in response to some signal from his men.

"Watch out," Hyongwoog cautioned me when we were alone. "Jeechul can be an ugly customer. He is the one who kicked Minister of Education, Dr. Bomnin Kim, in the groin making him collapse to the floor for entering five minutes after His Excellency had sat down for our morning conference. What indignities men will put up with to feed at the table of power! I myself had just arrived as the Chief walked in. Traffic had been backed up for miles due to the new subway construction along Hyoja Boulevard. Jeechul didn't know or care about that, living at the Blue House. Would Park have allowed him to offer such insolence to me? I often wonder. Power makes one forget one's debt. If I hadn't crossed the Han with my 500 paratroopers at 1 a.m. on May 16, 1961, he wouldn't be where he is now."

The language barrier was insurmountable and except for labored contacts and probings for mutual courtesy's sake, the two groups, Korean and non-Korean, separated like oil and water as the party ripened, each settling down to more comfortable conversations among themselves. A circle of Koreans had formed around His Excellency to match wits in ridiculing President Carter who had in a recent press conference confirmed his campaign pledge to withdraw US forces from Korea and cut off aid to Junghee Park's regime. One of them was Donsun Bag, who commuted half around the world between Seoul and Washington, D.C., with whom I had a strange bilingual conversation a minute ago. Though I kept answering in Korean, he carried on in his English, ungrammatical and unidiomatic, yet spoken with native assurance and pronunciation, R's rolled and dentals liquified. Hyongwoog, my Virgil, explained the presence of the man at the Blue House, though a mere rice merchant with no official status whatsoever.

"He is no relation to the Chief, either. He must have learned to speak English as a houseboy at American barracks during the war, when his father died. His enterprising mother went into the rice business, at first in bags carried on her head, then truckloads and trainloads. Soon her Miryoong Enterprise imported rice from Southeast Asia and the US. In time she got him into Georgetown University and supplied him with enough funds to get him invited to the Korean Embassy parties where he met US politicians who were soon on a first-name basis with him, calling him Rice Bag. He couldn't graduate from Georgetown but got a commission much more valuable than any earned degree, rice purchasing agency for Junghee, and began performing miracles. By bribing US Senators, Representatives, Governors, and other officials he put pressure on the Department of Agriculture to sell the surplus rice in the storage silos of Louisiana 20, 30, maybe 50% below the stated markup, though he alone knows for sure. The hundreds of millions of dollars saved were then transferred to a slush fund at the Blue House. Naturally Junghee Park loves him and calls him Honest Donsun. But whenever I see his oily smile, I know he has a pot of gold stashed away somewhere for himself."

Hadn't I heard the expression Honest So and So elsewhere? Of course, in Honest Gwon of Molinbeck and

Honest Han of Major Buckley, which had transformed the very meaning of the word honest in my lexicon. So the plain-dealing peasant soldier Park had his honest Bag, too.

"What do you think of President Carter, Archer?"

I heard the pointed question. It was President Park himself. All eyes were on me, putting me on the spot. Not too long ago the papers had reported Carter's speech to a group of National Merit Scholars, America's top high school seniors, congratulating them on the one hand but exhorting them, on the other, to be compassionate and grateful thinking of the many other bright young people who could not be there with them that day because, disadvantaged and deprived, they could not develop their full potential. Contrary to what these men were saying about him, Carter must be a man of great integrity and exceptional perception to speak that way to teenagers puffed up with pride and elitism. On the other hand, I didn't want to contradict and antagonize Park's friends more than necessary. Already I had winced a few times at the stab of a steely hate-filled stare from Lt. Gen. Giryong Yoon, Hyongwoog's Fashion Model, though I couldn't imagine how I could have offended him. My dilemma was averted by Gen. Wainwright who advanced toward us, accompanied by his aides.

"Thank you, Your Excellency, for the great party. I hope to have the honor of your presence at my place soon."

"Sure, General, any time."

"Now if you'll excuse me. I have to be up at 5 a.m. to drive up to the DMZ and review the frontline troops."

"Of course, General. Have a good trip. I hope you like your stay in Korea."

"Oh, absolutely. I feel at home already."

"I hope Mrs. Wainwright gets here soon."

"Any minute, Your Excellency. But she can take her time. I am enjoying my vacation from her."

The men laughed. Junghee followed his departing guest of honor to the gate to see him off.

When we were alone, I asked Hyongwoog about Gen. Giryong Yoon's strange hostility toward me.

"Because I am your friend," Hyongwoog said. "I wanted to drop him from the final list of coup participants but Junghee wanted him in, a former aide of his. On the eve of the coup we were at a tea house by Seoul Station, all in fatigues, ready for action, when Giryong showed up, perfumed, in a polyester officer's uniform he got on a recent trip to the US. I asked him if he was with us and he smiled, as if the whole thing was a big joke. I almost plugged him right then and there. He could have undone everything. All he had to do was run over to the Army Headquarters and squeal to Chief of Staff Doyung Jang, a distant relation of his. He said he was with us but, pleading his unfamiliarity with the Seoul situation, promised to lend his moral support in the background. Can you imagine that, moral support to a group of desperate men? I could see through this opportunist, who wanted to sit on the fence before jumping off to either side. I told him to change to fatigues and come to Junghee's house in Shindangdong. That night, torn in a hundred different directions, I could not confirm whether Giryong had showed up at all, but one thing is certain. I did not come across him at any phase of the real action. The paratroopers I led crossed the Han, overcame token resistance from the curfew patrol and accomplished the bloodless coup. Still it had been a touch and go situation, because the nearby divisions at Soowon, Anyang, and Samdug could have marched against us, the 24th, not to speak of the frontline divisions highly mobile and prepared. They could have decided to advance on the capital and contest the prize of supreme power. But we moved fast, surrounded Doyong Jang's residence, while he was still in sleep, and made him acknowledge the coup. In fact, he was offered Chairmanship of the Supreme Council, the titular head of the junta. By 6 a.m. on May 16 the success of our coup had been reported on the wire services at home and abroad. The mob started coming in droves, opportunists and climbers, and sure enough Giryong was among them, smartly dressed and manicured as usual.

"As soon as I got my CIA post, Col. Giryong Yoon wasted no time to come knocking at my door. Recalling our friendship he asked me to take him on as my deputy or whatever. Politely I told him that I couldn't start packing the Agency with my personal friends. That was the beginning of his mortal enmity toward me. His antennae probed for a weak link, which turned out to be Yongsug Bag, Class 5, Military Academy, Chief of the Army CIC, Counterintelligence Corps, and a member of the Supreme Council, somehow convincing him that nobody turned him down without drawing Junghee's ire. Yongsug Bag made Giryong head of the Seoul CIC Branch. Giryong soon managed to turn this modest position into a real power base before which the entire capital trembled. It wasn't long before Giryong pushed out his benefactor and took over as head of CIC, promoting himself to Brigadier. Of course he couldn't have done it without Junghee's support. Giryong's ambition began to soar from then on and he went around posing as heir apparent to Junghee Park and badmouthing me at every turn. I ignored him, not wishing to stoop to his level.

"Giryong and I clashed openly over the attempted coup of Choongyon Won, Commander of the 3rd Division at Samdug, who plotted to march on Seoul and overthrow the government on the pattern set by us. But it never got off the ground because there was a traitor among the conspirators, a Major Yee who blabbed all about it to Army CIC, giving Giryong the first crack at the investigation. When the matter reached my desk - I had my own sources of information in spite of jealous hoarding by Giryong - I advocated its minimization by keeping it under wraps as an internal breach of Army discipline. On the verge of paralysis by daily demonstrations everywhere opposing rapprochement with Japan, the country just couldn't handle another full-blown treason case, but Giryong would have none of it. Here was an opportunity to prove to the world and His Excellency once and for all the superiority of CIC over CIA.

"I was willing to sit this one out and let Giryong get all the credit and publicity he wanted, but soon intervention became necessary as he got out of hand thirsting for blood. His particular targets were General Shin Han in command of the 6th Corps and General Ilgwun Jung, the Prime Minister. To support the fantastic scenario that Choongyon had consent of Han to mobilize his Corps and enforce martial law and of Jung to head the new government, Giryong was 'collecting' evidence left and right, arresting and torturing their aides, secretaries and orderlies. Only when I persuaded Junghee that proof of such conspiracy would encourage more coup adventurers as it would demonstrate the weakness of his power base, the support of the Army everybody took for granted, did he order Giryong to stop. Of the nine arraigned, which did not include Han or Jung, only Choongyon Won and Indo Bag got death sentences, the rest going free with reprimands. You may be sure how Giryong must have hated me for that.

"Though he did not quite carry it off, Giryong had made his mark by the Choongyon Won Incident, and began to act as if he owned the world. Somehow he managed to overawe Army Chief of Staff Yongbay Kim and took control of the Bureau of Personnel, putting his men at all major Army posts, commanders of divisions, corps, and armies, making Giryong the most powerful man in the Army. Openly he recruited and consolidated an elite circle within the Army consisting of the class of 1950 of the Military Academy and graduates of the later regular 4-year curriculum, organizing picnics, seminars, fellowships, which cost over $50,000 a shot from the funds he got by shaking down the businesses. What did it all mean? His ambition. After tasting power he wanted to be top dog. Created by Junghee Park as a counterweight to me mainly and also as an informal watchdog over all the other power agencies, Giryong was not content with his derivative position. Though I knew what Giryong was up to, I couldn't do anything just then. North Korea was on a war path, sending boatloads of agents to our beaches. But through his own sensors Junghee must have felt the need to curb Giryong. He replaced him by Jaygyoo Kim, another Gyongsang boy, my successor at the Agency, as head of CIC. But Giryong wasn't turned out into the cold exactly. With a third star he was sent to the cushiest job in Vietnam, where he could make all the money he wanted in the safety of the rear. Now he commands the praetorian guard,

Capital Security. Mark my word, Junghee is making a big mistake, because this customer is devoid of gratitude and will bite the hand that feeds it."

My friend's inside narrative only confirmed my suspicion. The great edifice of government, with its laws, courts, and armies of servitors, empowered to grant or deny life to millions, was in truth nothing but a whimsical, arbitrary business, determined by greed, malice, gall, chance.

"You didn't do me a favor exactly in recommending me for this job or whatever I've got here," I said.

"I didn't, honest to God. I had no idea Junghee would be so taken by you. I thought he would just shake your hand and send you on your way with a medal or two. It must be your Gyongsang accent, as I said."

XI.
Bronco Rider

I was in his usual retinue of some dozen attendants when President Junghee Park set out on a tour of the front one morning. We were in three cars, preceded and followed by motorcycle security. After a lunch stop at the 5th Army, whose commander Gen. Dugjoon Oh was in line for the next Army Chief of Staff, our presidential party headed east.

"I want to see the Ranch," Junghee said.

He was referring to Liberty Ranch, located 100 miles northeast of Seoul in the middle of the Iron Triangle, where the wounds of the war were still visible after these many years - abandoned trenches, bunkers, bomb craters - the proximity to the DMZ discouraging settlement and development. The owner of the ranch had served under Junghee in the Army but his principal qualification for operating the ranch that supplied beef and dairy products to the Blue House was his origination from Gyongsang.

An Army detachment guarded the facility and a team of experts from the Ministry of Health oversaw every phase of production to insure fresh and sanitary delivery to the Blue House.

"The movie people are here doing a film, Your Excellency," said the officer on duty, saluting smartly.

"Who are they?" Junghee asked.

"Mr. and Mrs. Kim, that is, Director-Producer Jonghag Kim and Actress Nanyong Song, of Jongnan Film, Your Excellency."

At her name my heart skipped a beat. So finally I was getting to see the goddess who had taken my soul by storm with her movies. I had forgotten about her lately but the name brought back all the sweet and hopeless memories that had tormented and kept me awake nights. Would the real person be as enchanting as the celluloid image or would she be a disappointment? Almost outstepping the Chief, I went in the direction indicated by the officer.

About fifty people were packed in a circle around some object in the middle, so preoccupied that they weren't aware of our approach. Finally, alerted to the high one's presence, the group parted, revealing a horse on its side, beating the air with its legs, bleeding in the nose and mouth, writhing and squealing in agonies of death, while its rider with a cracked skull was being carried away on a stretcher to a hospital. The script had called for the hero's horse to slip and fall, throwing the rider off, while he was fleeing from a Japanese ambush, but the enactment had been too realistic. The horse had crashed on its chest, throwing the hapless rider to the ground head first, a double for the leading actor Jingyoo Kim. The movie, Lone Independence Fighter, was based on the life of Patriot Jwajin Kim, fugitive from the Japanese police in Manchuria, the Wild West of Korea in the 30's under Japanese occupation.

"Do we have your permission to put the beast out of its misery, Your Excellency?" asked Director Kim, coming forward.

"By all means," Junghee said. "I am sorry you had an accident. I would have loved to watch you at work."

Junghee was a devoted fan and patron of the Kims and had arranged the necessary government loans to set up their Anyang Studio and Seoul Film School on the south bank of the Han.

"Nothing would have pleased us more, Your Excellency," Jonghag said. "But this just about scratches the day off, because we can't continue with neither horse nor rider."

"Can't you shoot something else in the movie?"

"No, Your Excellency. We came prepared for only this scene, which is a full day's project. There is no alternative but to pack up and go. We'll keep you posted on our schedule and will be honored to have your presence any time."

There was a stir in the ranks of people before Junghee as they parted to let someone through. It was Nanyong Song, more stunning in person than on screen, a sun that eclipsed all other constellations into obscurity, fresh, vital, scintillating. Coming to a stand by Jonghag's side, she made a curt but cordial bow of her head to their distinguished patron.

"This is an unexpected honor," she said in mellifluous Jolla accent that jingled like a silver bell.

"The pleasure is all mine," Junghee said. "What a pity you can't shoot more!"

She turned to the rancher in the crowd and asked, "Can't we find another horse, sir?"

"I have a stallion but it's unbroken," he said apologetically. "None of my hands have been able to ride the monster. Bitted but not saddled, it bucks and kicks something awful."

The consensus was that the bronco should be looked at anyway. The rancher led the company to an enclosure behind a barn. At the approach of such a crowd the piebald horse with a flowing mane neighed, reared, and kicked menacingly, straining at the rope tied to a post in the middle and noosed around its neck. One look at this wild creature was enough to cower the stoutest of heart.

"Who will ride the steed for His Excellency?" somebody shouted like an auctioneer inviting bids for the crown jewel.

The ranch hands cringed back, no doubt remembering painful previous encounters. Nor did any of the soldiers in the detachment or anyone of the presidential party volunteer: equestrianism was not exactly a popular sport in post-War Korea.

"I wish I were twenty years younger," Junghee lamented.

Then his eyes fell on me and his sun-burnt, rugged peasant's face broke into a big, mischievous grin. "Would you like to try, Archer?"

Without waiting for my answer, he turned to Nanyong and asked if I would do as the jockey. Jonghag was farther away talking to the ranch owner.

"We can shoot, profiling his face from some distance, so it won't matter," she said, looking me over appraisingly, apparently seeing me for the first time. "But has he ridden a horse before? We don't want another accident."

"I will ride him no matter what if the lady finds me suitable," I blurted out, blushing to the roots of my hair.

Startled by my Jolla-accented Korean, resurrected by her example, she shot a glance at me for a sign of mockery but, finding none except utter abashment and confusion, nodded approval. Everybody's eyes turned on me, the electric charge buoying me up over the fence before I knew it. I went behind the horse to a spot calculated to provoke his kicks. Missing them by an inch I circled the post, until the animal got the rope wound around it so tightly that it almost strangled itself. Reversing the direction I made him unwind a little. Just as he breathed easier and was positioning himself to kick, I got on his blind side and pushed my shoulder against his rump when all his weight happened to be on one hind leg. The big animal tottered and shrieked painfully as the tether caught his fall almost snapping his neck. He stood puzzled and quiescent, head drooping in shame, as I cut the rope with a knife handed to me by a ranch hand.

"You are like me, mixed and spotted," I crooned softly into his ears, running my hand over his mane and withers, to which he submitted without a protest. But his docility had been temporary and deceptive. When I led him out of the enclosure and got on his back, holding the reins, the fight returned to him with renewed vigor. He reared and bucked ferociously to unseat me. Remembering the bare back riding I had practiced on the sly at the orphanage I hung on like the devil, clasping his belly tightly with my legs, and drove him into a nearby stream with sandy shoals which neutralized the violence of his kickings and wrenchings. Of course the whole crowd was closely following us, including Junghee Park, who had told an aide, I learned, to shoot the beast in case my life was in real danger. When I judged the violence of the animal's resistance to have peaked, I turned his head away from the river bed. As soon as we climbed up the other bank, he shot off like a bullet raising a cloud of dust. By the time we returned to the waiting and cheering crowd, my mount was ready to do anything I wanted, including the makebelieve overthrow of his tamer. Metamorphosed into another double of the main character by the able makeup and costume people on hand, I took the fall credibly enough for the camera and the five-minute sequence was used without much editing in the film released a few weeks later.

This totally unplanned, insignificant appearance as a substitute double was the beginning of my movie career. Jonghag called me at the Blue House and asked me to play a part in their next movie Star-Crossed, a wartime romance between a downed American fighter pilot and a Korean girl, who shelters and takes him to the UN lines.

"Nanyong will be the girl and you the pilot," Jonghag said.

"Do you think I can act?"

"I won't be asking if I am not sure. I have an instinct about this. You are perfect for it. I have already spoken to the President, who gives his blessings. Come to our studio tomorrow morning. We'll go to the location from there."

This couldn't have come at a better time, because I was actually looking for an excuse to get away from the Blue House, where the very air I breathed seemed tainted. On many occasions I felt stabbed by the edge of suspicion and jealousy on account of my physical proximity to the supreme power, though I derived from it very little advantage but free room and board.

For example, every time Gen. Giryong Yoon came calling at the Blue House - and he did far oftener than his duties as Capital Security Commander would seem to warrant - he deliberately snubbed and insulted me, walking directly into me in the hallway, almost knocking me over with his strong cologne, if not by bodily collision. I half contemplated standing my ground and bumping him off as I easily could with my superior physical size, but at the last moment I thought better of it and stepped aside, begging his pardon, which he never even acknowledged, striding on into the Octagonal Office. I stood watching this phenomenon, wondering not so much at his provocative behavior as at His Excellency's sanity in suffering, nay, apparently inviting, the company of such a pompous prick. Nauseated by the very idea that the likes of Giryong Yoon should consider me his rival for the high one's favor, I was glad to get away.

But the more positive attraction of the proposal was of course being near Nanyong Song, my revived passion. It was like a dream come true. Didn't Jinny Bay predict my meeting the lady of my dreams? She must have meant Nanyong, for I had no other lady that I had dreamt of, nor would I ever that I could foresee. Jinny must be right, the blind seer, Queen of Moodang, psychic of psychics, with such a loyal following. How lucky of Alan to be taken under her wing! They must be very happy together. I should look them up one of these days. But, then, Jinny said there was trouble with Nanyong. What kind of trouble? As if it needed to be spelled out. How right she was again, for Nanyong was off limits, a star loved by the whole nation, spoken of with awe even by Junghee Park, who had the reputation of whistling up and bedding down any woman he fancied, but, above all, married, apparently happily, to the country's top movie director and producer with numerous awards and honors under his belt. I meant nothing to her. If she were to learn about my love for her, she would be annoyed and feel insulted: calculation was at the core of love and one did not love someone unless that person promised some advantage, like wealth, position, talent, none of which I could boast. Even if I had the world to offer and proved irresistible to her, her marriage would stand in the way, insurmountable. Jonghag would fight for her and the law would protect his right. She belonged to him and I shouldn't covet her. Adultery was sin and its penalty used to be death. Yes, the warning lights flashed all right. The wiser course was to stay clear, to forget all about her and think of her only as some unobtainable object to be admired at a distance, like the moon or sunset. Perhaps I was asking for trouble by accepting this job and exposing myself to the temptation of hope.

But another voice overrode that of caution and urged me to go forward and seize what fate was throwing in my way.

Jonghag might be married to her but he did not own her. An individual had a right to choose, especially in matters of the heart, no matter what his or her station in life. Just as he could have a concubine or girlfriend stashed away somewhere, and I recalled reading some gossip about him somewhere, she could have a lover and that could very well be me. Nay, I could replace him and become her husband. Let the better man take the prize! The difference of some years in age between us did not matter. History had many celebrated marriages between an older woman and a younger man, Napoleon, 7 years junior, and Disraeli, 15 years or so. Yes, I would let her know that I loved her, telling her to look beyond my present obscurity to the resplendent future, especially with her participation and contribution, though I hadn't the foggiest how specifically that could be accomplished. I was sleepless with anticipation and left for their Anyang Studio at first light.

The first day of my new career, if it were to be that, began somewhat inauspiciously, mostly aimless waiting around in the swamps near Inchon where I, an American flier, had supposedly parachuted according to the screenplay I was given to read, while the camera crew lugged their equipment about and took their sweet time trying various angles. When everything seemed ready, and I thought we were finally getting into action, the cameraman shouted "Halt", and angrily ordered one of his assistants to bring the other bag of films from the truck parked nearly a mile away on the road. The bag he had with him was the wrong one. But, directing in the absence of Jonghag, who was in Seoul supposedly straightening out some overdue bank loans, Nanyong Song displayed amazing patience with the failings of her crew. None of the temperamentality commonly associated with beautiful women and prima donnas. Besides she was capable of attention to particulars, compassion for individuals.

"It's hard at first to get a clear picture of what's going on, or how everything fits in," said she, coming over to me, as if she had read my mind.

"How do you keep track of all these fragments so they add up?" I asked. "It's like visualizing the cathedral from the brick lying around in heaps. To have all the disconnected pieces in your mind and arrange them toward a unified whole seems uncanny, a feat requiring some colossal brain, not unlike that of God creating the universe."

"We have a few gimmicks to prop up our divine omniscience," she said laughing. At her bidding an assistant brought the director's shot chart, which revealed at a glance the structure and organization of the whole movie. There were a total of 57 cuts, that is, scenes or units of continuous filming. Mine was among the first, preceded by the aerial shots of an American fighter plane being hit by antiaircraft shells and spinning out of control after my ejection.

At this time the cameraman shouted the all clear.

"Off you go, Archer," Nanyong sent me off with a pat on the back. "You are on."

With the whole crew watching, the simplest action seemed weighted down like trying to move in water, but I freed myself from the entanglement of cords and started running for the top of the hill. There was no time to gather the chute and stow it away: the local Communist militia was heading my way. With one camera tracking me and another panning the posse downhill, which went berserk upon discovery of the torn parachute, I had to scamper away painfully dragging a sprained foot, credibly getting cut and bruised by the brambles and stones on the way. That was one day's work.

The next day the location was Mt. Triangle. I had crawled to an isolated mountain hut and collapsed at the doorstep, until found by the daughter of the house, Nanyong in a countrified blouse and skirt and youthful like a nineteen-year-old. With a scream she calls for her parents and they carry me inside. It was bright day but with the darkened lenses and lighting tricks the film portrayed twilight. After vain efforts to get my bearings and come to my feet, I pass out for good. Nanyong takes charge of me from the beginning, applies cold packs to my head and face, and nurses me anxiously, crying and praying all night. Slowly I mend but my presence creates great tension in the household. First of all harboring an enemy flier is a capital offense. In fact, the militia comes around, asks about me, and searches the house and its surroundings. But they don't find me because the family has hid me cleverly in a cave, the mouth of which is completely covered by bushes. But the strain of feeding and nursing me to health, especially when they don't have enough to eat themselves, as well as the constant vigilance against sudden raids and searches by the militia proves too much for the family, and the parents are determined to go to the authorities and turn me in. It is Nanyong who makes the heroic decision to shield me at all costs and lead me to the American lines. In the middle of the night she comes to my hideout and with some food she has taken from the kitchen we flee along the mountain ridge, often running smack into Communist patrols and checkpoints.

Throughout the filming I was more aware of Nanyong's physical nearness than the composition or artistry of the movie itself. I was often dizzy with excitement to be caressed and held by her hand with its long slender fingers, to notice her ivory skin under the fine down, and above all to be regarded by her large orbs of eyes, complete universes so full of tenderness and affection and devotion. Only if they were real, not acted! Hopelessly, inextricably I was in love with her. Nevertheless, at this point my passion for her was platonic, for the distant moon or sunset, and I knew no frustration. I had no design on her body yet. In fact, the thought never entered my mind. Still a virgin, I lacked carnal knowledge of women. I was contented and felt privileged to be near her, grateful to be touched by her or to smell her, if only to fulfill the requirements of the screenplay. Apparently the camera depicted my emotions for her with great fidelity.

"Your portrayal is perfect!" Jonghag exclaimed after a scene where we pledge never to part as we approach the front lines and get nearly separated by a barrage of gunfire. "You are a natural for romantic roles."

He had no reason to waste his compliments on me. Maybe I should go full time into acting and movie making. Maybe this was the career, the purpose of life I had been searching for but could not find. Korean folk music had been only a phase, a cause to champion for the sake of its practitioners, my Jolla friends. How were they, incidentally? Did Wansong leave for the US? Never. That glitch of his would always be there, unless perhaps I helped. I might just do that.

When released, Star-Crossed was a sensation and I was a star overnight. In subsequent movies I played a regular Korean lead, not an occasional foreigner. By suppressing the more pronounced Caucasian and accentuating the less Korean halves of my physiognomy, I turned into a handsome Korean male, thanks to Korean aesthetics regarding personal beauty. The ideal was to look Caucasian, because American (White) domination was complete in Korea, not only politically and economically but culturally. Everybody was crazy about Gregory Peck, Robert Taylor, Elizabeth Taylor, Deborah Kerr. Desirable were big, round eyes, high nose, sharply etched features, while held up for ridicule were the more typical native Korean traits, round face, low nose, lower cheek bones, narrow eyes, overall smoothness, flatness, delineated approvingly in classical Korean sculpture and painting. As a result Korean women paid a fortune to widen their eyes by creasing the epicanthic fold. By this standard I should be the handsomest man in Korea, but not quite: I overreached, which was perhaps worse than falling short. The excess, infinitesimal but critical in the skin deep business that is personal aesthetics, branded me a foreigner and needed to be toned down by makeup for my film appearances. It had to be just the right degree of Caucasianness, achieved by a full-blooded Korean, and of course Nan's face was the aesthetic optimum for women. Though glad at her being the beneficiary of the prevailing standard of beauty, I often felt sorry, even guilty at seeing so many Korean women crushed by an inferiority complex because they had smaller eyes, flatter noses, less than dainty mouths, which I considered just as acceptable, had the perception been otherwise. However, in no position to question or alter the aesthetics of a whole nation, I was just glad to be needed, to be at Anyang or wherever it might be on location with the film crews, wherever Nan was, the ruler of my heart, and threw myself head over heels into my new career, making one movie after another, Barley Hill, Red Stallion, Ondal the

Idiot, and so forth.

Before I forget I must mention another feature of my facial appearance, which improbably enhanced, rather than detracted from, its perception by my adoring Korean public: a cowlick I had trained to stray and hang down halfway over my forehead to hide a dime-size, quarter-inch deep depression I was perhaps born with and had been self-conscious about as long as I could remember. Boys at the Mercy Home used to taunt it as a "third eye". Everybody thought the forelock covering the defect one of my great assets, "distinctly Hitlerian, adding flair and accent to the face", as some columnists wrote in their reviews. I had no desire to be identified with the mad man of the century in any way, but he was held up as a model of masculine beauty among those generations of Koreans that had lived under Japan as Germany's ally. But since I couldn't get rid of it for the dreaded exposure, I had to keep it on, nay, flaunt it, in apparent subscription to the popular mystique.

Both Jonghag and Nanyong were great teachers and showed me how to walk, turn, speak, scowl, smile to maximize the dramatic effect. Though they deserved all the credit for so rapidly transforming me into a viable actor, in all modesty I must confess that I had a certain aptitude for it, too. No doubt my previous performance experience with my folk music friends helped. Add to this a certain amount of genetic predisposition, especially on my mother's side, as the sequel will show. Jong was a master of his craft, but Nan had a dimension he could not emulate: her character, her composure and detachment in time of crisis. Any work, involving men and equipment, is bound to have unforeseen breakdowns, slipups, hitches, no shows, but the movie industry seemed a solid sequence of such disasters, though I shouldn't complain, owing my initiation to one of them. So many things could go wrong. The camera might malfunction, the crane get stuck, or topple over with the operator on it, then the actors or actresses, even the supposedly good ones, wouldn't do the right thing. Each such mishap cost and set back the filming schedule days or weeks. Naturally Jong lost his cool and often broke into foul swearing, kicking walls, banging desks, throwing things, which of course didn't help. It was then that Nan took control, spreading her equanimity and serenity like a cooling, soothing salve over the inflamed skin. Soon everything would be set right and things could go on with minor adjustments.

In directing she got her point across so effectively that the scenes involving us seldom needed more than one take. Soon she planted in me an abiding passion for the complex and generalized art that was the film, not just the technical or artistic aspect of one department, such as cinematography, effects, or acting, but the whole business of putting people and things together, to function as an organic whole toward the grand, final product, the few minutes or hours of illusion that could rise to heights of the sublime.

On the pretext of some business errand in Pusan Jong put me in full charge of Moonbay, in which in addition to direction I had a principal acting role, or rather two roles, because the story was about two men, Moonbay and the narrator, who look alike, though unrelated biologically or in disposition, grow up together, go to the merchant marine school, command ships, and love the same woman, played by Nan, with the inevitable tragic consequences. Surprised, yet reassured by such a fictional treatment of coincidental resemblance, as it seemed to validate my own similarity to Alan, I played the two men's roles with a sense of deja vu, with surgical detachment, which didn't escape Nan's discerning eye.

"Did you have a twin brother?" she asked.

"Why?" I asked back.

"Because you portray them with such lifelike distinctness."

Only if I could tell her all about me and Alan!

"I was just following the script," I mumbled.

Most of the scenes were filmed in the Bay of Mokpo aboard a ship we had chartered for the purpose. Thanks to my relentless effort to increase efficiency, driving the crew to the limit of endurance, we could wrap up all the marine shots a week ahead of schedule. The crew had been sent home. Jong was still in Pusan. Nan wanted to visit her parents a couple of hours away from Mokpo and needed someone to escort her. I was only too glad to oblige. But first she had to fill the rented car with gifts for not only her parents but everybody in the village. We went from shop to shop, sifting and selecting. Relishing every minute of it, I wondered what Jong could be doing in Pusan that was so important as to leave this dear wife of his with another man. Did he think I was some kind of eunuch like those Chinese emperors left their women with?

We had to leave the car at the bus stop on the highway a mile away: the cart road cut across the field was not wide or firm enough for auto traffic. We hired an ox cart to transport the baggage, at the same time dispatching runners to herald our arrival. No notice could have been sent by mail because the visit was impromptu and there was no telephone in a five-mile radius. This was Haynam County, the southwestern tip of the peninsula, deepest of the deep Jolla south, intact from modernization. But my rising resentment at this fresh reminder of Junghee's Jolla discrimination soon melted away as I took in the unspoiled scenery, so poignant in its pristine beauty that it brought tears to my eyes. The water-logged patties, seamed by a network of causeways, burst with young rice greedily soaking up the energy of the July sun. The limpid Gaygog Stream, swollen by the recent rain, ran along the dirt road we traveled, with carp breaking the surface. The roadbed, strewn with clumps of grass, was washed out here and there, and forced us at one point to wade ankle deep, shoes and socks removed. The village of Shingiree, where Nan had been born, was perched at the edge of the patties in the foothills, towered over by the Moon Rise Mountains, with threads of waterfalls glinting through the foliage.

The whole village was at her parents' house, laughing, rollicking, shouting, all eager to touch or speak to Nanyong Song, their famous star. In her turn, greeting and handing out the presents, she didn't have the chance to introduce me to her parents properly. In her eighties, her mother, bent almost double, bustled about crooning and clucking contentedly. Her father, a bearded Confucian scholar and ramrod straight, did not take his eyes off me from the moment I stepped into the yard. Nan had told me that Jong had never been to see his in-laws. Maybe the poor man thought I was their movie producer son-in-law, a Caucasian to boot, another of the surprises his wayward daughter had been springing on them ever since she won in her teens an acting prize in a national contest she had entered without their knowledge or consent. He might have problems accepting me but I felt nothing but the warmest affection for him, for his wife, for the whole tribe of Nan's relatives. Only if I were what the old man supposed I was and could claim them all as my kin by marriage! Her conservative father had strongly objected to her going into the movies, but her debut had been facilitated by a distant aunt, Gyongja Jo, who had the connections, having been an actress herself in her time.

Back in Seoul the military presence we had noticed before leaving was even more in evidence, tanks, armored personnel carriers, tractors, armed men rushing about. Martial law was in effect to stem the rising tide of anti-Government demonstrations, demanding Junghee Park to step down, conceding to Daejung Kim in spite of the official election results that extended Park's military regime yet another term. Few countries knew how to change power peaceably like the Americans and Korea was no exception. The incumbent simply refused to vacate and had to be shoved out.

"Isn't it depressing to live under martial law?" I observed on our way to her house in Jungdong.

"Any coercion is," Nan said with a sigh. "But I guess one gets used to it. Syngman Rhee had his troops out like this to stop the students."

"Were you in the Student Revolution of April 19, 1960?"

"I didn't march in the front ranks, if that's what you mean, though many from my college did and got killed. But I have a good excuse. I was away on location, in Mokpo, filming Tears of Mokpo."

I had seen it. How I had cried with her as she portrayed the maiden left behind on the pier as her sweetheart sailed away to Jayjoo Island, back to his family, though his heart was really with her.

"Were you in Seoul or anywhere near Korea at the time?" she asked, again putting me in the dreaded dilemma. I wanted to tell her all about myself but I couldn't. Officially, I was still Dr. Archer Torrey, surgeon, from St. Paul, Minnesota.

"No, but I have read enough accounts of it to visualize the whole thing, as if I had been marching right among the columns."

Alan, my alter ego, had been in it. On April 18 columns of shouting students ran arm in arm down the streets, straight into the barricades. Troops opened fire and mowed them down, killing several hundred, but the students kept right on going. News of the shootings spread quickly. Next morning the population poured out, filling the streets from side to side, sweeping everything before them like a tidal wave. On his way to the Aran Ham Center, Alan got caught up in that wave. He marched along, buoyed by the human flood. He was way back in the rear, but had he been in the vanguard and faced gun fire, he would have kept going. Such was the collective momentum, that robbed the individual of the will to think or fear, molding him to the will of the mass, unspoken but unmistakable, unalterable, absolute, irresistible. As it was, the vanguard had reached the flash points a good mile ahead. After firing a few uncertain rounds the riot squads retreated, abandoning the first main defense perimeter at the intersection of Bell Street and Peace Boulevard. The second roadblock at Nayjadong crumbled. The third and last roadblock, drawn right at the entrance to the Blue House with tanks and manned by Syngman Rhee's hand-picked troops, withstood the first shock. Machine gun rounds mowed down the first wave of students climbing over the wall. But wave after wave kept coming, crashing against the roadblock, stepping over the dead.

Then everything was over. The mighty dictator lay in the dust, and so did his powerful servants and dependents. It was like watching an earthquake level proud buildings and monuments to the ground in one giant shrug.

"Yes, I believe you would have marched, in the forefront, at the flashpoint," she said reflectively.

"You mean get shot at? No, you don't know me. If at all, I

would be way in the rear behind a million others, ever ready even then to duck into a side alley at the first sign of danger. A born coward, I am afraid."

"One who can jump on a bronco at a moment's notice is not a coward in my book."

"That was different, for a different motive," I thought but couldn't voice it. I had to change the subject, quickly.

"What still puzzles me, though, is the rather tame ending," I said, with bitter cynicism.

"Of the movie, Tears of Mokpo?"

"No, I mean the Student Revolution. Syngman Rhee, assassin of so many dissidents and competitors, spiller of so much student blood lately, was allowed to retire to his Pear Blossom Mansion. The road from the Blue House to the Mansion was lined with crowds, all waving tear-stained handkerchiefs to the old 'Father of the Land', forgetting their hatred of him only the day before. It seemed the students had died for nothing. Putting all the blame on Giboong Yee, his deputy, whose family had committed suicide that morning and weren't around to plead for themselves, Syngman Rhee, the consummate machiavellian, had succeeded in reaching the sympathy of the people with his old man's stoop, while probably sneering behind their back all the time."

"How true! I never looked at it that way. I must confess I was among those who waved good-bye to him. We had returned to Seoul the day before, interrupting the filming. It takes an outsider to see what those inside can't."

After saying good-bye to Nan that night, I felt at a loss. There wasn't a place I could really call my own, certainly not the Blue House where I had never felt at home, which at this particular juncture was like a house in foreclosure. The few days away from its tension had been heaven.

I went to a phone and called Hyongwoog. He was home and asked me to come over. We talked late into the night, the martial law and dawn to sunset curfew our principal topics.

"Is it going to be another Student Revolution?" I asked.

"To answer that let's go to Sajig Park tomorrow where Daejung Kim is going to address a rally.

The road to the park was so congested that we had to leave the car at the Citizens Hall parking lot and walk the rest of the way. At least a million people filled the valley, in the roads, walkways, greens, among trees and rocks. It was my first experience of political oratory. His words came through like sunlight through rainclouds. With the first few sentences Daejung Kim had the crowd firmly in his grip, making them breathe and swoon with his every word.

"Maybe they were patriotic at the beginning as they claim," he said in mocking, lilting Jolla tones. "They couldn't bear to see the country go to the dogs, they say. That is a peculiarly jaundiced perception, if there ever was one, because most of us thought, with the tyrant Syngman Rhee gone, we were on the right track to democracy. What if we had some minor unrest and indecisiveness? What's wrong with a weak parliament a bit too eager to listen to our young heroes, the students? Didn't they earn the right to tell their elders what to do after unseating the despot with their own blood?"

A roar of approbation rippled through the crowd.

"But let us still allow their first motive as genuine patriotism, deluded and illusory though it may be. They have forfeited all claim to such noble sentiments by refusing to step aside for the rightful owner, the people, by continuing their usurpation for a whole decade and more, highlighted by greed and cruelty, by one scandal after another, currency reforms, stock market rip-offs, real estate speculations, bank scams, tortures and murders of innocent dissidents, climaxed by the latest barbarity, State of Emergency and Martial Law, brutally suppressing our righteous indignation at the travesty of a presidential election, this blatant fraud that insults the intelligence of the Korean people. Peaceful transfer of power through elections is a mirage so long as Junghee Park and his military men keep a stranglehold on our country. This evil force must be pushed out only by a matching force, by revolution, through a life and death struggle. I am willing to die a soldier in the sacred war to rid ourselves of dictatorship and set the country on the path to true democracy with equal rights for all."

The crowd thundered, calling on Junghee Park to resign

instantly. Soon chaos followed. Tear gas bombs popped everywhere and the riot police fell upon the scattering crowd swinging their nightsticks viciously. We barely outran a team of visored combat policemen and by back alleys and detours reached our car out of breath to find a newspaper extra stuck in the windshield. Daejung Kim, stabbed in the stomach, was in intensive care at the Scandinavian Medical Center.

Hyongwoog went to the nearest public phone and dialed a number. After hanging up he produced a 20 million won ($70,000) money order from his pocket and asked me to give it to Sanghyon Kim, Daejung Kim's secretary, waiting at a tearoom a block from the hospital.

Two days later Daejung Kim was flown to Japan by his friends more for his safety than for treatment. With him out of the way, Junghee Park felt secure enough to promulgate the Fifth Constitutional Amendment, known as the New Order, which in effect perpetuated his power, abolishing the National Assembly as a representative body. Angry demonstrations erupted nationwide, especially on university campuses. Giryong Yoon's Capital Security Command responded with chilling efficiency, manhandling and mauling the students, until 79 lay dead, enough to inflame the city into another revolution. But the outrage could not be reported for days by the muzzled press. When the full extent of the horror was known, it was already history that seldom provokes like the here and now. But even if the press had been in full gear and a crowd could have been fielded the size that had toppled Syngman Rhee in 1960, it would have been mowed down and swept aside like so much garbage by the huge tractors, front-loaded with 15 x 25 foot steel plates and positioned at strategic points of the city. The Park regime, product and beneficiary of a popular uprising, was not about to let another one be its undoing.

"I hate Yankee sonofabitches," Junghee swore, as soon as US Ambassador Marconi left after handing him Carter's ultimatum. "How dare Carter bully me like this, the head of a sovereign independent state?"

"He has the means, Your Excellency," Hoorag Yee said.

"By shutting off gasoline, for example, he can ground all our tanks, planes, and vehicles, and our million-man army will come to a screeching halt."

"Doesn't our Woolsan Refinery produce enough?"

"Just enough for civilian consumption, Your Excellency," Geeyung Jang said. "When the second phase is completed in about a year, we can supply our military, too. But the surplus has been earmarked for export to repay our foreign debts, which are ultimately American money."

"Fortunately, Carter can't do anything," Ilgwon Jung pointed out, "without authorization by Congress, which can be worse than quicksand, swallowing up everything in the morass of debate."

"What good would a delay of a few weeks or months do if the upshot is the same?"

"It won't be, if we get a good lobbyist to influence the votes, somebody who can change our image and impress the American public with the need for a strong government to counterbalance the ever-present North Korean threat and continue with what some call our 'economic miracle' lifting a nation of 40 million from the devastation of war to the height of industrial development."

"It may take some doing, though. Americans have a mental block against military governments," Geeyung Jang observed.

"But His Excellency's government is not military," protested Gaywun Kim, National Security Advisor. "He is as much a civilian as you."

"A former general is still a general in their eye," Jang remarked smugly, aware that he was the only nonmilitary man in the company, a fact often cited at his expense by his detractors. "That's what makes it military to the Americans."

"But, then, Carter was a Navy Commander," Jeechul Cha noted. "So was General George Washington, for that matter."

"That's a good point, Washington being a general," Junghee said, gleefully. "That's what we should point out to Americans, the fact that I have really no military ties. If I give over a division to another guy, that division is his, not mine.

The American people should know such basic facts of life."

"They are misled by the so-called opinion makers, journalists, writers, scholars, a bunch of liberals and eggheads, perpetual malcontents, who are however as venal as anybody, maybe more so because they are generally hungry. A buck or two spent wisely here and there will slant their views in our favor."

"What is our Embassy in Washington doing?" Junghee said irritably, who had been displeased with his current ambassador Jung-hoon Kim and thinking of replacement by his London envoy, Hyongwoog Kim's 'mousy runt'. "Isn't that their job?"

"What we propose can't be carried out officially," said Ilgwun Jung, a friend of Ambassador Junghoon Kim. "Our agent should be a private individual whose manipulations cannot be traced back to us."

"We may have just the right man, honest Donsun Bag," Junghee said, brightening. "If he can get rice deals at half price, he can do anything. Give him the assignment."

A silent fixture at many of these proceedings, I often had the illusion of watching a group of boys playing with a huge oversized ball, bigger than themselves, which they pushed or tugged every which way, without the least idea what the objective of the game was.

XII.
Daejung Kim Rescue

Stardom came with a price: I spent hours besieged by reporters at the Anyang Studio and whole pages were devoted to me with my picture in the newspapers and magazines. Fan mail arrived by the armful. They clamored to know more about my past, but I evaded their probing as best I could. I was just an American, from St. Paul, Minnesota, as my CIA-fabricated dossier stated, who happened to be at the right place at the right time to render some signal service to the President and then got into the movies, thanks to the Kims who discovered me. I watched out for any letter from my previous acquaintances, but no such mail turned up. In particular, I would have loved to hear from Alan and Jinny. Maybe they never read newspapers or magazines. Even if they did, my new name, plus my fame and glamor, must have made them dismiss the resemblance as coincidence. But wasn't Jinny supposed to be psychic? Perhaps they knew all about me but kept away for fear of embarrassing me. They need not. CIA oath or not, I would acknowledge them to the whole world, even if it meant the loss of everything I'd got. I meant to go to Moon Rock Island and look them up, but too busy adjusting to my new status I comforted myself with the thought that someday soon I would repay my debt at compound interest.

With me writing the English for him, Jong had been in correspondence with Robert Fenwick of Universal Studios, a voting member of the Academy, who finally invited him to

Hollywood to discuss the US release of Star-Crossed and its entry for the Oscar nominations. Prior to departure, he asked Nan to come along, expecting her to decline, which of course she did, alleging her boredom with business negotiations and the need to help me finish Reclamation then in the works. I urged her to go, sincerely, saying I could manage by myself. It seemed such a pity for her to miss a splendid opportunity to be in Hollywood, though she had been to the States several times already. At 22 she took a semester of screen writing and movie making at UCLA. Also with Jong she had been to Honolulu, Los Angeles, San Francisco, Chicago, Boston, New York, and Washington, when these cities hosted film festivals featuring their productions.

"No, I pass," she said decisively. "You won't lack for traveling companions anyway."

She had learned from reliable sources that Soonja, 21, who had appeared in a few of our pictures and had been seen often with Jonghag at restaurants and hotels, had a reservation already on the same flight with him.

"You mean Soonja?" Jong asked, his gills reddening a little.

"Yes."

"She just happens to be visiting her relatives in Los Angeles."

"I didn't say anything."

After seeing him and his mistress off at the airport, we left for Goonsan, Jolla, to work on Reclamation, the story of a single-minded farmer who wants to dam up a tidal flatland on the coast and reclaim it from the sea to turn it into farmland. At first work goes well and hopes rise high as the opposite branches of the dike extend steadily toward the middle of the inlet entrance. The end seems at hand when the opening is only ten yards apart, which however turns out unstoppable, a sore that refuses to close, letting the sea rush in and out at devastating speeds. The farmer-engineer tries everything he could think of. Mortgaging his last field, he orders a huge rebar net stuffed with boulders each weighing hundreds of tons, and drops it from a barge when the tide is at a standstill.

The cage seems to hold, wedged in the channel. Other barges that had been waiting drop their loads of rock furiously about the anchor, almost filling up the gap. But the tide has reversed, creeping in uncertainly, reluctantly at first, then roaring, pounding, like a hungry beast thirsting for its prey. The little plug is tossed aside and the accumulated weight of the sea rushes in, reclaiming its dominion over the mud flat. The rebar cage in particular is washed a mile inland, twisted and mangled in the mud. The sea pounds away at the other parts of the levee, first around the middle opening, then along the whole length, shaking everything loose. The disappointed developer throws himself into the waters when the tide is at its fiercest, as if to catch a runaway horse, and his body is never found. Nothing remains of his grand design, his dream, except piles of rock and dirt dotting the mouth of the inlet in a jagged line.

Back at the studio, having finished the film in record time, we suddenly found a lot of time on our hands. The next movie planned was not ready to go into production yet and we had better wait for Jonghag's return anyway. The sound stages were shut down and everybody was let go, the actors, camera crew, technical staff, extras. The whole campus was deserted like a ghost town. I went to Nan's office to say good-bye.

"Will you be here much longer?" I asked.

"I might as well," she said. "Are you heading to the Blue House?"

"I guess. But I am not crazy about it."

"Why don't you go to a resort like Mallipo and rest up at a beachside hotel? It will do you wonders."

I remembered Horace Beckett and his missionary crowd I had known from Alan's Fulbright Commission days vacationing there religiously every summer.

"Have you been there?"

"Yes."

"With Jonghag?"

"No, by myself. He was with somebody else."

"Another woman?"

She nodded.

"How long has this been going on?" I asked, indignant.

"Almost from the very beginning," she said with a sigh. "It was all my fault. When I started out as a teenager with my heart set on stardom, he wanted to sleep with me though a married man with two children. An established director and producer he seemed like the ticket to success. I held out for marriage and forced him to divorce his wife, for which he never forgave me. Almost the day after our honeymoon he started chasing other women."

"But that's wrong. Once he betrothes himself, he is yours and nobody else's. I can't understand why of all people you've put up with it all these years."

"Perhaps my Confucian upbringing which says a woman serves only one husband."

"Even when he is no husband?"

"Confucius was a man and wrote the code to suit his sex."

"I thought you were a Christian."

"About sin and redemption but when it comes to sexual morality, Christ is as male chauvinistic as the next fellow, denouncing adulteresses, never the adulterors, David, Solomon, and all the other seducers and polygamists who go scot-free, after a season of contrition, if that, for their multiple transgression. It is the universal lot of women to accept it."

"Not in this day and age, not for a woman like you. I insist that you fight the iniquity. It's your duty to your gender to be a role model and teach men to behave."

"Any idea how I go about it?" she asked, in a forlorn, hopeless tone.

"Can we go to Mallipo together?" I blurted out, voice trembling.

She turned her face away, big crystal drops rolling down her cheeks.

"Forgive me. It was presumptuous of me even to think..."

"You mean you don't want me, either?" she asked, brimming eyes hurt and reproachful.

"Oh, Nan!" I shouted, throwing my arms about her. "You know I want you more than anything in the whole world. I have loved you from the moment I first saw you in the movie

Rock Hill years ago. You are a gem, the most beautiful and precious. Nothing should hurt you. I'll love you and treasure you forever and ever."

"Even when I am old and bent like my mother?"

She must be thinking of her being older than I, somewhat paralleling the case of her own parents we had just seen. Nan's seniority, if I was conscious of it at all, only added to her charm. She was in that golden early middle age which in some women could be taken for youth in their twenties. In any case, would I change her for a twenty-year-old just because the latter had tighter skin?

"More so," I said, wiping her face, stroking her dark silken hair.

I dialed the Blue House and left the message that I would be filming in the Jeeree Mountains unreachable by phone. Junghee was apt to call me on location and ask what the story was about, how the filming went, who were in the cast, especially the actresses, if any of them were pretty and interesting enough to be introduced to him, and so forth. The real life story we were about to create was for nobody's eye or ear. We stopped for dinner at a restaurant in Soowon and arrived at the Mallipo Tourist Hotel near midnight. At the front desk we signed in as Mr and Mrs Butler from Chicago. With a few cosmetic touches, aided by dark glasses and a face net, Nan with her high nose and large eyes - which made her a striking beauty by any standard but especially in Korea - could pass as an American female tourist.

The bellboy took us up to our suite on the eighth floor. As soon as the door closed behind him, we were in each other's arms and made love, tentatively at first but explosively, with wild abandon, our pent-up passions breaking free. Stroking her skin, exploring her hidden recesses, sweet and fragrant, I could understand why Anthony relinquished the empire to hold on to Cleopatra. I loved and worshiped Nan with all my soul and could have died contentedly that very moment.

We looked out on the bay bathed in the morning sun, the sparkling white sand, fresh and clean like God's first creation, the surf breaking softly into sinuous ripples at the edge of the gentle slope of beach, the concave coastline bounded by rocky headlands, the little island covered with rocks and pines standing sentinel at the mouth of the bay. This picture of cosmic perfection was still perfected by the crowning piece, Nan in her naked glory. I knelt before her and raised my hands in adoration, enclosing her fingers. I loved her to distraction. How fitting that I should have surrendered my virginity to her! I swore that I would know no other woman, for she was my total fulfillment, my deity, to whom I would owe my lifelong loyalty to the exclusion of all others. Anything else would cheapen the meaning of the ecstasy I had experienced with her, its absoluteness, uniqueness. Jehovah was right in being a jealous god. With one difference in my case: the devotion was entirely voluntary, neither required nor asked for.

When we returned to the Anyang Studio, an urgent message waited, asking me to call a US number, collect. I looked to Nan inquiringly. Was it Jonghag about to tell me off, maybe even challenge me to a duel? How did he find out so fast? Nan shrugged with unconcern. He wasn't the type, nor did he have cause. It was Hyongwoog that answered at the second ring. I had no idea he had been out of the country.

"What are you doing in America?"

"I had to get out before they got wise to my dealings with Daejung Kim, which would have been any minute after they arrested his staff. Junghee is out to get Daejung, anybody connected with him, anybody from Jolla. My agents report that something fishy is afoot to do away with Daejung once and for all."

"You mean kill him?"

"Yes."

"Isn't he in America?"

"He was, rallying Korean Americans and getting an ovation at a joint session of US Congress. He is now back in Japan, whipping up support for his cause, especially among the younger Japanese politicians who are pushing for a trade embargo and other sanctions against Junghee's government. Junghee and his lunatic advisors are in a frenzy and see a spy or traitor everywhere. That's what makes your continued stay at the Blue House inadvisable."

"I was on my way to pick up my things and move out anyway."

"Good. In an emergency call Al Edwards at the number I gave you before. He can arrange your exit from Korea in a hurry."

"Do you think it may really come to that?"

"I hope not, but who knows? My political asylum in the US will soon be reported worldwide. If anything happens to Daejung Kim, I'll tell the whole world, testify before the Senate Foreign Relations Committee all about Junghee's dealings, rakeoffs, shakedowns, pogroms against Jolla people, US rice scams, secret funds, Korean lobby in Washington. He'll hate me and my friends."

"In case I must leave, can I bring along a passenger?"

"Who?"

"Miss Nanyong Song."

"I see. Jonghag is still in the States?"

"Yes, with Soonja Gang."

"Nanyong Song won't be in any personal danger, you know."

"Now she is because people will know about our relationship."

"Of course. I think one extra passenger won't make any difference, especially such a beautiful one. Give her my compliments."

I wanted to say good-bye to Junghee regardless, but he was closeted in the Octagonal Office with strict orders not to be disturbed. I walked down the marble-floored hallway and turned right into the West Wing heading for my room when through the door of the Operations Room I heard Gen. Taksang Hwang, Deputy Chief of the Secret Service, shouting into the telephone, "So the Jolla Dog Shit is tight and snug in the sack? ... Did you leave North Korean cigarette butts and cartridges in the hotel room? ... Drive carefully. I don't want you to spoil anything at this stage ... The rendezvous with the Golden Dragon is at 16:00 hours. That gives you some time. Call me as soon as you get aboard the Dragon. Wait about two or three hours out of harbor before dumping the sack overboard...."

I knew exactly who he meant by the Jolla Dog Shit. I didn't have a minute to lose. The Golden Dragon was the 200-foot, 700-ton speed boat, capable of 40 knots though registered at 10, equipped with the latest electronic detectors, built at Hyongwoog's special order to foil the nautical infiltration of North Korean agents. I didn't wait around to find out where the Golden Dragon was to anchor, though that piece of information was vital. Al or Hyongwoog would figure that out.

And they did. The rocky west coast of Japan didn't have too many harbors to speak of and an air and surface search by the US Forces Far East and Japanese Coast Guard disclosed the destination of the Golden Dragon to be Kanazawa, a small fishing village. A white van pulled up at the dock where the Golden Dragon was moored and disgorged a group of men in the red-trimmed white uniform and hat of the Imperial Hotel, who pushed down the pier a room service cart with a large cotton sack on its lower shelf hidden behind its skirting drapery, an entirely unnecessary precaution as nobody could see the cart or its load through the liveried entourage surrounding it. In that disguise they had entered Daejung's suite, disarmed his bodyguards, surprised him in the bathroom, and sprayed him unconscious with ether. The cart, its top still full of the undisturbed food, was loaded into the van waiting in front of the freight elevator on the street level. They were in and out of the hotel in less than 15 minutes. But as soon as the Golden Dragon with its new passengers and cargo weighed anchor, a US Army Cobra gunship hovered above, ordered Daejung's release from his confinement, and escorted the boat all the way back to Pusan, where the alerted press, foreign and domestic, was waiting at dockside.

XIII.
Exile

At our request Nan and I were put down at Manhattan, the premier city of the US, for accommodation at $3,000 a night in the Royal Suite of the Waldorf Astoria Hotel. I absolutely needed this reinforcement for proper introduction to my father's country, like looking up relatives I had never met before and must impress. Unfortunately, I couldn't tell Nan my compulsion, absurd as it was.

"It's a city one has to see in style," I said, "at the peak of one's prosperity, not to be stared down to insignificance by the skyscrapers from their impersonal, pitiless heights."

"You and your goofy notions!" Nan said, tapping my forehead.

She went along with this one-time extravagance, especially since Langley was willing to foot the bill.

We walked down the steps of the hotel into the street, to be immediately swallowed up in the multitude of pedestrians, white, black, yellow, all kinds of shades in between. There was nothing unique about my blood mixture in the melting pot that was the US. Faces closed, minds preoccupied, the fast-stepping humanity did not give us a single glance. America was a huge millrace that sped on, where one either kept up or got swept under. In the efficient, schematic jungle of steel and concrete I saw myself as an antediluvian, more at home in the slipshod, haphazard environment of Korea with its smells, poisons, sores. But as we saw more of the city, doing all the touristic things, taking the ferry to Wansong's Statue of

Liberty, the Circle-Line Tour, Apple Double-Deck Bus Tour, riding the elevators to the top of the Empire State Building, stopping at the Metropolitan and Guggenheim Museums, Lincoln Center, Carnegie Hall, Rockefeller Center, Broadway theaters, driving across the Brooklyn Bridge, George Washington Bridge, Lincoln Tunnel, and other marvels of engineering, riding the subway trains, sauntering in Central Park, eating at the great restaurants, I began to relax and felt at home.

How wonderful not to be noticed, either as a celebrity or as an oddity! No head turned in my direction as in Korea. I still recall a woman walking toward me on a country road near Boochon with a heavy load on her head, a sleeping child strapped to her back, her eye fixed straight ahead in total concentration. Not even a gun going off behind her ear would have made her bat an eye. When I went past, however, she came to a dead stop and executed a 180 degree pivot of her head, perhaps permanently dislocating her neckbone. All because of my anatomy, before my fame on screen. It was of course worse afterwards. By and by, without being consciously aware of it, I had learned to live with and even enjoy the attention I got in Korea. My first notice of its absence in the States came with a shock of withdrawal but, as I said before, the relaxing realization sank in. I was no longer the odd one to be singled out and stared at. Nor Nan as the star. New York was just too full of people to notice anybody, however stellar. Forgetting the ubiquitous watching eye, we could be ourselves, dance or whistle, be the unobserved spectators for a change. Losing ourselves in the crowd, we basked in the luxury of anonymity. But not for long. Hyongwoog took us to his house in a suburb of Washington, D.C., our address during the weeks of Koreagate hearings on the Senate floor.

Naturally, Hyongwoog was the principal witness and had a whole lot more to tell and my role was strictly supplementary and corroborative, but between the two of us we came up with enough hard evidence to institute the Koreagate investigations, convict several US Federal and state officials, including Congressmen and Governors, discredit prominent columnists and writers, condemn the corruption of Junghee's government, and forever tarnish the image of Korea, a sly backhand artist rather than the gentleman of the Far East victimized by superpower struggle.

Not taking it lying down, Junghee Park had Jongsob Han, Washington correspondent of the United Press Korea, supply false information to the Washington Post about our escaping with $300 million, which was in turn quoted as 'authoritative' by all the papers in Korea. I was prepared for the hard names they called us, but not for the innuendos and slanders leveled at Nanyong. It devastated me to have to drag her name through the mud, but she was game for it: "You don't get to be somebody without a stomach for jealous gossip from everybody."

But the real venom was unleashed by Donsun Bag, the Rice Bag, who took out a full-page ad in the New York Times, denouncing Hyongwoog and me as two ingrates and turncoats in the most colorful and violent language imaginable. However, soon indicted by the US Attorney's office, this master slanderer had to leave the US precipitately for Seoul, where he was given a hero's welcome and allowed to retire on the millions he had embezzled. But we had little cause for joy, for his place was taken by a worse customer, Anthony Kim, a New York attorney with a Harvard Law degree, with whom my friend Hyongwoog's acquaintance went back some time.

"When I headed the Agency," he said, "this character came to me repeatedly, asking for a job, expecting an automatic endorsement for a high position at the Blue House."

Upon verification, however, every one of the professional appointments and research commissions listed in his vita turned out to be false. Apparently he equated application for a job with appointment or commission. The only things genuine about him were his Harvard law degree, New York attorney's license and a colossal ego, as if writing a thesis by regurgitating others' theories and correctly answering the multiple choice or snap essay questions in the bar exam made him the world's greatest intellect. Unfortunately, most of those in Junghee's government thought so, semiliterate generals with barely a high school diploma who got their stars through the attrition of war and had a complex about degrees and titles. Hyongwoog was ready to give the impostor the boot but so many of his colleagues were impressed by Anthony's credentials, for whatever they were worth, that Hyongwoog ended up funding him to set up a Korean Institute for Communist Bloc Studies in New York. Not a single paper or report came out of that Institute during Hyongwoog's tenure at the Agency. To make the investment good Hyongwoog gave him extracurricular work from time to time, such as spying on suspected anti-government elements in the Korean American community, for which he displayed greater aptitude.

One night this man came to Hyongwoog's house. Not suspecting what a thorough blackguard he was, the FBI agents guarding the house let him in when he flashed his attorney's license.

"I'll break you for this," he said, snapping open his briefcase and taking out newspaper and magazine clippings ceremoniously, his husky voice at its raspiest. "You may get away, though I don't know for how long, with all the lies about your former boss President Park, Korean CIA, Donsun Bag, and others, but not with calling me a KCIA stooge. Are you that dumb? This is personal libel. I am a licensed lawyer. Don't you know lawyers are almighty in this country? I'll send you both to jail but before that I'll make you cough up some of the loot you have smuggled out of Korea. I'm suing you for $100 million each."

"Good," Hyongwoog retorted. "That will give you a chance to really practice your profession for a change."

"What is that crack supposed to mean?"

"Let's just say in the past you have distinguished yourself in other activities than courtroom advocacy."

"Like what?"

"Like defrauding Mrs. Yoonchul Gwon of a million dollars."

By bribing Giryong Yoon, Gwon's United Steel made a fortune as a prime contractor for the Seoul Subway construction. To save Gwon from going to prison when Giryong fell, his wife grabbed at straws and applied to Anthony, who happened to be in Seoul at the time, waving his New York attorney's license as usual and promising asylum in the US. For retainer and expenses he collected over a million dollars from her. Meanwhile her husband remained behind bars as securely as ever, and Anthony, who had allegedly left for the US to promote her cause, didn't even bother to return her long distance calls. Crying bitterly, she had been going everywhere asking for help to get her money back from the con artist.

"You believe the ravings of a crazy woman? It's your prerogative, of course, but if you publish it, as you did the other stuff, the damages will double."

"Thank you for the warning."

"My clients and I are willing to meet you halfway, if you stop treading on our toes and retract."

"What have we got to lose?"

"Maybe your lives. You've heard of the long arm of vengeance, especially that of a supreme ruler with unlimited resources. Your death may come suddenly, violently, when you least expect it, in a bullet, a knife, a bomb, poisoned food, or what have you."

Not every visitor was as unpleasant as Anthony Kim. Cerviet, the Frenchman from my FLI days, came and insisted on taking all of us, me and Nan, Hyongwoog and his family, to his 5-bedroom house in Virginia just across the river where his wife had dinner waiting for us. I had run into him the previous day as we left the Capitol after the day's proceedings and were heading to the garage where our car was parked. Commercial attaché at the French Embassy, he looked a prosperous official used to authority now. His wife, a plain dowdy woman as I remembered, was a dashing businessperson and operated three or four children's clothing stores. But the story of their present prosperity was a small-scale modern epic.

His parental home they had come to stay in France was a small farm about a hundred miles south of Paris but his parents and the peasant community could not accept a Korean woman among them. The couple had to move to another province and work at a count's castle as domestic servants.

After a year of this Cerviet went to England in search of better opportunities, leaving his wife alone in France. That was when he sent the postcard to us in Seoul. Not knowing anyone and not speaking French her life was in many ways worse than incarceration but she stuck it out for two years until her husband called her to England. Eventually Cerviet wanted to go to America. When his petition was presented, the American officials in charge of immigration leaped out of their seats and almost handcuffed him. So eager were they to add Gallic blood, at the top of the priority list along with Anglo-Saxon, to the US melting pot that they would have kidnaped him, had he betrayed the least hesitancy about his decision to immigrate. Pointing out that the quotas of Englishmen and Frenchmen had been seldom filled, they made no secret of the statistical importance the Cerviets represented. To prevent him from changing his mind they promised him immediate job placement and hinted at some cash bonus up front. This was too good to refuse. The next day Cerviet took his wife to the American Embassy in London and introduced her to Robert Tatum, the officer in charge, who had been waiting for them.

"She cannot be your wife," Tatum said.

"What do you mean?" Cerviet said, puzzled. "I married Renee at our consulate in Seoul. I have the documents here to prove it."

He produced the notarized license and certificate. Tatum, who prided on his good French, pretended total ignorance of the language and refused to even look at the papers.

"It can't be legal," he said, shaking his head.

"What is not?" Cerviet asked.

"Your marriage."

Cerviet challenged Tatum to verify the seals and signatures, but Tatum seemed to go deaf and remained cold and morose. Finally, he rose and made several telephone calls to his superiors, who all concurred with him. Uncle Sam, preacher of universal brotherhood and equality, was firm on the racial issue: that was biology and had nothing to do with democracy, equality of the races, and other American ideals set forth in the Constitution.

"I am sorry," Tatum said, "but your wife has to go through the Korean immigration quota, because nationality means not just one's citizenship but his or her ethnic, genetic background. That's the spirit of the law."

Cerviet had to go alone to America, leaving his wife by herself in England for eight months. Once in America he found plenty of un-American lawyers who differed from the official interpretation of the law and took up his cause as their own. To avoid an apparent widening of the issue and embarrassing repercussions Tatum and company quickly shipped Renee Cerviet across the Atlantic, at government expense. America had been good to Cerviet after all. He found a job at the commercial section of the French Embassy in Washington and saved enough money to buy a condominium near work, which he then sold at a profit to buy the present house with a view and a gorgeous backyard with many leafy trees that gave the impression of a private forest.

The only flaw, if it could be that, was their lack of children. They had tried various ways, short of artificial insemination the very idea of which repelled them, but had no luck.

"We don't miss anything," Renee said. "We have our work during the day and each other at night. Who wants those brats to get underfoot? It's enough to have to deal with them at the stores."

In token of his concurrence Cerviet put out his arms to her, who ran into them. Forgetting us, the couple embraced and kissed passionately like two teenagers. Not to be outdone, I picked up Nan, swung her once, then pulled her in for a smacking kiss, sending her into peals of laughter. Like most Korean men raised under Confucian culture where the Western concept of romance was unknown and sex was a weakness and evil to be abstained from manfully and indulged in only for procreation, Hyongwoog was rarely demonstrative of his tenderness to his wife but, overcome by love in the wind, he held out an arm to his wife, who, however, rebuffed him with a severe frown, indicating their children in the game room next door.

After reading about me in the papers Wansong Char flew

all the way from Honolulu and waited three hours on the Capitol steps to meet me. He had no way of finding out how to get in touch with me or obtain a pass to sit in the gallery of the hearing room. We were overjoyed to see each other. He had finally made it to his dream country, US of A, thanks to a phone call I had placed from the Blue House to the Foreign Ministry. After two years he was not disillusioned yet. He couldn't be, because he apparently had the best of all worlds, operating a Korean music and dance studio in Honolulu for Korean Americans, recent immigrants as well as descendants of the early immigrants who had come as sugarcane workers to Hawaii. But even if he lived in the most bigoted ghettos and skinheads tapped their forehead with the heel of their palm or stretched the corners of their eyes with their knuckles to taunt him "slope head" or "slant eyes", he would still rationalize and cope with that better than the Jolla prejudice from his own people back home. He had news about our mutual friends at the Center, whose remodeling and expansion was finally complete, five stories with a 900-seat auditorium. I had helped with the design and permit process, as well as the financing needed. Choran had her sixth child. Ilsob, whom I had placed at the Catholic Medical Center for dialysis when diagnosed with kidney failure, had died recently. Gwaryong was doing poorly. Weak heart or something. The folk musicians from Jolla still remained poor, living from day to day, hand to mouth, without recognition from the Korean community at large. Anger boiled inside me, mingled with sorrow for my departed friend Ilsob and apparently soon to depart Gwayryong and all the others languishing in the chains of degrading poverty and social indifference. They were true artists, real gems, the salt that kept our artistic sensibility from going bad, and yet Korea treated them like dirt. Leaving the restaurant, Hyongwoog was sincere in asking Wansong over to his house but Wansong refused and left for Honolulu that night.

The US Senate hearings out of the way, we didn't have to stick around in Washington, though Hyongwoog wanted us to weather the storm together at his house, fortified by his own bodyguards as well as electronic surveillance and FBI protection: through his old contacts Hyongwoog had confirmed that Junghee had a contract out on both our heads. But we had to decline. Though a likable man and a good friend, his lifestyle in the US did not agree with ours. Perhaps driven by the need to thumb his nose at any notion that he might be remorseful about his defection or fearful of its consequences, he had grown lavish and showy, gambling thousands of dollars at a throw, golfing for hours, partying incessantly. Everybody in town knew where he lived and how to get in touch with him. Compulsively gregarious like most people in public life, he couldn't stay away from the crowd and indeed went out of his way to attract more. His 10-bedroom Tudor house with a tree-lined driveway in the exclusive Washington suburb was the scene of sumptuous nightly dinners to which he was determined to invite at least once every notable Korean American doctor, lawyer, engineer, businessman, professor he could find through the Korean Directory or otherwise, sometimes paying for their air fares from as far away as Los Angeles and San Francisco.

It was among these guests that I met Dr. Charles (Chansoo originally) Hong, a neurosurgeon in New York, with whom I developed an enduring friendship. His wife Jane (Jungay) and Nan had gone to school together in Haynam, and had been close until Jane went to the US to study. Halfway through medical school she met Chansoo from Gwangjoo and gave up her career to be a wife and mother. What woman wouldn't? From the moment of our first meeting I never ceased to be amazed and delighted by his wit and erudition in such diverse fields as aerodynamics, history, art, and literature as well as medicine. His brilliant mind seemed to inject new insight into the most commonplace and trivial.

Few of the invitees ever refused, as they were curious to see how Hyongwoog Kim, the Trotsky of Korea, lived. Invariably he recited to them the corruption and evil of the Junghee Park regime, Park's betrayal of the original coup ideals, his ingratitude to the coup heroes, especially Hyongwoog himself. All this was coming out in his memoirs, so damaging that they would "fix Junghee once and for all," for which several Japanese newspapers were already vying for the rights. Junghee's agents were trying to stop him from writing them with all kinds of threats, but he was determined to publish the "ugly facts."

"Granted I had a share in them," he conceded. "But I was naive. I believed by overthrowing the Myon Jang regime we could clean up politics and set the country on the road to prosperity."

Of course Nan and I were in his captive audience: it wouldn't do for us to seem to shun his guests when they all knew we lived there. We were desperate for privacy, to have a quiet day or two to ourselves, but there was always something planned or coming up. This was particularly so on Sunday, when we had to go to church with the Kims. Like 90% of Korean Americans Mrs. Sungmee Kim belonged to a church, ready made to gratify their social craving. Here the immigrants could meet their own kind, laugh together, envy or despise each other for their past or present, air out and probe for weaknesses in others to reaffirm their own worth, and generally feel alive, not stifled as in the mainstream America, with which they interacted only marginally, at arm's length, across the language barrier and cultural unfamiliarity. There were over 300 Korean churches in Washington and its environs, to which a couple more were being added every month, determined to catch up with 1,000-plus in Los Angeles and 500 in New York, with a choke hold on first-generation Koreans, barring them from assimilation to America, the country of their adoption.

Lately, Washington First Korean Presbyterian, whose pastor was Sungmee's uncle or something, had expanded tenfold in membership, mainly to ogle us as we arrived in the limousine, to crowd around us as we got out, to fight to usher us to our seats, to get near us and start a conversation by hook or crook, invite us to lunch or dinner, to interminable birthdays, weddings, anniversaries, where we exhausted ourselves, repeating the same answers to the same questions. We tried to refuse politely, then firmly, but the Kims committed us anyway. Because we lived in their house, we were like their children and were expected to go along with "parental" decisions, family projects.

After trying in vain to dissuade us, he sent us on our way, pressing on us a money order for $100,000 and reiterating his invitation to come back any time, considering his home our own. He was sincere, of course, because he had an open, generous soul, and would have shared the shirt on his back with his friends. We accepted the money as a loan, though he meant it as a gift: we hadn't brought any of our own money when we were spirited out of Korea. Al Edwards, now transferred to Langley in charge of the Far East Section, had made arrangements so we could charge all our expenses to CIA, but we had been reluctant to make use of the offer. We were too grateful to the US for its hospitality already.

It wasn't difficult to get lost in the vastness of the continent. With only a road map as our guide, we hopped on our brand new Oldsmobile and drove at a leisurely pace to all the different parks, sights, monuments, and cities, crossing and recrossing the continent. When it got dark we drove into an inn, lodge, motel or hotel, made love, and talked until the wee hours of the morning. There was so much to catch up on and learn of each other, something we couldn't do easily in Korea, and time stood still. Sometimes we stayed indoors without stirring for days, ordering the room service to bring our food. Or we would set out in the middle of the night and drive for hours without stopping. Following no schedule or routine we did everything on impulse. At an unmarked crossroads we would turn left or right at whim and end up in a dirt road that led nowhere. Laughing, we backtracked and explored the other fork. We were two children totally liberated from worldly care and months passed as if it were yesterday.

There was one element of conflict, however: my alleged origin from St. Paul, Minnesota. I knew I had to cross this bridge someday, but whenever the subject came up, I put it off, not from any motive of deceit, but by inertia. Soon further evasion became impossible. We were heading for the Niagara Falls after Mount Rushmore when Nan wanted me to head for the Twin Cities.

"Are you ashamed of me or something?" Nan demanded, when I started making excuses. "I want to meet your relatives and friends, see the house, the streets you grew up in, the schools you went to."

"The truth is, Nan," I had to confess, "I didn't grow up in St. Paul or anywhere else in the US. I was born and raised in Korea, not knowing who my parents are, nor who I really am."

So after these many years I told her all about the strange twists and turns my life had taken, the brindled tapestry of four names, Chundong Bag, John Heyman, Alan Heyman, Archer Torrey, four lives.

"My poor, poor dear!" she kept exclaiming, eyes flowing. At the end of the narrative, she got hold of herself and spoke with calm resolution. "Let us look for your parents if it takes our lives to do so. For starters let's hold a press conference and tell the world who you really are. Somebody will recognize you and come forward, somebody who knew your father or mother, maybe even themselves if they are still alive."

"No, I am content to leave things as they are. In fact, I don't know how to handle a father or mother who shows up at this late date after dumping me like garbage, whose only credit is a stray sperm or egg, manufactured trillions a microsecond in those ubiquitous testicles and ovaries."

"Your resentment is understandable, but they may have had no choice. Remember there was a war on at the time. Let's give them a chance before we condemn them. It is not good to hate anybody, particularly your own parents. It's like hating yourself. I am amazed that you turned out normal."

"Let's take it easy for a while, though, at least until this exile business blows over. Even then I would have reservations. What about the legal consequences of my going back to being Chundong Bag? I am worried not so much about myself as for Alan Heyman of Moon Rock, who may be prosecuted by one or the other government."

"He can't be touched under the statute of limitations, though I don't see what crime he could be guilty of. What a story! I want you to work up a screenplay based on their life. That's the first movie we'll make when we get back. Let's call it Jinny Bay."

"You miss the studio and the screen, don't you?"

"So do you."

"Let's call Hyongwoog and see how things stand."

We went into a drugstore to look for a pay phone. It was Nan who saw the headline with Hyongwoog's picture on the front page in the newsstand: "Hyongwoog Kim, former KCIA Chief, missing and presumed dead." I dialed Al Edwards.

"He went to Zurich, Switzerland to draw from his account," Al said. "On these trips he didn't want us to tag along. Even if he did, our FBI agents couldn't have operated on foreign soil. I have reliable reports that a dozen athletic types had arrived from Seoul the day before, allegedly to attend a Korean cultural conference, though later inquiries showed no such event going on in Zurich or elsewhere nearby. The rumor is that they kidnapped him and took him to Junghee Park, who cut him up to pieces in the basement of the Blue House."

This happened a week after his 3-volume memoirs had appeared under the title The Image of a Despot.

Our Oldsmobile had already logged 70,000 miles on its odometer and looked it. But it had served us well, taking us wherever we wanted to go. We had been all over the US, two or three times, crisscrossing, doubling back, soaking in the energy and spirit of the soil, farmlands with thick stands of corn and wheat, rivers, mountains, lakes, primeval forests, wide straight four-lane or more highways of concrete or asphalt, each mile of which must have cost as much as building a 50-story highrise. In late August we were heading for the Yellowstone National Park to watch Old Faithful spout one more time, when the radio announced Junghee Park's murder by his CIA Chief Jaygyoo Kim, apparently in a brawl at dinner. Jeechul Cha, Secret Service Chief and fitness buff, also present, was among the shot and killed. The three girls who had been sitting in the men's laps screamed and jumped away for their dear lives, but two got shot, though not fatally. We weren't interested in the sordid details of his death. Free at last, we could go home to pick up where we had left off. Turning our back on Old Faithful we drove to the nearest airport.

XIV.
Moo Moo Film

Among the first to welcome us back to Korea was Jonghag. We shook hands and embraced cordially. There was no rancor, no outrage. Though Nan and I had become lovers while she was still married to him, which made us technically adulterers, we all knew he had deliberately pushed us into the relationship, the sooner to gain his own freedom from Nan, the insanity of it aside, and he wasn't so small or irrational as to deny it and act the deceived husband or betrayed friend. While we were away in the US, Jonghag had found obliging lawyers and had his marriage to Nan annulled, so he could marry and live with Soonja who had just given him a son. Feeling he had been the offender rather than the victim in the situation, he was apologetic about what had happened and generous in the financial settlement, giving Nan her half share of their equity. This was enough money to make a down payment on the former US Air Force hangars in Boochon being auctioned off. The balance, 90% of the bid price, was owed to the bank, owned by Doohwan Jun's government. We had to go into more debt for the conversion into movie studios. Fortunately, Star-Crossed, the first movie that had launched me into stardom, was still bringing in substantial income and kept us from going under.

However, in naming our movie company Nan and I had our first and only serious argument as a couple or as working partners. She wanted to name it Chun Dong Bag Film, urging me to retake my old identity and renounce the fake American one, Archer Torrey. I was willing to do the latter, especially since CIA didn't care any more, but balked at the former, readoption of my old name.

"You want it ridiculed as Churn Dung Bag?" I asked. "Besides I don't want to be reminded of those awful days. I hated Director Bag, that orphanage ghoul, and won't take his name. Nor will I belong to the same family name as Junghee Park whom I heartily despised."

Despite the widely varying spellings, Bag, Bak, Bhak, Pak, Park, Pahk, they were the same Korean name. Perhaps it was uncharitable to hold grudges against a man who had died so wretchedly, but it was not easy to forgive a man who had tried to kill us. Even if I could do so on our account, I certainly could not on account of the others, for his unremitting persecution of Daejung Kim, for doing away with Hyongwoog's life and those of many others.

"I must have a name that I like, that characterizes and identifies me uniquely."

"Any ideas?"

"What about Moo Moo, the character for 'nothing,' for both the personal and family name?"

"Preposterous! Nobody has heard of such a name!"

"That's the idea."

Despite Jinny Bay's prophecy and Nan's determination to look for my parents or relatives by aggressive publicity and search, I had by now no illusions about finding them. My GI father probably didn't even notice or remember the face of the woman he ejaculated into, and she in turn forgot or tried to forget all about me after turning me over to the lady in blue scarf, a neighbor or a distant relative to whom I had meant nothing despite my infantile fixation on her. My untraceable lineage was a blessing in disguise. I was destined to be a unit complete in itself, alpha and omega. What was more fitting than a family name shared with nobody else. The monosyllable moo "nothing" jumped out as a natural choice. Similarly with the first name. A monosyllabic personal name was a rarity in Korea to begin with and nobody in his right mind gave "Nothing" to his children. By being Moo Moo I was absolutely unique. No directory in Korea and maybe in the world would list another person by that name. Of course there was the homophonic Hawaiian muumuu and the English onomatopoeia of a cow's low, but since my sphere of activity would be Korea and the language Korean, the uniqueness of Moo Moo as a name would be unchallenged.

"My, aren't you a vain man!" Nan chided but acquiesced at last, and Moo Moo Film was born.

At her insistence, we went to the Mercy Home but found it erased, a textile plant standing in its place. Director Bag had died of a stroke some time ago, and none of his children could be located. Nor any of the former employees or orphans brought up there. So much for the dynastic dream Bag had cherished!

Back in Seoul we were up to our ears with the production of GI Orphan, when word came that Star-Crossed had been nominated for the year's Oscar in the best foreign film department. All three of us were invited, Nan, Jong, and I, to the award ceremony.

"Go by yourself," Nan said to Jonghag. "We have our hands full with our new film. Besides the credit should go to you, the director and producer."

"I couldn't have done it without you guys," Jonghag said honestly.

"We have made expensive commitments with thousands of people, including a division of the Army. You go for all of us and let's hope we win the Oscar. Take Soonja and your son with you."

Star-crossed didn't win the Oscar. Meanwhile we completed GI Orphan and submitted it to the Cannes Film Festival but its reception at the box office in Korea was disappointing.

"I am sorry it's not a commercial success," I said, reading a half-hearted review by Jiyong Jong, a film critic with the Joson Ilbo, who had earlier hailed me as a meteor on the Korean film horizon. Even the most intelligent people didn't care to be probed or disturbed as to their innermost emotional axioms. Koreans simply never had to be tested or challenged as to racism unlike Americans or others who lived in racially mixed societies. Racial minorities were more of an oddity like creatures in a zoo or science museum than a problem to be faced and dealt with on a daily basis.

"When we win the Cannes," Nan said indignantly, "they'll all change their tune and slobber at our feet."

"In the meantime we have to pay our bills," I said.

"We'll take a second mortgage on the studio."

She was referring to our 200-acre studio at Boochon. As a last resort before this drastic step Nan decided to call Dongsoo Yee, Chairman of the Gwangjoo Textile Group and a long-time fan of hers, respected for his integrity, whose financial empire had survived the Park regime's hostility to the Jolla people. He was not home at his Seoul residence.

"We can't reach him in Gwangjoo, either," his wife said anxiously. "All Gwangjoo phone lines are down. There seems to be some trouble brewing there. Mr. Yee went last week and was due back yesterday."

And big trouble it was. How prophetic Soogun Yee had been, for if Junghee Park was a jackal, his successor Doohwan Jun turned out to be a hyena many times more grabby and vicious. In the post-assassination scramble for power one man stood out at the head of the pack, Brig. Gen. Doohwan Jun, National Security Commander at the time of Junghee's death. Seizing Jaygyoo, the assassin, minutes after the act with the authority of NSC, Jun became the virtual ruler of the country by making the acting President Gyoohwa Chay appoint him Martial Law Commander and Chairman of the Joint Investigation Board looking into the alleged conspiracy behind Park's assassination. Though the impulsive, personal nature of Jaygyoo's crime became apparent, the Board stayed on to be the Grand Inquisitor, spreading terror through the land, arresting and imprisoning without a warrant anybody suspected of treason. By this means Jun, whose appetite for supreme power was whetted and unquenchable by now, eliminated all possible contenders one by one, whether formerly pro-Park or otherwise. For example, Jongpil Kim, Junghee's nephew-in-law, chief architect of the 1961 coup, and widely regarded as heir apparent to Junghee, was stripped of all his possessions, "accumulated corruptly," and sent out of the country on indefinite leave. The opposition politicians, imprisoned, fined, or disenfranchised, fared worse. In particular, Daejung Kim, against whom Jun inherited his late patron's provincial hatred, was sentenced to death for inciting student demonstrations with North Korean money.

Outraged by this harsh verdict against their hero the citizens of Gwangjoo, capital of Jolla Province, staged a citywide demonstration calling for the immediate dissolution of JIB and restoration of democracy, as well as the release of Daejung Kim. Jun responded by upgrading the peaceful demonstration to rebellion and sentencing Daejung Kim, who had been in prison all this time, once more to death for instigation of the unrest. So was set the stage for a pogrom, a genocide of unparalleled proportions. The ugly, long-suppurating sore of Jolla prejudice finally burst open, discharging a river of bloody pus.

A division of paratroopers was dispatched with orders to quell the revolt as expeditiously as possible, stopping at nothing. After encirclement the troops attacked, tanks and armored cars plowing into the ranks of demonstrators and foot soldiers in full combat gear opening up with assault rifles and automatic weapons. In shock and disbelief, the whole city rose in self-defense, in real rebellion. Even the city government and police sided with the demonstrators and opened the armories so they could defend themselves against the murderers. But of course there was no contest. Those that didn't get run over or gunned down were rounded up to be bayoneted at the public squares. When no further resistance remained afield, a cleanup operation was launched to destroy evidence of the crime. The bodies, collected by garbage trucks, were taken to the dump, sprayed with petroleum, and burned until identification became impossible. The smoke and stench from the massive cremation of some 10,000 bodies hung over the city for days.

But nobody, certainly no newsman, could go in or out of the city, sealed off hermetically by the besieging army. Even afterwards so thorough was the censorship enforced under martial law by the Jun government that, despite the whispered rumors and suspicions, the country remained largely ignorant of the full extent of the massacre. It was from Al Edwards, who came to investigate the matter personally for his government, that we learned all about it down to its horrid detail.

Putting aside everything we went into the production of Shattered showing the dashed hopes and lives of a young couple caught in the tornado of the Gwangjoo Revolt, Nan playing the girl and another up and coming young actor the murdered hero, a civil engineer with the City Public Works Department who drives a tractor into the path of a tank to keep it from mowing down rows of Buddhist monks kneeling in prayer at the entrance to City Hall Plaza. My role was limited to directing, which was an armful. Halfway through Doohwan Jun's agents pounced on us, suspending our movie license and foreclosing on the Boochon property. The only thing we were permitted to operate was the old Seoul Film School, a losing proposition quitclaimed to us by Jonghag. However, with characteristic resilience, Nanyong had plunged herself heart and soul into its management, making it the best in the field, though frankly I didn't see much point in training professionals, in an oppressive political system like South Korea, for a profession they couldn't practice freely.

I was in my office at the School working on a screen play, when Nan tore into the room, shouting and waving the newspaper ecstatically.

"We've won the Cannes!" she shouted, waving the newspaper ecstatically. "GI Orphan is the Best Picture of the year, the best in the whole world! I am so proud of you, darling. You've done it."

"No, we have done it, together."

"I love you, my sweet. I am yours to command, so happy to be your woman, to be part of you."

Her embrace was crushing, her kiss fervent. We could have made love right then and there on the couch or on the floor, had it not been for the stream of faculty and students coming to the door to congratulate us. Predictably, the media now raved about the film's searching inquiry into 'marginal existence,' 'the human soul on edge,' etc. In a big ceremony at the National Theater just completed on South Mountain, Doohwan Jun designated us Intangible Cultural Treasures of Korea, which entitled us to a lifetime pension of $2,000 a month each, most timely as our finances had sunken low. But did it mean reinstatement of the license and return of the Studio?

"No," said the florid letter from his Minister of Culture and Public Information unequivocally. "Your titles and pensions are in recognition of your past accomplishments, for the honor you have brought to the Korean film, but renewal of a revoked license is a separate issue to be determined according to strict official guidelines."

Shouldn't recognition of a job well done necessarily entail encouragement of the same? We wrote one more time to Jun to meet us so we could appeal the illogic to him personally but received no further reply. Trapped in limbo, we were not all that excited about GI Orphan climbing to the top spot at the box offices throughout the nation. Under receivership we couldn't touch any of the profit rolling in. The government was realizing handsome returns on its investment of small monthly pensions to us. Moreover, the Cultural Treasurehood exacted a heavy price in an unexpected manner.

In the fine print we had neglected to read Treasures were forbidden to leave the country together, if they were man and wife. If a trip was unavoidable, as in the present case when somebody had to be in Cannes to receive the award, only one could go, while the other remained at home or went to a different place so they wouldn't be together abroad at the same time, lest the couple, so united, should decide to defect, thus causing flight of Korea's resources to a foreign country. Though it could be any foreign country, the law, originally drafted under the Syngman Rhee Regime, primarily targeted North Korea, the obsessive enemy and rival of the south.

"But the law applies to married couples," I pointed out, "and not to us. We are not married."

"The whole world knows you as man and wife," said the

official in the Passport Section, Ministry of Foreign Affairs, smiling.

"We just live together but are not married, legally."

Somehow we had never thought of marrying perhaps because what we had was so complete that we had not felt the need for change.

The official knit his brow in thought, made a phone call, then said, "Well, it's a mere technicality, absence of your marriage documents. In a special case like this we look to the spirit of the law, beyond the letter."

But while this impasse continued with the Korean government, something happened that totally eclipsed any annoyance or inconvenience we might grumble about: the Soviet shootdown of the KAL jumbo jet killing all the 169 aboard. Among the victims were none other than Jonghag and his young family, who had boarded the doomed plane at New York where Jonghag had attended a film seminar. Angry demonstrations and rallies raged throughout the country, bitterly but futilely denouncing Soviet brutality, without fear of government suppression for a change. Our personal sorrow was beyond measure. Nan cried and so did I. It was a rotten thing to happen to anybody but Jonghag was certainly the last person such tragedy should strike. So was his two-year-old son and Soonja, who we learned was pregnant with his second child at the time. I would be forever in Jong's debt not only for my initiation into the film but for his gift of Nan. I had meant to tell him that and thank him, but I would never have the chance now.

There was a call from Cannes to confirm our arrival schedule. We decided that Nan should go. The Korean Airlines was arranging a ship funeral in the waters off Sakhalin where the plane had crashed and wanted me to attend. KAL thought and I agreed that it might offend the sensibilities of Jong's surviving relatives to see Nan, his divorcee, at his funeral. Besides Nan would shine at an award ceremony, whereas I would be a clumsy dolt most likely. On her way back from Cannes she could stop at Hong Kong and sign the sisterhood papers with the China Cinema Academy owned by the Chinese theater magnate Hungchang Wong, under which our School would get an infusion of a few million dollars a year for hosting some 200 students and faculty from the Academy. She would be met and shown around on arrival in Hong Kong by Samho Hyon, our Hong Kong agent. A distant cousin to Jonghag, Samho had played a few minor roles in the earlier Jongnan films, then moved to Hong Kong ten years ago to be the Jongnan agent and distributor for Hong Kong, China, the Philippines, and Southeast Asia. Though Jonghag was no longer in the picture, Nanyong and I had let him stay on as our agent.

Nan called from Hong Kong.

"At the Hilton," she said. "They have been decent enough to get the top floor with a good view of the harbor."

"So how was the trip?"

"Unbearable without you."

"I miss you too. Tell me about the ceremony."

"The president of the Cannes Board of Directors himself introduced me as the Star of the East, who has saved the hero, you, obviously in reference to our first movie, Star-Crossed. I had a standing ovation. Then, your absence, as well as its cause, was duly noted to the indignation of the congregation."

"How did they find out?"

"They are not dummies, must have their sources of information. All one has to do is pick up a Korean paper. I think some form of protest is on its way to Jun from the Board."

"I wish it weren't, because it wouldn't do any good. He is impervious to public opinion, especially outside opinion, and will become only more obdurate, daring the whole world."

"But he must care what other people are saying, especially movie makers of the world, stars, directors. Doesn't he go to the movies?"

"Maybe not. So what did you do afterwards?"

"I was bombarded by requests for interviews by the media of France, Italy, Germany, US, everywhere. But I declined and hurried out of the city next morning. I was boiling mad with Jun for not letting you come but couldn't express it. I didn't want to lie, either. Escape was the only rational thing."

"Too bad you couldn't take your time to sightsee. The Mediterranean puts on an orgy of scenic beauty thereabouts, I heard."

"Sightsee without you?"

"Well, we'll be together next time. So have you signed the papers?"

"No, this Hungchang Wong character isn't here, called away to Manila or somewhere unexpectedly, they said. I was so mad I almost turned around to take the next plane to Seoul. Samho and Wong's servants beg me to stay and wait. As if I had nothing else to do but hang around for someone out of town indefinitely."

"Maybe you could sightsee and do some shopping?"

"Not without you. If Wong doesn't get here in three days, I am out of here, contract or no contract."

But it had been a whole week since that call and she was still held up in Hong Kong, waiting for Wong. She had to hurry back to Seoul because the spring term was beginning. In her absence her aunt Gyongja Jo, who had been on stage and supported her career, was Acting President, but matters often arose that Nan should attend to. Also I had appointments to keep in the States but couldn't leave until her return. Yet it was not easy for her to decamp in high dudgeon, either: Wong had paid for her first class ticket, including the Cannes portion. In fact, he had paid for my ticket, too, so I could use it for other flights, including the one I planned to make to the US. Who said money couldn't buy loyalty? The phone rang at my school office. It was 3 a.m., one hour ahead of Hong Kong, where Nan was calling.

"You should be home in bed," she said, reproachfully. "What are you doing this late?"

"Touching up the Mayoress of Koreatown to show to Fenwick."

That was the new title of Jinny Bay with venue shifted to the US. Cutting out all references to the moodang or Moon Rock Island, lest we should embarrass Alan and his friends, I had injected a new element, the Soviet downing of the KAL plane, suggested by Jonghag's death. In the final version the hero, still haunted by her memory, goes back home to the States, where he takes years to finish law school and pass the California bar. After setting up shop in Koreatown, Los Angeles, he works mostly free for Koreans, earning just enough to get by. At a rally in Koreatown, protesting the KAL incident, the hero hears the honorary Mayoress of Koreatown deliver a fiery denunciation of Soviet barbarity. Her audience spills out into Olympic Boulevard in demonstration, which results in their arrest and imprisonment. Alan bails them out and gets to know the Mayoress better, whose checkered career, including her escape as an infant from Wonsan by LST in the care of strangers, convinces him that she is the partisan leader Jinny Bay's daughter, if not her reincarnation. Learning through his contacts that she is under FBI surveillance for suspected North Korean connections, he persuades her to chuck everything and go away with him with a new identity, Jinny Bay.

"What are you doing up so late yourself?"

"I am tired but can't sleep. I miss you so terribly I am going out of my mind. I dialed thinking nobody would answer but hoping you would be there, too. So hang up and go to bed."

"In a minute. So you are coming home tomorrow?"

"I wish. Wong is not here yet. Samho has an idea, though. You go to America, take care of business with Universal and NBC, and come and pick me up in Hong Kong."

"But I haven't got the passport yet."

"Everything has been arranged. If you go to the China Airlines counter at the airport tomorrow, you'll find your first-class ticket waiting and your passport, too, 7-day single-entry, which can be extended and converted to multiple in the States. According to Samho, overseas consulates are generally lax about it, but recently there has been an overhaul in diplomatic personnel and the left hand really doesn't know what the right hand is doing. So will you go to the airport?"

"All right. Wait for me and we'll have a bang of a reunion in Hong Kong."

Left alone after hanging up, I tried to go back to work,

but couldn't, restless with misgiving. I shouldn't have let her go alone abroad. What if something should go terribly wrong like an accident or foul play? A celebrity was fair game to all crackpots. Suddenly I visualized her face being covered by ether-soaked rag. How easy and quick it had been with Soogun, a man in superb physical condition! She was only a fragile woman, just barely 100 pounds. The very idea made me shudder. I couldn't live without her. I picked up the phone to call her back and tell her to be careful and ask Samho to provide some kind of protection like a bodyguard before she left the hotel to go anywhere in town. But, then, what good did all his bodyguards do to Daejung Kim at the best hotel in Tokyo, the city that boasted the lowest crime rate in the world?

The door of the next room slammed shut with a loud report that rang down the empty corridor, followed by the shuffle of the lame custodian making his nightly rounds, a Korean War veteran Nan had taken pity on and hired, perhaps in memory of her own brother who had fought and died in the war.

"Are you all right, Mr. Moo?" Insoo Bang asked, knocking at my door.

"Yes, I'm all right, Sgt. Bang," I replied, replacing the phone.

"It will be daylight soon. You had better turn in."

"In a while. I have work to do. Thank you. Good night."

The door pushed in and the short wizened man limped into the room dragging his bad leg. No one looking at this wreck of a man would have suspected that he was a fearless maverick, a crackshot who could shoot down a bird flying 1000 feet away, and had won a fistful of medals, having served in the Army from day one of the Korean War.

"Are you working on the story of General Intrepid?" he asked, plopping into a chair.

General Jintay Ham, Bang's CO during the war, single-handedly entered and knocked out a Red Chinese battery of guns on a strategic hill in the Iron Triangle that had pinned down several American and Korean regiments including the one he commanded, helping secure the whole Triangle for the UN side and fix the DMZ several miles further north than it would have been in the Armistice signed a few days later ending the 3-year-plus bloody war. For this the already much-decorated man was awarded the Hibiscus Medal and promoted to General, posthumously, because he hadn't survived his victorious solo mission. His distant cousin and chauffeur before his death, Bang wanted to immortalize him in a movie, and I had agreed, giving it the tentative title, General Intrepid. But so far I had only a series of unrelated combat episodes, which defied a dramatic personal focus. In particular I needed to motivate his last act of bravery, plainly suicidal, far too much beyond and above any man's call of duty. He had to be made more human and plausible, with a family, complexes and quirks, but Bang had not been all that forthcoming in this department, as if a touch of humanity might sully his hero's image.

"No, I was working on something else," I answered frankly.

"I have recalled more details, so you can start right away."

"You've given me enough hand-to-hand fights, ambushes, patrols. I need to know your general as a person, like you and me. Was he married, for example?"

"Did I tell you I had fallen asleep on my watch when the Reds fired their first rounds on the morning of June 25, 1950?" he asked, as if he had not heard my question. "Not that it changed anything. The night before I had a drop of sojoo, just enough to warm my bones, because it had been raining and chilly at the border. In a wink I was up on my feet in my trench and peered into the darkness outside, wondering what had awakened me. The leaves crackled in the pelting rain and the swollen stream set up a throaty bubble. I wasn't left in doubt for long. A flash of gunfire lit the woods and shook the ground. More fireballs mushroomed and peach and yellow trajectories furrowed the sky crisscross. The earth convulsed, upended and spewed fire. Huge Soviet-made tanks tore through the woods like rampaging dinosaurs, vomiting fire, trampling down bushes, kicking up mud, rock, and roots...."

I must have dozed off. When I woke, the sun was high up in the sky and I was on the couch under a blanket where I often took a nap in the office. The old man must have carried me across the room because I had no recollection of going there myself. I called China Airlines and found that they had a plane leaving for the States in two hours.

Everything was in order as Nan had said. Samho must be somebody to have such a pull from a thousand miles away. The passport specified my errands in the US, Universal Studios at Hollywood to arrange production of Mayoress of Koreatown and NBC in New York to negotiate the North American release of our films in videocassette with English subtitles.

From LAX I drove straight to the Korean Consulate General on Olympic Boulevard in Koreatown, Los Angeles, for a six-month extension and change to multiple entry, fully expecting refusal on account of some secret memo from the Foreign Ministry in Seoul. Luck was on my side and the consul, recognizing me from my films, stamped the approvals off without a second thought.

"I saw your movie just before coming here last week," Consul Yee said. "I applied for overseas posting to get out of Korea and breathe fresh air and ended up here in the smog basin."

After thanking him I drove back to LAX and flew to New York to take care of NBC first. Dr. Charles Hong met me at JFK. After our return to Seoul following Junghee's assassination I had been in touch with Charles, calling him from Seoul, ostensibly to get his input on a plot or character but really for his offhand remarks and quips so apropos and humorous that I always felt refreshed and slightly intoxicated afterwards. Charles took me to their delightful 5-bedroom apartment on Riverside Drive, Manhattan, where he lived with Jane and two children, Elizabeth, 12, and James, 8. For dinner we went to the newly opened Diamond Mountains, a gem of a restaurant with elegant decor and delicious cuisine on 32nd Street at Broadway. Back at their apartment, we were duly entertained by Elizabeth, an accomplished cellist with a

Carnegie Hall performance to her credit. In addition, she was an excellent student with a near perfect SAT score, taken five years ahead of her age. Naturally she was being courted by Harvard, Stanford, Yale, and others, as well as Juilliard. When I expressed my admiration of her talent and the bright future ahead of her, she said, to my surprise, that she wanted to be a movie director like me, and I tried to dissuade her.

"Why waste your brain power?" I said. "Do something more original and creative in science or art."

"But the film is an art," she declared.

"Secondary art at best. There isn't a single thing that's original about it. Everything is derivative. Take the plot for example. In most cases the story is already conceived and written down by the novelist, which the screen writer adapts to the medium. Original screen plays are an exception."

"What's secondary or derivative about adaptation? The moment you change or modify a single motif you are creating, like translating from one language to another. That's what Shakespeare did, lifting whole chunks of action from popular London magazines."

I had never looked at it that way.

"But in the movie there is one degrading element, the market place. Each project costs a lot of money and must pay. The commercial motive dominates every decision."

"The same may be said about every human activity or product, because it must have some utility, enough for people to pay good money for it, or it is simply eliminated. That's the whole history of survival and evolution."

I had heard of prodigies in music, mathematics, or even languages, but not in subtle reasoning and practical wisdom that came with maturity, with years of living, but there she was, a Socrates at age 12!

I called Nan at her hotel. It was 11 p.m. New York time, noon in Hong Kong. Should I have called her earlier, at the airport as I got off the plane, or at the latest when I got to Charles' apartment, before going to the restaurant, or all that entertainment and chat?

"The party you want has checked out," the receptionist

said.

"No, she coulnd't have," I said irritably. "It's Suite 3412."

"I have the right party, sir."

"Is there a forwarding address or phone number."

"No, sir."

Repeated inquiries yielded the same answer. Instinctively, I knew something was amiss. I dialed Samho, who had been in touch with her all along and should know how to get hold of her, even though she had left no forwarding address or phone number with the hotel. Only the answering machine came on. I left the message to call Charles Hong's New York number but couldn't wait around indefinitely. Calling the second time, I told the machine to have Samho meet me at Hong Kong Airport. Dropping everything, I hopped on the next plane bound for Hong Kong.

The flight from New York made it to Los Angeles in good time, but my connecting flight to Hong Kong was not until 4 p.m. I had six hours to kill. Fenwick was gracious enough to squeeze me in, though our appointment was not until three days later.

"It's dynamite," Fenwick said, squeezing my hand as he seated me on the sofa in his Hollywood office. It was our first meeting, though we had written to each other many times. I liked his frank, open face, clear, intelligent eyes.

"There is just one suggestion I want to make, if you don't mind."

"Go ahead."

"Let's give more scope to the battle scenes in the retreat from Lake Jangjin. They are always good theater. I am surprised you didn't exploit them."

I agreed, realizing how budget-conscious I had been, Korean style, cutting out these vital scenes, reimposing on the screen the spatial strictures of the stage. The screen writer would be Paul Kalustian who did Manchurian Warlord and The Battle over Japan, among other credits. Moo Moo Film would be coproducer and I would direct as well as play the lead as Alan Heyman opposite Nanyong in the role of Jinny Bay. I couldn't wait to tell her about this break we had wanted all along, a debut into regular commercial film in America. But where was she?

"Your screenplay won't go to waste, either, because Paul can use it. If he had to start from scratch the fee would have been double. As soon as he finishes in about two weeks, we'll have a preproduction conference to get the ball rolling. Where are you staying?"

"I am in transit at the moment bound for Hong Kong to find my heroine who seems lost somewhere out there."

"What do you mean by lost?"

"Well, I don't exactly know what to make of it. She has left the hotel without leaving a forwarding number or address, which is not like her. I got through to our agent's answering machine and gave my arrival time, but I am not sure whether she or he got the message."

"Maybe she went to stay with a friend."

"When I talked to her last, she had no such plans. Otherwise she would have told me. I fear the worst."

"Such as?"

"Robbery, kidnap, or what have you."

"Nonsense. Hong Kong must have police. She'll probably surprise you at the airport. Go get her by all means. We need her. Just in case of trouble, let me know. I have some influence with the State Department, which will apply the pressure wherever necessary."

After parting with Fenwick, a little cheered by his optimism, I took a leisurely ride into Koreatown, there still remaining some time before my flight, looking at the cityscape as it would come through the eyes of Alan Heyman in Mayoress of Koreatown. The streets, dominated by Korean signs and free from the graffiti and trash of downtown Los Angeles, gave the illusion of a Seoul suburb. Koreatown! Who would have imagined Korea to rise from the ashes of war like the phoenix of the legend on the soil of North America?

I parked my rented car and went into the Korean Food Court at Western and Eighth for late lunch. No sooner had I sat down at a table with a bowl of nangmyon than four men came over, one of them Vice Consul Shim of the Consulate who had stamped the extension on my passport at Consul Yee's direction. Relieved to run into me like that, they asked me to come with them after lunch to the Consulate to see my pal Yee. I declined the invitation on account of my Hong Kong flight leaving in a couple of hours. That's when they told me straight out that I couldn't go to Hong Kong and demanded my passport. Thinking fast, I told them that I had left it in my room at the Century Plaza Hotel from which I hadn't checked out yet. I had stayed there before and was familiar with its topography. Besides it was on the way to LAX. I had the distinct impression that the men were boxing me in as one of them went to the phone to call Yee. A few minutes later Consul Yee himself hurried in out of breath. Saying his job was on the line, he asked me to take them to the hotel and give back the passport. They followed in a blue Lincoln Continental with a diplomatic license plate. I knew I couldn't shake them. But luck was on my side again. At the Avenue of the Stars on Olympic, their car got blocked by another that had cut in before them and had not made the left turn as the arrow changed to red. Pulling up at the front entrance of the hotel, I gave the bell captain a $20 bill and asked him to keep behind my rented car the blue Lincoln Continental with four Korean diplomats just pulling in from the street. I waved to my pursuers before dashing into the lobby. Quickly I went downstairs to the mall level and exited by the back door into Century Park East. At a public phone I called a cab, which showed up instantly from the stand in front of the hotel on the Avenue of the Stars, where my consular friends waited, certain that I would return to my rental car with my luggage and travel documents. At the airport I went to a Hertz counter and returned the key, giving the location of their property.

XV.
Missing

The long line at the Hong Kong Customs and Immigration showed no sign of shrinking. Couldn't they provide an express counter for travelers like me with nothing but a briefcase for luggage? Until I got into the lobby, after clearing the customs, off limits to the public, I wouldn't know whether Nan was there to meet me, having gotten the message I had left on Samho's machine. What could have happened to her?

A fashionably dressed man walked into the customs auditorium through an employees-only door, with a uniformed airport security guard deferentially in tow. He surveyed the lines of people, until his eyes spotted me, then strode directly toward me, smiling broadly.

"I am Samho Hyon," the man introduced himself, offering his soft hand. "I got your message just in time."

I had talked to him over the phone but this was our first face to face meeting.

"Where is Nanyong?" I asked.

"I'll take you to her. Let's clear out of here."

The side door he had come in led us to a freight terminal where a police car waited, which took us to Samho's Benz in the parking garage.

"You seem to have connections everywhere," I couldn't help remarking.

"I've lived here long enough. Any trouble with the passport?"

"No, it worked out just as you had predicted, except

in LA..."

I decided not to mention the latest encounter with the consular staff in view of other priorities.

"LA? So you stopped at Hollywood. Is Universal going to produce Mayoress?"

"Yes, with Nanyong as the lead, but where is she? Is she all right?"

"Of course. She is staying at Mr. Wong's villa, palatial with maids and servants. You'll like it."

"I was going out of my mind because I couldn't reach her. She should have left a number I could call."

"I guess in the haste we forgot."

"Haste?"

"Yes, she has been busy shopping and sightseeing. Do you still plan to return to Seoul?"

"Where else?" I retorted, at the oddness of the question. "Seoul is my home."

"Home is where you are fully appreciated and can be most productive."

"Where do you suggest?"

"North Korea."

"Are you serious? I doubt they have films there at all or know the meaning of artistic expression."

"On the contrary, they greatly value the medium, which is in fact top national policy priority. The leadership is committed to its improvement to world-class quality, so its products can win international prizes and recognition. I have been personally contacted by Ilsung Kim and Jungil Kim to sound you out and extend their invitation to come to North Korea and make films there. If you are agreeable, they'll provide you with all you need and give you a free hand."

Temper frayed from a long cross-Pacific flight, sleepless and restless over Nan's safety, I hardly heard the terms of this serious proposal, which sounded like some idle talk for talk's sake, singularly out of place at this juncture.

"Let's get going first," I snapped. "I can't decide without Nan's approval anyway, because she goes where I go. I doubt she would agree, though. Her brother was killed during the war by the Communists and she has some horror stories to tell about Communist atrocities."

Her oldest brother had been a Lieutenant in the South Korean Army during the war and that, as well as the land they owned, had made them "reactionaries" targeted for elimination by the Communists. Her family went into hiding and survived the raids and searches by sheer luck. But her officer brother she loved dearly was killed in action, redoubling her hatred of the Communists. She still had two older brothers, one a teacher and the other a civil engineer, and a married sister, all living in Seoul.

"Atrocities are mutual in war," Samho reasoned. "Isn't Mayoress of Koreatown a case in point? The war has been over since a long time ago. We might as well bury our hatchets and think of uniting Korea. You can play a vital role in this process through your films. You agree on the primacy of Korea's unification, don't you?"

How corny this term "primacy"! In fact, all the clichés Koreans ventilated at the drop of a hat on the subject of unification only cheapened its moral imperative.

"Yes, but can we talk about it later? Let's first start the car and get going."

"In a minute. I have to know your answer right away because they are waiting."

"What answer?"

"Whether you will come and work in North Korea."

"Negative in that case," I said, annoyed by his importunity.

"Is it ideology?" he persisted.

"Don't be absurd. I haven't bothered with such rubbish. It's a matter of conditioning, of getting used to and feeling at home."

"But you haven't been there and don't know what it is like. I thought you of all people would welcome the opportunity to explore the unknown."

"We are talking about a place I can call home, not a summer camp. From what I have heard, I don't think Communism would agree with me. The West with all its inconsistencies is still my style. My juices flow more freely here. It's as irrational but decisive as one's preferences for a mate or a house to buy. Now if you won't take me to Nan, I'll take a cab. Just give me Wong's address."

"Okay, okay, I'll take you to her," he said, backing the car out.

He got off the main road and turned into a spur through a wooded area. As we turned a bend, a construction sign blocked the road, which he saw in time and braked abruptly. Simultaneously four long-haired men jumped from behind the trees, surrounded the car, and yanked open the doors.

"Give up all your money," one of them said in broken English putting a knife to my throat.

"Take it," I said fumbling for my wallet.

Before I could turn to see what they were doing to Samho a plastic sack was pulled down over my head. I shouted for Samho but my voice was muffled in the sack that now enclosed my whole body tightly and was tied at the feet. Soon I was suffocating. A slit was being made above my nose with a knife, the sharp edge almost cutting my face. Before I could fully savor the fresh air, the sweetest I had ever breathed, an aerosol hissed, emitting a powerful spray right into my nostrils. It was diethyl ether, the stuff I had used to recapture Soogun Yee. Was it divine retribution catching up with me?

With superhuman willpower I held my breath despite the bursting lungs. Hadn't KCIA used the same chemical to abduct Daejung, Junghee's nemesis? So these men were not ordinary bandits but KCIA agents out to get me. But Junghee was dead and Doohwan had more than evened up the score between us, I had thought. Was my passport violation such a terrible crime? The men carried me in the sack through the wood and walked on the beach, their feet sinking in the sand. Above the sough of the surf rose the chugging of a motor boat to take me to sea for dumping, just as they tried with Daejung in the Sea of Japan. They almost succeeded, except I stumbled on the plot and alerted Al Edwards in time. So I had saved Daejung but could I save myself! Even if somebody could alert the US CIA about my predicament, no Cobra would rush to my rescue: I was no Daejung Kim. Dumped overboard, the bag would impact the water so hard that it would probably knock me out instantly. Upon waking, if I did, I would breathe in the sea water and drown in a matter of seconds, thence to float around and be devoured by the scavengers of the deep. I had come close to death before but never with such overwhelming immediacy and constriction. There was no room to debate or contemplate. I tried to shout but no voice issued. Perhaps I was dead already, the soul lingering for sentimental reasons before its final flight to the gathering place to be with other disembodied souls, countless as the stars, yet distinct and whole in their separate individuality since the beginning of the species, among whom I would no doubt meet Mother, for all souls are transparent and declare their identity without shame, soon to be joined by Nan.

"Is the comrade doctor aboard?" somebody shouted in strongly accented North Korean, interrupting my melancholy thoughts. So these were not South Korean CIA agents but North Koreans kidnapping me for their film program. Evidently Samho had betrayed me to them but instead of resentment I felt gratitude, remembering my resignation a short while ago to being dumped overboard. It was literally a new lease on life. Besides Samho had done his bit to persuade me to go voluntarily to North Korea. I wondered what the means of my transportation would have been, had I agreed. Probably the same route, except for the unpleasantness of being bagged and gased. But then I would have had to walk instead of being carried, the ultimate luxury.

They were shouting that water was leaking into the boat. There was a splash of somebody jumping off. I felt my body being hoisted out of the boat and deposited on the deck of a freighter, where the sack was ripped open. Arms and legs relaxed and eyes closed, I pretended to be unconscious while being carried to a room. A sharp needle punctured my arm. The shot accelerated my heart beat. Slowly I opened my eyes. On one wall of the room hung a magnified portrait of Ilsung Kim, which kept expanding until it filled the room, the whole ship, the sea. I closed my eyes to block out the illusion.

When I opened my eyes again, it was morning. I was wearing the same suit I had worn in Hong Kong with the wallet, pocketbook, handkerchief, and other things intact, except my passport. It wasn't where I had it, in the inside breast pocket.

"My passport is missing," I said to the short-haired young man who had been watching me.

"They should all be there," he said with a shrug. "You can take it up with my superiors."

"Where am I?"

"On a ship."

"Can I see your superiors?"

He led me to a cabin next to the bridge, where a short, plump middle-aged man came forward, arms raised as if to embrace me, face lit with a big smile, in contrast to his forbidding attire, the buttoned-down Mao suit, or "people's uniform" as it was called in North Korea. Perhaps my presence aboard as prisoner represented a mission accomplished with attendant rewards. It wasn't clear whether he was the captain or some lower-ranking officer.

"How do you feel?" he asked, squeezing my hand he had grasped without my encouragement.

"Are you the captain?" I queried, disengaging my hand.

"No," he said unruffled by the challenge of his authority. "He is busy running the ship. I am the Party worker assigned aboard. It is my pleasure to inform you that you are on your way to Pyongyang at the call of our Great Leader Ilsung Kim. Please be seated."

"What have you done with my passport?" I asked.

"My comrades will return it after checking out according to law," he said. How incongruous that he, clearly operating outside the bounds of any law, should be mentioning law!

"Is Miss Nanyong Song all right?"

"Who is she?" he asked, his geniality erased.

"Let's not pretend. She is in Pyongyang, too, isn't she?"

"I heard a rumor," he said slowly, dwelling on each syllable, "that a Miss Song had been assassinated by South Korean CIA for working with our people in the cause of national unification."

Obviously he was reciting from a memorized text, palpably false: Nan had never worked for any political cause. Still the words like assassination and CIA were ominous enough. Could they have done away with her in the process of abduction because of her resistance or because something went unexpectedly wrong? I clammed up for fear of getting more disconcerting gibberish, and asked to be taken back to my room to brood over my fate.

Constant radio communication was maintained between the ship and Pyongyang control as we sailed north toward the Korean peninsula. Two days later the ship was within the boundary of the Yellow Sea but wherever I looked, there was nothing but emptiness. Suddenly, on some mysterious orders from the control, the freighter stopped engine in the middle of the ocean. The answer was not long in coming. On the distant horizon to the northeast a small speck appeared, which grew steadily into a hovercraft, skimming the waves. As soon as it pulled up alongside, I was lowered to its deck, then led into the so-called cabin with a slanting floor where I was made to lie on my side sandwiched between two men. The strange design must have something to do with the streamline. For the first time I had a full view of the freighter I had been on all this time. From bow to stern it was painted black, except for the name Construction in white at the bow. I never found out what happened to the freighter, whether it followed us to a home port or returned to ply the waters of the China Sea for some more contraband.

XVI.
North Korea

The hovercraft traveled all night, shaking, bumping, growling. Sleep was out of the question. The torture seemed endless. Finally the sky paled to the east, silhouetting the land masses. Past Cape Long Mountain of the Chong Shim fame, I was transferred to yet another transport that had been waiting at anchor, a white-painted yacht much roomier and cleaner though slower, which entered South Port at the mouth of the Daydong about eight a.m. Avoiding the public piers, the yacht docked at what looked like a private one connected to a factory.

Every part of my body ached, head, neck, shoulders, arms, and legs, as if I had been beaten mercilessly. It took an effort to stand up, let alone pick up the legs and move. Groggily, half supported by the captain of the yacht, I went down the gangplank and stepped on North Korean soil, unpaved, frozen and black. No doubt it would turn into a quagmire in summer. The waterfront was lined with low-lying structures, probably warehouses, though none of them bore any signs, either of names or numbers, jealously guarding their identities, their secrets behind the closed doors. Traffic was light, except for occasional freight trucks and pedestrians. Only aboard the vessels tied to the docks there was some activity, cleaning, loading, unloading. A few fishing boats were leaving port.

My guide took me to two men by the side of a black Benz parked on the other side of the street, both in people's uniform.

"Welcome," said one of them, a strikingly handsome man, extending his hand and taking mine, but not giving his name. "I hope the journey was not too taxing."

"You have now come to your socialist motherland," declared his companion, a saturnine character, slowly, deliberately emphasizing 'mother,' as if excluding my non-Korean paternity. He didn't mention his name, either. Like the unmarked warehouses, anonymity seemed the dominant feature of the land.

Only much later was I to learn that they were the duo of Research, the North Korean synonym for Intelligence, Joosong Kim and Mangee Yee, in the order of appearance, assigned to me by special order of Jungil Kim. Opening the back door Mangee gestured me to get in. I did and he followed. Joosong rode in front next to the driver. I wanted to but didn't dare ask where Nan was, for fear of hitting a dead end like the ship's Party worker. Likewise I suppressed the curiosity about my destination or the whole purpose of my abduction.

After about ten minutes on the paved highway, encountering practically no traffic, the car detoured onto a dirt and gravel road and passed a highway construction crew at work, an army of laborers, thousands of them. To the cadence of some martial tune that blared out of an amplifier, they stepped in unison, carrying bags of cement, pails of water, loads of sand and gravel, shoveling, mixing and pouring cement, with no sign of modern road working machinery such as loaders, rollers, cement mixers. But their spirits were palpably high. Group physical labor always exhilarated its participants, unless excessive or slavish. Neither from what I could observe. Perhaps it was too early in the day. The car got back on the main road to drive another short stretch, only to get off again. Until it reached Pyongyang, a distance of 10 miles or so, I counted no fewer than four such interruptions.

Miles and miles of black frozen dirt, dotted with patches of snow drift here and there, alternated with villages that looked like little fortresses, a red fence surrounding several homes, walls whitewashed, roofs gray, doors sky blue - just dabs of wild bright colors without scheme or harmony. One ubiquitous feature was the huge billboards that popped up everywhere, at the entrances of villages, in the middle of the fields, on mountain sides, "Hail to Our Great Comrade Leader and Chief Ilsung Kim!," "Long Live the Glorious Korean Labor Party!," "War of Speed," "War of Annihilation," "Absoluteness," "Unconditionality," and so on, some of them hardly making sense.

Taller buildings began to appear as the car got closer to Pyong-yang. My guides proudly pointed at the new concrete pavements, Thousand League Horse Boulevard and Paradise Avenue, flanked by six-story buildings so alike that they might have been stamped out of the same mold.

"Residential apartments for our workers," they said.

Most unusual was their exterior finish, high gloss tile with large colorful designs, more appropriate for public baths or swimming pools. In consequence every building was a powerful reflector in the sun, zapping and blinding unwary eyes, but my captors didn't seem to notice. From every rooftop sprouted huge billboards praising Ilsung Kim as hero, patriot, and father of the land.

"Where are the people?" I asked, pointing at the deserted streets.

"They are at work," Joosong said, staring at me reproachfully. "Nobody has any business to be out and about on the street unless they are in the transportation industry. Our socialist republic has no loafers, loiterers, vagabonds, no homeless or unemployed."

He must know about the post-Vietnam army of homeless in the streets of New York, Los Angeles, or Seoul. We zipped right through town without stopping or slowing down. Out of the city, the car picked up speed even more, as if we were late for an important appointment. Then, about half an hour later, the vehicle careened into a side road, squealing and almost turning over. We whisked past a checkpoint, its keepers, armed and uniformed soldiers, standing well out of harm's way as they waved us through: the driver hadn't even slowed down. I suspected some kind of long-standing feud between driver and roadside sentry regarding each other's authority, the former scoring in the latest round. The road became narrower with sharper turns, forcing even our impetuous driver to decelerate.

Suddenly we were driving along the bank of a large reservoir, the sight of which took my breath away. The rippling surface had the most wonderful calming effect. What was it about a body of water that affects the spectator so deeply, if not our subconscious recognizing the home where our life had originated eons ago?

A massive concrete wall, topped by a barbed wire concertina, blocked our path. The gate was barred by a suspended traffic arm, painted white. From the shack emerged two sentries, guns drawn. After looking at us suspiciously, they separated, one coming to the driver's side, the other to the opposite, to eye each of us with the minutest attention, annoying our driver and my two other escorts no end, as they endured the scrutiny, swallowing their hurt pride. Finally, the barricade swung up and let us through. The long driveway, bordered by a lawn of trees, led to an elegant and dignified building quite unlike any of the eyesores I had seen in Pyongyang, as if from a different age or country.

"This is the guesthouse for foreign heads of state and other VIPs," Joosong explained. "You'll be staying here, compliments of our Beloved Comrade Leader Jungil Kim."

"Do I get to see him?" I asked.

"No," Mangee said. "Why do you want to see him?"

"Because I have questions he may be able to answer."

"You address all questions to us."

"Where is Nanyong Song?"

"Don't ask questions about other people," Joosong admonished. Before I was ready to retort that she was my better half, he reasoned, sententiously, "In our Republic every individual carries out his assigned tasks and has no curiosity beyond them."

"What are my assignments, then?"

"For now you are billeted here."

Mangee drove off, leaving me in care of Joosong, who proceeded to show me around. Entering at the front door one stepped on a tongue and groove hardwood floor, varnished honey gold. A door in the hall opened, revealing a spacious conference room, floor covered with black-trimmed red carpet, walls decorated with huge portraits of Ilsung and Jungil Kim, and a round table in the middle surrounded by arm chairs. The game room next door had a pool table and a few settings for card playing. On the opposite side of the hall stood the swinging doors to the dining room with tables and chairs as in a Western restaurant. There were also offices, a library, and a theater equipped with a movie projector, screen, and audio system that could easily pass for a state of the art recording studio in Manhattan. The wide staircase in the back, directly facing the front entrance, divided at the intermediate landing and doubled back upstairs to the corridors sided by individual guest rooms.

"This is yours," my guide said, opening a luxurious suite. The king-size bed had a head table, reading lamp, and a stereo and radio set, and the bathroom came with a deep tub, a sauna enclosed in fragrant cedar walls and glass door, and a lavatory with a marble top and sink, a huge mirror and a complete set of male toiletries.

"Don't drink from the tap," Joosong said, when I turned a handle.

"How do I drink then?"

"Drink from here," he said, pointing to a bottle marked Vitality Water with a cup next to it on the counter. "The tap water may be too strong for you."

Actually it was too strong even for the natives, because North Korean water supply, unfiltered and unchlorinated, was full of escheria coli, as I learned later, though Joosong didn't spell out the contents of his euphemism. Sold at a few outlets in town, the bottled water was consumed exclusively by the privileged classes. The ordinary citizens had to boil the tap water, unless they chose to take chances.

"Look over here," called Joosong, anxious to divert me from my shock over the undrinkable water, noisily opening drawers in the dresser and pointing at socks, shirts, underwear, cuff links, and nail cutters. "You'll find everything you need here."

"I know the shirts won't fit," I said. "I have to custom order all my shirts."

With a 17-inch neck and 32-inch arms, I had a short reach for a big man, a definite disadvantage if I were a boxer.

"Try them on. I bet they are your size."

"I will some other time," I said.

"No, try now," he insisted.

I yielded and was amazed at the fit.

"How did you find out?"

"We have ways of finding out. You are worth the trouble."

This information was both flattering and disturbing. I was used to being stared at in South Korea because of my Caucasian features, but this was like being stripped and examined in public. How much did Big Brother know about my intimate details?

"By the way can I have my passport back if you are through with it?"

"I don't know anything about it. However, I'll make inquiries."

"Let me have it back, because I may need it when I leave here."

"You just got here, so don't talk about leaving."

That was a rather transparent ploy to discover their intentions with me and of course didn't work. After a bath and a sauna, which seemed to thaw out all the aches and kinks out of my body, I climbed into bed between the clean sheets and didn't wake, until Joosong came to ask me to dinner. It was dark already and lights were on.

"Three waiters, three maids, two male chefs, one projectionist, and one chauffeur are on the staff exclusively to look after you," he said, coming downstairs, obviously expecting me to be impressed and grateful.

My unresponsiveness could have disappointed or even angered him but I didn't care. To be waited on hand and foot for such basic needs as eating and sleeping was not my idea of human dignity. As soon as we sat down at a table in the dining room, a bowl of nangmyon was placed before me.

"We know nangmyon is your favorite dish," he said triumphantly.

"It is," I said, approving.

One bite and I lost all appetite. The buckwheat noodles were soggy and didn't have the stringy chewiness when freshly prepared, belying the reputation of Pyongyang as the nangmyon capital. There were other dishes, some quite tasty, which however did not make up for the disappointment over the substandard nangmyon.

Back in my room, I indulged in another bath and sauna to shake off a touch of the chills and the fatigue that had seeped into the bones. I got in bed, expecting to fall asleep immediately as before, but sleep did not come. What did they really want of me and where was Nan? She must be all right, because I was all right. They must have her in safe keeping somewhere to spring on me as a surprise. Obviously, they didn't mean to harm me. They wouldn't, if they wanted me to help with their film program, as Samho had said. Only if he had impressed upon me the lengths to which they were prepared to go to secure that help, I would have saved all of us a lot of trouble. There was no need for resort to force. It wouldn't have taken much persuasion, either, because we were being stifled in South Korea. Even if Nan should balk at first for sentimental reasons, she would have come around in the end. Why did they kidnap her first instead of waiting for me a few days? Besides, with her in their power, they could have just told me so and I would have walked to Pyongyang, to hell, of my own accord. Because they didn't want to take chances? A typical case of bureaucratic paranoia and bungle! Now that the harm was done, they could right it by bringing us together as soon as possible, like tomorrow. Knowing the size of my shirt, they must also know how indispensable she was for my creativity and productivity, my very existence. We would have to be taken together or not at all. If they were serious about our help, they wouldn't keep us apart long. We were each other's inspiration, were awesome together. And she made it all possible.

XVII.
Assimilation

My first morning in North Korea was ushered in by Joosong's shouted invitation to breakfast in the dining room downstairs. Our entrance was greeted by the bright smile of a good-looking waitress, doing obeisance. I bowed in return, which turned out to be gratuitous.

"Have you had a good night's rest, Comrade Deputy Chief?" she asked, addressing my guide exclusively as she straightened herself. After all, he was a handsome man and a Deputy Chief to boot, though I had no idea how high a rank that was. The object of her interest acknowledged with a mere nod and a grunt. He could have been a little more gracious, but the more amazing thing was that the girl wasn't even aware of the slight and went merrily about her business of setting the table. Who said a Communist society was classless?

Though there were only two of us, at least ten seemed expected, judging from the spread of base dishes, sauces, relishes, condiments, kimchee, salted and preserved anchovies, dried fish, and so forth. A cart was wheeled up to the side of our table, displaying over 30 bottles of liquor and wine - American, European, Red Chinese, and a few North Korean brands such as Ganggay wine.

"What would you like to drink?" Joosong asked.

"I don't drink," I replied.

The effect the announcement produced on my auditor was something close to shock. His mouth opened in astonishment and did not close for a few seconds. Big Brother's research seemed way off here, because I had made no secret of my dislike for the substance, even to Junghee Park who drank whisky by the bottle and treated refusal to drink along with him as high treason. Maybe drinking was such an integral part of their life that the North Koreans assumed it universal. The main course arrived, a mixture of Korean, Chinese, and Western entrees, overwhelming by their quantity. Feeling no appetite, I asked for toast. Whether to spite me for my finickiness or from ignorance, what they brought was bread steamed, not toasted. I had to let go after a few heroic bites into the mush.

Back in my room after the meal I tinkered with the dials on the radio by the bedside and succeeded in locating South Korean broadcasts. Quickly I lowered the volume so it wouldn't be heard outside, in case it should constitute some kind of crime. Listening to the familiar programs I had the illusion of being still in Seoul. The TV didn't work at all during the day. At nightfall one channel flicked on, only to show singing and dancing by performers in military uniform.

"I must do something," I said to Joosong when I saw him next morning. "This indolence is killing me."

"This is not indolence," he corrected. "A period of retreat and contemplation is essential for your assimilation to our society."

"How long is that?"

"About a year."

"A year!" I shouted, unbelieving.

"At the minimum, that is," he qualified.

I stared at him, still unbelieving. It didn't make sense to idle me that long: the film was indifferent to the color or creed, even "ideology," of its handler.

"Don't I do any work in the meantime?"

"Read the books in the library!"

As if they were what one might properly call books. The holdings in the library were such pitiful stuff as Immortal History, Foothills of Mt. White Head (Baigdoo), March of Suffering, Crossing and Recrossing the Yalu (Amnog), all dedicated to the glorious leader and his family. Not a single book could be found on Marx, Lenin, or Mao Tsetung, let alone Tolstoy, Dickens, or other literary classics. After pretending to read a few pages, I put them back on the shelves.

The next day Joosong brought a book with a nice blue cover, entitled Compendium, said to be the textbook published by the Central Committee of the Party or Central Party for short.

"Read it and take notes," he said.

"Why don't you read it to me?" I said. "I can understand better that way."

"All right," he agreed with alacrity, for he was vain about his voice, a not unpleasant baritone, which however got raspy and shrill as he got carried away. But I didn't mind the distraction, because the material didn't deserve even desultory attention. The book claimed that as a third grader Ilsung Kim wrote a play called Joonggun Ahn Shoots Ito Hirobumi, which was performed at school with himself playing the lead. Ito Hirobumi was the Japanese foreign minister, instrumental in the annexation of Korea to Japan at the turn of the century, for which he had earned himself the undying hatred of Koreans. Patriot Joonggun Ahn followed him to Harbin, Manchuria, where Ito was meeting the Russian foreign minister, and shot him dead. Promptly caught and executed, Ahn becomes enshrined in the grateful memory of Koreans for generations to come. So moving was the play young Ilsung wrote that not a single eye was left dry at the end in the whole theater. At age 14 he crossed the Yalu and went over to Manchuria with only his school bag, swearing not to return until his fatherland regained independence. This coincided with the day the Korean Labor Party was born. Age 20 saw him as a major anti-Japanese resistance leader. Listening with eyes half closed, I wondered how they could even think of marketing such crude stuff totally lacking in plausibility. Suddenly the reading stopped.

"Sit up and pay attention with eyes wide open," Joosong shouted. "Your posture is all wrong."

"But I can concentrate better, sitting more relaxed."

"Nonsense. What you look is what you are. Sit up straight

as I told you and take notes."

Mercifully, there was lunch and a two-hour siesta, instituted since the Vietnam War, I was told, in which North Korea had allegedly fought on the side of the victorious Viet Cong, to counterbalance the sizable presence of South Korean mercenaries in the employ of the US. The siesta was mandatory and enforced nationally, which was probably necessary considering how late at night everybody had to work, often past midnight, as I found out.

The moronic reading routine resumed. The passages now dealt with the Selfhood Doctrine promulgated by Ilsung Kim adapting Marxism and Leninism to the realities of Korea. More concretely, it called for political independence, economic self-sufficiency, and military readiness. The whole doctrine was so trite that I wondered how it could be elevated to the status of a distinct national policy and ideology. But then what dogmas were free from inanity?

When Joosong came to the end of a chapter, I ventured to ask about Nan again, though I had been rebuffed before.

"On the ship that took me here a Party worker told me that Nanyong Song was shot to death by South Korean CIA as a collaborator of the National Unification Front. Can you comment on that?"

"No, because I know nothing about it."

"She is here, isn't she?"

"Why do you keep pestering me with that line of questioning? I told you I don't know."

Joosong shouted so loud that the maid came running in fright, thinking she had been called for something she had done wrong. After sending her packing with another fierce shout, he faced me squarely, face reddened and swollen, lips quivering, fists clenched. I thought he would take a swing at me for sure but he gained control of himself by degrees. I had no idea he would be so exercised. I decided to leave the subject alone, but began to really worry about her now. Obviously my hosts had a different time table than mine about bringing us together. Was I wrong in supposing that she was all right? If they treated me like a VIP because of my film expertise which they hoped to exploit, they should bring us together, the best working pair. The sooner the better, because unemployment was that much loss to all the parties concerned. It simply didn't make sense that they should procrastinate our reunion if it was feasible. What if she was really dead? I shuddered at the thought and violently rejected it. On the other hand, she might have been kidnapped and added to Ilsung Kim's harem. "I will kill the bastard," I swore furiously, though I didn't know how to go about such a task in the strange limbo I was in.

"Don't be angry, Deputy Chief," I said in conciliation. "She is my sweetheart."

"Let's call it a day," he said, stomping out of the room, unmollified.

A few days after that outburst Joosong put me in the black chauffeur-driven Benz that was a fixture of the guesthouse and took me on a guided tour. The first on the schedule was a bronze statue of a young couple on a winged horse prancing skyward from a base 20 meters high. If the statue itself did not affect me much because I wasn't a connoisseur of plastic form exactly, its location on the hill top met with my total approval as it commanded a good view of Pyongyang and the countryside to the north.

"It is the Thousand League Horse of the legend capable of running a thousand leagues a day," Joosong explained. "The statue commemorates our Great Leader's call on all of us to work like the Thousand League Horse to restore and rehabilitate our country devastated by the War to Liberate the Fatherland."

That was the official designation of the Korean War.

"The Americans destroyed everything in sight with their barbarous bombings and shellings," he added, "but the will and energy of the people united under our Great Leader has made our fatherland a model of industrial and technological progress throughout the world."

Though bursting with pride over its achievements, he let slip the admission that such a simple task as mounting the bronze statue on its base had presented almost insurmountable problems because North Korea did not have cranes or jacks heavy duty enough to do the job.

The next stop was another immense statue on a concrete base overlooking a scenic bend of the Daydong River. Glistening gold, it showed Ilsung Kim in a traditional Korean tunic, his right hand waving a red flag above the heads of a large crowd. This was the famous Longevity Lookout, the highest point in Pyongyang.

"Is it solid gold?" I asked.

"No, gold electroplated. It's 25 meters high, 3 meters higher than the sphinx of Egypt."

The guide stationed there made us stand at attention and bow deep at his shouted signal to the gilded figure of the Leader. Leading us around the statue he broke into a passionate oration about "our Great Leader Ilsung Kim fighting the Japanese imperialists for the liberation of the fatherland...." His voice in falsetto quivering, eyes filling up with tears, he cut such a pathetically comical figure that I could barely suppress laughter.

We returned to the guesthouse for lunch and siesta. At 5 p.m., which was not the close of the day but the beginning of another full day within the day, Mangee showed up at the hotel to join his friend in escorting me and resuming the interrupted tour. I dreaded the prospect of another statue, but this time it was the Longevity Art Theater. The remarkable frequency of "longevity" in the nomenclature of practically every public object argued only one thing: the aging dictator's preoccupation with mortality. He had eliminated all possible competition and feared no coup or other man-made calamity that might undo him, except prosaic death by age or sickness that cut down the lowliest peasant as well as the mightiest conqueror. What if in his frustration to get the Herb of Immortality Emperor Chin of China had quested in vain, the latter-day emperor of North Korea should decide to destroy the rest of the world by setting off a nuclear bomb? There seemed no effective safeguard against such dementia in autocracies dependent on a single man's absolute power, to whom devices of mass destruction were so readily available thanks to modern science and technology.

The performance in progress was by the North Korean orchestra that was soon to leave for Red China on a goodwill mission. A symphony was followed by violin solos, string quartets, vocal solos and choruses. They sounded quite good, notwithstanding my expectations to the contrary. The auditorium was filled except for the front rows in the middle, where one man sat enjoying a wide berth. Some bureaucrat, I thought, whose importance however became manifest soon enough. Whenever he clapped, those in the back clapped, too, but when he did not, nobody dared to show any reaction, pro or con.

As soon as the concert was over, blown-up images of Ilsung Kim and Jungil Kim flashed across the screen in front of the curtain. The lone government inspector stood up and the whole theater rose from their seats. At the same time the entire cast of the orchestra left their chairs and climbed on the stage to face the audience and shout, "Long live our Beloved Comrade Leader!" Next moment, to my total surprise, these venerable-looking musicians, in their 50's and 60's, began jumping up and down like little bunnies. Waving to the left and right in acknowledgment of this demonstration, the government censor left the auditorium. But the shouting and hopping continued for a few minutes even after his exit.

"Who was he?" I asked.

"Our Beloved Comrade Leader Jungil Kim," Joosong said, scandalized by my ignorance.

"Who are the others?" I asked, pointing at the audience, still unable to get over my feeling of outrage and embarrassment at the degree of debasing adulation the orchestra and audience were prepared to stoop to as a matter of course.

"All Labor Party cadre. This art theater has only VIPs as clientele," he said, obviously expecting me to be impressed by the exalted company I kept. But they might as well be manikins, devoid of emotion or thought, because I could not get near them, shake their hands, or talk to them. I was quarantined, kept at a safe distance from them, with Joosong and Mangee standing or sitting between us like a shield.

After the crowd had left, I was introduced to the Director

who personally led us on a tour, showing off the stage equipment imported from Japan, and the recorder, projector, and other machinery and parts imported from West Germany. Nobody seemed to notice the inconsistency of such wholesale reliance on foreign goods, especially from capitalistic countries, with the declared Selfhood doctrine calling for economic self-sufficiency. The theater had a separate TV broadcasting room for the Longevity Channel, again "all built and installed by West German technicians." The Director went on to boast that the theater took only a year to complete.

"Nobody would believe construction on this scale would take only a year," he added. "But the staff at the Soviet Embassy behind the theater knows, because they have watched it go up from the ground up, something they couldn't dream of accomplishing in a million years."

So North Korea openly bashed its big brother Russia across the border. In spite of his patriotic pride I couldn't help noticing a hairline crack running down the back wall, which could be the first sign of structural failure. I peered anxiously at the vaulted ceiling over a hundred feet across, unsupported by any column, and fought the impulse to run out, ducking the hurtling debris of steel and concrete as the whole roof broke apart and crashed down over our heads. On the other hand, it could be imperfect curing, structurally harmless. They must have engineers who checked out these things before occupancy and periodically afterwards. Or did they? Oh, well, if Jungil Kim spent whole hours in it, who was I to be concerned?

It was already dark when we came outside, just in time to see a changing of the guard, goose-stepping off, swinging their arms, past the spectacular fountain in the square before the theater, the plumes rising as high as the building, lit in dazzling, kaleidoscopic rainbow colors. They really knew how to keep that show going right.

"I have some more matters to attend to here," said Mangee, dismissing Joosong and me and re-entering the theater.

I hoped there would be more sightseeing but was disappointed. My education in the Ilsung Kim lore resumed next morning, solid two hours going into the so-called 'studies,' those wretched books glorifying the founding father of the land.

However, there was a variation. After the siesta two movies were shown, one Korean and the other Russian, with the prefatory remark, "personally selected by our Beloved Comrade Leader Jungil Kim." My first reaction was incredulity. Both countries made films with total disregard for the audience. Allusion, implication, subtlety were unknown concepts. One and the same theme, subordination of the individual to the Communist state, was articulated and reiterated loudly and at tedious length, in strict adherence to the philosophy: quantity makes quality. The majority consisted of two parts, but some ran on for 20 parts, each part two hours long. If one made films like this in South Korea or anywhere in the West, he would be out on the street in no time. I began to reappreciate the virtue of accountability to the paying public. At least it kept these indecent blimps off the market.

"Why do you pamper me with food and movies like a child?" I asked one day.

"The movies are not for fun," Joosong replied acidly. "They are for your education and edification."

"They don't teach me anything."

"Because you have the wrong attitude."

There were exceptions, however, like the Soviet film, The 41st, a masterful treatment of the conflict between love and duty, made in the post-Khrushchev era of defreeze. After shooting 40 rounds, deliberately wide, at a White Army officer bearing an important message to his regiment, Mariotka, a woman partisan and sharpshooter, captures and escorts him to the Red Army Headquarters. Shipwrecked at an island on the way, Mariotka falls in love with her prisoner, an educated aristocrat, who tells her about Robinson Crusoe she has never heard of before. One day a ship approaches, a White Army ship, and he runs to it, shouting, in spite of her warning. She shoots the 41st and final round that kills him and is overcome with grief. It was singularly moving, proof that art will blossom in any clime or soil, however unlikely the subject matter. But my admiration seemed to shrivel at my mentor's chilling observation: "Pay close attention to the moral: no mercy to the traitor even if he may be a lover."

The North Korean film Sea of Blood was an outstanding portrayal of the resourceful Korean woman in adversity. The heroine's family crosses the border into Manchuria fleeing Japanese colonial oppression in Korea but the Japanese police execute her husband for his subversive activities. Her young son is also murdered by the Japanese for not betraying a partisan hiding in their house. One day, hired by the village alderman, she carries a letter to the Japanese police but is intercepted by partisans, who discover that the alderman is accusing her and others of sedition, a capital crime, in the very letter she is to deliver. In picking her as messenger of her own death the alderman had counted on her illiteracy. Chagrined and burning with revenge, she learns to read and write to become an effective partisan herself.

"I like the picture better than any," I told Joosong when asked for my opinion. "The sequence showing her, a woman past her prime, struggling with the alphabet is quite affecting. But the music and dialogue seem to work against the emotional current of the drama. Moreover, like other films it suffers from the basic problem, overt didacticism, which thwarts its potential to touch the hearts of the audience. Why don't you explore other themes that should be moving as well as educational?"

"For example?"

"Love would be one. However anxious you may be to impress the importance of revolution on the people, add the element of love, which makes the Soviet film Fortyfirst Shot so much more powerful."

Dispensing such basic suff, I half anticipated Joosong to explode in anger at my audacity of mentioning a theme like love, perhaps considered decadent and taboo in the spartan culture of North Korea. He remained a full minute in thought, betraying no hint of his reaction. Knowing his temper, I expected anything. He had asked for advice and I had given it to him. If he was too sensitive for even that degree of candor, I might as well clam up and never say a word, however he might prod for advice. Communists just never meant what they said. Fortunately, there was no blowup this time, just brooding.

I asked for and was granted the incorporation of exercise into my daily routine. They let me walk along the trails in the woods near the house, provided two or three on the domestic staff went along. I welcomed their company, pretty and personable young women in their early 20's. But I noticed a bleached look in their faces, caused by excessive use of face powder without foundational cream. The primal motive, to attract and lure the opposite sex, operated as powerfully here in Communist paradise as elsewhere, except it had miscarried in this instance.

On one occasion I asked them if they had seen a beautiful lady with a Jolla accent, describing Nan. Their answer was unanimously negative. Nor were they being untruthful, either. In this isolated society, where lateral communication was nil, one simply never learned anything beyond one's immediate surroundings. A byproduct of this inquiry was the discovery that there was no anti-Jolla prejudice here. These young women, born a decade or more after Korea's division in 1945, had nothing to relate to Jolla as a province. Even between the provinces of the north, Pyongan and Hamgyong, I couldn't detect any sign of conflict: the radical resettlement program carried out on a national scale to cauterize local or other attachments that might intrerfere with undivided Ilsung Kim allegiance had done away with regionalism of the kind seen in the south, except for a universal desire to live in Pyongyang, the capital, where the aristocracy lived. If any still survived, it didn't function in the invidious, virulent fashion as in the south: poverty and fear of the central government had a wonderfully equalizing effect.

"Do you live in Pyongyang?" I asked.

"No, in the country," the prettiest of them answered regretfully. "We are teachers at nurseries in the country and were suddenly called by the Party to work here."

They hoped that this selection, a compliment to their good looks, engaging personality, and Party loyalty, would eventually lead to permanent residence in Pyongyang.

My relaxed attitude and tone and more probably my foreign face must have disarmed them to come forward with as much confidence as they did. I was the stranger on a train they chanced to sit next to but would never meet again and need not fear for possible repercussions.

"Where are we?" I asked.

"Chestnut Grove," they replied, "named after the many chestnut trees growing all around."

Beyond that, untraveled strangers themselves, they had no idea whether we were south or north of Pyongyang. Everyday I tried to walk a total of 20 miles, measuring my speed to see how well I did in one hour on level ground and uphill, respectively, so I would be in shape to escape when a suitable opportunity presented itself. The thought of escape had come to my head as naturally as old hat. My life had been one long series of escapes from all those little prisons that had tried but couldn't hold me, Mercy Home, Lingga Island, Blue House. In comparison, Chestnut Grove should be a piece of cake. But soon realities disabused me. For one, I no longer had the boundless, reckless physical energy of early youth. My body lacked the stamina, maybe forever compromised by the repeated abuses it was subjected to - the starvations, deprivations, beatings in its formative years, the frostbite that nearly killed it or rather did kill so it got reborn as John Heyman, the gas inhalations, ether at the hands of my hosts lately, anthracite fume before that.

Even the modest ambulatory goal I had set myself at Chestnut Grove proved too much. Age and decrepitude had crept up on me unawares. Mistaking the fast pace of my work for exercise and equating my youthful figure and slimness with fitness I had never conceded I was getting old and flabby like everybody else. Nevertheless I was determined to build my body up again and make a run for it whenever there was the slightest chance. I owed them nothing, my North Korean captors, however obliging they might be with room and board. Until their supreme offense of kidnap was redressed, everything they did from here on only compounded their culpability.

One day I was chewing a caramel when I bit a piece of metal. The sticky candy had pulled the gold crown right off the anchoring stub of tooth. My guardians had me taken to the Flame Hospital near the Common Gate in Pyongyang for treatment. Except for the soldiers on sentry duty I didn't see lines of patients that should crowd a hospital at this time in midmorning. Later I learned that this was the hospital for the families of the Politburo members and Party chiefs. The Director of the hospital received me cordially enough and suggested a general physical, as well as the necessary dental work. Accordingly I was herded through all the departments, internal medicine, ophthalmology, neuropsychiatry, pathology. The facilities, up to date and clean, seemed to go to waste for lack of patronage. The party cadre must have extremely healthy families or the hospital was closed for the day to shield me from public view, which did not make sense. The dentist reattached the crown using equipment manufactured by Siemens of West Germany.

"How do you feel about getting free medical and dental care in the socialist fatherland?" Joosong asked on our way back.

I couldn't reply, struck by the aptness of the Korean saying satirizing a doctor who "makes a person sick to prescribe the cure." Though he stressed the word free, the medical picture of North Korea, as I learned later, was far from being as rosy as he had described. There was no doctor at the primary level, village or myon. Only a medical assistant recklessly prescribed herbal medicine. To hide the unavailability of modern medicine, such as antibiotics and vaccines, its effectiveness was publicly vilified: Western medicine didn't agree with Korean physiology and caused too many side effects. If not cured at the primary level, one went to the county hospital, which was so crowded that people generally ended up buying medicine privately. For the Party cadre, however, medical care was abundantly available as at the Flame Hospital. No wonder Ilsung and Jungil's close associates, enjoying all these privileges, should show absolute loyalty and unquestioning obedience.

Timing myself on my daily walk, I realized that my first priority was a map. The one in the encyclopedia at the library was too small to be of any use. Moreover, the encyclopedia was not complete, publication having stopped after the first volumes filled with the lore of Ilsung Kim and his genealogy, k in Kim being the first letter in the Korean alphabet. No other encyclopedia existed in North Korea than this one, published with the blessings of the Central Party. The implication of the bobtailed encyclopedia was clear: knowledge began and ended with Ilsung Kim. A cursory perusal of its pages demonstrated that even this knowledge was fiction of the most fantastic kind than fact.

Apparently he had visited every corner of North Korea in person and effected, single-handed, not only Korea's liberation from Japan but also the country's post-war recovery and progress. He did the latter, for example, through grassroots personal visits to every North Korean village and township, called "hands-on local guidance". The number of local guidance encounters was astronomical, requiring perhaps an army of Ilsung Kim clones, but nobody, least of all the editors of the encyclopedia, seemed to be aware of the absurdity. No matter. I eagerly devoured the articles describing the alleged trips because of the accompanying drawings and maps so as to obtain a workable composite of North Korea. I was soon disappointed. The maps, too schematic or too detailed and fragmented, were not to scale and did not interrelate with each other. Nevertheless I studied them closely every night, filling in the missing joints and contours and working out an escape route.

It was August. Cicadas chirped noisily in the dark green foliage outside. I had been in North Korea over six months already. With the escape plan firmly in mind, I wanted to see as much of North Korea as possible and importuned the Deputy Chief to take me sightseeing, which had stopped after the two statues and Art Theater. Finally the green light came through and I was taken to Panoramic Viewpoint, the birthplace of Ilsung Kim, Revolutionary Museum, Memorial to the Victory of the War to Liberate the Fatherland,

Agricultural and Industrial Exhibition Center, and the like, all monuments to the idolization and deification of Ilsung Kim.

The Museum of the Korean Revolution, completed in 1972 to celebrate Ilsung's 60th birthday, stood 6 stories high and housed 90 exhibit rooms with a total floor space of 50,000 square meters on a lot about 20 acres wide atop Longevity Lookout. The front of the building above the central entrance was mounted by a colossal representation in multicolored marble of the sacred White Head Mountains. The porch, supported by two columns reaching clear to the roof, was also in massive marble on a lavish scale. The museum was always crowded, but on the day of our visit the congestion was quite extreme even by the museum's standards. Some 40 student and worker groups happened to be visiting from different parts of the country at the same time, which forced my guides, apparently under orders to conceal me from public view, to extraordinary expedients, ducking in and out of side doors ordinarily locked.

Against the wall facing the entrance to the main lobby stood a sculpture of Ilsung Kim sitting on a pedestal, flanked by artificial pines, before which every visitor had to bow. At the entrance to the first exhibition hall hung a huge map of Korea dotted with little bulbs that lit up to indicate the location as a tape recording narrated his revolutionary activities. The Ilsung Kim saga went back to his great grandfather Ungwoo Kim, who had allegedly burned and sunk the American imperialist pirate ship Sherman, a merchant marine that had sailed up the Daydong in 1866 looking for trade. This event was celebrated as the first landmark victory in the century-old or longer history of struggle against imperialism. A big oil canvas depicted Ungwoo directing a crowd to load up barges with firewood, to be torched and towed to the stranded Sherman, a distinctly unheroic motif for a combat in my estimation, yet elevated to a historic moment for the nation. The next rooms traced the revolutionary accomplishments of Ilsung's grandfather Bohyon and his father Hyongjig. The remaining 80 or more rooms presented in chronological order the brilliant revolutionary work of the

Great Leader himself.

As a boy of 7 during the independence uprising of March 1, 1919, a sacred date for Korea, South included, Ilsung allegedly took part in the long march to Pyongyang alongside the adults shouting independence. This picture was followed by another in which his mother gives the young boy two pistols bequeathed by his father when he died, the future leader listening attentively to his father's deathbed testament and will as conveyed through his mother's lips. Photograph after photograph detailed every stage of Ilsung's maturation. But, surely, they were photographs of later dramatizations, using actors and actresses, with recent camera technology, unknown in the '20's, though passed off as the real thing on the unsuspecting public, just like the two pistols, enshrined in a glass cage under the picture, purporting to be those very ones Ilsung received on that momentous occasion so long ago, though obtainable for a few bucks maybe at a pawnshop. But, then, the same kind of hoax was common practice in the early newsreels of the US, staging a trench war in Europe or a volcanic eruption in the Caribbean, as the case may be, in the back lot of their New York studio.

Not content with creating its own domain, fiction set out to invade and alter fact. The spaces between the pictures displayed scraps from the Donga Ilbo and other dailies, allegedly published in Seoul to report Ilsung's achievements. For example, a newspaper photograph showed a big crowd at Seoul Railroad Station on August 15, 1945, the day of the country's liberation from Japan, waving banners and placards that read "Long Live General Ilsung Kim." In reality, as an examination of the back issues will verify, the original had read "Long Live Korean Independence" with no mention of Ilsung Kim, alias Sungjoo Kim, 34 years old, formerly a major in the Korean Brigade of the Soviet Red Army, who nobody had heard of at the time either in South or North Korea.

On the way to the War Memorial Museum, dedicated to the Memory of the Victory in the War to Liberate the Fatherland, a massive building located on Victory Road in the heart of Pyongyang, Joosong repeated his admonition to "pay close attention to the exhibits memorializing our destruction of American imperialism and South Korean puppetry under our Great Leader's guidance."

We were met by an officer guide in his 50's, who took us to a black and white picture and shouted, "Look at the Yankee son-of-bitches surrendering with a white flag."

Indeed the American military jeep displayed a white flag, but this was to mark it as the jeep transporting the American delegation to the Armistice Conference held in Gaysong in North Korean territory, before Panmoonjum in the no-man's land became the permanent site for further armistice talks. Out of context it served the guide's interpretation excellently. He went on to accuse the US and South Korea of launching a deliberate and premeditated attack on peaceful North Korea at daybreak on June 25, 1950. So this was still the official line, that the south, not the north, had started it. How, then, did they square it with the other official line that called the war "a war to liberate the south from US imperialism"? As evidence of the long preparation and conspiracy for invasion by the US and South Korea the guide pointed at a blown-up photograph showing US Secretary of State John Foster Dulles and Korean Defense Minister Songmo Shin on a tour of inspection at the 38th Parallel on June 24, 1950, South Korean soldiers in camouflaged combat fatigues of US make pointing their M1's and carbines northward in their bunkers, another supreme example of decontextualization.

After the Museum we were on Liberation Boulevard, an artery of Pyongyang. Again I was struck by the light traffic, seldom more than two or three vehicles in the entire stretch of road at one time. Our car stopped at the Common Gate Subway Station, dome-shaped with thick concrete walls. Following my guides, I took the sets of down escalators that kept going down to the bowels of the earth, literally, for they were laid at depths in excess of 150 meters.

"We are safe here even in a nuclear war," Joosong said.

I almost asked him if he really knew what he was talking about, fallout, environmental pollution, genetic mutation, but forbore. There was no question that it was the cleanest subway

I had ever seen. The trains were kept in mint condition without any graffiti or litter, still a distressing memory from my days in New York and Washington, D.C. This was not surprising considering the small number of passengers that made use of it, at least at the time we were there. In fact, more people were employed running the system than riding it. Every train had three or four women who did nothing but wipe off fingerprints from windows or door knobs. Most remarkable was the great number of chandeliers hanging like stalactites from the ceiling. Both Ilsung Kim and Jungil Kim had a passion for chandeliers and fountains, which were therefore apt to pop up wherever feasible. The fountain might be a problem to squeeze into a subway, but the chandelier was perfect. As a result the gawdy monstrosities hung from the ceiling as many as could be fitted in. The floor, walls, and supporting columns were all marble. Instead of the ads that cluttered the walls of a New York subway, every available space was covered by mosaics of the Great Leader and Chief. The piper had to be paid one way or the other.

The station guide seated me and Joosong in the special coach attached to the engine. Noticeable was the white slip cover over a seat ahead of us.

"That's where our Great Comrade Leader and Chief has once sat," the guide said.

By now I was immunized to such criminal waste and absurdity.

"Where are the passengers?" I asked.

"It's not the rush hour yet."

I seriously doubted that these immaculate cars ever filled up to capacity even during the rush hour.

As months passed without any indication of what they intended to do with me, I grew restless and asked Joosong again to arrange a meeting with his boss Jungil Kim.

"He is too busy to see you," he answered after staring at me a long time as if he couldn't get over my effrontery. "He'll see you in good time, after a period of education to assimilate you to our Republic. What will you talk to him about if you should see him?"

Were they serious about brainwashing me with the kind of crude and transparent method they had been using on me? So this good-looking but cerebrally stunted Deputy Chief must be an intellectual, psychological hotshot chosen to remake me. Let them keep their illusions. The first thing I would have asked Jungil would be what he had done with Nan, but remembering Joosong's irritation with the subject, I decided to skip it. He glared at me for not answering, but I didn't care.

I maintained my daily jog up and down the hill, measuring my speed and endurance, always in the company of one or two on the domestic staff. One day, however, nobody was waiting for me at the entrance. I made enough noise to announce my departure, but nobody came out to follow. Maybe it was a chore they would rather do without. I began climbing the hill in back of the guesthouse to see how far uphill the fence extended from this lower end near the reservoir. The incline became steeper but the fence, now of barbed wire nailed on posts, kept rising with it, until at the very top it dipped as the ground did, a Wall of China that circled the whole mountain. What was even more disconcerting was the presence of guards patrolling the entire perimeter at short intervals. They must be gotten out of the way by some diversion before I could scale or break through the fence. Explosive ordnance would do the trick, like a grenade, which could be tripwired. Even some rounds of rifle ammunition would do, because I could shake out the powder and rig a detonation device with a battery and wire or a kerosene-dipped fuse. I had picked up bits and pieces about ordnance from the dozens of war movies and documentaries I had made. But the question was where I could steal them. The soldiers would be instantly suspicious of my approach. Maybe I should resort to the primitive method of setting fire with dry twigs, laced with kerosene, which shouldn't be that hard to come by.

"Can I have a bicycle?" I asked one day.

"Why?" Joosong said.

"For exercise."

"Isn't walking enough?"

"It gets boring. A bike would be fun."

"I'll see what I can do," he said, like a parent harried by a child ever clamoring for new toys.

The bike came, a Japanese-made ten speeder, which I rode around the compound, growing more confident in the feasibility of escape with this added resource at my disposal. Apart from my own real life experiences, I had directed several escape sequences in the movies and felt sure of success. I would sneak out of the house in the middle of the night after everybody went to bed, push the bike to the hill top avoiding the men on watch, cut through the wire fence using the file attached to my nail cutter, and run or bike as the terrain permitted, putting as much distance between me and the compound as possible by night, then hide and sleep behind a bush, under a culvert, or in a barn during the day. Exit from North Korea was to be by either of the two alternatives. One was to hitch a ride on a Shinujoo-bound night train from Pyongyang, get off at Soonchon, head north for the Yalu River past Gaychon and Ganggay, then cross the river at Manpo to Manchuria, where by hitchhiking at night on trains and hiding during the day, I would work my way to Hong Kong somehow. The other was to go to the White Head Mountains, kayak down the Tumen (Dooman in Korean), cross over to Russia at Moopo and continue on to Nahotka via Vladivostok, courtesy of the Trans-Siberian, then find the Japanese consulate and petition for asylum and passage out of Siberia to the Free World.

After supper one day I went up to my room and turned out the light, pretending to go to bed early. A little after 8 p.m. the housekeeper, a woman in her late twenties, opened the door of my bedroom, confirmed my being in bed, and bade goodnight, as was her custom. As far as I knew, she did not return in the middle of the night to check me out. Immediately after she left, I kicked the sheet off and swung off the bed, undid the lids in the back of the radio and stereo, and extracted the food I had been storing - biscuits, candies, rice cakes, dried anchovies. I waited a few minutes, trying to calm my pounding heart. Nothing stirred in the pitch dark night. The whole world seemed to be holding its breath. I groped downstairs, food bag in hand, tiptoed to the conference room, and listened for any talking or snoring, before pushing the door open and entering. A window behind the sofa yielded noiselessly to my push. My body still had enough agility and I vaulted over the sill to the ground below. I looked for my bike but it was not where I had left it, nor anywhere else. Somebody must have figured out my intentions with it and might be watching me at that very moment. My hair stood on end, momentarily expecting a blinding search light to turn on and a barrage of gunfire to shred me. The wisest thing was to retreat to my room as if nothing had happened, but my feet seemed glued to the ground. With perspiration and effort I took steps towards the window, pulled myself up into the house, and crawled upstairs. Putting the food back in its old storages I lay down in bed, swallowing tears of disappointment.

One day, playing with the radio dial, I caught a news cast from South Korea. I had missed the first part, but I could tell it was about my disappearance, somewhere in Japan where my passport had been discovered, the reporter said. So that's why they had hung on to my passport. The motive was clear: North Korea didn't want both Nan and me to vanish in Hong Kong. Japan was a good choice because it was where Daejung Kim had been abducted and South Korean CIA might be suspected of foul play again. This firmed my plan to flee to Vladivostok or Nahotka in search of the Japanese consulate.

"May I have a map of the peninsula and Manchuria?" I asked Joosong the next day.

"Why?"

"I want to look up the places where the Leader had fought the Japanese."

"The Great Leader," he corrected me. "Don't ever omit the honorific."

"All right, the Great Leader."

The map he brought, published on the 30th anniversary of the Korean Labor Party, was too simplistic, indicating only those places of Manchuria where Ilsung was allegedly active. Nevertheless I was excited to confirm the relative position of Domoon on the Korean side of the Tumen, from which my river-crossing to Russia was planned. The only problem with this route was that as I got close to Domoon I would have to negotiate several high mountains, including the White Head, the highest peak in Korea with an elevation of nearly 9,000 feet. Even if the food problem could be solved, by pilfering from homes on the way for example, those mountains might be perilous with steep cliffs and ferocious beasts like tigers and wolves for which the northern country was famous. I looked wistfully southward to the DMZ, heavily guarded and sown with land mines, and therefore ruled out from consideration previously.

It was September, the season of clear blue skies and cool refreshing breezes after the humid summer months. Out on my usual walk after supper one evening I happened to pass a corn field and remembered that Ilsung Kim had survived, according to legend, on one ear of corn a day during his guerrilla days. Quickly I broke off a few ripe ears, husked them, then popped the kernels off the cobs for even distribution among my pockets, so no bulge would show. In my room I emptied the pockets and trasferred the corn to the inside of the radio and stereo cabinets. It would take many more trips like that to garner enough provision for the many days or weeks on the run.

Temperature plummeted, giving a foretaste of the winter. The fallen leaves crackled underfoot, whispering death and desication. I stood for hours watching the V-shaped formation of migratory birds flying southward. The dark surface of the reservoir in the distance was a void symbolizing my utter hopelessness.

My light summer clothes were no protection to the chilling weather and I welcomed the tailor who brought materials to make my winter clothing. I ordered two suits, black and brown. For an overcoat I selected gray camel fur, which would serve me in good stead, should I escape via Red China where gray was the dominant winter color. In addition orders were placed for a kerchief, hat, and boots. The Soviet style hat had a visor and pull-down flaps for ear muffs.

My food program added to the pile chocolate bars and

walnuts handed out at movie time. One day I opened the radio cabinet to check on my granary of corn and was dismayed to find the kernels sprouting from the heat of the transistors. I should have dried them first. Plainly the corn was useless and had to be all junked, but its great quantity presented a problem. I began flushing little amounts down the toilet, but either the piping was inadequate or the corn had swollen inside the pipes. The toilet got plugged up in no time and would not flush. Using my hands as a makeshift plunger I managed to unclog but had to go easy on the flushing, only a few grains at a time. The harvest was almost over and I would not get another chance to secure a supply of corn. I decided to resume filching at siesta time when all activity ceased for two hours. From the kitchen I lifted handfuls of ordinary and glutinous rice, as well as salt and boxes of matches. For utensils I gathered empty cans. The ceramic bowls on the kitchen shelves were definitely unsuitable for the intended trip.

I eagerly waited for the winter cold to freeze the rivers, so I would not have to swim them when I should make the break. One day the KBS news cast said South Korea was willing to open diplomatic negotiations with Red China, following the rapprochement between that country and the US. In January next year the US was to open an Embassy in Beijing, which meant that I wouldn't have to travel too far for my freedom. To see what kind of protection the winter clothes and boots gave me, I slept in them one night on the concrete deck outside the room and found it feasible, though uncomfortable. I did not catch cold even, except for a headache and a sniffle in the morning.

My study of the maps suggested a northern route - a drive by car to Jungjoo, then hitchhiking on a train to Goosung, Sangjoo, and Soopoong where the dam was astride the Yalu. The driver of the Benz at my guesthouse always left the key in the ignition. After supper he played sotta from 8 to 11 with the movie projectionist, cook, and maids, never even so much as looking out. Car theft was unknown in North Korea. Simply there was no market for stolen cars, because nobody drove, except a few specially trained professionals. The road sloped downward from where it was parked all the way to the gate and the car could coast to the shore of the lake on neutral. Those in the room would not hear a thing. During the three hours the driver sat at his cards I figured I could reach Jungjoo, where the car would be pushed over the bank of a nearby reservoir and I would start going on foot. From the encyclopedias I had studied I could put together a detailed map of the Jungjoo area and could visualize the reservoir fringed by cliffs as if I had lived there for years. Reservoirs were just about everywhere, closely guarded, to ensure local irrigation and water supply. No wonder guesthouses and villas requiring security were located next to them, to kill two birds.

The South Korean broadcast played Christmas carols, overwhelming me with nostalgia. There was no further delaying my departure. I tied a pair of pants at the ankles and stuffed both legs with the food I had been hoarding. The result was like an inflated life jacket, which could be worn slung over the shoulders. The space under the sofa in the living room, never disturbed by a broom as far as I could see, would serve as the hiding place. All I had to do was wait for the reservoir to freeze, for then it would be cold enough for the rivers to freeze too.

In the meantime I watched the movies diligently and pretended to write serious commentaries from the socialist point of view. Pleased at this change of attitude, Joosong asked me one day to write a New Year's message of congratulations to the Great Beloved Comrade Leader. I wrote down Happy New Year in my best calligraphy, in classical Chinese.

"What is this?"

"New Year's greetings."

"In our Republic we have discontinued the use of Chinese, according to our Selfhood Principle."

Indeed that was commendable. With the most scientific phonetic alphabet in the world there was no need to incorporate Chinese characters into writing, as they still did in South Korea.

"All right. I did out of habit. I'll write out in our script only."

"Still that kind of stereotyped, formal greeting is not enough. We need a long letter, expressing genuine good wishes from the bottom of your heart."

"Can you show me a sample?"

"Sure."

He brought and set out before me a published collection of congratulatory letters written for the various holidays, April 15, Double 9, and New Year's Day. Amazingly, some were by foreign visitors, students from Africa learning Selfhood and crews of ships that had docked in North Korean ports. How these total strangers to the language could have come up with such compositions, with modifiers pages long, piling one superlative after another, which took 10 minutes just to read, was beyond my imagination, though the incongruity didn't seem to bother the publishers a bit. Among the various domestic masterpieces one stood out, the one written by Ilsung Kim's niece's husband, Party Ideologue Minsang Yoon.

"Dear Comrade Chief Ilsung Kim, the great ideologist and theorist, creator of the eternal and immortal Selfhood Principle which shines high and bright in human history, illustrious iron general of hundreds and hundreds of battles, leading to victory the two revolutionary wars opposing Japanese and American imperialism, and great strategist of revolution who has restored light to the fatherland and set a shining example for all nations in their struggle to liberate themselves from colonialism and lead the world to revolution...."

That was just for openers. I tried but could not get over the nausea at such fulsome, naked, barbarous flattery. Did grown-up men do such things in earnest? As I copied, my own style of writing, South Korean spelling and phraseology, kept creeping in unawares, which Joosong caught each time and made me write over on a new sheet of paper. My hands and arms ached from the labor, but Joosong wouldn't allow me to rest. I had no option but to concentrate and get it over with. It was daybreak when the composition was over, seven sheets long, that finally met with his approval, for he carefully folded and put them away, as if the trash were million dollar bank notes, adding: "Our Great Leader and Chief is history's great gift to mankind that comes along in 5,000 years."

Now why didn't I think of that, "history's great gift to mankind, etc."? Next time I had to write another letter like this, I should incorporate it. Presumably there was no jealous copyright in this religious community.

"Even Mao Tsetung and Chou Enlai of China came running to him bowing from waist down thirty feet away when they met him," Joosong went on. "In the whole world nobody is revered as widely and deeply by everybody as our Leader."

My cynicism turned into awe and wonder. Joosong was a decent, intelligent fellow in no way different from me, and yet really believed in the utter rubbish he was reciting.

XVIII.
Joyride

On December 19, ten months after my stay in North Korea, the reservoir froze over, but I decided to wait a little longer, reasoning that flowing rivers would perhaps take longer to freeze. On the evening of December 29 I went to bed after supper at 7:30. The servant double-checked my presence in bed and went away, her last inspection for the day. Luckily a strong wind was slapping the sides of the building. At 8 I got up and stole downstairs. In the driver's room the card game had started already. I pulled out my baggage from under the sofa in the living room and slid out the door. When I reached the car, somebody was heard leaving the driver's room. I flattened myself to the ground. The wind rose and howled. At a bush a few feet from me the man loosened his belt and took a leak, its pungent odor teasing my nose. The man hurried indoors, shuddering. Shaken by the closeness I did not get to my feet for a while. A gust of wind whipped up and crackled the dry leaves. I opened the car door to find the key in the ignition as expected. Turning it enough to read the gauge I found the tank only half full. Perhaps that was enough to take me to Jungjoo. Putting the gear in neutral I released the hand brake and the car began coasting slowly. The driveway curved left and soon met the shore drive, which was far enough from the house. I turned on the ignition and the headlights. Half a mile down the road I arrived at the guard post. Seeing my Caucasian face, the sentry saluted me and raised the barricade at once. The second checkpoint with no barricade was a breeze: like my driver, I didn't slow down and was duly saluted off.

Not a single car moved in the pitch black night but the trips back and forth from Chestnut Grove had oriented me enough to the lay of the land. Accelerating to the full I soon reached the capital, its streets empty of cars or pedestrians. Without difficulty I was on what I believed to be the Pyongyang-Shinujoo trunk line. Often speeding 100 miles an hour I arrived at a fork, which had no sign. To discourage unauthorized driving as in the present case North Korean roads provided no obliging guideposts. My quandary was relieved by a farmer passing by, who directed me to take the right branch to go to Pyongsong. He must come from the field where he got tied up in some work that had to be finished, however late. Night work was taken for granted here and the concept of overtime did not exist. Wondering at my Korean he must have thought I was a cultural attaché or something at one of the embassies. I was on my merry way again, but soon the asphalt gave way to gravel, which was not in the script and bewildered me considerably. The only possible explanation was that the farmer had given me wrong directions. Could the hardworking man play a practical joke on me, a harmless sranger who had in fact lavished sympathy on him?

Suddenly, out jumped another farmer into the road, forcing me to veer sharply to the right and skid on the gravel. The car struck a tree, spun, and jumped over the causeway into the wayside paddy. The frightened farmer had melted away into the darkness. I turned on the ignition and tried to back out. The engine of the new Benz responded but the front wheels were stuck in the mud and kept spinning without purchase. A tractor was lumbering by. I went up to the driver and asked him to pull me out. Thinking me a high-ranking foreign dignitary in distress he consented, attaching a chain to the rear bumper. The car was back on the road, but the back fender, crushed in, was digging into the rear wheel. With the tire iron and jack from the trunk I managed to separate the two. I could drive. Barely thanking the tractor driver for his trouble I retraced my course, noticing it was 10 p.m. At the same time I remembered asking for Pyongsong, not Pyongwon as I should have. Depressing the accelerator to the floor I whizzed past Pyongwon and Sookchon, not too far off from the Chongchon River. A narrow one-lane bridge appeared and a soldier waved to me to stop, but I drove on, unheeding. Luckily there was no oncoming traffic. That's what I thought, but on reaching the other side I found five trucks waiting and shuddered at the close call. My driver's egotistic style of driving was valid only to an extent.

From here on the road was covered with large gravel the size of fists or bigger but I squeezed 60 miles an hour out of the battered vehicle, until the worsening snow forced me to slow down. Half an hour on the road brought me to Jungjoo Railroad Station, its front decorated by a huge portrait of Ilsung Kim. I had to turn right here to head for the Soopoong Dam, lying athwart the Yalu, the northern boundary of North Korea. On the way I was to dump the car into a reservoir near Goosong. But to my right I noticed a railroad track which had no business of being there. I must have taken the wrong right. The car was put in reverse but acted funny. The right rear tire had a flat but there was no spare in the trunk. Even if there were one, I wouldn't have been able to change in the darkness. I had no choice but to dump the Benz. Bag slung over my shoulder, I followed the railroad track, feeling the vicious bite of the below zero night air, until a bridge loomed ahead.

"Halt, Comrade!" shouted the sentry who had been warming himself over a fire.

Pretending not to have heard I kept walking across the bridge. In the bitter cold the soldier remained hunkered over the fire without giving me a chase. Suddenly realizing that he could not only arrest me but shoot, I sprinted the balance of the span out of breath.

The track led to a small country station, its single platform stacked with crates weighing a ton each. There were spaces between them and I squeezed in to get out of the driving wind and wait for a train going north to the border to hitchhike. Noticing the inch-deep snow covering the crates, I became aware of my parched throat. I scooped up a fistful and shoved into my mouth. The sharp stab of pain overrode any sense of relief. It was past 11. I was lucky to have come this far. The car would not be found until next morning and I would be many miles away by then. While answering the call of nature, I stuck a finger into a crack in one of the crates and felt the smooth hard surface of a rocket. My hairs stood on end. If any of the boxes, crudely nailed together should break apart and spill its contents, the whole pile would blow up everything in a mile radius till kingdom come.

In search of a safer hiding place I saw at the edge of the platform a huge crane that fed coal to the locomotives. Just as I was about to climb up to the operator's cab, the cadence of a steam locomotive could be heard approaching in the distance. With the bag tied to my back I waited near the track, in a good position to spring aboard, though my limbs began to shake uncontrollably with cold, the gloves, boots, overcoat, and fur cap covering my head and most of my face seemingly useless. The train got closer and the bright headlights sliced through the darkness. A slow freight train, it slowed down even more going through the substation, perhaps in deference to the piled explosives. It was easy to seize a handle and yank myself up over the side of an open car loaded with mineral ore. Rearranging the stones near the side I built a makeshift foxhole to fit in and lessen exposure, but the wind cut like a razor blade. Shouldn't I have stayed at the Chestnut Grove guesthouse lying in the warm bed and enjoying the food they served? I tried to stay awake, remembering my old brush with death through freezing after the escape from the Mercy Home, but was soon overcome by sleep.

"Wake up, Comrade," somebody was shaking me, the train conductor.

I sat up and stared at him blankly, not comprehending the situation. In sleep I must have thrown out a leg over the side, which came to the train man's notice.

"Please get off the train," he said politely, probably in awe of my well-dressed appearance.

Begging his pardon, I jumped off and backed away in the direction the train was going. The locomotive started moving again, belching a thick cloud of steam that engulfed the whole train and provided a screen, behind which I jumped aboard right behind the locomotive. The steam from the engine would be thickest here, I reasoned. Like the others this car was also loaded with ore stones. Then I realized I had left in the other car my bag with clothes and food. I had absolutely nothing and would soon be obliged to beg for food somewhere. My watch, the only article of any value, indicated 9 a.m. Would anybody give me food in exchange for the watch?

The train slowed down to a stop at the next station. Three uniformed station personnel headed for the car I was on, climbed over the side, and started pulling me down. My presence had been reported to them by the railroad security guards posted at intervals along the line. Most North Korean railroad lines were single track and such security was necessary to prevent collision, if for no other reason. The sign on the station building said Shinonchon, one station before Sagjoo. A few more stations and I would have been at Soopoong right on the border with Manchuria. On the platform in front of the building stood a police man, my bag at his feet.

"Pick it up and follow me," he ordered.

Exhausted and hungry, I dragged it on the ground.

"Pick it up and carry it," he shouted.

"I can't. It's too heavy."

"Shut up and do as I tell you."

In the police shack next to the station a police captain sat rubbing his eyes as if he had just been awakened.

"Are you the fellow who abandoned the Benz?" he asked, looking over the papers on his desk.

"Yes, I am."

"You are all black."

I ran my hand across my cheek and felt the sandy grains of black soot, that had spewed out of the coal-burning locomotive. A look in the mirror revealed a pathetic chimney sweep I could not recognize. The police captain had a basin of water brought to wash away the caked dirt and soot.

"Can I go to the restroom?" I asked.

The police chief nodded to a subordinate, who took me

outside to a shack put up by slapping together a few rough boards. Squatting down over the hole I pulled out the map in my breast pocket and tore it to shreds, lest it should indicate a deliberate escape plan with a correspondingly heavy penalty. By the time I reemerged I felt strangely at ease, resigned, almost cheerful. With great interest I studied the police chief, a perfect real life model for a slow-witted local functionary, his basic good nature and friendliness struggling with his sense of office and self-importance. I almost asked for his name, address and phone number, so I could use him in my next movie, when I realized the hopelessness of such a fantasy. They would now perhaps shoot me for ingratitude, treason, espionage, or whatever. The phone rang and the chief's nondescript face tightened with tension. After hanging up he opened the knapsack and looked through.

"Even glutinous rice," he said surprised, ordering his subordinates to handcuff me.

Overcome with weariness I began dozing but was awakened by a loud bang. Having slammed the door shut, Joosong fixed me with a hate-filled stare. Without a word, he led me to a helicopter, waiting at a nearby elementary school, which took off the moment we got on and landed at a small airfield near Pyongyang. Blindfolded, I was put in the back of a jeep and taken to a room in a government building. The blindfold was removed and disclosed a fat police chief at a desk with Joosong seated next. Paper and pencil in hand, they pointed to another chair for me to sit, facing them.

"Comrade," the fat man opened the session with a shaky voice. "You went considerably north past Jungjoo, North Pyongan Province. You must have mistaken the road."

I kept silent, it being not clear whether he was making a statement or asking a question.

"Answer whether you lost your way or that's where you intended to go," Joosong snapped, losing his temper.

"I went that way," I said, not wanting to hide anything.

"Why?"

"I decided I could not live here."

They took down my every word, then went out. Four

guards came in to watch me. After a while the two men returned, and the four watchmen left the room.

"Was the New Year congratulatory message all a lie?" Joosong asked.

What an inane question! Perhaps they had telephoned Jungil or Ilsung Kim, who could not believe that a writer of those fervent words of praise and devotion could turn against them. Were all dictators so naive and gullible?

"Answer!" the fatso screamed.

Did they seriously want an answer?

"I wrote it because I was told to write it. Actually I felt like a jerk to be heaping such unctuous flattery on people I haven't even met once in my life."

For a long minute the two men stared at me and at each other, as if they couldn't believe they had heard right, then busily wrote down their separate versions of my answer before exiting the room. The four guards promptly took their places inside the room. Obviously my interrogators were conducting a direct phone conversation with Jungil Kim, who must be telling them to ask certain questions and have my answers relayed back to him. The two returned and the four goons went out.

"Where did you plan to go?" Joosong asked.

"Hong Kong."

The two left the room with just those two syllables. Another change of the guard and the two returned with the next set of questions.

"How did you plan to get there?"

"Hitchhike on trains."

"Hitchhike?" the fat man asked.

"Yes."

The two men wrote down the answer and left the room, to return with another question.

"How did you plan to get food?"

Obviously they hadn't opened my bag yet.

"Every station has a pile of grains, doesn't it?"

This absurd time-delay three-way conference call went on for over half an hour before the jeep took me to Pyongyang. It was past 3 p.m., December 30.

As usual, the streets were dead with no sign of life, human or otherwise. The jeep stopped before a two-story building, marked Rehabilitation, a police jail belonging to the Pyongyang Community Security Department, on the waist of a hill in a Pyongyang suburb.

The cell block we entered had rows of rooms on either side of the hallway where interrogations were being conducted. Inside an unfurnished room, as a crowd stood in a circle watching, I stripped and put on a heavily padded and quilted prison uniform. Locked up in a numberless solitary, I realized the total helplessness of my situation. They could rub me out like a bug and nobody would be the wiser.

The floor was wet, cold, and dirty. The toilet in the corner was shaped like a flushing type, but the bowl had a rubber pad with a pull string stopping the bottom instead of water. There was no water tank and the only supply of water was drips, three times a day, a couple of minutes each time, from a rusted pipe protruding from the wall and bent downward just clearing the head of the sitter. Since this was all the water the room was going to get, the inmate had to be extremely frugal with its use, brushing the teeth or washing the face or other parts of the body with the first drops, and letting the slop collect in the bowl, into which he excreted before pulling the string and flushing down everything. Little water went far with this method but it was impossible to keep the stopper or the pull string clean, which were simply exposed to dry, befouling the room for a long time. The wall opposite the iron door had a barred window, which showed a patch of sky but did not let in any sun. The door had two openings, a peep hole at the top and a food slot at the bottom. The jailers, armed with pistols, walked up and down the hallway at irregular intervals.

I shouted and told them I was hungry. A young jailor came to the door and looked in a long time, his eyeballs rolling up and down, left and right, before walking away without a word. It was past meal time and I did not expect anything, but after a while the jailer returned and pushed in an aluminum bowl of rolled rice, corn and beans, cut like sushi, together with an unusual spoon, its handle lopped off at the base to prevent self-injury by the user, I was told later. There was no soup or other side dishes. With the first bite my teeth chomped on a stone, taking away all appetite. After the bowl was removed, two jailers standing on each side of the door read out the rules:

"Until bed time the inmate must remain seated erect, both hands on his lap, eyes wide open and looking straight ahead, no part of the body moving...."

Whenever I closed my eyes or shifted my weight, the guards shouted "Violation!" To perform the offices of nature one had to raise hands and obtain permission. I realized this enforced Zen was much more effective in breaking down one's spirit or resistance than beating or any other form of torture, as the latter involved some interaction. Total insulation from other humans simply went against the grain of the social animal. What did they want with me? I had done the most natural thing, attempt to escape from unlawful detention. Did they expect me to be grateful and loyal simply because they had fed and slept me?

At 10 p.m. the bell rang announcing bed time. Now I could move. Diligently I kneaded my cramped legs to bring back the circulation before laying myself down between four blankets spread on the floor, which however did not keep out the encroaching cold. I bit my teeth down hard to stop their chattering but now my whole head and body shook. Sleep seemed out of the question but fatigue got the upper hand.

When I opened my eyes, it was morning and my two jailers were watching me like some curious specimen. It was a grim New Year's Day ushered in by stone-mixed grains and salt soup, and a volley of foul oaths tapped out across the hall. No meal was to be free from stones the size of soy beans and the soup, the thinnest and clearest imaginable with nothing in it, except one or two pieces of overboiled turnip or cabbage floating lonesome occasionally. There was no hint of soy bean paste, the universal Korean soup stock which supplied the necessary protein cheaply. When water trickled down the rusted pipe, I cupped it in my hands and wetted my face, without the benefit of soap or towel. The only way to dry myself was using the sleeve of my quilted jacket. Instead of a tooth brush or paste coarse-grained salt had to be rubbed on teeth with a finger.

The wind blew fiercely one night, buffeting the roof and sides of the building. One of the guards pacing the hallway stopped at my door.

"Wouldn't a wind like this blow away the shacks in South Korea?" he asked.

I merely smiled. On another occasion a jailer asked whether anybody could purchase chocolates in South Korea.

"Yes, anybody can with money."

"Not the Party cadre and top government brass?"

"No, anybody can, even a toilet cleaner, shoeshine boy."

"No!" he said, unbelieving.

"Can I ask a favor?"

"What is it?"

"I want to eat an egg a day."

"I'll see what I can do."

Days passed but there was no sign of either the jailer or the egg. I could not stand the growing hunger and the visible weakening of my body from lack of nourishment. A total of six guards, not always the same ones, took turns in watching me 24 hours a day in three shifts, two at a time. No other prisoner seemed to merit as much attention, but I didn't know whether to resent or rejoice in the distinction.

"Would you kindly tell the Deputy Chief who was in charge of me to come and see me?" I asked one of them.

Of course nothing came of it. With the big stones saved from my food I marked the passage of time, one stone put on the window sill for each passing day. Ten days passed but still there was no Joosong Kim. The eight blankets and thick quilted clothing assigned to me did not keep out the northern cold which averaged 20 below zero Celsius. My repeated request for eggs fell on deaf ears. I began to fear I would soon weaken with no immunity and die of some vile disease. When the jailers were not watching, I began carving on the concrete wall with the bobtailed spoon an epitaph to myself, "Moo Moo died here," but it took several days just to scratch even a single stroke.

On the 25th day a jailer came to my cell and told me to step out. A jeep drove us to the office across the yard, where Joosong Kim was waiting with the Chief of Police.

"What did you want to see me about?" Joosong asked first.

"To tell you I have erred grievously," I said, head down, contrite. "I didn't understand Comrade Jungil Kim's intentions."

"Beloved Comrade Leader Jungil Kim," corrected the Police Chief.

"Right. Beloved Comrade Leader Jungil Kim. I have repented."

The two men busily took down everything I said as before.

"Have you anything more to add?" Joosong asked icily.

"Give me an egg a day. My health is going fast."

I could not think of anything more to say. The two left and soon three weeks went by with no news or egg.

My right big toe itched unbearably from the frostbite I got while riding the open train. I kept scratching until it got infected. Also I suffered from diarrhea which didn't seem to stop. A week later a doctor arrived and gave me a vitamin shot and a Soviet-made bowel hardener and antibiotic called Mitin, Russian for mycin. For the first time I felt better, psychologically, at least. Perhaps they didn't mean to kill me after all. Otherwise they wouldn't be wasting valuable medicine. This reflection revived my spirit wonderfully. To live for whatever purpose was good.

A month later Joosong and the Police Chief came again and I asked about Nan, but Joosong denied any knowledge of her as usual.

"If she is still alive, bring us together," I appealed urgently. "We make a good team and will work for the Great Leader and Chief and Beloved Comrade Leader with everything we've got. I wanted to escape for selfish reasons but have now resolved to sacrifice the small for the big, namely, the revolutionary task of making first-rate movies for the Republic."

They left with their notes and did not reappear, but the doctor was in daily attendance. The shots he gave me were some kind of tranquilizer, perhaps to quiet me down so I didn't harm myself. The constant guards seemed to serve the same purpose, never taking their eyes off me. But there was no relief from hunger. After supper one night a scraping sound came from the door. A rice pot was squeezed in through the slot with a half-inch layer of rice stuck to the bottom. Throwing a blanket over it and myself I ate the rice greedily, picking every grain, licking the bottom, until I stopped, struck by self-disgust at this reduction to an animal. Who had given me the extra food? Obviously one of the guards. I tried to discover his identity by making tentative signals to each of my six guards but none of them reciprocated with a confirmatory sign. To the very end the good Samaritan remained anonymous. It was a one-shot deal and not much quantitywise, either, but restored my faith in humanity. No matter how lowly my existence, I still belonged to the species capable of compassion which was human and therefore divine.

In March Soviet multivitamin pills were issued to me. The jailers who brought them examined them closely with great curiosity.

"Is it true you don't have to eat any other food with these pills?" they asked.

"No, they are mere supplements. You have to eat," I explained.

"Do they have them in South Korea?"

"Yes, everybody is overly health-conscious and takes a lot of these."

"You mean party cadre."

"No, any Joe Blow on the street."

They could not believe it. Suddenly in the next cell a jailer shouted to his prisoner to speak more clearly, which however had no effect on the addressee who mumbled on inarticulately. The jailer mocked and jeered him in a language he would not have used to his dog. Across the hall another jailer swore at a prisoner, telling him to sit up instead of lean on the wall with eyes closed. Loud slapping followed. Still from another source came a barrage of oaths accusing the prisoner of being worse than a pig, because a pig could be slaughtered for meat and hide but the prisoner was just consuming food doing no good to anybody. The prisoner, convicted of some economic crime, was being reprimanded for asking more salt soup.

One day the jailers took me to the office to give me a haircut. It was out of the question to ask for any particular style or to be squeamish about my Hitlerian cowlick. The end result was an extremely short cut, a quarter inch at most, which of course disclosed the forehead cavity, but in the general exposure and unsightliness that particular blot probably didn't even register. Still I would have liked to look at myself, but no prisoner was allowed to look at a mirror, perhaps out of kindness. When I returned to the cell, my guard on the shift smirked and I knew I must look a sight. His buddy being absent, I told him briefly how I had ended up there and pointed at the epitaph traced on the wall.

"Please show it to Miss Nanyong Song," I pleaded.

"Is she your wife?" he asked sympathetically.

"No, but closer than a wife."

"Mother or sister?"

"No, but even closer."

"Don't you have any other relatives?"

"No, none whatsoever."

"Don't worry," the jailer said. "They won't let you die, if you have been brought here to make motion pictures."

I wished I could be as confident.

Rats had unrestricted access to the cells especially at night. One morning I found one of my shoes missing, and was told that the resident rats must have made off with it. Giving me another pair, my keepers instructed me to guard them well because none more would be issued. In the absence of a cabinet or dresser, the only way to safeguard them was to put them under my head like pillows. Also I had to sleep with the extremities of my body tucked in securely under the blanket, particularly the toes, said to be favored by the rodents for nibbling. Perhaps the prison authorities raised them: when nothing promising was in sight, the rats regularly went for the prisoner's excrement, making sewage disposal that much less of a problem.

It was April and the grip of cold was relaxing. One day my jailers opened the iron door and told me to step out for a sun bath in the yard, dotted with yellow flowers, whose exquisite charm brought tears to my eyes. Savoring the sweet, soft air I stretched my arms and legs, which spread a wonderful exhilaration throughout the body.

On April 9 I was told to take a shower at the staff bathroom and get into the old clothes I had escaped in, washed and ironed. At the warden's office were waiting my old acquaintances, Joosong and the fat Police Chief.

"May I speak first?" the Police Chief asked Joosong, who must outrank him. Joosong nodded.

"You are guilty of destroying public property and attempting to escape out of the country, and should be executed, but we are giving you another chance to work for the fatherland."

I thanked him sincerely, who bade me and Joosong good-bye outside at a waiting black older model Benz, obviously replacement for the one I had wrecked. The confinement had lasted exactly 100 days. I felt as if I could dance and sing with joy.

"You look a sight," Joosong said, breaking his silence till now.

I smiled sheepishly. The car drove past Chestnut Grove for about 20 minutes. A big billboard by the wayside depicted Ilsung Kim giving a personal hands-on demonstration of rice planting at a collective, an example of his "local guidance." We turned right at the billboard and continued on an unpaved road, encountering more examples of "local guidance." At a checkpoint over the hill we were waved through and stopped at a two-story house, neat but a cut lower than the Chestnut Grove guesthouse. Sentry posts at key points of the property were equipped with powerful search lights. Joosong took me to the living room, where the servant had brought a tray of cookies and apples. I devoured them.

"I am sorry to have caused you trouble," I said to Joosong, when the edge of hunger was blunted. "You seem stressed out."

He was skin and bones, having lost at least thirty pounds. I must have been his responsibility, in which he had failed miserably, losing face with his beloved leader.

"I want to talk to you man to man," I said.

"Fire away," said Joosong, curtly, still bitter about the setback in his career caused by my joyride.

"I have made up my mind to live in North Korea, making films for our leader. But I am a man and need female companionship. Let me meet Nan. At least tell me whether she is dead or alive. If she is dead, I will forget about her and look for a new woman."

It was of course a ploy to discover her whereabouts but wily Joosong did not fall for it.

"I told you already I don't know anything about her," he said impatiently. "Now forget about her and write a letter of apology to our Beloved Comrade Leader Jungil Kim."

Straining the resources of the Korean language for panegyrics to the great leader and phillipics of denunciation to my wretched self, I took three days to finish it, though only five pages long. I had to be supercautious, knowing that everything I wrote down would be analyzed and scrutinized under a microscope for any sign of mendacity by a team of experts, including Jungil Kim.

The first floor of the house had the living room, equipped to show movies, kitchen, and dining room. My bedroom was on the second floor across from the library and aide's room, from which they could keep me under observation. In my room were the personal things I had left behind at the guesthouse in Chestnut Grove. Here I had no say about what I would like to eat as I did at Chestnut Grove, Korean, Japanese, Chinese, Western, or whatever I wanted. The meals were strictly Korean on a reduced scale, rice with a few side dishes. Joosong came around a couple of times a week. On one of these visits he dropped off the three-volume History of General Ilsung Kim's Struggle against Japan.

"Read them and write down summaries," he said. "When I come, I want to hear you read them to me aloud."

"Yes, sir," I assented, suppressing my dislike for reading

anything aloud, the most distractive thing as far as I was concerned making concentration impossible.

There was no ambiguity about my status here: I was a prisoner and was not allowed out of the house, even to go into the yard. Only on his visits Joosong took me out for a walk or a sun bath. In addition to the numerous guards a fierce German shepherd was let loose on the property at night.

A few days after my arrival a big dinner was served to celebrate April 15, Ilsung Kim's birthday. Joosong brought a bottle of champagne and the cook served up pig's feet among other delicacies. We drank to the health of the Great Leader and Chief Ilsung Kim.

The house had about 200 books, mostly on Ilsung Kim's life and work. Some of them turned out to be encyclopedias with map insertions, which I began to study as at the other house, to execute my escape plan again. I had to escape no matter what. Any kind of restraint or confinement triggered this automatic reaction. Copying down the attached maps and putting them together I discovered that I was at a place called Wonhungni in a northern suburb of Pyongyang. July was chosen as the time, because with the corn ripe in the field I wouldn't have to weigh myself down with a grain bag as before.

TV and radio were preoccupied with the world pingpong championships to be held in May at Pyongyang, minus the South Korean team whose entry had been denied by North Korea. Everybody was welcome, except the kinsmen from the south. To please Jungil Kim I proposed to make a documentary of the championship games, but a few days later Joosong brought a negative response. Undaunted, I volunteered to edit the documentary film, whoever should make it, but this was denied too. As it turned out, I was glad I didn't have anything to do with it. The North Korean telecast was the most prejudiced, one-sided affair, showing only those games where North Korea was winning. Besides the North Korean spectators were extremely hostile to the foreign teams, especially American. Even the by no means impartial sportscaster had to admonish his home crowd to be more civil. They openly taunted and swore at the foreign visitors, showing themselves up to the whole world as crude hicks devoid of sportsmanship. The other radio broadcasts I could switch on, South Korean KBS and Japanese NHK, were not so chauvinistic and at least covered the whole field.

It was July. Birds sang and cicadas chirped in the green hills and fields, lush with life, as if the bleakness of winter had been a distant memory. Thinking it wise to take along a supply of food regardless, I saved the French toast I got for breakfast, dried it on the window sill to a crisp, and stored it away on top of the water heater in the bathroom next to my bedroom. From the kitchen I borrowed small quantities of salt, saying I needed it for my arthritis. I even stole three match boxes. Extra caution was necessary as things were much scarce and more strictly guarded here.

All summer long that year it rained heavily day after day with lightning and wind, which was welcome to me as just the kind of weather I needed for another attempt at escape. The rain would muffle footsteps and force the sentries into their shacks. But of course the condition had to prevail after bedtime, 10 p.m. July 15 turned out to be that kind of day. About 11 p.m., timing my move with the lightning and thunder and carrying a backpack of food, clothes and extra shoes I stole softly downstairs. All the windows on the ground floor were barred, except the one just above the airconditioner in the kitchen. Both the cook and maid were in deep sleep, undisturbed by the rainstorm. Climbing on the frame of the airconditioner I slid the window open and cautiously looked out to see if the coast was clear, when an ominous snarl startled me. It came from the watchdog that had crawled directly underneath out of the rain. Quickly reclosing the window I got off my perch and went back upstairs to my room. Any future plan would have to include the elimination of the canine obstacle I had overlooked.

XIX.
Hide and Seek

In the absence of central heating every room in the house was separately heated by two or more portable electric radiators on wheels which were stored away during the warmer months in a closet in the room. I had noticed that the aide's room next to the library and two doors away from mine had a particularly spacious and deep closet for its three radiators behind the desk facing the door.

A little before dinner a few weeks later I crawled into the space in back of the radiators with the bundle of dried toast and salt I had accumulated. The doors did not close tight because my body was pushing the radiators out but nobody would notice the gap on account of the desk in front. My plan was to lead the sentries and the dog away from the house in ever widening circles to look for me once my absence was noticed. The house and compound left unwatched, I would slip out, hitchhike on a train to Wonsan, Gowon, Chongjin, Woonggi, Sosoora, and then Nahotka in Russia as before.

At 7 p.m. the cook went up to my room to announce dinner, doing what the male housekeeper normally did, who was away on a four-day vacation. Not finding me in my room, she went to the library, then to the aide's room where I was.

"Teacher, Teacher," she shouted into the empty room, not noticing anything untoward about the radiator closet as expected. Closing the door behind, she scampered down the stairs to report me missing. About an hour later a large company of armed men arrived and searched the house inside out. Several came into the aide's room, tapped the walls, the ceiling, looked behind and under the desk, and even opened the radiator closet, but did not bother to look behind the radiators. Some were heard going to the roof.

The officer coordinating the search described me on his walkie talkie and ordered a team to cover the area to the east of the Daydong River. In the hallway he directed a squad to turn over the empty kimchee pots in the backyard.

"Use the dogs and look everywhere," he ordered.

I feared they might bring the dogs into the house, but they didn't. Squeezed tightly and locked in fetal position I couldn't stretch my legs. My back ached and sides cramped. Things were not going as I had planned. Instead of the circle of search widening, leaving the center in a vacuum, the guesthouse had become the search headquarters, to which more and more personnel converged with cordless phones and radios, shouting and receiving orders all night long. In particular, the aide's room where I hid served as command post, where messengers and team leaders came in and out with their reports and instructions.

To ease the growing hunger I chewed pieces of the dried toast sprinkled with salt, but the discomfort from the full bladder intensified with every passing minute. About 3 a.m. the room was temporarily vacant. I slipped out to the bathroom in the hallway and urinated into the sink, avoiding the commode which would have to be flushed. I opened the tap a crack and wetted my parched throat from the trickle.

Out the window I saw powerful search lights turning on and off all around the house, giving the illusion of night and day rapidly alternating. Seeing another contingent of security personnel enter the house, I trotted back to my covert.

The second night came around. I was desperate with thirst and the need for excretion. At 4 a.m. I slipped out again to the bathroom in the hallway and drank a little from the tap. This time I had no choice but to sit on the toilet. The next problem was disposal. If I left it, they would know someone had been there, but if I flushed it, the sound would alert them also. As I stood undecided, dogs started barking. Quickly I pushed the handle and returned to the closet. Nobody could have heard the usually thunderous flushing noise above the insistent canine chorus that continued for some time.

On the fourth day the housekeeper's voice could be heard around the house. He must have cut his leave short.

"See what the sonofabitch had taken with him," the officer in charge told him who stood in the aide's room. "Look through all his personal things."

"Yes, comrade," the young man said, leaving.

About two hours later he returned to the room.

"Everything is there, except for one thing, his nail cutter."

He must have a complete inventory of all my personal belongings.

"What about his clothes?"

"The clothes he used to wear are all here, but his winter suit and boots are missing."

I had figured it would take at least two months to cross the border on foot, by which time it would be cold. To prevent their police dogs from getting my smell I had also washed all my underwear, socks, shirts, and towels.

In the afternoon, humming monotonously, the housekeeper entered the aide's room to tidy up the mess left around by the searchers. To close the curtain he stepped on top of the desk. The humming stopped. He had seen the gap in the door and knew. Silently he got off the desk and ran out of the room. There was no point in staying in the hole to be dragged out. I crept out and sat on a chair just in time to face the mob that crashed into the room. The leader in his thirties, whose voice I had heard so much and recognized at once, told the people to clear out and leave him alone with me.

"Why did you put on this stunt again?" he asked, politely, almost indulgently.

"I can't live like this. My girlfriend has disappeared and I am not allowed to work, only eating and sleeping like a pig."

"You were on probation. Everything would have worked out all right in time."

"I had waited long enough."

"You'll have to wait longer now."

When I expressed my desire for water to wet my throat, he ordered the housekeeper to bring a bottle of soda, which was so refreshing I felt I had never tasted anything like it before. A while later a thin man with the rank of Deputy Chief of Police entered.

"You are guilty of treason and an attempt to escape to a foreign country, punishable by death," he said.

"I am a South Korean and want to go home," I said. "How could it be a crime?"

"You are a resident of this community and must obey its laws."

"I was brought here against my will and don't belong here."

"You are a fool," he said, losing his temper. "The Constitution says South Korea is part of the fatherland, too, though illegally occupied by the bandits, Americans and their running dogs. You are a North Korean citizen."

A while later Joosong Kim showed up. After staring at me balefully without a word, he went out of the room accompanied by the police deputy chief. I asked the housekeeper to go after Joosong and ask him to take me to prison after a few days I would need to recuperate from my latest ordeal. The housekeeper returned to report that Joosong had already left the house. My repeated request for a meeting with Joosong was ignored. They did not haul me away to prison at once and at supper time the housekeeper came as usual to ask me to dinner downstairs.

It was the same dining room but everything else had changed. The food on the table was prison fare, salt soup and mixed grains boiled. The diet had skydived from Grade 10 for Politburo or Party chiefs to Grade 1 for prisoners, the lowest rung in the North Korean hierarchy. Ordinary citizens ate somewhere around Grades 3 or 4. Security around the house had been beefed up with about two companies of policemen and five or six police dogs. A new triple concertina of barbed wire was installed along the fence surrounding the complex with a thin wire woven through it to sound the alarm at the slightest disturbance. My heart sank. Escape was impossible.

My self-confidence was gone. Perhaps I should forget about escaping once and for all. But vegetation for the rest of my life was unthinkable. Maybe I should really work for Ilsung and Jungil Kim and make films. But would they let me now? I had tried to run away twice, especially after such fervent words of repentance and renewed allegiance following the joyride, enough to make even the most trusting skeptical about my sincerity. Perhaps I was the epitome of mendacity and ingratitude, beyond redemption. What could you expect from someone of my background, an abandoned, unloved, warped orphan? I had to concentrate on regaining the confidence of my keepers so I could have complete freedom of movement again. That meant renouncing any thought of escaping, until nothing could go wrong, until the odds were 100 to zero in my favor. But this resolution did not last long. Next moment I was toying with various desperate measures, such as setting fire to the house and running away during the confusion.

Shut up in my room I no longer had visitors, except the housekeeper who came up three times a day to announce meal time. On the third day they replaced the Soviet-made radio on which I could hear South Korean and Japanese broadcasts, with a North Korean set which had a fixed dial tuned permanently to Radio Pyongyang as at every ordinary North Korean household. In spite of these restrictions the continued residence at the guesthouse began to revive my hope that everything might turn out all right. Perhaps Jungil Kim was prepared to overlook the whole caper as a childish prank. After all I hadn't even left the house. But all these wishful thoughts ended three weeks later with the arrival of the fat Police Chief of my previous acquaintance who handcuffed me, ordering the domestic staff to pack up my clothes and effects.

"You are to be taken to a place where you will be punished for your great crime," he said.

This sounded ominous, like the place of execution. I was prepared for anything by now. It was after nightfall when we left the house. The Benz drove through a forest where soldiers were engaged in some drill. Otherwise we encountered no pedestrian or residence on the way. Neither the police chief nor the chauffeur spoke a word.

"Can you loosen the handcuffs?" I asked, unable to bear the pinch.

They did not reply or comply. We came out into open country and made good speed along the paved road, until we entered the city, the streets lined with buildings. The car stopped before an impressive four-story building, Pyongyang Police Headquarters. In a large waiting room on the fourth floor I was seated on a sofa directly before the usual portraits of Ilsung and Jungil Kim on the wall. About 30 minutes later I was taken downstairs and turned over to two other men, who led me outside to a jeep.We drove a long time through the darkness, across the Daydong River, past fields, up mountain roads. The handcuffs bit painfully into my wrists and I renewed my request to relax them but there was no response as before.

About two hours later the jeep went past a school yard and parked before a white three-story building, the Politburo Prison for political and ideological crimes. My escorts dropped me off at the admitting room where the man on duty called me to his desk and asked my name, age, address, and occupation. Things must have really changed. Before they had hushed about my identity. Even the cook at the guesthouse did not know who or what I was, but here they made me shout out my name and occupation. I must be in the dump to be junked for good. In another room I was issued thin gray summer prison clothes, in which I was formally indicted and charged before a judge. At about 10 p.m. I was taken down a hallway flanked by cells with barred windows and solid doors as at the Police Jail. The floor was cold, against which the four blankets, two underneath and two on top, proved useless. The thin summer clothes did not help and at night I shook with the chill unable to sleep, though it was early August. Besides a dog tied in the courtyard kept barking all night.

Day broke. Prepared to be rebuked for the curiosity, I asked a jailer where I was. Fortunately, he merely smiled and passed by without answering. The jailers had to be addressed by the inmates with the utmost honorifics, but the latter were regularly referred to by the former as assholes, creeps, jerks. Breakfast arrived, a mixture of corn and soy beans and salt soup with a hint of greenery, long thin blades of bear grass. The bitter taste of the soup came from the paste used as stock, which was acorn ground with the skin on instead of the usual soy bean.

After the meal I was summoned to the warden's office. Sitting at the head of the long table opposite me with two others to my left and right, the warden asked how I had ended up here and listened to the recital of my woes from Hong Kong on with unshakable calmness. The others were equally dead pan. If they heard it for the first time, mine was just one of the many international abductions routinely carried out as a national policy and they weren't hearing anything unusual. More probably, they knew all about it from my extensive file in front of them, no doubt containing my autobiography, and were just going through the routine. At the end of the interrogation I asked the warden for extra blankets and clothes, but he merely stared at me without saying yea or nay.

Though it was still summer I shivered miserably back in the clammy cold cell especially after sundown. Maybe it was my steadily declining health. From the unresponsive way the warden had taken my request I despaired of anything coming out of it but the next day a quilted jacket and a thick cotton comforter finished with coarse canvas were put into my cell, which made the cold a little more bearable afterwards.

The wakeup bell went off at 5 a.m. and the inmates had to sit up in 'meditation posture,' whole body straight, eyes fixed on the wall in front, and hands resting on knees, as at the Police Jail. Immediately after breakfast at 7 the meditation posture was resumed and continued for three hours until a three-minute break, which was used stretching and massaging the kinked and cramped limbs and parts of the body. Time was up again for the resumption of the Zen posture. After lunch at 12:30 the same posture had to be maintained until the 6 p.m. supper, which ended in 10 minutes. The Zen returned and remained in effect until 10 p.m. when the bell rang for bedtime. In addition to the 3-minute break the rigor of the Zen position was relieved by a 20-minute sunbath, given at different times for different inmates and as necessary as food to burn off the itchy skin irritations that set in almost immediately without exception in the foul atmosphere of the cages. So of the 17 waking hours exactly 16 went to the Zen, the remaining hour being the sum of the 30 minutes for the meals, 9 minutes for the rests, and 20 minutes for the sunbath.

Reputedly Buddha arrived at his Enlightenment after meditating in the Zen position for months under a linden tree. Perhaps I didn't attain nirvana but I sure could meditate and rewrote Mayoress of Koreatown along the lines Fenwick's screen writer might have done it. Page after manuscript page appeared on my mental retina as on a computer screen, in which I could write in and make changes. Ecstatic at the discovery I welcomed the Zen punishment and decided to write many more screenplays as soon as I was done with the one in hand.

I came down with a bad case of diarrhea from eating the unknown stiff grass in the soup, which was never meant for digestion, for it always came out whole in the stool. The jailers gave me some stool hardener, which however had no effect.

The jail had over 300 inmates but the cells were so constructed as to prevent their meeting or view of each other. Consequently everybody was totally cut off from company except that of the jailers. Similar care was taken in administering the 20-minute sunbath at the sunning shed in the yard, a row of about 20 rectangular concrete boxes, unroofed so as to be observable from the watch towers, and entered by a wiremesh door on one side. The sunning schedule was spread out throughout the day according to the number of users and the direction of entrance or departure varied each time to minimize contact coming and going. In fact this was so cleverly and strictly administered that in the whole time I was there I never saw anybody passing my sun room while I was in it, nor did I pass one that was occupied as I arrived or left. Everybody brought along his bedding, which was dusted and sunned, and also laundry to be washed at the tap in the room during the 20-minute occupancy.

Once a week the inmates underwent a unique physical examination, which consisted of taking off all clothes and sitting up facing a wall with a blanket thrown over themselves, until the jailers came, looked through the clothes, removed the blanket, and told the inmate to stand up and bend over so they could look into his anus. Of course its primary purpose was to degrade and break the inmate, not to find anything wrong with him. The untrained jailers were apt to miss even the most glaring symptoms of a disease, unless brought to their attention specifically.

About a month later I was moved to another cell on the other side of the hallway. Under its wooden floor ran a pipe which passed hot steam three times a day, making the room warm. But this advantage was offset by the discomfort posed by an army of bugs that crawled out from under the boards through the cracks. The commode in the corner had a square wooden seat, which however could not be sat on. Huge exotic bugs ringed the rim, each refusing to give up its territory even when sat upon. When power went out, which was often, candles were lighted. I used the softened wax to stop up the cracks in the flooring to block the bugs but was severely reprimanded for wasting the valuable resource, candle wax.

It occurred to me that if I were engaged in writing, I would necessarily be off the Zen posture. The question was whether they would let me write. There was only one way to find out.

"May I see the Warden or whoever is in charge of me here?" I asked a jailer one day.

"What about?" he asked.

"I want to have permission to write."

"What about?"

"My crimes."

"Let's see what I can do."

The next day they brought me paper and pen. I had guessed right. They let me sit any way I wanted while I wrote. Why didn't I think of it sooner? After the Zen freeze it felt like ultimate freedom, beyond which I need not aspire to more. This time I went about the writing deliberately, taking my time, to prolong my freedom as well as manipulate my readers with the content of the written matter. A whole week went by to complete 50 pages thanking Jungil Kim for his favors and repenting the misguided, short-sighted attempts to escape, a most heart-felt display of contrition mobilizing the confessional language of Augustine, Francis of Assissi, and all the other saints, for I was sincere in my denunciation of those attempted escapes, stupid, halfbaked capers.

I kept asking for a meeting with the warden or somebody in charge, partly to see how my new writing was received, partly to discover what they wanted to do with me. Three weeks later I was taken out of my cell to his office that resembled a recording studio with soundproofed walls, though no recording device was visible, not that it mattered one way or the other. When the door closed, the room was eerily quiet. The man behind the desk was middle-aged, slightly paunchy.

"Have some cigarettes," he offered.

"Thank you, but I don't smoke."

"As you wish, Comrade Moo," he said, not at all offended. "Why do you want to see me?"

"To ask if our Beloved Comrade Leader Jungil Kim has read my confessions," I said.

"I am sure he has."

"What does he say about them?"

"I can't speak for him."

"May I write about the films of North Korea?"

"Sure," he said, lighting a cigarette. "I know you can make films. Last week we had a showing of your movie Evergreen as part of an educational program for the Party cadre. It was a splendid work."

"Thank you," I said, touched by this recognition.

It was made shortly before our American exile about loyalty at work. A junior executive in a large construction company is tempted to set up his own company on the strength of a big job he gets through his salesmanship, but he chooses to report it to his company and see to its successful completion in spite of an unappreciative and meddlesome board of directors. It would be suitable even in North Korea.

So he knew all about me and Nanyong for we had directed

and played in it. All those who had seen the movie with him must have learned our names, too. Did they also know that I was rotting in jail or was my warden friend the only one privy to it?

"I know the song Yellow Shirted Guy featured in the movie," he said, before I could ask him about Nan. "Would you care to hear it?"

Without waiting for my reply, he began singing. To my amazement he sang, off tune, all the five verses sitting behind his desk with his eyes fixed on me. I was so embarrassed that I kept staring the whole time at a Japanese electric shaver on his desk. Vanity made such fools of us!

Joosong's reactions on the subject of Nan still fresh in my mind, I left his office without asking about Nan. I didn't want to jeopardize his goodwill. More paper and pen were brought to my room, so I could resume writing, taking my time as before and weighing every word. I wrote conjuring up the image of Jungil, so I shouldn't ever lose sight of my reader. Knowing that Jungil had something to do with every film produced in North Korea, I listed and praised the positive achievements, which weren't too numerous and were easy to remember. I was on my 30th page when the guard who had been watching banged the door open and jumped in.

"Don't mix Japanese in our language," he shouted, grabbing the sheets and shredding them to pieces. I had forgotten about the eradication of Chinese characters in North Korean writing, which the guard mistook for Japanese. As much a creature of habit and a snob as the next fellow, I kept intermixing the characters in my Korean writing, while intellectually castigating them. The guard's patriotic outburst had a happy outcome as far as I was concerned, for I could take another 15 days to finish the 50-page letter, proposing as diplomatically as possible a wider base for movie material than the personal exploits of Ilsung Kim. This time it took some effort to write that much, because I ran out of material, there being a limit to padding and rehashing.

Completion of the letter meant resumption of the Zen posture. Though sorely tempted to shift my weight or stretch my limbs, I dared not. Swift penalties were exacted for any violation in the form of reduced food rations, from which I wouldn't be exempted in spite of the warden's recognition and cordiality toward me.

One day I heard an inmate on his way to execution yelling, "Fucking assholes, you'll get it all back in double, triple measure." It was the first time I heard an inmate swear with such raw honesty and vigor and affected me powerfully. The jailers fell on him and gagged him with rags, but he spat them out and shouted his maledictions even louder, until a brutal kick to his groin crumpled him to the floor. His short-lived, pathetic defiance was heroic. Emaciated, reduced to the state of an animal, he had yet enough spirit to go to his death like a man. Would I?

Toward the end of November, a month and a half after my last letter to Jungil Kim, the warden called me to his office, raising my hopes, but all he wanted to know was the cast of characters appearing in my movie Barley Hill.

"Miss Nanyong Song was the leading actress," I said.

"Who were the others?" he asked.

"Jingyoo Gim, Unjin Han, Gumbong Do, Janggang Hu,..." I reeled off, disappointed at his evincing no further curiosity for Nan.

"Tell me more about their personal particulars, starting with Miss Song," he said.

So she was alive! In spite of his seeming casualness he could not conceal his pointed interest, I concluded elatedly, only to be crushed by the next question why. Could it be that Ilsung Kim was exploring some common topic in his attempt to win her over, because even he, the dictator, found rape an unacceptable alternative?

Another agonizing month passed but no word came from Jungil. The New Year was beginning, my third year in North Korea, with no prospect of release. Late in the afternoon on January 5, a bitter cold day, a tall jailer brought to my cell my brown suit wrapped in a bag and told me to change. The zipper had been removed from the fly, forcing me to tie the belt below the holder eyelets. The jailer shouted impatiently, raising his hand as if to strike me. This dashed all my hopes for release. Surely he would have treated me with more respect, if I were to be set free. Handcuffed, I was led out to the yard where a jeep was waiting with two policemen. As soon as I got on, the jeep roared off, leaving behind my abode for the last several months.

"Keep your head down," they said to prevent my seeing anything outside. Five minutes later we stopped at another prison yard. My two escorts left, leaving me with the driver in the car.

"Where are we?" I asked the driver, more to make conversation than with any serious intention of inquiry.

"The best hotel in the world," was his cynical reply.

The two policemen returned and led me to a building through an arched iron gate. At the entrance the jailers, holding down officer ranks, took over and put me in my cell. The floor was papered with cement sacking and the toilet was in an enclosure by the door. An inmate assistant, chosen among the convicts for good behavior, brought my supplies - shoes, long johns, facial and laundry soap, towel, tooth brush and powder, three aluminum bowls, basin and bedroll. The worthy, more arrogant than the jailers themselves, told me how long each item was expected to last - 10 months for the shoes, 6 months for the towel and soap, and so forth.

"No new ones will be issued before their time," he warned.

The day's routine was also spelled out - wakeup and roll call at 5 a.m., breakfast at 7, lunch at 12, and dinner at 6, with a flexible 20-minute daily sun bath and a bath every other week. Hung on a wall was a sheet of paper with the house rules written in India ink and brush - no talking to other inmates, strict maintenance of the meditative position, and so forth. But the calligraphy was the most artistically pleasing I had ever seen. It must have been some convict's hand. What a talent to be wasted!

At meal time a jailer came around with an inmate assistant pushing the food cart. The jailer ladled soup into a bowl and the assistant spooned up rice. I was amazed at the high quality of food - rice boiled with corn and topped by a slice of pork and soy bean paste soup with a lump of pork fat. This was real meat in months. To get maximum mileage I cut the slice of pork into small pieces and chewed each a long time, savoring the creamy sensation at my tongue tip. Any concern I might have had regarding cholesterol was a luxury long forgotten in conditions of absolute want. They even handed out candies or cookies as dessert occasionally. No sooner was the meal over than the meditative sitting posture resumed, making me meditate indeed. Did Jungil give me up as beyond redemption or did my letters of contrition and my proposals for improvement of North Korean film, whose merits must be clear to any expert, find their mark at last? At one moment I rode high on the crest of hope and the next I sank into the abyss of despondency.

At 10 p.m. the bed time bell rang. A jailer stopped at my door to peep in and clang another lock shut outside. Steam passed through the pipes under the floor with loud pops like gunshot reports, but the floor took a while to warm up. The cell, dimensioned for an average Korean male, was not wide or long enough for me and I could barely lay myself down diagonally. The wakeup bell rang promptly at 5 a.m. After dabbing my face with water from the basin I settled into the eternal sitting position until breakfast came, which was again quite as substantial as supper.

In addition to the "sun bath" there was a real bath with water twice a month, which, however, turned out to be a big disappointment. The large tub in a room at the end of the cell block was filled with steaming water literally at boiling point but there was no cold water tap to cool it. All I could do was fill a basin with the scalding water, dip my finger tips in it and quickly withdraw them, spread the moisture over different parts of my body, and rub down vigorously. By the time the water in the basin had cooled tolerably, my time was up. Of course, under the strict segregation rule, I was there by myself, except for my escort, the inmate assistant.

"Why waste heat like this?" I asked.

"To prevent waste of water," he replied. "Otherwise

everybody will be splashing and rinsing."

What a strange logic! Back at the cell the barber, another inmate assistant, brought a razor and hand mirror. The reflection on the unclear mirror was a total stranger, thinned to the bones and hairy like an ape, valleys cutting deep into my face on both sides of my nose.

Every morning at 11 a.m. the prison doctor went down the rows of cells, holding a chest of medicines and shouting, "Sick anybody?" From every room the response was affirmative, stomachache, headache, flu, indigestion, and an assortment of pains. But after a cursory look at the complainant the doctor walked on without slowing down. To make him stop and answer even a simple question one had to pretend as if he was on the point of death.

In March the sun became warmer and a small bird piped on the wall of the prison. I had put on more flesh and was no longer ravaged by hunger, occasionally leaving a piece of pork or pollack uneaten.

The whole of North Korea was in a cleanup frenzy to get ready for Ilsung Kim's Birthday, and the prison was no exception. I was given a bag of plaster powder to be mixed in water and applied to the walls and ceiling of my cell with a brush tied to a stick. But without the use of a proper fastener the dried coat of plaster came off like dust, whitening clothes or everything else that came into contact. Now it was impossible to lean on the wall, making the house rule against it quite superfluous. The next day cement sacking was handed out with glue to paper the floor. When the glue dried, a can of varnish was supplied to put a gloss on the sacking. But the varnish was as thin as gasoline and no matter how many coats were applied, no glossy surface emerged. In the meantime the fume from the chemical was overpowering especially in the absence of ventilation. I began vomiting and running a fever. No wonder the prisoners called the Birthday "April Torture". However, I expected my release or something unusual to happen on this day because a few days before a strange jailer had come to take my pictures.

Meanwhile, this day on which I had pinned so much hope

came and went like any other day. In some ways the holiday was worse than other days: we had to remain cooped up in our cells without the sunbath outing because most of the prison staff were off. But hope eternal sprang up and I reasoned that Jungil Kim wouldn't be so stupid as to let me rot in jail for ever after taking so much trouble to get me. The delay was just another insurance to secure his investment, to burn out any vestige of the West in me.

Early in July the investigator in charge of me arrived from the Politburo in Pyongyang, a balding man in his forties who looked open and good-natured.

"How is your health?" he asked.

"Good," I replied.

"Any questions?"

"Yes. Has the Beloved Comrade Leader Jungil Kim read my letters?"

"Of course he has."

"Can I then write to him again?"

"Yes. I'll send paper and pen."

When I returned to my cell, I found writing materials waiting for me already and took ten days to write a 30-page letter, begging for news of Nan's whereabouts.

"If she is dead, let me visit her grave with wine and dried pollack to comfort her soul. I'll then forget about her and serve the fatherland with all my heart...."

But the investigator who had promised to come back for the letter did not show up for nearly two months, dashing my hopes for early release and preferential treatment. Finally he arrived on August 15, Liberation Day, but his first words were full of complaint: "It's a holiday but I had to come all the way here because of your letter. It had better be good."

He didn't even bother to read and told me to seal it, then put it in his pocket and went away without saying good-bye.

The summer heat was unbearable. Mosquitoes bit day and night. Vicious blood-suckers, they forced me to stay awake whole nights catching them. My record one night was 237. The only defense was a towel covering the face with a small aperture at the nostrils, however uncomfortable this might be in the sultry night. I noticed that the insects came in waves. The first wave hit at around 7 or 8 p.m. but did not start feeding immediately, merely scouting the field and making mock dives and attacks designed to provoke the intended victim. Then, about 10 or 11 p.m., when the victim succumbed to sleep, exhausted by the futile skirmishes, the main wave arrived to feed in earnest.

In this heat it was sensible to take off clothes completely especially while sunbathing, but this was forbidden. North Korea was as prudish about nudity as a Puritan burgess. From long imprisonment my skin had developed itchy white patches which the sunbath helped some, but my groin, wet from sweat, itched as badly as ever. The mercurochrome supplied by the prison doctor only burned the skin off and did not cure the itch. So during the sunbath I furtively opened my drawers to expose the affected area to the sun without being noticed by the jailers. A few days of this treatment brought on a marked improvement. Unfortunately I was discovered in this act by a jailer one day who taunted me as a dirty masturbater.

It snowed continually in December. After a snowfall we were turned out, one person at a time, to shovel and sweep the snow. It was hard work but much preferable to being frozen in meditative posture at the cell. Snow was particularly heavy on Christmas Day, which had of course no significance in North Korea. I was glad to get out and sweep the snow. The fluffy powdery stuff, untrodden by human feet, was the epitome of purity and sanctity that needed no further embellishment. Then, noticing that the jailer was not looking, on impulse I loosened my belt and let out my urine to write "Merry Xmas", a behavior I am hard pressed to explain. If I had any lingering reverence for Christmas, I sure had an odd way of showing it.

It was New Year's Day, a year since my transfer from the Politburo jail. There was no such thing as special pardon or amnesty during or around New Year's Day, but again hope sprang up and now I expected release on February 16, Jungil Kim's birthday.

In my dark unventilated cell, barely 20 square feet wide, not able to sit or lie down at will, I could not think of human rights, dignity, freedom, creativity. Survival alone mattered.

A blade of grass or an ant busily searching for food seemed a monumental miracle. During a sunbath I built a rampart of dirt around an anthole to protect it from flooding. It was a thriving colony and its workers hauled in loads many times their size, a whole butterfly at one time, the bodies of their own dead now and then. I noticed other inmates shoring up budding grass. A vine started to creep on the ground and in vain I looked for a means of training it up the wall. The next day somebody more ingenious than I had come up with a solution - a piece of thread one end of which was tied to the vine and the other end to a sliver of wood smaller than a toothpick anchored in a chink in the wall.

It was July again. One hot muggy afternoon I was walking back and forth in the sun room for exercise, ignoring the perspiration, when the inmate assistant named Chay signaled to me to come closer.

"Word may come down any minute for your release," he whispered. "So dress up and be ready."

This left me stunned, the meaning of his words not sinking in for a while. I couldn't eat supper, the excitement robbng me of all appetite. I waited and waited and stayed up all night, but the summons did not come.

"Why did you lie to me yesterday?" I yelled at Chay when he showed up in the morning.

"Lie about what?"

"That they would release me."

"I said any minute. It could be today, because it didn't happen yesterday."

Of course nothing happened that day or the next or the day after that. I had been disappointed many times before but this time I felt literally crushed. I couldn't pick up the pieces again and go on living, hoping. It was better to end my life, if I were to rot in jail. The best method seemed to be fasting, especially since it would be a drawn-out affair which was bound to attract Jungil Kim's attention. If it didn't because he had no intention of retrieving me from the living hell, then I would let the fast take its course and end my life, which would be no loss.

After supper one day I made up my mind to start the fast from breakfast next day but morning came with such ravenous hunger that I decided to postpone a few days and stow away candies to sustain me for three days, the length of time I intended to fast, long enough to come to Jungil's notice. By now I was going through with this adventure entirely as a means to force the issue, not for suicide, even as a remote possibility. I wrapped 15 candies in scratch paper and glued the packet on the underside of the toilet seat using boiled rice. The momentous day arrived but again the overnight fast weakened my will and postponed the execution until lunch time. In the meantime I ate all the cookie crumbs I had been saving in the cell, as well as licking the bowls and dishes of the breakfast clean.

The fast began at lunch. The jailers took away the untouched bowls of rice and soup without much notice, perhaps thinking I had lost my appetite, but when the supper tray was found untouched, they began to suspect something.

"Why don't you eat?" they asked.

"I have made up my mind to die," I answered.

"Suit yourself. You'll soon be begging for food."

Noting my breakfast still untouched next day, the jailer said derisively, "So you still refuse to eat?"

"Let me talk to my investigator," I demanded.

"We'll let you talk to him after you starve a month."

Before taking the bowl of rice away, he turned it upside down to see if the inside had been hollowed out. In fact, driven by hunger I had thought of the very thing but had desisted just in case. After two days I was exhausted, though I had eaten all the candies. No longer caring what they might do to me, I stretched out on the floor, abandoning the meditative position. On the third day I could not raise myself to sit on the toilet. At mealtime the jailers put in food regardless of whether I would eat or not. The aroma from the dishes drove me insane. Hot breath puffed out of my throat as if my whole body was on fire. At night I secretly crawled to the toilet and drank the dirty water in the bucket but there was no relief. I no longer had strength to sit up and answer the roll call twice a day, in the morning and at night. In the meantime the jailers had been loud in denouncing my fast so the whole block knew about it and the inmates were all rooting for me as I found out later. On the fifth day my consciousness blurred and by nightfall on the sixth day I lost it completely. It was Assistant Chay who found me lying in my own mess, unconscious, I was told. The doctor came rushing to administer a shot. I began to revive slowly the next morning. Eyes closed, I could hear them talking about me.

"His toes are wriggling, so he isn't dead," somebody said.

I opened my eyes a crack and saw strangers standing around me, apparently highly placed officials. After they left, Assistant Chay brought me rice gruel and egg patties. Propping me up he told me to open my mouth. I bit down my lips and refused, but Chay wheedled and coaxed me like a child, and put a spoonful into my mouth. The food went down my throat as into a powerful suction pipe. I was back among the living. Apparently my strategy had worked, though it had taken a little longer than I had expected and nearly killed me.

"I had no idea you are so important," Chay said reporting on what had happened after I passed out. "The high and mighty prison officials were scared shitless when they thought you were really dead and ran around like poisoned rats."

"Who were here while I was out?"

"You peeked and saw me, didn't you?"

"Yes, but who were the others?"

"A new investigator and the Chief of Political Security, the almighty Chief himself, who would not be coming around for no mean starving prisoner. So you must be something. I've tried to fast before, but nobody paid any attention. After hearing that a man lasted at most ten days, I begged to be fed after three days. If it's someone they want alive, they'll force feed gruel through a straw stuck in the throat."

Until I recovered my strength, Chay came to me daily with gruel and other nutritious food, as well as much valuable information. After a while I could go to the sun room and one day heard someone tapping on the wall from the other side. I reciprocated with three taps of my own, thinking it was another inmate showing his approval of my defiance. The exchange of wall tappings went on for a few days but suddenly I became suspicious that this might be a trap and stopped.

At night jailers on duty had calls from their families, mostly their children wishing to hear their dads' voices before going to bed. No jailer had a private phone at home, so their families had to come to a public phone and call them at work. Nevertheless the soft loving chats, though one-sided, were sweet and deeply affecting. I both envied and pitied these men who were as much prisoners as we. How much more comforting and bearable my condition would be if I had a family to think of, if I knew who my parents were. Where was Nan? If fortune brought her back to me again, the first thing I would do would be start a family, a dozen children, even if it meant transplanting a whole new womb into Nan, who hadn't conceived since an unlicensed back alley abortion she had in the first year of her marriage to Jonghag, whose child she didn't care to bear, having no love for him. How wonderful it would be to be related to other human beings biologically! That was true immortality. As it was, my death would be total and final, leaving no trace behind.

I was put back on my previous diet of rice, pork, pollack, and soybean paste soup. But stones still abounded in the rice, some as big as beans, ruining my teeth. I got wiser and poured the hot water they brought along into the bowl of boiled rice and stirred the contents with chopsticks, until all the stones settled to the bottom. Now I could eat the top layers of rice at ease. But the method was not fool proof. One day I took a bite and heard an ominous crunch. I spat out everything in my mouth. Later feeling with my tongue, I found half of my right lower molar missing. What I had thrown out was part of my tooth as well as the stone. The broken molar began to ache and wiggle. I could not eat and the pain was excruciating. There was no dentist at the prison and my request for an outside dentist did not produce any results. On the third day the prison doctor took me to the sun room, and told me to open my mouth and look up, so he could extract the stump with a pair of pliers.

I obeyed. Without further ado he took a grip and yanked out. The pain stopped my breath. A weaker man would have easily gone into shock and heart seizure. The bleeding wouldn't stop and the doctor told me to bite down a wad of cotton. Only on the third day the bleeding came to an end.

For some time I noticed bunches of hair falling off my head and feared I might go bald prematurely. Whenever I ran my fingers through my hair, handfuls came off. Attributing it to malnutrition I asked the doctor to give me some vitamin pills but the worthy fellow said that loss of hair was part of the aging process and could not be prevented or reversed by vitamins. Assistant Chay happened to be by and heard about the problem.

"Do you use the laundry soap to shampoo your hair?" he asked.

"Yes," I said.

"Stupid. Your hair is not canvas."

The veteran inmate was wiser than the doctor. A few months after I stopped using the soap, hair started to grow back. The facial soap, given once every six months, was too precious for shampooing, as it was hardly enough for the face, but dirty hair was better than none at all.

Of course tap water was not fit for human consumption and even prisoners had to drink boiled water. Inferior quality was something every North Korean took for granted in life.

Through Assistant Chay I learned that I was staying at Politburo Prison Number Six, which incarcerated only political prisoners, critics and ideologues opposed to Ilsung Kim and his son, serving 15 or 20 years without formal trial, often without the knowledge of their families. They were teaching at a school, or working at a factory or office, or resting at home, when picked up by unidentified characters declaring themselves to be from the Party. Once imprisonment here was known, their wives came with divorce papers for their signatures, because otherwise their families would be relocated to the boondocks losing their jobs and connections.

The Sixth was divided into special and ordinary cellblocks. I was in the special block with about 60 cells housing about 90 inmates who enjoyed good food and were exempt from forced labor. Our only requirement was that we examine and reform our consciousness and ideology. The prisoner would be released and allowed to serve the fatherland again if judged reformed.

Otherwise, he would be sent over to the common block on the other side of the wall, a living hell with nearly 2,000 inmates packed 30 or 40 to a room, who worked from before daybreak to long after sunset in the nearby coal mine until they dropped dead. Almost all the common inmates asked to be put on the physically demanding excavation detail, because they would be given a piece of pork fat, a spoonful of cooking oil, and a stick of toffee a week to keep up their strength. Otherwise a common inmate lived on corn and other coarse grains boiled together, salt soup with some greens, and absolutely no meat except once a year on New Year's Day. But even this meager allowance was apt to be appropriated by the upper echelons of prison administration and an inmate was lucky to have a piece of intestine. Naturally the prisoners clamored to be put on the unloading detail when supply trucks came, for they could glean some droppings, if not purloin, from the sacks and barrels though that was risky under the watchful eye of the jailers. If the ingesting end was subhuman, the voiding end was even more degrading. The common inmates had to line up for hours to use the single toilet in their shed. Because of the congestion in the morning not everybody could relieve himself before going to work and did so on the road or at work when the guards were not looking. In winter they suffered from cold in their cells, and many lost their fingers and toes to frostbite, their only protection being overalls and underwear. Socks were unheard of and their feet had to be wrapped up in pieces of cloth they could scrounge here and there. Bathing, whether in the sun or in the tub, was unknown, and so was soap, even the depilatory laundry type. Unlike the south North Korea did not practice torture. If they did not like someone, all they had to do was put him in one of the 30 or so common prisons scattered around the country. If it was a confession they wanted, they got it quickly. Otherwise the convict worked for a few years and died, life expectancy in these hell holes seldom exceeding ten years. It was a chilling revelation and as nothing came of my fasting caper I momentarily expected a transfer to the common block.

Another New Year's Day was over. I had been in North Korea four years, three of them in prison. Gradually I was losing hope of ever seeing the outside world. Even more alarming was my growing resignation and apathy, not really caring any more whether I got out or not.

XX.
Tayoung Yee, the Historian

On January 8 the jailer brought a prisoner in his mid-70's to my room as cellmate. His addition seemed to doom my chances of gaining freedom, because they wouldn't expose me, a kidnap victim, to a companion if I was to be released at all.

"I am Professor Tayong Yee, the historian," he introduced himself.

It was the first time I met anybody so free and open with his name or occupation, whether in prison or out. Another unusual thing about him was his being allowed to bring with him a small writing table and an envelope full of documents, writing paper and pencil. I was glad of his company but the professor with his scholarly paraphernalia presented a serious space problem. The cell was simply not big enough. Finally, after repeated requests, we were moved a few days later to a bigger room next to the bathroom. But just as we moved in, the rusty steam pipe under the floor sprang a leak, filling the room with vapor. We had to wait in another cramped cell for a whole week while the pipe was being fixed. As soon as we went back to our proper room, the professor settled down to writing whatever came to his head from morning till bedtime. I couldn't imagine his writing anything of value, but what amazed me was the uniform deference shown to him by the jailers. He was promptly supplied with any amount of paper he wanted and exempt from the meditative posture or the rule prohibiting conversation. The jailers simply looked the other way, when he talked to me which was often and long.

Professor of History at the Military Academy and official historian of the Labor Party Yee had authored History of Power and The Korean People's Struggle for Liberation, which had served as textbooks in the North Korean curriculum and been quoted in the scholarly bibliographies of the West. Especially his second book, The Struggle, a passionate denunciation of Imperial Japan as well as other powers that sought to aggrandize themselves by enslaving weaker nations, had served as an inspiration in the 60's and 70's to the South Korean students demonstrating in opposition to Junghee Park's "humiliating talks for normalization of relations with Japan."

Suddenly, he lost his professorship and position with the Party and was sent to the Shinyang Paper Mill to work as laborer for a whole year before his commitment to the common block at Prison Six. He was glad to sign his divorce papers so his wife and children could go on living in Pyongyang but to this day, after serving ten years, two of them at hard labor, he didn't know what had caused his downfall. Up to the last minute he had every assurance of acceptance and approval of his work. Perhaps this was just a test of his loyalty by his Chief, to see if he was worthy of higher trust. Was Job more patient with his God?

Late in April Professor Yee and Assistant Chay had a quarrel over a razor blade. We had one issued every other week so we could shave ourselves at bath time but since it served the whole block, it dulled fast and pulled rather than shaved the beard, especially for those at the tail end of the line. Nevertheless it was Assistant Chay's job to pick up and account for it when we were through, for it could be a dangerous weapon, especially for self-injury. On that day Yee and I happened to be the last users and Chay came to collect. Finding half of the blade broken off and missing, Chay accused Yee of hiding the missing portion to use for scratching out errors in his writing, which Yee vehemently denied. Our cell was turned upside down ten times and our clothes and bodies thoroughly searched but the half blade did not turn up. The search of the other cells and inmates did not produce it, either.

I knew Yee must be the culprit because I clearly remembered using the whole blade and he had used it after me. For the world I couldn't figure out where he could have hid it, nor did he ever tell me.

However, he proceeded to give me quite a lecture on blades. Though labeled Fragrance Mountains to give the appearance of domestic manufacture, they were in fact all imported from Eastern Europe, because North Korea did not possess the know-how to make sheet metal thinner than one-fifth of a millimeter. That's why North Korean cans were as thick as pots. Indeed I recalled my taking two cans for my aborted escape, thinking how substantial they had felt. North Korean steel technology was so primitive that its only export was pig iron. Then at one point an upsurge in patriotic pride caused a suspension of its export until North Korea could manufacture salable iron products. Czechoslovakia, the chief importer of North Korean pig iron, had to order 100,000 axes to satisfy the new export regulation. As soon as the shipment arrived, the Czechs took out the handles and melted down the heads to make their steel.

"I thought you were a historian, not a materials scientist," I observed in admiration.

"I know a lot of other things that you wouldn't even dream of," he said. "One of these days I'll tell you something that may have a direct bearing on your parentage."

"What is it? Tell me right now."

"In good time but not now."

He wouldn't budge from this position, compelling me to curb my burning curiosity in the possible transition from Double Nothing to something. After all what could this old jailbird know that I didn't already? My life had been given worldwide publicity, especially since GI Orphan won the Cannes. I didn't hide anything in the hope of my real parents or relatives coming forward with the information I sought, but nobody had come forward. In spite of his advanced age the old man was given to grandstanding and posturing. Perhaps he wanted to keep me in suspense, to gloat in his power over me as the possible oracle of my origin. Not wishing to give him the pleasure, I pretended disinterest and eventually forgot all about it.

The winter was particularly severe that year and power outages were frequent, which meant no steam and freezing temperatures for the inmates. Predictably, hydroelectric power, North Korea's main supply, was low in winter, and what electricity there was had to go to the industries. But I felt the shortages, caused by wholesale waste compounded on a national scale, could have been avoided. For example, I noticed from the sun room bare wires in direct contact with the eaves, increasing the loss factor to 99%. Another anomaly was that the telephone wire was as thick as the electric. It was a wonder that the phones worked at all.

About 11 a.m. in the middle of December a jailer came for me and told me to follow him. Passing three doors beyond the usual interview room, he led me outside the wall of Prison Six and headed for the white three-story building that housed the administration. It was the first time in two years that I saw the whole compound, which was completely surrounded by a high concrete block wall, rough with slumped mortar at the joints. We crossed a bridge over a moat to the administration building. The office I entered had plenty of sun and noisy with the steam rushing through the radiators. About five minutes later a man in people's uniform stepped in who must be highly placed from the obsequiousness shown to him by the prison staff.

"Would you live in North Korea if Nanyong Song were with you?" he asked, startling me with the abruptness of the question.

"Yes, sir," I answered with alacrity. "I am an ordinary man who needs a woman above anything else."

"But she isn't your wife."

"Because of the distorted lifestyle in the capitalist society. If she and I are brought together again, the first thing we will do is get married. I am sure she wants it that way too and in any case I can persuade her. I have resolved to live conforming to the pattern of stable family life set down by the Party. Through prison life I have learned the true meaning of the Korean Labor Party, which deserves absolute and unconditional-al loyalty. Previously, spoiled by capitalism, I questioned such obedience, but now I know better. To accomplish the revolution we have to follow our Leader and Chief unconditionally."

"How can you contribute to the revolution?"

"By making pictures with a heightened class consciousness. The pictures I made before tended to blunt the class consciousness of the masses, playing into the hands of the capitalists. My new pictures will be totally different. I have repented my errors thoroughly and feel like a new born man, ready to go into the battle front of revolution."

The official, soft spoken and gentle but deadpan like others of his ilk, didn't show the slightest sign of his emotion one way or the other. I might have been talking to a tape recorder that merely asked a set of questions and recorded my responses with mechanical fidelity. The hour long interview ended with no indication when or whether I would be released. I returned to the cell depressed, not so much at the uncertainty as at my transformation into a parrot, mouthing 'revolution,' 'class consciousness,' and other terms like gospel truths and furthermore believing them, at least at the time.

"He is a special envoy from Jungil Kim," Tayung Yee said after making me go over the details. "Your release is imminent."

"I hope you are right."

"I know I am. Do you recall my promise to give you information regarding your parentage in good time? Well, that time has come. I am convinced that you are the grandson of Dr. Josef Minsky, the world-renowned naturalist who served briefly as Minister of Agriculture in Syngman Rhee's cabinet before the war. Do you recognize the name?"

"Of course. Every child has read about him in the history book. I was particularly intrigued because he was a Caucasian and yet was allowed to hold down such a high rank in Rhee's government. But why not make Douglas MacArthur my grandfather if all we have to go on is my Caucasian appearance? There are two or three billion of them running around."

"Didn't you say you were left at the Mercy Home

orphanage in Daegu?"

"Yes."

"Were there many other mixed race orphans?"

"Not by the time I was old enough to know what's what. But it's possible there had been others."

"Even if there were a hundred others, nobody else would have had the high order of intelligence to be a Minsky. Wait. We are trying to determine a geneology and false modesty will only get in the way. You are a genius, let's face it. Your IQ must be 200 or higher."

"I never had it tested."

"Well, they don't tell everything anyway. But your mastery of the secondary curriculum in less than a year and your ability to teach yourself whole new languages and disciplines in a matter of months is a typical Minsky trait. Remember nobody is superior to his biology and genetic coincidences are rare. I'll tell you all about the Minskys and judge for yourself whether they are your ancestors or not."

• • • •

In the first decade of the century Josef Minsky, a Russian Polish biology major just out of college, came to Vladivostok and married Gisoon Bag, the daughter of a Korean fur dealer, Daybay Bag, Treasurer of the Provisional Government of Korea in exile at Shanghai, to whom every patriot worthy of the name owed a helping hand. As he was frequently away from home for months at a time, the young couple gradually took over the business and built it into a fortune. Following the defeat of the White Army, in which Josef commanded a division, the Minskys immigrated to Korea in 1921, of course hiding their relationship to Daybay who was on the most wanted list of Japanese police. Ceded an abandoned logging camp in Gayma Plateau, "the Roof of Korea" as it was called, the backdrop to the coastal strip around Chongjin where Pastor Doochan Ham, a relative of Daybay's and a patriot, had his enormously influential church, the Minskys built a ranch to hold and process wild animals hunted, trapped, or collected under a general license for the zoos, museums, and laboratories all over the world. Soon the Snow Country Ranch became famous. In his true element, the primeval forests of Northern Korea, Josef's homing instinct for the rare find grew ever sharper, for which the universities honored him with doctorates.

The Minskys had one son, Anton, and the Hams a son and two daughters, the younger of whom, Haran, practically grew up with Anton on the ranch a short walk from her father's church. Anton liked Haran well enough, but he also had a crush on her older sister, Aran, several years his senior

"Aran Ham of the Aran Ham Center for Folk Music in Seoul!" I exclaimed, amazed.

"Right," Tayong said. "I won't be surprised if they've named one after her, because she has rescued Korean music from the quicksand of memory and oral tradition, not to mention her family's generous endowment for the cause. Upon graduation with top honors from the Pyongyang Conservatory of Music she returned to Chongjin to be music director at her father's church, declining lucrative recording and film contracts. The fame of the Chongjin Presbyterian Church was due as much to her incomparable music as to her father's eloquent preaching."

It wasn't long before Haran went around broadcasting, "Anton loves my sister!" The grownups smiled indulgently. Haran went right up to Aran herself and blurted, "He loves you, Sis." Anton felt crushed and expected the offended lady to chastise him publicly for his presumption, but she never let on that she had heard anything untoward and went on giving him the special music lessons deemed necessary by his guardians to round out his education.

Late one night Pastor Ham called at the ranch and after a hushed conference with his parents told Anton to come along to the church. Anton obeyed, certain that the moment of reckoning had come for his unholy feelings toward the sisters. The pastor led him through the side door into the sacristy, where a dignified old gentleman came forward and warmly embraced Anton, declaring himself Daybay Bag, who had risked by coming there not only his life but that of everybody else. It was an emergency. A courier had to be sent immediately with messages and funds to the Provisional Government. Anton had to be it. Though only 18, he was over 6 feet tall and big boned thanks to his Slavic genes. Receiving his itinerary and instructions from the two patriarchs, Anton realized how close the Hams had been to his family and was smitten by a new sense of guilt and shame. Romantic attachment to even one of the Ham sisters would have been like incest or worse, but he was guilty by a double measure.

But he was not allowed to dwell on this line of self-recrimination. Put on the train bound for Shanghai next morning via Wonsan, Seoul, Pyongyang, Dantung, and Beijing, he was to travel over 10,000 miles clear to the other side of the world. After delivery at Shanghai, he proceeded directly to Princeton Theological Seminary to which he had just been admitted in spite of his total lack of formal schooling. On the first day at the nearby elementary school in Chongjin he was ogled at relentlessly by the whole school, even when he went to the bathroom. Unable to relieve himself, Anton came home crying, pants soiled. That was also the last day he attended a class in Korea. His parents enrolled him in a one-student home tutorial, ordering textbooks from grade one to 20 in a dozen languages they jointly commanded. So began his unusual schooling. He might be spared the anatomic curiosity of his peers, but was driven into one intensive course of study after another. Paranoid that their son might not be getting enough, his parents preferred to err on the side of excess. Fortunately, endowed with a brain like a sponge Anton absorbed everything these anxious pedagogues drummed into his head. Dr. John Beach, Director of the Good Samaritan Presbyterian Hospital in Chognjin, wrote about him to his alma mater. After appropriate exams proctored by Beach Princeton was convinced they had an outstanding candidate.

During the few years it took him to get his doctorate in theology with emphasis on history, World War II ended and Korea was liberated from Japan, only to be divided and occupied. Targeted for extermination by the new masters of North Korea, the Minskys and the Hams fled south by sea, with some 400 others of the Chongjin Presbyterian Church, quite a daring escape which got written up in the Western press as Exodus of the 20th Century. Incidentally, this saved Aran from unwanted marriage to Ilsung Kim, who had long desired her since her Conservatory days in Pyongyang and exacted her consent to marry in return for the release of her imprisoned father.

In South Korea the Minskys and Hams were far from being the typical refugees, uprooted and dispossessed. Pastor Ham's new church, 'Star of the East', begun as a makeshift tent near Seoul Station, grew so explosively that soon it had to be moved to a new building on the slope of Mt. North. KBS importuned Aran to sing on the radio and the College of Music offered her a chair. Haran became a movie star, celebrated for her role as the betrayed wife in Sunset. General John R. Hodge, US Military Governor, asked Josef Minsky to head the Department of Culture and Education. Syngman Rhee, hand-picked by the US as President of the Republic of Korea to end the military government in 1948, asked Josef to stay on in his cabinet as Minister of Agriculture and Forestry, but they didn't get along, primarily because Rhee found Gisoon, Josef's wife, a threat. Everybody still remembered her father Daybay Bag, though he was not around: he had disappeared some years before near Harbin while meeting a contact, presumably betrayed to the Japanese police and tortured to death. Had he lived and returned to South Korea, he would have been killed or jailed on various trumped-up charges like the other returnees from Shanghai by Rhee, who fabricated and guarded the myth that he had been the only patriot to bring about the country's liberation.

After his resignation, Josef and Gisoon immigrated to the US and settled in New York, joining Anton who was teaching Far Eastern history and culture at New York University after graduation from Princeton. Hired as collector and naturalist for the New York Museum of Science, Josef found an opportunity to return to Korea in 1950 on an assignment to capture the elusive dwarf owl Bugoog Bird, whose haunting two-tone monody one heard in the quiet of a summer night from the woods high up in the hills deep into the night. Koreans had lived with its song for thousands of years, and poets had written about it, but nobody had seen or studied the bird itself.

During his hunting days in the wilds of Korea Josef had fallen asleep exhausted under a larch. When he woke, the sun had set but a half light lingered. Suddenly a small yellowish brown bird, looking like an owl and about the size of a bull-finch with two tufts on its head came flying up from the canyon below, alighted on a branch of the larch, threw its head back, and sang, projecting the sound like a ventriloquist to distances so out of proportion to its size or appearance that unless he had seen from the beginning he wouldn't have credited the nondescript creature with the music. At another time he happened to be by a nest of these birds he now recognized by sight. After a suitable time he returned to steal the nestlings but found the nest abandoned. On this trip Josef was hopeful of success because he had been in correspondence with a Buddhist monk of long acquaintance who reported sighting a nest of these owlings not far from his hermitage in the mountains of Haynam.

At 4 a.m. on Sunday, June 25, 1950, the People's Army attacked on a broad front along the 150-mile border, 38th Parallel. By Tuesday Seoul was like a stirred beehive, shells from howitzers crashing into town and everybody in a frenzy to cross the bridge over the Han and flee south. The American Embassy had been calling on all foreign nationals to report to Inchon for immediate evacuation by a chartered Norwegian freighter, but Josef Minsky was in the mountains catching his bugoog bird, unreachable by phone, radio, or messenger. Bombs and gunfire flashed through the pitch dark night and flying shrapnel hissed in the pelting rain, but the crush of refugees heading for the river showed no sign of abatement. Shortly past midnight the ROK Army Corps of Engineers blew up the bridge, causing dozens of vehicles to plummet into the swollen river. Street fights had broken out all over town, rifle shots punctuating machine gun bursts.

Next morning on Wednesday the sun rose in total

unconcern over the rainstorm and pandemonium of the previous night. It was a changed world, red flags fluttering noisily atop the City Hall and Capitol, and Ilsung Kim's and Stalin's portraits, still wet with paint, draping the sides of buildings and walls. Soviet-made tanks roared up and down the streets, chewing up the asphalt and firing random rounds. The victorious soldiers marched by, heads held up high, arms swinging, to the cheers of the crowds. House to house searches began for enemies of the people, government officials, businessmen, landowners, to be shot and thrown into ditches.

Everybody who had been in the Exodus from Chongjin was rounded up and imprisoned, beaten, or shot. Josef Minsky, arrested in Gwangjoo with a cageful of the bugoog birds, was shifted from one temporary prison to another with other foreign internees, diplomats and missionaries. Taken by train to a camp near the Soopoong Dam on the Yalu, they were detained for three years until their repatriation at the end of the war, that is, for those who survived, one out of five. Josef's birds didn't, dying almost immediately, nor did Josef himself, who died of tuberculosis in the last month. Pastor and Mrs Ham were among the first to be captured and dispatched by the vengeful conqueror, Ilsung Kim.

Ignorant of their parents' fate the two daughters remained in hiding for some time but were eventually tracked down. Aran was kept under close watch at Ilsung Kim's mobile field camp. With a group of other film and entertainment people Haran was at the Mapo Prison and taken north when MacArthur recaptured Seoul in September. Near Pyongyang, while the group scattered in the dark during an air raid, she managed to escape to the UN lines and met Anton Minsky, who had joined the war as an officer in KLO, a special commando arm of the Eighth US Army formed for infiltration behind the enemy lines, in the hope of finding and rescuing his father and friends. Married on the spot, they made their home in Pusan, the wartime capital.

Soon after her marriage Haran had a letter from Aran asking her to obtain information about KLO and overall US Army plans through Anton who had access to the top echelons of MacArthur's Headquarters because of his linguistic and other expertise.

"Dear Sister," Aran appealed. "I ask not for my sake but for the lives of our beloved parents and Dr. Josef Minsky, Anton's father, who will die if you do not comply."

The next KLO detachment, led by Anton himself and airdropped near the Soopoong camp, was ambushed and decimated with no survivors. In the meantime ROK intelligence, which had Haran under surveillance for some time, convicted her of espionage and treason. Her execution was delayed however because of her pregnancy. It was the second year of the war, which had become a minor World War with over a million Red Chinese committed on the side of North Korea and a matching UN Command on the opposite side. As the front line stabilized more or less around the waist of the peninsula, Aran was transferred from a guarded guesthouse in Antung, Manchuria, to another in Shinujoo on the Korean side of the Yalu, where Ilsung left her unmolested after finding his attempts to win her as futile as ever. One day Aran learned about Haran's terrible sentence through someone loyal to the family. With his help she slipped out of the house she had been detained in and crossed the front, still fluid at the time, with other agents being infiltrated south. Upon arrival at the Army prison in Daegu, she found Haran already executed after premature delivery of a baby boy by Caesarian section, butchery rather than surgery because it was immaterial whether she died of hemorrhage and blood poisoning or a bullet wound. Aran took care of the infant, until Ilsung's agents caught up with her. She placed her nephew in an orphanage prior to her transportation north by her abductors who had no allowance for excess baggage, the mixed-race child, and had in fact explicit orders to do away with it.

"How do you know all this?" I asked at the end of his narrative.

"I was Ilsung Kim's personal secretary as well as chronicler at the time," he said. "That didn't mean I could chronicle everything but I had to know pretty much everything connected with Ilsung's life, public and private. He took me everywhere he went. I was in Chongjin with the groom's party for the wedding that never took place. I still remember him falling apart and bawling heartbroken when he learned of his bride's flight. He had really cared for her. The rage and vengeance came later."

"But why did Aran write to her sister and force her to commit espionage?"

"She never did."

"You said she did."

"Somebody else did, me. I had a gift for penmanship as well as writing and it wasn't hard to forge after studying some of her writing samples."

"You are the lowliest of lowly vermin."

"I deserve your contempt, but I was merely doing my job the best I could. To date Aran has been spared knowledge of the forgery or the deaths of her parents and Josef Minsky."

"What happened to Gisoon Minsky?"

"I don't know. She was living in New York. Probably she is dead by now."

"Where is this lady Aran?"

"In a well-guarded mansion somewhere with all the comforts she could desire, including musical instruments and books."

"As Ilsung's wife?"

"No. He has a wife, Sungay, whom he married soon after his return to Pyongyang without his intended bride. Sungay was then his secretary and was good to his infant son Jungil left motherless after Jongsoog died in childbirth."

"Then Aran Ham must be his concubine or mistress."

"No. With all his power he couldn't swing that. He is not known to be a respecter of feminine virtue particularly but in her case he seems to observe an uncharacteristic code of honor."

"Does he visit her?"

"Once a year on her birthday to ask her whether she has changed her mind about him and about working for him like everybody else, only to be told that she hasn't. It's an annual ritual, comical or solemn, depending on how you look at it. You must give him credit for constancy if nothing else."

"Did she leave the child at the Mercy Home?"

"I am sure that's where she left you because you say so. You are a Ham-Minsky and she will confirm it."

"I doubt she could recognize me after all these years. I don't think I could. Nothing remains of her image, except a jumbled blur. Nevertheless, if I see her, maybe it'll all come back. But how can I see her?"

Though skeptical, I couldn't help being hopeful. Perhaps my abduction to North Korea was preordained so I could meet Aran Ham. How I wished she were my real aunt, as Tayong Yee said!

"You'll have a chance. You are being freed to make films. Persuade Jungil to produce subjects that use Korean music and ask for an authority in the field, which she is. They are all getting on in years and Ilsung Kim might just let her go, letting bygones be bygones."

Late in February, two months after my interview with what Yee described as Jungil Kim's personal envoy, the guard told me to take a bath, though I had taken one a few days before. When I stepped out of the bathroom, Assistant Chay was waiting with my old clothes, all washed and ironed. As soon as I changed, discarding the prison garb, the jailer took over and led me directly to the conference room in the front of the building, where two officials in people's uniform, sitting at one end of the table, directed me to take a seat at the other end. One of them, thin as a stick, drew out of his valise a rectangular cardboard.

"Pay close attention to what I read," he said, holding up the cardboard above his head. "We forgive your grievous crimes, so you will have another chance to work for the Selfhood Fatherland to the utmost of your ability. Signed Jungil Kim."

To be free at last! Disappointed so often, I couldn't believe its reality when it came and stared me in the face.

"Come and follow us," the same official said, leading the way.

"Can I say good-bye to my cellmate?" I asked hesitantly.

"You want to go back to your cell?" he asked unsympathetically.

"No, sir."

I followed without another word, telling myself that some day soon I would surely return and visit with Tayong Yee, who had suggested the possibility of my transition from nothing to something, from Moo to Minsky, however improbable. I would repay him by arranging his release at the earliest opportunity. I owed it to him. But such fickle stuff is gratitude made of that once outside, caught up in the whirlwind of events that followed, I couldn't come and visit him at Number Six, let alone arrange his release.

A Benz parked in the yard drove out the gate as soon as we got in the back, with me in the middle. The two men flanking me did not say a blessed word as we drove past collectives drying corn. We passed a small country train station and a cement factory before entering Pyongyang.

"I hear you have reflected on our revolution and your mind has been reformed," said the thin official.

"Yes, one hundred percent."

"When we get to your quarters stand before our Great Leader and Chief's portrait and swear your allegiance loudly and solemnly."

"I will."

We drove through town and stopped at a two-story Politburo Guesthouse, staffed by a dozen cooks, maids, and other servants, a close replica of the guesthouse in Chestnut Grove. Shown to my bedroom upstairs I flung myself down on the bed, luxuriating in its cleanness and softness, amazed that my feet didn't touch the walls when I stretched out full length. I could sleep without waking for a week.

"Come downstairs for your lunch," the thin man said.

"Yes, sir," I said, jumping up.

All the rooms in the house had mats of colorful design instead of rugs on the floor. In the dining room on the right wall hung Ilsung Kim's color portrait, before which I came to attention and shouted, "I thank you deeply, Great Leader and Chief, for showing me, a pathetic creature that has lived in ignorance of the meaning of revolution and your far-reaching wisdom and benevolence. I swear to give my heart and soul to you, Great Chief, the sun of our people and pole star of world revolution, and to discard my old capitalistic ways and live meaningfully for the people and working classes."

After watching my performance closely my guides told me to sit at the table, loaded with good food, not dreamed of in No. Six. They kept urging me to eat and I wasn't loath to oblige. When I finished what was placed before me, the maids brought in something different, which I was again asked to consume. This was the other extreme, the stuffing torture, and I could barely stand up when they were finally done with me. In the living room I sank into the sofa like a stone, asleep.

After the nap I turned on the Hitachi TV set in the room but the reception was appalling, ghosting and streaking, to which I called attention.

"Look," the official said after a quick adjustment. "It works okay when I tune it but goes wrong at your touch. Even the set seems sensitive to the pollution of capitalism, ha, ha."

"But it's still ghosting," I said after a glance at the screen.

He looked between the set and me a few times and said, "It's your eyes, not the set." Five years of staring at the opposite wall only three feet away had ruined my vision.

I was fed voluminously again the next day and the next, and my cheeks filled out visibly and biceps put on flesh. All of a sudden, I noticed my right anklebone swelling to the size of an egg and a yellow spot forming in each eye. My resident counselor took me to the South Mountain Hospital, a 7-story modern structure about 20 minutes away by car, a cut lower than the Flame Clinic though used exclusively by the families of Party bosses. After a general checkup and various tests the doctor said everything was okay.

"What about the swelling and the dots?" I asked, aghast.

"They'll go away in time," he said, without any explanation of the clearly abnormal symptoms. Perhaps he simply did not know because of the crudity of his diagnosis or training. Unable to verbalize these thoughts I came away, fearing that something might be gravely wrong with me. How ironical to be set free only to be struck down by some vile disease like immune deficiency!

My counselor took me next to the barber shop at the Pyongyang Inn, said to be used exclusively by foreigners. There must be precious few foreigners because all of the six brand-new chairs remained empty the whole time I was there. But the reason soon became clear: the barber cut hair only one way, his way. No sooner had the cloth been fastened around my neck than his clippers plowed across my pate, leaving a deep furrow.

"You should have left some hair in front," I said mournfully.

"Leave it up to the barber comrade," my counselor and watchdog cautioned.

I ended up with a crew cut, the dominant male hair style in North Korea. Diligently but futilely pressing the bristle of hair down to cover the exposed Third Eye, I swore I would never let a North Korean barber near me unless he gave his word to leave that part alone.

"What will you say if you met our Beloved Comrade Leader just now?" my guide asked on the eleventh day after my release.

"I don't know. I have never thought about it."

"Imagine he is right here in front of us and think of the right things to say."

Try as I might, I couldn't come up with suitable dialogue on such short notice, though I had known all along that I would meet Jungil some day. Nobody, not even Junghee Park, had been so important that I had to rehearse the conversation in advance before but I might have to here in North Korea, dealing with characters like Jungil Kim.

"We are going out to eat," my companion said coming up to my room in the evening. "Something mighty nice may happen to you tonight."

My heart started pounding. So it was happening after all, the long-awaited meeting with Jungil Kim. What should I say to him? All the flowery phrases I had rehearsed after my guardian had planted the idea in the afternoon seemed to have taken flight. The imprisonment had done wonders to my autonomic nervous system. My intellect might still despise the likes of Jungil Kim but my reflexes cringed in abject servility even at the mention of his name. We waited, my companion looking at the clock as anxiously as I. It was quite late, past 10 p.m. when two men in their 50's arrived, one in military and the other in people's uniform, both mellow with drink, and told me to get into the Benz they had brought. Obviously they were well acquainted with my case.

"How did you figure you would escape with a face like yours that can be spotted anywhere?" one of them said in a bantering mood, reminding me of the same observation made to me by the older boys at the Mercy Home. Except this time I took the warning to heart, my spirit of rebellion completely quelled.

"Why don't you try again and rot away another five years?" the other said.

I smiled like an idiot, masking the shiver down the spine. Never again would I risk the chance of imprisonment in a North Korean jail. About ten minutes later we stopped at a three-story building with many Benzes parked in front. A guide led us down the long hallway covered with a deep-piled carpet. At a door they all entered, telling me to wait. A little later the guide returned and beckoned me to come in.

XXI.
Reunion

I walked into the middle of the hall where a party was in progress. Suddenly all faces turned to me and an applause broke out, bewildering me. Then I heard a woman scream, which sounded familiar. I looked intently and saw her rooted to a spot trembling and pale, supported by a few men around her. Could it be really her? A deathly quiet reigned as I stepped closer, squinting. It was her, my Nan. At one bound I pounced on her and clasped her in my arms, her soft warm body as fresh and sweet as I had always known it, as if I had never left her side. We could have remained so locked forever, deaf to the loud applause, oblivious to the flash bulbs exploding wildly like fireworks. The months and years of misery and degradation evaporated in the white heat of our undiminished passion and love for each other.

"This is our Beloved Comrade Leader Jungil Kim," Nan said, pointing at the round-faced chubby man with an innocent, boyish charm and disarming air of candor. Yes, he was the same man I had seen at a distance in the Longevity Art Theater.

I bowed deeply and he put out his hand for me to shake.

"Let's take a picture together," he said standing between us.

"Comrades," he said turning to the roomful of people, "meet my new movie advisor."

A big round of applause followed. Seating us to his right and left he said aloud so everybody could hear, "Let's make an honest couple out of you and set the wedding date as April 15, our Great Chief's next birthday." This was greeted by hand clapping, laughter and some suppressed ribaldry.

"Beloved Comrade Leader," I said on impulse. "I have been denied her bed for nearly six years and, short of a remand to No. Six, nothing will stop me from climbing it long before April 15. So please marry us now according to the prerogative of every ship captain, magistrate, or head of state."

"Moo Moo!" reproached Nan, blushing and hanging her head with embarrassment, while the chiefly male crowd responded with a loud expression of approbation.

"So be it!" Jungil said. "Stand before me holding hands. I pronounce you, Moo Moo and Nanyong Song, husband and wife. Live happily, and work for the fatherland. Now you are married. This is your wedding party."

The company crowded around us and expressed their best wishes, all quite sincerely in spite of the extreme brevity and informality of the ceremony.

"Are you disappointed by the simplicity, my dear bride?" I asked Nan when we were alone.

"Of course not," she answered cheerfully. "We have had no less than the Crown Prince of a nation wed us, my lord and husband."

It was past midnight but the party showed no sign of letup. Flushed with drink, red eyes almost popping out of their sockets, Jungil was his best convivial self.

"Has the doctor lifted his ban on your drinking since I saw you last?" Nan asked him.

So she had been seeing him. She knew about his doctor's orders. How much more did she know about him?

"Let him go to hell," he said. "It's a special day and I'll drink no matter what he says." Then, turning to me, he asked, "Do you object to your wedding guests drinking?"

"No," I answered. "Forgive me for not joining, Beloved Comrade Leader, but..."

"It's I who should be asking forgiveness for playacting so long, making you suffer all this time."

At the same time Jungil pulled my hand to his lap and gave it a squeeze, an odd gesture as apologies went but effective in defusing and neutralizing, at least for the moment, all my pent-up resentment and antipathy toward this author of so much mischief. I had laughed hearing about a farmer wetting his pants upon holding South Korean President Doohwan Jun's hand in a receiving line, but I was wetting my pants too, in a manner of speaking.

"Look!" he said, in a loud voice for all to hear, putting an end to my bemusement. "We haven't touched her and are turning her over whole to you. We Communists are clean and pure that way."

The audience exploded with hand claps and approving shouts.

"Thank you, sir," I said, truly grateful, for this had been the most agonizing concern of mine the whole time I was in prison, recalling the promiscuity of Junghee Park, Doohwan Jun, Syngman Rhee, and just about any politico in South Korea, in power or out. I had read with deep mortification about the colorful escapades of Daejung Kim, for whom I had risked my life, during his one-year residence at Harvard, narrated by his favored women.

The band struck up on the stage that faced the head table and the party guests rose to dance and sing. Immediately I was made the target of enforced drinking. Jungil poured out a glass full of Hennessey cognac, which was followed by another glassful from Ginam Kim, publisher of the Labor Daily, Jaygyong Gil, Deputy Chief of Foreign Affairs, Jungnin Kim, Chief of Liaison with South Korea, a spectacled man in his 50's who said he was head of the official news agency Korea Central News, and so forth, who all said solemnly, as they poured:

"Let's be loyal to our Beloved Comrade Leader."

I remembered Gil from the wire dispatches some years before my abduction as the North Korean diplomat expelled from Sweden for smuggling. His continued employment and preferment in government service could argue only one thing: Jungil's endorsement of his conduct. Jungnin Kim had also been featured frequently in South Korean papers because of his subversive activities.

One character was remarkable, Ingoo Cha, Deputy Chief of the Arts, for taking down notes and following Jungil Kim around like a cocker spaniel, always on the verge of stepping on or getting stepped on by his master's heels. Destined to have many run-ins with me, he suddenly reminded me of Professor Tayong Yee at No. Six I was almost forgetting who must have been at Ilsung Kim's beck and call likewise. I should start somewhere to engineer his release but I did not know where. Any rash move on my part would not only draw unnecessary suspicion to myself, especially when I was only on probation, but prejudice his case even worse.

I was shocked to hear "Tears of Mokpo," "Yellow Shirted Guy," "Carmellia Girl," and other decadent songs of the capitalistic south, sung by these leaders of Selfhood Revolution at the personal order of Jungil who showed his intense enjoyment by rocking his body side to side, jerking his shoulders up and down. How could they fail to perceive the incongruity? Nan, to whom I had looked for an explanation, didn't seem surprised at all, apparently used to such partying.

"Mr. Moo is not feeling well," Jungil said to Ingoo Cha, noting my blood red face and throbbing neck. "Take him upstairs."

Nan was trying to argue herself out of a request to sing. The walls and ceiling swayed dangerously when I rose, supported by Ingoo Cha. The room upstairs was unique with a row of beds apparently designed to accommodate party casualties like me. As soon as I lay down, I fell into deep sleep, from which I did not wake until an hour later when Nan came up with Deputy Chief Haysong Gang to take me back down to the party, loud and merry as ever. Jungil's sister Gyonghee's handsome husband had a talent for singing and gave a moving rendition of a Soviet aria I had never heard before. The most accomplished dancer was Jaygyong Gil, perhaps thanks to his diplomatic services abroad.

"I apologize for my lapse," I said, taking my seat next to Jungil.

"Did you rest up?" he asked.

"Yes, I am all right now."

"Let's watch a movie then."

When Jungil rose, all the others rose too. Waving them back to their seats, he led the way to the auditorium next door, followed by four of his aides, Nan and me, and a news camera crew who trailed us, taping our every move. The film was a 30-minute documentary on North Korea's awesome military might. What was there to stop Ilsung Kim from making another venture like the first Korean War before his death, if the reward appeared to be a quick victory? The thought was chilling. When we returned, the party was still going strong. Drinking and eating continued until 3 a.m. I was completely overcome with fatigue.

"Take the couple home by my car," Jungil said, calling Ingoo to his side.

Mellow with drink and in the best of mood, Jungil came to see us off to the front door, a courtesy he seldom extended, Nan told me.

"Take them to the honeymoon suite," he told the chauffeur.

Though anxious to find out what had happened to each other, we decided to keep quiet until we had absolute privacy. About 40 minutes later, halfway between Pyongyang and Soonan, the international airport, the car left the main road and got into a lane that turned and twisted sharply through thick stands of trees and ended at a gate in a high concrete wall with a fortified guard box on one side. An armed sentry saluted smartly and the solid iron gate slid open ponderously. Inside to the right stood another guard box. The driveway resumed through a wood of pines, firs, lilacs, and beeches, seemingly in primal condition. The car came to a stop before a huge sprawling mansion.

"My God," Nan cried. "This is Jungil's villa where I stayed for nine months when I first arrived five years ago."

It was even more luxurious than the guesthouse of my first residence. The servants led us to the living room immediately to the right of the front door, where a table was set laden with cognac, dried fish, fruit, and other hors d'oeuvres. But food was far from our thoughts. After appropriate apologies to the staff, we went directly upstairs to our bedroom.

"What have they done to you?" Nan cried, throwing her arms around my neck. "You are nothing but skin and bones."

"You should have seen me before my release," I said.

"Animals!" she shouted but, remembering, lowered her voice and pointed at the vent in the ceiling that could easily conceal a listening device.

"Let's take a bath together," she suggested, aloud for the benefit of our possible auditors.

"Splendid!" I replied.

The door firmly closed behind us, we undressed wordlessly and ran into each other with wild impatience. Crying, laughing, we talked all night.

As I had surmised, she had been kidnapped like me at Repulse Bay, where she was lured by a female guide our Hong Kong agent Samho had engaged for the purpose. In her case, however, no ether had to be used because she passed out the moment the North Korean thugs surrounded and put her aboard the boat. When she stepped ashore at South Port, Jungil Kim himself was waiting to meet and escort her to the villa, where she was left in the care of an army of servants, including resident ideology instructors who made her memorize the biographies and songs glorifying the father and the son, until she almost added the Holy Ghost. Like me she had to watch and critique movies everyday. On New Year's Day and on the birthdays, February 16th and April 15th, she had to write those wretched congratulatory letters, the stress of which knocked her out for weeks. From the villa she was transferred to other houses of slightly lesser dignity, but on the whole her treatment had been consistently VIP for an abductee and prisoner. Staying at the best hotels, traveling first class, she was taken to see the great sights like Diamond Mountains on the east coast, Fragrance Mountains to the north, and Mt. White Head with its crater, Lake Heaven and Earth.

Next morning, when we came downstairs long after noon, I was staggered by rows of suitcases, trunks, and boxes, all containing Nan's clothes, shoes, belts, cosmetics, purses, and other personal belongings.

"Where did you get this royal trousseau?"

"Jungil gave me to wear to his parties like the one last night."

"How many have you been to?"

"Dozens of them."

"Nan, tell me the whole truth. I'll understand...."

"He hasn't made a pass at me, if that's what you are thinking, nor his father to whom I am yet to be introduced. He was telling the truth when he said they hadn't touched me. North Korea may be a prison but not a bordello. I've met several foreign women, Chinese, French, even Syrian, all abducted more or less like me, put to language instruction or other use, but not prostitution. In fact, North Korean puritanism can be carried to an extreme."

The Moonhee Yoo incident was an example. About a year after her arrival Nan watched a North Korean movie Story of a Cell Leader describing partisan activity. The story was nothing to rave about but the main character, about 25 years old, was outstanding in personal charm and acting skill. Nan wanted to find out more about her but couldn't learn even her name, because no credits were given in North Korean films. Except for Ilsung Kim and Jungil Kim nobody had the privilege of becoming famous. She asked Haysong Gang for her name. This man, always asking for Nan's comments on North Korean film and seemingly receptive to her candid, often harsh criticism, merely pouted his lips and did not react at all this one time when she had nothing but unreserved admiration. Two years later Nan saw her again on TV in Maid of the Diamond Mountains, playing the role of a revolutionary worker from girlhood to old age, and in Our Homeland, where her supporting role as the main character's wife outshone everything else, turning the tawdry political propaganda into a bright gem. Intrigued, Nan wanted to see more of her work and wanted to meet her in the worst way, but her films were discontinued after that one showing, contrary to the North Korean practice of a hundred or more reruns of any successful production. Months later the same titles were announced on TV and Nan eagerly waited for her appearance, but her roles were taken over by other actresses with ruinous consequences. Only much later she learned from somebody in strictest confidence that she would never be able to meet Moonhee in person.

Born in Gaysong she was a dancing prodigy and became the protégée of People's Actor Chul Hwang in the early 60's. A year later as the main character in the musical Patriotism she became a star overnight, desired by all men. After studying at an acting school in Czechoslovakia she married Hosun Yoo, a ranking movie director, and had three children. But scandal dogged her even after marriage. With a warm, kindly disposition she sincerely wished she could oblige all her suitors and tempters, which was a legion. In the late 70's the Congress of Film Workers staged a public condemnation of her morals but she defied her male accusers, naming the dates and occasions when they themselves sought to seduce her. For the trouble she was banished to the boiler room at the February 16 Film Studio to work as an oiler. Reinstated after a year she appeared in Maid of the Diamond Mountains and Our Homeland but the Party had her watched closely and found that she was dating a young man employed at the Pyongyang Radio Station. His father, a big shot in the pro-Communist Korean Japanese Federation, had him sent to North Korea to discipline and wean him from his dissolute ways in Japan. But with his father's money and influence the young man could live luxuriously in Pyongyang, driving around in a flashy limousine and dazzling Moonhee with expensive gifts. On a winter day the young couple made love and fell asleep with the heater on in the limousine. The youth was dead of asphyxiation and Moonhee, unconscious, was rushed to the hospital where two weeks of intensive care finally brought her around.

One day all film workers were ordered to assemble and were taken by buses to a shooting range out of town. Soon a jeep drove up to a post at the end of the range. A blindfolded woman was pulled out of the vehicle and tied to the post, screaming names and accusations though inaudible to those at the other end.

"People's Actress Moonhee Yoo is being executed in the name of the people for wanton lewdness," the public address system announced, followed by a volley of gunfire. Her body slumped, full of holes spouting blood. The spectators cried in shock and her husband, who had come without suspecting anything, passed out. All he had been told earlier was that she would be taken home from the hospital as soon as her condition permitted. All her films were taken out of circulation and burned, and her pictures in magazines and pamphlets cut out or blacked out. Banished to the countryside, her widowered husband was allowed to return after a year and a half. Everybody who had been there at the execution was ordered to hold their tongue about what they had witnessed on pain of similar punishment. So Nan's informant was taking a considerable risk in telling her all this gruesome story, too horrible to believe.

"But if Jungil's interest in us, in you had been purely professional, shouldn't he have brought us together as soon as possible?"

"I know. It beats me, too."

Our speedy reunion would have given him many extra years of valuable service and could have even won us over completely, removing the motivation to flee. But whether acting on his own or by bad advice, he had kept us separated, ignorant of each other's whereabouts, forever alienating us and intensifying our hostility toward the private fiefdom of the Kims.

The next day Deputy Chief Haysong Gang called to tell us to come to a party within the hour.

"Doesn't he believe in sending out invitations ahead of time?"

"Never. He figures everybody would be flattered by the invitation, no matter when."

Nan was to wear a blue chima and white jogori.. Her big wardrobe now made sense. In a few minutes a Benz drove up and took us to the same party room at the Central Building. More or less the same men were present but there were considerably more women than before, all in blue and white like Nan. One of them came over and introduced herself as North Korean representative to the North-South Meetings being held at Panmoonjom.

"What's the occasion?" Nan asked, pointing at their dress.

"March 8, Women's Day, celebrated all over the world," she replied. "Don't they in South Korea?"

"No."

"Well, they are always reactionary there."

Every woman's seat had a gift from Jungil Kim, a small music box made in Japan. Other than Jungil's sister Gyonghee and her husband we were the only married couple and seated as before to the left and right of Jungil. These Communists, including Jungil himself, didn't seem to believe in displaying their spouses in public, maybe considering their existence a sign of weakness. After the obligatory food courses the guests left their seats and moved around, holding their glasses of drink. The room was noisy with laughter and conversation. Jungil led me to the back.

"What kind of films do you think we should produce?" he asked.

"The Immortal Collection, our Great Leader and Chief's biography, provides excellent material," I said. "However, the episodes should be made into action films like American Westerns rather than chronological narratives."

Before he could react, a shout came from the stage. Members of the all women band jumped up and down on the stage, bunny rabbit fashion as I had witnessed before, chorusing "Long live Beloved Comrade Leader!"

Jungil waved his hand in reply, somewhat impatiently, as a sign of dismissal, but their enthusiasm would not abate.

"You know all this is fake and pretense," Jungil said, suddenly turning to me and grasping my left hand, which seemed to throw a new light on the man, lonely and bitter, the victim, rather than the diabolic architect of the bizarre hell North Korea was with its inverted values. The chorus of hymns would one day turn into a roar of condemnation, the same adulating crowd clawing him like the Furies. Jungil must know this and yet was powerless to change.

We were asked to another party the very next day. Nan said she had gone to parties back to back often, and I hadn't believed it. They seemed to party every day, day and night. When did they ever find time to do any work? It was the same Central Party Main Hall, where Jungil was surrounded this time by military men of general rank.

"It's the birthday of Armed Forces Chief General Jinoo O," Jungil said, indicating the gentleman seated between us. Nan sat to the left of Jungil.

The first toast was proposed by Jungil, which was followed by many more by the other participants with the predictable effect of loosening up the tongues and raising the voices. In a few minutes the party grew so loud that one had to shout to be heard. Jungil seemed his confident ordinary self again with no hint of the cynicism shown to me the night before.

"No political pressure will be applied to your work," Jungil said when we were alone. "Just make quality films for the unification of the fatherland."

"We will, Beloved Comrade Leader," I said. "Personally, I like to work with history, because we can become objective and analytical, detached from our present interests."

"I agree."

"We should also broaden our horizons by exposure to the outside world. Why don't you host international film festivals in North Korea as they do in the south?"

"That's a capital idea. Let's make good films and hold events like the Asia Film Festival. In a few days I will have you both over to my office to work out the plans."

Suddenly Jungil rose to his feet, shouting "Army uniform!", and left the room. All the others jumped up and followed him out of the room. Soon they all returned wearing an army uniform with a colonel's epaulette, a demotion. Nan and I were the only ones in civvies. After a look at Nan's blouse Jungil ordered an aide to bring her an army coat. That left me the only civilian but Jungil didn't try to change that. Pulling me to the side he showed me a huge star sewed on his sleeve, distinguishing it from all the other uniforms.

After another toast everybody, except Jungil, Jinoo and

me, went to the space before the stage and formed a circle to march clockwise to the beat of the band, Nan in the comical outsized military jacket stepping along with the rest of them. As a person came nearest to Jungil he or she shouted "Eyes Left", turning the head sharply and saluting. The shout and salute came in rapid succession, one every second, and as many as there were marchers. Standing next to Jungil I was saluted to as well, which was embarrassing. I could not help seeing an analogy between this miniature review and the jumping and shouting display of the female band members the other night, branded fake by Jungil. The distrust forced him to degrade his followers to the level of puppets. After circling a few times around the hall the company returned to their places at the table. But no sooner were they seated than Jungil jumped to his feet shouting "Navy uniform". All went upstairs to change into the white uniform and the circling "Eyes Left" started again as before. Of course Jungil's had a star sewn on its sleeve for all to see.

Dancing and singing followed the review. Those designated went on stage and sang mostly South Korean pop songs. Soon Nan was asked to sing, as at other parties she had been to before.

"Wait," Jungil said, following her to the stage. "I want to conduct the band myself."

She sang "Student Boarder" and "Parting" with deep emotion that moved the listeners. If there was such a thing as a born star, she was it, lighting up on stage before an audience, any audience. It was my turn. For this exigency I had one song rehearsed, "Song of Hope", but on impulse changed the words to suit the occasion, complimenting the aging general Jinoo O, the birthday man, on his continued vigor and alertness.

"I can make a clean sweep all the way to Pusan in one week," he said when I took my seat next to him, quite drunk from all the glasses he had accepted. "I am only waiting for the order, which might come any minute...."

Instantly I regretted revising the song, which wasn't meant to inspire him or anybody else with such martial zeal.

One morning Ingoo Cha came to the villa and told us to

get ready to leave for a tour of the Film Library, greatly exciting our curiosity. The first thing we would look into would be Sunset starring Haran Ham, my mother according to Tayong Yee. The Library stood on a hill in the middle of Pyongyang behind an iron gate closed to the public.

Immediately recognizing our guide, the sentry opened the gate and led us to the front door where Director Soontay Bag waited. At his office Bag briefed us on the holdings and organization of the Library, very easily the world's largest of the kind. In the 3-story building about 100 meters long with perfect temperature and humidity control, a staff of over 250 recording voice artists, technicians, translators, subtitle writers, and projectionists maintained a thorough videocassette catalog of some 15,000 films, indexed by title, country of origin, and year of production, giving the cast, producer and director, and synopsis for each entry. Jungil, the unquestioned authority on the film in North Korea, had personally supervised the compilation of the 1,100-page catalog for the Library and the recording and printing of translations and subtitles for more than half of the foreign entries. Except for those exchanged through FIAF among Communist nations most of them had been pirated or stolen. Old films making the rounds at third-rate theaters out of control of the distributors might be bought at junk prices, or projectionists might be bribed to make illegal copies in black and white instead of color in the original. One important service rendered by the Korean Japanese Federation was acquisition of Japanese films this irregular way. That's why the Library had most of the films by Shojiku and Toei, where control was lax, but only few of Toho. The primary function of the Cultural Secretary at a North Korean embassy abroad was film intelligence and collection. Soontay Bag, Director of the Library, spent half his time overseas obtaining the pirated and stolen editions, flown home in diplomatic pouches marked "No. 100 Material," hands off to everybody, the status given to top weapons and industrial intelligence by other countries. Such thievery never caused any problem because the stolen property was not shown to the public, necessarily excluded for fear of ideological contamination.

"All the films you make from now on will be stored here, too," Ingoo said, pointing at the North Korean section which naturally took up most space. The film was the single most potent cultural force in North Korea, the shaper of its psyche. Printed on North Korean currency were movie stars and scenes. The whole country had to watch a Party-recommended release day and night. Collections of quotations and theme songs had to be memorized for competition in periodic contests. When I heard a sentry at our compound reciting a whole sequence of dialogue from Moon Tip Island, the latest fare, I thought him a nut but many others were doing the same thing. This particular movie was about the heroic North Korean garrison on Moon Tip Island at the entrance to Inchon Harbor dying to the last man fighting off the onslaught of MacArthur's amphibious armada in September 1950, but the potentially good material was botched, all drama and realism drained out. Not even once did an enemy plane or ship flash across the screen, as the garrison members blustered away one by one shooting at an invisible foe. But this atrocity, which would not pass muster even as a school play, was touted as a great work and was apparently received so.

We were amazed by the completeness of the South Korean holdings, which included all those we had ever made or appeared in. A quick search through the catalog showed Sunset, produced and directed by one Bomson Yee, 1950, with Haran Ham as the female lead.

"Can we check out some of the pre-war productions?" I asked.

"Of course," Soontay said, but not before getting a nod from Ingoo.

To avoid suspicion Nan and I checked out 17 titles along with the one we really wanted. After the main storage building we were taken to a newly-finished underground facility next door with a network of compartments connected by aisles and gangways.

"For storage in case of nuclear war," Soontay said.

Fortunately despite what Armed Forces Chief Jinoo O said the other night, such war must not be imminent from the still empty spaces.

On the way home we were taken to the Daydong Shop for foreigners, located next to the Pyongyang Inn on the shore of the Daydong. Well stocked with electronic products, cameras, clothes, cosmetics, food stuffs, mostly Japanese made, the 2,000 square foot store was busy with about 30 Korean Japanese buying presents for the relatives they were visiting. Welcome were US dollars, Japanese yen, West German marks, British pounds, and other Western currencies. In contrast the currencies of the Soviet Union, Red China, and East European countries were not accepted at all, which seemed supremely ironic.

"Exorbitant! Highway robbery!" were the shoppers's comments on the prices.

We never found out how bad they really were because Ingoo picked up the tab, urging us to feel free. I picked up a solar transistor radio and a mini-cassette tape recorder, which was to prove of enormous value later on, and Nan a sewing machine and an electric iron like a good housewife.

As soon as we arrived home, we mounted Sunset on the projector. I was struck by the charm and vivacity of the much wronged heroine. The theme was the infinite sacrifice a Korean woman is capable of making for her men, first her husband who, graduating from medical school in Japan with her help, promptly shacks up with a concubine, his cultured Japanese nurse, then her son who turns out to be a Red terrorist in South Korea after Liberation and is executed, and lastly her grandson, a fractious infant dumped on her lap by its remarried mother, to whose rearing the heroine dedicates her declining years. Only the actress's innate gaiety and spirit, which couldn't be faked or acted credibly, carried the story through, infusing the depressing role she was cast into with hope, with faith in life eternal.

"Is she your mother?"

"I don't know. But she is a good actress."

"She is terrific. I now remember my aunt Jo telling me about her as the first lady of the screen at the time. They were closely associated, worked in the same company, until it went belly up, though she was vague about it."

Gyongja Jo, the one who had helped Nan get into the film, had been left in charge of our Seoul film school in our absence. I briefly wondered what might be going on with her and the school while we were away all this time.

"You know, Moo, the more I look at her, the more she looks like you, the cast of her cheekbones, forehead.... I am sure you are her son."

"Nan, you are as bad as Tayong Yee. By that standard half of the Korean female population may be my mother. Let's face it. It's one in a million shot and the old man, batty from long imprisonment, was just fantasizing, though well-meaning. Besides I am not sure whether I want to give up my genetic freedom, my potential brotherhood to all mankind, east and west, to be somebody's son, grandson, or nephew. It's like a king abdicating his empire to retire to a cottage. This obsession with one's so-called 'roots,' what I call 'genetic complex,' is as reactionary and destructive as Nazism. Survival of the world depends on transcendence of biocultural egocentricities. We all belong to the gene pool, descended from Adam and Eve in the Garden of Eden, the megaplate of tectonics before Earth split up into continents."

"Are you putting up these ferocious defenses against possible disappointment now that you are inches away from finding out what your genetic identity is?"

The next day Jungil called and asked us to critique a play My Homeland based on a popular movie and performed at the Great Pyongyang Theater, the largest in North Korea. Unlike the fast-paced movie, the play was a dreadful bore, poorly organized and executed. The height of absurdity was the last scene where a real life steam locomotive roared onto the stage, a 100-ton mountain of steel belching steam and black smoke, with a load of homecoming partisans. They did it by laying a whole new track to the theater and opening up the back wall. I could have thrashed the person responsible for the idea. The stage was not meant for such realism. Obviously not guessing what we thought of him Dan Yee, the director, thanked us profusely for honoring him with our presence.

"You must be from Seoul," Nan said, noting his accent.

"Yes," he said, sadly. "I came here with the others during the Inchon Retreat of September 1950."

He must have guessed we had come north against our will, too.

"Was Haran Ham with you by any chance?" Nan asked.

"Yes, as a matter of fact. We were on the same truck that pulled out of the prison yard. We drove only at night because of the US Air Force but that was no guarantee of safety. One night a squadron of Corsairs attacked us, setting the truck on fire. We all jumped out of the truck but were too weak and sick to run away, especially with the guards keeping sharp watch, rifles at the ready. Not Gutsy Haran Ham, though, as she was called. She upped and ran into the bush nearby. The guards opened fire and we heard a woman's scream. That was the end of Haran Ham, I think. Why do you ask?"

"Oh, just curious. We happened to watch an old film with her in it."

"Sunset? Isn't that a gem!"

Though appreciating what he could tell us about Haran Ham, I had to write an honest report, which scotched the play.

But professional integrity, at least mine, was a flexible thing, as I soon found out. Not too long later another request for review came over the phone. Again we went to the Great Pyongyang Theater in the company of Ingoo Cha and Injoon Bayg of the White Head Mountain Creative Group to watch International Conference of Bloody Outrage, the story about the secret emissary Joon Yee sent to the 1919 Hague Peace Conference by the deposed Korean king to appeal his country's case to the world body, of course without the permission of Japan which had annexed Korea in 1910. Unable to make himself heard, so the legend went, Joon Yee dashes onto the podium and slashes his stomach open in protest before the delegates. Unfortunately, assuming too much of the audience's knowledge, the play failed to provide crucial background information either about the loss of Korea's sovereignty to Japan or about Yee as a credible character, who ranted and raged from beginning to end. Not only was it a failure as a historical play but lacked a good story line. But this presented a serious dilemma because the playwright was said to be Ilsung Kim, who could not make a mistake. I ended up praising the play, though despising myself for the cowardice and duplicity.

Nan became sick, anticipating the congratulatory letter on April 15, Ilsung Kim's birthday, which we had to finish jointly. This year's birthday was special because he was 70 years old, the Korean milestone in venerability. Of all the events and monuments marking this occasion the Selfhood Tower should take the cap, visible from all points of Pyongyang and many miles around, as it rose on the shore of the Daydong dominating the skyline. Modeled after and yet designed to surpass the Eiffel Tower of Paris the all-stone structure rose from a base of 70 solid blocks of stone, each the size of a house, and used a total of 25,550 pieces, the product of 365 multiplied by 70, the number of the glorious days Ilsung Kim had graced the earth with his life, obviously without reckoning the leap years, to make up its height of 170 meters, easily the highest stone monument in the world and higher than the sphinx by nearly a hundred feet. Unlike the Eiffel accessible to the public, however, special authorization was necessary to enter and climb the tower. Accompanied by Gang and Cha, Nan and I entered the door at ground level and saw the facing wall covered by congratulatory marble boards sent from the trade unions and leftist organizations of over 100 nations praising the Selfhood ideology. The elevator took us to the top, where the whole city of Pyongyang and the surrounding countryside lay at our feet, a truly breathtaking sight, almost erotic in impact, the blue ribbon of the Daydong sinuously curling about the city from the mist-hidden hills in the east down the fertile coastal plains to the Yellow Sea in the west. We were horrified to learn that 200 lives were lost in building the structure, obviously because of inadequate equipment and primitive technology, but our mentors seemed to think the sacrifice a fitting tribute to the greatness of their chief.

I went to the eye clinic at the Red Cross Hospital, reputed to be the best in North Korea, but all the doctor did was prescribe some ginseng pills. Once compromised, my sight did not return to normal and I had to wear glasses, especially to watch movies. These days we were checking out four or five films a day from the Library, mostly Russian or East European.

One day with some trepidation we took out the American film Papillon together with movies of socialist countries. We had seen Papillon in Seoul, where it was a box office hit for months, but wanted to see it again, to have some fun along with work. But we figured wrong. The movie brought back painful memories of my prison life and left me trembling in cold sweat.

"Nothing they do for us will ever make up for what they did to you," Nan said in angry tears. "They'll pay for it dearly. Let's get out of this hell."

"Only when the odds are 100% in our favor," I said.

"But that may be never," she said, despairing.

For months there was no word from Jungil. Only later we learned that he had been in China, persuading Deng Shaoping and other octogenarians, all opposed in principle to dynastic succession, to make an exception in his case, but in the meantime we literally quaked with fear thinking that he might have changed his mind about us. We might be enjoying our fool's paradise, ignorant of an imminent banishment for life to a distant collective farm or coal mine in the border country. So helpless and degrading was the feeling of total dependence on the whim of a dictator.

Naturally we were relieved when Jungil called one night at about 10 p.m. asking us to come and see him the next day at his office between 5 and 6 p.m. A day's advance notice, a record of sorts for him! We stayed up all night preparing notes on our production plans for his approval. Foremost on the list was the Legend of Chong Shim so we could ask for Aran Ham and the Emissary of No Return, an adaptation of International Conference of Bloody Outrage, to which I had given A plus to flatter the author, Ilsung Kim. I was going to make it a first-rate movie, partly to atone my venality, partly to facilitate our escape by insisting on filming it on location outside North Korea.

There was one other thing we planned to carry out during

the interview, to record our conversation, getting him to admit our abduction, whatever leading questions we might have to ask. We needed this to clear ourselves when we should reach the West because we learned that the South Korean press was reporting our case as voluntary defection, a couple of turncoats who had switched sides for some personal gain. We had to disprove the fable with some material evidence. Though frightened by the risk involved, Nan agreed to take charge of operating the miniature recorder purchased at the tourist store, the size of a king-size cigarette pack, by stashing in her purse and pushing the buttons at the right moments. We had to leave the lid of her purse open for it to work but we could hide it under her handkerchief or tissue without much loss. Adapting to different distances and positions, we practiced for hours long past midnight. In case of discovery we were to say that the recording was for our later reference so we could carry out his wishes more faithfully.

Ingoo came to pick us up in Jungil's limousine promptly at 5 p.m. Nan saw to my outfitting, a bright-colored necktie in a burgundy suit, tailored in North Korea. For herself she had picked a white two-piece dress with an orange blouse, matching the white square handbag with the recorder in it. She was as beautiful and enchanting as ever and I couldn't help feeling a grudging respect for Ilsung and Jungil's basic decency in leaving her alone. I could almost forgive them for all the other injury they had done to both of us.

The guards at the arched gate bearing the emblem of the Labor Party saluted and let us through to the next guarded gate. The driveway continued and the limousine pulled up at a three-story granite structure, called Central Party Committee Building. In spite of the identical name it wasn't the same place where the parties were held. Apparently many other buildings went by that designation and I wondered how they kept them apart. The only rationale I could think of for the plural nomenclature was confusion of outsiders, spies, though I couldn't imagine how they could operate here at all even without such added precaution. A soldier with a pistol in his belt sat at the front door. My heart sank, thinking he might frisk us or search our possessions. But this sentry also jumped up and only saluted. The elevator took us to the third floor. The door opened and Jungil Kim stood with a big grin and outstretched arms in a dark gray people's suit. A news cameraman was busily taking pictures of our meeting and followed us as Jungil led down the hallway to the big door of the reception room. After half a dozen pictures Jungil waved the cameraman away and motioned us to enter. Ingoo, who stood hesitating, was ordered to wait outside.

The room was only about 1,000 square feet with a rectangular desk at one corner and a round glass table in the middle with chairs and sofa around it, but the wall to the right of the desk had a bank of six TV monitors. At the touch of a button KBS came on. It was news time. Another click brought on the Drama Hour of MBC featuring Mija Sa.

"Let's talk for about an hour before going to supper," he said, switching off the TV and seating himself on the sofa. We took the chairs facing him. A waiter about 30 years old brought in soft drinks in covered glasses on a tray and set them on the table before us.

As planned, Nan put down her purse at her feet and pushed the recorder button, pretending to take out her handkerchief. Jungil began speaking rapidly like a machine gun in a high-pitched voice. Once begun there was no stopping him, carried away by the flood of his own words which couldn't be marshaled neatly into grammatical sentences. Repetitions were numerous and tense and honorific endings were omitted or garbled. He was the opposite of most other people, collected in private conversation but flustered in public speaking. At least what we saw of him at the parties and ceremonies was a dignified man behaving and speaking with a high degree of self-possession, thoroughly aware of his impact on those around him. Why he should be so rattled before us, a mere captive couple, was quite beyond me. Did the film mean so much to him?

Unsolicited, he was trying to explain why he had to resort to force in bringing us over to North Korea, though not without lengthy and numerous detours as he vented his frustration over the stymied North-South normalization talks and the many causes that had contributed to the decline of North Korean film, counterproductive and wasteful bureaucracy of socialism, diplomatic isolation, misdirection of energy, and so forth, at times displaying scathing self-criticism.

"Our film industry needed someone to pull it up by its bootstraps," he went on. "We had your films, and knew about your Cannes award and exile in America, but it seemed unlikely you would come here on your own. At this time our Hong Kong contact intimated that you might not be averse to leaving South Korea...."

"Was it Sam...." I tried to ask, still rankled at the man's treachery.

Raising his hand like a traffic cop, Jungil stopped me and forged ahead, "In fact, you were very unhappy with the film policy of South Korea."

"That's when they revoked our license," I said.

At this time the waiter brought more drinks and changed the ash trays, and none of us spoke until he withdrew.

"But you know how it is to depend on others," Jungil said. "Our operatives at contact level are clumsy and lack tact, as you have experienced."

The phone rang. Jungil picked it up, barked irritably into it, "Later," and hung up.

"I need someone to speak with authority, to speak out, teach and correct by example."

"But criticism may not be taken kindly," Nan said.

"Don't be afraid to speak out," Jungil said. "I'll back you up all the way. This brings us to the next point, your presence and activity here. I want you to tell the world that South Korea has no real freedom, no democracy, too much government interference in your work, which is true, isn't it? You have said so yourselves. Tell them you have left superficial freedom to seek true freedom, to enjoy freedom of creativity. This, rather than your kidnap, would square better with your privileged status here."

I glanced at Nan and she winked back ever so slightly to signify that the recording was going well and must have gotten that part.

"I had some concrete proposals," I started to say.

"Good," he said, looking at his watch. "Let's talk until 8, no, until 9:30."

"Then may I?"

"My men say I ask too much. I chew them out and they hang their heads but the next moment they come back with the same old stuff. Unless we revolutionize, in ten years we'll fall so far behind we would be last among nations."

"But the Film Library...." Nan tried to comment.

"There's good reason for not releasing foreign films, American, Soviet, even Chinese. The contrast will overwhelm us, like a kindergartener taken to a college class. On this trip to China Yaobang Hu confided to me about the problems they face there upon opening doors after the death of Chairman Mao, who had insulated China for fear of Western contamination. No infusion of new and advanced technology. The first thing the young ones learn is to grow their hair and beard long. If we let go and show all the Western films, pretty soon nihilism will sweep over the nation.

"I have instructed Deputy Chief Ingoo Cha to see that you head a new corporation with authority over the existing Studios and Creative Groups. Make them work and compete, cut out dead wood, bring out new talent, build a whole new industry. Time somebody had kicked them in the butt. Our directors should learn by watching you in action. Our actors have no chance to grow. Some talented people may appear now and then, but after one or two works they bottom out or burn out, because good looks and raw talent can take them only so far."

"Maybe the fault lies in favoritism," I said. "First thing I'll ask Deputy Chief Cha is to call together all the entertainment people, so I can choose from among them, not limiting my choice to film actors as such."

"A director cannot use a talented actor if he or she doesn't belong to his own Studio," Jungil said. "Otherwise he won't hear the end of it. To overcome this problem we had an actor pool organized to recruit actors on a wide national basis but they keep using only those they latch on. Those that don't get picked never get picked. This is the weakness of socialism."

"Of all societies," I felt obliged to note.

"Right," Jungil agreed. "South Korea is dominated by Mija Sa and her gang."

"Nor is it a bad thing necessarily," Nan observed. "Stars need a long period of incubation, well, most of them anyway."

She was referring to my relatively short apprenticeship, which Jungil caught.

"He is an exception," he said. Then he turned to her, and said, "You are perfectly right and exemplify your theory. And what a fine example to boot!"

His admiration for her was so frank and spontaneous that I could have jumped up and hugged him as my own brother. He might as well be, well, at least a platonic half cousin, if Aran Ham was my aunt as Professor Yee said. By the same token Ilsung Kim with all his hangups might not be quite the monster, if he was capable of such constant devotion to her over these many years.

Forgetting his original schedule to talk for only one hour before supper, Jungil kept talking, not knowing when to stop. The side of the cassette on which we had been recording, good for only 45 minutes, had run out a long time ago. Of course there was no question of pulling out the tape and turning over for the other side. Only later Nan realized she could have excused herself to go to the ladies' room and changed the sides, but in the charged atmosphere of the moment such expediency did not come to her mind. However, nothing of substance was lost, because what followed was just a rehash of subjects already covered. In unfinished, often incoherent sentences, Jungil charged on at the same speed with undiminished passion, never giving his listeners a chance to respond. Used to passive acceptance by his audiences, he simply didn't know the meaning of conversation.

Apparently assigned to the task of reminding his boss, Ingoo came into the room and tried to attract his attention, but each time Jungil ordered him out irritably. Muttering, Jungil kept chain smoking cigarettes, stubbing them out after two or three puffs. However, there was one interruption Jungil tolerated throughout our meeting. The waiter came in at the rate of every ten minutes speciously to empty out the ash trays and change the glasses. In hindsight, he must have been Jungil's bodyguard making sure of his safety. Jungil's one-sided conversation continued for two more hours. Ingoo entered one more time only to be shouted at for the trouble. But after his exit for the last time, Jungil seemed to calm down a little and the meeting became more of a dialogue.

"As you know we have two studios, Korea Art Film and February 16," he said. "I want you to set up another one."

"In that case could we name it Moo Moo Film?" I asked, an impulsive thing of which no sooner had I said it than I became ashamed for its transparent egotism. Was I unconsciously testing Jungil to see how far he could be pushed, a risky business, because naming a major national company after an individual, unless he was Ilsung or Jungil Kim, was unthinkable?

"Good," Jungil said without hesitation. "That's as good a name as any. I appoint you, Mr. Moo, president, and you, Mrs. Moo, vice president."

"As our first project may I suggest filming on location Secret Emissary of No Return, a variation on the play International Conference of Bloody Outrage, so as to exploit its dramatic potential to the full?"

Again, suspecting nothing, Jungil assented without reservation.

"As you know, Patriot Joon Yee died on July 14, 1919," I said, seizing the opportunity. "If we mean to do the film, we have to start shooting right away. It's late October now and soon all the leaves will be gone in the Hague. But how can we get there having no diplomatic relations with Holland?"

"Go to an East European country which has access to Holland and commission a camera team there to do the job," Jungil said. "Take a trip to Russia and Eastern Europe in a few days. I'll deposit $2 million in the Bank of America so you can draw freely for your overseas activities. You'll see how wretchedly these Russian and European beggars live."

Nan and I were dumbfounded. He was really putting money where his mouth was. I was no less amazed by his contempt for his socialist allies. Decades of International Communism seemed to have intensified rather than softened nationalistic rivalry.

"You know what the recent Unaligned Nations Conference held here wanted?" Jungil asked with triumph in his voice. "A film festival in Pyongyang next year. If we arrange it to precede the Asia Film Festival in Seoul, we can steal the thunder."

"That wouldn't be easy," I said cautiously. "Nonaligned countries are in fact underdeveloped countries mostly of Africa, whose film industries are primitive or nonexistent. While going ahead with the Pyongyang Festival as decided, we should invite Japan and other advanced countries of Asia and the West to dignify the occasion."

"President Moo, that's a capital idea. I cannot agree more heartily. What Western countries do you have in mind?"

"The US above all."

"But we have no diplomatic ties with the US."

"We can go through countries that have them like Japan for example. They'll be happy to relay the message. I have a few acquaintances who can get the ball rolling, if you'll allow me to contact them."

"By all means, but how do you propose to contact them?"

"By phone maybe on our trip to Europe."

"Splendid! I hear your offices are ready for occupancy," he said, rising. "How soon do you want to move in?"

"Tomorrow."

"Splendid!"

Our meeting had lasted three hours. Ingoo was called in and instructed to get our passport pictures ready right away for our imminent travel. It was past 9 p.m. but right away meant just that, right away. Cha drove us to the photo lab in another building, still open at this hour perhaps for just such exigencies, before taking us to the Central Party Building with the large partying hall where Jungil was waiting at the front door.

"Where do you get all the energy for these late hours of work?" I asked, walking by his side down the hallway to the elevator.

"Doctors tell me my body is ten years older than my age," he said. "But hopefully it is designed to wear out longer than normal. I always work late unless called away by other duties."

Perhaps the parties we had seen him in were these other duties, as necessary as his work proper to get the tension out of him, if they did. Waiting at the restaurant on the third floor were the top film brass of North Korea, Ingun Bang of the White Head Mountain Group, Sooam Gil, in charge of the film in the Party Art Department, and Myungjay Yee, Deputy Chief of the Ilsung Kim Documentary Film Studio. Soon the waiters set out a sumptuous American steak dinner, during which Jungil announced the creation of Moo Moo Film and our appointment as President and Vice President, telling them to give us full cooperation.

Back at home we were thrilled to pieces by the success of our recording. The gamble had paid off. There was enough solid evidence here, admission by the ultimate authority himself, to exonerate us from any charge of defection in spite of our special privileges, such as foreign travel and film activity. Armed with this we could bide our time for escape, collaborating to the full, making good films, even having some fun in the meantime. Suddenly Jungil appeared pitiable, a victim trapped in the self-admitted contradictions of socialism and grasping at straws. The only real regret we had over the evening was our inability to have him help us meet Aran Ham right away but we were sure we could arrange it unobtrusively in time as we eased our way into the inner workings of this enigmatic country.

XXII.
An Outlet

At the reception room on the second floor of the Korean Art Film Studio were waiting Ingoo Cha, the heads of the Studios and Creative Groups, and the Administrator of Moo Moo Film, resurrected eight years after its closure by the Doohwan Jun regime of South Korea. After presenting the shooting plan of our first project, Secret Emissary of No Return, with its plot divisions and scenes, including the shots to be taken overseas, I asked for the photographs of all available North Korean actors and actresses to choose the cast from. On the model of the earlier Moo Moo Film I proposed a staff of 230 to produce about 40 works a year. But when I mentioned the numbers, they all looked at each other, as if I had cracked a dirty joke.

"With only 230 people you may have problems in operating the studio," Sooam Gil spoke out at last. "The Korean Art Film has 1,800 people and produces about ten a year at most. With 230 you will never get off the ground."

"Our Beloved Comrade Leader has instructed us," Ingoo interposed, "to leave everything to President Moo. Let's not voice objections at this meeting. Just listen to what he has to say and follow."

"No, I am perfectly open to suggestions," I said. "Perhaps I am overlooking something. Let me have a look at the organization chart of the Korea Film."

Sooam spread it out on the table. The payroll included not only personnel in production proper but those working at the nursery and other auxiliary facilities such as porters to fetch food rations and other supplies, which seemed superfluous. So for now the personnel issue was left on hold. After eating the lunch packed from home, we put in a requisition for 10 cameras, 3 editing machines and one crane. The equipment, all West German-made, arrived next day except for the crane. Soon enough, however, I discovered how insufficient 230 was for the work I wanted done, fundamentally because of the built-in inefficiencies. For example, if I needed lumber to build a set, which normally one phone call would take care of as need arose in other economies, I had to requisition a whole year in advance so the government could earmark the allocation in the budget. Even then only uncut logs were released, which the studio had to cut and mill to size. So for lumber alone I needed one man to estimate what we would need for the next 12 months, one man to write out and turn in the requisitions using the right forms, one man to contact and put pressure at the right places to hasten the shipment, several people to transport it to the mill for cutting to specifications, and so forth. Before I knew it the staff tripled to 700.

On the morning of October 24 Gang and Cha told us to get ready to leave the next day handing our passports and an envelope. The official diplomatic passports of the People's Republic of Korea in a burgundy jacket had our names spelled out accurately in English and Korean. The envelope contained $20,000 in US currency and 20,000 Russian rubles, "pocket money" personally allocated to us by the Beloved Comrade Leader.

"We'll be visiting East Germany, Hungary, Yugoslovia, and Czechoslovakia via Moscow," said Cha and Gang, beaming, unable to conceal their elation over being chosen to accompany us.

Nan left at 3 p.m. to get her hair done and prepare her wardrobe, but I remained at work checking out the new equipment. When I got home, which was late, I found Nan still packing, skipping around like a child on the eve of a picnic.

"I feel like a butterfly out of the cocoon," she said.

"What's the big deal?" I said, disguising my own

excitement. "You've been abroad before."

"This is different. I thought I had come here to die, separated from you forever. But we are together and can travel together."

We were up nearly all night, packing, repacking, talking, laughing, remembering something, changing our minds. Next morning Gang and Cha arrived with their own baggage. I put on a dark brown suit but after hours of headstart Nan was still unclad and miserable.

"I don't have a thing to wear," she declared.

"But, darling, the closets are full of your clothes," I observed.

"None of them is suitable for fall wear and travel."

How familiar it sounded! Things must have gotten back to normal, I thought, vacating the room to wait for her downstairs and keep our travel companions company. She ended up wearing a buff corduroy two-piece, a beret of the same material, a green wool scarf of her own knitting, and brown boots, which made her look like royalty.

Though the only international airport in North Korea, Sooan was a modest three-story terminal with only two planes I could see. We went up to the VIP counter bypassing the general passenger gates and waited half an hour while exit paperwork was handled. A car took us to the waiting plane, there being no jetway. Our party was ushered to the first-class section, which had only two other passengers, both foreigners. As soon as we got seated the plane took off, a medium Soviet Aeroflot passenger model.

There were two ways of leaving Pyongyang by air, via Beijing and via Moscow. The latter was the only option open to Koreans, because Beijing took only US dollars, Japanese yen, British pounds, German marks and other internationally recognized currency, but not Soviet rubles, of which North Korea somehow had an abundant supply.

The direct nonstop 8-hour flight arrived in mid-afternoon at Moscow International with an ultramodern terminal built by West German engineers for the 1980 Olympics.

"The crowd never came," was Cha's wry comment,

referring to the US boycott that year.

In contrast to the modernity of the building the entry procedure took us right back to the stone age. At one table two young immigration officials, in their early 20's, did the checking, taking on average 15 minutes per passenger because they had to feed everything, passport and entry forms, into the fax machine for authorization by headquarters. Fortunately our diplomatic passports dispensed with the customs inspection, which would have otherwise delayed us twice as long. In the lobby we were met by Ambassador Higyong Kim and his secretary, who took us directly to the Moscow Hotel, said to be the best in town, where a whole suite had been reserved for our party. With foreigners as its exclusive clientele the hotel took only dollars and other officially recognized foreign currencies, which the ruble was not, the coin of the realm, and one entered the front door only by presenting the room key. But the lobby crawled with prostitutes who somehow managed to get in and kept winking at the Korean men, taking them for well-heeled Japanese tourists bent on having some fun. Though rated first class, the hotel did not have any room service and for breakfast one had to line up at the cafeteria for self-service. But in compensation the food cost almost nothing.

After resting a day, mostly sleeping to shake off the jet lag, we left by Aeroflot next afternoon and arrived three hours later at East Berlin. Hyojoong Gwon, a short middle-aged man, met us and presented Nan with a bouquet of roses, before taking us to the Metropol Hotel, built recently and deservedly rated superclass with facilities and services comparable to the best in the West. A resident of East Berlin and with no direct connection with the Korean Embassy Gwon was in charge of procuring Western goods for Jungil from West Berlin or other Western capitals, to which somehow he had unlimited access. He also turned out to be the chief broker for the sale of Boeing helicopters to North Korea that had caused such a storm in the Western press. I could guess that Samho Hyon of Hong Kong was another such buyer in the Far East. Before leaving Pyongyang Jungil had given us Gwon's name, saying we could get him to buy anything we wanted, an offer Gwon reiterated, but we couldn't think of anything. For now I was content after supper to luxuriate in the sauna in many years.

Next morning we took a walk around the hotel, looking for streets that might suit as location for the Joon Yee story. Turning the corner at the end of the block we saw the Stars and Stripes fluttering on a flagpole before a big building, the US Embassy with two Marines standing guard at the gate. It was like stumbling into a long lost relative.

"Did you see that?" Nan whispered, nudging me, as Ingoo walked a few feet ahead. Leaning in that direction she seemed on the point of breaking into a run for the building.

"Don't you even think it!" I warned, pulling her back. "We are still in the Communist bloc."

At the Gate of the Brandenburg Palace which separated East and West Berlin we posed and took pictures. The rest of the day we spent sightseeing, Nan buying a few clothes. A total of three days was spent visiting points of interest in and around Berlin, the palace of Frederick II, Potsdam, the site of the Big Three Conference toward the end of World War II where the division of Korea was sealed, and the Depa Studios, formerly Upa Studios, where fine films used to be made.

A short 40-minute flight took us to Prague, Czechoslovakia. Ambassador Jayryong Jee took us to the Prague Intercontinental, another superclass hotel where they had two adjacent rooms reserved for us on the sixth floor. The only problem was that the Secretary, who had come along with the Ambassador and undertook our check-in, apparently for the first time at a hotel like this, went all over the place but the front desk where it was done, making us wait in the lobby for nearly an hour. Shortly before getting there Ingoo had asked for our passports saying he needed them for hotel registration but did not return them after the check-in. Of course he could keep them for all we cared. As a rule upon arrival at a foreign airport he would give them back to us for the entry procedure but collected them for one reason or other. From their room he and Gang watched our door day and night, and darted out to follow us whenever we left our room.

"Let us know beforehand when you want to leave your room," Ingoo said, making no secret of their watchdog status.

When we went downstairs for dinner, the space before the restaurant door was again packed with prostitutes who made overtures openly to the men, ignoring Nan's presence. Gang, who had traveled abroad often, observed sagely, "They can be had for $100 but be careful. They are all spies." I wondered who he wanted to warn. It couldn't have been me, arm in arm with Nan. Maybe it was Ingoo and himself, both of whom I caught more than once throwing wistful glances in their direction.

About 10 p.m. after supper Nan and I went to Gang and Cha's room and placed a long distance call to Gyongshig Kim in Tokyo, a graduate of the Seoul Film School, at the same time pushing the speaker button so my companions could hear too, according to the modus operandi tacitly agreed upon. It was daybreak Tokyo time.

"Sorry for waking you, Gyongshig."

"Who is this?"

"Moo Moo."

There was a brief pause as he digested this bolt out of the blue.

"Is that you really?"

"Yes. Don't you recognize my voice?"

"Yes, of course. Where are you?"

"Prague. I apologize for not letting you know sooner."

"What's going on? We all thought you were dead. The other day we had a memorial service showing GI Orphan."

"Thank you for remembering me. I'll tell you all about it when we meet. In the meantime can you help me get in touch with Kintaro Okabe?"

Kintaro was a leading Japanese film critic who had become a good friend ever since he first came to Seoul to interview me for his Asahi Shinbun column, and would be an invaluable ally in effecting Japanese participation in the Pyongyang Film Festival Jungil wanted. When I called him at the number Gyongshig gave me, Kintaro was so shocked he couldn't talk coherently. It was he who had taken charge of my memorial service, believing I had been killed by KCIA. Incidentally, we spoke in Japanese, a language remarkably similar to Korean in grammar and pronunciation as French is to English, which I had picked up in a few weeks using tapes. My auditors, old enough to have gone to school before Liberation and fluent in Japanese, heard nothing objectionable in our conversation.

"Can you come to Prague to discuss the details of the Festival if I send you the round-trip ticket?"

"Sure, but entry visas are difficult to get from Czechoslovakia. What about Budapest, Hungary? Hungarian visas are easy to obtain. It so happens that I will be there in December for the Japanese Film Week sponsored by the Culture Ministry of Hungary."

"Good. I'll send you the ticket right away and we can set the date of our meeting by phone again."

Next morning we all went into the streets of Prague to see if we can shoot our film there. Typically, I had been eating and sleeping The Secret Emissary, writing and rewriting the dialogue whenever I had time, on the plane or in the hotel room. With well-preserved old buildings Prague seemed to have just the degree of antiquity we needed to substitute for the Hague, off limits to us, except for Joon Yee's tomb and the exterior of the Hague Conference building which would be filmed by a third party. In the afternoon we went to visit the National Barandov Studios as arranged by the North Korean Embassy. The only such institution in Czechoslovakia it also happened to be the oldest in Europe boasting a half-century history and widely used even by the Western bloc nations for its excellent facilities and inexpensive rentals. The celebrated film Amadeus, for example, was almost entirely shot here.

With Secretary Kim of the Embassy as interpreter I explained my plan to the directors of the studio and asked for assistance with equipment, extras, sets, and costumes. They consented on the spot. Compensation would be on a cost basis with details to be ironed out at the next meeting of working level personnel. We were all elated over our extraordinary luck. After the conference the head of the studio took us on a tour. The first thing that struck me was the great number of historical films being shot.

"We are all doing what you are doing, staying away from contemporary subjects to avoid Party or government interference," was his frank answer.

Back at the hotel I directed Ingoo to call Pyongyang and have them send immediately the three actors Nan and I had picked prior to our departure from among hundreds of photo candidates to play the roles of the three emissaries Joon Yee, Sangsol Yee, and Wijong Yee, as well as the camera crew, stage manager, and 150,000 feet of film. The next day we had the producer, art director and stage manager of the Barandov come to the hotel to go over the story of The Secret Emissary of No Return and negotiate the sending of a Czech camera crew to the Hague to take pictures of its streets, the conference building, Dutch windmills, and Yee's tomb at a cemetery.

On November 4 I was told that the people and film footage we had requested had arrived from Pyongyang exactly as we had specified. It had been only four days since our call. They really got things done if they put their minds to it. That afternoon a Czech cameraman came to the hotel to find out what I wanted. Drawing pictures and using Secretary Kim as interpreter I went over the list of the scenes to be shot and explained how they fitted in the story, giving him copies of the screen play translated into Czech by Kim working day and night.

"Please have everybody involved in our project read and study it," I asked the Czech, wishing that I knew the language to determine the quality of the translation.

"Gladly," he said, scanning it without a questioning pause or scowl. Perhaps Kim was the rare breed, a true bilingual, and everything was all right.

Nan and I went shopping with a light heart. The country was famous for its leather goods and our first stop was a shoe store. The merchandise was excellent in design, workmanship, and quality. We bought enough shoes and boots, 15 pairs altogether, to last us several summers and winters, but the bill came to only $100 US. Nevertheless, grateful for our patronage, the store manager threw in several extra heels for each pair.

In the evening we went to dinner at the Embassy and met the actors and staff from Pyongyang. My heart sank with dismay at the size of the man who was to play the role of Sangsol Yee, a near pigmy. The photos we had seen had been mug shots, not showing the rest of the person. Only if they had told us about it and made a suitable substitution! But the rigidity of the system, which rewarded only blind obedience, discouraged such initiative. Things might get done quickly but rollercoasted to disaster once gone wrong. There was no time to switch and we had to use him camouflaging the defect by camera trick the best way we could.

After giving the crew a tour of the proposed locations, notably the North Korean Embassy, chosen for its spacious reception room, and the Prague Community Cemetery, Nan and I took the two cameramen to a department store and bought them safari jackets with big pockets for their rolls of film, lenses, and other gadgets, which had been bulging all over their people's uniforms. Though unnoticed except for the credit in the finished product, they were most visible in the filming process, and there was no point in making them more outlandish than they already were in a foreign city. But our behavior came immediately under attack.

"In our Republic nobody is allowed to give or take gifts without special permission," Ingoo said.

In vain did we try to explain our motive. What we had done was close to high treason, encroaching on the prerogative of the father and son to give presents of substantial value like apparels. Apparently warned against it or aware of the legalities involved, though that hadn't stopped them from taking them, the cameramen never wore the jackets during the whole time we were there.

On the historical day of cranking in, the first after a suspension of many years, I personally took shots of the cemetery, already deep in fall colors. We needed summer scenes and I couldn't trust the camera crew, with or without the safari jackets, to make the right selections. It took quite a bit of looking and I had to lug the camera all over the park, taking a lot longer than scheduled. When we returned to the hotel late, Nan told me what she had overheard Cha telling his buddy Haysong Gang and Ambassador Jee.

"He said once you pick the right camera angle you should stick to it and get on with the shooting, not wander back and forth like a blind mouse."

This was just one example of the hints and criticisms he had been dropping around to discredit me.

"I would have to straighten him out soon before he wrecks the whole project," I said, disliking the thought.

Next morning we went to an ancient building in town to shoot some scenes for the Peace Conference. Though the Conference building itself would have to be photographed in the Hague, its surroundings could be captured here. But whenever I positioned my camera at a likely spot, a car or a modern building was apt to intrude into the lens, making it impossible to complete the shot. After shifting around a long time I had to return without taking a single shot, hoping to have better luck the next day. At the hotel was waiting an invitation from the Embassy to attend a birthday party, Nan's, which neither of us had remembered.

Tired and frustrated, we would sooner be left alone rather than showered to death with attention. But that was not to be. Jungil Kim might be thousands of miles away in Pyongyang but his watchful eyes seemed to be staring right down at us from the four walls of our Prague hotel room.

Accompanied by Haysong Gang, Ingoo Cha, and the three actors playing the secret emissaries we drove to the Embassy. After a toast to the health and longevity of the father and son, the drinking began in earnest, each guest emptying a full glass and refilling it to give to another, which could not be refused according to the venerable Korean etiquette. The result was general inebriation in a short time. When the conversation came around to the shooting sequence that day, up rose Ingoo Cha from the table, to walk to and fro self-importantly before facing me.

"We lost a lot of face today, hopping around with the camera as if we didn't know what we were doing before all those foreign spectators," he said. "By your indecision you were tying up the Barandov people too, who had to stand around doing nothing. They are expensive. We cannot afford to have this repeated."

"I see your point," I said as calmly as possible. "But I had no choice. I had to exclude extraneous stuff like a 1980 Volvo."

"Don't make excuses," he said, growing arrogant.

Things had come to a head. If I backed down now, the little man would be all over me. Slamming the table with my fist I rose.

"I quit," I said. "You take over. I'll give a full account of everything that happened today to our Beloved Comrade Leader."

I wasn't all that upset nor would let myself be riled up by the likes of him. Actually I was amused at myself, a democrat by profession reacting every bit like an autocrat intolerant of criticism or debate. Ultimately, debate was valid only to a point and superior knowledge had to prevail to avert disaster. But then how was my forcefulness different from that of Jungil Kim's, who had to abduct us? Not by much perhaps. Anyway I didn't have the luxury of a philosopher to straighten out all the wrinkles in the logic. The world was a huge collision course of a billion animated particles with their own perceptions and wills, and the weak had to yield to the strong. I simply had a job to do and it was imperative that a chain of command be established early on to get anything accomplished. Jungil had assured me of his full support in everything and this might be the time to test it.

"Deputy Chief Cha," Haysong Gang interposed, "get hold of yourself. You are out of line."

So it seemed Gang in charge of intelligence had more clout than somebody in charge of art, however close he might be to the fountain of power.

"Control yourself, Deputy Chief Cha," added Ambassador Jee more hesitantly, embarrassed by the flying tempers at his table but too awed by Cha's connections to assert his hostly authority. The others all sat at a loss with downcast eyes. Mumbling apologies, Cha returned to his seat.

Straining to the limit we finished shooting all the likely urban outdoor scenes of Europe we needed for The Secret Emissary and could leave Prague by night train on the fifth day arriving in Moscow the next morning. Though billed first class the 50-story Ukraine where we checked in was premodern in many respects. For example, the elevators were not automated and run by those awful middle-aged women who, upon reaching the lobby, were apt to chat on with their buddies or walk off to take care of their personal needs, thinking nothing of the guests who had been waiting ten to twenty minutes. Gang and Cha, both avowed Communists, bitterly denounced this corollary of Communism.

I wasted no time to make arrangements through the North Korean Embassy for a visit to Mosfilm, the top Soviet film studio known for its size and quality work at least in the Communist bloc. While waiting for transportation, Cha came up to me in a gait that was a strange cross between a strut and a crawl.

"As head of my country's art program I should have been given more advance notice," he pouted. "A sudden visit like this lacks formality."

"Formality be damned!" I retorted. "All we want is see the place and get some ideas, not hold a ceremony."

"In any case because of the informality I cannot act as representative of the North Korean film industry. You do it. I am to be your assistant on this occasion."

Was this punctilio or punk? I didn't care. There was no time to argue about it anyway.

"Be my guest," I obliged.

Mosfilm was only half an hour from the center of Moscow. An elderly uniformed guide met us at the front door and led us to the office on the third floor where after the introductions the Deputy Director and Production Manager proceeded to brief us on Mosfilm operations. It became clear that the two studios of North Korea, Korean Art and February 16, had both been patterned after Mosfilm. Another close parallel was that its staff of over 3,000 produced less than 20 movies and about 30 TV series a year.

"I heard the Soviet Union produces 150 or 200 films a year," I said. "If Mosfilm makes only 20, where are the rest made?"

"Every republic of the Soviet Union has a studio of its own," the Deputy Director said. "Nineteen altogether, which make up the rest."

"How do you employ your actors?"

"Some are retained on a full time basis but most are contracted each time as needed."

What was surprising was the attachment of a whole division force of infantry, artillery, cavalry, and armored units to the studio, not for its defense or security but for use in making military films. It was a division of actors, not of soldiers, an extravagance only socialism could afford.

Since Khrushchev Soviet film had moved away from political propaganda, going big into spectacles and classics, such as Tolstoy's War and Peace, Resurrection, Anna Karenina, Dostoyevsky's Crime and Punishment, Brothers Karamazov, and even Shakespeare's Othello, Hamlet, and King Lear. In my opinion, however, they were going about it all wrong, ignoring the basics of film and the needs of the audience. Their one common denominator was incredible length, 3 or 4 parts on average, some going on for 10 or 20 parts. For example, the Hollywood version of War and Peace was only two and a half hours but the Soviet counterpart was over nine hours and downright boring.

"Why do you make them so long?" I asked. "I heard Western countries have difficulty fitting them to their theater or TV schedules."

"We have quite an argument going on about this among ourselves," said the Production Manager who had been on the sidelines so far. "We want them short but the higher-ups, the politicians, want them long."

So North Korea was not alone in having considerations other than artistic or professional determine film production. A tour of the facilities followed. The floor area under the roof exceeded 50 acres. They simply never did anything small. I asked how a studio of such vastness could locate so near the heart of the city, and the Deputy Director pointed out that the city had expanded since the studio was built. Population explosion was just as serious here as elsewhere. Though big in size the buildings were old and the annexes and additions were unmistakable afterthoughts and impulses, the whole lacking unity or plan. The equipment was mostly antiquated and inefficient, but nobody seemed to care.

We returned to Pyongyang on Nov 17 after winding up our three-week tour of Eastern Europe and Russia and plunged directly into filming the rest of The Secret Emissary since winter and snow would make outdoor work impossible. The first domestic location was chosen as Ogdol about an hour's drive west of Pyongyang, where its wall ruins resembled Seoul's South Mountain closely. The sequence dealt with Sangsol Yee, one of the three emissaries, bidding goodbye to Joon Yee as he left the country first. Everything was just right that morning and I was finished with the scene in one hour to the surprise of all those curious and still skeptic among the staff and onlookers. When I returned to the Korea Art Film Studio after the shooting, its Director and other officers asked me what had happened at the site that brought on the cancellation. We pushed relentlessly to meet the deadline Apr 15, Ilsung Kim's birthday. But one snag after another began to surface, such as the total absence of costumes especially for the palace scenes. Proletariat-oriented North Korea had had no call for realistic depiction of royal or aristocratic lifestyles. No book or picture could be found in the libraries nor anybody who remembered what they looked like. There was no time to send for the requirements from Japan or South Korea. Nan and I ended up designing the costumes, selecting fabrics, and drawing pictures of hairstyles from our memories.

But we were quite helpless with another hurdle, court and folk music of old Korea to provide an authentic audio background. Like its southern neighbor, North Korea had known nothing but Western music since Liberation in 1945, though mostly of the march and pop song variety, looking down on the native tradition as backward or decadent. The time had come to change all that. At the next meeting with Jungil I meant to bring the matter up and simultaneously introduce the topic of Aran Ham. But when we met him a few days later, he caught us off guard with a totally unexpected surprise, putting to flight all other thoughts we might have had.

"It would look better to give the world the impression that you live and work in Eastern Europe, coming to Pyongyang occasionally on business. Not only will it stop all their speculation about your personal freedom but also provide a handy springboard for our inroads into the West. So why don't you go back right away and set up a suitable base in either Yugoslavia, Czechoslovakia, or Hungary. While there, you may also check out the designs and facilities of their studios for the Moo Moo Studio we are building."

Accompanied only by Ingoo Cha, visibly more deferential to us now, Nan and I left for Prague on the last day of November to sign a formal contract with the Barandov Studio, take European interior shots for The Secret Emissary, prepay the cameraman leaving for the Hague shots, and also meet our Japanese friend Kintaro as we had promised each other on the last trip.

The moment we checked in at the Moscow Hotel where we had stayed before, I called Kintaro in Tokyo to set the place and time for our date, Budapest Hilton 10 days later on December 10, sometime during the day as soon as we registered and confirmed our rooms. Upon arrival at Prague by the next flight I signed a contract with Barandov paying $100,000 down as deposit and another $20,000 for the Hague expedition which left that very afternoon. There was some sunlight left yet and I didn't feel like going into a hotel in Prague, when I had three countries, Czechoslovakia, Yugoslvia, and Hungary, to explore as the possible site of our base of operations.

"Let's take a train ride to Belgrade," I proposed.

"I'll ask the Embassy and see what's available," Ingoo said.

We boarded the train at 7:50 p.m. The first-class sleeper

was clean and comfortable but we were not allowed to rest: crossing the border between Czechoslovakia and Yugoslavia we were awakened twice by the immigration and customs officials of the two countries and were unable to go back to sleep until the train pulled in at Belgrade early afternoon.

The city was full of life and energy. Department stores were piled up with goods of all kinds and enjoyed brisk business. Shopping was fun in Belgrade rather than a hassle as in Moscow. Unlike their standoffish Russian counterparts the salespeople here greeted customers with a smile and tried to sell, their pay determined by how much they sold. On his visit to Pyongyang Tito had allegedly advised Ilsung to leave service industries to the private sector. Tito practiced at home what he preached abroad. Another endearing thing about Tito's Yugoslavia was the total absence of his idolization: there were no statues, monuments, or billboards immortalizing him. In fact, his power and presence was unseen and unfelt. This perfectly normal state of affairs in the West or West-oriented country came as a complete surprise to us coming from North Korea, worshiping Ilsung Kim as a way of life.

Next morning we went to visit the Yugo National Film Studio. Here again Ingoo wanted to hide his identity and acted as my aide, though enough notice had been given to suit the dignity of an emperor. On about the same physical scale as Mosfilm or Barandov, the studio nevertheless produced twice as much, 40 films a year, with only 230 employees, which number happened to be exactly the same as I had proposed originally for my studio in Pyongyang, contrasting with the 4,000 at Mosfilm. Things were done with greater efficiency and flexibility. Unlike Mosfilm or its carbon copy Korea Art Film, one didn't have to put in requisitions a year ahead, and could order lumber or paint by phone. Costumes, tools, and other supplies were stored in two warehouses each about 10,000 square feet, and only four women took care of them, whereas about ten times as many men would have been needed at Moscow.

After four days in Yugoslavia we left on December 8 by plane for Budapest, Hungary, and checked in at the Hilton.

True to its reputation as the pearl on the Danube, the city with two million residents, the largest in Eastern Europe, was bewitchingly beautiful. The blight of Communism seemed to have spared this showcase, but not entirely. Noticeable among the pedestrians were shabbily dressed men or women lugging huge suitcases.

"Soviet tourists on their shopping spree," our Hungarian guide said contemptuously.

He might as well, because Hungary had the highest standard of living in Eastern Europe, higher than that of Czechoslovakia, since the adoption of the free market system in 1970. The streets of Budapest were lined with stores owned by private citizens. Anybody could be an entrepreneur hiring up to 15 employees and paying taxes. As a result 15% of the nation's industry was privately owned.

"Do Hungarians travel abroad a lot, too?" I asked.

"Yes," the guide said. "We have no restrictions when going to a Communist bloc country, but travel to the West has a limit, once every other year."

"For fear of ideological contamination?" I asked.

"Nonsense," he snorted. "It's to save our foreign exchange. Our currency is valued awfully low against all Western currencies. That's why many retirees immigrate to our country from the West, especially the US."

"Those with Hungarian ancestry?"

"Not necessarily. The word is out that our country is a paradise for senior citizens and people with fixed incomes, and they are coming in droves, Germans, Jews, Chinese, you name it."

"As diplomats we have of course no restriction on foreign travel," volunteered our interpreter, the Secretary from the North Korean Embassy, perhaps feeling the need to show off his superiority. "On a diplomatic passport one can cross the Austrian border without a visa."

My ears pricked at this gratuitous information. Vienna, which was West, was only three hours away by car. This decided my choice. Budapest had to be the purported East European base for Moo Moo Film. Besides, Hungary had quite a reputation, disproportionate to its population of 10 million, for the quality of its film with a few Cannes and Oscar awards under its belt. The secret lay in the ideal productive atmosphere in which the film artists worked: the state bankrolled every project but did not interfere with its execution, the directors and producers alone doing whatever they pleased.

At the Hilton we went for dinner to the restaurant on the lobby level, clean, cozy, and warm. A quartet of portly violinists, probably in their eighties, went from table to table playing the Hungarian Fantasy, Danube Waltz, and other romantic tunes. Soon they came over to our table and began to serenade us. To give them a tip Nan looked in her bag but finding no Hungarian money she looked at me and Ingoo in consternation.

"My bag!" shouted Ingoo, jumping to his feet, face drained of blood.

Next moment he dashed out of the restaurant and I followed. It was the bag with all our money, passports, and other documents for the trip, which he normally carried with its loop wrapped around his wrist. Shortly before entering the restaurant he was sitting on a sofa in the lobby reading newspapers and must have come away without the bag. We saw the hotel security standing watch by the sofa guarding the bag and waiting for its rightful owner to show up. After a brief inquiry as to its contents, they returned it to Ingoo, who bowed repeatedly in gratitude, almost weeping. Had he really lost it with all the money, he would surely have been fired, if not beheaded, however close he might have been to Jungil Kim.

Next morning we went to visit the famed National Mah Film Studio, a recently completed ultramodern building with soundproof glass walls. Each room was equipped with a sophisticated system of curtains, somewhat like the sails of an ocean-going schooner, to maximize the use of natural light, obvitating many problems of artificial lighting such as glare and spotting. Other equipment and facilities were also well designed and maintained, giving us valuable insight into the plans for Moo Moo Film.

On December 10 we didn't budge from our room, waiting for Kintaro. Except to answer calls from Ingoo who wanted to confirm our presence in the room, we didn't go near the phone, so as to leave the line open just in case our Japanese friend should decide to call first. Our anxiety mounted as there was no sign of Kintaro even after lunch that had been sent up by room service. At 3 p.m. a light tap came from the door. It was Kintaro. All three of us embraced and wept without uttering a word. Eight years had passed since our last meeting in Seoul, but at age 65 he was as hale as ever.

"We were so worried we wouldn't see you," Nan said, wiping her tears.

"I looked for you since morning," he said. "The front desk gave me Room 609 as yours, but when I went there, somebody else answered the knock."

"That's next door, my buddy Ingoo's room," I said. "What did you do?"

"I was so embarrassed I walked away back to my room, and decided to wait for you in my room. Not hearing from you, I went down to the lobby again and was given the correct room number this time."

"Were you surprised to hear from us?" I asked as we sat down in the sofa and chair around the coffee table.

"Not really," Kintaro said. "The artist goes wherever he can work best. I wouldn't have put up with the caprices and meddlings of the South Korean military. So you like it better in North Korea?"

"Jungil Kim has promised to keep his hands off our work, and that brings us to the crux of our meeting. He wants to host a film festival in Pyongyang next year. Japan, the US, Britain, and other Western countries would most probably boycott it. This is where you come in. With your influence you can persuade them to participate."

"What have they got to show as host country except their propaganda trash, unless of course you've been busy and made a hundred movies since we saw each other last?"

"We are finishing our first movie."

"Your first? I thought you had a productive environment."

"The fact of the matter is that we just got started...."

"Shh!" Nan cautioned, pointing at the air conditioning vent, intercom, and chandelier and motioned us to move to the corner by the window.

"I always gave North Korea the benefit of the doubt whenever I heard about these abductions," he said, shocked, after listening to our narrative. "It was just inconceivable that they could be used as a national policy by any government, simply because this sort of thing can't be kept under wraps for ever."

"Only in an open society like the US or your country," Nan corrected.

"What I can't get over is the insanity of making you rot in jail all these years instead of exploiting your talent."

"Maybe to cower me for good so I won't attempt another escape. They have succeeded because I won't even think of it until the odds are 100% and nothing can go wrong, which probably means never. So please keep everything you've heard today to yourself. Our future contact will be strictly on business, to promote the festival."

"There is just one more thing we want to ask you," Nan said, handing him the tape recording of our first meeting with Jungil and the black and white pictures of Jungil shaking hands with her as she landed at South Port. "Keep the tape and pictures for six months and if you don't hear from us, release them to the Japanese and South Korean press."

"Gladly."

The reason for this request was that we still did not know what Jungil's real intentions were or how long he would use us for his purposes. In case we should die like so many anonymous prisoners, we wanted the world to know about it.

"Anything else I can take with me, like messages or letters to your folks and friends in Korea? I can mail from Tokyo or deliver personally in Seoul where I am going next month to attend a meeting of the Organizing Commission for the Asia Film Festival."

"Why didn't we think of that? We'll tape letters so you can take them to Tokyo and give to Gyongshig who'll know what to do. He has the addresses."

Fearing customs inspection or other trouble at Kimpo Airport, we decided to tape in the middle of the rock music cassettes bought in Belgrade. Our recording took the whole night, as Nan's crying had to be erased. In case the tapes should fall into Jungil's hands, he would learn how miserable she was, our protestations to the contrary notwithstanding, but whenever she tried to speak choking tears and sobs overcame her, which I could not quite eliminate by editing.

Back in Pyongyang we found the costumes we had ordered before departure made all wrong and unusable. After a nationwide search the Studio came up with a 71-year-old seamstress, who had come north with her husband during the war but had kept her Seoul dialect intact and wore her hair in a bun on top of her head in the old style. Glad for the opportunity to reuse her skill, she made the clothes over in a short time.

To recruit a permanent staff of actors for Moo Moo Film we had placed an ad in the Labor Daily and selected about 30 from among the hundreds of photographs submitted before our departure. I asked to call them together for an interview. Promptly 60 showed up, none of whose faces corresponded to those on our list.

"What the heck is going on?" I blew up in a rare display of temper.

"But those you had chosen had either bad health or undesirable background," the Administrator said.

The truth was not difficult to guess. Setting aside our choices, the Party came up with its own favorites, for it had to retain control over an important profession like movie acting, highly visible and glamorous even by Communist standards. Who were we to quarrel? Maybe it was just as well. We wouldn't be held responsible if anything went wrong. Photos never told the whole story as in the case of our short emissary and face alone did not make a star anyway. Also there was no time to make an issue of it and go through the selection process all over again. We picked 30 from among the 60 and 20 more from the graduating class of the Film and Drama College.

It was the end of the year, the dread time when letters of loyalty had to be written to the father and son, a duty from which no citizen was exempt whatever his station in life. Leaving the composition to Nan I devoted myself to finetuning the script of The Emissary. On New Year's Eve we were invited to the New Year Show to "wish the Great Chief health and longevity" at the February 16 Culture Palace which had 6,000 seats. Exhausted from the day's work all I wanted was a shuteye at home but I dared not stay away, for absence would be immediately reported and be given all kinds of sinister construction. As expected, the audience consisted of the top men of the land, including Ilsung Kim and foreign dignitaries, all sedately dressed and conscious of their elitist positions, but the performers were elementary school children doing adult roles in plays that showed Ilsung Kim liberating the fatherland from Japanese imperialism and winning victory from the Americans in the War of Liberation to secure North Korea as paradise on earth. Now and then Ilsung Kim's face flashed across the giant screen at the back of the stage, whereupon in total disregard of the show in progress the audience broke into thunderous applause, in which Ilsung himself joined enthusiastically, grinning from ear to ear as he stared at his own face.

From 9 a.m. next day we were among the thousand guests at the Silk Embroidery Hall, Ilsung Kim's residence, for the New Year's Day Breakfast. Every table was loaded with great food which however got cold and uneatable by the time the host got through with his New Year Message, a whole hour long. Across from us sat Dokshin Chay, formerly South Korea's Minister of Foreign Affairs, who had defected to North Korea after immigration to the US. His suit creased by the huge Ilsung Kim Badge given to him in return for whatever secrets he could sell to North Korea, he nevertheless looked seedy and fidgety, not at all like the conquering general he once was as Commander of the South Korean Expedition to Vietnam and heir apparent to Junghee Park until replaced by Doohwan Jun.

"Don't pay him any attention," whispered Haysong Gang, our mentor.

Poor man! He was already treated like trash. All he had earned for his trouble was the Ilsung Kim Badge and perhaps a lifetime pension at some third rate apartment.

"We would look very much like him after a few years," Nan said on our way home. "We've got to get out of here."

"I know but let's wait for the right moment, which is bound to come. When we are in Austria or some other Western country out of reach of North Korea, we'll make our move."

"Wouldn't the US Embassy in Prague do just as well?"

"No. Didn't you see the Czech guards at the Embassy? I don't know the exact legalities involved but so long as we are in an Eastern bloc nation North Korea could exert its pressure and get us back. But Prague is close enough, only a few hours by car from Vienna, don't you remember the man from the Embassy saying? So be patient. We are getting there."

While going through the inanities of New Year, we had to get ready to leave for Prague on the 4th of January to wrap up the foreign shots for The Emissary.

"The actors tell me they don't have any suitable luggage to bring along," Nan said. "But I think we have a solution: the bags Jungil Kim has sent his presents in."

"How many do you have?"

"At least a dozen."

"Are you sure he had no ulterior motives?"

"Oh, Moo, I am not his type. Besides he had to boast his purity to you, remember?"

We called our secretary Jayil Kim and told him to collect the bags from the house for our traveling companions but no amount of persuasion would move him once he learned they were the Beloved Comrade Leader's gift bags.

"Don't worry," he said. "Everything will be taken care of."

On the morning of the 4th we left on our third trip to Prague with 15 others, the 3 male actors to play the emissaries, 2 female actors, cameraman, assistant producer, lighting technician, make-up artist, and so forth. Immediately after takeoff the Korean Civil Airliner began playing General Ilsung Kim, Jangbayg Mountain Spirit, and other patriotic North Korean songs, though some of the passengers were not

Korean. Settling into our first-class seats Nan and I closed our eyes in stoic resignation. However, we were mercifully distracted by the lunch which consisted of sushi, barbecued beef, kimchee, and dried slices of pollack. Unlike the Soviet Aeroflot planes which had flown direct to Moscow on our previous trips, the Korean plane stopped at Irkutsk for refueling. All the passengers had to deplane and walk to the terminal, a jetway being a luxury unheard of here. True to its reputation as the coldest spot in the whole world, the air sliced our faces like knives. I raised my gloved hand to my nose to scratch and heard it crackle like crackers at the touch: the moisture in the passages had all frozen up. It was amazing that a whole city of people lived there putting up with that kind of cold. But I learned that they loved winter, the healthiest season, because no germ survived the temperature. Flu and other maladies returned in spring and summer.

We got back on the plane but a short flight later were ordered to deplane again for entry procedure at Novoshibirsk on the western edge of Siberia, a level plain with steppes, swamps, lakes, meandering rivers and tributaries as far as eyes could see, all frozen solid. But we were not done with entry procedure, which was repeated all over again at Moscow. I couldn't imagine a more blatant form of the Fly Aeroflot, Buy Soviet policy, openly discriminating against non-Soviet flights. At the baggage claim Nan and I were astonished by the yellow Samsonite traveling bag every member of our party retrieved, "on loan from the Traveler Store," which rented out bags and clothes to party cadre or foreigners traveling abroad.

Arriving at Prague next night we checked in at the International Hotel, decidedly second-rate compared to the Intercontinental Nan and I had stayed on our last trip. But even this was too expensive and only four of us stayed, including Ingoo Cha and the assistant producer cum guard, the rest going to sleep at the Embassy quarters.

Work began at daybreak next day. At the Barandov Studio I examined the shots taken at the Hague by the Czech cameraman and was relieved to find them exactly as I wanted, Patriot Joon Yee's tomb, Peace Conference Building, and others. Unlike the weather-beaten crumbling tombstone that used to appear in Korean history textbooks, the pictures showed a brand new monument along with a flower stand and a bust of Joon Yee in marble, recently commissioned by the South Korean government bowing to outcries of indignation at home.

That night we called Gyongshig in Tokyo.

"Have you received our taped letters from Mr. Kintaro?" Nan asked anxiously.

"Yes," he said. "I've already forwarded them to Seoul and you'll be getting their replies soon through the Korea-Japan Federation."

"Is everything going to be all right?"

"Of course. Nobody can fault you for writing to parents and relatives, nor them for receiving from you."

We sincerely hoped he was right and there would be no repercussions on either side.

Outdoor shots having been taken care of on the previous trip, our shooting this time concentrated on interior sequences, notably at the hotel where the emissaries had first checked in, the boarding house they had to move to to save money, the auditorium at the Peace Conference Building, International Press Club where they held a press conference, and parties at the US, Japanese, and Russian embassies in the Hague, where they tried in vain to win the sympathy of the delegates by appealing personally. Korea was a colony of Japan, the rising sun of the East, and these emissaries from the former King of Korea had simply no standing. Whenever a particular setting was called for that could not be mocked up authentically inside the sound stage, scouts were sent out all over town in search of a suitable building. The Barandov people couldn't have been more cooperative. Moved by the Czech translation of the screen play, which gave them an insight into Korean history, scarred by foreign invasions and occupations as numerous and traumatic as Czechoslovakia's, they were eager to help, identifying the foredoomed cause of the Korean emissaries as their own.

Every morning we were up at three, checked out the

filming equipment and material, and left after hurriedly downing Japanese instant noodles brought from Pyongyang to be on location by 7. Everybody had sandwiches for lunch and worked on without letup for days. Winter in Prague was as freezing as anywhere else and presented a serious dilemma for the occasional outdoor shots still remaining. Since the Hague Peace Conference was held in July, the actors had to sit or lie down on frozen ground wearing only summer clothes, drink ice water before speaking or just move lips without speaking to prevent the camera from catching the white puffs of steam exiting their mouths. The dance party at the Japanese Embassy was a real problem, as it required the appearance of dozens of Oriental women in kimono. We could hustle up and fake the kimono but not the wearers, as we had brought only two actresses from Pyongyang. The only alternative was to mobilize the wives of the Embassy staff, who however knew nothing about Western ballroom and were too shy to stand straight, let alone dance, before a movie camera.

"The Party wills it," the Ambassador ordered sternly, quelling their open rebellion, but it was a tall order transforming a bunch of uncoordinated housewives, however willing, into tolerable dancers in a few days.

At the end of the day the rushes were examined at random to see how they had turned out. Only the cameraman, lighting, art, makeup and other technical people need be involved in this process, but everybody else clamored for a peek, including Deputy Chief Ingoo Cha and the actors. Once admitted each participant had to look at this or that shot more particularly, adding this or that comment. What would have been over in a matter of minutes lengthened to hours, making up my mind to exclude the supernumeraries. Notified of this decision, Ingoo was predictably loud in objection.

"The Beloved Comrade Leader was explicit about all of us participating in the review process," he said.

"He was referring to the final work print, not the daily rushes," I countered, refusing to yield.

According to the time-honored tradition Joon Yee, leader of the group, commits harakiri, suicide by cutting up the abdomen, at the Peace Conference before all the delegates to protest their indifference to the Japanese annexation of Korea and becomes the Secret Emissary of No Return as his body is left behind to be buried in a Hague cemetery. What really happened was that he died shortly after the conference, stricken by grief and mortification at having failed his dethroned king. The truth by itself was tragic enough, but Korean imagination had to add the additional touch, harakiri. Probably it was his surviving companions that reported that way upon return home, in their heightened state of mind perceiving little or no difference between the two modes of death, and their countrymen readily adopted it, never bothering or wishing to check for veracity and printing it as fact year after year in government-sanctioned textbooks, both in South and North Korea. Ilsung Kim, alleged author of our original script, apparently believed it to be authentic, as did the rest of North Korea, immune to critical inquiry. Lately, however, some South Korean researchers happened to be going through the minutes of the Peace Conference and, finding no reference to the sensational event, were ready to go about rectifying the omission, until the truth dawned on them, forcing them to publish it with as much temerity as impugning immaculate conception by Virgin Mary. From the movie-maker's point of view, the legend made a better story with unlimited potential for dramatic exploitation, the heroic, if pathetic, resolution of the little man from the hermit kingdom, bewildered and heart-sick at his futility in a foreign city, to write in blood the anguish and indignation of his countrymen, the momentary shock and horror of the spectators, who go back to business as usual, quickly dismissing the unpleasant episode, and the unrelieved sorrow of his grieving family and nation.

The climactic scene of his suicide had to be shot with lightning celerity. The Prague Railroad Union Building, selected for the Peace Conference, was booked solid for a whole month for New Year dance parties by various groups. Who said Communists didn't have fun in their lives? After much importuning we finally prevailed on the management to let us use it between shifts and after hours. Naturally it strained everything, especially when some 400 Czech extras were involved. Hired to play the delegates dressed in unique national costumes, they had to be told through an interpreter exactly how and when to sit down and stand, speak and make other moves, all to be filmed within one or two hours before the next party guests arrived. It seemed so hopeless that several times I threw in my towel, but Nan rose to the occasion, getting hoarse from shouting instructions to the actors, cameramen, makeup personnel, and extras, a whole ocean of them. Finally the impossible was accomplished and at the end of the allotted time the sequence was complete. Similar pressure applied to the scene at the emissaries' boarding house on January 27, one day before departure from Prague. The Czech technicians left after their eight-hour day and Nan and I had to finish up with only one lighting man skipping supper and sleep: we had to leave town first thing next morning for Moscow to catch the Korean Civil Air flight. Otherwise we would have to wait another week.

When we returned to the hotel exhausted long after midnight, we found the mirror that used to hang above our headboard in our suite lying shattered on the floor, probably because somebody had knocked it off leaving in a hurry on hearing our footsteps.

"Somebody was trying to remove a listening device from behind the mirror," Nan said.

"It must have been Ingoo," I reasoned. "Remember how I asked him on the first day we arrived to change to another suite because this was too small to accommodate conferences with our staff and Czech technicians but giving this excuse and that he wouldn't oblige?"

"The bastard!"

I called Ingoo and pointing at the pieces of glass asked him to report to the police at once.

"Burglars!" he said, faking surprise. "But let's forget it because you haven't lost anything."

"But our privacy has been invaded. We feel violated."

"Police investigation will hold us up and we won't be able

to leave in time for the plane."

He had a point there. We couldn't afford even an hour's delay. All the feverish work at the last minute just to make the flight would have been for naught. We only called the domestic staff and had the mess cleaned up, considering ourselves lucky for not having discussed anything compromising in bed other than work. The bug might have been a blessing in disguise as it could have strengthened Jungil's confidence in us.

As our Civil Air plane approached Pyongyang next day the PA system again blared away with the General Kim Song, followed by the announcement:

"Patrons, you are soon to arrive in Pyongyang, capital of the glorious Selfhood fatherland, where lives the Great Leader and Chief who leads world revolution. Pyongyang has Panoramic Heights, birthplace of the great Chief, Selfhood Tower, and other sights...."

The same message was repeated in broken English with untranslated Korean words such as Joochay for Selfhood, which was probably just as well as it vitiated the offense by being unintelligible. We were met at the airport by the Moo Moo Film staff and a pair of brand new Benzes, one silver and the other green. We knew at once that they were from Jungil who had asked us offhand just prior to our trip what our favorite colors were. We had named them thinking he wanted to give us some clothes, not Benz 600's, especially when we already had an almost new one.

"The man is trying to chain us down with favors and presents," Nan said.

"A chain that may be harder to break than one forged in steel," I said.

"Not for me. Nothing can make up for the six best years of our lives he has taken away from us. Besides for a man trying to please he has very little tact, flaunting his birthday all over the place, especially before you who has no real birthday to call your own?"

Both cars had 5-digit license plate numbers with the prefix 216, denoting Jungil's birthday, February 16, assigned only to a handful of his most trusted servants.

"Darling, you don't have to convince me. I was the one he put in prison, remember? Which car shall we take?"

"I don't care. Let's take your color."

We were heading for the silver Benz when Soggyoo, Party Secretary of the Film Section, came running and said, "Mrs. Moo, your car is over there."

"But I want to ride with my husband."

"No, you ride in your own. That's our Beloved Leader's wish."

"Let's meet at home," I said, taking her to her car.

"By the way," Soggyoo said, "there is mail waiting for you at your office."

"From where?" Nan asked shrilly.

"Japan."

It was a manila envelope of letters from Nan's relatives and friends in Seoul via Gyongshig in Tokyo. This was news from home in eight years and affected us as powerfully as if we met them in person, though for fear of official displeasure either in the south or north the writers were all reserved and factual.

"Forgive me, Mom and Dad!" Nan cried bitterly. "I always wanted to be your comfort and support, not sorrow and pain, in your old age."

Her father had suffered a stroke the day she was confirmed missing. After weeks in the hospital he was brought home, left side paralyzed, in the care of her mother who had been crying day and night over her double calamity.

But not all the news was bad. Her brother Namgyoo had become full partner in the engineering company he had been working for and was developing a big housing project in Yongnamgoo south of the Han. His wife was expecting their second child. Also upbeat was the letter from Gyongja Jo of the Seoul Film School.

"All your friends and fans are overjoyed to discover you are both alive," she wrote. "Wherever you may be, I know you will benefit mankind through your work. We try to carry on your work here as best we can. We are no longer at the old campus by the river which had been turned into a golf course. We relocated to a vacant lot further south in Soowon where the land was cheaper. Enough of your friends came through with donations to build the new school, named Moo Moo Film Academy, which has had good luck with an enrollment of 1,500. Maybe the bank did us a favor by foreclosure. We turn away many more than we take in, 10 to one. The acting career is becoming as prestigious as the law, medicine, or pulpit. Besides the school has an extra drawing card, your illustrious names...."

"How could they take away the Boochon campus like that?" Nan asked in disbelief and indignation.

"Doohwan Jun is a greedy bastard," I said. "Do you still think we should go back to the den of thieves?"

"He won't rule forever."

"They are all alike, Syngman Rhee, Junghee Park, Doohwan Jun, you name it."

"But our folks and friends are there. Where else can we go, unless we take all of them away with us?"

"Why not? South Korea is no good for them anyway because they are from the persecuted minority of Jolla. We should arrange their mass emigration."

"To be another minority in, say, France?"

"Who wants France? Remember Cerviet's problems with his old folks? I was thinking of the US, which has nothing but minorities. Besides in Koreatown of Los Angeles they'll be in the absolute majority and won't have to speak a word of English, going to Korean groceries, Korean doctors, Korean churches. The more I think about it, the more I am convinced the US is our next home."

"But is it free from corruption, injustice, and prejudice?"

Hadn't I known at close, smelly range the Molinbecks, Hesslers, Keans, Whitwalls, all the sundry and shady crew, just as grabby, conniving, and prejudiced as the rest of the biped species, to have any illusions about one country above another?

"No place on earth is, darling. But in the US we can yell out loud about it, make a big stink, which eventually leads to a measure of correction, like Civil Rights legislation, Watergate, and Koreagate. Not perfect but enough to keep the worst under control, which is a whole lot more than what one can do anywhere else."

From our office window next day we noticed a motorcade of about 40 vehicles entering the compound with Ingoo Cha in the lead.

"From our Beloved Comrade Leader for the exclusive use of Moo Moo Film," he said.

They included one mobile home complete with 3 bedrooms, kitchen and bath, one bus with a large conference room, 5 limousines two of which were convertibles, 3 huge commuter buses, 15 miniature buses, 10 trucks, 3 jeeps, and 7 cargo vans. The mobile home and bus were German Benzes, the limos US Fords, and trucks Japanese Nissans, all expensive models.

"The mobile home is for your personal use when you are on location," Ingoo added.

The entire staff assembled at the auditorium for the presentation ceremony. Ingoo went up on the platform and delivered a passionate speech.

"In spite of the cold weather our Beloved Comrade Leader personally inspected each and every vehicle before they were sent out here. Let us do our share by working hard and producing good films that will bring joy to him. It was his particular wish that you obey and aid President Moo in his great work."

From each department a representative stepped forward and shouted at the top of his voice, "We have erred grievously in the past but will in the future work harder and repay our debt, bearing in mind our Beloved Comrade Leader's kindness and thoughtfulness."

I had no idea what kind of error they were referring to. In any case they must have rehearsed many times over, because the words they used were identical, though I, the titular head, had no knowledge of it. Jungil Kim's munificence only reminded me of my own impotence and vulnerability. The finale was the singing of the Ilsung Kim and Jungil Kim Songs, all the five verses of each.

"The ceremony is over and you may leave," Soggyoo Yee told us.

"Isn't the rest of the company being dismissed?" I asked.

"We have still some unfinished business," he said.

Outside the auditorium we heard them shouting slogans.

"They are decent enough to spare us," Nan said.

"Maybe."

"Why maybe? Can you stand more of that?"

"No, but by the same token we are being excluded. We'll never be part of them."

"Who wants to be?"

"That's true."

A few days later Jungil called us to his office.

"Have you been listening to the South Korean news lately?" he asked as soon as we sat down.

"No, sir," I replied, noticing that we hadn't for some time, not even Nan, the South Korean radio addict, who couldn't go to sleep unless she listened a couple of hours to broadcasts from the south. Domestic shots for The Emissary took us everywhere, to field camps and country inns. By the time we got home, we were so tired we barely had time to say goodnight to each other, let alone sit up to listen to the radio.

"It's their news time," Jungil said, switching on MBC.

The whole program was devoted to the funeral of the 17 killed in Rangoon by a bomb, placed by North Korean agents in the eaves of the pavilion at the Auong Cemetery where Doohwan Jun, on a state visit to Burma, the first on the itinerary to the several nonaligned nations of Southeast Asia, was to lay a floral wreath. The switch had been pushed a few seconds too soon, just as Jun got off his limousine and was walking down the path lined by his principal cabinet officers and aids. The mourning crowd suddenly erupted into anger and tore through the streets of Seoul shouting vengeance on Jungil Kim, named as the mastermind by the captured agents.

"Mad dogs!" Jungil spat contemptuously, switching off.

However, the incident had serious consequences: North Korea became a paraiah even among the Third World countries which used to look up to it for moral leadership.

"We don't have a foothold left in Southeast Asia any more," Jungil conceded. "But who cares about backward Southeast Asia? We'll go through Europe and reach the world market with our films. This is where you come in. I appreciate your weeks of unremitting toil in the cause."

"Thank you," I said. "But there is so much more to be done. We need technical assistance from Japan, America, and Hong Kong. In the past they would have come at my invitation but after Rangoon I don't know."

"What's done is done," Jungil said, grinning disarmingly. "Maybe money would help. Spend whatever is necessary to make connections abroad. We just have to get out of the bind we are in."

"I want to call Samho Hyon of Hong Kong first of all," I said. "He has the phone numbers of my contacts in Hong Kong and the US. Also I have a few other things to ask him about."

"Sure," Jungil said with a knowing smile. "He is a smart operator and has been my purchasing agent for years."

As if I couldn't have guessed. I almost asked how much Samho got paid for selling Nan and me but refrained. The same thought must have crossed Nan, as evidenced by a twitch in her face at the mention of the traitor's name.

"You had better make the call from Beijing," Jungil said, "because a call from Pyongyang would expose you immediately. Who are the contacts?"

"Wong Film in Hong Kong, Dr. Chansoo Hong of New York, because he was our agent in dealing with NBC, and Robert Fenwick of Universal Studios in Hollywood, who has the screen play for our Mayoress of Koreatown. It would be great publicity to produce it jointly with Universal."

"How does the story go?"

"It's narrated from the point of view of an American Korean War veteran, critical of the way his government and General MacArthur handled the war and haunted by the memory of cruelties committed by the US Army against the Korean people."

"The US government would allow such a film to be made?"

"Of course. Self-criticism is the staple of American movies. Nothing is sacred, sex, family, morality, religion, patriotism, certainly loyalty to a current administration."

"But isn't that suicidal?"

"On the contrary, openness and debate strengthen America."

"Hm," Jungil fell pensive. "Go on and tell me the story, in detail, omitting nothing."

So I became a regular Sheherezade, entertaining my prince with a night's tale. I concentrated only on the screenplay, and made no connection between the main character and Alan Heyman, my alter ego. In spite of my strenuous exclusion of extraneous matter, my narrative was way longer than the movie itself and lasted until near daybreak. I had to work in the scenery, background, and occasional commentary, impromptu of course, rising to the supreme challenge of converting a skeptic into a backer and investor, who would hopefully propel us to the US for our ultimate liberation. Without seeming boastful I must report that I held his attention to the very end. In fact, he was rapt and hung on to my lips as if his life depended on it.

"Let's produce it by ourselves" Jungil said, when I finished.

He wanted to hog it all. I felt a sinking sensation of defeat in my heart: I had done my job too well.

"But think of the advantages of joint venture with Universal," I pointed out. "Apart from ready accessibility to its vast worldwide network of distribution, the publicity we get from working with Universal, perhaps the most visible US company, is something money can't buy and will provide the springboard into the West you want in a grand way."

"Are you sure the US government will allow it?"

"Freedom of expression is guaranteed by the Constitution."

"Even if you prevail upon the US government, the South Korean puppets will do their damnedest to stop it."

"There is no love lost between the US and Doohwan Jun. Just to spite him the US might do exactly the opposite of what he wants."

"Will we get credit?"

"I'll see to it. Besides if we film at Wonsan, Lake Jangjin and the hills of Gayma, the credit will be written all across the film, the best advertisement for our scenic resources. The whole world will be beating at our door to come in for sightseeing."

"They are all on the east coast, aren't they?"

"Yes. Is that a problem?"

"Currently the area is off limits to tourists for fear of military espionage. But on strict verification of employment I guess we will let the Universal people in."

After taking Nan home so she could get some sleep before she went to work, I headed for the airport with Soontay Bag, Director of the Film Library, to make the long distance calls. The 50-seater Civil Air two-engine propeller plane shook violently throughout the flight making me so sick that I had to run to the nearest restroom the moment we touched down at Beijing Airport. Afflicted with constipation I took a while going about my business and was not quite prepared for the banshee that tore in, shouting my name.

"What's the ruckus all about?" I asked, opening the compartment door a crack.

"Oh, sorry!" Soontay murmured, withdrawing shamefacedly but not forgetting to check the security of the windows.

Instead of going into town we checked in at the airport hotel and called Samho at the number Jungil gave me. I had never dreamed that I would be calling this traitor. Apparently alerted by Pyongyang he was expecting my call and greeted me brightly.

"I hear you are going great guns over there," he said.

Could he possibly expect me to thank him for the favor? I restrained the impulse to shout and tell him off.

"Do you have the phone numbers I need?" I asked evenly.

He gave them instantly.

"I assume the $500,000 from the sale of our films to Malaysia is safe in our account at the Sumitomo Bank of Hong Kong."

"Well, it's been withdrawn to pay for expenses."

"What expenses?"

"I had to print more copies of your films for export."

"To where?"

"The Philippines, but I didn't get paid because the guy fled with Marcos. There were other expenses after your departure, too, to silence the press and discourage official inquiries. And of course there were office expenses. The rent is phenomenal here."

So the funds we had counted on when we got out did not exist. I should have known as much, dealing with a thief. Without another word I hung up and called the US numbers. Fenwick was away at the Antarctic, doing a documentary on the erosion of the ozone layer. I left with the secretary my name and a Moscow address, an apartment rented by a North Korean student, which Jungil Kim wanted me to use for communications with the outside world.

The call to Dr. Chansoo or Charles Hong had better luck. He answered himself at the first ring.

"Is it really you?" he said after a pause. "I've somehow known all along that you were alive contrary to everybody's opinion and have been holding off NBC for your final signatures authorizing the release."

"Go ahead and sign for us. You have our power of attorney."

"I wish you could be here and do it yourself. Where are you calling from?"

"Beijing."

"Give me your address so I can send to you."

"Actually, I am just visiting here. I'll give you my Moscow address."

"Moscow? Did you find relatives in Russia or something?"

He seemed to have an uncanny telepathy, because my possible Russian ancestry had just crossed my mind, too.

"Not one in a million chance."

"Now if that is not bigotry. After all Russia had Dostoyevsky and Tolstoy."

"But the present generation is another breed, capable of

shooting down an unarmed civilian airliner and content to wallow in inefficiency and corruption."

"What are you doing there then?"

"It's a long story. Maybe we should meet somewhere like Budapest. I'll send you the round-trip ticket."

"I can afford it. Just name the date."

"I'll write you as soon as I know for sure."

Only if I could ask Chansoo to get a call through to Al Edwards, who would spring us out of North Korea by hook or crook, the way he did out of South Korea. But I dared not breathe his name, a nonfilm personality I'd have to explain to Soontay listening in, which was probably well-known to the North Korean intelligence community. Why hadn't we thought of Al sooner, the most logical choice? We should have given the tape recording and pictures, our 'material evidence', to Al, the professional cloak and dagger man, not to Kintaro, an amateur. In hindsight our escape plan proceeded haphazardly in fits and starts without direction. Overawed by the terrible consequences of offending whimsical despots, we simply couldn't think straight or look ahead. Maybe it was not too late. When Chansoo came to Budapest, we could ask him to get the evidence from Kintaro to Al, who might need it to commit the machinery of CIA to our rescue.

Incidentally, by now Nan and I were agreed that the US was where we should defect and live and work for the rest of our lives, the country of the Statue of Liberty, the country of the elder and younger Minsky's choice, my possible kinship to them aside. We were both too deeply disillusioned with South Korea to make it our next abode. Besides to opt for South Korea was to reject and betray North Korea, the human and physical reality of which had grown on us and touched us viscerally in spite of its cruelties and inanities. Only by turning our back on both, would we be true to our total Korean heritage. Besides, in my case, I had a non-Korean admixture, Russian or otherwise, that cried for acknowledgment and endorsement. I had to live the life of a mixed-blood in full, with a vengeance, battering down the fortresses of exclusion worldwide, built on differences in race, culture, nationality, province, family. The US was the ideal base of operations for this self-imposed mission. Scarred and ruptured by racial tension, as well as struggle between rich and poor, the universal theme, the US was yet unalterably committed to diversity and tolerance, for the alternative was self-destruction. Its destiny was mine and Nan's, to be the pathfinder for the two Koreas, for wherever there was strife, contention, division. As soon as we got to the US, we would get busy producing films dedicated to the theme of Earth Village built on the rock of transcendent, common humanity.

From Beijing I also called Gyongshig in Tokyo, thanked him for transmitting the letters from Seoul, and asked him to head the Tokyo branch of Moo Moo Film.

"Gladly," he said. "I have all the time in the world after my recent resignation as Director of the Association's Culture Department."

"Was it under duress because of your contacts with the Federation on my behalf?"

The correspondence between us and our friends in Seoul had to be routed through the Federation, that is, Korea-Japan Federation composed of pro-Communist ethnic Koreans in Japan, which alone had access to the ships that went back and forth between Japan and North Korea.

"Well, maybe, but it was about time I had left. It's sickening to see all that bickering going on among Koreans living in a foreign country where the natives treat them like dirt anyway."

"But the Koreans are natives, too, like yourself."

Gyongshig's grandparents had immigrated to Japan in the 30's under a Japanese policy to assimilate Koreans and Gyongshig had been born and raised in Tokyo, except for his education which was in Seoul.

"Yes, but the Japanese never accept us and don't even give us citizenship."

Japanese racism was as fierce as Korean. Perhaps all these racially homogeneous nations had this problem. But racial bigotry was no guarantee of love within the race itself. At a motel in Montana during my American exile I had heard an

Afro-American comic say on TV, commenting on the strife in Northern Ireland, "They got to invent niggers, if they ain't got them already." Jolla bashing in South Korea was a case in point and so were the goings on in the Korea-Japan Association. Composed of ethnic Koreans in Japan allegedly sympathetic to South Korea and opposed to the Korea-Japan Federation, the Association was second to none in infighting. Again the merit of the American experiment stood out like a beacon that beckoned. With all its racial and human problems, the US was still the most tolerant of societies. At least it was honest about them, and tried to do something about them, to bring about equality and freedom for all, even though it might end up as lip service only. Others simply didn't even bother with the lip service.

"Your starting salary will be double what you got paid at the Association. As your first assignment I want you to buy and ship to me traditional Korean costumes including long bamboo pipes and horse hair stovepipe hats and all the tapes you can get of pansori and folk music, recordings of artists at the Aran Ham Center, Choran Bag, Sonhee Kim, Gwaryong Shim, Ilsob Hong..."

Tears sprang to my eyes at the mention of my old friends, and I couldn't speak for a while. Our paths had naturally parted, but I owed them my formative years, my artistic development. Prevented by other priorities, I hadn't made a film dedicated to their art and lifestyle yet, as I had sworn. For many of them it or any other form of recognition from the world would come too late.

"Hello, I can't hear you. Are you still there?"

"Yes. I need those folk music tapes urgently to finish the film I am making."

"Okay. Also you'll soon receive some newspaper clippings about you."

Upon return to Pyongyang I found the clippings, one of which was an article, 'A Tribute to Moo Moo's Art' in the Josun Monthly by Sangpil Shin, the last person from whom I expected any kind of tribute. He had been the most vocal critic of me, hating everything about me. What could account for this aboutface? The so-called tribute was in fact an obituary and I was referred to as the late Moo Moo. Death was a wonderful reconciler that ended all rancor and jealousy.

XXIII.
Work in Earnest

Nan and I were back to the grind. Whenever Jungil talked enviously about the high caliber of actors in South Korea, we assured him that North Korea had as much potential that only needed to be brought out. As we actually started working, we found ourselves eating our words. It was easier said than done to search out and bring up new talent. One major stumbling block was the North Korean aesthetics of feminine beauty. Perhaps thanks to Selfhood, North Korea retained the older values and preferred plumpness, roundness, flatness, thin eye line, subdued skeletal structure, the opposite of what they went for in South Korea. My opinion of the latter being what it was, I should be happy with what I found and go along with it. Not so. In the eternal dichotomy of head and heart, mind and body, intellect and instinct, or however it might be characterized, come time for action, the latter won out: as much a Pavlonian dog as anybody else, I behaved exactly as conditioned, the South Korean or Caucasian way, with inevitable conflict. Sonhee Jang, a waitress at the Airport VIP Lounge, 20 years old, with a slender body and three-dimensional oval face, had come to the notice of Nan and me at once but we heard no end of crabbing about our poor taste until she later played the star role in Spring Fragrance. We ran into the same kind of resistance with Gumsoog Bag, 21, a dancer, who eventually starred in Promise. Of course, discovery was one thing and development quite another, and we didn't really need all that negative feedback in the arduous process of training and refining a recruit.

North Korean idiosyncrasy affected the rest of feminine appearance. Young women took pains to bind up and flatten the shameful protrusion of their breasts. Even in mid-summer they wore long-sleeved jogori. Their skirts had buttons instead of zippers and a large waistline designed to cover up, not show off, the feminine contours. The overall impression was dowdiness. Panties were unknown and women wore instead a sort of shorts. Everytime she went abroad Nan brought tons of panties and brassieres for her staff who, however, took to the gifts with reluctance.

The recruits had to be taught the basics, how to walk, sit, smile, put makeup on. Many times women wearing skirts would be found with their legs spread apart to be severely scolded by Nan. We took care to take as many of our people with us as possible on trips abroad to expose them to the outside world and make them more sophisticated, Westernized, that is. Invariably Nan bought more fashionable skirts and pants for the women, which they wore gladly while they were traveling, but took off the moment they got back on home turf.

"The Party forbids it," they said.

"It's all right," Nan assured them. "I have the Beloved Leader's personal guarantee."

But they wouldn't wear them, fearing criticism from their peers.

If acting was a problem, speech was even worse, because the North Korean actors had cultivated a slow, mannered style somewhat as in a period play. One actress could not synchronize with her own lip movements in the picture and after many tries Nan, a natural voice actor as well, had to speak for her. By an Ilsung Kim directive North Korea had so-called 'cultured standard,' a hybrid of Pyongan and Hamgyong dialects, but Nan would have none of it.

"The scene is Seoul and we need to speak Seoul dialect," she insisted and had her way.

Though rigid like this, North Korea was human after all and men and women loved and often star-crossed affairs surfaced, which meant trouble, maybe not as terrible as in Moonhee Yoo's case but just as serious, because in North Korea there was no such thing as private life. Mihwa Bag, 19, recruited and trained for the lead in Separation, had the potentials of a great star. By and by her affair with a young violinist in the bachelor apartment building next door became known, subjecting her to a hearing before the Party Ethics Committee. Pregnant already, the frightened girl took some drug which caused her to bleed profusely. Still in the ICU, she was handed notice, banishing her to the country. We tried to intervene, arguing that what she did on her own time was strictly her own business, but the Party was adamant: private life was public in North Korea, because what affected the individual affected society at large. If nothing else, I learned at least one truth in North Korea, the relativity of every truth, the contingency of every axiom. Privacy, as sacred as life, freedom, and pursuit of happiness in the West, was a point in question. The Party ideologue fairly bowled me over with the evil of privacy and individualism, responsible for the divorce, distrust, isolation, fragmentation, desolation of Western life. The best we could do was to keep her in Pyongyang working as a cleanup woman for outdoor sets at the Korean Art Film Studio.

We almost lost Yongshim Im that way, a new girl for the lead in The Jetty, based on the mammoth landfill project on the west coast, turning the vast tidal mudflats into a giant agricultural and industrial complex, the Yellow Sea held off by a dike parallel to the coastline and five miles into the sea starting at the Bay of Light in the estuary of the Daydong and a system of locks enabling oceanliners and tankers to sail from South Port into the Daydong, with arterial highways, bridges, and aqueducts crisscrossing the area. Since the west coast of Korea had the worst hydrographics in the world with tidal differences exceeding 30 feet, the sea many fathoms deep, the enterprise, on a scale equaling the greatest engineering feats of history, deserved to be immortalized in film. I was particularly intrigued by the project, because it was such a contrast to the tragic one-man undedrtaking I depicted in the south with the film Reclamation. Though largely documentary, the film had a story line, a young couple, both engineers on the project, falling in love through mutual dedication to work. Yongshim was the female engineer.

One afternoon the head of the New Talent Scout Department came to us and accused Yongshim of having an affair with Namsoo Jung, a lecturer at the Film College, married to Shinay Jo, a member of the White Head Creative Group, often cast in the role of Jungil's real mother Jongsoog Kim.

"She's got to go," he said.

"But we need her for the role," Nan said.

"We cannot show favoritism," the official declared solemnly. "She must be made an example of."

"If you must send away anybody," Nan pointed out, "send away the man, who is equally culpable, if not more."

"We have to follow rules," the man insisted.

But the ruling hierarchy was perfectly capable of bending the rules when convenient. In fact the present situation involving Yongshim was the direct result of such rule bending. When urged by the Party to get married, Shinay pointed at Namsoo, though, already engaged to another girl, he had rebuffed Shinay's advances before. Since Shinay was valuable, the Party decided to eliminate the weak and drove out Namsoo's fiancée. Chafing with hurt pride at the shotgun marriage, Namsoo had decided to pick an affair with Yongshim. Nan had a talk with Yongshim, a sensible girl after all, who quit seeing Namsoo, placing her career before her feelings.

One day, noticing two of her female employees engaged in heated debate, Nan asked them what the trouble was. Neither of them came forward with an answer at first.

"She is due for a physical with the gynecologist but doesn't want to go," the married one of them said at last.

"But she isn't married. Why should she go to the gynecologist?"

Further inquiry revealed an alarming fact. In North Korea every woman, married or single, had to be examined as to pregnancy and virginity on a regular basis for the official record. Without our knowledge all our unmarried female workers had been so screened. Armed with such intimate knowledge, knowledge that most mothers don't have of their daughters in the West, the authorities could smugly dispense their wisdom, telling their trapped women who to marry or when to get pregnant. It was this kind of unchecked self-righteous power, perpetuated in the name of virtue and chastity, that begot such excesses and atrocities as the Moonhee Yoo Incident, Big Brother gone berserk, whose truth I couldn't believe at first and which, if nothing else, forever alienated us from North Korean society.

A week later Chansoo Hong's cable was forwarded from our Moscow address: he was sending his wife and daughter with the papers to the Budapest Hilton some time between March 16 and 19 because he couldn't be spared from his hospital. That was just as well because it would be a real treat for Nan to be with Jane or Jungay again and also for us to see how Elizabeth, the genius, had turned out.

The whole Moo Moo Film crew as well as Nan and I drove ourselves to the limit and by March 13 the Emissary was finished, a month and two days before the projected deadline. Jungil called to congratulate us and ask for an immediate preview. Present at the auditorium of the Central Party Building were Jungil, Ingoo, Sooam Gil, Injoon Bayg, and Myongjay Kim in charge of Ilsung Kim documentaries, the top men in the film bureaucracy of North Korea. Though gratified by their exclamations of approval as the film unrolled, I was unhappy with the slow tempo of dialogue, which could not be speeded up overnight for more realism, unless Nan and I did all the talking.

"I am totally satisfied," Jungil said, coming over and holding both our hands. "There isn't a single thing to find fault with. It was like watching a European film. I'll report to the Chief immediately."

We all went upstairs for dinner, which was preceded as usual by many rounds of toasts, making everybody tipsy.

"Why isn't your name among the credits?" Jungil asked.

I had made Nan director and omitted my name altogether, mainly to punish myself for the sycophancy of picking the story as my first work in nearly ten years simply because it was Ilsung Kim's work.

"Vanity, sir," I said pretending candor. "I'll put my name in next time when I make a better film."

"But you couldn't do any better. There isn't a thing wrong with it, as I said. I insist on your name being mentioned."

So the credits had to be changed to read: Nanyong Song, Director, and Moo Moo, General Supervisor. In any event this was the first time credits were shown at all in a North Korean film. A typical North Korean film would go directly into action without a preamble whatsoever in writing. In medias res for sure. As a result no North Korean knew the names of any actors or other personnel involved in making the films they had watched umpteen times. Actors had only faces, no names. If their film became famous, the actor came to be known by the name of the character he or she played in the film. Yonghee Hong, who became the darling of every North Korean because of her role in Flower Girl and whose face was printed on the won bill, the North Korean currency, was known only as Flower Girl, her name in the picture, not by her own name which nobody knew. This was all part of a radical plan to prevent anybody from getting known to the people other than Ilsung or Jungil, because fame of any sort could become the focus of opposition and revolt. It was the simplest but the most effective means of disarming dissent, not known or tried by other dictators, perhaps more effective than a total ban on firearms, because without a known personality to rally around and converge upon, not enough force would be packed to unseat an existing regime. The Korean Kims were astute enough to have discovered and put to use this truth with unfailing consistency. Naturally it took some talking to incorporate credits into our films.

"It's not for personal fame or aggrandizement that we need them," I argued. "It's to make everybody involved feel responsible for their part in the film. Our Republic is the only one in the whole world that makes films without credits and we'll become the laughing stock if we went out like that into the world market, not unlike walking down New York's Fifth

Avenue with no clothes on."

Always sensitive to outside opinion, Jungil gave a grudging nod. This was a turning point in North Korean film making, however, because from here on every release by Moo Moo Film had credits at the beginning and those by the other studios had them at the end.

"You know our comrades are like the proverbial frog in the well," Jungil whispered to Nan and me during the post-preview dinner, "seeing only the little patch of sky overhead. Trapped in bureaucracy and party influence, they are egocentric and obstinate. Don't mind them. Just push ahead according to your own convictions. I'll back you up totally."

Perhaps he was referring to the friction I had experienced with Ingoo Cha, his acknowledged film counsel, who, either at his boss's order or because he had overheard this conversation, cornered me in the hallway as we were leaving, to beg our pardon for his ignorant interference. I put him at ease, praising his loyalty and inviting his frank opinion on any issue in the future.

Jungil went on to promise the use of his personal helicopter and plane for our transportation to shooting locations. We took him up on this offer and made good use of the chopper and 40-seater prop plane from the next filming on.

Another important corollary of the dinner was Jungil's authorization on the spot of Moo Moo Film Headquarters at Budapest, which enabled us to leave next day, accompanied by Sooam Gil, to meet Jungay and Elizabeth Hong in Budapest, not forgetting to take with us a print of The Emissary to show to the Barandov Studio staff at Prague on our way back.

Immediately after checking in at the Budapest Hyatt we called Jungay. It felt as if we were free already just to be able to dial direct without having to go through an operator as in North Korea. They were not at the Hilton, because the airline had goofed and made the reservations with the Danube Intercontinental, to which we drove at once, of course accompanied by our inalienable companion Sooam Gil. After confirming the room at the front desk we went upstairs, leaving Gil at the lobby. Nan and Jungay ran into each other's arms and cried for a long time.

"Hi, Uncle Moo," Elizabeth held out her hand with the elegance and grace of a reigning monarch. She was a young lady of 20, in her last year at Harvard Medical School. Her dignity and maturity, combined with beauty and youth, gave me a pang of regret at the passing years. I was getting on and there might not be enough time left for me to do any really meaningful work.

"So you will be a neurosurgeon like your father?" I asked.

"No, I'll probably work at the National Institutes of Health doing AIDS research."

She had her future assured, but frankly I was a little disappointed. All the promise and potential for heady adventure and experiment seemed to have gone out of her. I had always thought of her as setting the world on fire, ranging the stratosphere with the freedom of a disembodied spirit, like Batman on his wings. Perhaps it was my ignorance of the infinite challenges in medical research, but her chosen career suggested too much solidity, security, respectability. There was of course no mention of her preteen infatuation with the film, from which I had tried to wean her. Now that I had succeeded, I felt as if I had cut my own throat.

In spite of their US citizenship Jungay had been mortally afraid of coming to a Communist country and taken the most roundabout way getting there. After flying to Geneva, they took a sightseeing bus to Rome, a cruise ship to Athens, then a train to their final destination, Budapest.

"What has happened to you?" Jungay asked.

"Shh!" Nan said, going over to the door to make sure that nobody stood outside eavesdropping. Still mistrustful, she stuffed towels in the cracks around the door before taking them to a corner of the bedroom and filling them in on all that had happened.

"It just blows my mind," Elizabeth observed, shaking her head incredulously. "How can they think they could get away with it in this day and age?"

"They have been doing that quite well," Nan said, recounting the episodes of other abductees she had met or heard about.

"But for a whole government to engage in such crime...."

"It's a gang, a bunch of hoods, not a government."

"Why don't you just walk out with us?"

"It's not that simple. For one thing, there is our guard dog watching the elevator downstairs this very minute."

"Then let's take the stairway to the basement and slip out by the garage entrance. I can't imagine your putting up with these gangsters even for a minute."

"We can't blame him for not wanting to make a move until nothing can go wrong. They've done a number on him with all those years in prison."

"Poor Uncle Moo!"

"It's not so much my own personal phobia as my concern for Nan's safety."

"My husband says that the Hungarian Red Cross would give you sanctuary, if you went to them."

"You don't know their system. Nothing can shield someone the Party wants. We have to curb our impatience and wait until we are out of reach of the North Korean Communist Party. The right moment may not be too far off, though. Jungil wants us to launch into the West, including the US. We have his okay to produce or at least initiate negotiations to produce Mayoress of Koreatown jointly with Universal."

"How exciting! When you arrive in the US, you can just go into any store or home, and ask for help."

"In the meantime, I want you to do something for us. Look up the film columnist Kintaro in Tokyo, and ask for the stuff we've given him, which he was to publish if he didn't hear from us otherwise in six months. That was three months ago."

"What was it?"

"The tape recording of our conversation with Jungil Kim in which he admits his complicity in our abduction and some pictures of Nan taken with him at South Port, where he was waiting as she got off the kidnap ship. They'll convict him before any court of law. Give them to Al Edwards at Langley, who would know what to do with them, so the US authorities would be able to help us escape or at least expect us when we do."

"Does this man Kintaro know we are coming for them?"

"No, I had better call and tell him. Better yet, I will write a letter for you to take to him. He is a good man but may be offended at this seeming withdrawal of trust."

After signing another set of papers regarding copyright for the NBC releases, I settled down to compose a diplomatic letter to Kintaro, while the girls went on with their talking, often interrupted by tears. Before parting, with the vanity of a maker I asked mother and daughter to come with us to the North Korean Embassy to view The Emissary.

"No," Jungay screamed. "We won't go near that den of bandits."

After putting them on the Athens-bound train next morning we left for Prague. At the Barandov we had a preview with its directors and staff who, having participated in the production, were naturally curious how the film had turned out. They seemed impressed, especially by the fact that we had taken a total of two months to finish after we left.

"It would have taken us a year at least," one of the Czech directors said.

"Our leader Jungil Kim is pleased to invite all of you to a big party in Pyongyang to show his appreciation of your cooperation," I said.

"We are delighted to accept," he said.

Upon arrival at Moscow a few days later we headed for Leningrad, Petersburg now, to take a few shots from the old capital of Czarist Russia for inclusion in The Emissary. The train left us in a 30 below zero temperature, which made it tough going to film the old Korean Legation building that had briefly housed the envoy of the Korean king at the end of the Yee Dynasty to the Russian court. Back at Moscow Nan came down with a bad flu that ruled out her return trip to Pyongyang.

"Why don't you go on ahead by yourself?" she said, barely able to speak through her stuffed nose and scratchy throat.

"I can't leave you alone in a strange town."

"I won't be alone. Ambassador Kim's wife is here all the time. I'm surrounded by more Koreans here than in Korea. Besides I am in your ancestral land, remember?"

The cold did not subdue her sense of humor.

"One-quarter only, if that. Even if I am hundred percent Russian, I have renounced it forever. It's just not my type."

"Anyway the final editing can't wait, so go."

Reluctantly I had to leave her in the Moscow Hotel with reassurances of tender care from the Ambassador's family and staff. Back in Pyongyang I called her several times a day, perhaps surpassing in the few days the total number of long distance calls made from the whole country in a month. Except for Jungil and a handful of men at the top few had access to overseas lines, and that only for official business. Besides, calling one's wife to shower her with endearments was perhaps not in the machismo code of the ruling North Korean hierarchy. But I didn't care. She was my official business, my only business, my entire reason for being. My sweetheart was bedridden in a foreign country and needed comforting with my voice, if not with my physical presence.

I came home late as usual one evening and was informed by the servants that Jungil Kim had called me several times and left the message that he would call again. His hotline rang in a few minutes, before I finished changing.

"You are late," he said.

"I had to add a few finishing touches to The Emissary before the official release and work on the productions."

"I called because the Puppets have made a public announcement of your story. I'll send with someone the video cassette recording of the KBS and MBC telecasts. Please give me a call back after you look at it."

Haysong Gang turned up in about half an hour and we went to the projection room. It was a bizarre mixture of half truths. To improve its international image through the film North Korea recruited us, who, disaffected by our business reverses in South Korea, jumped at the opportunity and defected, betraying the country that had raised and honored us. To cover up the crime, however, we invented a scenario of our abduction to be spread by the North Korean agents, Gyongshig, Kintaro, and the Hongs, the spokesman for the Ministry of Security concluded. What a fantastic, incredibly stupid, cockeyed reasoning! On the other hand we couldn't have it any better, as it exonerated Jungil from the charge of abduction and hopefully put him at ease, relaxing his vigilance regarding our continued presence and service in North Korea. Apparently South Korea didn't get the Jungil Kim tapes, which must be safe in the hands of US intelligence as we wanted. It was just possible that US CIA might be deliberately orchestrating the hoax to facilitate our return. Maybe South Korea was in on it, too. Either way it served our purpose.

"It's a crisis situation," Jungil said, calling me instead of waiting for my call as soon as I finished watching. "My guess is the friends you wrote to must have reported to the Ministry of Security. Anyway we cannot take it lying down. Let's launch a counteroffensive."

"But I don't see any reason for alarm," I pointed out. "They are thinking the way we want them to think."

"That's true, but let's go a step further and convince them you are not even here in North Korea. Is Mrs. Moo still in Moscow?"

"Yes, she hasn't gotten over her flu yet."

"That's good. I mean we can turn the misfortune to our advantage. It so happens that a Japanese NHK reporter is visiting Pyongyang now, who might be asked to call her at Moscow, so she could confirm your regular sphere of activity as Eastern Europe."

"I'll call her and brief her on what's happened and what answers she is supposed to give."

"Good. To back up our story you may also leave first thing tomorrow morning and hold a press conference in Budapest or Belgrade, making sure to invite reporters from Western as well as socialist countries. Show them how free you are to move about and what blasted liars the South Korean Puppets are."

I tried to call Nan from the house but the operator said the line was out of order and not expected to open up until next morning. It was too late to call Jungil about it and I let it go at that, thinking that perhaps Jungil wouldn't have had time to contact the NHK reporter either. Haysong, who had left the house after my phone conversation with his boss, showed up at daybreak. He couldn't have had more than a few hours of sleep.

"There is a plane leaving right now," he said, handing me my South Korean passport they had taken away previously. "The reporters may want to look at them as evidence."

So the passport with my picture that was found in Japan before to induce the belief in my abduction thereabouts must have been a copy of this original. Or was this the copy? At least I couldn't tell.

Our plane stopped only briefly at Moscow, giving me barely enough time to call Nan from the airport.

"How are you feeling, darling?"

"Better. I am up and about. So I guess I will live yet."

After bringing her up to date on the latest developments, I told her to join us at the Budapest Hilton next day after talking to the Japanese reporter who should be most cordially invited to visit us in Budapest where we were on a filming assignment. After checking in at the hotel, Haysong and I went straight to the North Korean Embassy to make arrangements for the press conference. The Press Secretary was an able man, fluent in Russian and Hungarian, who undertook the necessary press releases and personal phone calls to the correspondents.

Like a teenager waiting for his first date I was all in a flutter until Nan arrived next day, visibly thinned and touched by a hint of fragility that made my heart ache with longing and solicitude.

"How are you, my precious?" I said, enclosing her in my arms.

"Middling," she said.

On the way to the hotel I learned that the NHK reporter in Pyongyang wouldn't buy her story about our European domicile and kept badgering her with penetrating questions about how exactly we had ended up in North Korea. It was all she could do to put him off until a face-to-face interview with another NHK colleague of his, one Moto Masao, to be dispatched to Budapest from Paris.

"Let's stop here," Nan said, indicating the Matis Cathedral, a white Neogothic masterpiece with soaring spires, where the Hungarian royalty had their coronations through the centuries.

"Do you mind?" I asked Haysong.

"No," he said. "I'll wait out here."

The interior was even more ornate and awesome, lofty ceilings that seemed to touch the heavens, supported by magnificent columns, exquisite carvings in stone decorating every inch of the walls, stained glass windows each of which could hang in the best museums. The grandeur and sanctity of the place seemed to make a convert out of an infidel like me, as I kneeled next to Nan in prayer.

When I went up to the front desk and asked for messages, the clerk handed me a telex printout in Romanized Japanese, which read: "The interview is not newsworthy, so return to Paris after going through the motions not to hurt the party's feelings." The clerk must have confused my name with the NHK reporter's. We sat on a bench in the lobby to wait for him. Half an hour later an Oriental man in his 30's walked into the lobby, followed by a Caucasian cameraman. Intuitively knowing him to be the intended recipient, I went up to him, introduced myself, and gave him the cable.

"How come you have my personal message?" he asked in embarrassment.

"I guess we both have too many m's and o's in our names."

"I am sorry. Since I'm here anyway, why don't we go to your room and take some pictures of you?"

After posing in our suite for the pictures with the Danube below as background, we sent them on their way. It was a big letdown, having come all the way from Pyongyang and Moscow specifically for the meeting, but in a way we felt relieved at not having to stage an elaborate lie. The press secretary reported little success in rounding up other foreign correspondents to make a press conference. Budapest was a backwater off the limelight of world attention and only stringers worked for the various news agencies on occasion.

"Belgrade has some resident correspondents," Haysong said after calling the Embassy there.

So off we went to Belgrade like hunters going after their game. The drive took seven hours. We chose the Intercontinental because its auditorium was ideal for a press conference. To stress my unofficial status in North Korea I declined the offer of the North Korean Embassy and made arrangements with the foreign press through Correspondent Bag of the North Korean Central News, though any knowledgeable person would know that one was as much an organ of the North Korean government as the other. Everything looked rosy and a big press turnout seemed assured, until we went to the hotel office to formalize the oral agreement we had regarding the use of the auditorium.

"I know nothing about such an agreement," the Yugoslav woman in charge said. "All meetings of political nature like this must have a 15-day preapproval by the police."

"It's no political meeting," I said. "It's just a press conference about me and my wife, both private individuals with no governmental or other organizational affiliation."

"Makes no difference."

"Consider it a small party of friends."

"Then you don't need the auditorium."

"Our room is just a bit too small."

"Sorry. No meeting without a prior permit."

At the police headquarters we explained our situation and asked for permission to hold the conference next day, but the answer was still negative. Briefly I thought of asking the North Korean Ambassador to intervene for what good it might do, which would however explode our elaborate pretense of private status. It was an absolute deadend. My previous good opinion of the country evaporated before this irrational, contemptible inflexibility over nothing. No wonder the patchwork of nation Tito had labored all his life to put together and consolidate broke apart into so many warring sovereignties scarcely before his body had time to get cold, their jealousies and hatreds as primitive and implacable as Evil itself, though held at bay by his towering personality while he lived and undetectable to a superficial observer like me.

On the day of the conference I stood in the lobby feeling stupid like the fool I was who had invited the whole town to his one-room hut, while Haysong was negotiating with the front desk for a switch of our accommodations to the largest available suite. By 10 a.m., the appointed time, over 20 reporters showed up. After explaining the problem, I asked them to come up two or three at a time to our room, which should be all right with the Yugo police. Disgusted at the prospect of delay most reporters took off, but still some remained, AP, Reuters, Tanyug, the Yugoslavian agency, one Ozaki of the Japanese paper Yomiuri who had come from Bonn specifically for the conference, and of course Correspondent Bag of the Central News. A suite was finally made available, to which we all went up.

"Is that all you have to say?" asked the tall AP reporter after listening to my statement refuting the announcement of the South Korean government.

"Yes, the truth is simple," I said.

Grinning, he stood up and walked out of the room. The others started asking questions aimed at deciding the defection or abduction issue, except Bag of Central who diligently scribbled away in his notebook.

"Defection, of course," I said, "though I would rather use an expression like exercise of my human right to choose wherever I want to live. The repression of South Korea, especially with regard to the film, reached such a point of harshness that we had to get out and came to live and work in Europe."

"What route did you take?"

"From Hong Kong we went to West Germany, where a friend of ours suggested that we visit North Korea. Comrade Leader Jungil Kim met us in Pyongyang and offered to bankroll our film productions with no strings attached, an offer we could not refuse. Ever since we have been living and working in Europe."

"Why Europe?"

"Because we want to be more cosmopolitan in our outlook and activity."

"Did your being half Caucasian have anything to do with it?"

"Perhaps. Korea is racially homogeneous and people like me tend to stand out."

"Why have you been silent all these years?"

This was a question to which frankly I had no answer to date. Why did Jungil let me rot in jail for so long instead of using my expertise right away?

"I felt my life threatened by South Korea, especially following the disappearance and presumed murder of the former KCIA Chief Hyongwoog Kim, an outspoken critic of the military regime, so I lived in West Germany incognito a few years."

"Miss Nanyong Song disappeared a few days before you. Where was she?"

"I sent her to West Germany first to hide at a friend's house."

"Where is the main base of your activity in Eastern Europe?"

"Budapest. Moo Moo Film has an office at the Hyatt Hotel, downtown Budapest."

This was a lie but I could not hesitate and give the game away. Fortunately, none of them asked to examine our passports, which Gang had put in our possession for presentation in case of demand, to verify our alleged entries to West Germany. If they had, the falsehood would have been exposed at once. Not only did they bear no European entry stamps but they had expired more than five years before. So as in other human situations one fumble was matched by another and somehow things worked out all right in the end.

Next day we hurried back to Budapest and took a one year lease on Room 602 at the Hyatt Hotel in the name of Moo Moo Film. With Haysong listening close by, I called Gyongshig in Tokyo and the Hongs in New York, apologizing for the charge of espionage leveled against them by the South Korean government. Ironically, not subscribing to Korean newspapers the Hongs learned about it for the first time from me and laughed. They couldn't care less.

"The Barandov people are here," Jungil said, praising us for a job well done when we reported to his office upon arrival in Pyongyang.

"Thank you, Comrade Leader," I said. "But I am not totally pleased. Budapest is a bit too East European for our Westward thrust, not having even a resident foreign press corps."

"No problem. Change to Belgrade."

"I was thinking further west than that, Vienna, Austria, for example," I said, my heart skipping a beat. In Vienna we could seek asylum at the US Embassy.

"Why not?" he said after a short reflection. "Let's work it out."

Because of my sudden trip abroad the public preview of The Emissary, scheduled for Ilsung Kim's birthday, April 15, was given on April 25 at the People's Culture Palace with an audience of over 2,000 representatives from all walks of life. Just before the showing we were asked to go on stage with the Barandov guests for recognition. As General Supervisor I had to give a short speech.

"My wife and I are happy to be here in our homeland, though by force of circumstances we live and work in Europe. Without the cooperation and assistance of our Beloved Comrade Leader Jungil Kim we couldn't have taken the Korean scenes on location here. Our European colleagues are ecstatic about our beautiful mountains and rivers and our rich culture and heritage. We hope to make more films like this and visit more often, because our bodies may be over there but our hearts are always here."

After the applause subsided, a 30-minute documentary was shown about us and Moo Moo Film, which at one stroke exploded the mendacity of my spiel about our European residence, because Nan was shown residing at Jungil's villa, visiting zoos, sightseeing, and finally reuniting with me at

Jungil's party to live happily ever after at his villa as his permanent guests, not at all temporary visitors like the Czechs. As if to drive the last nails into the coffin, the commentator observed with exaggerated emotion at our reunion scene, "What a joyous reunion after six years of separation!" So we could not have lived together in Europe all this time as I had said! What would all these people think about me? I would have gladly crawled into a rat hole if I could find one. My only hope was that they were so used to bald lies and inconsistencies that mine would simply wash over without registering.

Immediately after the premiere Haysong Gang and Ingoo Cha steered us upstairs to the third floor conference room to meet the waiting reporters, some 40 strong, including foreigners, a full-scale press conference by any standard, all arranged without a word to us, just as we had been left ignorant about the documentary and the speech I had to make before the preview. Did Jungil have such an unbounded faith in our unrehearsed, spurt of the moment performance or was he still testing us, not caring what wrong things we might say?

To my amazement none of the correspondents, trained to scent the least inaccuracy or inconsistency, referred to the contradiction between my speech and the documentary. The only possible explanation was that they didn't understand my speech and so didn't notice the inconsistency. One Japanese reporter wanted to know what we had to say about the South Korean government's version of our departure and I gave an essentially identical answer as at Belgrade, perhaps a little more scathing.

"Doohwan Jun has a short memory and forgot all about his persecution of us eight years ago. We didn't leave because we wanted to. We were pushed out."

When asked about the North Korean film industry I was quite open in my criticism to give the appearance of our freedom.

"In the absence of challenge and competition complacency and stagnation are apt to set in. With its equipment and facilities North Korea can easily make over 100 films a year, not the 20 or so at present."

Only three or four people did all the questioning and the others, apparently hustled there just to make up the quorum, merely took notes or just looked on.

While filming The Emissary, I had been thinking about the next movies long before Jungil's unexpected endorsement of Mayoress of Koreatown, and had decided as the first choice on The Escape, based on the short story by Sonhay Chay, the socialist writer of the 20's. In the story a farm youth, crushed by exploitation and poverty, packs up and leaves Korea with his old mother and wife, crossing the Tumen into northeast Manchuria, the favorite destination of other Korean immigrant farmers like him at the time, where he hopes to develop wasteland, only to find that there is no empty land waiting for him to develop. The land leased from the Chinese landlord does not yield enough to support his family in spite of his backbreaking work. His whole family hire themselves out, doing odd jobs around other people's homes, but they often go without food for days. Realizing that honest people like him are the victims of a system which must be destroyed to make room for something more equitable, he leaves his family to join a revolutionary group.

In spite of its transparent and somewhat insistent ideology the story was quite moving, but my primary motive in the selection was to impress Jungil with my socialistic sympathies. It wouldn't hurt to make him feel that I was really one of them and let his guard down, so we could make our escape more easily. Perhaps it was the height of hypocrisy to pose as a socialist when all along I regarded socialism a naive, impracticable idealism that failed to take human greed into account. But I felt any action on my part justified when dealing with Jungil, who had given us cause and provocation first. Besides socialism was certainly a useful corrective to the excesses of capitalism, as witnessed by the welfare legislations of every country in the West.

As the hero's mother, Nan wanted to use Yonshil Kim we had met earlier with other semiretired luminaries like her, most of whom had come from the south following their husbands or lovers before or during the war, attaining Distinguished Service Actor or People's Actor status. Yonshil did not have a phone at home and there was no way to get in touch with her except by writing or sending a messenger. Instead, after getting the directions from the studio staff, Nan and I set out for her house late one afternoon, curious to know how a People's Actress, the highest rank in the profession, lived in North Korea. Besides we had a private message to give to her. She and her husband, Hayil Gang, formerly with the Donga Ilbo in Seoul, had two daughters they had left behind in the hasty retreat of the People's Army following the success of MacArthur's amphibious landing at Inchon in September 1950. During the brief recapture of Seoul by the Red Chinese and People's Army in January 1951 they returned to Seoul to look for them but could locate only their younger daughter. The missing older daughter was none other than Gayja Kim, a popular singing star who eventually immigrated to the US and had been in touch with Nan from time to time.

Yonshil lived on the second floor of a five-story walkup near the Korea Art Film Studio of which she was a member. Though delighted to see us she was a bit flustered at our unannounced visit. Apologizing for the poverty of her place she asked me to wait outside and took only Nan inside, a 300 square foot efficiency, the kitchen directly facing the cluttered entry way, with an old refrigerator and TV, but no bathroom.

One had to go to the communal one somewhere in the middle of the hallway. Her husband, who had turned to screen writing after their defection and belonged to one of the Creative Groups, was still at work, past 6 p.m., though he was close to 90. Before she opened the door, she had been under a comforter, which still remained spread out on the floor.

"Please put your feet underneath," Yonshil said. "The whole building has been freezing like this for days since the hot water pipe broke."

Indeed, the floor was icy. Pulling the comforter over her feet and legs, Nan unwrapped her presents, coffee, sugar, dried pollack and beef, and Yonshil beamed with pleasure.

"We haven't had coffee in years, which was particularly hard on my husband, who had to have coffee, cups and cups of it. That's how we had met, in our family coffee shop in Myongdong."

"How is your daughter you brought with you here?"

"She was sickly during the war and died soon afterwards," Yonshil said with a sigh. "I heard Gayja is in America. Do you know anything about it?"

"She and her husband bought a shopping center in Koreatown, Los Angeles, and live comfortably."

"Hush! Don't tell anybody I have a daughter living in America."

In her 80's Yonshil had a touch of rheumatism in her legs but was eager to take the part and acquitted herself well when the filming started showing up for work before anybody else. We had to rush into this project, though The Emissary was not quite finished, because of the many cold weather scenes: the hero leaves his homeland with his mother and pregnant wife on an ox cart whipped by a snow blizzard and his family, including the just born infant, almost freeze in the unheated hut, while he looks in vain for firewood in the Manchurian wilderness. It was mid-April and there was no time to lose, because we would otherwise postpone seven or eight months until the winter, which was out of the question.

The male lead chosen was Changsoo Chay, in his mid-forties, an exceptionally talented actor, perhaps the best in the Orient, who instantly understood and gave a full measure of the intended character, taking it to higher dimensions of imagination and feeling. Born in any other country, he would be the rage and sensation, but here in North Korea he was nothing but a salaried hack.

So we had the hero and his mother but was still short of the most crucial member, his wife. Literally, scores were tested but none was satisfactory. In desperation, Nan wanted to look up Jongbog Moon, recently promoted from Distinguished Service to People's Actress, who had come north during the war with her lover Chol Hwang, the stage actor and a married man. She had a younger sister, Jongsoog, a well-known character actress in Seoul, with whom Nan had collaborated in several pictures.

"She should be all right if she is at all like Jongsoog," Nan said hopefully.

"But she is so much older, in her sixties, or is it seventies?"

"Age doesn't matter. You can fix her up to look like a blooming damsel. Besides they say she has kept herself remarkably well."

There being no phone as usual, Nan set out one day for her place at the Longevity Boulevard Apartments, to which Jongbog had moved recently, a step up as the complex boasted the largest and spaciest accommodations among the numerous residential developments in Pyongyang. But the building had no elevator and Nan had to walk up a steep stairway to her fifth-floor unit, a hazardous proposition because there was no banister and the runs of the steps were so narrow that she had to plant her highheeled foot sideways each time. It was more like climbing a ladder than ascending a stairway. The landing was part of the narrow hallway flanked on both sides by apartment units, before each of which lay spread the usual semicircle of shoes to save that much space. Jongbog's at the end of the hallway was no exception: the entry way, about 40 square feet and crammed full of boxes, bundles, books, and other sundries from floor to ceiling, had absolutely no room to spare for footwear. The toilet was in the kitchen and the two bedrooms were so small that a kingsize bed would have filled them. There was no living room.

Jongbog seemed to melt with pleasure at the sight of the presents Nan brought, cosmetics, soap, shampoo, underwear, socks.

"What is it?" Jongbog asked, picking up a square tin can.

"Sesame oil," Nan answered.

"Sesame oil?" she exclaimed, her eyes wide with wonder. "I haven't tasted it in a dozen years."

Nan had brought the can, made in China, that Jungil had presented her before. The only available cooking oil in North Korea was corn oil, which was in short supply also.

"My son lives with me, 21 years old, from my second

marriage," Jongbog said. "How is my sister Jongsoog?"

"She is a star and well off."

"Really?" Jongbog said unbelievingly. "It would be nice if she were here like you to enjoy the freedom of our socialist fatherland."

"Why should she?" Nan retorted somewhat sharply, irked by her ignorance. "She lives in a big house with a car, VCR, microwave oven, telephone, everything she could possibly want. You have nothing like that though you are a People's Actress."

"Does her husband work for the Party?"

"No, she isn't even married and has done it all by herself."

I knew Jongbog wouldn't work out but Nan wanted her anyway.

"Her face has that depth of pathos we can't find in anybody else."

"Yes, but the role requires someone capable of vitality and passion, too."

"Let's use her for the grieving mother in Gwangjoo Is Calling. Maybe we can start on it right away. Jungil would love it."

That was a revised version of Shattered, based on the Gwangjoo massacre, which had gotten us into so much trouble with Doohwan Jun. So while preparations were being made for The Escape, we shot Gwangjoo, using some of the film strips and stills smuggled out of Korea that Gyongshig had obtained and sent to us recently. The two-hour semi-documentary was finished in record time, two weeks. Ecstatic over the result, Jungil had hundreds of copies made for distribution to foreign governments and organizations as well as to ethnic Korean groups all over the world. Here was his opportunity to expose the cruelty and corruption of his rival in the south. The film was shown in all the major cities of the States, for example, courtesy of Samho Hyon, kindling a storm of outrage among Korean Americans that was soon to translate into Jun's downfall.

"We have no choice," I said. "You have to be Changsoo's wife, Nan."

"No, I am too old for the role."

"But you said yourself that age...."

"Nobody is superior to his or her biology, didn't Professor Yee of No. Six say? Anyway I have made up my mind to do directing and nothing else, so long as I am held here against my will."

"But this is a means to gain the freedom we want."

After much coaxing she half consented to put on makeup and go to Peony Peak to stand before the camera. The rushes convinced me that she and Changsoo would make the perfect couple.

"Darling, there is no doubt about it. You are a star through and through, still in your prime. I can use you for many more years."

"No, this is the last time I'll act."

"Okay, darling, whatever you say."

That afternoon, while checking some equipment at the recording room of the Korean Art Film Studio, we ran into Mihwa Om, another People's Actress from the south, with whom Nan had a special relationship: Mihwa's mother, the Costume Lady as she was called, had been Nan's designer as long as she lived, and was given a great funeral by her when she died. The old lady used to hold Nan's hand and shed tears, thinking of her daughter, Mihwa, the Red defector. Apparently her acting career was over and she now worked as a voice actor.

"How can I repay you?" Mihwa said, crying.

"No, she was like my own mother and I owe her a lot more," Nan said.

"I have to be further in your debt, let alone repay you. It's impossible to make ends meet with many dependents. My husband died recently, the one I came north with during the war. Could you hire one of my daughters at your studio? I hear its employees get better food rations and preferential treatment."

"Let me see what I can do, but we have no control over personnel. All my husband or I can do is make recommendations to the Party which decides. Let's hope for the best."

Nothing happened in Mihwa's case, though we had put in a word. She was just one of the nameless unprivileged millions trying in vain to arrange a competing edge for their own young.

By the time we were ready to take the first shot of The Escape it was the end of May and gone was the snow of yesteryear, putting us in a dilemma. The studios simply did not have adequate snow machines.

"There was snow at the White Head Mountains even in July when I went there," Nan remembered.

Inquiries revealed the presence of snowdrifts at White Head and we flew in Jungil's chopper and two-prop plane with all our equipment and staff and landed at the airstrip at Three Lakes, designated as a historical site just to commemorate Ilsung Kim's stopping there for a drink of water while fighting the Japanese. The snowdrifts were still there but one had to be careful stepping on them, mostly hollow shells with the inside melted and gutted out. Making do, we took shots of Nan gathering firewood in midwinter, subjecting her to the severest physical ordeal she had experienced in her whole career before the camera, as she had to hold a bundle of firewood on her head with one hand and pull another with the other, slipping and falling in the snow and whipped by the storm coming from the helicopter hovering overhead, which turned out to be more powerful than any fan we could have rigged up, perhaps too powerful. Nevertheless she was game and in spite of the cold and wetness we both enjoyed filming on this grand scale, except for minor irritations.

Before leaving Pyongyang we had asked the effects people to pack bags of artificial snow made from crushed styrofoam for the snow sequences. When the time came and the bags were opened, out tumbled flock.

"I asked for styrofoam, not flock," I yelled, losing my temper. "How are we going to make it look like snow?"

"We couldn't find such material," the man who had been placed in charge said.

"Call Pyongyang and tell them to get it right away."

"But there is no phone."

"Go down to the county seat. They must have a phone

connecting to Pyongyang."

After a while he and several others returned to report that the only phone connection was through three or four exchanges with different switchboard operators.

"We gave the message but don't know whether it will get through correctly."

Operator A would give the message to Operator B for relay to Operator C and so on until Pyongyang was reached but the final message was apt to be quite different from the one at the starting point. Obligingly they gave an example. Not too long ago another film crew had their camera break down on them at the mountains and sent an urgent message for a new camera. But so thorough was the distortion during transmission that the Korean Art Film Studio in Pyongyang was in an uproar because they thought somebody had been killed in an accident. I knew they weren't pulling my legs. Nationwide, phone communications were nonexistent or deplorable. What few phones there were didn't work properly, with about 90% of the incoming calls at our offices alone being wrong numbers. Since I couldn't imagine the country being so backward in such basic technology, my only conclusion was that the situation was a deliberate creation on the part of the Party to isolate individuals and communities, though it was a typical case of cutting off the nose to spite the face: as in the present case the Party couldn't get anything done when it wanted to. No wonder Jungil had to have hotlines and direct lines separately installed everywhere for himself and his associates.

On the way to the airstrip on the fourth and last day we stopped for a tour of the Ilsung Kim Historical Site, culminating in renewed oaths of allegiance and group pictures before his statue. Many of them, including Nan, had been there already but one couldn't have too much of a good thing, moral, spiritual rebirth by pilgrimage to the holy place where the Great One had his inspiration and recreation. After return to Pyongyang we left by train next morning for Hayjoo to shoot rice transplanting scenes.

The unrelenting pace of work with little or no sleep seemed to take its toll on my body. One morning I simply couldn't get up, all my muscles aching with the slightest motion.

"What you need is a good long rest," Nan said, though she knew it would be catastrophic to the shooting schedule with so many people involved, not only us, the studio people, but the numerous governmental and other organizations and individuals in transportation, administration, agriculture, etc.

"Maybe I can get an instant rejuvenation by sauna or massage," I suggested.

After some run-around Nan found out where I could get the treatment and had me taken by my secretary to the People's Culture Palace, a huge concrete dome 150 meters in diameter and 50 meters high, at the center of Pyongyang. To enter one had to take off and shelve his shoes and put on slippers set out on both sides of the entry way. Beyond the gym with various athletic equipment spouted a most gorgeous fountain in assorted colors centered around an illuminated pole. The annex next to the building housed an olympic-size swimming pool, off limits to the public for use exclusively by swim champions who worked out daily for competition abroad.

Along the perimeter of the Palace were appointed public baths, saunas, and beauty parlors. With tiles and fixtures imported from Scandinavia and Japan the baths were on a lavish scale, well surpassing the famed Roman baths, perhaps to compensate for the absence of private baths at home. However, like many other such grand facilities dedicated to the people and meticulously maintained, they were very much underused and mostly empty, boggling my mind. Why go to all that expense for so few?

We went by the elevator to the fourth floor, which had rows and rows of private baths and saunas. After a bath and sauna I went to the massage parlor on the same floor with half a dozen beds, all empty.

"Is it always empty like this?" I asked the young masseur.

"Yes, during the day," he said.

"When do they start coming?"

"After supper, late at night."

"Who are they?"

"Party cadre, Federation Koreans from Japan, foreigners,

diplomats, students, or other visitors and their families. The foreigners come Wednesday and Saturday, when no national is allowed. "

This happened to be Friday, which however didn't mean much because most people worked seven days a week anyway. Moreover, even if they had the leisure, the working masses, making 60 to 70 won a month, simply couldn't afford the private bath or massage, 10 won a shot.

After completing domestic scenes I checked out the sets and costumes available at the Korean Art Film Studio for the Manchurian shots, which account for two-thirds of the film, and found them awkward and unconvincing. This was an unexpected setback, because we thought we could fake Manchurian scenery and hadn't planned on any expedition across the border. Off limits and closely guarded, though directly north of Korea, this region couldn't be entered either overland or by air without special permission from the Red Chinese government in Beijing through high-level diplomatic channels. Then, in the nick of time, somebody told us about a Friendship Film Delegation to Red China being organized by the Ministry of Culture. We asked for our inclusion, solely to explore the feasibility of filming in Manchuria or somewhere suitable in China. The last thing we wanted was to give the impression of muscling in, but that's what we ended up doing. The previously formed delegation, headed by Yaybong Moon, a People's Actress and others from the Korean Art Film Studio, was dissolved completely to make way for us and the Moo Moo Film staff, except Yaybong Moon herself, a fine actress in her seventies, also from the south, with an impressive record to her credit, though like her peers she now had minor and infrequent roles in wretched military films only.

We were met at Beijing Airport by our Red Chinese hosts who took us to a luxurious restaurant for dinner. After staying overnight at a hotel near Tiananmun Square we were taken on a tour of the city, beginning with the Forbidden Palace, which had been a dream of mine. The buildings were on a scale that dwarfed anything found in Korea, but lacked meticulous attention to detail. Perhaps a jewel was destined to be small. That evening the Deputy Chief of Red China's Ministry of Culture hosted a dinner at a traditional Peking duck restaurant. Thanking him for the hospitality I expressed my admiration for the care the Red Chinese had taken to preserve historical buildings and monuments, which were largely absent in North Korea.

"Would it be possible to come here for the historical films we want to make in the future?" I asked.

"Any time," the official answered genially. "We will be honored and hand over the key to the city. Film it as much as you want."

"We may want to film other parts of your country, too, like Manchuria. Our two countries have been so close historically that practically every major event involved each other."

"Of course. That's why we had to intervene when the US Forces invaded Korea. Our whole country is open to you from end to end."

The next day we visited the Beijing Film Studio and saw some more of the city I hadn't seen the last time I came to make phone calls - the streets, alleys, and sidewalk bazaars that had sprung up everywhere with the new official encouragement of entrepreneurship. The more I saw of Beijing, the more evident became the truth of the cliché, Nothing is new under the sun. I should have known better by now after seeing America, Russia, and Europe, but for some strange reason I had always had a China mystique, which, sadly, the trip helped strip away.

True to their word the Chinese officials gave us permission to travel to Northeast Manchuria, a sensitive military and industrial complex. One surprise awaiting us at Changchun was its Film Studio, the oldest and most prestigious in China. Originally established by the Japanese, it had been the only studio in the whole of China for some time and produced many excellent works. During the Korean War when most of North Korea was under continual aerial and naval bombardment, its film people were evacuated to Changchun and continued working at the studio. Yaybong Moon had been among those refugees and her inclusion in the delegation was to thank the

Chinese authorities for their cooperation during the hard times. Unfortunately, the personnel were all new and young, to whom the Korean War was something they read about in history books only.

"We are currently making a movie which takes place mostly in Manchuria during the 30's and would appreciate it if we could film it here on location," I said.

"Sure," the Director of the Studio said. "But I don't have the final say on this matter. The Film Joint Venture Corporation in Beijing does, which hopes to earn foreign exchange by collaborating with foreign film companies."

Well, there was no subtlety here.

"Of course we will pay our way," I assured him.

So instead of coming home directly to Pyongyang as we thought we would, we had to go back to Beijing to ink the contract for the filming of The Escape, which had to be called a joint venture, though all it amounted to was just permission on their part for us to enter and take pictures.

After returning to Pyongyang we got our equipment and people together, about 30 in number, and left for Changchun, which had to be via Beijing. The small plane servicing the Beijing-Changchun route was almost filled up by our crew. Seated in the so-called first-class section up front, Nan wearily dropped her head on my shoulder.

"Where are we going to bury our bones, moving around like dust blown in the wind?"

"Let's look at what's right in front of us and not think too far ahead. Take a nap and you'll feel better."

The new provincial capital Changchun was not suitable for the old Manchurian scene we wanted to portray and our hosts suggested Koloon about an hour and a half by car from town. After loading up the men and equipment on five rented trucks we were ready to depart when word came that to go beyond the city limits a permit must be obtained from the Department of Public Peace three days in advance.

"But the Corporation in Beijing has made the arrangements so we can start right away," I protested, though I knew it wouldn't do any good.

"Sorry, sir," said the bureaucrat in his blandest Chinese manner. "It is the law and we have to obey."

We had to wait around for three days fuming, but when we got there at last, I felt it had been worthwhile. We were instantly transported to rural Manchuria in the 30's as if time had stood still - clusters of straw-thatched homes dotting the plain, narrow dirt roads best traveled by foot or ox carts, open air market places at crossroads.

The first shots were about the hero's scrivener business he sets up on a mat spread out by the roadside, which of course fails. Though it was June, the script called for snow-covered midwinter and a fan had to be turned on to spray a mixture of salt and lime for snow. But the hardship the actors endured can be imagined: not only did they inhale all the salt and lime dust but perspired like fish, all wrapped up in padded and quilted winter clothing and fur.

But soon something totally unexpected threatened to scuttle our entire operation. The whole countryside had turned out to gawk. With the help of the local constabulary the crowds were pushed back but in a few minutes into filming the viewfinder would reveal a rustic head or two inching in, followed by their bodies, ruining the footage. Keeping the rubbernecks back was harder than directing the actors or getting the right angles for the camera. Nor could we be too harsh with them, either. Most of them were ethnic Koreans who had walked long distances just to watch us. Whenever their eyes met those of the harassed film crew, their faces lit up with patriotic pride and joy. Of course they followed Nan like a swarm of bees their queen, and Nan didn't have the heart to turn them away.

"We heard it's a Korean filming company," one middle-aged man said to Nan. "So we got up at dawn, packed our lunches, and walked twenty miles."

Now and then he stole a glance at me, the only jarring note which however could not change and indeed sharpened the overall Korean timbre.

"That's a mighty long walk," Nan said. "What type of work do you do?"

"We are farmers."

"Can you up and leave your farm work like that?"

"Work is always there, but you don't come around everyday. We Koreans are all proud of the great work you are doing here."

Only if he knew how grueling movie making was. The scene where Nan lashes out at the Japanese police hauling her husband away, until she gets knocked down had to be done over 20 times, Nan getting black and blue from the real blows that fell home, because her counterparts did not know what they were doing. I was ready to scream and pack up, but she stuck it out, patiently redoing everything, until we got it all right. Though the going was rough at times, all the Manchurian shots we needed were completed in 12 days and we returned to Pyongyang to take one last scene, the blowing up of a train by the hero, which could not be readied before we left. The effects engineer had waiting for us a real train, not a mockup, wired up with explosives to go off at our pleasure.

"But this is destruction of property," I objected.

"We have the Party's okay," he said.

It was insane but we had to go ahead and blow up the perfectly serviceable train. There were half a dozen movies on the immediate agenda, not to speak of Mayoress of Koreatown, and we had to leave soon for Karlovy Vary, Czechoslovakia, to attend the 24th International Film Festival in which The Secret Emissary had been entered, the first such venture for North Korea in a dozen years. Begun in the 50's the Festival, held each year in Karlovy Vary and Moscow alternately according to the Charter, had as much prestige as those of Venice or Cannes in the West and was certainly held in the highest esteem in the Eastern bloc. About 50 countries entered each time, including Western countries like the US, France, West Germany, Italy, and Japan. For the main competition only one entry was allowed per country, but there was no limit on noncompetitive exhibitions and some countries presented three or four. In our case we had just The Emissary for the competition and none for the other, as nothing else was ready for exhibition.

Apart from Nan and me our delegation consisted of Soontay Bag, Director of the Film Library, the three male actors who played the emissaries, two actresses also in the film, four actors of the White Head Mountain Creative Group who played the roles of Ilsung and Jungil Kim and their mothers respectively, and an interpreter. From the moment of arrival our women attracted attention, looking like exotic dolls in their colorful traditional dresses. To our chagrin, however, most of the delegates, even those from the Eastern bloc, did not know where Korea was and greeted us as Chinese sporting some ancient costumes. As usual, we slept and ate and went to meetings and shows as a body like school children herded around on an excursion in a strange city, and any thought of escape was out of the question. We couldn't contact any member of the US or Japanese delegation separately.

On the day our entry was on, the show time drew near but the auditorium was practically empty, filling us with a sickening sense of defeat. Lacking experience, we realized only too late we hadn't done anything by way of publicity, whereas the other countries had plastered the area with their posters. Somehow we had been naive enough to think that the Socialist event would be more orderly than that, free from such unseemly display as capitalistic advertisement. As a result few knew about us and the tickets for general admission had remained mostly unsold. Even the delegates, who had free passes, stayed away. However, present among the handful of viewers was Dr. Brosch, the noted Czech film critic, who chaired the Judges Panel, making me feel a little better.

"Bravo!" he said, coming over to Nan. "It's a remarkable picture and unique in having a lady as director. Would you please come to the Directors' Panel meeting tomorrow?"

"Thank you," Nan consented gladly.

That night we prepared a ten-minute speech entitled "The Film and the Woman Director" and had our interpreter translate into French. The presentation was received with enthusiasm.

I made sure we saw as many of the entries as possible during the competition. What was noticeable was a tendency toward sensuous depiction verging on pornography among Eastern bloc productions, which however failed to generate much interest, whereas Western films with conservative themes and portrayals were more popular. The theater was sold out for the US, French, and Italian entries, both competitive and non-competitive. The Italian actress Monica Vitti was mobbed by reporters and fans wherever she went.

At the reception hosted by the Soviet delegation at the hotel, Brosch came over to Nan, patted her on the back, and gave a wink. Intuitively we knew we were in the winners' circle. When the votes were in on the last day, Nan won the Best Director's Award. It was a truly exciting moment and the usually sedate members of our delegation broke their reserve, hugged each other, and wept.

"We did it," Soontay Bag said, pumping my arm, his eyes teary. "Our Beloved Comrade Leader will be delighted. You have justified his confidence in you."

His personal loyalty to Jungil was touching. Only if I could share it!

"Thanks. We should encourage him to venture boldly into the world market, especially the West."

"I am sure he is already thinking along that line."

Emboldened, I called Chansoo Hong of New York to ask if he got the tapes and photos from Kintaro to give to Al. The answer was negative.

"Kintaro wouldn't hand them over," Chansoo's wife said.

"Did you show him my letter?"

"Yes, but he said he would have to talk to you first, a suspicious man."

In a rage I called Tokyo and got Kintaro.

"I couldn't," he said. "Anybody can forge a letter. I didn't want them to fall into the wrong hands. The South Korean media was saying Mrs. Hong is a North Korean spy."

"She is a friend of mine I trust completely."

"Well, it's too late anyway, because she and her daughter are in the US. I tell you what. Why don't I hand them back to you, so you can do whatever you want. I will be in Budapest at the invitation of the Culture Ministry of Hungary which is hosting a Japanese Culture Fest in September. By the way congratulations on your award."

Didn't they have a Japanese Film Week only a few months ago? Hungary seemed really stuck on things Japanese, but then who wasn't these days? In spite of its anti-Japanese fulminations North Korea thought nothing of buying from Japan all the ramen, instant noodles, it consumed, not to speak of radios, TV sets, vehicles, even furniture.

"Thanks. We'll meet in Budapest, then."

Before leaving Karlovy Vary we had two press interviews, one with Weekly Post and the other with Asahi Shinbun, both of Japan. Japanese interest in North Korea had always been considerable. On both occasions I repeated the same scenario agreed on with Jungil, namely, Nan's and my defection from the oppressive military regime of South Korea to work freely in Eastern Europe, with plans to get established in Western Europe, most probably Austria. The Asahi reporter had come along with a friend, Professor Nosuke Fuji of Meiji University who taught cinematography. At the end of the interview they presented me with a Nikon camera and asked us to have lunch with them.

"Good," I said. "Let's walk into the restaurant here."

That was the hotel where the Festival was going on and most delegates were staying.

"No," they said. "Let's go to the Moscow Hotel about 15 minutes away."

I could guess why they insisted on going elsewhere. They wanted to see if we were as free as I claimed.

"Please do not follow," I told Soontay Bag whose presence at the interview the Japanese had been keenly aware of.

"I understand," Bag agreed readily.

Perhaps he felt secure because he was holding our passports. Or perhaps he felt that after winning the award we wouldn't be so stupid as to leave our laurels, the privileges and favors that awaited us in Pyongyang.

From Karlovy Vary we proceeded to Budapest to check in at the Hyatt, Room 602, to give more substance to its lease as Moo Moo Film Office. The itinerary called for our stopover at

Vienna to open an account with an American bank and look for a suitable place to anchor Moo Moo Film for our forays into the West. As we were about to depart next morning, thinking that perhaps this might be the moment we had been waiting for, Soontay Bag put the brakes on as if he had read our minds.

"This trip you would have to make alone, President Moo," he said.

"Leave Vice President Nanyong behind?"

"I am afraid so. We might run into South Korean CIA which may seek to harm the lady."

"But she is an integral part of Moo Moo Film and her opinion is vital in any decision."

"The more reason we should think of her safety."

They were determined to hold her as hostage in case I should not return, and there was no point in arguing. I was escorted by Bag and four North Korean Embassy employees who never left my side until I quit Austria. Three rooms had been reserved at the Mojur Hotel in the suburbs of Vienna, mine in the middle so they could watch my every move. We must have been quite a sight, an inseparable pentagon of five Oriental angles and a Caucasian center, marching up and down the streets and in and out of the buildings.

Austrian bureaucracy, as helpful as any elsewhere, gave us the runaround, dispensing the requirements piecemeal. We had to go back to the North Korean Embassy to obtain an ordinary passport for me because the rule did not allow a diplomatic passport holder to register a film company. But we returned to the Ministry of Trade only to find out that I needed an Austrian national as partner as well as supply an Austrian address of not less than two years. This required another trip back to the Embassy, where consultations and phone calls came up with an Austrian businessman, Helmud Pandler, who had extensive business dealings with North Korea, for the partner, and the home address of Hosang An, the Commercial Attaché of the Embassy. After the registration we went to the Vienna Branch of the Bank of America to open a business checking account for Moo Moo Film with me as the only authorized signer, making an initial deposit of

$2,100,000. It would be a couple of weeks before the printed checks would be mailed.

"No, we'll pick them up," I told the bank clerk and made arrangements with Attaché An for the pickup.

Though it was raining cats and dogs, a crowd met us at Pyongyang Airport to mark our triumphal return. We went directly to Jungil's office and showed him the videotape of the Festival and some other portions of our trip.

"Take a videotape like this whenever you go abroad," he said, "because I don't get to see any of the outside world."

He actually sounded envious, this all powerful man!

"Sure, Comrade Leader," Nan assured him.

Not too long later we had a report from Budapest about Attaché An's inability to get the checkbooks from the Vienna Bank of America. When he signed a form as requested, the bank clerk pointed out the discrepancy between his signature and mine on the record. Instead of simply explaining that he was doing a favor for me, he panicked and bolted out of the building, fearing he might be arrested for fraud or something. This laughable conduct by a senior diplomat was a good indication of what North Korea's isolation was doing to its citizens, even its privileged classes. They had no perspective, no savvy, and ran scared at the slightest noise or shadow. However, we welcomed the news as it gave us another excuse to visit Vienna soon.

But no such excuse became necessary. A four-page article with our picture appeared in the Japanese Weekly Post, under the title "Kidnap or Defection?", which in essence exonerated Jungil from any mischief about our detention in North Korea. Jubilant, he had us over at his Central Committee office and talked away for two and a half hours on just about everything that came to his mind.

"You should spend more time out of the country and each time make your presence there visible. It was good to set up shop in Vienna. As soon as you go back there, throw a big party inviting all correspondents, even those stationed in Bonn, Paris, or London. I'll deposit $3 million more in your account so you can draw freely as you see fit."

We were floored at the offer but I had to strike the iron while it was hot.

"Thank you, Comrade Leader. But for those functions my wife should be present, too. Her input is valuable in everything but above all her absence would be the first thing these Western reporters would notice and ask questions about."

"You are absolutely right. When the Vienna office is ready for full operation, you should both be there. But the South Korean CIA menace exists and cannot be discounted. We can't do anything to relax our guard. The Puppets are still so hostile that they twist around everything we say or do. During the latest normalization talks with them the Chief offered our plentiful mineral resources for development by their unemployed. They could come and mine all they wanted, free of charge. After all we are all Koreans and this way we get to keep everything in the family. But they wouldn't take it, suspecting all kinds of imaginary traps. His next proposal was arms reduction to relieve the crushing defense burden. One million is too many mouths to feed for Doohwan Jun and the Americans end up putting clothes on their backs and shoes on their feet. The answer was again negative, because they think we'll keep our discharged men in some holding pen instead of sending them home to their families and farms."

I made a halfhearted gesture to remind him that he was digressing from the issue at hand, Nan's inclusion in the next trip to Vienna, but of course he didn't notice, nor would he have deflected an inch from the spate of oration once loosened, even if he did.

"After his visit here Red Chinese President Yaobang Hu asked me why we don't go for tourism, which brings in a lot of cash without much outlay. Eastern Europe has been doing it all along and so have Russia and China. After three years in the business, Hu bragged, his country netted $700 million. Long before our conversation I had been thinking about opening up the east coast and building hotels until Byongshig Kim, Vice President of the Federation, came over and told me what he had heard from his contacts at the Japanese Ministry of Defense: an interoffice memo said that as soon as we opened up, thousands of agents would be sent over disguised as tourists and discover within one month everything of value about our military installations, in far greater detail than they can learn from the satellite pictures. They talk about it openly. So agreeing with Hu I had to point out that his country is big and therefore can afford to open up to tourism without exposing the vital parts but ours is small and the coastline short, most of which is heavily fortified, and once the tourists start coming, especially the Japanese, it's like disarmament. Hu saw my point, but suggested a tourist course connecting Beijing with the Diomond Mountains to accommodate the many visitors to Beijing who want to go on to see the famed sight. Build a few hotels there and we would have our money back in one year, he said. Of course all these concerns would be academic once unification is achieved."

"What keeps you from doing it? Will Russia or China oppose?"

"No, they are so busy watching each other that they would both sooner have a unified and peaceful Korea along their borders."

"I know for a fact that the US would sooner wash its hands of South Korea, too."

"The only power that would see us divided is perhaps Japan, because united Korea would be a threat to its dominance in Asia. I believe you are right about the US having nothing to gain by the division. Its continued military presence in South Korea is merely to please Japan."

"But surely that motive is not strong enough to intervene and stop any actual steps taken by South and North Korea toward unification."

"No."

"Then why don't you just walk over and shake hands with Doohwan Jun and be done with it?"

"It's not that simple. You see he hates my guts for the Rangoon business. Besides he is not free, just as I am not, to up and hug me, even if he is man enough and willing, because all the lackeys that surround us - alas, we can't do without them like a carpenter helpless without his tools - have woven a tight knot of tangled interests they would rather die safeguarding than give up. Everybody wants to make sure he keeps his property, bank account, his pot of gold in any deal that comes along."

"Then unification will never be a reality in our lifetime."

"You never know. Sometimes things come to a head like earthquake."

"We should pray for such earthquake then."

"I am quite a fatalist when it comes to earthquakes. One can do only so much. Next month a group of US reporters will be here primarily to discover whether North Korea is willing to throw its doors open and if it is not, who of us are opposed. They won't know that I had to put up quite a fight to just let them in. When their questionnaire was presented to my comrades, they were incensed by its offensive inquisitiveness and were almost unanimous in turning them down. I persuaded them that the foreigners would be impressed by our self-reliant economy. We have been making our tanks and planes all by ourselves, as well as our trucks, tractors, jeeps, and sedans, whereas South Korea has to import the engine even for a motorbike. Their vaunted Hyundais are all assemblies of foreign parts. Only 40% is made in South Korea, unlike ours made 100% here. The reporters will compare our products with South Korea's, maybe a little rough around the edges but all Korean and solid. Through long belt tightening we have constructed a firm military and industrial base. Now it's time to improve general living standards, just as Deng and Gorbachev have come to realize and we'll come out ahead in this department, too. The only problem is the younger generation. When I went to China, Deng confided that the first thing the youngsters went for when the economy was liberalized was long hair. In our case it seems Japanese nylon socks."

"This is by the way," said Nan, "but can you allow our women to wear pants? Many have told me that the skirt presents an unbearable hardship in the extreme cold of North Korean winter."

"They can't wear pants?" Jungil asked, surprised.

"College Disciplinary Teams point them out and humiliate them publicly."

"I saw European women wear blue jeans, that canvas material. Now if you have long legs like European women, blue jeans or any pants look great, but with Oriental women, fannies almost touching heels, they look awful. So I joked about it and my comrades must have interpreted it as total ban."

"Even for short-legged women pants can be designed to look sharp and elegant."

"Elegant or not, I have no objection. Let them wear pants. Let's start with the Moo Moo Film staff."

"What if the Disciplinary Teams harass them?"

"I'll forbid them. I wish I could show the American reporters The Emissary with English soundtrack. Do you suppose we could have one dubbed in by contacting NBC before their visit?"

"There is no harm in trying. I'll send a copy to them right away via Gyongshig in Tokyo so he could express mail it to New York."

"Good. How is the deal with Universal on Mayoress of Koreatown coming along?"

"They are enthused about shooting here. As soon as we wrap up the pending projects, we'll ask you for their visas. Or maybe we should go there first to Koreatown."

"No, let's have them over first. Our people are still new at overseas travel and are apt to behave like country bumpkins. In the past they might go to Moscow Festivals and return home without seeing a single foreign movie, because they don't know where to sit or when to rise. You see our comrades know only how to look pretty wearing good clothes but don't know how to talk and socialize with poise. Even the Russians are just as bad, churlish hicks, hanging back, like back alley dogs. All socialists are like that, I am afraid."

"The more reason they should have the experience and exposure," Nan said. "America is just the place."

"Maybe some European country first, because they should get exposure in small doses. Too much, as they will in America, will overwhelm them."

"Americans are an informal, genial people, very much open and accustomed to different lifestyles. In fact, the more authentic or exotic, the better they like it."

"Like watching circus animals. No, we'll have the Americans over and try to mock up Koreatown here as much as possible and if necessary, let's first explore some European location."

I signaled to Nan to desist. Obviously Jungil had a change of heart, wisely, about sending us to the US, though he had been eager to do so when he first heard the story. So the easy one-step asylum at any house or store next door, as it would be in the US, was not to be ours.

"I am now convinced," Jungil went on, having changed the subject, "that we should send abroad films, not sports teams. One good film does more to change our image than ten soccer or pingpong teams. Do they give you all you need at Moo Moo Film?"

"Our people must get preferential treatment, because everybody wants to work with us. But please do not make it invidious. Sometimes it gets quite embarrassing."

"Did they paste on the semi-reflecting mirror inside your cars?"

"Yes, thank you."

"Deputy Chief Ingoo Cha asked me about pasting the pellicle on and I told him not to come for authorization to go to the bathroom. All the Deputy Chief had to do was just put it on, if you wanted."

Jungil, like others in positions of power, always named his servants by their titles, perhaps a comforting reminder of his own elevated status.

"Actually it was necessary because we sometimes change inside our cars."

"I'll have architects over to design a new house for you. Do you prefer one-story ranch style or two-story American Colonial?"

"We really don't care," Nan said. "We are happy where we are."

Jungil's villa, though at some distance from town, was

quite adequate but Jungil thought otherwise.

"It's too far from work," he said. "Besides it's only a villa. You need a permanent residence. I have found a perfect spot in town near the studio. The house will be designed to suit all your needs, so you will be completely at home. As film makers you will certainly need a good size viewing room and also large living room and dining room to entertain guests in style, especially foreign guests."

We really didn't want him to go to the expense and trouble of building a home for us where we had no intention of living but any strenuous refusal on our part might give the game away.

"Thank you, Comrade Leader," Nan said. "Build the way you like it and we are sure to like it, too."

Soon after this conversation Nan had to leave for Prague via Moscow leading a team of Moo Moo Film staff to settle the account with the Barandov Studio and also to make a new film. We owed the Studio 1.5 million rubles for the rentals and expenses incurred in making The Emissary, which was almost as many dollars at the official exchange rate between Russian ruble and North Korean won. Embassy employees were sent across the border to Austria, where rubles were dirt cheap, as much as five rubles to a dollar, to purchase the amount of rubles required. The result was an expenditure of only $300,000, a discount of 80%. The new film, Separation, also to be made at the Barandov under her direction, was about a North Korean family separated during the war, one sister marrying a Czech officer on the UN Armistice Commission to live in Prague and one brother going south and eventually immigrating to the US, their reunion coming about through their children who take summer classes at the University of Paris.

I had to stay behind to add some finishing touches to The Escape and shoot the Korean scenes in Separation. Ten days later, accompanied by Soontay Bag, I left for Vienna to pick up the checkbooks at the Bank of America and follow up on the registration of Moo Moo Film. As soon as we arrived in Vienna I dialed Room 602 of the Hyatt Hotel, Budapest, where Nan should be waiting for my call. Nobody answered. I tried many times more, but there was no answer. This felt like Hong Kong all over again. Soontay inquired at the North Korean Embassy and found that she was in the hospital with a severe abdominal pain, a symptom she had from time to time. Putting aside everything, I flew out of Vienna to Budapest and went to her room at the hospital.

On this trip she had the first attack the night she arrived at Moscow. When a tranquilizer gave her some relief, she left for Prague with her crew as scheduled, refusing admission to a hospital for examination. Driving herself and the crew to the limit she finished the Prague shots including the climax, the reunion of brother and sister after 30 years. Having sent the staff home she flew to Budapest to meet me, but no sooner had she checked in at the hotel than she had to be rushed to the hospital with another attack of pain and fever.

"It hurt so bad, the guts twisting and wrenching, that I thought I would die for sure this time," she said. "I couldn't help screaming. I screamed and screamed for you. The nurses must have thought I had turned bovine."

We laughed but before I knew it, I was trembling for her safety and praying fervently to God not to let anything happen to this brave good woman. "Strike me down instead, Lord!" I bargained.

She was discharged later that day. Her gallstone couldn't be operated on because of her weak health. The date of surgery was set a month later. Our gloom lifted somewhat when we found waiting at the hotel an invitation to attend the 28th London Film Festival opening on November 15, exactly one month after her scheduled operation. Unlike other competitions this was strictly on invitation only. The Executive Director or his representative went to various international film meets, looked over the winners, then sent out the invitations to the chosen from among them.

"It's perfect. You'll have recovered sufficiently to come along by then. London, England! That's the other America on this side of the Atlantic. You realize what this means?"

"Too good to be true. I bet Jungil will throw a monkey

wrench somewhere, though."

"Even he must realize what an honor this is. The offer is too good to refuse. Let's get everything squared away to make November 15 the D-Day."

As the first step to this end, I called Chansoo Hong of New York, ostensibly to ask him to speed up English dubbing into The Secret Emissary in view of the London invitation. Of course Soontay Bag was at my side, listening to every word I said.

"I got through to Fenwick at Universal and told him all about your plans about Mayoress of Koreatown," Chansoo said. "His co-producer Al is particularly interested. They are ready whenever you are."

"What a coincidence that your daughter's wedding is on November 15," I said, resorting to the code we had agreed on when Nan and I met his wife and daughter at Belgrade, Elizabeth's wedding to signify the day we executed our escape. I was to use it, when the speaker phone was not on and the other party could speak freely. "Only if it was in London, I could attend."

"It could be earlier. Didn't you say you are setting up shop at Vienna? The US Embassy there has been apprised as well as other embassies including those in Russia and Eastern Europe, just in case."

"You can't blame the young ones for being impatient to jump into the marriage bed. But they can wait two months, I am sure. The young man sounds terrific. I hope you don't become a jealous father. Returning to Fenwick, is he willing to come to North Korea for Mayoress of Koreatown?"

"No, Universal can't find any insurance company to underwrite the trip. Not at this moment anyway."

"A group of US reporters is visiting North Korea soon."

"They are a different breed and will go to hell for a story."

"I understand. Good-bye, then. Congratulations again on Elizabeth's wedding. Tell her we'll send some gifts, maybe from London."

Nan and I took a walk around the hotel past the Matis Cathedral, when she clung to me affectionately, yet with uncharacteristic shyness.

"I have something particular to discuss with you," she whispered.

"I am all ears."

"Wait until we get to our room."

I hastened my steps, almost carrying her in my arms, glad that her gallstone had not impaired her senses otherwise.

"It's not that," she said, laughing, when I locked the door and was kicking off my shoes. "Honey, we have lived in sin without a proper wedding."

"What do you mean? We had a ceremony performed by the highest officer of the land."

"But not sanctified before God. Before they cut me up, let's go to the Cathedral and take our marriage vows anew."

I caught myself before bursting into laughter, remembering my desperate prayer at her hospital bed only a few hours ago. After all she was getting a major surgery, with all its terrifying disclaimers about the outcome, in a foreign country.

"Let's. It's a splendid idea."

We went out and looked for gifts to be exchanged at the ceremony, platinum rings inlaid with diamond. With Soontay and Soggyoo on our heels, though it was 5:30 a.m., we walked up the steps and sat down in the venerable building where Daybreak Mass was in progress.

"Father, please pray for us," I said after the service to the aged priest.

"Sure," he said in fluent English, leading us to a confessional booth. "About anything particular?"

Neither of us had courage enough to say it was our wedding.

"Just bless us and pray for our souls," Nan said.

He prayed for us so fervently and sincerely, eyes closed, hands joined, and brow knit, as if we were his own children in trouble, not a couple of strangers passing by, that we felt guilty about pulling out our rings and placing them on each other's fingers on the sly.

Leaving Nan behind to wait for the surgery, I left,

accompanied by Soontay, for Vienna again to take care of the unfinished business. I got the checkbooks without any problem. The North Korean Embassy had done some research and found a company that sold office services as a package. Three or four secretaries handled phone calls, appointments, telex messages, and other correspondence for thirty or forty companies. Gyoohyang Chay, Secretary of the Embassy, was to check once a week for messages and mail. For a fee of about $200 a month it was as good as having one's own regular office.

Next morning I flew back to Budapest to rejoin Nan and also rendezvous Kintaro. Staying at the same Hyatt as we, he brought to our room the tape recordings and pictures in the original pouch we had given him.

"Scout's honor," he said. "I've never opened it and don't know what's in it."

"Weren't you even curious?" Nan asked.

"Yes, but I gave you my word to keep it for six months and then publish unless I heard otherwise from you. If I opened any sooner, the temptation to publish might have proved too much for me."

"You are a true man of honor."

"It's more like cowardice. I couldn't trust myself enough to hold the secret once I learned what it was."

That evening we were invited to dinner with Kintaro to the home of Gosha Helents, the famous Hungarian film director and recipient of a Special Director Award at the Cannes, who had a Japanese wife and had been a long-time friend of Kintaro's.

"I'll drop you off and wait outside until you are through," said Secretary Chay of the Embassy, our driver.

"No, that's not necessary," Nan said. "We won't be able to enjoy ourselves, knowing you are waiting outside in the dark."

"No, it is my pleasure."

We couldn't dissuade him. Of course he was acting under orders to keep an eye on us. I almost pitied him and wished I could tell him that he needn't worry because we weren't planning to make our escape in Budapest.

Our host, who had not been told the whole story to avoid unnecessary complication at this stage, made no secret of his contempt for North Korea.

"Defect to North Korea of all places?" he shouted unbelievingly when in the course of the dinner we mentioned our flight from the military dictatorship of South Korea. "How can you breathe, let alone work in a society like that? Not too long ago a Hungarian TV crew went to Pyongyang to do a special report on North Korea. Everybody they interviewed said, 'Our Great Chief and Leader'. My God, great chief and leader in this day and age? We have heard you have many thousands of years of history and culture behind you. How could you allow yourselves to sink that low?"

I sat there, smiling like a fool, instead of telling the truth to an honest and bright man like Gosha, whose art I truly admired and whose friendship I would have valued more than anything else.

Nan had the doctor's permission to go home to Korea and return for her surgery four weeks later, with strict orders to rest. She wouldn't leave, however, until she bought enough material to make costumes for Spring Fragrance, including bolts of lace: North Korean fabrics didn't hold up, sagging miserably when worn. I sent her on ahead because I had to stop at Beijing to present to the Joint Venture people an outline of Genghis Khan, my first non-Korean project, and find out where a thousand or more horses might be mobilized at one time for the battle scenes.

XXIV.
Revelations

When I returned to Pyongyang, I found Nan in the midst of a corps of seamstresses making costumes not only for Spring Fragrance but seemingly for all time. So engrossed was she with the work that she didn't notice my entrance.

"How could you be so reckless? Don't you realize how sick you are?"

"I am all right. We want to finish all the films before the London deadline, don't we?"

"Yeah, but not at the risk of your health."

"I am actually having fun, which is better than boredom."

She was her usual headstrong self and wouldn't budge. There was no other way but to resort to some artifice. I called Jungil.

"Congratulations," he said, referring to the London invitation. "Draw up the roster for the delegation right away."

"I have already, Vice President Nanyong and me, and six others, two male and two female actors, one cameraman, and one director. But I am calling to enlist your help in making sure my wife gets her rest."

"No problem. I know exactly where she can get her seclusion and rest. She'll commune only with nature, strolling, boating, fishing to her heart's content."

"Sounds great, but with all due respect, who will bell the cat? I can't get her off the building, though it's past five already. I don't suppose you have any such wifely obstinacy to contend with."

"Don't I! What saint or statesman doesn't? Anyway in your case I think I know just how to deal with the problem. I'll drive over myself and take you both to the place. We can all use a change of air."

He hung up before I could decline out of courtesy. Did he really chafe under domestic tyranny? I had never met the lady but from Nan's description of her she had once met on one of Jungil's birthdays at their home I couldn't imagine a wife more submissive and pliable. On the other hand, looks could be deceiving. Whether real or affected for dramatic effect, the man's vulnerability to Xanthippean truculence at once humanized and endeared him, at the same time stabbing me with a pang of guilt about our impending London defection.

His motorcade consisting of three identical black Benzes arrived in 15 minutes. With characteristic energy he bounded up the steps into the building and met us at the Costume Warehouse.

"Vice President Nanyong," he said coming up to her. "We don't have a minute to lose. Drop everything because a state of emergency has arisen and I have to take both of you at once to a safe place."

Leaving Pyongyang with us in the same car with Jungil the motorcade rounded Mt. Daysong and drove over an hour down an asphalt road southwest, then into a side road between pear orchards heavy with fruit. The sentry saluted smartly at a checkpoint before the embankment, which bounded a seemingly endless reservoir, dwarfing anything I had seen including the one by Chestnut Grove, formed by evacuating a whole county. Across the reservoir, clear like a mirror, rose the hint of a roof or two above dreamy green foliage at the water's edge.

"Well, what is the emergency, Comrade Leader?" Nan asked, fearing no less than a coup d'etat.

"I'll tell you when we stop," Jungil said, maintaining a grave face.

She kept looking at me for a clue, while I kept my face averted, trying my best to suppress laughter.

The cars pulled into the driveway of a two-story shake-roof house, built entirely with ten-inch logs, surrounded by towering birches and firs, through the sylvan interstices of which glinted the surface of the lake.

"How do you like it?" Jungil asked, leading the way.

"How absolutely beautiful!" Nan said. "We haven't seen anything like this before. What's the place called? Where are we?"

"The whole area is restricted and only a few people know of its existence. Let's go inside and see if everything is in order."

Four servants held the front door open, bowing as we entered. The wide hallway on the ground floor was flanked by a recreation room with billiard and card tables, dining room, library, and indispensable theater. The ten-foot wide stairway with rosewood banisters spiraled upward to the bedroom suites. The one assigned to us had a delightfully appointed sitting room with large windows opening directly on the lake, a sauna, and a bathtub equipped with a jet circulator.

"Will you please rest here?" Jungil said, leaving. "Go fishing or swimming in the lake. There is a pier in the back. I'll have to rush back to Pyongyang to see if the state of emergency is over."

He dashed off before Nan could say good-bye, let alone ask questions.

"You sly devil," she said, turning to me when we were left alone. "You knew all about this."

"Not at all. I am as surprised as you are."

"You are a bad liar but I forgive you. It's heaven. Let the studio go to hell. Let's stand here and feast our eyes on the scenery, then sleep for three days without waking."

While she lay in deep sleep, I left early next morning for the studio to complete the simultaneous production of Spring Fragrance, Salt, and The Jetty before D-Day. There was absolutely no time to lose with the first one. It was fall already, whereas the swing scene and other crucial sequences had to be filmed before the leaves turned color. In spite of all this haste the grass had browned and needed spraying. For the Seoul scenes where the prince graduates from school and passes the highest government examination, I had to take the entire crew to Gaysong just north of the DMZ, the only city in North Korea where old buildings were preserved. The sequence where the hero, disguised as a beggar, comes to visit his future mother-in-law, the disappointed and disdainful snob, required track shots. I took them myself, lugging the camera on my shoulder and closely following the brisk and comic interaction of many actors. Then, apparently tired by the weight of the camera and overwork in general, I dropped the sound-recording unit to the ground, the first such accident. Fortunately, no damage had been done to the machine but I was mortified and frightened. The years of imprisonment could have wrecked my metabolism beyond repair, dooming me to tottering old age and helplessness prematurely. Momentarily the black specter of Death seemed to rise up to smother me in its enormous embrace.

But I wasn't allowed to wallow in morbid self-pity for long. By night train I had to take a crew to the Jetty, the newly-built sea wall enclosing the gigantic reclamation project near South Port. Returning from the Jetty late one evening I suddenly realized I hadn't been to see Nan, that only about a week remained before her departure for the surgery. Catching a catnap now and then on location or at the office I simply hadn't had the time. I told the chauffeur to head for the reservoir.

Her days had consisted of fishing, watching movies, reading, and strolling. The morning was generally taken up by fishing. Unlike her previous experiences in South Korea where she would dip a line into the overfished water and wait for hours like a fool to bring up nothing, she was busy hauling up here, detaching the fish from the hook and putting them in a clean tub of water for release the next day. The abundant fish caught the moment she dropped the line. For one thing she was the only fisherman in the whole reservoir. For another, unbeknown to her the grounds keeper scattered boiled silkworm pupas into the water before she got to the fishing pier, so the area teemed with schools of jumping fish. Pleasantly tired after two or three hours of 'fishing' she returned to the villa to watch the movies. After lunch she walked in the garden or on the bank of the reservoir which ended in a headland of wooded cliffs.

On the fifth day, feeling an impulse to explore she took along a female servant, and kept hiking up the hill following a barely noticeable trail through the woods. Apparently under orders not to leave the guesthouse except to open a door or sweep the yard, Gumsoog didn't want to stray farther, but Nan pressed on, assuring her reluctant and timorous companion that she, Nan, would be responsible. After nearly an hour of climbing they reached what looked like the crest, only to find that it was the lower rung of an ascending series of crests. Looking down she saw the other side of the slope falling away more steeply to the edge of the reservoir culminating in the headland that bounded the embankment and hugged a cove in the coastline with a sandy beach gleaming in the sun. On the shore through the leafy wood could be discerned the outline of a house, resembling the one she was lodging at but strangely forbidding. Impelled by curiosity she decided to investigate. Next day she went through the wood, parallel to the embankment, and climbed from her side of the headland.

"Look at my hands," she said, showing cuts and bruises, fortunately healing with no sign of infection. "At the top of the ridge I looked over."

"How could you?" I was really upset with her. "We should lock you up."

"But listen to what I found, an elegant beach house built with logs like this, with a patio opening on the cove."

"Who cares? You are not supposed to...."

"It's a guarded prison, a chilling sight, from which I was turning away when I heard a song float out of the house, a woman singing Spring Fragrance to her own gayagum accompaniment. I was spellbound. It was the most exquisite voice, better than anybody's I've heard, Sonhee Kim, Choran Bag, the best from your Aran Ham Center crowd. I remained glued to the spot long after she had finished, vaguely hoping to catch a glimpse of her. My patience was finally rewarded. She came out to walk on the patio, in a mauve coat and a blue scarf tied over her head fluttering in the chilly evening wind blowing in from the lake...."

"Blue scarf?" I almost shouted.

I must have forgotten to mention this detail to Nan, perhaps because it was so obvious to me.

"Did you get a good look at her face?"

"No, it was too far. She wasn't young but was tall, her carriage straight, graceful, and dignified."

"She is the lady who left me at the orphanage."

"Aran Ham?"

"Whoever. Show me the place."

"You mean right now?"

"Yes."

"You are as bad as Jungil. Why don't you wait until tomorrow and ask him to take you to her or bring her to you, saying we've heard her and need her for Spring Fragrance right away?"

"She may not be Aran Ham. Besides I can't wait that long."

"Not even one night?"

"No."

"We can't go in there. The front gate in the fence is guarded by armed sentries."

"That's the landward side of the house, isn't it? What about the cove side?"

"It is left open, but I saw some kind of barrier across the mouth of the cove, too."

"That's no problem. You are talking to the swimmer of the Gulf of Siam, remember?"

"But you were many years younger and hadn't been through Prison No. Six."

How true! I remembered my dropping the audio unit of the camera the other day.

"To get caught snooping might mean another term in No. Six."

"I'll just have to be careful and will be in and out in no time. Darling, I've got to do this, even if it's the death of me. I've waited all my life for this. I have to know who I am."

"What happened to all that talk about genetic freedom?"

"Hogwash!"

At the end of the embankment I waded into the lake, icy cold in spite of the makeshift wet suit Nan had put together. In easy long strokes I rounded the headland and swam for the cove, watchful for any submerged trip wire or alarm device. Nan had been right: a stainless steel wire net, held up by sturdy poles driven firmly into the lake bed, stretched half a mile across the entire length of the opening, the top sticking a couple of feet above water and mounted by a motion detection strip. There was no question of pulling myself over that. To go under it I dived but the net, contoured to the bottom ten feet deep at places, had no opening. I was on the point of turning back to return with a wire cutter and waterproof flashlight, when the last desperate dive and search revealed a trough underneath wide enough for passage, formed by erosion after installation. Having marked its relative position for exit later, I dived and emerged on the other side.

Dripping, I came out of the water and cautiously climbed the beach. A row boat was tied to a short pier. A ten-foot high concrete fence, topped with barbed wire, enclosed the property, except for the open lake side. I crossed the stretch of level ground and reached the patio where Nan had seen the lady in question that afternoon. If I had any uncertainty as to where the object of my quest might reside, it dissolved next moment: a sweet, unearthly, siren-like soprano, accompanied by the wail of a three-stringed ajang, floated out of the lighted upper window that was left open. I stood rooted to the spot in admiration, long after the song had ceased. My years of apprenticeship at the Aran Ham Center, eclectic, dilettantish, downright wasteful from a pragmatic point of view, had a purpose: to enable me to recognize and appreciate the caliber of her music.

The sliding glass door to the patio was not locked but entry that way might be noticed by the servants moving about downstairs. I climbed and stood on the awning made of wood that projected a few feet over the patio doorway. I reached up and grabbed the sill plate of the window from which the singing had come. Slowly I pulled up and looked in.

My singer was not in the room. With a powerful jerk I vaulted myself through the window, almost crashing into the music stand. Except for the opposite wall against which a canopied king-size bed stood, all the wall spaces were taken up by shelves on which were arranged drums, ajang, flutes, gayagum, gomungo, cymbal, and music books, more like a museum of Korean music than a lady's boudoir. I was on the floor picking up sheets of music that had blown off the stand by a whiff of wind when startled by her sudden appearance behind me.

"Mother!" I gasped.

"I have no son," she said, staring at my face.

"Don't you remember the Mercy Home?"

In one bound she put her hand on my forehead, pushed aside the cowlick, and felt the crater with her finger.

"You are indeed my nephew, my sister's son," she said, bursting into tears and embracing me. "We were out for a walk in the market place that day. I was as happy and proud as any mother as you toddled alongside holding my hand. Then this pompous horrid old bigot, all dressed up in traditional suit and stovepipe hat, came up to give us a once-over. 'Is this human or beast?' he spat, at the same time stabbing your forehead with the point of his stick. You fell screaming, blood gushing from the puncture. The wound healed but left this permanent dent."

"So you are Aran Ham," I said, noting her family likeness to Haran Ham in Sunset in spite of the silvery hair and crow's feet.

"Yes, your mother Harman's sister. They murdered her. It's a painful story and you had better brace for it."

I let her tell the story, which confirmed what I knew already from Tayong Yee. She pulled out the family album, positive proof of their erstwhile existence on earth, Grandfather Josef towering over Syngman Rhee at the latter's presidential inauguration, Grandfather Doochan leading a joint worship service at South Mountain Plaza, my father and mother in Pusan during the war shortly after their marriage. He was my father all right, Anton Minsky. I had his eyes and nose, but her lips, my mother's, pert and playful. Though resembling closely, the sisters contrasted like black and white, one somber and austere, the other bursting with merriment. What fun it would have been to have grown up with Haran for mother and Aran for aunt! Remarkable among the memorabilia Aran kept was a long letter Haran wrote to my father shortly before the War, before their marriage.

"My dear Anton, I never seem to give you a chance to answer my letters. But so many things happen so fast here I just can't wait. Of course that doesn't change the fact that you are a beast not to have written. But I forgive you. You must be busy with your research and teaching. How your students must adore you!

"Well, my friend, you are not the only genius around. I am a movie star, playing the betrayed wife in Sunset. The whole nation worships me, wants to take my pictures, get my autograph, hear me talk about any stupid thing. I didn't know being a celebrity could be such a nuisance. I am asked to be everywhere at one time, to address this meeting or that, to dedicate this building or that bridge. Lately, at the entreaty of the Ministry of Public Information I read on the Poetry Hour of KBS. I didn't know my voice had a 'gripping power and drama' that just thrills my listeners to pieces. The discovery seemed to make up for the years of my inferiority complex about not being able to sing like Aran. My voice is certainly not as musical as hers as you know and as I am painfully aware, but perhaps it is capable of a different order of music, as prose is different from verse and yet can be art. But what wouldn't I give for that 'celestial' quality of her soprano, as you once put it, as the whole world raves about it, justly. She sang at the National Theater last Friday and she was divine! Di-vine! I am so proud of her. Please love and cherish her with all your heart, because such love is pure, beautiful, spontaneous, good like the blue sky, the dew on the blade of grass on a summer morning, the echo of the bugoog owl in the valley at night, for which your father's quest has begun in earnest. He is determined to trek and capture those mysterious woodland songsters, though perhaps their mystery had better be left alone.

"What an irony! I love you and yet I am telling you to love someone else. I don't even have the luxury of jealousy like other unrequited lovers because my rival happens to be my dear, poor sister. My heart is fit to burst thinking of her fate. Who would have thought that her talent should be her undoing, that her song heard only once should plant such an implacable passion in the Demon's heart, compelling him to sneak into the guarded dormitory of the Pyongyang Conservatory and almost succeed in kidnapping her? What a trauma it must have been for her! Of course I didn't know anything about it then. She had never been quite the same after that and had to retreat to Chongjin. Sungjoo Kim was not crazy enough to follow her there, knowing that the Japanese police were waiting with her as decoy, but after Liberation he came directly to Chongjin to press his suit, while at the same time waiting for word from Chichikov, the Soviet Military Governor in Pyongyang. As a professor of Far Eastern history you must know all about Sungjoo Kim, alias Ilsung Kim, but maybe you don't. The whitewash had been so complete. Anyway I am giving you an absolutely reliable eyewitness account. Maybe you can use it in your next book."

What amazing tenacity Truth had, for it will out somewhere, sometime, in all its stark totality, no matter how often or long twisted, mutilated, eradicated! The voice from beyond the grave continued:

"Sungjoo and his band of so-called independence fighters, marauders in fact preying more on Korean immigrants in Manchuria than the well-armed Japanese Kwantung Army, which soon chased them off into Siberia, had been recruited in the Korean Brigade just being formed at Khabarovsk under the Soviet Far East Command as a guerrilla unit for infiltration into Korea to harass the Japanese border garrisons. Hard-pressed by the German invasion of Russia the Soviet Army had the Brigade shifted to the home front, especially in the defense of Stalingrad, where it acquitted itself well enough to come to Stalin's notice. At the end of World War II Stalin picked Sungjoo and his pals as his native agents to run the newly-won Soviet territory, North Korea. Their credentials, junior officers in the Red Army, in their early 30's, healthy, unschooled ruffians with police records, recommended them to Stalin better than doctorates from Harvard or Oxford. Popular leaders like Manshig Jo, 'the Ghandi of Korea' as he was called, were imprisoned and murdered, while returning patriots from the Provisional Government were blocked entry. Landowners and intellectuals, people with any claim to respectability, were rounded up, killed or sent to the coal mines. Communist hostility toward Christians was particularly virulent. In Ujoo the whole congregation of a church at worship was taken to a cliff and pushed over. When families and friends went to collect their broken bodies, they were set upon and dispatched with bamboo spears. The horrors were repeated everywhere, forcing the Christians to flee south in droves, risking capture and death. Father, imprisoned, was waiting for trial by people's court.

"In the meantime the Soviets went on to ram the band of hoodlums down the throat of North Korea. Sungjoo Kim's name was changed to Ilsung Kim, a legendary independence fighter who was no relation or acquaintance to Sungjoo. Everybody knew he was a back alley scrapper from Pyongyang with many unsavory deeds like rape and robbery to his credit, an impostor because the real Ilsung Kim would be over 60 if he were still alive, not a ruddy 34-year-old, but that kind of detail didn't bother the new leadership. The most incredible bald-faced lies were fabricated and recited, as if we North Koreans had no memory or intelligence. The impostor's portraits were hung everywhere alongside Stalin's, to which the whole nation had to stand up and bow, singing hymns of praise and thanksgiving for Kim's fictitious battles and triumphs over the Kwantung Army. After beating down resistance sufficiently, Chichikov sent the green light to Sungjoo or Ilsung restlessly waiting in Chongjin. Installed in power the new ruler of the land asked for Aran's hand, his wife having died recently after giving birth to Jungil. Rejected, he threatened to hand over to the executioner our Father spared to date for the purpose. When Father found out what the price of his release was, he gave his okay to the exodus from

Chongjin, urged by his elders and deacons but held off till then because of his determination to die rather than leave North Korea."

So Jungil and I had come within a hair's breadth of being cousins. I was overcome by a strange sense of helpless entrapment and doom. Without my knowing it my life had been entwined with that of the Kims, the last people in the world with whom I could have wished for such affiliation, so intimately that dissociation from them seemed impossible without snapping the tangled skeins.

"Her performance the other night was broadcast in its entirety on KBS, no doubt reaching the ears of the Evil One who will besiege her with yet another wave of calls, letters, and signs reminding her that she was his forever and he would come and get her soon. Can you imagine the man's gall? Not only was the engagement coerced, because Aran would never have consented except to save Father, but the wedding itself had not come off, there being no bride. There was no marriage, no consummation. He has since married his former secretary Songay and Aran is here in the Free World away from his clutch, and yet he considers her his. For once I am grateful for the 38th Parallel, the Iron Curtain, for keeping him on the other side, except I don't understand why the US and ROK governments can't seal it off really tight and stop his awful messages from getting across.

"Anton, I need you here immediately. Not for my love for you because I've become quite stoic about it but because of an emergency. Bomson Yee, producer and director of Sunset, has run away with all the funds and an actress named Gyongja Jo, whose talent must shine more in bed than on the screen."

Nan's aunt and the one we had left in charge of the Film School in South Korea! A small world indeed. Who would have suspected such a scandal attaching to the pillar of probity and wisdom to whom we turned for moral as well as practical guidance! And she hadn't disappointed us yet. A reformed seductress no doubt. Whatever had happened to this Bomson character?

"The rotten bum! He had the nerve to make passes at me,

too. See what perils you expose me to by being away. Of course he got nowhere with me. Nobody had been paid and the creditors were about to tear the studio down to pieces. I put in all my money and borrowed from Aran and everybody else to hold off their fury for a while. The studio must be saved and the filming now under way must be finished, not only because it is going to be a hit but because it is the most important chapter in the annals of Christianity, in modern Korean history, in our lives, yours and mine. It is about our exodus from Chongjin, in some respects grander and more heroic than its Biblical counterpart. The Israelites, though more numerous, had the advantage of being a closed group, safe from encroachment by the Egyptian society at large. But here we had to plan and carry out everything in the milieu of a church, by nature open to the public, to all comers off the street including Communist agents and agitators, of whom we had a legion. Over half of the membership had melted away, openly recanting Christianity and adopting Communism. But even among the avowed loyalists there might be informers who would be glad to report the mass flight for a reward. Each participant had to be closely screened, because in those days it was hard to trust anybody.

"But one traitor was easy to spot. You remember Elder Wansog Shin, the shrill-voiced demimidget with the ego of an elephant, who couldn't open his mouth but to spit some venom, except when he prayed aloud during the Sunday morning service for the congregation which the elders took turns in doing. Such silvery words rolled off his tongue that the congregation was moved to tears of contrition or raptures of thanksgiving. Hearing him in this role one would never have associated him with his other persona, a jealous, mean, backbiting snake. His constant complaint had been that my father was too autocratic and ran the church as he saw fit disregarding the elders' counsel, which meant his, the only dissenting voice. The Shins still kept coming to the church for the sole purpose of spying on us. Dame Shin poked her upturned nose everywhere, sniffing for a shift in the wind and visiting each member's home on one excuse or other. Her three sons had all become important in the Communist regime, the oldest heading the Dockworkers Union. Instead of repaying the church members for helping them in their poverty, they turned informer against them and were instrumental in the arrest and imprisonment of many. Everybody agreed it was the Shins who had informed on the Ans, the family that used to decorate the altar with fresh seasonal flowers, who were all ambushed and killed by the border patrol while trying to escape to the south, though they had taken a supposedly safe route and a reliable guide. Captain Heegyoo Mo's ships, warehouses, and other interests were first to be confiscated by the Communists because the Shin boys, who had been given employment by him, had access to everything he owned. Perhaps this flagrant treachery of the Shins was the catalyst that bound the rest of us in an unbreakable bond, preventing leakage of the plot and seeing it through.

"From the beginning overland passage had been ruled out on account of our multitude. Besides it appealed more to us to go by sea as the parallel was obvious with the biblical Exodus. We had decided to steal back one of Captain Mo's ships, the Sea Queen, past due and expected back at port momentarily with a load of lumber from Hwayryong. Deemed seaworthy enough for our number, it had aboard some of the captain's trusted former employees privy to our plan. Meanwhile the groom's party had arrived in pomp and style by special train from Pyongyang with a large entourage of friends, musicians, security and service personnel. Invoking the old tradition that it was bad luck for the groom to see the bride before the wedding, we had put off his impetuous advances, but to make sure of his bride he had an armed guard posted at our house, while rollicking prenuptial carousings went on at the hotel. The anxiously awaited Sea Queen was finally sighted rounding Cape Boar's Head just before the wedding day, its waterline coming down to the cabin portholes. Maneuvering round other shipping to dock it careened and almost capsized. Though outraged at such abuse of his beloved ship, Mo felt reassured of its capacity to transport all of us.

"The signal went forth and everybody began to gather at the appointed place, an abandoned warehouse by the dock, dropping everything they might have been doing so as not to incur the suspicion of the neighbors. At our house the sentry was easily put out of the way by plying with drinks. But Dame Shin was a problem, who hung around speciously to help with cooking and other preparations but in reality to keep an eye on us, obviously at the groom's behest. Only when Dr. Dongwon Sung came to ask my father and the rest of us to visit and pray for a church member dying of tuberculosis and asked Dame Shin to come along too, did she leave in a hurry, afraid to catch the disease. You remember the gentle doctor, of whom you had been quite jealous at one time, who sang in the choir and continued to work at the Chongjin Presbyterian, refusing the offer from the Seoul National University Medical Center, to be near Aran, though without encouragement from the lady whose heart had closed to the male world since her attempted kidnap. Without his timely improvisations an undertaking like ours, however well planned, would never have gotten off the ground.

"The Soviets patrolled the coast diligently from their base in Chongjin, an oval bay with a narrow opening seaward flanked by the headland to the north, and a long breakwater to the south, its shoreline sawtoothed with piers. The plan called for departure at 2 a.m. shortly after the first night patrol returned and before the next set out, which would give the Sea Queen enough head start. Athwart the mouth of the bay a string of barges was anchored, loaded with firecrackers and sparklers set to go off after we were well on our way. Your father's knowledge of explosives came in handy here. I had no idea he was a general commanding a whole division in the Czarist Army.

"Well, I must run. I am counting the days and hours before you get here. Beware. This time I will be shameless and ravish you. In the meantime please write. If I don't hear from you soon, I'll disown you forever. Love. Haran.

"I almost forgot the main purpose of writing this letter. I went to see my sister-in-law Soyong dance the Swan Lake at the City Auditorium. After the performance she wouldn't join the family for coffee or a snack, pleading a headache. I was curious and followed her, leaving the others. What should I see but her getting into a sedan with Saybang Hong, the attorney and Member of the National Assembly! I was shocked. Should I tell my family what I saw? Above all, should I tell Jintay?"

With a shock I recognized the name, Colonel Jintay Ham, the hero of the unfinished General Intrepid, and CO of Sgt. Insoo Bang, custodian at the Film School, still alive and at his post the last time we communicated with Gyongja Jo.

"Oh, my poor brother Jintay," the voice from beyond continued, "not suspecting anything, sweating it out at his lonely outpost on the 38th Parallel in defense of his country and home! What kind of home is that? He should never have married her, a dancer whose legs are just too shapely and long for her own good. The weight of this terrible secret is stifling. I wish you were here to give me sage counsel as you used to sitting under the chestnut tree behind your house. Do not tell me I am putting too much into her meeting the attorney. It cannot be harmless or innocent. No decent married woman with her husband away at the front or away from home for any reason at all goes around at night meeting other men, especially a well-known lothario like Saybang Hong. I have checked around and confirmed that my sister-in-law is a trollop, who is going to destroy Jintay, destroy our whole family. Never have I felt such a sense of doom. All our accomplishments and successes of the past have been undone, blotted out by this shame. Surely we didn't come south for this. Oh, how I long for the carefree, idyllic days when everything made sense, life was innocent and pure! Do you think we'll ever be able to go back?"

We were both silent with a sense of doom. So here was the missing motivation Sgt. Bang wouldn't supply, that had driven poor Uncle Jintay to suicidal intrepidity. How blind I had been to be surrounded by so many vital links to my identity and ancestry and yet remain ignorant of their significance all this time! Looking at him, Uncle Jintay, in his wedding picture, standing tall and handsome in Army Captain's uniform next to his ravishing bride, Soyong, who could have suspected the fatal flaw in the union?

"His orderly used to tell me so much about him, bugging me daily to do a film on his military achievements."

"What's his name?"

"Insoo Bang."

"I know him, a distant cousin on our mother's side. Did he mention Jintay's marital problems?"

"No, not a word. I didn't even know he was a blood relation to his hero."

"That's commendable loyalty. On the other hand, he owes it to him. He would have gone to prison for beating up a cop, not to mention other infractions, hadn't Jintay intervened and enlisted him in the Army to shape him up. The day before Jintay's death Bang drove him to Daegu for an emergency meeting at the Army Hqs. On the way back to the regiment they made an unannounced stop at the house where Soyong was staying. Jintay found her in bed with her lover. Waiting outside in the jeep Bang heard the pistol shots but Jintay had not been charged with the murder of the adulterous pair because Bang hadn't told a soul about the fatal detour, except to me when I ran into him by chance in Daegu."

"What happened to my grandmother Gisoon Bag Minsky?"

"I don't know. Cooped up here I have no way of knowing who is alive or dead or what goes on in the rest of the world. But there is something indestructible about that lady and I wouldn't put it past her to be not only still alive but hale and well at the age of 91, she was exactly 25 years my senior, owning a good chunk of Manhattan by now. It was her entrepreneurship that had built the previous Minsky fortunes in Vladivostok and Chongjin."

"I'll make inquiries through a friend of mine in New York."

"Perhaps you had better wait until you are safely back in the US yourselves. Ilsung or Jungil Kim shouldn't have an inkling of all this."

"But it's been decades since, long enough to neutralize the

stubbornest grudge."

"Not this man Ilsung's. On my birthday he comes around every year, with gifts - these books and instruments are from him - to ask me whether I had changed my mind."

"And he doesn't try to force himself on you?"

"I'll kill myself the instant he does and he knows it."

"He loves you. At least you must give him credit for that."

"It's more like the compulsion of a madman who, determined to tame an untamable bird, cannot admit defeat either by letting it go or killing it."

What an expensive cage he must build and maintain to indulge his obsession! Though I understood her bitterness and hatred, I couldn't help feeling a grudging admiration, mixed with pity, for Ilsung, who could have been my uncle, who was human after all.

"Does he ask you to sing?"

"Every time he comes here. But I won't sing for him."

"What about the rest of the world?"

"It's the same as singing for him, because he controls everything, radio, TV, theater. I wasn't alone in refusing to bend to the despot's will. After kidnapping him north during the war, Ilsung repeatedly asked Gwangsoo Yee, the Tolstoy of Korea, to head the Party Department of Culture but Gwangsoo, malnourished and minus one lung from tuberculosis, would have none of it and chose to raise potatoes and corn in the Gangwon mountain village to which he was banished, not writing a single line, until one summer day ten years later he fell with a stroke and died."

"Couldn't he temporize a little, go along with the powers that be, and continue to be productive and creative, rather than deprive posterity of his genius altogether?"

"No, because artistic creativity comes with integrity, a degree of intractability, obstinacy if you will."

Was that peeve or willpower? Either way I knew I was not capable of it. Coupled with my basic cowardice I was just a hired hack ready to sell my soul to the next highest bidder. The exalted name of artist I could not arrogate because I really never created anything. As I told young Elizabeth Hong at one time, all my plots, passions, poetry and drama had come from the pens of writers like Gwangsoo. I was just an adapter, technician, manager. Only people like Gwangsoo or Aunt Aran were the true creators, who would rather die than be compromised. But, then, as Elizabeth put it, wasn't translation or even the slightest variation a creative act? No, I was again looking for an excuse to duck out of the truth about myself.

"Hating him for his obstinacy Ilsung had his body buried in the ground nearby wrapped in a mat without even the dignity of a coffin but that unmarked grave will be exalted above all the proud monuments of Ilsung Kim, destined to tumble down and be trampled underfoot."

"Aunt, will you sing to be free, to get out of this hell?"

"How do you propose to manage that?"

"I want you to sing in Spring Fragrance. I'll simply ask Jungil for you, saying Nan and I heard you sing. He knows we are dissatisfied with the tapes we can get from South Korea, and will do whatever we say is necessary to make it a first-rate film."

"Do I get to see this girl Nan, your wife?"

"Of course. Boy, isn't she in for a surprise! She is a great girl and I love her very much. You'll like her."

"Has she given you any children?"

"No, we have been too busy and haven't felt like raising a family...."

"Well, you have no time to lose. You are the only one left of the Hams, Bags, and Minskys."

Without meaning to be deceptive, I didn't want to prejudice her against Nan unnecessarily by telling her about Nan's inability to conceive.

"I have been reborn through you, Aunt," I said. "Thanks to you I know who I am, who my parents are. But the discovery of my biological identity leaves me even more convinced about the basic soundness of my Manifesto on Genetic Bondage propounded in an interview I had with a Japanese newspaper. We can't afford to seek immortality through procreation. The globe is overloaded with homo sapiens. I can hear earth groaning under our combined weight.

We have a crisis on our hands, population explosion. We simply can't keep adding billions of Chinese, Russians, Africans, Hindus, Japanese, Koreans, jostling for space and going at each other's throats. Our very survival depends on containing this explosion by emancipating ourselves from genetic bondage, from the tyranny of roots, by adopting a new morality or consciousness about the species, the gene pool...."

"The pool can use some chlorination, by injection of the superior Ham-Minsky genes."

"Unfortunately, every Chinese, Slav, German, Ethiopian, Mexican, Japanese, however retarded or ill-favored, has the same conviction."

"We are talking about us, the handful of Hams and Minskys, not the billions out there. I hope your wife has more sense than you. In fact, I demand that you stop this nonsense about population explosion and work on your duty right away. Otherwise there is no Spring Fragrance or anything else. Give me your word."

"All right," I promised, not knowing how to make it good. But promise was one thing, delivery another. In time maybe I could make her come around and see the light. I had unbounded faith in her intelligence, though she might belong to the pre-crisis generation.

"Whatever happened to Dr. Dongwon Sung, my father's rival for your favor?"

"Poor man! He was caught tending the ROK Army wounded at the Seoul National University Medical Center the day the city fell. Dispatched to the front to tend the People's Army casualties this time, he was killed in the Nagdong River Offensive. What a waste! Had he lived, he would have been a famous saint, though fame was the last thing he sought. Unlike many of the so-called great men, he always did his good deeds for their own sake, not to be known and rewarded for them by others, sometimes even the beneficiaries themselves. He was a genuinely good person. War is a terrible thing to cut down so many good people in the bloom of youth!"

"Did you love him?"

"No. As your mother points out, I had a phobia of the

male sex."

"Even my father?"

She was thoughtful for a moment.

"He was probably the most brilliant man I've come across. Naturally I was flattered by his attention, but I couldn't really encourage him, knowing how attached my sister was to him and how right they were for each other, agewise and temperamentally. When you were delivered to me, a bloody little lump torn out of her womb, I felt you were the son I could have had from him."

"You are my mother, because that's how I've always known you. I'll call you Mother if you'll let me."

"No, don't! I'll always be your aunt and that's close enough. What matters is not what you call but how you feel about someone. In any event, never, never forget your own mother, my poor bright-eyed Haran, whose merry laughter still rings in my ear. Such innocence and gaiety! Such cruel, insane waste!"

Tears choked her. Never would I tell her about the letter forging her handwriting that had led to her sister's undoing.

"Mother! Aunt!" I cried, holding her frail body in my arms. "You are her continuation. She lives through you, through me, through her art. She is immortal, beyond the reach of this madness, Divided Korea. Let's get out of here before it destroys us all."

For fear of drawing suspicion we decided to postpone a visit to Chongjin and the Snow Country, the birthplace of my parents, until a suitable opportunity should come along, which wouldn't be too long: the area would be perfect for Salt, based on the short story by the leftist writer Gyongay Gang in the 30's about a family driven by poverty from their home near Chongjin to Manchuria across the Dooman. When the Japanese kill his father on suspicion of underground connections, the eldest son leaves home to join the underground ignoring the entreaties of his mother and wife to stay and look after the family. At this time the Japanese ban the import of salt into the area to choke off anti-Japanese insurrection. To support her family the mother joins a band of village salt smugglers, who get ambushed by the Japanese but are rescued by the Korean guerrillas under the generalship of her own son, the mother now understanding his decision to follow a greater cause.

When we mentioned to Jungil our need for Aran Ham's music, he told us to go and ask her ourselves, wishing us luck. We went, accompanied by Ingoo Cha, entering the grounds of the mansion by the sentry-opened front gate. With convincing reluctance for Cha's benefit she agreed to cooperate, after exacting an official document guaranteeing her freedom, artistic and personal. Both father and son were only too glad to sign anything to make her work again. I now understood why the best musicians in the south did not hesitate to yield her the first place in their profession. Age had only ripened and perfected her art, giving it greater depth and originality. With her in charge of the sung narrative I worked furiously, driving the crew to the limit, to finish Spring Fragrance before Nan's departure for her surgery in Budapest so I could go with her, and also to find an excuse for Aunt's inclusion in the London delegation. But haste made waste. The movie couldn't be finished in time and Nan had to go by herself for her rendezvous with destiny. The lead actress, a loan from the Korean Art Film Studio, slipped and fell off the swing, requiring immediate hospitalization for compound fractures. Her personal suffering and loss aside, we were back at square one, all the shots taken with her in them useless because she was not expected to be able to walk again, let alone act. The urgency of the situation silenced any objection to my nomination of Sonhee Jang, the VIP Lounge actress, as replacement, who fully justified my choice in the sequel, though during the period of breaking in I often doubted my own sanity and sorely missed Nan's assistance, who had a way with these new girls.

But the catastrophe brought an unexpected boon as byproduct. Aunt Aran proved once more the maxim about the separation of art and artist. From her forbidding presence, remote bearing, contempt for romantic or sentimental frivolity, understandably from her own traumatic experience, neither I nor Nan nor anybody else suspected the riotous comical genius that could enliven her rendition of the Love Song in Spring Fragrance:

"Love, love, my sweet love,
Comely and fair in every way,
Viewed from left or right,
From front or back,
At all hours of the day and night,
Bringer of joy, lifter of spirit,
My love, my all...."

Which immediately suggested itself as the theme song for a modern-day adaptation of the Idiot Ondal tale, that had appeared in one of our earlier works in South Korea. The new version had a village youth, mistaken and taunted as a halfwit for his good nature but appreciated by his sweetheart for what he really is, a bright man capable of dedication and concentration, who succeeds as a shipwright, winning not only the Ilsung Kim medal for achievement but the grudging acceptance and approval of his still skeptic in-laws. While waiting for the still bewildered Sonhee to shape up for her lead role, I produced the comedy without even a screen play, letting everybody ad lib along the general idea. The whole company, including Aunt Aran, thought we were fooling around just to while the time away. When edited and stitched together, the result was a rollicking, uninhibited, fun-filled hour and a half, sustained yet by a sound moral that would pass muster with the strictest Party censor or stuffiest Puritan. When released, Love, Love, My Love became an instant hit with everybody on the street, singing or humming at home or work the Aran Ham Tune as it came to be known, because her name had been given top billing. The theaters got literally mobbed all over the country and scalping appeared for the first time in North Korean history, a ticket fetching 10 won, 10 times its nominal value, which was incredible considering the average worker's monthly income of 60 or 70 won. Since Liberation the word 'love' had disappeared in North Korea and a movie with this word in its dialogue had been unthinkable. So this was the first film ever made with the word recurring with a vengeance not only in the body of the movie but in the title itself.

The success of Love inspired me with yet another short-order fare, The Railroad, with the theme of one maiden being courted by two young men. Predictably, a love triangle was taboo in North Korean films. All treatments of relationship between the sexes were simplistic reductions, the only invariable element of complication being that the boy prove himself to win the girl by becoming a Hero of Revolution or Hero of Work. It was about time all this had changed, though I didn't dare go as far as to take on adultery. The participants were all unmarried and the heroine's dilemma is resolved by one of the suitors nobly conceding to his friend and going on to become a Heroic Railroad Builder, suggesting that one may lose love to gain honor. But any potential offense that might linger was elevated and ennobled by Aunt Aran's Work Songs, traditional farmers' songs from different provinces resurrected with the infusion of her lilts and twists that made the old singsong folk melodies jump and gallop like a young horse grazed on juicy summer hay. The movie, filmed in one day at the site of railroad construction on the Jetty, was well received. By the time Spring Fragrance was finally released about a week afterwards, the name Aran Ham had become a byword for Moo Moo Film, the fame and recognition which was so deservedly hers.

So far nobody had an inkling of our relationship, which was exactly what we wanted.

"What did you do to make the old songbird come out and sing again like that?" Jungil Kim asked, calling me at the office shortly after Spring Fragrance, apparently suspecting nothing.

"Nobody would pass up a chance to be in the movies, as you must know."

"Others have tried with the same ploy to no avail."

"Maybe she realizes she is getting on and it's either now or never."

"Isn't she awful to work with?"

"No, though set in her ways, she makes no problem. Frankly, if anybody could write music and sing like her, I'd put up with her worst tantrums."

I almost succumbed to the temptation to ask him to add her name to the London roster, but forbore: it might alert any number of his sensitive nerves. We had all agreed among ourselves that we should forget London and wait for a more opportune occasion, which we decided should be our visit to the Bavaria Studio in Munich, West Germany, world-renowned for its special effects facilities, to film Chong Shim, with music by Aran Ham, a rearrangement of her doctoral symphony. We already had Jungil's tentative approval of the idea. North Korea simply did not have the technical know-how to plausibly depict underwater scenes which account for most of the action in the movie: the hereoine of the legend who sells herself to sailors to be thrown into the sea as a sacrifice to the gods, so that her blind father would regain his sight with the money, is taken as soon as she hits the water by mermaids to the undersea palace for royal recognition and feasting before being sent back to earth to rejoin her father, no longer blind.

"Did you hear from the hospital how Mrs. Moo's operation went?"

"Yes, it was a success. The head of the department, a surgeon of international repute, took up the scalpel himself."

"She was lucky to have had the symptoms break out while in Budapest so they could be correctly diagnosed and treated. Yesterday I was talking to Dr. Jin Nam, Director of the Flame Clinic, who frankly admits that Hungary's medicine is way ahead of ours, even Russia's. Still it was brave of her to go through a major surgery all alone in a foreign country."

"She wouldn't hear of my coming along, saying my work could not be interrupted."

"What an example of dedication! I hope she will be back with us soon."

"She is recuperating well and will be ready for the London trip."

The mention of London seemed to stop him short, or did I imagine it? The Festival was to open in a week but no word had come down about our preparations for departure, making me wonder whether the trip was still on. Our entry was to be shown toward closing, 12 days after the opening date, so we still had some time for that, but if we were to be there at all, we might as well from the beginning, mixing with other countries' delegates and seeing what they had to offer. However, determined not to betray any anxiety or eagerness on my part for trips abroad, especially to Western countries, I did not refer to the matter again, waiting for him to make the first move. But he did not.

"By Golly," he exclaimed, changing the subject, in childish ardor, perhaps faked, "won't the puppets in the south turn pale with envy when we spring Spring Fragrance on them at the Seoul festival!"

"What festival?"

"Last time we sat down with Doohwan Jun's envoys to talk about normalization, we agreed on cultural exchange as the first step, which means film. We conceded as much as to let them have the first round in Seoul."

"When is it going to be?"

"It was supposed to be New Year's Day, but with them you never know. At the last minute they are apt to develop cold feet and come up with an excuse to put off."

XXV.
Last Hurrah

On December 15th, the opening day of the London Festival, the first team of the delegation, totaling 24 members left for Moscow led by Ingoo Cha. I wanted to leave a few days later separately and join them after picking up Nan at Budapest. Ingoo was to arrange the visas for the entire delegation from the British Embassy in Moscow. What puzzled me was that the delegation had expanded many times the original number requested, 8, seeing that the first team alone had 24. It wasn't difficult what function the excess number played. Three days later, still in Pyongyang, I heard that, visas refused by the British Embassy in Moscow, the advance team had flown to Vienna to try their luck with the Embassy there, though I couldn't imagine what good it would do. Weren't they all under the same British Foreign Office obeying the same directives?

In Budapest four days later, I was relieved to find Nan at our Hyatt suite discharged from the hospital two weeks before and getting housecalls.

"She is recovering well without complications," said the doctor, leaving after his daily visit. "I'll check back tomorrow."

"Wait a minute, Doctor," I said. "She might have to go somewhere tomorrow?"

"Where?"

"Vienna and London."

"Out of the question."

"But the Chief of Surgery assured us that she would be

ready to travel by now."

"I don't know anything about that. No matter what may have been said before the surgery, I am in charge of her post-surgical recovery and I forbid it."

That was final.

"I won't go without you, darling," I said to Nan after he was gone.

"Don't be silly. You go on by yourself. With Aunt Aran in Pyongyang London was not meant to be the place anyway. I'll be ready for Munich and Vienna."

The phone rang. It was Ingoo from Vienna reporting that no visa had been issued yet. It was the 24th, nine days into the Festival.

"It doesn't make any difference, darling," I told Nan, after hanging up, "because nobody is going anywhere."

Two days later, visas still pending, we called the Hongs in New York. The phone rang a long time without anybody answering. We wanted to check on any new developments in their liaison work. Also we were to notify cancellation of "Elizabeth's wedding," and ask in some oblique fashion for information on Gisoon Bag Minsky, my grandmother. As it turned out, we ended up doing none of these. When Jungay finally picked up the phone and recognized our voice, she had a bombshell to drop on us.

"Chansoo is in the hospital with liver cancer," she said, sobbing.

It was some time before Nan and I got over the shock and called the hospital. Under heavy sedation he couldn't talk to us. The news seemed like an omen dooming our plan to escape, dooming everything in life. Wasn't he the picture of health and fitness, the epitome of moderation, discipline, good sense, and humor, everything intended to promote long life? What chances did the rest of us have, living irregularly, impulsively, under constant stress? Or could it be that his life was too well regulated, too perfect, with a hint of hubris? But that meant repudiation of reason, any attempt at rational management. We might just as well revert to instinctual, bestial existence.

Leaving Nan behind I left for Vienna the next day in the company of Soontay Bag. As soon as the Budapest Embassy car crossed the Austrian border, we were greeted by three or four Koreans, who looked vaguely familiar. Following them to their waiting car, everything came together at last. Their leader was none other than Hogun Im, Deputy Chief of Research from Hong Kong who had led the team that abducted us. The young fellow next to him was the one who had stuck a knife to my neck, minus the wig. What a cozy reunion! The young man grinned from ear to ear noticing my recognition of him, as if he expected me to pat him on the back for a job well done.

"They are all waiting for you at the Embassy Guest Quarters, President Moo," Im said.

"Are you coming with us?" I asked.

"Yes," he said, unable to conceal his pleasure.

Our visas came through on the morning of the 28th, one day before the viewing of our entry. The delay of over ten days was caused, it turned out, by a fierce diplomatic skirmish between South and North Korea regarding our entry into Britain. We arrived at Heathrow Airport 7 p.m. and were met by three representatives from the Festival Executive Board and half a dozen Korean students, from South Korea of course, who had volunteered to interpret, guide, and run errands for us, disregarding the risk of their government's displeasure.

"This is an insult," Ingoo Cha blustered, learning the second-rate status of the hotel reserved for us. "It is beneath our dignity."

The reservations were changed to the Tower Hotel, which was top class, where we unpacked. I found myself completely surrounded. The rooms to the left and right were taken by my guards and so were those across the hall. But this was not enough. I had to double with Actor Yoonhong Kim, who had played the role of the secret emissary Wijong Yee in the movie. Whenever I left the room, several followed, boxing me in, even when I went to the post office to mail videocassettes of my films and two boxes of wild ginseng to Chansoo on his deathbed in a New York hospital.

The next day, the viewing scheduled to start at 6 p.m., I went shopping in the morning with my usual retinue, Hogun Im one of them. After picking up some clothes for Nan and me, I stood at the shortest line and put my things on the counter at the register. Hogun, who had come right behind me, dumped an armful of merchandise next to mine. There was no separating stick and I tried to push my purchase away from his, but he nudged and winked at me, meaning I should pay for his, too.

Arriving by a chartered bus in good time at the National Cinema where The Secret Emissary of No Return was to be shown, we found all tickets sold out and dozens of Korean students standing around, unable to get in. Instead of apologizing for our inability to secure their admission, Cha saw this as an opportunity to make a political speech:

"Young generation of Korea! In your socialist fatherland you can study free of tuition. Nobody starves and everybody lives happily and harmoniously following the leadership of our Great Chief Ilsung Kim..."

He blustered on, insensitive to the jeers of his audience, bright students probably from well-to-do families or on scholarship, who couldn't possibly be impressed by free tuition or freedom from starvation.

The 500-seat auditorium was packed full. Halfway into the show Ingoo and Hogun came to my seat and started whispering so loud that I was obliged to take them outside to hush them.

"Whatever it is, couldn't you wait until the show's over?"

"No, it's an emergency. We have important information about some Puppet intellectuals trying to embarrass you during the question and answer period following the presentation with trick questions like the historical inaccuracy of depiciting Joon Yee's death as harakiri. What answers will you give?"

"Leave it to me. I know exactly what to say. In fact, there isn't a single thing they can ask about the film that I cannot dispose of to our advantage."

I was quickly becoming a braggart like my captors. Indeed

on the issue of historical accuracy I was going to plead artistic veracity, often truer than factual, but no such question came up. Perhaps the movie was moving enough to silence the factual skeptic. A few foreigners and a Korean woman asked about the wisdom of using the cinemascope, obsolete in other countries, the poor quality of the subtitles, and the availability of the film in videocassette. Blaming the Eiga Corporation of Tokyo for the poor translation in the subtitles, I promised a better version soon to be made available in the US by NBC. About the cinemascope I could only mumble that it was better suited to spectacles and crowd scenes. From the beginning I wanted to use the standard 35mm which lent itself more readily to TV and overseas exports, but was overruled by Ingoo Cha, who claimed that Jungil liked the wider screen.

When I finally emerged from the theater at about 9 p.m., a group of about 200 Korean students who had been waiting outside waved goodbye to me sadly, as if in commiseration, making my eyes wet.

The bus had gone half a block when Ingoo suddenly told the driver to stop and started yelling at three reporters who had got on, Changnay Bag of the Donga Ilbo, Jayhoon Yee of the Joongang, and Hanggyoo Mang of the Associated News, all with large circulations back home.

"Gentlemen," I called, following them out. "Come to the Tower if you want to talk."

Trained to overlook insults, they showed up by taxi almost at the same time as we arrived at the hotel. I led them into the restaurant where our people had taken a block of tables to order their supper.

"Aren't you wasting your time?" I asked.

"We don't mind, if you don't," said Bag.

"This interview is going to be so different that you won't be able to print it."

"Try us."

"Have you reported that thousands of Gwangjoo citizens, as many as 10,000, have been killed by Doohwan Jun's paratroopers?"

"We are foreign correspondents, stationed overseas, and

don't deal with domestic news."

"Have you seen my film Gwangjoo Is Calling circulated in all overseas Korean communities?"

They shook their heads, lying.

"Doesn't your conscience bother you to watch the perpetrators of the atrocities serenely carrying on as if they haven't done anything out of the ordinary?"

I could see them squirm uncomfortably.

"Will you allow us to ask questions, too?"

"Shoot."

"Is Jungil Kim a vegetable as reported as a result of a car accident?"

"See how hopelessly misinformed you are. He is as healthy and alert as any of us here."

"It's not our fault if we don't know too much about him," Mang said. "All he has to do to put an end to such speculation is hold a press conference like this."

"I'll tell him so when I see him next."

"Do North Koreans accept him as his father's successor?"

"Absolutely. Ilsung Kim has made him his heir, not because Jungil is his son but because the people follow him as an able leader with a far-reaching vision. Remember that dynastic succession has been in fashion longer than any other form of succession in human history because of its built-in continuity and stability."

"How are your film activities in North Korea?"

"Absolutely free. I have made more quality films in the short time I have been there than all those I have in South Korea. For example, Spring Fragrance just completed is something I could never dream of making in South Korea because of the costs. It's a paradise for movie production."

"Only for you," said Yee.

"Quality has a better chance of recognition there than in the south."

"Why isn't your friend Nanyong Song with you?"

"She is my wife."

"Congratulations! Why isn't she with you, then?"

"Do your wives go everywhere you go?"

"No, but she is your star and should have come with you to an international event like this. We have reliable information to the effect that she is held back as hostage so you won't run away."

"See how wrong you are again. We are free to go anywhere we want. Our main sphere of activity is Eastern Europe centered at Budapest, where she is now recovering from her gallstone surgery. You can confirm it by calling at the Hyatt or calling the hospital."

"Don't you want to come home to Seoul?"

"Naturally I miss Seoul. It was my home. I would like to visit but I fear reprisals from Jun worse than ever now that we have released Gwangjoo Is Calling, completing its earlier version Shattered he suppressed, which is sure to pull him down and trample him underfoot with as little mercy as he has shown to his innocent victims."

"Are the Diamond Mountains as beautiful as they say?"

"Words can't describe them," I said, recalling Nan's visit there a few years before, though I hadn't been there myself. "It's absurd you can't come and see them for yourselves, your heritage, every Korean's heritage. The whole peninsula is, south or north of the DMZ. This half century of crime, dividing one nation, got to stop. Don't you hear the wailing of those millions, killed since the division of 1945, whose ghosts won't be laid until the country is unified, their sacrifices redeemed? Lift up your eyes above your immediate divisive interests and catch a glimpse of United Korea, bathed in splendor."

"Are the men in your company all film people?" asked Bag, cutting me short.

"No, some of them are security people protecting me from Jun's assassins."

During the two-hour conference Ingoo Cha and Hogun Im took turns to remind us every five minutes of the lateness of the hour. Parting with the journalists at last, I felt truly sorry for their being in a profession that made them put up with all that abuse and humiliation. My pity turned out to be very much misplaced, however, for it was they who had felt sorry for me all along. Later in the US I saw a newspaper article on this conference by one of the three reporters, saying that I had the word 'hopeless' written on my palm, flashing it secretly to them when my guards were not looking, an absolute untruth. I thought they would be a cut above the others, being London correspondents and all that, but they were just as bad, always spicing up or lying outright for the sensational effect. Nevertheless the interview or immediate publications about it in South Korea did not create any problems for us in Pyongyang, which was all that mattered for the moment.

Before sending the reporters off I arranged a little treat for them: posing with the pretty North Korean actresses for commemorative photos, so these warm bodies might replace or modify their image of North Korea as a cold, sinister monster.

At 5 a.m. next morning my roommate Yoonhong Kim shook me awake and told me to get ready to leave.

"Are you mad?" I shouted. "We just got here. Go back to sleep."

"Deputy Chief Ingoo Cha told us to get ready," he persisted.

The door flew open and the author of the insane directive strode in himself.

"What's this nonsense about leaving?" I demanded. "The Festival is in full swing now and we should make the most of it, participating in all the activities. Good manners alone require us to say goodbye to the Executive Board before we leave."

"We have said goodbye to the Board already," said Soontay Bag, stepping in.

My room was filling up like Victoria Station.

"The tension has reached a crisis point," said Hogun Im, who had also slithered into the room. "We have wire taps on the Puppet Embassy."

They were adamant, apparently carrying out a plan made a long time ago, though no word of it had been communicated to me, head of the delegation. All the decisions were made without me, a mere figurehead. I certainly had no hankering for power and they could have it for all its worth, but I resented being helpless to prevent such utter waste born out of ignorant paranoia. We left the hotel at 7 a.m., our stay in London totaling 36 hours.

To catch the weekly Korean Civil Airliner we had to stop at Moscow. It wasn't my first experience of this mammoth of unreason but I felt it more acutely now that I was implicated through the quarter of my blood. The single purpose of the airport terminal was to offend and exasperate the visitor - complicated entry procedure, lengthy baggage retrieval, universal discourtesy. The same pointless procedure was repeated over and over and each person in authority, whether immigration, customs, schedule information, or directions, did their work with maddening deliberateness, not caring in the least how long the lines got before them. After two hours of standing in line I was finally next. Ahead of me a European male was being looked over from top to bottom and asked all kinds of irrelevant questions. Muttering, he put a cigarette to his mouth.

"Where do you think you are smoking?" the young immigration official barked, looking up from his desk.

"I wasn't smoking," the passenger shouted back. "I just put it to my mouth."

The crowd around us burst into peals of laughter, which rippled through the whole building and set the rafters vibrating for a long time, many not knowing what it was all about, a relief they all needed. I wondered why any sane man had to come to Russia at all and put up with all the indignity.

"This is the weakness of socialism," was the sententious observation of Ingoo Cha, who was right behind me.

I didn't dare join in. For all I knew he might be setting up a trap. Even if he were sincere, as I had no doubt he was, I might intrude in a sibling feud: they might revile and curse each other passionately, yet be totally intolerant of the mildest criticism from an outsider, which I still was, would ever be.

After the immigration we had to go through another 30 or 40 minutes at the baggage claim. Baggage carts were in such short supply that one had to follow the carts in use in hopes of getting them when finished. Our suitcases weighing a ton each from all the wild shopping we had done in London, we definitely needed the carts and several of us ran after them, only to return empty handed, the last users giving them up to their favorites, which did not include us from North Korea.

But my frustration and anger at the airport evaporated: waiting at the hotel was the greatest prize I could hope for.

"When did you get here, love?"

"Yesterday."

"What happened to all the strictest doctor's orders?"

"I don't know. They let me travel the day after you left."

"I see. In the Communist world medical opinion is not strictly medical. So the South Korean reporters were right after all when they said you were being held back as hostage. I laughed at them and lectured them about prejudice."

"Well, who cares. We are together and I am healthy. The day before yesterday I went to West Berlin to get new lenses for my glasses. As soon as we crossed the boundary, my escorts, three North Korean Embassy men and our Party Secretary Soggyoo Yee, took positions around me as if we were entering a combat zone. They were mortally afraid some Korean might recognize me, though I was as well camouflaged as could be, wearing dark sunglasses and short-haired wig. Walking here and there in search of an optometrist shop, I noticed an Oriental couple coming toward me. When we were about thirty feet apart, the woman's eyes widened. I turned my head aside, but heard her saying to her husband as we passed that it was me, Nanyong Song, and her husband telling her that it couldn't possibly be because I was in North Korea. I felt as if my heart would burst, not being able to own up and greet and embrace my own countrymen in a foreign city. After that my guards bugged me so much that without visiting any other place I had to hurry back to East Berlin."

Anxious though we were to return home, we had to wait three more days for the flight. Making the most of our enforced sojourn she went to the nearest District Service Center with Secretary Yee of the Embassy as interpreter to shorten the skirt she had bought in West Berlin. After waiting one hour in line, Nan was able to turn in her skirt to the clerk, who told her to return two days later. Nan went back on the appointed day for her skirt. Another receptionist was there, the previous one nowhere in sight. When presented with Nan's claim check the girl brought back the same old skirt, unaltered.

"You haven't done a thing to it," Nan said, suppressing her anger.

"I don't do anything," the girl shot back. "I just hand over what those in the back give me."

"I didn't bring it to be just looked at."

"Come inside and put it on to show me what's to be done."

In the fitting room Nan waited 30 minutes with the skirt on, but the receptionist did not come to her and kept gabbing away with her friends. Unable to wait any longer, Nan raised her voice and called the girl.

"It can't be altered, so take it back," she said after a cursory look at it.

"Why can't it?"

"Because there is a backlog of previous orders."

Nan unleashed a barrage of invective aimed at the girl and Soviet system in general, colorful enough to start World War III. Wisely, Secretary Yee did not translate and consoled her.

"I am used to it," he said with a bitter smile. "To live in Moscow one has to be under anesthesia."

All the shops had salesgirls who chatted on among themselves. When a customer went in and asked for something, they said "Nyet" and went right on talking. To merely go inside and pick the stuff one wanted, one had to stand in line. When our turn finally came and we were allowed to go in and look for the desired merchandise, we were left entirely on our own in this search: there was no guide or directory. If we couldn't find anything, either because the store didn't have it or we didn't know where to find it, it was our tough luck. If we found something, then again we stood in line at the cash register to prepay for the item, where, as may be imagined, the greatest congestion occurred, because the cashier did her sums with abacuses or in the head unaided by computers or calculators and had to start all over again because she got the figures wrong. But you are not done yet, even if you get through this hurdle by some miracle: the receipt has to be taken to another window for the clerk to give you the goods. Simply there was no sense of responsible work and inferior quality was the order of the day, but nobody knew any better and made no attempt to improve.

Next day we went with Interpreter Yee to the Farmers Market, a sprawling warehouse, one of the dozen or so in Moscow where farmers brought the crops raised from their privately owned plots. In the Soviet Union a farming household was leased about an acre of land which they cultivated on their own time after work at the collective. Whatever they got out of the private lot they were free to sell at the market, crowded and noisy like the South Gate Market of Seoul and abounding in produce, fruit, meat, honey, cheese, flowers, and clothes. Hoarse from outshouting each other, the sellers were excited and in high spirits. One man, a Tartar, offered me a handful of peanuts to taste.

"Just taste," he said, grinning confidently. "You don't have to buy."

The marketplace was a veritable kaleidoscope of ethnicities and nationalities, White Russians, Central Asians, Southerners, Northeast Asians.

"Doesn't he look like a Korean?" Nan asked me, pointing at a peddler of sweet potatoes in his 40's.

"Yes, I am a Korean," said he, overhearing.

"Imagine running into a Korean in the middle of Moscow," Nan said. "Do you live near Moscow?"

"Near Vladivostok," he answered.

"That's the other end of the continent," I said, thinking he might be living at the very spot where my grandfather Josef built his first ranch.

"Imagine running into a White Russian who can speak better Korean than me," he said in surprise.

His Korean was a bit rusty.

"Why did you come so far?"

"Because business is good here. It took me 15 days to get here by train with all the merchandise, which includes my neighbors' who are all Koreans. I'll be on my way back as soon as I sell everything."

"How long have you lived in the Far East?"

"From my parents' time. They've all died."

"How about your own family?"

"I am all by myself. My wife ran away because she didn't care for my extended trips like this as a traveling salesman."

So there were certain constants in human relations, no matter what the race, politics, or culture.

"I am sorry," Nan said.

He laughed as if he found her sympathy comical.

"You can't be from North Korea," he said, noticing how well dressed we were. "Do they live well in South Korea?"

"Yes, they do," Nan said, not caring what Secretary Yee standing nearby might think.

Wishing to give him some business, she picked a bagful of his goods and asked for the price, but the merchant refused to be paid.

"It's on me, my gift to you, beautiful lady," he said, gallantly.

Thanking him for the compliment Nan stuck the bills in his pocket before dashing off.

Next to the Farmers Market, on the other side of the partition, stood the Collective Shops, which were almost empty of custom. The contrast was most striking. Prices might be lower but poor quality prevailed. For example, cabbage and other produce were still caked with dirt. Even when prospective customers came by, the shopkeepers didn't bother to look up, let alone shout their wares. Predictably, the private plots, less than one-tenth of the total Soviet acreage, accounted for one-third of Russia's annual food supply. All that vaunted collective technology and mechanization amounted to nothing, because plants grew better with the owner's tender loving care. The Soviet government had to tolerate this much concession to capitalism, contrary to the basic tenets of socialism. The Utopian society envisioned by it simply did not work. The colossal failure of the Soviet experiment was a sad commentary on human nature. Human beings will be human beings no matter what with their greed and selfishness. No amount of appeal to ethics, idealism, or religion will change this basic reality and all social and economic planners had better take this axiom into account, like gravity or mass in physics. As it is, Russia had become a vast serfdom, an entrenched caste system, with power concentrated in a few who lived beyond the wildest extravagances of the old Russian aristocracy Bolshevism set out to destroy.

Days passed after our return from Europe but Jungil did not call though the year was ending. On New Year's Eve Ingoo brought Jungil's message, asking us to come to his office at 4 p.m. by his limousine to be sent to our office. It was just like Jungil to come down with a summons like this at the last minute. It being New Year's we had gone home earlier than usual, but had to hasten back to the office to meet our transportation, a Benz 600 in which Ingoo was waiting.

Jungil met us in his conference room with the long table, but this time with Ingoo at one end next to him and us at the opposite end. In a light mood he talked rapidly just about everything that came to his head, movies, the latest scandals in Seoul, including Yoonhee Jung the TV star's adultery. Of course we had come armed with our tape recorder but the value of the recorded material looked doubtful. However, more relaxed, he didn't quite monopolize the conversation as before and permitted our input now and then.

"The Great Chief was very pleased by Spring Fragrance and wants to meet you on New Year's Day tomorrow," Jungil said. "It was during his tour of the countryside when he wanted some diversion that I showed it to him. After watching it, he said you really know how to make movies."

"Let's not forget that Aran Ham with her music makes all the difference," I said, seizing the opportunity. "Her genius will show to real advantage in the forthcoming Chong Shim to be shot in Munich."

"Sure. Have you made arrangements with the Bavaria Studio?"

"I am going to meet their representatives soon in Berlin."

"For years the Chief has been receiving and reading your moving letters, Mrs. Moo," Jungil said, making Nan wince. "Each time he wanted to meet you but something came up or his underlings slipped up, preventing it. This time he wants to see you tomorrow morning without fail. When you meet him, just show your determination to work hard for the great fatherland and he would be most encouraging. How many prints of Spring Fragrance have we made?"

"Six, Comrade Leader," Ingoo said.

"Shouldn't we get more printed in Japan?"

"Yes. We need about 200 more, enough to send to all the ethnic communities as before with Gwangjoo Is Calling, except this time it is in color and deals with our folklore and music with no political overtones. They should learn about their rich heritage and tradition."

He turned the conversation to the South and North Korea talks currently under way.

"I thought we had an agreement in principle, cultural exchange to begin with New Year, but again they have cold feet, as I predicted. They will think about the date and let us know. Now who will be denounced by history for blocking unification? Anyway, the first cultural item we will show will be Spring Fragrance, which will stagger them, make them really sit up at attention."

"Chong Shim would be even better," I had to keep plugging.

"Sure. Can you get it ready that soon?"

"I'll try to get the next available spot at the Bavaria Studio. In London I told the South Korean reporters all about the movie, whetting their appetite as it were."

Was it diplomatic to talk about the London affair?

"Talking of London," I decided to speak out, come what may, "I couldn't understand why after spending so much money and taking so much trouble to get there we had to slink away at break of dawn like a bunch of deadbeats run out of town, a conduct, the Executive Board might think, unworthy of an invitee to the prestigious Festival."

My worry was fully justified by the event. The film Salt with Nan as principal actress won the Best Actress Award at the Moscow Film Festival next year and I expected another invitation from London, but it never came. Once was enough for the Executive Board to be caught in the South and North Korean crossfire.

"I am satisfied with everything, the Festival, the press conference," Jungil said. "But remember that the reporters were actually the pawns of the Security Ministry and were feeling you out. Instead of filing stories with their home offices, they were reporting to the Ministry directly, giving their impressions and assessments. You succeeded in baffling them. They said you seemed to be speaking your mind freely unlike the so-called defectors reading from a script, but on the other hand you couldn't because you were surrounded by guards and your wife was held as hostage. All this came out in the 23 communications intercepted between London and Seoul. So from now on they shall see you both attending international conferences freely."

I could not believe my ears: he was practically pushing us into freedom.

"Why don't you travel yourself while the Chief is still alive," I changed the subject to hide my excitement. "Once you take over power, you may not be able to get away at all."

"Be my eyes and ears in the meantime," he said. "Whenever you come across something unusual, videotape it and show me. I'll rely on your judgment. One can't be everywhere and see everything in life anyway."

On New Year's Day we went to the annual New Year party at Ilsung Kim's residence on Mt. Silk Embroidery. At the first checkpoint we were about to step out of our car for inspection, when somebody came running to tell the sentries to wave us through. At the front entrance a guide met and took us directly upstairs, dispensing with double and triple inspection. In the anteroom were Politburo members and Party and Administration heads of ministerial rank, some of whom we had met at Jungil's parties. However, from the large number of strangers it was clear that the two centers of power, father and son, had different sets of adherents. Among those who came over to shake our hands were Defense Chief Jinoo O, Foreign Affairs Chief Yongnam Kim, Deputy Premier Songchol Bag, Chief of the Interior Jangyop Hwang, and

Research Chief Jongsoog Hu, the Iron Lady as she was called. After waiting about ten minutes the Chief of Protocol came in and led us to the Reception Room. As we were entering, somebody ran up to us to give the tip, "The Chief is hard of hearing, so speak a little loud when you address him." I almost suggested a hearing aid, but of course held my peace.

In the middle of the reception room, about 300 square feet wide, stood Ilsung Kim, formerly Sungjoo Kim, in dark blue suit and grey necktie, who could have been my uncle, with two or three aides and his wife Songay in blue velvet skirt and coat, his former secretary. Little did they suspect how much I knew about them! This was the first time Nan or I had come so close to the supreme ruler, still ruddy, almost youthful, and in good health in spite of his 70 odd years. Stepping in front of them we bowed.

"Happy New Year!" Ilsung said first, offering his pudgy hand.

"We wish you health and longevity, Great Chief," Nan said loudly, shaking his hand.

I mumbled something to that effect, too, but not as loud. With us to his left and right he faced the camera. Seated on the sofa, flanked by us with Songay next to Nan, he let more pictures be taken, in all of which the First Lady was studiously excluded. Did his superman image require disssociation from a frailty like a wife or could it be that at heart he disowned his expedient alliance to Songay, his former secretary and babysitter, considering himself really married to Aunt Aran, the small detail of the unwilling bride aside? Our miniature tape recorder was spinning faithfully in Nan's bag which, growing bolder, she had put between her and Ilsung instead of on her lap.

"Are you okay after the surgery?" Ilsung asked.

"Yes, thank you, sir," she answered.

"The operation was in Hungary?"

"Yes."

"Your works are all excellent, Secret Emissary, Spring Fragrance, Escape, and what else?"

"Love, Love, My True Love."

"What?"

Nan repeated and he repeated after her, nodding and grinning. Couldn't she have mentioned some other titles like Separation, Jetty, or even Gwangjoo Is Calling instead of Love, Love, My True Love? Was it possible that she, a scion of Eve, was flirting with the most powerful man in the land? Power was always the strongest aphrodisiac. Utterly groundless though such suspicion was, I found myself becoming actually jealous, as if I were still in prison, perhaps realizing my impotence and vulnerability. If he wanted her, I had no means of stopping him, the autocratic warden of North Korea, a prison except in name.

"What are you working on now?" he was addressing me.

"Mayoress of Koreatown, Salt, and Chong Shim, among others, sir," I said.

"What are they about?"

While I explained, reconciling as best I could the antithesis of synoptic clarity and dramatic detail, Songay and Nan chatted amiably as if they had known each other for years. Later she told me that the First Lady, speaking for her husband, wanted more films made based on historical material. But that's exactly what I had been telling Jungil in my letters from prison. Could she or her husband have read them and influenced my release? As might be expected, Nan promptly told her that we had a score of projects exactly along this line, beginning with Genghis Khan.

"We want peaceful unification," Ilsung Kim said to me at one point. "This year there should be more contact, but those in the south are thinking of joining the UN as two separate Koreas, though that's the surest way to perpetuate the division. Our position is that we leave our systems alone, have two governments but one nation, like a federal entity, which singly joins the UN. That way at least internationally we are not permanently divided. But they won't listen. Reagan is not helping either, referring to us as two Koreas to please Japan."

Unlike Jungil who struck his listener as unstable if energetic, the father spoke unhurriedly with the degree of self-assurance and authority only a man in complete control was capable of. He was so persuasive in fact that I would have probably believed his every word had I not known him for what he was, Sungjoo Kim, the back alley bully and would-be raper of my aunt, the mass murderer of my kinsmen and of many more millions. Indeed you've come a long way, Sungjoo, my inner voice said condescendingly. But then who hasn't? Haven't I, Churn Dung of the Mercy Home, now face to face with the mighty one? Doesn't a guy have a right to change, to a second chance? Whatever his past, he could have become a new man, with new ideas which could be the salvation of the land. Even if he hadn't and was indeed the Demon incarnate denounced by my mother, couldn't he be saying the right thing? Should the text be thrown out with the author? All the tension and nervousness had departed and I felt strangely at ease, serene, receptive, perhaps because I felt superior to him, knowing so much about him without his suspecting it in the least.

"So for this Federated Korea," he continued, "we may come up with a brand new name like Goryo, or Gogooryo, or even Bagjay, but not Shilla, because that little viper nation induced Tang to attack and destroy her neighbors, critically shrinking our living space from Manchuria to the peninsula. You know your history, don't you, President Moo? When we have this Federation, tension will ease out gradually and one can travel freely from south to north and vice versa. But it's beyond me why Doohwan Jun and his moneyed pals want to play into Japanese strategy and keep Korea divided forever."

"Why don't you offer something radical, something the south can't refuse, like total abdication?" I said. "You will gain a permanent place in history, even if you may shorten your rule by a year or two, if that."

"In your work," he went on, not comprehending or pretending not to comprehend, "stress that we should be one nation and unify. We can't go down in history as the generation responsible for dividing the country bequeathed to us whole by our ancestors. We should tolerate the coexistence of two systems in one national framework. The Chinese have been doing it for 100 years with Hong Kong. When I went over this time, Deng Shaoping said before he gets too old he will unify China peacefully, leaving the capitalistic system of Hong Kong alone. So you see coexistence is not infeasible. We should do like the Chinse. We are not after each other's throats here. What do they mean by defeating Communism? Will they be satisfied only if they kill off their 20 million brethren in the north?"

At this point the door opened and members of the Politburo marched in to wish him health and long life.

"Happy New Year," he said, shaking each well-wisher's hand.

"Let's meet again soon," he said turning to us after he was done with the Politburo.

Conversation with him continued off and on as others trooped in to pay their respects. All in all it lasted a total of 75 minutes, when the Chief of Protocol announced that it was time for him to step into the party hall. All rose and headed for the hall, where the less exalted invitees had been waiting for hours in some cases. Following close behind, I noticed him lumbering with shuffling feet, the unmistakable sign of old age. The meeting had revealed how keenly interested Ilsung was in our work. But, then, why hadn't Jungil arranged such a conference with him sooner? Could it be that Jungil considered us competitors and a threat? Or was he still testing us? In any event our meeting him face to face in this fashion meant our initiation, for whatever its worth, into the innermost circle of real power in North Korea.

The party did not begin until Ilsung Kim was done delivering his usual hour-long New Year's message. But the participants took to the cold food with seemingly genuine gusto and raised toast after toast. When Ilsung Kim rose from his seat at the end of the party, a thunderous applause shook the building. As soon as he stepped outside the hall, somebody ran up to the platform and took the microphone.

"I have a surprise for you all," he said. "Thanks to the special favor of our Beloved Comrade Leader Jungil Kim you are all invited to a viewing of the film Love, Love, My True Love by Moo Moo Film at the People's Culture Palace."

At the mention of the title the whole auditorium rocked with laughter even before he was quite through with the announcement, attesting to the popularity of the film, which provided just the right kind of comical relief the strained atmosphere had needed.

The next morning our meeting with Ilsung Kim was carried on the front page of the Labor Daily, a boost to the morale of the Moo Moo Film staff.

The Executive Board of the Cannes Film Festival to which we had submitted Spring Fragrance through the North Korean Delegation at the Paris UNESCO Headquarters wrote back saying Cannes did not consider musicals, a debatable classification. Soon afterwards another letter came through the same channel from Pierre Chambard, the influential French critic and a member of the Executive Board, expressing his regret at the Board's decision overriding his dissent and desiring an interview for a column in Le Monde. He was willing to come anywhere I designated.

Predictably Jungil jumped at this opportunity for another favorable exposure of North Korean film.

"Meet him in Budapest," he said. "That's where your office is anyway. Going all the way to Paris, his territory, would look as if you are begging."

"How right you are!" I agreed.

Since I had no excuse to bring Aunt Aran along on this trip, there was no point in going all the way to Paris. However, to insure Aunt Aran's inclusion on the Munich trip Nan and I deemed it wise to build up some prefilming publicity for Chong Shim. We had Aunt Aran perform and record the entire opera she had composed, which would provide the music for the movie, with dialogue to be dubbed in later.

On February 20 Nan and I left for Budapest accompanied by Soontay Bag and an interpreter, taking with us the Chong Shim music recording and the prints of our films produced so far in North Korea. Apart from the meeting with Chambard Nan was due for a checkup at the hospital where she had the operation. I was pleasantly surprised by Chambard's complete familiary with our work before we came to North Korea. Delighted to get our new prints he gladly undertook the introduction and possible performance of Aunt Aran's operatic symphony.

"It so happens that the Director of the Munich Philharmonic is a good friend of mine," he said. "I am sure he would give it a close look. Its debut may be arranged at the Philharmonic while the movie is being shot at the Bavaria Studio."

It had been a cordial and frank discussion between professionals on a wide range of artistic, technical, and economic problems and new directions and challenges in movie making. Chambard had enough material to write an insightful article on Korean and Asian film and we had the publicity we wanted. Soontay Bag, our chaperone, was so pleased with the interview that he extended on the spot an invitation to Chambard to visit North Korea, all expenses paid, which Chambard accepted with pleasure.

The next day I ran into Gosha, Kintaro's friend, who wanted to show me a four-hour documentary he had made recently describing a medical breakthrough in cancer treatment. I was out of my depth in the first part that detailed the biochemical process experimentally arrived at by a team of Hungarian researchers, but the second part was quite impressive, as one happy patient after another reported cures or remissions. The treatment was effective especially with cases detected early. I called the Hongs at once and, though skeptical, Elizabeth arrived the next day with Chansoo's urine sample. We drove to the Research Center 200 miles away from Budapest by a car loaned from the Embassy. When the urine analysis showed that Chansoo's case was too advanced for treatment by their method, we all felt crushed, as if we had received our own death sentence. Elizabeth left for home the next morning with a bottle of the new drug to try on her father anyway because she had nothing to lose. Chansoo died a few days afterwards.

In March we stepped up on the filming of Salt for submission to the 14th Moscow Film Festival opening at the end of June. From the start, however, we had so many problems that I almost thought it was jinxed.

Poor acting was one, which was nothing new but became acute especially because we were in a hurry. Used to posing and declamation few actors could give the degree of realistic but subtle and flexible portrayal I wanted. With their preconceptions and settled mannerisms they were harder to direct than a bunch of kids for a school play.

The Cultural Language was a hassle as usual. The screen play called for Hamgyong dialect, but the writers and production managers were afraid to deviate from the standard, fearing the censor. Again Nan and I had to change the whole dialogue.

Since the burden of the story is carried by the mother, the unlettered widow who joins the village band of salt smugglers to support her family and at last understands the greater cause her son is fighting for though at the cost of neglecting his family, her role required a star caliber actress, though the male actor, the son, need not be anybody special. I looked high and low, but there wasn't anybody I was really happy with. Nan had to be it, though she had been operated on only five months before and was still under treatment for postsurgical intestinal adhesion.

Like Escape the primary setting of the film was Manchuria. After taking some preliminary shots at the Pyongyang studios we left for Beijing on March 26 with a staff of over 30, and faked the Manchurian scenes in the suburbs of Beijing with the help of the Beijing Film Studio.

Employed as a maid in a Chinese home, the heroine is raped by the master and gets pregnant. But rape and birthing were taboo in both North Korean and Chinese film, and the crew kept backing away, saying they would get into trouble. Nan and I had to literally push them in front of the camera, reassuring them that we would take the blame, not they. No North Korean actor had seen or been trained in a raping role and couldn't put on a convincing act with Nan, who had to go through the same sequence over and over.

The film had children of 7 or 8 years old appearing, which would have been no problem in North Korea but presented a major hurdle in Red China where children were an endangered species and hard to get under the one-child per couple policy. Families simply wouldn't offer their children to be filmed, as if standing before the camera involved some kind of wear and tear. One scene called for crying children. After training them to cry on cue, we would start cranking the camera, only to have angry parents jump in and snatch them away shouting at us. Nan had to go over and explain the whole rationale through an interpreter, before we got the children back. While doing all this, she had to undergo medical treatment. I couldn't help admiring this wonder woman of a wife and considered myself the luckiest man in the world.

In Beijing, as elsewhere, we stayed at a hotel and the crew at the Embassy quarters. But the honor came with a price tag. Our original understanding was that they would come to us at the hotel for conferences but in practice we ended up going to them because they didn't. It wasn't their fault, either. Unless they moved as a group, individuals were not allowed out of the Embassy compound and special permission had to be obtained each time to come even for important official business. At one time I called the sets and arts people for an urgent conference at the hotel but they didn't show up long after the appointed time. Unable to wait any longer, I left my room in a state and stood before the elevator, jabbing the down button. The door opened, and who should I see but all five of them huddled inside, staring at me surprised and making no move to step out. They had arrived half an hour ago and been closed up in the box, going up and down, because they didn't know how to get off.

Finally filming was over and during the two days we had to wait for the Civil Airliner I wanted them to go on a tour of the Great Wall, but Soggyoo objected, quoting a Jungil Kim directive according to which friendship between China and Korea might suffer if Koreans saw this symbol of conflict between Old China and Gogooryo, the Korean Empire in Manchuria. Of all the inane directives attributed to Jungil this must take the cap. I couldn't imagine a single Chinese who might be offended by a Korean seeing the wall, constructed nearly two thousand years ago, but we had to let it go at that. Only Nan went to the Great Wall, while the rest were sent to the various old palaces in town, including the Forbidden City.

Upon return to Pyongyang we mobilized the same helicopter and plane used when filming Escape to go to the White Head Mountains for the winter shots. We couldn't justify Gayma Heights, my parental home, as originally hoped, because the local contacts reported no sign of snow there this late into the spring.

"A suitable opportunity will present itself for sure," Nan said. "Besides it wouldn't be the same without Aunt Aran to show us around."

Aunt had no role in this particular movie and we couldn't easily ask her along without drawing unwanted attention.

Fortunately the high altitudes of White Head still retained impressive snow drifts. For the scene where the heroine fords the Yalu with bags of salt on her head Nan had to immerse herself up to her chin for hours in the swift current of the freezing river with chunks of ice floating by, to the awe and admiration of the entire crew. Though pressing on with work I was afraid the strain might prove too much for her so soon after her operation. It did. By evening she was feverish and the doctor had to be flown in from Pyongyang. Fortunately, by next morning her temperature went down. I called for a day of rest, but Nan wouldn't hear of it. It was the last scene of the film, taking place in a snow-covered wood. After an injection Nan came to the selected location and acted before the camera from 8 a.m. to 2 p.m. treading the snow drifts at below-freezing temperatures. Fortunately, soon large flakes of real snow began falling, making the shots most realistic. The forced march under Nan's inspiration paid off and Salt was completed by May 8.

I called Jungil to set a preview date so he could see it before sending it off to Moscow, but he said he didn't have to see it and told me to forward the first print to Moscow right away. He would view another print of it some time later. Indeed there was no time to lose because the deadline for entries had long past. Someone fluent in Russian had to be found immediately to carry it personally to Moscow and ask the Board for its entry in spite of the delay. The next day a spare print was delivered to Ilsung Kim, whose praise of the film as a realistic depiction of the Korean people's suffering in Manchuria stopped any grumbling there might have been about some of its unorthodox elements.

Nan left two days before the opening date, July 1, for participation in the 14th Moscow Film Festival leading the North Korean team of 15 people, including the actors, screen writer, and Soontay Bag. Though Salt was slated to be shown on July 2, I was in Korea until June 30 shooting Korean scenes for Chong Shim to get it ready for the Munich trip and making a copy of Sunset in case none was available outside North Korea.

Begun in 1959 to "promote peace and friendship among nations through the art of film" the Moscow Film Festival was held every other year alternating with Karlovy Vary and had this year 107 nations entering with over 100 works in the competitive division and 400 noncompetitively. Nan and I stayed at the Moscow Hotel which hosted the Festival in its auditoriums and conference halls.

From early morning on July 2 our people were busy with the procedure involved in putting on the show and preparing for the reception to follow. Recalling Karlovy Vary I was worried there might not be enough interest in our entry. Close to 4 p.m., the show time, crowds began arriving in big waves packing the auditorium. The movie began on the nose. Not a sound came from the audience. Nan and I feared that our affluent Western viewers with a completely different set of cultural values might be offended by the extreme poverty of a Korean immigrant family, chased from one place to another by Japanese colonialism in Manchuria during the 30's. But as the movie progressed, we could feel the audience responding positively. A thunderous applause broke out when the showing was over, which grew even louder when the spotlight was directed at our box according to custom blinding Nan and me. Only then I drew a sigh of relief. In the lobby we were assailed by autograph seekers congratulating us on the work. Our reception drew an unexpectedly large crowd. Sensational were our actresses, wearing gold-trimmed and embroidered Korean dresses bought in Seoul a month before through Gyongshig. The guests stood in lines to be photographed with them.

While the Festival ground on, I went to West Berlin with Soontay Bag for three days to meet the representatives of the Bavaria Studio to negotiate the filming of Chong Shim, explaining to them what we wanted done. A formal contract would be signed and payments made at a later date. Meantime the rest of our group participated in the group tours provided by the Festival host. One of these was a trip to Leningrad, popular among the visitors not only for its cosmopolitan atmosphere resembling Paris but also for its exemption from the no alcohol law enforced in Moscow since Gorbachev came to power. Particularly relieved were the North Koreans who stocked up on cases of vodka for the next dry spell.

Another popular tour was the visit to Chekhov's birthplace. So many wanted to go that five buses had to be chartered. A two-hour ride down a two-lane country road took us to a checkpoint, where without any explanation the vehicles were detained over an hour. Finally some of the more vocal passengers went up to the tour leader, who said he didn't have our passes required to go through the checkpoint.

"Didn't you know we need them?"

"We got them all right but forgot to bring them."

"Where are they?"

"At the office back in Moscow. Don't worry. Somebody has been sent to fetch them."

That meant a roundtrip of over 4 hours.

"Those of you who want to wait for the passes may, but those who don't need not."

"What do we do then?"

"Go back to town," the guide said without the least sign of remorse.

Most passengers were hopping mad and opted for the return, leaving only a busload of diehard Chekhov fans behind. Later those who had been patient to the end said that Chekhov's house was in a wood less than a mile away and clearly visible from the checkpoint where the tourists had been stopped. Of course it never occurred to the tour organizers that such a detail might have been of interest to their customers.

On July 12, the day of awards, the grand prix for the best picture went to the Soviet film dealing with indiscriminate Nazi massacres as I had expected, because it was the 40th anniversary of the end of World War II and some anti-Nazi film was bound to be chosen. In the best actress category Nan shared the top spot with Hungary's actress, but in the runoff Nan was voted Best Actress unanimously. We barely managed to make our way out of the auditorium to the lobby through the crush of well-wishers and popping flash bulbs. The press was waiting, including ABC TV, asking Nan what she felt on this momentous occasion.

The Pravda and other major newspapers came out with glowing reviews for Salt and its star Nanyong Song. The Pravda said:

"The charm and passion of the actress who plays the hero's mother heighten the climax of the drama. This difficult role is played with moving, vivid, and masterful artistry. Above all, the film is moving. It belongs to the Korean people and portrays the deep emotions of Korean life. The oppressed people gradually awakening to class consciousness is successfuly handled through unique screen composition..."

For all the wrong reasons for sure, but they liked it and that's all that mattered. The farewell party was held at the Kremlin in a huge magnificent hall with gigantic chandeliers where the most important ceremonies had been held through the centuries. The entire back wall in white marble was filled with the names of distinguished workers of the Revolution. The dinner tables groaned under the weight of food, but the prohibition was in force and no drop of alcohol could be had to the discomfort of many. With that extraordinary Russian sense of timing the band was playing military marches. Only when the guests, all experienced party makers, shouted their preferences, did the band switch to a waltz to which everybody paired off dancing.

The entire film industry, if not the whole city, greeted our arrival at Pyongyang Airport. The award, a major victory by any standard, was given extensive media coverage.

"Our Beloved Comrade Leader is very pleased by your accomplishment," said Ingoo Cha. "He'll call and arrange a meeting to congratulate you in person."

A whole week passed but neither the call nor the meeting came about. Jungil's secretary phoned to say that he was tied up. This was just as well. The less we saw of him, the less guilt we would feel in going through with our plans for departure. West German visas had been applied for, including one for Aunt Aran, and we could leave early next year for the mid-February filming, the earliest available time, at the Bavaria Studio. Except for official contacts we deliberately avoided communication with Aunt Aran for fear of betraying ourselves unwittingly. Nor did we have time for anything other than work, tying up all the loose ends before our final departure from North Korea, our home for nearly ten years.

In August we saw the preliminary print of Promise directed by someone on our staff. The story was promising, a young woman dedicating her youth to the cause of war as a phone operator, but everything else about the film was awful, acting, scenery, dialogue, cinematogrphy. To redo it, Nan took the staff to Bakchon, North Pyongan Province. The Party Secretary suggested bringing the mobile home with bedrooms, kitchen and bathroom, but Nan left by car, saying she would sleep with the rest of them, only to find the mobile home parked and waiting for her when she got there. In the middle of the day she entered it to use the facilities and found it as hot as a sauna. Its airconditioners did not work, though we had asked for their repair repeatedly. North Korea didn't have a technician to fix these Benz products, we were told. Overcome by a heat stroke she had to be sent to Pyongyang with a fever of 103 degrees. But as soon as the fever went down a little she was back on location working at a pace the others couldn't keep up.

At the end of the first day she called a conference to coordinate plans for the next day. Nobody showed up. After waiting a whole hour she had the chauffeur take her to the inn where the crew were staying, a three-story concrete walkup. As usual, the unlighted stairs had no banister and she had to climb to the top floor feeling the sides of the stairwells. At her knock the door opened, overwhelming her with the stench from the room. The tatami mats, covering the floor from wall to wall, were so full of black moldy holes that Nan couldn't find a place to sit. The lone occupant, an actress understudy, offered her a pillow. There were supposed to be four other women, including People's Actress Yonshil Kim.

"Where are the others this late?" Nan asked.

"After supper they went down to the stream for a swim," she said hesitantly. "It's so hot."

Just then Nan was distracted by bugs crawling about on the floor and let out an involuntary scream.

"Why don't you leave the window open?" Nan asked, panting from the stench and heat of the enclosure.

"Then we'll get all the smell from the pigsty right below the window," the girl said, though Nan couldn't imagine anything being smellier than the room itself.

It was understandable why the others had taken off to the stream and weren't returning. After waiting as long as she could for the late bathers Nan conceded defeat and returned to the mobile home to fall into deep sleep in many days. She was awakened at 4 a.m. by loud Ilsung Kim songs blasting out of the public address system. They were so loud she was literally shocked out of sleep. The songs were followed by a reporter who shouted at the top of his voice what county had overaccomplished beyond its production quota and what work lay ahead for the day, and so forth. She was told this was done every morning to wake people up.

From early summer we had been busy filming Iron Eater, a monster movie based on the legend about a child whose diet was metal and who kept growing and growing until it was bigger than the proud palace of the corrupt king and crushed it and its inhabitants under its weight, and Gildong Hong, Korea's version of Batman and Robin Hood combined, Gildong flying about to aid the downtrodden. Though no great lover of supernatural fare, I felt this diversion from our solidly realistic repertoire necessary to make our Chong Shim project seem less extraordinary. To execute both films credibly, however, it soon became plain that more special effects were necessary than available in North Korea. I decided to invite the specialists from Toho Film of Japan and the Bruce Lee Company of Hong Kong. Apart from the obvious benefits to be derived from importing superior foreign technology, this move was intended to demonstrate to Jungil one more time that the movie trade knew no boundaries, political, cultural, racial, its craftsmen trotting all over the globe wherever need be, so he would not be tempted for any reason to revoke his previous authorization of our Munich trip for Chong Shim. When contacted, however, neither group wanted to come to North Korea with its unsavory reputation, especially since the Rangoon bombing by Jungil's agents. I had to give my personal guarantee of their safety over the phone, which ironically they took more seriously than the official one. Double pay in advance also helped. Six Japanese, including Director Nakano, the first man in special effects in Japan, and nine Chinese martial arts experts arrived in Pyongyang at about the same time.

To forestall their disappointment at the closed and regimented life of North Korea I had them taken directly to their quarters, the guesthouses on our compound, where with Jungil's permission the security personnel were allowed to put away their weapons and uniforms and wear civilian clothes as long as the visitors were around. The guests were impressed by the neatness of the city and beauty of the scenic sights but it didn't take them long to catch on. Particularly distressing to them was the total absence of recreational facilities, restaurants, bars, dance halls, brothels. With nothing but work to do they drove themselves to the limit and completed the contracts in half the time it would have taken ordinarily. We had the pleasure of sending them home with their virtues intact to their wives, whose virtue was of course a separate matter and none of our concern.

Chambard wrote from Paris:

"My friend at the Munich Philharmonic is on vacation in

the US but I was able to show Aran Ham's work to Rudolf Kelsen, the famed Director of the Vienna Symphony, who was so taken by it that he is including it in next year's spring concert series opening March 1. I had no idea Korea had such musical genius. Rudolf ranks Aran Ham with the best, Mozart, Verdi, Puccini, Beethoven. I have written an article in Le Monde about it, a copy of which is enclosed, but I want to interview her and do full coverage when you get here..."

I felt I was dreaming. I could have died that very minute with no regret, with a sense of fulfillment, knowing that I had been instrumental in bringing to light this great gift to mankind, Aran Ham. My heart was bursting with pride for her as a Korean, as a kinsman. How extraordinary that she was my aunt, my very own aunt, who had saved me, a premature infant, from certain death. I owed her everything.

With Jungil's blessing, I went to East Berlin accompanied by Soontay Bag and Soggyoo Yee to finalize the Chong Shim deal with the Bavaria Studio. At the Palast Hotel I finally met the legendary Dr. Zuet Debauer, who did the art work for Never Ending Story, among other credits, and Mrs. Fleming, world-renowned for her costume work, who designed for Liza Minelli in Cabaret. The preliminary drafts and designs according to the guidelines I had given before were excellent, showing how well we had communicated. The contract was signed, on condition that neither of them would delegate their work, and paid $400,000, half of the total cost, $800,000, $100,000 a day. It was a bargain, because I had expected it to run twice as high.

Everything went without a hitch. Most of the films projected for the year were in the editing or finishing stages, and nothing stood between now and the trip early next year to Munich and freedom. Jungil called us at our offices a few times and even once at the hotel when we were on location at Gaysong near the DMZ shooting scenes from Gogjong Im by Myonghee Hong, but didn't propose a meeting, which was fine with us as we really didn't have time to spare in our marathon schedule to wrap up before we left.

At 4 p.m. on New Year's Eve Ingoo Cha came to my office

greatly excited.

"Our Beloved Comrade Leader sends presents to all the workers of Moo Moo Film," he said in a tremulous voice. "He was so pleased by the two films, Iron Eater and Gildong Hong that he ordered the presents sent right away."

It was in character for him, an overgrown child artistically, to be so taken by such juvenilia. But, again, the reasons didn't count; the end result did, his continuing to like us and leaving us alone to finish up. Three trucks entered the gate, loaded with the presents. Of course the whole gang, 700 strong, had to assemble at the auditorium for the 'transfer ceremony' where Cha recited the list of gifts: 50 deer, 400 pheasants, 200 wild geese, 200 boxes of tangerines. The geese had been smoked but the deer and pheasants had just been killed. The tangerines had come from Japan.

"Our Beloved Comrade Leader is pleased with the good work you are doing and asks you to keep it up next year under the direction of President Moo and Vice President Song."

Some of the audience were so moved, either by the gifts or by Cha's peroration that they wept. Representatives stepped forward from the ranks to swear allegiance aloud and the whole assembly sang all the five verses of each of the Ilsung and Jungil Kim songs. The Administrator, Party Secretary, and Supply Director got together to work out an equitable distribution. But North Korean equity on this as well as other occasions was strictly hierarchical. The upper echelons got a whole deer or a whole case of tangerines each, but those at the lower rungs received one pheasant or a few tangerines at most. While the gifts were being handed out, some workers couldn't contain their joy and broke out into impromptu dancing. We were told the next day by the Administrator that it had taken them the whole night doling out the gifts. The cost in manpower and time could be imagined with the supply and rationing of products operating along similar lines on the national scale. At least with gifts I would have had a 700-way equal split of everything, but that was not how socialism based on equality worked. It had its own esoteric method of implementing the ideal, which however was not totally free from disaffection. For example, those who had worked close with us received more and were joyful. Sonhee Jang who had starred in Spring Fragrance got a whole deer to the envy of many who complained that as a newcomer she didn't deserve so much, though she might be a star.

On this New Year's Day the customary reception at the Chief's Palace was not held, prompting our speculation that he might be seriously ill. With some 40 key members of the studio we had our own celebration at our office. Drinks flowed freely and food was plentiful. Though a New Year celebration, it was meant to be a farewell party for those who had worked with us closely and diligently. We almost cried, thinking of all the trials and triumphs we had shared, how these good people had given their utmost to work. Our hearts ached at the prospect of separation.

After New Year's Day we began to wrap up our affairs in North Korea one by one. To those we had recruited and trained we gave the last pointers, the trivial but crucial tips in acting and film technique that only experience teaches. It was customary at this time to go over the achievements and accounts of the previous year. All production came to a halt as the various departments held their review and analysis sessions. Going from one group to another Nan and I gave lectures and seminars, emptying out all our accumulated knowledge. Perhaps noticing the intensity and depth of our presentation many of them insisted on videotaping everything, to which we consented without hesitation.

To avoid any suspicion that we were contemplating permanent departure, we went to the construction sites of Moo Moo Film and our new residence. Most of the studio buildings were up and only some more mechanical work remained to be done, which might take a long time, however. Delayed repeatedly because of material shortfalls the new target date was April 15, Ilsung's birthday. I felt guilty to see soldiers forced into the labor shivering with cold and warming their chapped hands over briquette fire. The studio was very easily the largest in the world with a total floor space of 65 acres, three sound stages of several acres each, two about half as large, 6 recording rooms, 5 auditoriums, property warehouses, production offices, and 300 rooms for general storage. To prevent voltage drop during filming or recording a 2,000 KW transformer was installed. An apartment building was attached behind the studio to accommodate employees working overnight. The cranes, cameras, lighting, furnishings, window treatments, plumbing, and elevators were imported, the total expenditure of foreign exchange close to $100 million. Our house, about 200 meters away from the studio complex, was also nearing completion in the ultramodern ranch style Nan had picked out from an American architectural magazine.

Nan and I gave away as many things as we could to our employees and friends, clothes, cosmetics, shoes, hats, gloves, and accessories. Some time ago Nan had obtained from Jungil exemption from the general ban against gift giving on the pretext that acting was a special profession whose practitioners had to look more sophisticated than the general populace. Since this was January, when gifts were normal though from the father and son only, our giveaways did not attract particular attention.

We began packing our luggage and carryon items. Curiously there was very little we wanted to bring from North Korea, except some of our pictures and tapes of conversation with Ilsung and Jungil. Apart from the print of Sunset we didn't want to take any copies of our movies, which would have filled a trunk. We had to be selective about our photographs, thousands of them, which obviously could not all be taken.

It was a cold but clear sunny day. Nan and I led Aunt Aran in brown fur coat and blue scarf down the sandy beach to the waiting helicopter we had signed out ostensibly to look for a suitable location for our first project of the year, Sunggay Yee, the movie based on the life of the founder of the Yee Dynasty, known to be a native of Gayma Heights, my ancestral homeland. The helicopter put us down on the rim of a canyon with a breathtaking view. A few miles to the east lay Chongjin, the naval base, the starting point of the Exodus of the Hams and Minskys and other church family. The canyon was at the foot of the high country, Gayma Plateau, the roof of Korea. The snow country unfolded like Shangrila in all its purity and grandeur, unspoiled, unaging. Rolls of shimmering peaks rose and marched away majestically into the mist of the distant skyline.

With Aunt Aran between us we walked down the road cut into the crystalline rocks glistening flesh red or purple through the towering primeval pines and firs that swayed under the weight of their white canopies. Below the steep cliffs of feldspar the path followed the arrow-straight stream outlined by a three-foot thick ice cover between jagged banks of gneis, lined with larches, oaks, poplars, leafless and hoary but vibrant with stored vitality. The unfreezable stream bubbled under the ice cover resounding like a gigantic instrument that filled the valley with a soothing hum. An arch over the road bore the sign, Gayma Livestock Collective, replacing the old one, Snow Country Ranch.

The basin was dotted with buildings and fenced yards so planned as to blend and harmonize with the surroundings, the whole giving the effect of an open air cathedral. The steep sides formed the walls, the stream the center aisle, the stables and barns, pens, sheds and feeding lots on either side the pews. The homes of the residents, built upstream on the higher ground, formed the steps to the waterfall at the head of the stream, the altar. Did my grandfather, a scientist, an independent, freewheeling thinker from all accounts, build this temple to worship Nature like the Stonehenge or Pyramid, except, unlike the others, his served a pragmatic end as well? A clever man bargaining with his God and coming out ahead!

"Even Ilsung has sense enough to leave everything as he found it," Aunt said. "They built it all by themselves, your grandparents Josef Minsky and Gisoon Bag, who had come from Russia empty-handed. The valley had nothing in it but an abandoned logging camp."

"Which was their house?"

"There!" she pointed at a log house of about ten rooms, with the sign Collective Office above the doorway, at the highest point in the canyon on one side of the waterfall. "That was your father's room closest to the fall. The noise never bothered him. In fact, he said he never heard it."

"This is the third log house I see," Nan said.

"Where do you think Ilsung got the idea for the other two?" Aunt said.

Just behind the house soared a tall chestnut tree, under which my father and mother must have played. What wouldn't I give to bring them back to life and have them revisit their childhood home with us and retrace their sweet memories!

XXVI.
D-Day

The itinerary included Budapest, West Berlin, Munich, and Vienna, which meant three Western cities and therefore three opportunities to effect our escape. In West Berlin we had Jungil's permission to attend the 7th Berlin Film Festival beginning in the middle of February, though we were not participating. South Korea was and we disdained to compete.

At 9 a.m. on January 29 we got into our separate Benzes to the shouted chorus of "Be back soon safely!" from our domestic staff lined up in front of the house. It was with a mixed feeling that we left Jungil's villa, our home for the last three years and more. On the one hand we didn't want to return, but on the other we already missed its luxury, prestige, and the devotion of our servants who openly wept, waving. Our entire baggage consisted of two suitcases, one for each of us, the sum total of our decade long stay in North Korea. As usual we were driven straight to the planeside. Placing my hands on his shoulders I thanked and said goodbye to my chauffeur who had taken me everywhere in cold or heat, night or day, taking utmost care of my comfort and safety. Nan was doing the same thing to her driver, except she seemed to be crying. I hoped he wouldn't take it extraordinary and report it. We met the rest of our group, 27 altogether, two thirds of whom were security personnel. We looked for Aunt Aran but she was not among them. Our hearts sank. Could Ilsung have had a last minute change of heart? In a few minutes, however, a stately limousine, perhaps Ilsung's own, pulled up right by the stairway so she could mount the steps directly ahead of anyone else. Finally, she was being accorded the dignity that was long overdue. Suppressing our impulse to shout and embrace her, we greeted her most formally and correctly and she in turn nodded to us in her distant, chilling way, as she ascended past us.

Seeing us off were the top echelons of the North Korean film bureaucracy, Party Art Chief Dongho Yee, Film Library Director Soontay Bag, Party Secretary Soggyoo Yee, Chief of Administration Inam Byon, and others. Bidding bon voyage warmly and sincerely, they seemed dearer, no longer the insidious tools of oppression and imprisonment. At most they were fellow prisoners who had no other choice. The Civil Airliner took off shortly after 10 a.m. Through the window the mountains and rivers receded, gleaming in the morning sun. We fervently prayed for God's protection of our 20 million countrymen trapped there in unbreakable chains, unable to get out like us. As if to dramatize the fact, the p.a. blared away with the Ilsung Kim Song, "The bloody trail on the ridges of the Jangbayk Mountains..." as soon as the plane leveled off after a short climb. However, this execrable tune was strangely nostalgic and even sweet to my ears that morning.

We were pleased to find Aunt Aran seated by the window on our side in the first row of the first class cabin, two rows away from us. One row ahead of us on the opposite side sat Deputy Premier Songchol Bag, whom I had met a few times at various functions but never really had a chance to talk to and get acquainted. In our complex state of mind, neither Nan nor I caring to start new acquaintances, she had her eyes closed in thought, head resting on the back of the seat, and I was bent over the screen plays of Worhyang Gay the Courtesan of Pyongyang and Songs of Old Man Chay, which had been assigned as next projects to the junior directors of Moo Moo Film before we had left. But Bag kept turning his head in our direction, trying to catch our attention. Finally, shortly before the plane touched down at Moscow, he came over and asked where we were headed.

"To Berlin and Munich," I said. "Where are you bound

yourself, Deputy Premier?"

"Bucharest to attend the Rumanian Communist Party Congress," he said, twisting his lips in distaste. "The same old tedious business. I wish I could be doing what you are doing. I like your work a lot and hope to see more of it."

I was touched by his candor, most unusual for a man of his high position. He would have bared his soul if we could talk more. Was it my Caucasian face, the permanent stamp of strangeness, that disarmed his customary caution, or did he know that all his secrets were safe with us who wouldn't be back in North Korea again?

They put us with Aunt Aran at the Moscow Hotel, though we had not asked for it. Things were obviously working in the right direction. Except for the guards who took the adjoining rooms, the rest went to the Embassy quarters as usual.

In Budapest the first order of business was the contract on Genghis Khan I had procrastinated long enough. We had decided to go ahead and sign anyway. Perhaps Jungil could find somebody to finish the project or perhaps we could offer to come and finish it after our defection, if he was man enough to take it. At the present stage it was crucial that it be signed so as to fill up our agenda for the next two or three years. The total came to $26 million, about a third of what it would have cost to do elsewhere. A deposit of $5 million was paid by check drawn on the Moo Moo Film account with the Bank of America, Vienna.

The next day we had a cordial phone conversation with Helmud Pandler, our Austrian partner, who would meet us in Vienna in March and finalize our joint partnership.

"I have read about the forthcoming Philharmonic performance of Chong Shim," he said. "I'll have it recorded in full and try to distribute. The cost will run around $20,000 for about 30,000 copies. Any objections?"

"Of course not. Shall I send the check over?"

"No, I'll pay and you can reimburse me for your share. I'll have all the receipts and vouchers in triplicate for your deputy, Secretary Chay of the Embassy here."

"Thank you."

"Any idea when the film itself will be completed?"

"Shortly after the trip to Munich. It's just a matter of editing and putting together for the final print at the studio in Pyongyang."

"You know it may not be a bad idea in the future to do the final assembly here. I know studios you can rent for practically nothing."

"Great. We'll discuss that when we get together."

He was our partner strictly at the distribution end, making copies of our originals and marketing them, but I wouldn't mind having him as partner all the way from the production end, too. Maybe he would underwrite half of Genghis Khan, but I would need Jungil's okay on it, which would be never under the circumstances.

February 16, Jungil's birthday, was nearing and we would have to hasten to write the congratulatory letter if we wanted it to reach him in time.

"Let's forget it this time," Nan said. "We are abroad, busy with our work. He would understand."

"He would appreciate it even more therefore," I insisted.

"You do it then. It's a torture to pile up one flattering lie after another while plotting betrayal."

Betrayal indeed, because except for the initial crime, to which he was driven by necessity perhaps, he had been good to us, putting his trust in us. On this trip he had deposited $25 million in the Moo Moo account, to which I alone had access. More people would have trusted their wives rather than large sums of money like that. On the other hand, I had to steel myself, conjuring up the haggard, bleached faces of the political prisoners slowly dying at Prison No. 6 and the 20 million others, who just lived in a bigger prison, ground down by toil and idolatry.

"Let's work on it together, psyching ourselves to it, expressing our genuine good wishes, because we like him and thank him for the many good things he has done for us. That is in the past, and we are not lying about that. Just forget about our plans for the future, which is uncertain and unknown anyway."

"That's sophistry and you know it."

"But I thought it was you who wanted to leave, not so much me."

"We have your aunt to think of now."

"The more reason why we cannot afford any slipups. We shouldn't feel guilty about the letter, which is necessary to insure 100% success of our plan, if for no other reason."

We devoted the next two days to the composition of a long, fervent congratulatory letter, which was sent to Pyongyang by special messenger.

Accompanied by Party Film Instructor Dognam Bag Nan and I left Budapest and met our party, including Aunt Aran, who had been left behind, at Moscow Airport to catch the Aeroflot to East Berlin. The first thing Nan did upon arrival in Berlin was to buy new clothes for all our actresses and dancers to put them in the peak of fashion. Though she would have taken Aunt Aran to the most expensive couturier in town, she didn't feel its necessity. The sheer elegance of the blue silk dress Aunt Aran had on, designed and sewed by herself, could dignify even the Queen of England.

That night we called Jongay Hong and asked her to come to West Berlin to meet us during the Festival. She sounded as if she had gotten over her bereavement and agreed to be there. We wanted to give her the pictures and tape recordings to lighten ourselves in case we had to make a run for it. Also she could warn the US authorities of our impending action, with an increase in our number by one, Aunt Aran.

"Could you also find out about the whereabouts and circumstances of a Mrs. Gisoon Minsky, maiden name Bag?"

"Widow of Dr. Josef Minsky, Minister of Agriculture and Forestry under Syngman Rhee?"

"Do you know her?"

"Of course. She is the grand matriarch of the New York Korean community and a member of my church. Why do you want to know?"

Overcome by this information I was speechless for a few seconds.

"Never mind about her for now. You have told me enough.

I'll call you back."

Nan and I went to Aunt Aran's room with a pair of boots, gloves, and a mink coat, the need for which must be self-evident to our guards. The February temperature in Berlin was near zero.

"We'll just leave things where they are," Aunt Aran concluded. "We know all we have to know, that she is alive and well. To have her come here or anywhere, even if she is willing and able to make the journey, would only complicate matters. When we are in the US, we'll see her to our hearts' content. I hoped but didn't seriously think I would see her in this life again. I haven't survived my prison for nothing."

"Golly, I can't wait to see my own grandmother in flesh."

Any indecision or sense of guilt I might have had about leaving North Korea evaporated. It was my birthright and duty to establish and reconfirm my ancestry, my roots. Even Jungil must understand that. Hadn't he applauded Separation, denouncing South Korea for not doing enough to rejoin the families separated by war? If I told him outright about my grandmother, he might just grant me a leave of absence to go see her on humanitarian grounds alone. But who was I kidding? The kidnapper would never let his prize go. He would certainly hold Nan and Aunt Aran back as hostage if he let me go at all. Most probably he would try to lure my grandmother into his clutch, too, using us as decoy.

Our security, tight as it was, was beefed up by a dozen more burly types, ostensibly Embassy personnel but most probably dispatched from Pyongyang specially for the occasion, one of whom introduced himself as President Sunghwan Chun of the Film Supply Corporation, whose existence I hadn't heard of before.

Crossing the border from East to West Berlin the eyes of our guards glittered in alertness. The suite at the Hyatt had two bedrooms with a sitting room in between. We occupied one and Aunt Aran the other. Our guards stayed in the room across the hallway, with the door left ajar at all times, flouncing out after us whenever we went anywhere. The other members were put up at the Embassy as before.

An invitation was waiting from the Mayor of Berlin asking the three of us to attend a 6 p.m. reception at the Hilton, a 15-minute drive from where we were. Sunghwan Chun had us get into the backseat of the Embassy car, himself taking the seat next to the driver. Another car, maybe a rental, followed crammed full with other buddies of his.

The party was already in full swing with representatives from the 100 or so participating nations. Somebody tapped me from behind. It was Chambard, looking most distinguished in a black tuxedo.

"You look like the Duke of Normandy," I said admiringly.

"It's silly but as head of our delegation I am supposed to dress up. Incidentally, how did you know I was a duke?"

Of course I had no idea he had been one.

"It shows like the color of your skin. Blood will assert itself."

"You are a fine one to talk about blood after all that philippic against genetic bondage?"

"Where did you hear about it?"

"From Enoki of Asahi. I have read his article, which made such good reading that I translated it for Le Monde."

During an interview with Enoki in Budapest some time ago, before confirmation of my parentage, I had held forth at length on the global necessity to eliminate obsession with one's 'roots', genetic bondage, the root cause of all the destructive, divisive passions.

"Forget it. It was just a phase. There is somebody I want you to meet, my, eh, Miss Aran Ham, with whose work you are already acquainted."

"The Puccini of the Orient. What an honor, Ma'am!"

Soon Aunt Aran was holding court with Enoki, Kintaro, Gosha, Metternich of Austria, and others, with me as the happy interpreter. Only if I could tell them that she was my aunt!

I happened to notice walking in the door Jimi Hwang, Nan's protégée who had become the top star of South Korea after we left, accompanied by her sister-in-law Bokhee Cha, the singer. They had come straight from the airport, not at all expecting to see us.

"Have you been all right, Big Sister?" Jimi said, holding Nan's hands, eyes filling with tears.

"I have survived," Nan said. "Glad to see you doing so well."

"Luck is with me so far. Since you left, I have established Jimi Film, which has produced 30 movies already. How are you, Director Moo?"

"Fine, working like an ox."

"You look great. That reminds me. Please come and watch Oxen I star in with Chunil Jin to be shown three days from now."

"We won't miss it for the world," Nan said. "How are our friends?"

"All doing well. Unhee Chay got the best actress award at the Asian Film Festival held in Seoul, and Gumnyu Doo got reunited with her twins' father. Did you hear about Mihay So's affair with Jino Yoo?"

"No."

"The scandal dominated the gossip columns for months. They both got divorced from their spouses, and got remarried, but the children were a problem, especially with the new one they had between them. With that kind of rocky start the marriage didn't have a chance. So they are now drifting back to their former spouses, who had in the meantime developed other attachments of their own. Oh, it's a holy mess all around. Do they have anything like that in North Korea?"

"Humans will be humans everywhere," Nan said, not knowing which was worse, brutal suppression or holy mess.

"Call me at my room, Big Sister," Jimi shouted as she was taken away by the South Korean Consul General in West Berlin, an arrogant brute who didn't even apologize for the interruption. "We have a lot to catch up."

At 9 p.m. we left the lobby, fully expecting the cars with our bodyguards to be waiting at curbside, but they were not in sight. We went up and down the block, but they seemed to have vanished without a trace. Then we found them across the street, too busy to notice us: they were being questioned by a squad of West German police.

"This is the moment we have been waiting for," Nan whispered excitedly. "Let's grab a taxi and drive to the US Embassy."

"Are they open at this hour?" Aunt Aran asked.

"We'll just tell the Marine guard that we are seeking asylum."

I was about to hail a taxi, when I realized that none of us had foresight enough to bring along our passports or any of our luggage with the photographs and recordings, which would have been odd indeed.

"Not this time," I said.

Nan and Aunt Aran silently followed me across the street, crestfallen. The police, spotting unsavory-looking characters watching for hours the entrance of the hotel where an international event was in progress, had pulled them over to the other side and found them carrying firearms. Showing our invitations by the Mayor, we vouched for them, Embassy employees detailed to our protection that night.

"You may go, but we have to take them in for further questioning, because firearms violation is a serious matter," the police sergeant said.

Serious indeed, for why would they carry them except to use on us, shoot to kill, because after so much investment Jungil Kim would rather destroy us than see us fall into the wrong hands.

Next morning the Secretary of the North Korean Embassy called to thank me for my intercession, saying that they had all been released after verification of their diplomatic status. Neither of us referred to the single most important circumstance, their possession of lethal weapons.

The next day being February 16, Jungil's birthday, we all went back to East Berlin for the luncheon at the North Korean Embassy. In the middle of the dinner the Ambassador silenced everybody and ceremoniously presented Nan with two roots of mountain ginseng, sent specially by Jungil Kim. No sooner had the party resumed than it was interrupted by another loud announcement.

"Our Beloved Comrade Leader wants me to relay this message," said Ingoo Cha facing me. "Carry on according to your convictions. Also a sum of $2.3 million is being sent by special courier for deposit in your Vienna Bank of America account to be drawn on at your discretion."

After this we still couldn't go on with the luncheon, because an employee came hurtling down the hallway and burst into the room to say, "Long distance call to President Moo from our Beloved Comrade Leader in Pyongyang."

I ran to the phone following him.

"You got the ginseng all right?"

"Yes, just now. Thank you, Comrade Leader."

"They are for your wife, genuine wild roots found deep in Gayma Heights, with unbelievable medicinal power."

Could he have any idea what Gayma Heights meant to Aunt Aran and to me other than as the provenience of these wonder herbs?

"Thanks. And thank you for the money, too."

"Would that be enough?"

"More than enough for some time."

"Ask for more if you need it."

The money and the ginseng bewildered us. It seemed as if he was trying to overwhelm us with kindness, reading our minds. But any sense of guilt on our part was shattered by Jungay Hong's arrival at our West Berlin hotel, with some more news about my grandmother.

"She is 91 but looks and acts as if she is only 50," she said. "As owner of the 50-story Star Building and the Peninsula Mall in downtown Manhattan, she is easily the richest Korean American and is known to be an easy target for all kinds of freeloaders and swindlers. Every foundation, charity, scholarship, or movement automatically puts her name down at the top of the donor list to be solicited. The Korean Embassy in Washington, D.C., the umpteen Consulates all over the US, and even the Korean Government in Seoul itself consider her as a regular revenue item in their annual budgets. She was the one who came up with the cash to pay down for the purchase of the building on Fifth Avenue at 52nd Street when it suddenly came on the market for the Korea Trade Center. She might as well, I guess, because nobody can take money with them on their last journey. I should know. Poor lady, she is all alone, with no children or grandchildren to give her money to."

My heart yearned for her. Only if we could fly to her this very minute and tell her that she was not alone, that we were her kin.

"Well, when you go back, could you tell her that she has some kin still left," I said, seeing no harm in saying this much though we had agreed with Aunt Aran, who was in her room, not to complicate matters by telling Jungay in advance.

"However, don't tell anybody else about it," I added, as a precautionary measure.

"Oh, don't worry," Jungay said, with a chuckle. "Even if I tell, nobody would believe it, including the lady herself. There have been many pretenders over the years claiming to be her grandson or granddaughter, practically every mixed-blood kid from Korea, with fantastic stories and proofs, all lies and fabrications. You see there couldn't be any grandchild involved. Her only son Anton got killed in a miscarried attempt to rescue his father from a North Korean prison and her daughter-in-law, Haran Ham, the enchanting star of Sunset, married to Anton, was executed, according to best available records, immediately upon sentencing for espionage. But you can't blame them for trying. Wouldn't you, if you stood to inherit all that wealth?"

She fell silent to stare at me for a few seconds, then at Nan.

"He is not claiming to be Gisoon Minsky's grandson, is he?" she asked Nan with a half smile.

"No," Nan said. "Actually, he shouldn't have mentioned this at all, because it's a secret to be told her directly to protect the parties concerned."

"So this mysterious descendant of Gisoon Minsky lives in North Korea?"

"Something like that but we are not at liberty to say more."

"That's a fine way to treat your bosom friend, Nan. I thought you had trusted me with something even more valuable, like these pictures and recordings, your very lives."

Knowing exactly what pressure points to push, Jungay should have been head of KGB rather than a physician's widow. Capitulating, we knocked at Aunt Aran's door to get her involved in the disclosure.

"Why don't you make the break right now?" Jungay said after learning the whole truth. "You are in the West. I'll wait outside with a taxi which will take us to the airport. We'll be in New York in seven hours."

"No, we can't," I said. "They are in the lobby watching the elevators."

"We can go down to the parking level or better still take the stairway."

"They are watching our door across the hallway 24 hours."

"Maybe we can trick them or bump them off."

"We just can't take that kind of chance, especially with the ladies involved."

"I am game," Aunt Aran declared suddenly. "Aren't you, Nan?"

"Yes."

"I think you are using us as an excuse."

"I won't be taunted or goaded into taking unnecessary risks, especially by you whose safety I can't jeopardize seeing that you are the only living witness to my identity as a Minsky. Didn't you see the artillery they carry around? They are itching for an excuse to use them. I never seriously considered West Berlin as a possibility, a small enclave in solid Communist territory crawling with North Korean agents who are so at home here that they may even stop the plane taking off with us in it. In Munich or Vienna where they are aliens and powerless, it will be much safer."

"All the US Embassies have been alerted," Jungay said. "They didn't know about Miss Ham but she would be welcome of course. It's just a matter of walking into any US Embassy compound. The one here near the Brandenburg

Gate may serve the purpose just as well."

"If we can break away from our shadows. The more I think about it, Vienna looks like the best candidate. Our friends will continue to be alert in Munich, because West Germany is almost like the States with American military bases and has no formal diplomatic relationship with North Korea. Austria is different. Though pro-West, it is formally neutral and North Korea maintains an Embassy. If nothing happens in Munich, the more likely place, their guard will relax by the time we get to Vienna. Still we'll need some help. Why don't you call Pierre Chambard in Paris? I have his number. Tell him all about our intention to flee."

"Can you trust newsmen?" Jungay objected. "They would sooner sell their own mother to grab a headline."

"She is right," Nan said. "If any of this leaks out and Jungil suspects anything, we are done for."

"I wanted to hedge our bet."

"I don't think it's necessary. Al Edwards knows his business. Remember how he spirited us out of Seoul using the UNC chopper?"

"Tell him it will most probably be in Vienna, unless things are really favorable in Munich in which case I will let him know. Ask him if there is a number I can call direct other than the Langley one?"

"I will when I get back."

"No, do it at your hotel and let me know. Maybe we should devise a code. Have him call me as an AP correspondent asking for an interview. Jungil wants good press and does not look too closely when it's a call from a reporter. The interview can be set up to exclude our captors and snatch us away. He can work out the details and let me know. We'll follow his directions."

We divided the hundreds of pictures, cassettes, and above all Aunt Aran's invaluable albums, letters, notes and diaries in two large shopping bags, with gift wrapping paper arranged prominently on top. Jungay carrying one bag and Nan the other, we went downstairs with our faithful tail in tow, all riding cozily in the same elevator. Two other men rose from chairs seeing us step into the lobby. At the curb I paid the cabby to take Jungay to her hotel. Later she called to say that the AP reporter was away for the weekend but would get in touch with me when he returned next week by calling me at the Budapest office. Jungay left that afternoon. For fear of incurring suspicion we didn't see her off at the airport.

Next morning Nan called Jimi at her hotel, who was still asleep at 9 a.m.

"Are you going to be presented on stage after the showing?" Nan asked.

"Maybe. Why?"

"I want to bring you a bouquet."

"Thanks."

"Maybe we can have dinner afterwards or at some convenient time for you."

"I'll have to consult Director Jongsang Kim who is arriving tomorrow."

He had worked as an assistant director for us at one time and we had helped him with his career.

"Good. Let me know. I am sending you the pictures we took together at the Mayor's party."

Jimi's curtness and evasiveness, in contrast to her effusion the day before, should have tipped us off but, always looking at the better side of people, we attributed the change to the early hour and kept making fools of ourselves. After hanging up Nan had a few prints made of each photo and sent them to Jimi by one of our guards.

On the day Oxen was to be shown, we asked for the best florist in town and ordered two huge bouquets of roses. Just as we reached the Palast Theater and got out of our car followed by two guards, each holding one of the bouquets, we noticed Jongsang entering the front door, a pink tie in a beige suit, a pencil of moustache above his mouth, hair slicked, cocky, insolent. When we called out, he turned but quickly averted his face and kept walking away as if he had not seen us. The little ingrate brought back the memory of my loathing for the narrow, intolerant, calculating South Korean mentality, nauseating me, dispelling any lingering uncertainty I might have had as to where we should go to live after North Korea. For sure it was not going to be South Korea, my birth in it a mere accident to be set aside.

"Let's get out of here," I said to Nan.

"What do we do with the flowers?"

"Throw them away. Give them to the ushers. I don't care."

"But we are here and can't back out. Besides I've promised Jimi."

Our faithful companions, undisturbed by our snub, took the seats to our left and right, the bouquets in their laps. The action in the movie never got off the ground and it was a torture to sit through the pedestrian progression to its insipid end. The lights went back on but Jimi was not to be seen anywhere in the theater, nor Jongsang or anybody we knew.

"Dump them in there," I told our friends, indicating a trash can.

"No!" Nan intervened. "We can't stoop to their level."

We found an usher, a dimpled German damsel, and unloaded our flowers, though she was doubtful she could find the intended recipients.

"Cook and eat them, if you can't find them," I said.

She looked puzzled at me for a while, then broke into a tingling laughter, saying "The gentleman is funny!"

Half of the passengers on our Lufthansa plane were our people, 53, of which the Moo Moo Film personnel proper accounted for only one third. The bus took us directly from Munich Airport to the Bavaria Studio. We were all quartered at an office building which had kitchen facilities on the ground floor, offices on the second, and guest rooms on the third.

"Didn't you reserve any hotels?" I demanded.

"We didn't," Sunghwan Chun said unperturbed. "For security reasons. Besides this is closer to the filming area."

That was true. We could walk to it in five minutes. But of course the primary reason for quartering us at the studio was to insulate us from outside contact and prevent defections. The guards were everywhere, around our rooms, in the hallways, at the entrances, and on the sound stage itself while we worked. Unless something unusual happened, we had to rule out Munich.

Filming began immediately. The aquarium and other sets were not exactly as I had expected and required some modification but on the whole the shooting went well without a hitch, Aunt Aran putting forth inspirational performances. With the able technical help from the studio staff, we could truly enjoy the work as never before, relieved from the many distractions of nitty gritty, as if we were the audience under the spell of the music, fantasy, the sheer beauty, tenderness, gossamer-fine texture of the whole wonderful fable, so outrageously unreal and yet so credible, as all true art was.

But our enchantment was rudely broken by our guards following us everywhere, to the dining room, dressing room, dark room, projection and recording rooms, even to the restroom. On the third floor of the building where we were quartered two men sat at a desk set up in the hallway opposite our rooms. When our door opened at any time, up they rose to their feet, ready to follow. I learned later that they had all been handpicked by Jungil from his own personal security staff. Unable to bear this close watch, I decided to have a talk with Sunghwan Chun, their hancho.

"Why do you fellows follow us even to the restroom?" I asked him. "Are we prisoners? I am so ashamed I can't face the German studio personnel."

"We didn't mean to distress you," he said apologetically. "But we are here to protect you, not to watch you. If anything should happen to you, we'll pay dearly for it. Numerous phone calls came through from the moment we got here. When we pick up, some Korean asks how long the filming would last. We ask him who he is and he hangs up. This has been going on daily. Obviously this is the work of Puppet Ministry of Security dogs who are bent on some mischief."

I could have told him that nobody meaning to do real harm would be going around disclosing himself to the victim, but there was no point in showing him up. Though he would not admit it, the real source of their tension was the Munich police car parked right below our dormitory windows the moment we arrived, perhaps because the studio had asked for extra security knowing that we were from North Korea. Whenever we went by it on our way to and from the studio, our guards would position themselves on that side, almost shielding us from the policemen in the car, perhaps fearing that we might run over and ask for asylum. The thought had crossed our minds but had been ruled out: all three of us might not make it to the squad car and even if we did there was the distinct possibility of a shootout between our captors and would-be liberators.

"I know you have a job to do," I said, "but don't make it too obvious, at least when the studio people are around."

"We'll try," he said.

He kept his word and the surveillance became less obstrusive afterwards. The filming ended in ten days to our satisfaction. The rushes convinced me that Zuet Debauer had outdone himself especially with the undersea shots, the mermaids carrying Chong Shim to the palace at the bottom of the sea, her reunion with her long-dead mother, and her triumphal return above sea borne on a water-lily pad.

After paying the balance due and thanking them for their help we left by night train and arrived at East Berlin at daybreak. In the afternoon the North Korean Embassy chartered a tour bus and showed us the city, Brandenburg Gate, Berlin Wall, and Saxon House of Orlenburg, a former Nazi concentration camp about an hour to the north.

"How do they compare with those at No. 6?" Nan asked, as we walked down the cellblock.

"These are luxury hotels," I said, without exaggeration.

Each cell had labels giving the names of the inmates, each distinguished by a biography and a bouquet of flowers. They had more space, more light, more air than the political prisoners composting at No. 6 and other North Korean jails. Suddenly I recalled the haggard face of my cellmate Professor Yee and the promise I had made to secure his release. With a harrowing sense of guilt I realized I had not even thought of him, let alone done anything for him, since my release. Now it was too late. I would be leaving for Vienna via Budapest and would rather die than be back in North Korea. Perhaps the poor man was dead by now, with all his encyclopedic knowledge, ever ready to juggle the facts and perfect the Ilsung Kim myth in eloquent prose.

Their combat duty behind the enemy lines, West Germany, successfully completed, all the staff, including our inseparable bodyguards, caught the next flight to Moscow on their way home, leaving only Film Instructor Dugnam Bag in sole charge of us, Aunt Aran, Nan, and me.

Among the bundle of messages and mail the front desk handed us when we checked in at the Budapest Hyatt was the all important message from Gregory Anderson of AP, asking me to call him at a Vienna number. Could it be Al himself? With Bag listening in, I dialed immediately hoping to hear Al's pleasant banter. It was a stranger with a deep bass that answered. I quickly got over my disappointment. Of course it had to be somebody else, not Al himself who should be directing the show from behind. Anderson, if that was his real name, wanted an interview with all three of us for his worldwide syndicated column.

"In fact why don't I meet you at the concert in Vienna?" he said. "Maybe we can sit in the same section."

"That sounds great," I said. "They have sent us complimentary tickets already, but I'll be glad to buy you one next to ours."

"No, that's not necessary. One of the perquisites of this profession is complimentary tickets. I am sure I can persuade them to seat me near you."

My heart was pounding and I could see that Nan and Aunt Aran knew what this meant without my telling them in so many words. So the US government had taken our case into its hands. It was just a matter of waiting a day or two. We were as good as being in the US already.

There was an invitation from Marco Moravia, Coordinator of the Venice International Film Festival, to attend the next meet in June.

"I have heard great things about Spring Fragrance and also your new film Chong Shim," he wrote. "Either will qualify nicely for our Musicals Division. Unlike Cannes we value this form of art highly and look forward to your participation."

We needed this boost to our morale, slightly crimped by the Cannes rejection. We may be leaving North Korea but our work had to keep winning, no matter who got the credit.

My telephoning was briefly interrupted by the visit of the North Korean Ambassador bringing flowers and bottles of wine to our suite and office, as he always did whenever we came to Budapest. But he was not the only one that showed such courtesy. Knowing our intimacy to the Kims ambassadors came and greeted us with flowers wherever we went.

With Bag still listening in, I called our Austrian partner Pandler to meet us in Vienna to sign the incorporation papers and take care of other business. My next call was to the Vienna bureau of the Asahi Shinbun to arrange another interview with Genji Enoki, this time to introduce Aunt Aran and possibly repudiate my by now well-publicized dogma on genetic bondage. Only his recording came on. After thanking him for his article, I hung up, saying I would call him again in Vienna. I also called the Kyodo Press to talk to Susumu Kuno, who had helped diffuse some jingoistic resistance to the release of The Emissary of No Return in Japan. Reporter Hasumi answered and said Kuno was in Scandinavia covering some international conference and would be back soon. Thanking Hasumi for all the favorable publicity given to the Moo Moo releases as well as The Emissary, I advised him of our arrival in Vienna for the Philharmonic debut of Chong Shim. I also had the pleasure of talking to Pierre Chambard in Paris, who assured me of his intention to be present at the Symphony Hall on the opening night.

"I'll bring other media buddies of mine," he said cheerily. "You'll get a big writeup about this."

On the last night, long past midnight when our friend Bag nextdoor should be asleep, we silently packed our baggage, taking only the videocassettes of our finished films and leaving everything else, clothes, books, screen plays, personal effects, and other valuables.

"It's awful to leave without saying goodbye to Secretary

Ilsug Yee and his wife," Nan said, in tears. "They have been so good to me, looking after me during and after my operation, never leaving my side. They were doing a job for sure, but they did so sincerely, from the bottom of their hearts. I'll be in their debt forever."

"Let's write to them when we get out."

"No, that will be their undoing."

"That's true. We'll just have to wait until Korea is united and all this madness of hostility disappears. That day will come as surely as the sun rises."

Prophetically, the sky to the east exploded in crimson, the huge, glowing half circle astride the silhouette of the distant mountains. None of us had slept a wink, but didn't feel tired.

At 8 a.m. who should knock at our door but Secretary Ilsug Yee and his wife!

"I am so glad to see you again," exclaimed Nan, leading them inside. "I was wretched because I didn't know how to send word to you before we left for Vienna."

"I have been chosen to escort you to Vienna," said Yee, in his 50's, round-faced, jovial, excited about the trip. North Korean embassy personnel simply never went anywhere after being posted to their respective stations unless there was a special order. In the last six years Yee had been in Hungary he had never been to Austria, though it was just next door. The Party must have high regard for his ability and reliability to have asked him for this important mission, which meant promotions and transfers to more important posts like Moscow or Beijing in store. They must think we were good luck to them, little suspecting the disaster to befall them in a few hours. How ironic that we should repay them this way!

"Let's tell him to fake a stroke or something and duck out of this," Nan nudged me when we were alone.

"Are you mad?" I almost shouted. "It's rotten for things to turn out this way, but we have no choice, darling. It's his fate, just as it is ours to see this through, come what may."

At 9 a.m. we all went downstairs to get into the two cars furnished by the Embassy, Nan and Aunt Aran in one car driven by Bag and me and Yee in the other.

"Get in, Mrs. Yee," I offered to the secretary's wife who stood on the curb waving goodbye. "We'll take you home."

"No," her husband interposed. "She can find her way home."

It was a two-hour drive to the Austrian border. When we were near it, I realized that I had left behind the tote bag with my passport and other documents strapped over the chair before the writing desk in our suite. How could I be so stupid? We had no choice but to turn back.

"Why don't we call the hotel?" Ilsug Yee suggested. "They might be able to help. In fact, my wife might be there?"

"Why?" I asked surprised.

"Oh, to clean up and tidy up."

That was a superfluity we had not asked for, because nothing needed to be tidied up and the hotel did all the maid work. So without our knowledge, either under orders from the Party or on their own they had been going into our room, a trespass normally resented but welcome in this particular emergency. It was possible that she might think it strange that we should leave so much of our stuff behind, including change of clothes. Most probably she would attribute it to our haste or some change in plans that required our return to Budabest to pick them up, though originally we were to fly directly to Pyongyang from Vienna after the concert. After all the hotel suite was our office and headquarters. Anyway we would soon find out what conclusions she had drawn and what actions she had taken. There was just the barest possibility, one in ten, that she would put two and two together and alert the right places. The question was how fast they could react. By the time they got through to Jungil and got the instructions back, we would be out of Austria, out of their reach. Hopefully.

Pulling into a small village near the border we called our number at the hotel. It was Yee's wife who answered at the first ring, as if she had expected it. There was a slight pause, obviously adjusting to my call, perhaps embarrassed at being found out.

"There is no time to lose," I said. "Can you call a taxi and bring the bag yourself?"

"Sure I can," she answered, slightly piqued at my doubting her ability to discharge such a simple task.

She sounded as if she didn't suspect anything. Even if she did, the errand would at least delay by that much any action she contemplated taking. While waiting for her, we saw and waved down the Vienna Embassy car with three Embassy personnel driving by in the direction we had come.

"We thought you had an accident," said Attaché An in charge of Moo Moo Film, Vienna, who had funked out of the bank when he couldn't get the checkbooks.

They had been waiting for us at the border three hours after the appointed time. To save time we all got in our respective cars, so we could take off the moment Mrs. Yee handed us the bag through the window. She arrived, got off the cab, and came running to my car with the bag. None of us budged from our vehicles, the American code of chivalry being unknown to Korean males. Taking the bag, I apologized for my forgetfulness and thanked her profusely for her invaluable service in the nick of time, all intended to monopolize her attention. The car started and we were off. There seemed the briefest eye-contact between husband and wife, Yee barely nodding in acknowledgment according to the Korean machismo.

After checking in at the Intercontinental I met Pandler at a lawyer's office to sign the incorporation papers and also hand him $500,000 to be credited to my share in the 50-50 partnership. With An in tow I went to the Vienna Branch of the Bank of America to maximize interest earnings, which An approved as wise. The manager came out and took me to his office, making An wait in the lobby.

"You have a healthy balance of over $20 million," he said. "That makes you one of our most valued customers."

"I want to talk about that. It's not earning much interest in checking."

"We could put it in a high-yield savings account and transfer as you need to checking."

"Can I phone in such transfers?"

"Sure. Just sign here please."

"That's real short," he said, looking at my signature. "I notice you did not supply your mother's maiden name. Maybe you had better put it down to prevent impersonation because phone-ins are involved."

"Impersonation?"

"Somebody might get hold of your checkbook and write out a big sum to himself, forging your signature, which seems rather simple, then make it good by calling in a transfer."

Proudly printing down the name Ham, I suddenly realized how vulnerable my checking account had been all this time. I had given An a whole stack of signed blank checks so he could write in the amounts and make payments when necessary. After my defection to the West, he or any of Jungil's agents were certain to use them and accuse me of having stolen the money.

"Can I make it more theft-proof by adding something to my name?"

"Like your middle name?"

"Actually it's my full name."

"Sure. I strongly recommend it."

On the new forms he provided, I put down, Chundong Bag Moo Moo John-Alan Heyman Archer Torrey Ham-Minsky. What a coincidence that Director Bag had the same family name as my maternal great-grandfather Daybay Bag! Maybe he was distantly related, though the chance was slim, Bag being one of the most numerous family names. Whether he was or not, I had no animosity toward him any longer. He was as much part of me as all the other names that composed me, and had unwittingly but prophetically pointed to my descent from the true patriot.

"Now that sure is not short," the banker whistled, smiling, as he retrieved the papers. "Which is the last name?"

"Ham-Minsky."

"The others are given names you go by?"

"At one time or other."

"Please be sure to sign each check exactly like this, omitting nothing, in that order."

"Don't worry. I won't forget."

At the Symphony Hall that evening we sat in the front row, Aunt Aran between us, Nan to her left and me to her right. To my right sat Gregory Anderson, a tall lanky man with his press badge on his chest. Immediately behind us sat Chambard, Kuno, Enoki, John Stone of UPI, Charles Blackmur of Reuters, André Richelieu of AFP, Richard White of the New York Times, and a few others, all wearing their press badges, seemingly unnecessarily because the management couldn't care less, but perhaps for the benefit of our North Korean companions who couldn't all sit as close to us as they would have liked, 15 of them, the top brass of the Embassy including Ambassador Geechul Hwang and his wife seated next to Nan, not counting those we didn't know about placed in various parts of the auditorium, especially at the exits. While waiting for the curtain to go up, we held a mini-press conference, Anderson calling the shots and busily taking notes.

Kelsen in white tuxedo stepped onto the podium to the applause of the expectant audience.

"Ladies and gentlemen," he said as the crowd quieted down. "We have the distinct honor of the presence among us of the lady who has composed the work we are going to perform this evening. It is my pleasure to present to you Miss Aran Ham of Korea."

He was looking in our direction and the audience broke into a thunderous applause. Briefly I was nonplussed, not having been prepared for this, and was about to tell Aunt Aran to stand up and take a bow.

"Take her up, both of you," Anderson said from the corner of his mouth, continuing to clap and smile.

As all three of us rose, Nan and I supporting Aunt, and started to head for the steps to the stage, Anderson handed me a note:

"Follow him backstage afterwards."

I looked up and saw a US Marine sergeant at the backstage entrance behind the orchestra, visible only from our angle, waving to us. The applause didn't weaken the whole time we made our procession to the podium. After helping her step up Nan and I stood to the side.

"Ladies and gentlemen, Miss Aran Ham, composer of Chong Shim."

She bowed deep acknowledging the affection of the people. The applause became explosive. Soon the orchestra rose to their feet, and the audience followed. Raising her arms she looked at her fans to the left and right, up and down, flashing her rare but most fetching smile, before taking another bow. She was no longer the recluse and prisoner, the songbird shut up in the cage by the lake for Ilsung Kim's personal pleasure and whim, but belonged to the whole world, the bounty of her genius to enrich us for generations to come. I saw her as the young woman in blue scarf, the image carved in my memory, the mother I had never known but always dreamed of, the apotheosis of womanhood, not the desicated remains of an unfulfilled, wasted life, but the radiant focus of vital and youthful energy and creativity, ready to explode into a thousand wonders. My heart was bursting with pride for her, tears of joy flowing freely. With the standing ovation still continuing, we slowly retreated along the aisle down the middle of the orchestra. Just as the door closed behind us the crowd hushed and the orchestra struck up the opening strains.

The Marine, preceded by an old guide of the theater, led us down a few flights of steps and out the back door used for delivery. We ran, Nan and I pulling and almost carrying Aunt Aran, to the US Embassy limousine parked in the dark, deserted alley, its engine running, lights on, doors held open, and a Marine chauffeur at the steering wheel. Nan went inside first to help Aunt in, me lifting her off the ground, when the metallic voice tore through the darkness, the voice of Ilsug Yee:

"Halt, traitors!"

Simultaneously I heard bullets hissing by. The limo jumped forward, doors banging shut with a jolt, and screeched out of the alley. The Marine Sergeant, who had jumped into the front seat, returned the fire spitting out of an automatic from behind an electric pole. As we got into the main street and turned away from the plaza in front of the theater, several North Koreans scrambled to their cars giving up their brief chase on foot.

"Give us all you've got, George," the Sergeant ordered.

The limousine was going 65 miles an hour but the needle was jerking up for more, when slammed by what felt like an antitank rocket.

"Sonofabitches!" the Sergeant swore under his breath. "The car is bullet-proof but it may still be a good idea to duck down."

At the same time, rolling down the window a little more and pushing his hand out he fired his 38, putting out the lights of one of the two fast approaching cars. He fired clip after clip at the other one still behind us peppering our rear, but kept missing.

"Do you have another pistol, George?" I asked. "I can get him from your side."

"Be my guest!" the driver said, pulling one from the holster under his jacket. "We should have brought a tank if we had known we'd run into this much firepower."

Reaching over to open the window on Nan's side I froze in my tracks at the sight of Aunt Aran slumped over a pool of blood on the seat.

"Bingo! Bullseye!" Sergeant Jim Watson shouted ecstatically, watching the stricken car behind us frogleap the side rail and tumble down the bank bursting into spectacular flames that lit the countryside.

With trembling hands I lifted Aunt and laid her on the back seat.

"Oh, no, not her, please no, oh God, no, please, oh God!" Nan moaned.

Glued to her pulseless hand I sat stunned, not hearing, not seeing, not knowing or caring where I was, where I went.

• • • •

Flaps down, throttle pulled back, eardrums popping, registering only the hushed swish of air friction, the 747 began its descent for landing at Kennedy Airport, New York, where my grandmother Gisoon was waiting, along with Jungay, Elizabeth, Al Edwards, and other friends.

"I have killed her," I cried, burying my face in my hands, freshly reminded of the enormity of my loss, smitten with guilt. "I tried to use her to establish my identity."

"No, you didn't. She was all set to come with us anyway."

"She would have lived many more years in the beautiful villa by the lake, hadn't I come along and given her ideas. I should never have disturbed her seclusion."

"What good is it to live a prisoner under guard and die unknown, unmourned, unremembered? She would have chosen this way, even if she had known the outcome in advance. Besides she is not dead, at least not in what counts most. Her immortal music is with us. Let's devote our lives to her sacred memory."

"How?"

"For starters we can make a movie about her life and art, the best we have made, not one but many, so the whole world will know her greatness and loss."

"What a rotten time to be born!" I said, crying, recalling the turbulence and violence Aunt Aran had lived through, colonial occupation by Japan, division and occupation by the US and USSR, war with millions of foreign troops, Red Chinese, American, and an assortment of nationalities seesawing up and down her land, bombings and shootings, massacres, vendettas, roving bands of men deranged with one ideology or other seeking out enemies and murdering the innocent, endless lines of homeless refugees wandering in the wasteland, cries of the orphans.

"The more power to the purity and beauty of her art!" Nan said, wiping my face. "Maybe her senseless death will so outrage and inflame the conscience of the Korean nation, north and south, that the dividing wall will come tumbling down, brothers and sisters trampling across the DMZ to embrace each other, and end the half century of fratricide. For that alone she would not have died in vain. As soon as we land in New York, let's establish a foundation, dedicated to her memory, to the memory of Haran Ham, Jintay Ham, Rev.

Doochan and Mrs. Ham, Josef and Anton Minsky, all those who have perished as victims of the Demon, Divided Korea. We'll name it Ham-Minsky Foundation."

"No. I think they would have wished for a broader name, to stand for all those that have fallen victim."

"But we can't name them all."

Suddenly remembering, I pulled the Bank of America checkbook from the valise and wrote out the full and exact amount from the balance slip handed to me by the Vienna branch manager, $21,625,239.76, payable to Cry, Korea, Cry!, an odd name for a foundation but the only one that came to my mind. I felt no arrogance or incongruity in identifying my personal loss and grief with that of a whole country, Korea, whose only fitting attitude for generations to come seemed lachrymosity.

"This is the first installment from her assassins," I said between sobs.

Nan made no attempt to stop my tears, as her own eyes turned into oceans fit to drown the two halves of Korea with their unending tale of sorrow.

Framed in the window was the Statue of Liberty, Wansong Cha's Lady in White, upraised torch pointing skyward, still promising a haven to the oppressed and downtrodden of the world, proclaiming America the Beautiful, the only country committed to such an improbable code of hospitality in the face of global congestion, pollution, hostility. Wasn't she naive, deluded, hypocritical, or simply outdated? Only if she would stoop down and feel the haven my aunt, my mother was getting - a bit too restful, too permanent, too cold!

"Why her and not me?" my tortured soul kept wailing in protest.